I was born in August 1984, and received my name from my dad who was, and still is, a fan of Doctor Who; it's a good job that I am also, and my mum along with older brother.

I studied Fashion & Textiles at college, where I did my final project on a story that I wrote. This is where my love for writing began.

As I have now finished my first book, I hope that tomorrow will bring even more inspiration.

Mirror Bound

Nissa Gordon

Mirror Bound

Vanguard Press

VANGUARD PAPERBACK

A CIP catalogue record for this title is
available from the British Library.

ISBN 978 184386 532 2

*Vanguard Press is an imprint of
Pegasus Elliot MacKenzie Publishers Ltd.*
www.pegasuspublishers.com

First Published in 2009

**Vanguard Press
Sheraton House Castle Park
Cambridge England**

Printed & Bound in Great Britain

To my mum, for everything that you have done for us all; none of us would be where we are today if it weren't for you. Especially this book, as you did all the leg work by posting everything off for me; so thank you with all of my love.

Chapter One

The high red lights flashed overhead on the corridor ceiling with the alarms sounding all around the ship signalling that they were under attack, officers ran to their posts careful not to bump into anyone else without even slowing down; they were all dressed in similar uniforms dark navy blue jackets and trousers with a high necked white shirt, which the sleeves flared out of the cuffs of the jacket. They themselves though weren't all the same; in fact they were all quite different; some of them had different coloured skin, from white, tanned, green to purple, even their hair was different colours; those who looked more human had different coloured hair but also markings like tattoos on the left side of their faces.

A small boy with flaming red crimson hair tried to make his way past the other officers. He looked around wide-eyed as if wondering what was going on; he was dressed similar to the officers but more basically as if in a training uniform; he just had the white shirt with his class badge on both sleeves.

Two older officers rushed past him from behind. He looked up at them; the one on his right had three long purple head tails almost down to his waist, the other had dark greyish skin almost black with his white hair tied back revealing his pointed ears.

"I can't believe that they would actually attack an imperial ship." The purple skinned man said angrily shaking his head.

"What's worst though is that they didn't have an escort." The dark-skinned man said. "We don't even have a full crew for something like this; it was only a training exercise which was why we were all out here in the first place. Now what are we supposed to do?"

"It'll give them a chance to do some real-life training." The purple skin man said, seemingly trying to sound positive about the situation.

The man with dark skin suddenly turned around as if he had only just noticed the boy following them; he seemed to take him in as if assessing him and what he was capable of.

"You can come with us; you could be of some use." The dark skin man told him. "What's your name kid?"

"Um... Aba'rian... Renji Aba'rian." He told them breathing heavily.

"Well, Renji do you think you're brave enough to help us out?" The purple skin man asked him smiling as he put his hand on his shoulder leading him down the corridor. "I'm Jerenzo and he's Osric."

"Captain Osric." He corrected him.

Renji nodded as he allowed himself to be lead down the corridor, wondering what they wanted him to do; when the ship shuddered suddenly as they were fired upon.

"Pirates of course, stupid in my opinion for an Imperial ship to be travelling in this part of space without an escort." Jerenzo told him.

"You've already mentioned that, I believe." Osric reminded him.

Renji looked between the two of them; he had studied both their races and from what he had learnt they kind of made an unlikely pair of friends; but they were, it seemed as though he had a lot to learn but he wasn't sure if this was how he wanted to do it.

He had imagined what it would be like to fight the pirates, and had talked about it with his friends, but he never really imagined that he would be thrown into something like this the first time that he left his home world; he didn't know if he would really be brave enough to go up against pirates, but it didn't seem as though he had a choice in the matter.

The door to their right slide open as Jerenzo directed Renji inside, he heard a lot of voices coming from inside the room; he didn't need to see inside because he already knew which room it was and it filled him full of dread as if it suddenly dawned on him what he was about to do, but he knew that running away wasn't an option.

The tall man in the centre of the group of security officers stepped forward so that Renji could see him fully, he looked as though he was in his late twenties but he couldn't really tell because he was a Tasian; his black markings swirling down the left side of his face, he had long black hair pulled back in a pony tail and his cold dark eyes looked upon Renji as though he was an unwanted pest.

"And who is he?" He asked.

"General Kasiya, this is Renji Aba'rian; we thought that he might be of help." Osric told him. "This imperial ship carries the future queen meaning that they'll be other children on board, his age; he should be able to slip past the pirates to find them."

"But even if he does get caught, at least he'll find out who the pirates have captured so far." Jerenzo added nudging Renji smiling at him, as Renji just looked nervously between him and the General who really did look as though he didn't want him there.

"Do you think you can find her?" General Kasiya asked him.

"Ye...yes sir." Renji said bravely, though truthfully he didn't have a clue what she looked like or where she would be on board the ship; he hadn't actually studied the imperial ships because they weren't really accessible to the public.

"We'll see." General Kasiya said as he walked over to him pulling something out of his pocket, he grabbed Renji's right arm and injected him. "So we don't lose you."

"Oh..." Renji said rubbing his arm as he stared at the General's back walking over to the transporter pad.

"Come on kid." A tall man said cheerfully as he followed his commanding officer onto the pad. He was human with fair skin and sandy brown hair with a kind face.

Renji looked at them all standing on the pad before he walked over and stood next to the man who had spoke to him, but General Kasiya stepped forward and put his hand on his shoulder to motion him to step back closer to him; Renji didn't look up at him but stepped back beside him just as the pad below them shone brightly and they all disappeared in a bright white light.

They reappeared a moment later in a dark corridor with the red lights still flashing above them but the alarms were no longer sounding as if someone had turned them off; Renji quickly looked around noticing that the wall console behind them was blown out from weapons fire.

"If you run into trouble contact us." General Kasiya told him walking off without looking back at him.

The other officers though didn't walk off but looked at Renji and then at their commander, they looked as though they were unsure about leaving him alone on board the ship which was overrun with pirates to actually look for the queen; which in fact was why they were also on board.

"Sir?" The human man said questioningly.

"Spread out in pairs, we need to find all those on board." General Kasiya told them. "I don't believe that the list of passengers was correct that we received it so when you find the crew make sure you have them confirm the list."

"Yes sir...but what about Renji, are we really to let him go off alone?" He asked him.

"It's safer if he does, he hasn't any markings but he still has red hair they won't hurt him." General Kasiya said over his shoulder, he held up a hand scanner. "As soon as you find her send us a signal."

"Um...yes...yes sir." Renji said looking at the other officers nervously before he turned around and walked off alone, he had seen the looks on their faces; they had been just as unsure about him going off alone as he had been, but of course he would do as he was ordered because that's why he was there to train as an officer for when he became old enough to serve properly.

Renji tried to imagine telling his friends when they got back to school how he bravely came on board to find the queen and rescue her, how General Kasiya had praised him and told him that he looked forward to the day that they would serve together as officers; he tried to think of these things but the dark eerie corridor and the flashing red lights kept reminding him how alone he was and just what he was really getting himself into.

He had only left the others five minutes before when he heard voices coming towards him; he stopped and looked around for somewhere to hide not knowing either what was behind the doors on this corridor; he reached out and pressed the square button on the small rectangular door panel. The door slide open ever so slightly so that Renji had to squeeze through the gap into the blackened room, hoping that they wouldn't notice the opening in the door or that there was anyone in the room, he didn't dare look behind as a thought that there could be someone there like from a horror program that his older brothers liked; he knew that his mind was only playing tricks on him because he was so scared but he couldn't help it as he had never done anything so scary in his whole life.

"They came on board somewhere around here, but they won't have a ship to go back to when we've finished with them." A deep voice said outside of the room.

"Neither will we if we can't get those damn kids." Another man said, but his voice sounded a lot harsher as though he was suffering from cold. "They said they can't get near it as though it's being controlled."

"Well that just confirms that one of them is a Tiania or she's somewhere close by protecting them." He said sounding somewhat pleased at this news. "Imagine what we could get for them all. We could clear the treasury out."

Renji risked looking out through the gap as the voices seemed to be moving away; they were both over seven foot and had shaved heads, they were dressed in ripped vests and black trousers with boots over the top of them. He waited until they were gone before he squeezed back out and went the way that they had just come from, hoping that he would be able to get to them before anyone else did; the only problem was not being seen and somehow convincing them that he was actually there to help them, would he if he was in their place?

Renji used the access conduits and work-ways to get to the lower decks, not thinking it was a good idea to use the lifts considering that when the doors opened there could be a pirate stood there.

He fell out of a crawl way fifteen minutes later breathing deeply and quickly looked around hoping that the noise of the bulkhead cover hitting the deck and echoing throughout the deck, hadn't attracted any unwanted attention after he had come so far.

Renji quickly went off to the left hoping that he was going the right way, he hadn't gone far when he felt immense heat coming from the next corridor making him stop for a moment before he went on bravely; there it was, just as those pirates had said but it had gotten much worse engulfing the whole corridor now. He stood there as close as he dare to the fire with his hand up cover his face because of the heat, but through the flames he saw her, a girl his own age.

"Are you alright?" Renji shouted over to her, but she didn't answer him. "I'm here to save you, is there another way around to get to you from back there?"

She didn't answer him again, but instead the fire started to fade somewhat; the young girl stepped forward taking hold of the hand of the other girl and walked forward through the flames.

"What the hell...?" Renji shouted alarmed at what she was doing, seeming to forget that she was a Tiania; as soon as she was clear of the flames he grabbed her hand not feeling the heat radiating from it as others do. "Don't do that okay...I mean...give me a little warning next time..."

She looked up at him without speaking as she followed him back the way that he had came, never letting go of her hand.

Kasiya and his team waited patiently for Renji to return; yes they had gotten his message that he was on his way back so soon, which had surprised them but when he saw Renji and the two young girls they just stared at him.

Renji stopped in front of them breathing deeply, though he hadn't let go of the young girl with long red hair or rather she hadn't let go of him; the other girl had pulled her hand free and rushed over to the officers wanting to go home.

The officer to Kasiya's left who was several inches taller than him and had short graying hair with green eyes set in a hard face, made to grab hold of her knowing who she was, but when his hand was only several inches away from her he quickly pulled it back.

"Damn it...she's hot, she nearly burnt my hand off." The man shouted at Kasiya, who looked from him to the young girl who had grabbed hold of Renji's arm seemingly not wanting to let him go.

"Perhaps she doesn't like you." Kasiya told him and then turned to Renji. "Stay with her."

"Um...yes...yes sir..." Renji said somewhat unsure...

Renji woke suddenly with a start, he looked around the darkened room frantically as if looking for someone but then felt the weight of someone holding onto his arm; but it wasn't the arm of the boy in his dream but that of a grown man.

He looked down at the girl beside of him holding onto his arm as though he was still in the dream, she looked just like her; her long red flowing hair framing her face; it could almost be her only if he knew that it wasn't impossible but she was the closest thing he would ever get to find to her again.

He carefully pulled his arm free of her grip, but at first she didn't want to so he tried a little harder and she finally let go of him. He threw back his side of the covers careful not to pull them off of her, not wanting to wake her; he swung his legs over the side of the bed his own long crimson hair tied back off of his naked muscular torso and then looked back at her sleeping there. She was a child, a six year old child who looked like his long lost empress; looking so peaceful just lying there. She was the only one who was different, yes he was a grown man now but he hadn't really changed that much his duty was still to her and his people; the only real thing that passed between them was time and ages, actually so much that he was partly afraid to tell her the whole truth, but he knew that one day he would have to tell her.

"You're distracting me as usual silly girl." Renji whispered as he stood up, his whole body shimmered and then he disappeared out of his bedroom; a moment later he reappeared outside on a very windy balcony.

It was still late or rather early in the morning, and the moon was still out though now low in the sky as if readying itself to surrender to the blazing sun that was waiting in the shadows to rise once more.

Renji looked out over the city that covered most of the land in all directions, the capital city of Drac'tear that seated the Dragon Senate; all the worlds within the allies governed somewhat by the Malarias Fleet and powerful worlds and their governors that back them. Somehow the city looked darker than the first time he had visited it as a young man, a bodyguard to the lost empire that no one dare mention nor support openly anymore; so much had changed and yet stayed the same. Those who were already awake or yet to retire for the night still went about their business, air cars, taxis and ships flew in the sky lanes high above the city though not the highest of the skyscrapers.

Renji stepped forward and leant on the railing just staring out at the city below him high above in the Senator's quarters, wondering if he was really doing the right thing by being here, if he was the right person for the job.

15

"Damn!" Renji shouted pushing himself up off the railing, and his hair changed to brown and grew back into his head becoming much shorter.

The red rays of the sun started to slowly glow around the Dragon Senate. It may be a mile away but because of its size he could see it clearly from the balcony where he stood; he knew with the raising of the sun that he should head back down before he was sent for but it seemed as though it was too late as the door behind him quietly slid open and a young man about his own age stepped out; or rather the appearance of his own age.

The man stood there unmoved, his dark hair gelled back in place his uniform pressed and perfectly presented; the buttons fastened to the top so it was almost impossible to breath properly unless one was used to wearing the uniform, his white trousers didn't have a mark on them and his high black boots polished so that you could see your reflection in them.

Renji didn't need to turn around to know who stood there waiting for him, scowling at his appearance; which he could never understand because he was allowed to wear whatever he wanted for bed, though cream coloured trousers with purple flowers running down the sides wasn't really everyone's taste.

"So it's that time already is it?" Renji asked turning around to face him.

"What are you some sort of animal?" The man asked him irritably.

Renji just looked at him for a moment, not really in the mood for him this time of the morning but knew that he couldn't really do anything to him.

"I heard the door idiot." Renji told him as he walked back in with his officer stepping aside for him. "Perhaps when I get back, you could do some more training to hone your skills; that's if you're not a total loss."

The man just glared at him as if he was wishing he could do terrible things to him, before he followed him back inside quickly getting in front of him so that he could call for the lift.

"Babysitting that little brat, and you still outrank me..." He mumbled though loud enough so that he would be heard.

"Perhaps the Senator thinks highly of his daughter so wants someone better looking after her." Renji remarked as the doors opened and he stepped inside. "Guard quarters."

"Please." The man said standing in front of him to attention.

Renji rolled his eyes as he leant against the wall, this isn't really how he liked to spend his mornings; he could definitely think of better ways than listening to his disgruntled officers complain about him, though he had to at least give the guard some credit for saying it to his face unlike the rest of them who were too afraid to say 'boo' to him.

The doors slid open and the officer stepped to one side to let Renji pass. He slowly stood up straight and walked out without looking back as the doors slid shut again leaving him alone to get changed, he went back to his quarters which were now empty and changed quickly to meet his officers in the Senator's living quarters below considering that he was probably waiting for him now.

Renji walked in to the main living quarters of the senator his boots not making a sound over the luxurious cream carpet beneath his feet, his long crimson hair gone for now, as it wouldn't really go down too well and would probably draw too much attention to what he really was. He wore a different uniform than the other security officers, as though he had made it to suit his own tastes; he wore a long black coat open which flowed behind him when he walked, he didn't wear the white trousers but black with a white shirt.

The officer who had gone to fetch him this morning walked in with another from the adjoining room. He didn't looked at all impressed when he saw Renji stood before them as the Senator came out behind them. He was much older than they were; his face already showed deep lines of ageing and grey hair had already started to set in to the hard-faced politician; his dark plum robes draped over his suit.

"Renji!" The young girl shouted as she ran out from the room behind the senator, her long red hair flowing behind her as she ran over to him which contrasted against her blue school dress; she flung her arms around his waist hugging him tightly as she looked back at her father. "Morning."

Renji smiled down at her before he looked back over at her father who was watching them closely.

"Victoria you shouldn't be so familiar with the guards." Her father told her.

"I'm sorry Senator Kentaro; it's my fault for encouraging her." Renji told him.

"Yes indeed." Senator Kentaro agreed.

"Come on Renji, I've got a trip today remember; that's why I'm up early." Victoria told him letting go of him though started to tug on his arm wanting to leave already.

"I'll just be a minute, go on ahead." Renji told her.

She smiled up at him as she let go of his hand walking off, while Renji stayed behind knowing that the Senator would want a word with him like he did every morning before he left with his daughter; anyone would think that he was paranoid that something was going to happen to her.

"I want you to stay with her, don't let her out of your sight; if anything happens to her then it'll be on your head do you understand?" Senator Kentaro warned him.

"Of course sir, I wouldn't let anything happen to her." Renji assured him turning to leave.

"You say that, but considering the recent attacks do you think that you would be able to protect her?" The Senator asked him.

"If you didn't think I was capable you wouldn't have assigned me to protect her in the first place...sir." Renji answered before he turned to leave without being dismissed.

He walked out of the room turning to the left, he saw her stood waiting for him at the end of the corridor smiling at him; he smiled back at her. "Toria."

"Are we going?" Toria asked him smiling as she reached up to press the button on the small console next to the door which called for the lift, it was a little high for her so she had to stretch.

"Of course." Renji said as he stood next to her waiting for the lift.

The doors slide open and Toria ran inside, she turned around smiling up at Renji as he walked in and stood beside of her; she grabbed his hand and leant against him. It was quite an odd sight really, he didn't really look the type to have a child hanging all over him, but he really did adore her.

Renji looked down at her, it was so hard at times seeing her here and with them when he would rather take more drastic action than sitting around babysitting while there was a war going on off world.

"Come on..." Renji said stepping forward as the doors slide open, but they couldn't leave the lift because a young boy was stood in front of them blocking their way; he had short mousey brown hair and brown eyes and was wearing a school uniform that Renji hadn't seen before. "Are you going to move, so we can get past?"

"Um...yes sir...sorry..." The young boy said as he quickly stepped aside.

"What're you doing here, these are private quarters?" Renji asked him as he rounded on him, though Toria still had hold of his hand smiling at the boy who just looked at the pair of them with a stunned yet surprised speechless look upon his face; considering that they didn't look as though they belonged together but here they were.

"Well...um...um..." The boy said nervously trying not to look Renji in the eyes.

"Well, come on; speak up we haven't got all day." Renji prompted him. "I'm very busy, so if you don't tell me I'll have someone come down here and throw you in the cells until I've got time to deal with your childish antics."

"Right, yes sir...Ber...Bernal Hallefal." The boy answered.

Renji just stared at him, the name did in fact ring a bell; he was supposed to know it though he just couldn't put his finger on why he knew the name. Well considering that Renji couldn't remember who he was he waved his hand for him to continue telling him who he was in more detail.

"Oh right...yes...I was sent here for my experience?" Bernal explained quickly, though he could see that Renji still didn't know who he was. "All the students in my year are sent out on work experience."

"Really?" Renji said stepping around him with Toria in tow; Bernal on the other hand just stood there staring after the two of them. "If you want experience, standing there like a dummy isn't going to get you any where."

"Oh..." Bernal said and then quickly ran after them. "Sorry sir..."

"You're here to observe; that means you watch only." Renji told him. "Don't interfere with the Senator and his daughter; her."

"Yes sir." Bernal said.

"That's mean Renji." Toria said.

"That's my job." Renji told her, before he turned his attention back to Bernal who was now walking two steps behind them. "You will address me as 'Colonel Aba'rian' or 'sir' and this is 'Lady Victoria Kentaro'…"

"Toria…I like Toria; remember you said that it suits me." Toria said smiling at him.

"Fine, only when her father isn't around are you allowed to address her as Toria, when he is Lady Victoria or Lady Kentaro." Renji continued. "Unless otherwise instructed."

"Yes sir." Bernal said stopping as they came up to another door, but Renji and Toria carried on walking as the door slid open for them; he had to run again to catch up with the two of them. "Where are we going…sir?"

"School." Renji answered.

"I've got a school trip today, I'm going to the Magic War Museum." Toria told him.

"Oh yeah, I've been there with my school." Bernal said thoughtfully. "But I'm surprised that you're going, aren't you a little young?"

"That's what I said." Renji agreed irritably.

"Father said that it would be good for me." Toria said looking up at Renji, but she could see that he didn't agree; in fact he looked quite annoyed.

An awkward silence fell over them all as they walked over to the air car parked in front of the shutter, it was the only vehicle in the garage which was just for Renji's use only.

The long white corridors of the museum were almost empty except for the students in Toria's class, there were pictures of the battles spaced evenly on the walls throughout with voice communication boxes below them, so all you had to do was press them and it would tell you about the picture.

Renji watched them from the shadows after leaving Bernal to wait for him in the air car outside. Four girls walked in with Toria behind them, they were all human and like Toria came from important families on the planet.

"My daddy said they deserved what they got." The girl at the front told them. She had short blonde bobbed hair and had silver stud earrings.

"It isn't normal…I mean what they can do." The one on her left said, her hair was a couple of inches shorter than Toria's but she was a brunette.

"Well…" Toria started to say but she just couldn't bring herself to say what they expected her to say. "I have to go to the bathroom."

Toria rushed off before she could be stopped, or they could offer to go with her; Renji watched her run down the side corridor and waited until in was empty before he followed her. She stood at the end of the corridor in front of a large painting that covered the wall, it was of a battle in space over a beautiful blue, green and purple world; though the Magic ships which were defending it were all but destroyed.

"I don't know how you expect to keep your friends if you keep running away from them like that." Renji said as he stopped several feet away from her. He looked up at the painting knowing what it was of and how many Magics had lost their lives that day.

"Renji…" Toria said turning around to face him. "Are they really bad people?"

Renji couldn't answer her instead he turned to leave; she ran after him taking hold of his hand as she always did.

"I'm sorry." Toria said looking up at him.

"Why are you sorry?" Renji asked her without looking down at her.

"It's…father said they're the reason why mothers dead and that he nearly lost me…" Toria told him. "It makes me upset when I think about it, but you…"

Renji stopped her suddenly. "'I'm not a Ma…"

"But you know about them, you're not like the others when you talk about them." Toria told him.

"Toria…this isn't the place…" Renji told her looking around making sure that no one was listening to them.

"I'm sorry." Toria said pulling her hand out of his. "I'll see you later…back at home."

Renji couldn't stop himself; he hated to see her upset. "If you're good I'll tell you a story about them."

Toria turned around smiling at him excitedly. "Really?"

Renji nodded smiling back at her, how could he refuse her when she smiled at him like that?

The doors slid open to the lounge with the lights on dim, Renji beside the door stood to attention as the Senator and his guards walked in.

"Father!" Toria said excitedly as she put her homework down rushing over to him. "I thought you weren't coming home tonight?"

"My meeting was cancelled." Senator Kentaro told her simply. "So how did your trip go?"

"Well…um…" Toria said not really sure what to say to him, considering that she hadn't really enjoyed it much.

"Yes?" Senator Kentaro prompted.

Toria couldn't look him in the face and instead stared at his feet, she knew she couldn't tell him the truth because she would be in trouble.

"It's simple enough to understand, they're a plague that needs to be destroyed before they destroy us." Senator Kentaro told her as though he knew why she wasn't speaking. "They killed your mother and almost killed you, do you think that good people would do that?"

"No…" Toria said as tears started to well up.

Renji stepped in between the two of them. "Sir she's young, and doesn't fully understand everything…"

"That's why we have museums, to make them understand why we're at war." Senator Kentaro told him. "Go to your room Victoria."

Toria ran to her seat and grabbed her homework before she ran past them all and out of the room without looking back at them.

"Her imagination runs away with her, as you are fully aware; I want you to set her straight if she asks you about them." Senator Kentaro told him sternly. "I know that she listens to you."

"She's just a child." Renji said.

"That's my point, children can be swayed by the smallest thing." Senator Kentaro told him. "Yes it may seem wonderful to a child in a story that someone has special powers but in reality it's very different; those people are capable of anything and she needs to understand that before she gets hurt."

"I understand sir." Renji said standing to attention.

Senator Kentaro waved his hand at him as he stepped around him, Renji though turned around and waited until the Senator and his guards had left the room by the opposite entrance.

When they had finally left Renji turned and followed Toria out. He wondered if it was such a good idea to go and see if she was alright but his question was answered for him as he noticed the door to his right was open; he slowly walked over to the darkened room and leant on the door frame.

He could hear her crying inside the room even though he couldn't actually see her, but he knew where she was; he stood up and walked into the room around the long dining table and chairs.

The floor to ceiling curtains were closed which made the room even darker and cast shadows from the light that shone in from the hall; Renji pulled out the end chair and sat down.

"Toria…" Renji said softly.

The curtains opened suddenly and she ran out from behind them and flung her arms around Renji who pulled her up onto his lap. He pushed her hair out of her face and then held her as she cried into his chest.

"You know I hate it when you cry." Renji whispered.

"I'm sorry…I didn't mean…to get…you into trouble…" Toria said crying hard into his chest.

"Hey, come one now…look at me." Renji told her lifting her chin to look up at him. "You didn't get me into trouble."

"But…" Toria said.

Renji smiled at her. "You can still hear my stories, only if you promise not to tell anyone."

"Really?" Toria said sounding a little brighter and started to wipe the tears from her face.

The computer beeped loudly on the desk by the window where the curtains were drawn back letting the late afternoon light into the room, over the furniture; there was a long black jacket thrown over the back of the chair to the table by the door.

Hot steam filled the adjoining bedroom as the bathroom door opened, Renji walked out with a towel wrapped around his waist, his muscular torso covered in droplets and his long wet crimson hair stuck to it and his back.

He threw the towel in his hand on the edge of his bed when he heard the beeping from his computer and walked through past his full length mirror and the wardrobe which was wide open into the main lounge over to his desk; he walked round pulling the chair out as he pressed the silver button on the top left corner of the screen turning it on.

An older man appeared on the screen. He had dark eyes set in a stern face shaped by his dark shoulder length hair with part of it pulled back away from his face; he was dressed in the uniform of the Malarias Fleet, navy blue short jacket with a white stripe on his right shoulder to his waist on his left.

"Kasiya, what can I do for you today?" Renji said cheerfully leaning back in his chair, making it appear as though he was actually sat there talking to him naked.

Kasiya just stared at him, seemingly unimpressed by his manner and his appearance.

"I hope that you're not talking to me naked?" Kasiya asked him irritably.

"Don't worry you're not my type." Renji assured him smiling broadly. "I just got out the shower, that's all."

"I have an assignment for you." Kasiya told him.

"What about Toria?" Renji asked sounding a little worried. "I don't want to leave her here alone."

Kasiya didn't answer him straight away as though he was considering his request, though really he was studying Renji's reaction.

"Ichigo Illiania will be watching her while you're on assignment." Kasiya assured him. "After all this time, we're not going to leave her behind now."

"Right yeah…sorry…" Renji said distractedly; he knew that Kasiya knew the truth, well perhaps not all of it but enough to keep him there. It was still hard when given an order like this and he had to leave her behind as though he was abandoning her.

Kasiya pressed several buttons on his side of the screen. "I'm sending you the information; and Renji are you ready to tell me everything now?"

"There's nothing to say." Renji told him sitting up straight his whole manner changing seeming to become quite serious. "As soon as Ichigo arrives I'll leave."

"Good luck." Kasiya said before he logged off without pressing the matter further.

Renji just stared at the screen for a while, this was when he doubted himself if he was really doing the right thing by keeping everyone in the dark and the whole truth to the situation knowing that it was more serious than any of them could really understand.

Renji jumped suddenly when the door beeped, he had been lost in his own thoughts instead of concentrating on his surroundings. He stood up and walked over to the door. He pressed the square button on the door wall panel and it slid open, stood in front of him was the twelve year old Toria; her long red hair tied back in a pony tail dressed in her school uniform, white shirt blue over jacket and knee-length skirt and socks.

Toria looked Renji up and down and smiled at him. It wasn't very often that she got to see him like this not that she minded of course though her father would probably kill him; she knew that she had known him since she was four years old and for a long time he had been like a big brother that she had never had but he wasn't family and that wasn't how she really saw him either not that she would ever tell anyone or him of course.

"I was…um…just coming to tell you that I'm staying with Annyetta for a couple of nights." Toria told him.

"Oh, right…I'll tell Ichigo when he gets here." Renji told her going back into his quarters, knowing that she would follow him inside; which she did making sure that the door slid closed behind her after she had checked that no one had seen her enter his room. "I have to go away for a while, but he'll watch over you until I get back."

"So where are you going?" Toria asked him, even though she knew he wouldn't tell her anything since he never did when he disappeared like this.

"That's classified, sorry." Renji answered as he went through to his bedroom, picking up the towel off of his bed before he went back into the bathroom.

Toria just stood there staring after him, she didn't know what to say to him because this was quite normal by now him going off though he always came back; to her, well that's how she liked to look at it.

"Ok then, have a safe trip…and come back soon!" Toria shouted through before she turned around to leave.

The bathroom door shot open in the other room and Renji rushed out to her almost tripping over the towel still wrapped around his waist, Toria slowly turned around trying not to laugh at him and to keep a straight face.

"What sort of goodbye is that?" Renji demanded. "You could at least say it to my face."

Toria smiled slightly as she looked up at him. "See you soon." Then she turned around and walked out, leaving him alone staring after her this time.

"I wish you would as well." Renji whispered to himself before he turned back around to finish getting ready.

Chapter Two

The sun shone in to the classroom that slowly started to fill with just human students, who looked as though they came from the most noble houses on the planet; they made their way to their normal seats talking among themselves about all the exciting things that had happened to them over the weekend while Toria sat on her own at the back of the class next to the glazed black windows; they let light in but that was all they did because you couldn't see anything in or out of them.

At the front of the classroom behind the teacher's desk was a large computer screen that interacted with the computer on the teacher's desk and all the computers on each table; there was one computer per desk.

Every desk was taken in the class except one; Toria sat there knowing that no one would sit next to her, not that she was bothered of course because it was easier that way, at least she wouldn't have to pretend that she was one of them.

The bell rang throughout the school and the teacher walked in. She was in her mid thirties her black hair already starting to show the white though not in her features she still looked quite young; she wore a full length dark navy jacket with a white shirt and knee length blue skirt like the girls in the class.

The teacher wasn't alone though, there was a young girl with her; she had short bobbed dirty blonde hair all perfectly in place which framed her pretty face and set off her sparkling blue eyes.

Whispering broke out throughout the classroom. It had been a while since they had a new student and a girl as well; they of course all wanted to know who she was and who her father was as though to make friends with her only on the basis of stepping up on the social ladder of the inner senate court life.

"Right then class, I would like you to welcome our new student; Siren Napea." The teacher told them. "She has transferred from off world, after her father was posted here. I hope that you will all get along…but where to put you? Oh yes, there's a seat at the back of the class next to Miss Kentaro."

Siren seemed to look through everyone as she looked to the empty seat at the back and at Toria as though she was the only thing that she was looking at and Toria definitely didn't like the way that she was looking at her; Siren nodded to the teacher before she slowly walked to her new seat walking past the rest of the class ignoring them all before she pulled out her seat and sat next to Toria without saying a word to her.

Neither of them had never met before, though you would never be able to tell that by the atmosphere that was radiating from the two of them as though neither of them wanted to be near the other.

For the whole lesson neither of them even spoke to the other, when the bell rang they both stood to leave the class but before any of them could leave the rest of the girls had rushed over to talk with Siren; of course Toria wasn't really interested so she made her way past them all.

"Aren't you coming with us?" Reanne asked Toria as she stopped her before she could get too far; she had permed shoulder lengthy brown hair and wore diamond stud earrings.

"I have thing's to do, sorry." Toria said pulling her hand free quickly walking off before she could be stopped again.

"Don't mind her; she can be like that sometimes." Reanne said.

"Yeah we'll show you around." Charlie said sounding annoyed by Toria's behaviour as normal; she had layered hair which was a little darker than Reanne's. "She's not...well she's a little odd at times...today's one of those times so it's best that you stay clear."

Siren listened to everything that they said to her though she didn't show them any sign that she was overly interested only taking in it seemed what they were saying when really she was summing them all up to what they were really after; and then it came.

"So who's your father?" Fallon asked her trying to sound interested but not too over interested, as if she didn't want to give her the wrong idea about why she was asking; though everyone wanted to know. She had light brown hair tied back in a neat pony tail and dark black eyes that seemed somewhat eerie, as though there was something dark inside of her watching you.

"Who does he work for?" Sherika asked her, she was always interested in things like that as was her father who liked to know what type of people his daughter went to school with. Well this was where they made all of their future ties in life so the more important ties the better. Sherika had pale grey, long white hair which she always wore in a braid completely pulled back out of her face; even though she said that she was human there was a thing about the colour of her hair, but no one ever really questioned her.

"Does it matter who my father is?" Siren asked them.

They all looked at her unable to hide their surprise or rather shock that she would actually speak to them in such a manner and especially on her first day.

"I mean, do I have to tell you who my father is or can't you tell by my surname?" Siren asked them pleasantly enough, before she picked her school bag up off of her chair and made her way past them leaving them all quite speechless; not that she seemed to care.

Thick black smoke clung to the air surrounding the blown-out office buildings, adding perfect cover for those hiding in the remains waiting to strike again; the eerie abandoned city that was lost decades before still seemed to hold a battle field even today.

The tallest building to the north of the cities and the most damaged of all the buildings seemed to have most of the smoke surrounding as though it was covering the building itself; those inside had to cover their mouths so not to breath in the smoke and so that they wouldn't be identified if seen.

Renji sat on the window with a blaster rifle in hand and watching over the city below him, though he looked different to normal; he had his natural coloured hair and its full length pulled back in a pony tail and his clothes were different as well. He was wearing a dark burgundy vest and his torso and arms had what appeared to be tattoos but they were real, natural markings which showed his family statues and also how powerful he was.

"There aren't many left now." Renji informed his officers.

There were half a dozen other men in the room with him, all of them had similar markings and wore the same clothes but none of them had red hair like his. Three were sat on the boxes watching the computers on the make shift table they had erected out of the metals left behind in the room.

The other two were stood at the far window keeping an eye on below and the surrounding buildings, watching for the enemy not wanting them to get too close.

"They aren't the problem though, sir." The man stood at the door told him, he had black gelled hair stuck up in strikes. "We still haven't found the lab yet, and we've been here over a week; perhaps the intel was wrong."

"We'll stay another day, until they've finished scanning the whole place." Renji told him nodding towards the men at the computer and then smiled suddenly. "Or is it that you want to get back to your new wife Helrin?"

"Well there's that of course, but also we don't want to compromise our positions either by staying away too long." Helrin answered.

"Yes…I to want to get back to Toria…she seems to end up in a lot of trouble when ever I'm not around." Renji said turning around.

"She seems important to you." Helrin said.

"I'd hate to see anything happen to her." Renji told them.

Several hours later and still nothing had happened, Renji stood up and stretched his whole body feeling somewhat numb from sitting too long; and of course he wasn't really the type to just sit around doing nothing.

"Come on, we'll have another look around Helrin; Losun take over here." Renji told them striding over to the door where Helrin was stood."

"I thought you had gone to sleep there." Helrin said smirking at him.

"I think I would have, if I stayed there any longer." Renji said as they walked out of the room, he threw the strap of the blaster rifle over his shoulder and got his hand scanner out of the back pocket of his trousers; he pressed several buttons and it started to beep with seven dots on the screen signalling the position of him and his men in the building.

"Do you honestly think it's in here?" Helrin asked him.

"Well this was one of the places it was supposed to be, we've checked out two so far." Renji told him. "There's only this and one more place that it could be."

"I'd like to know how you know so much, about all of this." Helrin said watching his reaction.

"I've been around a very long time." Renji told him.

"How long, is a long time?" Helrin asked him.

"Before the empire fell." Renji answered as he took the lead not really wanting to get into the matter.

"No way...so you actually know what all this really looked like before." Helrin said somewhat surprised.

"I've never actually been here before." Renji told him.

"You don't actually act like you been around for hundreds of years." Helrin told him as Renji pushed open the door to his left and went inside the room.

The room was covered in dirt and dust of decades past. As he walked over the dust covered floor he made foot prints disturbing the particles; there were two large tables with computers on them and several piles of computer sheets with faded data upon them.

Renji picked up the first three sheets and started to scan through them hoping to find something important, while Helrin started to open the filing cabinets behind him; every drawer was filled with data, that they didn't really understand themselves but knew why this world had been destroyed.

"Why couldn't they just store them on a computer chip?" Helrin said irritably. "How the hell is someone supposed to use this?"

"Hopefully, the computer chips with all of this research should be in the volt also; all we have to do is find it." Renji said calmly, though that wasn't how he was really feeling; this wasn't really his type of mission. He preferred a bit more action.

It was as though they had sensed how he was feeling as blaster fire ripped through the building above them echoing throughout the empty corridors shaking dust off of the walls.

"Well it looks as though they got bored as well." Renji said.

"Are we going to give them a hand?" Helrin asked turning around, but he noticed that there was a small gap in the far wall where the dust fell through. "There's something there."

"Where?" Renji asked as he looked over at Helrin who was pointing at the wall facing them, he walked over to it and put his hand against it. "It's warm...perhaps..."

He put both hands against the wall and concentrated his inner energy and then directed it at the wall, for an instance it disappeared and they both saw another room; they both knew that there wasn't a door to it in the corridor so it had to be a hidden room perhaps the one that they had been looking for. Renji tried again, this time directing even more energy at it to dissolve the barrier; the wall faded away as though it had never been there in the first place revealing a brightly lit computer storage room.

This was the cleanest room in the building, probably in the whole city as though the war hadn't affected it at all; there was no damage to the walls, ceilings and most importantly the equipment that covered the walls. It was hard to image standing in this room that there was blaster fire several rooms down the corridor, with both sides after the information locked away in this room, for so long.

"Well, I think we might have found it." Renji said as he stepped inside the room closely followed by Helrin. "Right we need to find the data chips."

Renji went to the left side of the room and activated the computer wall console; the lights lit up and showed him a map of the data storage room he was in along with information of what was stored in the buffers.

"This is it, get a copy"? Renji told him as he carried on reading through the open files as if he was actually looking for something for himself. He scanned through a couple of dozen quickly but his mood quickly changed to frustration again when he couldn't find what he was looking for. "Damn it!" Renji shouted hitting the console making the lights flicker somewhat from the force of his punch.

"What's wrong?" Helrin asked somewhat surprised by Renji's sudden change in behaviour.

"It isn't here…it was supposed to be here…" Renji told him. "A way to bring her back to me…"

"What? Bring who back?" Helrin asked now completely confused.

"Just get the copy!" Renji ordered turning around pulling his blaster rifle off and readying his weapon; he pressed the small button on the under side of the rifle. "We're moving out, we'll meet you back at the shuttle."

"Yes sir." A man replied through the com, along with several blaster shots. "We'll be back in five, sir."

"Renji out." He told them pushing the button, before he turned back to Helrin. "Have you got it all?"

"Almost?" Helrin answered. "Renji…what was it, you thought was here?"

"It doesn't matter now." Renji answered irritably, but he also sounded disappointed at the same time as though all his hopes had been on this mission and now they were dashed just like that.

"There are still hundreds of files, whatever it is could still be here." Helrin reassured him.

"We need to move out, they're moving in on our position." Renji told him.

Helrin pressed several buttons on the flat screen built into the table surface, and then two computer chips ejected from the compartments just above it; he grabbed them both and put one in his trouser pocket and handed the other over to Renji.

"Just in case the council isn't quick enough for you mate." Helrin told him as Renji looked down at it before he put his in his pocket. "Whatever it is, it seems pretty important to you…if you find it let me know."

Renji nodded as he turned to leave the lab, Helrin closed the door not wanting it to be found again. They held their weapons ready as they quietly left the room, not wanting to give away their positions but they were ready if there was a fire fight to get out of the building; he tried to concentrate imaging himself back at the shuttle but nothing happened he just stayed where he was.

"They've put up a shield, I can't transport out of here." Renji said. "We'll have to do this the hard way it seems, good job I'm in a bad mood."

"Good thing for us, but not so much for them." Helrin agreed.

They made their way along the dimly lit corridor, their blasters out in front of them and their scanners only showing them on this level though they both knew that they weren't alone in the building; then just as Renji turned the corner his screen flashed and started to fade until it completely blacked out.

"My scanners gone dead, they're sending out more than just the shield…but this way they might not be able to pick us up either." Renji said thoughtfully as he carried on down the corridor.

He could see the open door to the stair well, three doors away; though now that he was there he wasn't so sure that it was such a good idea knowing that it would be covered but it was also the only way out at the moment.

Helrin followed back to back, walking backwards bring up their rear; he wasn't going to let anyone get past him he had someone waiting for him back home. Renji reached forward and slowly opened the door his blaster in front, his finger on the trigger ready to fire at any sign of moment; and there it was a man moved slightly just below the railings. Renji opened fire not giving him a chance, he positioned himself behind the wall with the gap of the door open enough so that he could fire through it and still see the men on the stairs; while Helrin stood behind the door.

"On my mark." Renji told him. "One…two…go!?

Renji went through first firing down the stairs while Helrin shot up the stairs at the men marking them from the floor above. Renji pushed forward firing at the men before him as they carefully tried to step backwards down the stairs and return fire, but of course were not doing such a good job unlike Renji and Helrin.

Toria stumbled backwards out of breath pulling her school jacket off and throwing it behind her, not seeming to care what happened to it; though an upper classman caught it and stood on his own. He was tall for his age, taller than the other students stood around watching; he had short blonde hair and black markings down the left side of his face though he seemed quite amused by the two girls fighting before him.

Siren swung the practice sword above her head before she brought it down on Toria who blocked it with her right arm kicking her in the chest simultaneously knocking the wind out of her; the girls stood against the far wall behind Siren and screamed as they watched their classmates fight one another before their very eyes. The boys on the other hand were jeering them on as though they thought watching two girls fight was actually exciting.

"What the hell is your problem?" Toria demanded as she dodged another swing. She knew she had to concentrate because Siren wasn't like the rest of them she could really fight; and this was their second time at it and like the first it didn't seem as though it was going to end any time soon.

Siren swung at her again but this time she turned around moving towards Toria from the other side and grabbed hold of her, pulling her close.

"You're my problem." Siren answered before she kneed her in the chest.

Toria felt her whole chest contract as she made contact with her, it was as though she was training back home with Renji or one of the guards not with a girl her own age and size; she didn't have time to think of the reason why she didn't like her at the moment she had to concentrate on beating her somehow.

Toria blocked another hit, but this time she grabbed the training sword with both hands and pulled it out of Siren's hand; Siren stepped back as Toria brought the sword down on her this time and it seemed as though Toria was just as good as she was.

The students just watched the two of them not seeming to know what to do and surprised that these two young ladies knew how to fight so well, though every time one of them was hit the girls screamed as though every hit was a serious blow.

"What on earth?!" A woman said behind them her hands on her hips below her open jacket, her light greying hair pulled back out of her face somewhat astray as though she had ran down here after hearing what was going on.

They both stopped suddenly staring at each other and then turned around to face the woman; she didn't look at all pleased with either of them.

"Well...I never...in all of my years teaching, have I ever seen such un-lady like behaviour." She told them somewhat speechless, finding it hard to find the right words for them. "My office, right now; both of you. I'm going to call both of your parents??

"My father is off world until the end of the week." Toria told her calmly as she walked over to the lad holding her jacket.

"Well...um...I'll contact whoever is in charge of your care in his absence." She told her, making it clear that she wasn't going to get away with it all because her father wasn't here.

"Why don't you come try out for the club?" The lad told Toria, ignoring the teacher.

"Kyo!" The woman shouted sternly at him.

"Thanks." Toria said smiling shyly, but it didn't last for long as Siren grabbed hold of her arm and dragged her along towards the teacher. "I can walk on my own thank you."

"Well it didn't seem as though you could.' Siren said letting go of her suddenly after pushing her towards the teacher. "I apologies Miss Ricsan."

"That isn't enough, my office now...both of you quickly." Miss Ricsan told them.

They both glared at one another before they stepped around her and walked off towards her office, Toria still held her jacket in her hand not bothering to put it back on; Miss Ricsan slowly turned around and followed them both down the corridor with students staring and whispering about them both. They finally stopped outside her office and waited for her to tell them to go inside.

"Put your jacket on, and tidy yourselves up." Miss Ricsan told them. "Go inside and wait quietly while I contact your parents and guardians. Really...unbelievable..."

Toria and Siren watched her walk off before they both went inside, Toria started to put her jacket on as Siren closed the door behind them.

"This is your entire fault you know." Siren told her.

"What! You started it, again." Toria told her not finishing fastening her jacket as she stepped closer. "I don't get it, what's your problem?"

"I told you, it's you." Siren told her.

"I don't get it, I don't even know you…" Toria told her.

"It's what you stand for, you and your father." Siren told her.

Toria didn't seemed to understand at first and then she suddenly punched her in the face surprising them both, but even more so when Siren changed suddenly and blue and green markings suddenly appeared on the left side of her face, neck and leg.

"What do you think you're doing?" Siren demanded as she tried to change back to her human form. "How dare you!"

"What about you; just judging me, thinking that I'm one of them." Toria shot at her. "I have nothing against Magics…even though they killed my mother…I…I…still think it's wrong what they've done to you."

Siren just stood there, she didn't seem to know what to say to her; she hadn't been expecting such a reply nor did she know about her mother.

Toria turned around suddenly and pulled the chair out behind her and sat down, while Siren just stared at her before she too walked over to the other chair and sat down beside her.

"How…how can you think like that after what they did?" Siren asked her. "I lost my parents to the Malanas Fleet and I hate them all, for what they've done to us for all of these…I don't understand how you can be so forgiving?"

"What about those who took you in afterwards, they're not Magics?" Toria asked her.

"They're different." Siren said stubbornly.

"Perhaps…it's the same with me…perhaps I met one…" Toria told her, but looked somewhat saddened by it. "Perhaps he's really nice to me…perhaps he changed how I would feel about them…"

The door burst open behind them before either of them could speak startling them both, Renji stood in the doorway with his jacket in his hand and slightly red in the face; Miss Ricsan stood a little behind him as though she was too afraid to get any closer.

"What do you think you're doing, I'm away for two weeks…just two weeks and you end up in a fight!" Renji shouted at her as he marched into the office towering over the two girls.

"I'm sorry…" Toria started but he cut her off before she could finish.

"No, sorry doesn't cut it this time." Renji shouted at her.

"But…" Toria tried again.

"No!" Renji shouted at her. "I don't want to hear it. Come along, I'll deal with you at home."

"Can we at least drop Siren off at home?" Toria asked, knowing that she was risking a lot by asking a favour especially while she was in so much trouble already.

"What?" Renji said even more angry, now that she thought that she could still get away with asking something of him after what she had done. "Who?"

"It doesn't matter, I mean if it's too much trouble." Siren said quietly behind Toria.

Renji looked between the two girls, his temper seeming to fade somewhat as confusion set in instead.

"Wait a minute…" Renji said. "Weren't you the one who was found fighting with her?"

"Yes." Siren answered.

"We've just solved things now." Toria told him brightly.

"That's nice, fine." Renji said turning to leave. "Just once, just once would I like a peaceful day…remember that won't you?"

"Course." Toria answered as she stood up and grabbed Siren's hand leading her out of the room, passing their teacher who seemed quite speechless seeing the two girls seemingly getting along now.

Renji dropped Siren off and then took them back home, but neither of them spoke the whole time; nor did they when they got back into the apartment. In fact Renji left her and went straight to his quarters. He threw his jacket over the back of the chair and then carefully pulled his top off over his head and then dropped it on the floor revealing his torso which was bandaged and bruised. He sat down or rather flopped down on the sofa just as his door beeped though he knew who it was and didn't bother answering knowing that she would just come in on her own.

The door opened slowly and Toria popped her head around to see if it was clear to come inside. She saw him sat on the sofa and went in further; she stopped suddenly when she saw the bandages and how bruised he was before she rushed over to his side.

"Are you alright? I'm sorry that you got dragged to school as soon as you returned." Toria told him as she knelt on the sofa beside him. "Can I get you anything? Are you in pain?"

Renji smiled slightly at her, but she just looked at him worriedly; he put his arm around her and pulled her into his chest even though she tried to pull away from him.

"Just for a moment." Renji told her and with that she stopped struggling and softly rested against him not wanting to hurt him.

"Didn't your mission go well.?" Toria asked him.

"What makes you think that?" Renji asked a little surprised by the question.

"It isn't often that you get injured." Toria answered looking up at him, concern showing on her face.

"This isn't much; it's nothing compared to some of the injuries that I've had in the past." Renji assured her.

"You're lying." Toria said sitting up and poked him in the chest over his bandage.

"Aww…hay!" Renji shouted. "At least be a little more gentle will you?"

Toria leant back against the sofa away from him. "What if something happened to you…and I was left here alone?"

Renji was quite surprised by the question, as it seemed so was Toria; she hadn't really meant to say it out loud and suddenly jumped to her feet off the sofa.

"I'm sorry…I didn't mean…um…" Toria said nervously backing away from him as he tried to stop her. "You should rest…yes…um rest…I'll um…get us something to eat…"

Toria turned around and ran out of the room, leaving Renji to stare after her; but after the door had closed behind her he pulled out the data chip from his pocket.

"I would never leave you behind." Renji promised.

Siren and Toria walked down the corridor side by side, only the day after they were fighting one another and now it seemed as though nothing at all had happened; they both seemed quite a bit alike, meaning that they didn't really get along with the rest of the upstart students who thought that they were better than the rest of the galaxy all because they supposedly came from noble and aristocratic families.

"Did you get into a lot of trouble?" Toria asked her.

"Well, kind of…but not as much as I thought I would." Siren told her.

"What are you two best friends now, or something?" Kyo asked behind them, startling them both somewhat.

"Best friends is going a little too far, don't you think?" Siren said.

"She means, to begin with we're just acquaintances." Toria told him.

"Right…" Kyo said shaking his head smiling at the two of them as they carried on walking up the corridor though with him in the middle this time.

"Don't you care what people think of you?" Siren asked him suddenly.

"Hay!" Toria shouted at her.

Kyo just laughed at the two of them and carried on walking without answering her question, but in fact he had done.

"Come check out my club later right?" Kyo asked them both as he stopped turning around to face them. "At least then the two of you can fight as much as you want and you won't get into trouble for it."

"Well…I don't know if I would be allowed." Toria said nervously.

"What?" Siren said grabbing hold of her as she turned her around to face her. "Then how the hell do you know how to fight?"

"Well…um…that…well, I'll probably get into trouble for that when my father gets back…" Toria said avoiding eye contact with her. "As will…Renji…"

"Renji? Who's Renji?" Siren asked not sure what was going on.

"That guy who came to get me." Toria answered. "He's head of security at my place…and has been my personal bodyguard since I was four years old."

"No wonder you were so good." Siren said. "Being taught by that guy…if you didn't pick up what he was teaching you, he'd probably be quite scary."

Toria smiled brightly. "I guess he can come off like that, but really…he's lovely…"

Kyo started to walk off as the bell rang for the start of classes. "I'll see you later, stay out of trouble."

Toria waved at him. "See you later."

While Siren grabbed hold of her and pulled her along to class, also not wanting to be late but she also didn't want to end the conversation just yet.

"We're going to be late." Siren told her. "So this security guy?"

"Renji?" Toria said smiling, which Siren picked up on straight away.

"Yeah, Renji; do you think that I could train with the two of you?" Siren asked.

"I don't know...but, I guess I can ask him tonight." Toria said thoughtfully, though she wasn't to sure because he was unsure about training her sometimes and if there were two of them; but she would still ask him.

"Great." Siren said as she carried on leading Toria down the corridor towards their classroom receiving a few strange looks from the students who were watching them yesterday, then it suddenly dawned on her why they were staring and she let go of Toria's hand; Toria though just laughed and linked her arm.

"I thought you were like me, and didn't care about what others thought." Toria told her.

"That...that isn't the point....we shouldn't be walking like this..." Siren told her as she tried to pull her arm free, but Toria wasn't going to let her go. "Damn it already."

"You're losing your composure." Toria said smirking at her, which made her stop struggling suddenly.

As they both walked into the class room together, Toria still linking Siren's arm everyone stopped talking and looked over at them; of course by everyone's reaction and what had happened the day before no one had actually expected them to come in today as though they were best friends and as though nothing at all had happened.

"How's that for an entrance?" Toria whispered.

"You did that on purpose." Siren answered.

"This way's better, than them thinking that we're at each others throats." Toria told her letting go of her finally, so that they could walk to the back of the classroom between the tables; though as soon as they both got past the first table everyone started to talk again.

Toria smiled slightly to herself as she pulled back her chair and sat down next to the very ruffled Siren, who wasn't as pleased by everyone's reaction.

"Stop grumbling." Toria told her.

"You did it on purpose." Siren repeated.

"Get over it." Toria told her.

"I haven't even decided if we're friends yet." Siren whispered as the teacher walked into the classroom, and the rest of the students quietened down; but the teacher herself stopped suddenly and looked over at them both looking somewhat worried having them seated next to each other.

"Is it me or is she looking just at us?" Toria whispered leaning slightly over to her.

"No she is." Siren answered without moving her lips.

"Well...um...yes..." The teacher said distractedly as she tried to begin the lesson.

The entrance hall of the apartment was empty as Toria walked inside alone and pulled the hair pin out letting her long hair flow down her back; the walls were a soft lemon with large mirrors on both sides set above entrance tables against the walls, with elegant vases and sprays of flowers that could only be found off world in shades of blue, yellow and green.

Toria ran past the mirrors because she didn't like them and around the corner, right into something solid which groaned loudly as arms wrapped around her so that she wouldn't fall backwards.

"What have I told you about running?" Renji asked her as she looked up at him blushing deeply. "And right into me as well…how do you expect me to get better?"

"I'm sorry." Toria said as she tried to move away from him but he wouldn't let her go. This seemed to make her go even more red if it was even possible but there was something else; she could feel herself actually burning up from the inside as though her whole body was reacting to him.

Toria didn't know why, she just knew that she had to get away from him, she pushed him as hard as she could into his chest almost stumbling backwards as he let go of her groaning loudly once more; she didn't even look up at him as she ran around him as he tried to stop her wondering what had gotten into her all of a sudden.

"Toria wait!" Renji shouted after her, but she didn't stop.

Toria ran down the hall and pushed past one of the other security officers, not stopping to see who it was; she just had to get away from everyone. She locked her door behind her breathing deeply as she dropped her bag on the floor beside the chest of drawers and unfastened her jacket pulling it off quickly dropping to her knees as this hot wave washed over as though it was trying to consume her.

Renji calmly followed her but was soon stopped by Bernal, straightening his uniform.

"Did you see her, she just pushed me right out of the way and into her room." Bernal told him. "Has she had another fight?"

"No I don't think so." Renji said thoughtfully. "I'll deal with this; why don't you sort out the arrangements for this weekend."

"Yes sir." Bernal said standing to attention before he bowed his head slightly and walked around him.

Renji walked over to Toria's door and beeped her, but there was no answer so he tried it again.

"Toria! Open the door." Renji shouted through to her, but there was still no answer. "Toria, if you don't open the door; I'll open it myself."

"Go away!" Toria shouted through.

Renji just stared at the door. He had no idea what was going on she was fine a couple of minutes ago and she had never behaved like this before towards him; well not here anyway.

"Toria…I'm coming in." Renji told her as he pressed the door console but it just beeped at him, which told him that she had locked the door. "Toria!"

"Go away!" Toria shouted back as she looked over her shoulder at the door and pushed herself up, she struggled over to the door and put her hand on the door console which just melted at her touch; she pulled her hand away when she smelt the burning stepping back looking from the console to her hand.

Toria had no idea what was happening to her, she only knew that it hurt; her whole body seemed to be burning from the inside out, never had she felt such pain before. She somehow managed to strip off as she walked through to her bathroom and carefully turned the cold water on for the shower as she stepped underneath, but as the cold water hit her body steam erupted filling the room making it seem even warmer than it already was.

Renji was still trying to unlock the door when he heard the shower going in her room; he stopped what he was doing and rested his head against her door as if he suddenly realized what was wrong.

"I'm sorry." Renji whispered.

Toria stood in the shower for nearly an hour before it finally felt as though the cold water was having an effect on her. It went as suddenly as it had came; and now she was freezing suddenly from the water. She quickly turned the water off as she stepped out of the shower pushed the door out and grabbed her lilac bathrobe wrapping it around her tightly before she grabbed the nearest towel off of the rack beside the sink and wrapped her wet hair up in it.

As Toria walked past her foggy mirror she saw a shadow move in it behind her, she spun around but there was no one there so she grabbed another towel and wiped the dew off the mirror so that she could see through it clearly but there was nothing there now; she shook herself and went back through to her bedroom closing the door behind her, thinking that she really did hate mirrors.

She picked up her uniform off the floor and put it over the arched chair in the corner of her room which had a small side table with a lamp and several data pads on it, she slowly turned around and went over to her bed falling forward onto it before she crawled up to the top pulling the fur throw around her and bringing her feet up making sure that they were properly covered and closed her eyes wondering what was wrong with her.

…Half a dozen small fires suddenly sprung up around her, people started to scream behind; she looked over her shoulder as the officers stepped back away from her as though they were afraid of her. They were all wearing bluish jumpsuit uniforms and looked about six years older than she was, or so she thought as she caught a glimpse of herself in the reflection of the computer console; she looked about the same age as they were.

Her long reddish hair was tied back into two buns one slightly higher then the other, she was also wearing the jumpsuit which she was sure that she hadn't seen before but also at the same time felt as though she had.

Toria didn't know what to do as she stepped back herself not wanting to be too close to the fires, but there was someone behind her now holding her so that she couldn't move away. But with just his touch the fires seemed to get worst, but he still wouldn't let her move away from him or from the fires themselves.

Toria tried to look behind her at the person who was holding her but she couldn't see his face as though he was blurred out somehow, the only thing that she could make out is that he had long crimson hair tied back in a pony and his uniform was different to hers; he had a white top with a dark blue almost black jacket which fastened on the left side of his waist and the same coloured cargo trousers.

"Put it out." He told her tightening his grip.

"Let me go…I can't…" Toria told him.

"I won't let you go until you've put all the fires out." He told her as he pulled her closer into him so that she was pressed right against his chest.

Toria didn't understand this feeling, she knew who he was somehow and that she could trust him; his presence felt calming but also somehow overwhelming as though he was clouding her senses. It only seemed like a moment but she had lost her concentration on the fires which seemed to be dieing out until they were both suddenly engulfed by the flames; she could hear screaming behind her knowing that she should be screaming as well, why couldn't she hear herself screaming?...

Renji sat at the security desk with his feet up on the table, watching the security monitors in the small dimly lit room with Bernal sat beside of him looking over at him every so often.

"What?" Renji asked his annoyance sounding in his voice and showing on his face.

"Well, do you honestly think it's such a good idea to just leave her in there?" Bernal asked him finally.

"She'll come out when she's ready." Renji told him.

"But she's missing school." Bernal protested.

"I contacted them; I told them she wasn't feeling well." Renji told him as though this settled the matter.

"But…" Bernal tried.

"But nothing, she'll be fine." Renji told him taking his feet down to stand up and towered over him; he turned to leave with his jacket flapping behind him.

He walked out of the office and along the hall, there was no one else around because they were all off world with the Senator who hadn't contacted them once to ask how Toria was though that wasn't really anything new; he often went away for weeks on end without contacting her, but everyone still thought of him as the loving father, if only they knew the truth.

Renji just walked not realizing where he was going until he finally stopped outside of her bedroom. He found himself just standing there looking at the door hating being locked out of her life like this, that she wouldn't let him in to help her.

Toria was pacing back and forth in front of her bedroom door, her long hair down and almost to her waist line; she was wearing a knee length plain brown skirt with a matching waistcoat top and nothing on her feet. She still felt uneasy about what had happened to her the night before and also the dream afterwards, she didn't know what it meant or even if it was actually her; for now though she would just pass it off as a stray dream and that she wasn't feeling well.

Every so often she would stop and look at the door, she knew that she had to contact him so that he could get her out but she was worried at the same time because she didn't want anyone knowing what she had done; but the choice was made for her when the door beeped suddenly making her jump.

Toria looked at the door console knowing that she had to answer. "Yes."

"Toria?" Renji said sounding a little unsure.

"Renji…um…well…the lock…um…it's broke." Toria told him nervously.

"How did you break the lock?" Renji asked and then paused for a moment. "It doesn't matter, give me a couple of minutes."

Toria stood there waiting for him, wondering how he was going to open the door when she heard something hit the door outside of her room making her jump again; she saw something in-between the crack pushing it open wider and wider until finally she could see his face as Renji lowered the crowbar pushing himself in-between the opening and using his own body to open the rest of the door. Toria though ran at him flinging her arms around him before he had finished surprising him somewhat.

"I'm sorry…I…um…wasn't feeling well." Toria told him looking up and blushing slightly.

Renji smiled at her as he made his way into her room, she let go of him as he looked over the wall console which she had somehow melted.

"I'll replace that, so it'll be as good as new." Renji told her. "I already rang the school and told them that you weren't feeling well."

"Thank you." Toria said a little uneasy waiting for him to ask her about the console but he didn't, he left her and a couple of minutes later he returned with a tool box from the security office. "I'm sorry."

"What for?" Renji asked her as he knelt down opening the box.

Toria looked at him and then turned around and went over to her corner chair and sat down, she watched him replace the console wondering all the time if she should actually say something about what had happened; but instead she just shook her head telling herself that she had already decided that it was nothing. She just wasn't feeling well that's all it was, all it could be.

The classroom was slowly filling with students all talking excitedly about the weekend, well all those who were actually attending that was.

"I got a new dress." Reanne said excitedly.

"I know daddy said that he'd buy me what ever I wanted." Fallon said

Siren looked up at the girls talking, finding herself hoping that Toria would come in soon so that she wouldn't be on her own and so that they wouldn't come over to her so she had to pretend again that she was actually interested in what they were talking about.

"Toria what are you wearing?" Charlie asked her

"I bet your father got you what ever you wanted." Reanne said smiling.

"Of course he did." Toria answered as she walked into the classroom, her long hair down with the front parts tied back out of her face; she moved quickly past them all trying to get to her table but a lad stopped her.

He was the same height as she was and had blondish hair and green eyes. She tried to step around him but he put his leg up resting his foot on the opposite table so that she couldn't pass, his friends thought it was quite funny stood around them watching.

"What do you want?" Toria asked as politely as she could, even though she actually wanted to push him off of the table for stopping her.

"Saturday night, how about you go with me." He told her.

"I'm already going with someone, and she's a lot prettier than you are." Toria told him as she smiled slightly pushing his foot off of the table, while he just sat there speechless.

Toria walked over to her table and sat down beside of Siren, who was actually waiting to find out who she was actually going with.

"Well?" Siren prompted her.

"Well what?" Toria asked.

"Who are you going with?" Siren asked her. "And why did you say she?"

"Because she, is a she; Lady Annyetta." Toria answered smiling. "I've known her for a couple of years now, but she goes to a different school. She's actually really nice, though you would never guess that she was actually the same age as us because she acts really grown up all the time."

"You mean, compared to you." Siren corrected.

"No, I mean she acts really grown up; as though she really is an adult trapped inside a body of a child." Toria told her and then thought for a moment. "She doesn't even look the same age either sometimes, because of the clothes that she wears…what's the saying? She never just lets her hair down, and has fun."

"Unlike you who can have it at a drop of a hat?" Siren teased while still trying to look serious.

"So who are you going with?" Toria asked her changing the subject.

"My youngest brother Marcus, he's an officer so he said that he'll take me with him." Siren told her.

Toria sat there for a moment as though deep in thought before she spoke again. "I'll get Renji to pick you up on our way." Toria told her. "And I'll try and remember to ask him tonight about the training thing as well, considering that I forgot with not feeling well the other night."

"So what was actually wrong with you then?" Siren asked her.

"Truthfully I don't know." Toria answered while she fidgeted with her fingers and avoided eye contact with her.

"What's that supposed to mean?" Siren asked.

"Just what I said…I don't know…I…" Toria tried to explain. "I…I felt really warm…though I guess it was more than just that…it was more like burning, from the inside out…"

Siren just looked at her; she didn't seem to understand either from that short and strange description.

"It started when I was with Renji, but I've never felt like that before." Toria told her. "Yeah I get warm sometimes when I'm around him but that's because I get embarrassed sometimes…"

"You like him." Siren said bluntly.

"What? Well…yeah…I've known him along time; he's well kind of like a brother I guess." Toria told her trying to sound dismissive as though the whole thing didn't mean anything.

"No, I mean you like him." Siren said.

Toria pouted, as though given into her figuring it out. "It doesn't matter anyway, he's my bodyguard…my father's security officer…and I'm the little girl he's assigned to look after."

"If you say so." Siren said just as dismissively. "So fine; he's like a brother then."

"Right." Toria agreed nodding slightly.

Chapter Three

Light shun into Renji's dully lit living room though it wasn't a bright light considering the time of day, as it looked as though storm clouds were moving in over the city for a late afternoon shower; which was quite out of season but added to the mood that was consuming the planet at the moment.

Renji was sat at his desk going through the files he downloaded off of his last mission though his mood seemed to be changing like the weather outside was, as he flicked through yet another file. Then his computer beeped signalling that he had an incoming call interrupting his work; he pressed the flashing button on the screen making the files disappear and Kasiya appear on the screen in place of them.

"That was quicker than normal, were you sat waiting here?" Kasiya asked him.

"Well you said not to go far." Renji said dismissively.

Kasiya just looked at him as though he was up to something.

"Well? The confirmation for tonight?" Renji asked him.

"The target is confirmed." Kasiya told him. "Ichigo will meet you there when you arrive."

"Of course and yourself?" Renji said.

"I'll make contact with you before they make their move." Kasiya told him and then seemed to add as an afterthought. "Our scientists are going through the data files that you brought back, hopefully they'll be able to fine something of use."

"Do you honestly believe that?" Renji asked him.

"One has to believe, or one will lose hope." Kasiya answered.

Three security officers walked into the apartment lead by a very disgruntled young man with his hair gelled back into place; the other two were older than him and wore their helmets with the black visor down so that you couldn't see their faces.

"I'll go and find her for you sir, and reprimand Aba'rian for not bringing her to meet you." He told the Senator who walked in slowly behind them, followed by another two guards.

"She was probably out with her friends, choosing a dress for this evening." Senator Kentaro told him calmly.

"I doubt that." He mumbled to himself so that he wouldn't be heard and walked on ahead of them, but he hadn't gone three paces when Renji appeared at the end of the hallway.

"Good afternoon Senator." Renji said bowing his head slightly. "I apologise that we didn't meet you, but Toria was helping Lady Annyetta over with her belongings."

"You should have informed us that you changed the schedule." The security officer told him.

41

"You're right Leshato, but I was too concerned with the security and safety of Toria and Lady Annyetta." Renji told him. "I doubt that the Senator would want anything to happen to his daughter and the daughter of Lord Kitack while in his care."

"Quite right." Senator Kentaro said as he carried on walking with the other officers.

Renji stepped aside for him but Leshato stood his ground as though he was ready to pick a fight with him, until Renji grabbed hold of him suddenly pulling him out of the way as Toria suddenly ran around the corner and stopped in front of them smiling.

"Father, I'm sorry that I didn't come and meet you." Toria told him. "Annyetta's staying so I was helping…"

"That's alright, as long as you're alright that is all what matters to me." Senator Kentaro told her smiling slightly.

Toria smiled back at him as she stepped aside so that the security officers could go inside and so that she could walk by his side.

"So did anything interesting happen while I was away?" Senator Kentaro asked her.

"Yes, we got a new student; she's really nice." Toria told him as they went inside the apartment. "She's coming with us tonight as well with her brother…"

Leshato waited behind so that he could talk with Renji, who seemed to know what he wanted so also stayed behind even though he still had important things to attend to before tonight's grand party begun.

"Your behaviour towards Lady Victoria disgusts me." Leshato told him. "It always has done."

"I don't know what you're talking about." Renji said turning to leave, this really isn't a topic that he wanted to get into but Leshato stopped him as it seemed it was a topic he finally wanted to discus himself.

"I think you do." Leshato said. "She's a child and you're leading her on."

"I know she's a child." Renji told him walking off but Leshato followed him still.

"Her father has plans for her, and you defiantly don't come into them like that." Leshato told him.

"Really, and what would you know about his plans for her?" Renji asked him as he stopped and turned around to face him but he only smirked at him and begun to walk around him; Renji though grabbed hold of him and forced him up against the wall. "If you know anything I suggest that you hand over the information quietly, or believe me, when I'm finished with you; you'll beg me to finish you off quickly."

"Please…" Leshato said nervously even though he tried to hide it, his shaky voice unable to hide how he truly felt; he tried to push Renji away from him but of course Renji was much stronger than he was even though Renji was far older.

"She is mine…mine to protect, if any harm befalls her you will be the one who pays the price." Renji warned him as he let go of him and walked off as though nothing had happened between them.

Senator Kentaro's security officers stood on either side of the living room door in full uniform along with their helmets covering their faces, while Toria twirled around in front of Renji showing him what she was wearing; she had part of her hair up pinned with jewels and wore a one piece strapless trouser suit in midnight blue that almost looked as though it was a dress because there was so much fabric to the trousers.

"What do you think?" Toria asked him as she finally stopped twirling in front of him smiling.

"You look lovely." Renji told her.

"I'm sure the fine young men attending tonight will think the same thing as well." Senator Kentaro said stood at the entrance.

Toria wasn't the only young girl in the room, sat calmly watching the screen was a beautiful young lady in a flowing red and purple dress; her long purplish hair tied back in curls flowing down her back.

"Lady Toria you look lovely like Colonel Aba'rian said." Annyetta said smiling kindly at her.

"Though not as nice as you Annyetta." Toria told her smiling as she walked over and held out her hand for her. "Shall we go?"

Annyetta took her hand gently and stood, Toria lead them out of the room with Renji behind her watching the whole scene with a disapproving look upon his face.

"I don't understand those two." Bernal whispered beside of him as he quickly took his place.

"Um…" Renji said seeming to agree with him.

The air car flew through the traffic with ease as the air lanes started to become more crowded above them, though they were in the State Lanes which was only reserved for high official personnel. This particular air car had three compartments, the front for the driver and the security officers the middle for the senator and his aids and the back for his guests; tonight for Toria and her friends.

Toria sat with Annyetta and Renji on either side of her with Siren on the facing seat with her brother. Siren had her blond hair down as usual and wore a pale forget-me-not blue sleeveless dress to her knees with matching flat shoes.

Siren's brother sat beside of her very stiffly in his dress uniform, a black jacket with double red stripe down the arms signifying his command position; he was very handsome with short style sandy coloured hair and blue eyes, at least twelve years older than Siren was.

"So which unit are you assigned to?" Renji asked him.

"I'm with General Yang'erdart's regiment." Marcus told him.

"So you must be on leave, I mean considering how far the system is from here; isn't it a two week journey just to travel from here to there?" Renji asked him.

"Yes it is, it seems that you're very well informed about these matters." Marcus said watching his reaction very carefully but he never gave anything away.

"I may be a senate guard but I am also an officer in the Malarias Fleet" Renji told him. "This isn't my first posting."

"Really, so to which unit were you assigned?" Marcus asked him.

"The Burning Nastur." Renji said half lying.

"How interesting. It was destroyed along with several Magical ships." Marcus said thoughtfully. "Wasn't that about nine years ago?"

"Yes." Renji answered.

Toria looked at Renji as this, the date catching her attention but he didn't look at her as though he knew what she was thinking.

"That Magic Commander, I'm surprised that he let himself be destroyed considering that he was from the old empire." Marcus said.

"Well it seems that you are just as well informed as I am." Renji said calmly, even though he didn't really want to discuss the matter any further.

"Ren…" Toria started.

"Lady Toria, we've arrived." Annyetta told her.

Toria turned around and saw out of the window that they had indeed arrived at the Senator Empirical Hall, the beautiful palace alight in the night scene as though it was a floating jewel; the palace had one grand staircase to the front entrance and three to the rear. The palace itself was twelve meters off the ground held up by beautiful silver pillars of stone that were no longer found in the galaxy.

"Isn't it beautiful?" Toria said just as the door opened next to Renji and he stepped out and held the door open for them all.

Renji held his hand out which Toria took as she carefully got out of the car trying not to step on her trousers, which she somehow managed to do and smiled up at Renji as she took her place beside him waiting for the others.

Renji helped Annyetta out while Marcus got out on the other side of the car and helped Siren out of the car, who wasn't at all pleased with his behaviour.

"What do you think you're doing?" Siren demanded as they walked around.

"Well I just…" Marcus started.

"No, she's my…" Siren started, but stopped when she saw Renji holding out his arm while Toria had her back to him; she thought it was strange because he never spoke or did anything to get her attention she just turned around and took his hand and allowed herself to be lead inside.

"Is that normal?" Marcus asked. "You don't think there's anything…?"

"NO." Siren answered simply.

Marcus looked over at her, her answer might have been absolute but the look on her face wasn't so sure.

Annyetta turned around smiling at the two of them. "Are we following them inside?"

"Yes, yes of course." Marcus answered holding his hands out for both Siren and Annyetta.

Senator Kentaro walked in front of them with his guards beside him, Bernal and Lesharo walked behind the Senator and in front of Toria and Renji; Lesharo of course was quite displeased with the scene seeing them entering together.

Air cars line the plaza with officials entering, some welcomed the Senator while others ignored him; officers were there with their wives and partners; everyone wore such grand clothes and jewelry that was only seen on such occasions.

Senate guards stood at the bottom and the top of the grand staircase and stood at the entrances watching everything that happened, not letting anything slip by them.

A man walked over to their group in the same uniform, watching and listening to everything they said and did; he had short brownish hair that stood straight up but looked as though it had actually been styled that way. He seemed to look at Renji the same way that Lesharo did, but when his glaze fell upon Toria it soften somewhat.

"Good evening." The man said to the side of Bernal, which startled him making him jump.

"Ichigo." Toria said smiling at him brightly. "I didn't realize that you were attending tonight."

"What, Renji didn't tell you?" Ichigo said his reddish eyes glaring at Renji.

"No, no he didn't but we have been busy this week." Toria told him, she stepped around him and then suddenly grabbed hold of Sirens hand pulling her towards him. "This is my new friend Siren; she started the week that you were here last."

"Yes I think I remember, the two of you didn't get along." Ichigo said smiling slightly. "Well I'm glad that you sorted things out."

"Ichigo takes over from Renji sometimes when he's not here." Toria told Siren as Ichigo and Renji walked off talking.

"How long have you known them both?" Marcus asked her.

"Years of course, why?" Toria answered a little unsure of his question.

"No reason…" Marcus said distractedly as he watched them walk off. "I'll be back shortly." And with that he walked off in the same direction.

"Renji can be like that sometimes." Toria told Siren who looked annoyed with her brother.

"He just wants to make sure that his little sister is safe, and that she doesn't end up in the wrong crowd of people." Annyetta said.

"Which of course is easily done here, with everyone hiding behind a mask." Toria said as she began to walk, but she bumped into an older man before Annyetta could stop her.

"Well if it isn't Senator Kentaro's beautiful daughter." The man said as Toria looked up at him slowly. He was older than Renji but with the same kind of build with black hair and cold eyes; he was wearing his dress uniform and showing off his new star cross medal.

"Durant…" Toria said trying to hide her dislike of him, not that she was doing a very good job even trying that hard not that he seem to care much either.

"That's General Commander Durant Su-Ratnal." Durant told her.

"I'm not calling you that, for one it's too long and another, I'm not one of your officers." Toria told him.

"Lady Toria…" Annyetta tried to say.

"That's alright; I like a woman who speaks her mind." Durant said smiling at her.

"Really, from what I've heard about you; you don't actually like people in general speaking back to you." Toria told him.

"That's different, now come along." Durant told her as he grabbed her arm and tried to pull her along but she wasn't having it. "Now you don't want to cause a scene and embarrass your father, do you?"

"You're the one who's causing the scene and who'll end up embarrassed." Toria warned him before she kicked him in the shin.

"Damn it!" Durant shouted as he let go of her and those stood close by turned around to find out what was going on. "You may look like you belong here, but truthfully…"

"Is there a problem?" A man said as he came up behind Toria and placed his hands on her shoulders; he was also in the same uniform.

Toria looked up at him somewhat surprised by his voice, but at the same time she felt as though she knew him from somewhere but couldn't put her finger on it. He was very handsome though, dark shoulder length hair pulled back away from his face; he had dark eyes that seemed just as cold as Durant's but he smiled ever so slightly and Toria knew in that moment that he was nothing like him.

"General Kasiya." Durant said with dislike in his tone.

"He was acting intemperately." Toria told him as she turned around to face him.

"Yes indeed." Kasiya said as he moved in front of her so that she was no longer in-between the two men.

"I was only asking the young lady for a dance." Durant told him, trying to make himself out to be innocent.

"But you didn't even ask." Toria shouted at him trying to kick him again but Kasiya stopped her.

"This isn't the time." Kasiya whispered to her.

"Sorry." Toria said.

"What!" Durant shouted outraged at this as Renji walked back over quickly towards Toria and grabbed hold of her arm pulling her closer into him. "What the hell is this?"

"I think you have forgotten your place." Kasiya told him, and then added to Renji beside him. "You should get her away from here, now."

Renji stepped back as did Siren and Annyetta just as the side room exploded, he picked Toria up and threw her over his shoulder as he turned around and ushered the other two to quickly move.

"What're you doing?" Toria shouted as she tried to move, but he wasn't letting go of her.

"Damn it, stop moving or I'll drop you." Renji told her as he made his way through the panicking crowd.

There was another explosion this time above, the glass ceiling raining down; security officers tried to make their way through the crowds who were pushing past them towards the exists only caring for their own safety.

"What is the meaning of this?" Durant said as he started to push his way through towards the nearest security team. "This way!"

"Well someone is going to get it in the morning." Kasiya said calmly as he pulled out a hyper-injector and injected him in the arm.

Durant turned around as he felt a slight pinch in his arm, Kasiya stopped following him as two men appeared either side of him and grabbed hold of his arms.

"Magics!" A security officer shouted several feet away.

This didn't help the already panicked crowd. It just seemed to make them even worse; a dozen more Magics transported into the entrance hall.

A tall blue-skinned man appeared behind Renji though right before Toria's eyes, he was wearing the same jump suit in her dream and was holding a blaster rifle.

"Renji, behind you!" Toria shouted.

The man seemed surprised but only for a moment as Renji moved and pulled Siren out of harm's way, so that the Magic had a clean shot at the security officers just before them.

"Move." Renji told her pushing her along not bothering to look back at the man, but Toria did; he wasn't following them instead he had turned around blocking the exist that they were heading towards but he let them go.

"Renji, he let us go." Toria whispered but loud enough so that he would hear her.

"This isn't the time." Renji told her.

In front of him was Siren who was pushing everyone out of her way while keeping a tight grip on Annyetta's hand, but she was also looking around every so often for her brother who had just disappeared before all the chaos started.

"I can't see him anywhere." Siren said.

"I'm sure that he's well, Lady Siren." Annyetta said calmly.

"We haven't got time for small talk, through there." Renji told them as he pushed past them and leant against the wall behind a giant potted planet; the wall opened up as if it was a door onto a dimly lit corridor. "In there now."

Neither of them questioned him as they rushed inside leaving the chaos and screaming behind as the door closed seamlessly behind Renji, if they didn't know it was there they still would have believed it was just a wall. Renji reached out with his free hand and touched the wall which lit the torches all along the right side of the wall.

"What's going on?" Toria demanded as she started to struggled again. "Do you have any idea how bad this actually looks? It looks as though you've kidnapped us."

"Stop moving around." Renji told her.

"No, put me down." Toria told him, so he did; he dropped her.

She slide backwards and fell onto the cold hard floor at his feet, she looked up at him not at all impressed by what he had done and then she suddenly grabbed hold of his leg and then his arm and used him to help pull herself up; when she stood up properly she pushed him back against the wall and stepped forward.

"Now, why don't you tell me what's going on?" Toria told him.

"We don't have time for this." Renji told her as he pushed her out of his way and started to walk down the passageway alone. "You can stay there or come with me. It's up to you of course."

Toria watched him for a minute while her friends stared at her; they both knew that she cared deeply for him and that if she did decide to continue to trust him that they would also. Toria looked over at them both and nodded as she begun to walk, she walked ahead of the two of them but didn't make any effort to catch up to him.

Renji didn't need to look over his shoulder to know that they were following him. He did regret his actions and what had happened tonight but there wasn't really much he could do about it now; or was there?

They all walked for ten minutes straight in total silence which was starting to annoy Toria. She had finally built up the courage to ask him where they were going and marched over to him; she pushed him in the back so that he would look over his shoulder at her.

"Are you at least going to tell us where we're going?" Toria asked him.

"Now you're asking?" Renji said smirking at her, but Toria didn't look at all amused by his comment. "I'm taking you home."

"What?" Toria said somewhat surprised.

"The senator should be quite worried." Renji told her.

"Oh?" Toria said somewhat disappointed, which of course Renji noticed but didn't say anything.

"How long are these tunnels? How many are there? How did you know about them?" Siren asked him as she picked up her pace to follow them.

"It doesn't matter." Renji told her.

"Of course it does. Toria, tell him it matters." Siren told her.

Toria wouldn't even look at Siren, Renji looked over his shoulder again when she didn't say anything; he could see that she was confused about the situation but it just wasn't the time to explain.

"Just…come along…" Renji told them. "It isn't much further then I'll drop you all off at home. Lady Annyetta, you'll have to go home as well considering tonight's events."

"Of course." Lady Annyetta said calmly.

They walked on for another five minutes until finally Renji stopped, though it was at a dead end; he reached out again and stepped back as the wall once again opened up before them like a door onto a brightly lit corridor. Renji went out first to make sure that it was clear before he signalled for them to follow him; though Toria still wouldn't even look at him even though they were back in the central corridors.

Renji stepped forward towards Toria but she didn't move, even when he reached out towards her but he wasn't reaching for her but the wall behind her; as he touched the wall the torches went out and the door closed once again as though it had never been there in the first place.

"Vehicle storage is just this way." Renji told them as he turned around and headed off again just expecting them to follow him.

Toria was the first one to start walking, it was as though she was in a trance as she followed him but Siren wasn't going to have this any longer.

"You're just going to carry on following him like this?" Siren demanded. "Those corridors, you must have realized that the only way to access them is by Magic? This was once a Magic planet…"

Toria didn't say anything as she pulled her arm free and just continued following Renji. Siren though still went after her with Annyetta walking calmly behind them.

"Damn it, say something to him. This isn't like you." Siren demanded, but still she didn't answer; so instead Siren marched over to Renji and stopped him. "Look, look at what you've done. She trusted you and you broke that trust, do you even care?"

"I told you before that this isn't the time." Renji told her pulling his arm free and carrying on walking.

Siren though didn't follow him this time and stopped Toria as well before she walked passed her though she had to keep hold of her, Annyetta stopped of course because she was only following them because Toria was.

"We'll get back on our own." Siren told him stubbornly.

"It isn't as though I'm going to hurt you." Renji told her. "If I was going to do something, I would have done it before now."

"I don't care, I don't trust you, I don't even know you." Siren told him.

Renji was quickly losing his patience with her; he needed to get Toria back even if it meant leaving them behind here. Renji marched over to Siren towering over her and then suddenly grabbed hold of Toria's arm pulling her over to him wrapping his arms around her; his behaviour just pushed Siren a little too far, yes she was surprised but she wasn't going to let that stop her.

"She's coming with me." Renji told her as he began to turn around.

Siren focused gathering all of her strength from within her, she used both her arms as she forced the energy out of her body and through her hands creating a wave of water as though she was throwing it at him. The wave of water just erupted into a cloud of steam as it came just inches away from them both; Siren could just make out Renji smirking as he turned around and carried on walking with his arm around Toria's shoulder.

"You should be careful where you do things like that, and who you do them in front of." Renji warned her as he disappeared.

Siren ran after them through the cloud of steam but they were gone, she went all the way up the corridor and back again where Annyetta was waiting for her.

"He...he's disappeared and took Toria with him." Siren said numbly.

"What're you going to do?" Annyetta asked her calmly, as though this whole situation hadn't bothered her in the least.

"I want to believe that he wouldn't hurt her...but...damn it!" Siren said unsure what to do. "I can't turn him in, can I?"

"We should be heading back then." Annyetta said calmly as though that had settled the matter. "My officers will be here shortly, they'll take you home."

Senate guards patrolled the apartments in pairs; the doors were open to Senator Kentaro's apartment with two of his guards stood outside weapons in hand as Renji walked up the corridor with Toria at his side.

"Sorry it took a while." Renji said as he let Toria go in first.

Neither of the guards questioned him as to why he had taken so long, as they let him inside though he did hear them radioing through of their arrival. Toria went to turn left to go to her room but Renji stopped her and directed her in the opposite direction.

"Not yet…you have to speak to your father." Renji told her.

This statement seemed to bring her partly back to her senses as she looked up at him, what was she supposed to say to her father? Was this some sort of trick? Did they know what he was? Was this to see how loyal she was? Her head began to spin with a thousand and one questions as she allowed herself once again to be lead away by this man that she thought that she could trust with her life, now somewhat unsure if that trust had been misplaced.

Lesharo marched out of the living room stopping them in their tracks, Toria just stood there not looking up at him but at his feet; Renji grabbed hold of her quickly to carry on walking so that he wouldn't pick up too much on her behaviour.

"What happened?" Lesharo demanded as he followed them both back into the living room.

"That's what I would like to know." Senator Kentaro said as he stepped forward his guards stepping aside. "You should have stayed in contact with Lesharo."

"My concern was with Toria and her friends." Renji told him. "I made sure that they stayed out of harm's way."

"You threw her over your shoulder." Lesharo said through gritted teeth.

"It was the quickest way to get her out of there, knowing where she was; I didn't want her to get lost in the panicked crowd." Renji told him.

"It's inappropriate…" Lesharo began.

"Victoria what happened?" Senator Kentaro asked her.

Toria just stood there not daring to look up at Renji beside of her instead she took a deep breath before she looked up at her father.

"I was talking with Durant…sorry General Su-Ratnal…he wasn't being very nice…and tried to make me go off with him…" Toria told him. "Another officer came over to see if I was alright…along with Renji…but then the…um…first explosion went off…Renji grabbed me to take me somewhere safe and then he brought me back home."

"Really, are you sure that's all what happened?" Senator Kentaro asked her.

"You don't have to cover for him." Lesharo told her.

"I know that, but I don't need to…he didn't do anything wrong." Toria told them.

Lesharo didn't seem to believe her and even her father didn't seem completely convinced this time, but he still waved his hand for them to leave; Renji directed her out of the room.

"You should rest tomorrow, no need to worry about the meetings; they've been cancelled." Senator Kentaro told her before she walked off with Renji out of the room.

Renji walked up the hall with Toria just ahead of him, she stopped suddenly outside of his room which came first but she didn't turn around to face him.

"Toria…" Renji said softly.

"All I need to know for now, is; can I trust you?" Toria asked him.

"Always." Renji told her as he began to reach out.

"You'll tell me everything won't you one day?" Toria asked him as she looked over her shoulder at him.

"Would you prefer if I promised?" Renji asked her.

"Yes, promise me that you'll tell me everything…and…you won't leave here without me." Toria told him.

Renji smiled slightly at her. "I think I'd get into quite a bit of trouble if we ran away together."

"My father can't really say much if it's my choice." Toria said as she walked off to her own room. "Remember it's a promise."

She didn't really want to go off by herself but she also knew that he wouldn't tell her what she wanted to know; but hopefully he would one day. She stopped suddenly, why had he stayed all these years? What was he after? Was her father really up to something against the Magics? Would Renji one day betray her? No she had to believe in him that he would never do anything to hurt her. He cared about her; perhaps not like how she cared about him but it was enough, wasn't it?

"Tor…" Lesharo started but before he could finish even saying her name she had run off crying. "Damn it! I only said your name, you little spoilt brat; if it isn't him…"

Toria wasn't even listening to what he was saying as she ran off into her bedroom locking the door behind her, she looked around the room with her eyes full of tears clouding her vision when they fell onto a photo frame; she slowly walked over to the bedside table and sat down on the edge of her bed as she picked up the photo frame.

There were two photos in it, both of them were of her and Renji. The picture on the left was of her when she was just four years old in her summer school dress, she had only known him a couple of months but she adored him; but now she wondered if her feelings for him were real or if he actually did something to her so that she would trust him.

It was so strange looking at the two pictures, you could see how much that she loved him but that wasn't the strangest part it was that he hadn't aged even a day since they had met eight years ago.

"Damn it!" Toria shouted angrily throwing the photo across the room, it smashed against the wall falling to the floor in small pieces and the photo's set on fire. "You ruined everything!"

She turned over on her bed and started to cry again, but this time even harder than before.

Siren marched down the school corridor the other students, older and younger moving out of her way, not daring to stop her because she looked angry enough to attack them all. There were four older lads stood at the end of the corridor outside of the dojo watching those sparring inside as Siren approached them, two of them were human but the other two were Opurian's with dark skin and dreadlocks to their waist.

"Wow…do you believe it, she's really going at it." The Opurian on the left said.

"I can't believe a little girl like her could take on the captain." The other Opurian said.

"She hasn't yet." A younger boy said stood in front of them.

"Do you mind?" Siren said behind them. "I want to go inside."

"What another pretty girl coming to join the club?" The Opurian asked her as he looked her up and down.

"Just move." Siren told him as she pushed him out of her and marched inside, to find Toria sparing with Kyo in a small orange vest top and a short red and orange skirt. "What in the world is she wearing?"

"Not bad if you ask me." An older boy said as he put his arm around her shoulder. He had short gelled hair and blue eyes and was wearing his gym clothes; he smiled at Siren as she looked up at him.

"Do you mind?" Siren said as she lifted his arm away and walked onto the mats ducking out of the way as Toria almost kicked her.

"You're in the way." Kyo told her angrily.

"That's the point." Siren said as she grabbed Toria and pulled her off the mats. "We need to talk…in private."

"I don't feel like talking at the moment." Toria told her as she tried to pull her arm free but Siren wouldn't let her go and pulled her into the girls' changing room. "What do you think you're doing?"

"I could ask you the same thing." Siren said as she quickly looked around to make sure that they were alone before she started on the real reason that she was there. "You've been avoiding me all week, you won't talk to me in class and now look at you...what the hell are you wearing?"

"I don't like the gym clothes they have us wear." Toria answered.

"Well yeah, I agree with you on that...wait a minute we're going off subject." Siren said. "What's up with you? I know it was a big thing what happened; god, that lot in class haven't stopped talking about it all week. But it was different for you."

"I don't want to talk about it." Toria told her as she started to walk again, but Siren stopped her.

"Well I need to." Siren told her.

Toria looked at her somewhat confused, seemingly unaware of what she meant.

"What I did...in front of you..." Siren told her when she realized that she had no idea what she was talking about.

"What?" Toria said still unsure. "I don't care about what you did..."

"Well I do." Siren shouted at her losing her temper.

Toria pulled her hand free and started to walk off, but she suddenly stopped and turned back around to face her. "I wouldn't turn you in, and you must know that or you wouldn't have used your Magic in front of me. Oh and by the way, if I had turned you in we wouldn't be talking now; nor would you be still in this school."

"Fine, I just had to say it; you understand right?" Siren said.

"I'll see you later." Toria said waving as she started to walk off, but she wasn't going back to dojo instead she walked in-between the benches for the exit at the other side of the room; Siren slowly followed her.

"I bet you haven't even talked to him have you?" Siren asked her.

Toria opened the door and just stood there staring at her as Siren came up beside her.

"I told him that he didn't have to yet." Toria told her angrily. "It's like, what was I thinking; I don't really know him. Yeah I've known him for years, and I thought that I could trust him but really, he's only here for one thing."

Siren walked past her out of the door and into the busy hall. "If I

52

hadn't seen the two of you together, I might have thought the same thing; but not now. He does care about you."

"I'll hold you to that, for when he shows us why he's really here." Toria told her.

Lesharo made sure that he was last in the lift so that he could be the first one out, whereas Renji stood next to the Senator as they made their way up to the Senator's office in the main Harujon Senate Building; which housed all the officers and the small meeting rooms. This building though beautiful, in its own right was only a shadow of the main Senate Dragon Dorm, where the galactic senate held their meetings.

Renji's mood or rather his whole composure had changed since the weekend, as though something had happened to just him; of course there wasn't really anyone there that he could talk to nor could he talk to his friends about the situation, he just had to somehow get over it.

The doors slid open onto a dazzling bright hallway; Lesharo stepped out first with Renji and Senator Kentaro behind him. The windows to their right were floor to ceiling and slightly tinted, but still let in most of the light especially at this time of day when the suns were shinning into the officers' eye; the sound of their feet were muffled out by the luxury carpet beneath their feet.

On their left were the doors leading off around the corner, each one housed a senator and their aids; they walked on through the empty hall but could hear men talking around the corner that they were heading towards but they couldn't make out what they were saying nor who the voices belonged to.

Lesharo turned the corner first and everything fell silent when they saw him, though when they saw Senator Kentaro they seemed quite pleased and rushed over to him.

"Senator we were just coming to find you." The man said as he rushed over, his head was partly bald on top covered in brown markings to his hair line which was also brown and pulled back into a short pony tail; he was dressed in a knee-length robe and beneath it he wore a long v-neck shirt with trousers that looked as though they were two sizes too big for him.

The two aids behind him had the same skin tones as were they dressed similarly though they didn't wear a robe over their clothes; all three of them stood in front of Lesharo who was a foot shorter, he smirked at them as he stepped aside so that they could speak with the senator.

"Really, well it looks as though you've found me; Barertac." Senator Kentaro said calmly.

"Yes, well we have news; but you didn't hear it from us." Senator Barertac said. "The Raius system alliance are sending us a new representative, they say that he should be here by the end of the week; they also say that he isn't a Magic though he looks like one."

"Is that so?" Senator Kentaro said thoughtfully. "Well then, when he arrives we'll have to make sure that we give him a warm welcome."

"Um...yes sir...of course..." Senator Barertac said nervously.

Senator Kentaro stepped forward to carry on walking, Senator

Barertac moved to the side to let him past but quickly changed his mind when he moved towards Lesharo and moved to the other side along with his aids.

"He'll probably be a Magic, they sent one last time." Lesharo said as he followed beside Renji. "That didn't go down well, nor will it this time either."

"Shall I have a team keep an eye on him?" Renji asked.

"Yes, just to be sure." Senator Kentaro answered. "It's dangerous after all having a Magic in the Senate, they could get the other members to do whatever they want."

"Even though it's against their laws to use Magic against those who don't have it?" Renji asked.

"I doubt that's ever stopped them." Lesharo said.

"You think so?" Renji asked him. "Then why are they losing the war?"

"Because they're fools." Lesharo answered.

"Quite right." Senator Kentaro agreed.

Lesharo paced back and forward in front of the door to Renji's quarters growing more and more impatient having to wait for him, while it seemed that Renji took his time in the bedroom getting ready.

Renji seemed to be somewhere else, he couldn't keep his mind on what he was supposed to be doing; though it didn't help that he hadn't slept well for the past couple of weeks because he kept having strange dreams. He was only half dressed as he walked past the mirror, out of the corner of his eye he saw something which made him stop and look back; two blurred figures of a woman and man with long red hair worn down.

"Is that me...?" Renji whispered to himself as the image faded away.

"Damn it, how long are you going to be?" Lesharo shouted through.

"Relax already." Renji shouted back as he went over to his bed and grabbed his shirt pulling it on. "We don't have to be there for another ten minutes."

"The rate that you're going we're going to be late, even though I got up early." Lesharo told him.

"That's your own problem." Renji said as he fastened his shirt and then tucked it into his trousers before he sat down on his bed to pull his boots on. "Instead of waiting for me, why not get Toria."

"She doesn't listen to me, that damn brat." Lesharo answered.

"Well that shows that she has some sense." Renji said as he walked out of his bedroom finally dressed.

Lesharo stopped pacing smiling at him. "It seems as though you've also lost your place of favour with her lately, perhaps she didn't like being embarrassed the way you did. Personally I think that the way that you behaved was out of order as well. She's a lady after all."

"It was the quickest way to get her out of harms way." Renji told him again as he grabbed his jacket walking past his chair, Lesharo turned around opening the door as Renji pulling his jacket on. "It was a good job as well, considering that their target was General Durant Su-Ratnal; he was talking to her just before the first explosion."

"Is that Lady Toria you're talking about?" Bernal asked as he stopped just outside of Renji's quarters.

"What? Did you both come over to meet me?" Renji asked them somewhat annoyed by the fact that they didn't think he was capable of arriving at the meeting on time.

"She didn't take it very well, did she sir?" Bernal said as he followed them to the main living quarters. "It was probably the first time that she saw them...of course it doesn't give you a very good impression, especially when she always seemed so interested in them."

"Then this was a good thing, hay Renji; she finally understands why we're at war with them." Lesharo said quite smug with himself. "Though you would have thought that she already learnt this lesson when her mother was killed by them."

None of them had heard the door open behind them, not even Renji; but Toria was stood there. She had her long hair down and was wearing a knee length sleeveless dress, with a lilac under dress which was longer on the right hand side but also could be seen through triangular openings on the right of the dress.

"I'm glad that I can help you fill in your conversation gaps." Toria said surprising them all.

"Toria..." Renji started.

"Don't let me stop you, please do carry on." Toria told him as she walked forward and pushed him out of her way.

"Toria!" Renji shouted as he went after her.

"We'll be late if you don't hurry up." Toria told him.

"What?" Renji said irritably.

"I don't see why I need three guards to take me to the senate to meet my father." Toria said to herself.

"These are dangerous times that we live in." Lesharo told her.

Toria though didn't answer him she just carried on walking leading the way out to their hanger, this definitely wasn't how she wanted to spend her day off nor did she want to be around them at the moment especially Renji. She still hadn't worked out her feelings for him yet.

None of them talked until they arrived at the senate building, Renji got out of the air car first and held the door open for her but Toria stubbornly got out on the other side to Lesharo's amusement; Renji though wasn't amused by her behaviour slamming the door shut and marching around the other side.

"Go on ahead of us." Renji ordered.

"Come on." Lesharo told Bernal as he pushed him along.

Toria started to follow them but Renji stopped her, she turned around to face him, his mood fitted perfectly with the weather behind him; cold, wet and miserable.

"What do you think you're up to?" Renji demanded. "If you carry on acting like this, they'll think that something really is wrong."

"That's because there is." Toria shouted at him as she pulled her arm free and quickly rushed inside, but Renji was right behind her.

"This isn't the time or place." Renji said quietly.

"Then when...?" Toria asked him as she stopped just before the junction in the hall and turned around to face him. "I really did want to trust you, even though that you've lied to me all my life about who you really were...I get that you didn't think that you could trust me; but it's different now."

"Toria..." Renji said.

"I did trust you, I cared about you...but how do I know that any of it was even real?" Toria said sadly. "Lesharo was right, I should be angry with you and your kind; we're at war. They killed my mother and now you're after my father..."

"That isn't it." Renji said.

"What?" Toria said angrily. "Not my father and his business? You can't say that...that...it's...no..." As she seemed to realize that if it wasn't her father, then he really was there for her, really had been tricking her all these years and she had fallen for it.

"Toria, please; I can explain, but not here." Renji said quickly.

Toria shook her head as she started to step away from him. "No...stay away from me."

"Toria calm down." Renji told her as he reached out for her.

"Come any closer and I'll scream." Toria warned him, so he stopped; she turned and ran around the corner to her left almost knocking a man off of his feet not that she even stopped to see if he was alright.

Renji walked around the corner to go after her but stopped when he saw the man before him, he was the same height and had long beautiful reddish hair almost to his waist which was quite a contrast against his white suit.

"Was the young lady with you?" The man asked Renji.

"Yes, she's just a little upset." Renji answered.

"I'm..." The man started.

"The new representative." Renji said.

"Yes, Blaze." He told him.

"Interesting name." Renji said.

Blaze smiled at him suddenly. "I needed an interesting name to go with such an interesting place."

Renji just looked at him. "I do know that isn't a joke but your real name. Renji Aba'rian."

"Well it's nice to meet you Mister Aba'rian, I'm sure that we'll meet again." Blaze said still smiling at him as he walked away with his aids looking somewhat confused at Renji, who bowed his head slightly in respect but he carried on after Toria.

Chapter Four

Renji tossed and turned unable to settle, his sheets coming tangled and caught between his legs; and his pillow slipping off the edge of his bed as he turned again and knocking it off finally with his arm that seemed to be trying to keep something away from him.

...A teenage Renji marched across the landing platform his red hair much longer and tied up in a pony tail but gelled up and spiked. He was in his training clothes with a sword upon his belt, his black markings upon his forehead made him seem even more angrier than he was with his eyebrows disappearing as he glared at the woman he was approaching; the ripped vest revealing the black markings across his chest that ran down his arms, his dark navy blue trousers blending in well with his skin tones.

He was heading for the grand transport ship at the far end of the platform which was in fact the only one there, the transport was a metallic gold with a red dragon painted atop of it, reflecting brightly in the afternoon sunlight, soft purple and lilac coloured clouds above just out of reach with the settlement far below.

A young noblewoman stood alone at the bottom of the lowered ramp of the transport as if she was waiting for him, her reddish hair was braided and pinned up; her full length dull blue silver coat tailed behind her unfastened revealing a midnight blue basque and a dark stormy-blue full length skirt.

"I can't believe that you refused me." Renji said by way of greeting.

"There were reasons for my decision." The woman said calmly.

"Reason's, what reasons; I was in the top five of my class." Renji shouted at her.

"Yet you still haven't learnt your place." The woman said.

"My place?" Renji said mockingly as he stopped before her. "So I'm beneath you now, all because I wasn't born into a noble house?"

"That isn't what I meant." The woman told him. "I don't believe that you are suited to be a palace guard, that doesn't mean that I don't believe you to be an able warrior; far from it. But this isn't the best place for you, I'm sure that there's somewhere else that you'll be able to do a lot more than just guarding me."

"I don't understand." Renji said shaking his head. "I..."

"Stupid and bad tempered, well they'll definitely have their work cut out with you then." A woman said from the shadows on board the transport ship.

Renji looked up the ramp to see who it was as she stepped forward, she was the same age and height as the other woman but she wasn't dressed as a noble. She had short bobbed purple hair and a slightly round face with a cheeky smile. She wore a dirty-red coloured tight fitted long sleeve v-neck top with black leggings and knee boots with a blaster strapped to her right thigh and a sword on her belt.

She walked down the ramp never taking her eyes off of Renji nor did he as though he was transfixed on her. She stood beside the other woman.

"So are you interested?" The purple haired woman asked him.

'Interested in what? And who are you?" Renji asked her.

"Toria." She answered.

"She's one of my cousins." The other woman told him. "So you'll still be guarding a member of the royal family."

"She doesn't look like a Tiania." Renji said looking her up and down.

"And you're wondering why you're not suited to be a palace guard." Toria said as she stepped forward off of the ramp and then suddenly hit him in the arm. "Quit checking me out like that."

"I'm not checking you out...as if I would." Renji said defensively.

Toria stepped even closer to him and then smiled suddenly at him. "I don't mind; just perhaps don't make it so obvious."

"What?" Renji said now completely taken off guard, his cheeks blushed slightly because no woman had ever said such a thing to him before.

"If you'll excuse us, your majesty." Toria said bowing her head respectfully, Renji though was still staring at her as though he had lost all interest in anything else around him. "Bow your head."

Toria forcefully bowed his head for him and then grabbed his arm to lead him away.

"Wait Ollie..." Renji said though still allowing himself to be pulled away by the other woman.

"If you're going to call her by her first name, at least call her Olena instead of giving her a nickname...especially in public since she has guards on her transport, people can still hear us." Toria told him and then added more kindly. "It'll be alright."...

Renji woke suddenly sitting bolt up right looking around the room in a panic as if he was expecting to see someone there, but when he realized that he was alone in the room he flopped back down closing his eyes once more and fell into another deep sleep.

...An older Olena walked calmly up the corridor which was filled with guards that all stepped aside for her to let her pass except for one, Renji; who stood his ground not letting her pass making everyone else stare even though they should be used to his behaviour by now since he had always been like this.

"I know that she told you, now tell me." Renji told her. "Where has she gone? How long do I have to wait? You can't just give her to me and then take her away."

"What makes you think that she was yours to begin with?" Olena asked him calmly. "Perhaps it was all in your head."

"No...Ollie, I want her back now; I can't wait however long she expects me to." Renji told her.

"She told me once, that you don't wait for her." Ollie said with a sad expression upon her face and then walked around him. "It looks as though she'll be right about you...and here I told her to trust you more."

"Ollie...!" Renji shouted...

"Ollie!" Renji shouted as he woke sitting up suddenly.

Toria stood at the end of his bed ready for school but looking quite concerned. Renji though didn't seem pleased to see her stood there; Toria of course could see this also by the look on his face that he wasn't at all pleased.

"What're you doing?" Renji asked in irritation, as he flopped back down onto his bed, but there wasn't a pillow beneath his head, he reached over the edge of the bed feeling for it on the floor until he found it and pulled it up and put it under him.

"I live here...so I can go where I please." Toria answered him stubbornly.

"That's funny, but this isn't your room." Renji told her. "In fact it's a bedroom of a man who is far older than yourself. A lady of your station shouldn't been seen entering servants quarters."

"I'm leaving for school in ten minutes, and you're not even up yet." Toria told him, ignoring his last statement even though she knew he was right; but she still couldn't let it drop. "You've been like this for a while now...who...who's Ollie?"

Renji looked up at her. "Just someone I used to know, a very long time ago."

Toria turned to leave but stopped again. "I'll get the air bus to school...they're doing Magical incursion checks, so be careful."

Renji made to get out of bed but fell instead because his legs were still tangled up in the sheets, Toria couldn't help but laugh at him as he struggled to free himself and stand up.

"It's been a while, but at least I've finally got a smile out of you; even if it was at my expense." Renji said throwing the sheet back onto his bed, though he still didn't seem as though he was in a smiling mood himself.

"I know I'm just a child and there's so much going on out there but..." Toria tried to say. "It's hard sometimes...because I want to trust you and then other times I'm so unsure so angry with you, maybe it is because I'm so young...and I don't understand fully."

"That's fine, I don't mind you being confused; just come to me even if it's just to yell at me even if I'm not in the mood to listen." Renji told her. "Walking around in a bad mood doesn't really look good for me."

Toria smiled slightly before she turned to leave, her confusion was with him as well; so how could she explain that to him or anyone.

"Thanks for the warning." Renji said after her before she left.

A boy was thrown onto the training mats in the dojo, as he failed to block an attack his blue hair sticking to his sweet stained silver face; he tried to get to his feet as the other lad circled him, waiting. The other lad was human and from the year above him, he was quite well built especially for his age which he seemed to like showing off during practice because he never wore his vest top, as though he thought it made him look better.

"Come on Yerwan!" His friend shouted from the side lines.

"If you can't get up, I'll take that as your defeat." The older boy told him.

Talk erupted throughout the dojo, no one really liked training with him but with the competitions coming up they were all trying out for the ten competing spots; and of course this was the only way to do it.

The teacher didn't seem to mind the others talking nor the older boy's behaviour; he was six foot three dark-skinned with a shaved head, not a man to cross with. Toria walked into the dojo behind the teacher, her long hair was pulled back into a pony tail out of her face; she also wasn't wearing the school gym clothes but her own which of course none of the guys ever complained about because this was the only way that they would ever get to see her in such small tight-fitted clothes. The teacher seemed to know that she was there and turned around to speak with her; he towered over her not that she seemed intimidated by him, considering the type of men that she had grown up around because of her father.

"Good morning sir." Toria said pleasantly enough.

"You're late." He told her. "You've been a part of this dojo for two years now, and are finally up for one of the ten spots so you think that you can turn up late for practice and still make the team?"

"This isn't the only subject that I'm taking, sir." Toria told him and silence fell over the class room.

"It's your turn." He told her as he grabbed her arm and pulled her onto the nearest mat; the lads moving before they were even told not wanting to get into trouble themselves.

"All she had to do was turn up on time." The older boy said as he dragged the silver skinned boy off of the mat to the benches.

"Well she was right, she does have other classes beside this one." Kyo told him. "She isn't like you Greg who only thinks about one thing."

"I want her." Greg said suddenly.

Kyo looked over at him somewhat surprised by his remark. "I doubt that you're her type."

"I want to cage her up..." Greg told him.

"She isn't a wild animal." Kyo said somewhat disturbed by his friend's behaviour.

"Really, shall we see?" Greg said as they walked over to her, to watch her against the teacher. "She isn't like the rest of them here, that's what I want."

Kyo didn't understand him nor did he want to, but he did want to watch Toria against their teacher considering it had been a while since anyone had been pit against him.

"Now then, in your own time." The teacher told her.

Toria couldn't help but feel annoyed by his mocking behaviour, especially considering that she still also trained with Renji and the others back home.

"If I can beat you, can I have a place on the team?" Toria asked him.

He laughed at her, while the other students seemed stunned into silence by her question.

"'Course you can, that is if you can beat me." He told her smirking as he lunged at her to punch her but she had already moved out of reach and turned around, she kicked him in the ribs before she came to a stop behind him. "Not bad for a rich brat."

He turned around in flash and came at her again, but this time all she could do was block his blows because they were so fierce; she had to somehow get out from under him or she'd never be able to fight back properly.

Toria believed that it was worth the risk, as he made to hit her again she grabbed his left arm to stop him and kicked him again; but as she let go of him he punched her in the face knocking her off of her feet.

Toria's head spun as his fist connect, her skull felt as though it had shattered and a burning sensation ran from her head to her toes; though without her even realizing, her hair changed colour to a hot red.

"Her hair...that isn't normal is it?" Greg asked.

"I think it depends on the person." Kyo said surprised himself.

"Pretty trick." The teacher said.

Toria pushed herself up off of the floor, her face was sore but her whole body was burning with rage. She looked up at him her eyes a burning red, her annoyance with him plain to see by everyone, but then she suddenly smirked at him before she rushed him punching and kicking not giving way for him; not giving him an inch as she let her senses overwhelm her. Every time that she touched his skin there was a burning smell in the air and she left behind a slight burn mark upon his skin.

"Now, now...what are you doing?" He asked her, but she didn't answer him.

Toria ran at him but instead of striking him she jumped over him and turned around before she kicked him in the back sending him flying onto the floor, she landed gracefully behind him and walked over to him; she grabbed the back of his vest top pulling him to eye level and made to punch him in the face.

"Toria stop!" Kyo shouted at her.

Toria stopped suddenly at the sound of his voice, as if hearing it brought her back to her senses realizing what she was doing; she let go of the teacher and stepped back trying to avoid eye contact with everyone else in the class.

"I'll think about that place." The teacher told her from the floor.

Toria didn't say anything she just turned around and walked off the mat, the others clearing away for her but Kyo wasn't letting her go off alone and pushed past the others in his way so that he could go after her; when she was out of the dojo and the doors had closed behind her she ran off.

"Toria wait up!" Kyo shouted after her, as he also started to run. "Damn it, I only want to talk..."

Kyo looked over his shoulder to check that there wasn't anybody else around before he did it, he didn't even stop running as he concentrated hard imaging himself next to Toria and then on the school roof; he disappeared and reappeared beside her a second later wrapping his arms around. This time they both disappeared and reappeared on the roof top an instant later, Kyo let go of her almost stumbling backwards unable to hold onto her any longer.

"What do you think you're doing?" Toria demanded turning around to face him being hit in the face by a cold wind, she closed her eyes as she let the coldness wash over her.

"I could ask the same of you." Kyo said. "You do know that you could have really hurt him...and me; look I'm still smoking here."

Toria looked over at him, he was; his clothes were smoking slightly. She turned around and walked over to the edge standing just inches away from the railing but not daring to hold it, she was still so hot this burning inferno trying to consume her from the inside out and she had almost let it.

"So what's going on?" Kyo asked her. "I've never seen you like that before...is it because...I mean are you...?"

"I just lost my temper that's all." Toria told him turning around smiling reassuringly, but she wasn't sure if he bought it.

"Fine you don't have to tell me." Kyo said. "Just be careful."

"Thanks." Toria said.

Toria skipped classes for the rest of the afternoon and rushed home, not actually realizing that this will probably cause even more problems in the long run. She ran down the empty halls from the hanger bay to the lifts luckily not bumping into anyone on her way, only stopping in front of the lift which opened up for her straight away so she got inside.

"Kentaro quarters." Toria ordered.

The doors closed and started up as she took up pacing she was still too nervous to just stand there calmly. The lift seemed to Toria to take forever to reach her level and open up again to let her out; luckily she didn't have far to go from the lift to her quarters just a couple of steps and then she was inside and safe.

Toria didn't need to ask the computer where Renji was, she just knew; letting her feet take her to him leading her to the living room. She stood at the door watching him stood on the far side of the room checking the wall console. She dropped her bag suddenly and walked over to him; it didn't seem as though he had realized that she was there until she was only a couple of feet away from him and then he turned around to face her.

"What're you doing here?" Renji asked her.

Toria didn't answer him at first she just rushed at him and flung her arms around him and then she started to cry into his chest.

"Toria..." Renji said gently, he hated it when she cried; it always seemed to make him seem powerless in a way.

"I...I had an accident at school..." Toria told him.

Renji of course knew straight away what she meant grabbing hold of her and pulling her further enough away so that he could at least see her face, it was stained with tears but also the left side of her face was starting to bruise; Renji reached out to touch her softly.

Toria only allowed him to touch her for a second but it was a second too long as her whole body started to burn up once again and she moved away from him, afraid of herself and what she might to do him, as she had no idea what was happening to her.

"Don't do that!" Toria shouted at him startling him somewhat.

"Toria I can help if you'll let me." Renji told her.

"What? What are you talking about?" Toria said somewhat panicked as she stepped backwards, but as she did so the wall console behind Renji exploded suddenly. "What...what was that?"

"All you need to do is calm down." Renji told her as he stepped closer but still she backed away from him.

"How can I calm down when you're making it worse?" Toria told him.

Renji smiled at her suddenly amused by her comment. "I'm sorry; but if you'll let me I can actually help."

Toria just shook her head as Renji disappeared and reappeared right behind her, he grabbed hold of her and pulled her into him wrapping his arms around her tightly so that she couldn't break free of his grasp.

"Just this once...because you'll have too learn how to do it yourself." Renji whispered as he closed his eyes concentrating on her, on her body, the heat radiating from within her which was so intense; he finally gathered up all the extra heat within directing it to her hands using it as a focal point.

"It hurts..." Toria told him as she tried to struggle free.

"Just a little more." Renji told her as he took hold of her hands even though she tried to keep them away from him, he held onto them firmly as both of their hands were burning from the eminence heat; it took several minutes until nearly all of the heat was transferred to Renji but he still didn't let go of her. "You'll make this up to me one day."

Toria didn't say anything as she leant back into him and closed her eyes, he scooped her up into his arms and carried her off to her bedroom.

Renji had contacted the school telling them that she had come home early because she was feeling unwell and had apologized for not informing them straight away when he had collected her, and of course also made sure that everything was alright that nothing unusual had been reported about her.

When he had finally been able to get away, after making sure that she was alright, he had to leave the apartment for something important, but of course he didn't actually tell anyone where he was going only that he was popping out for a short while.

Renji was sat alone in a dark and dingy bar with a pint of blue lasis in front of him. He was still in uniform which made the other patrons stay away from him which looked kind of shady for cargo pilots, though it was after all a back street bar that they went to, to get away from the top brass.

The bartender looked like he was five times older then Renji and had every type of blaster that you could think of up on the wall behind him, his two bar staff moved up and down the bar serving the drinks not really putting much effort in to it as though they would rather be somewhere else; whereas those in the bar didn't seem to care where they were as long as they had a drink in their hands.

The door swung open and two young men walked in, on the left was Ichigo in his senate uniform and next to him was a tall handsome young man; they kind of looked as though they could be related in some way if you looked closely enough.

The young man was taller than Ichigo and had short reddish-brown hair which was more like Toria's. He was dressed in a uniform that made all the pilots look the other way and Renji shook his head as he picked up his drink not needing to look around to see who it was; he wore a brown short sleeved top with a metal plate across his chest blasters strapped to both legs over his black trousers and he wore high travel boots.

They both walked straight over to Renji and sat down facing him, Ichigo signalled to the bar keep that they wanted drinks as Renji put his glass down.

"I think we stand out enough without you dressed like that." Renji told him. "You should have just worn your proper uniform."

"So what did you want to talk about? I don't have long before my transport has to leave." The man asked him.

Renji didn't answer him as the bar staff came over with a tray with their three blue lasis upon it. He put them down in front of each of them roughly spilling some out of every glass; none of them said anything instead they just let him walk off so that they could talk.

"She's getting worse." Renji told them.

"What do you mean, she's getting worse?" The man demanded. "You're supposed to be looking after her."

"It's starting and it's only going to get worse...it's just a matter of time before they fully realize." Renji told them. "Baron I called you here because I'll need your help. We'll need a ship outside of the Fleet and I still don't have one...I mean after my last one was destroyed."

"Of course, anytime, anywhere; you don't need to ask just tell me." Baron told him. "We shouldn't have let it go on this long though."

"Why can't you help, I mean considering that she knows about you?" Ichigo asked.

"She doesn't know everything..." Renji said thoughtfully. "The problem is though, that I've still not been able to link the senator to Malevalus; only with Toria."

"That isn't enough." Baron agreed.

"How did they come in contact, are they still in contact...what're they going to do with Toria when she comes of age?" Renji asked.

"Five months and she turns fifteen, when she turns sixteen they'll move in and we could lose her for good." Ichigo told them.

"I won't let them..." Renji said before he took another drink.

"Are you willing to stop her though, incase they do get to her?" Baron asked him. "Could you kill her if you had too?"

Renji didn't answer him nor did he look at him, he couldn't; yes he had thought about it so many times that he's actually lost count but he still didn't know if he would he strong enough to go after her.

It was a good enough answer for them when he didn't say anything, they had already known that he wouldn't or rather couldn't do it, but they just wanted to confirm it for sure.

The stadium was full of students all divided into their own school colours on the four platform levels, the bottom platform was for the first round up to the quarter finals for each year group which the higher year groups would have their quarter finals on the next platform. Then it was the semi finals and finally on the top platform was where all the finals were held.

"I think I made a good choice by putting her on the team." The dojo teacher said beside Greg who looked as though he was in a very bad mood with his right arm in a sling.

"I can't believe she broke my arm, we're on the same team." Greg said for the tenth time that afternoon.

It was the one and only time that Toria had agreed to wear the school gym clothes, a short sleeved blue t-shirt and shorts; kind of pale considering what she would normally wear.

Toria blocked a blow from her opponent who was bigger than Greg, he didn't seem at all bothered that he was fighting a girl as long as he won; he had gold skin and a gold Mohican.

"Come on Toria! You can do it!" Siren shouted from the side lines.

One of the referees stopped just behind Siren and looked over to the direction that she was shouting at. He had quite a surprised expression upon his face at the sight that met his eyes. He reached into his top pocket and pulled out a hand com unit, then pressed the button on the side.

"Lasergut to Aba'rian." He said into the com as he stepped away from Siren, not wanting her to overhear.

"Yeah...Aba'rian here....it better be good..." Renji answered sounding somewhat preoccupied.

"Did you know that your charge is here today?" Lasergut asked him calmly.

'Yeah...I think she mentioned something about it." Renji answered. "Get to the point."

"Did you know then that she's competing?" Lasergut asked him.

"What?" Renji shouted through the com accompanied by blaster fire.

Siren turned around at the sound of Renji's voice looking around for him, well she knew that Toria hadn't told anyone what she was doing otherwise she wouldn't have been allowed to come; Siren though couldn't see him anywhere only the referee talking on his com.

"Damn it!" Renji shouted again, again there were several blaster shots in the background.

"I'll let you go, it sounds as though you've got your hands full." Lasergut said. "I just thought that you would want to know what she was up to."

Lasergut pressed the button on the side of his com signing off before Renji could say anything, but Siren was walking over to him; he turned around to face her.

"Is there something I can do for you?" Lasergut asked her pleasantly enough.

"Who are you? And why did you call Renji?" Siren asked him not at all bothered that he looked far stronger than herself.

"I was just letting the bodyguard know where his charge is. It's up to him now if he'll do anything about her being here." Lasergut said. "If it was me, I wouldn't let her out of my sight; he mustn't value his life too much."

"And just what is that supposed to mean?" Siren demanded.

"It's a grown-up thing." Lasergut said as he started to walk away.

"Will Renji turn up?" Siren asked loudly.

Toria heard his name and looked over towards Siren, wondering if he was there; but she shouldn't have let her guard down as the lad took full advantage of this opportunity, he kicked her in the chest and then punched her twice in the face. Toria stumbled backwards taken off guard, but she stepped back too far and slipped off the mats disqualifying herself.

"What a shame, why don't you come back when you can actually fight." The lad said smirking at her as he walked over.

Toria ignored him as she just sat there waiting for her vision to focus properly again and her body ready to move again. Siren walked around the mats to her after someone had told her it was over; she held out her hand for her.

"Thanks." Toria said as she took her hand and allowed Siren to help her to her feet. "Renji...you said his name...is he here?"

"What, no." Siren said. "Wait a minute, is that what distracted you?"

"Well, technically I'm not actually supposed to be competing." Toria told her. "So both of us, me and Renji would actually get into trouble; that's why I haven't told anyone because I don't want him getting into trouble."

"Then why didn't you tell him?" Siren asked her thinking that she was being stupid not telling him in the first place.

"He may train me, but he still wouldn't let me do something like this." Toria told her.

"And what was that?" Her teacher said as he marched over and near enough pushed Siren out of the way so that he could speak to Toria.

"Mr Centine..." Siren said as she balanced herself. "These things happen."

"No...no they don't...she was winning and then she just let him win." Mr Centine said a vein pulsating on his temple. "What did you fancy him or something?"

Toria pulled herself up and looked over her shoulder at him even more disgusted. "I don't think so."

Toria walked around him, not really in the mood now to listen to all the reasons why he thought she had lost and walked off with Siren.

"I didn't say that you could leave!" Mr Centine shouted after her, not that she paid any attention to him and even the other students turned around pretending that they weren't with him, as he was drawing way too much attention to himself.

Renji jumped over a half blasted away metal wall with a blaster in each hand firing at anything that moved while the two men behind him just watched, he moved forward and blasted a hole behind the mens' heads; all the colour in his face just faded away as he dropped his blaster and ran off. The other two men left looked at one another and also dropped their blasters and held up their hands surrendering.

"Good choice." Renji told them and then added to his own men. "Why don't you finish up here, I've got something to take care of."

Renji didn't even wait for a reply as he walked off swinging the blasters around before he replaced them in the hostlers on his thighs.

Kyo was doing really well. He had gotten all the way to the finals, Toria stood with Siren and with Greg hovering near by; they watched as Kyo threw his opponent to the ground.

"I knew Kyo was good, but I've never seen him like this before." Toria said.

"Yeah I know, at this rate he'll win." Siren agreed.

Neither of them noticed the commotion that was going on behind them until it was too late. Toria was suddenly pulled off of her feet and thrown over a very strong shoulder of a man with crimson hair.

"Damn it...put me down!" Toria shouted at him.

"Oh my." Siren said, she wasn't going to get in his way this time because he looked furious.

Everyone moved out of his way not even attempting to rescue Toria or find out what was going on, except for one stupid man.

"Hay, who do you think you are? She's one of my students, you can't just come in here and take her." Mr Centine demanded while Toria shook her head at him in disbelief that he'd be so stupid to actually get in Renji's way, while he was this angry.

Renji though didn't answer him nor did he even turn around to face him, he just carried on walking as though he hadn't heard a thing; the crowd once again moved aside for him not daring to get in his way as he made his way towards the exit. The doors slid open before them but as soon as they closed Renji dropped Toria to her feet. He had grabbed hold of her again by the shoulders before she had even regained her balance and near enough threw her against the bulkhead.

"What the hell, do you think you're doing?" Renji demanded. "Do you even care that it'll be me who'll get it?"

"He...he wasn't supposed to find out..." Toria said nervously.

"That wasn't my question." Renji said his anger sounding in his voice now.

"I'm sorry..." Toria said. "I didn't mean..."

"You mean you didn't think." Renji shouted at her. "You're not the only person involved when you get into trouble, why can't you understand that; there's always other people who'll end up worse off."

"I'm sorry..." Toria said.

"It's alright you saying that, but it's gone far beyond that now." Renji told her. "I could have carried on training you without him finding out...but now, nothing; I can't do it any longer...I don't even know if I'll have a job after this one."

"I'm sorry...Renji...I'm so sorry..." Toria said as she started to cry her body shaking as he held her against the bulkhead, she hadn't wanted him to lose his job, she didn't know what she would do if he would just suddenly leave.

"Don't cry..." Renji told her angrily.

"I...I'm...sorry..." Toria said as he suddenly pulled her into his arms, his anger disappearing.

"Damn it, I must be mad." Renji whispered as his anger disappeared.

"I...I'm sorry...Ren...ji..." Toria said as she cried into his shoulder.

"Really mad, but I'll sort it." Renji told her. "Just no more."

There wasn't a sound as Toria sat quietly on the sofa in the living room with Renji and Bernal stood behind her while her father sat in the chair facing her. They all sat in silence as they waited as though life in that room had stopped but just outside through the window you could still see the air cars flying by.

A couple of minutes later Lesharo entered the room through the open door with a smirk upon his face, seemingly quite pleased with himself; this of course didn't seem to sit well with Renji and Toria as they both knew that it couldn't be anything good if he was this happy.

"Master Utenro." Lesharo announced and stepped aside.

Everyone looked up at his announcement as a half giant walked into the room, he had to bend down slightly as he came through the door and then once he stood up again his head was almost touching the high ceiling.

Toria thought that his appearance looked more like a thug than a training officer. Toria sat there nervously not daring to ask if they were serious, but her fears were made true as her father spoke.

"Seeing that you have an interest in self-defence I've got you your own teacher." Senator Kentaro told her.

Toria looked at her father in disbelief and then at the half giant stood in the doorway now blocking Lesharo from view. She couldn't believe it, what was he up to? Perhaps this was his way to try and put her off the whole idea by getting her the strongest and most imposing teacher he could find.

"Senator with all due respect, we as her guards could train her." Renji said.

"Yes, that would probably be the best course of action but considering that you have been her guards for years you might go easy on her." Senator Kentaro said. "She needs someone who won't hold back, that way if anything was to happen to her if you weren't there to protect her she would be able to look after herself instead of wondering where she had gone wrong in her training."

"It isn't very often that she's on her own." Renji said knowing that it probably wasn't a good idea to argue back but he had to do something. He knew that she would never stand a chance against that, since even he sometimes had hard time against giants.

"Anything could happen, anywhere, anytime." Senator Kentaro said standing up. "These lessons will take place. It has already been decided. And Aba'rian I don't really see you training her, you've always been too soft on her."

"But father..." Toria said as she stood up.

Utenro reached forward and grabbed her by the wrist and pulled her towards him startling her somewhat as she stumbled taken off guard. His grip was so tight that she actually thought that it was going to break her wrist.

"We'll start our training now." Utenro told her gruffly as he pulled her along with him with ease. "You're like a little doll...hope you don't break that easily."

"Wait...!" Toria shouted as she was pulled away against her will.

Renji made to go with her but Senator Kentaro stepped in his way.

"I know that you've known her along time, since she was a child." Senator Kentaro told him. "Now I want you to remember something, your place as her guard; that is your only function here, nothing more than that."

"Yes sir." Renji answered.

"She is at an impressionable age, so I don't need her head being filled with nonsense; or unwanted feelings." Senator Kentaro told him. "I need my daughter at my side especially in these hard times; she needs to understand why the Magics are so evil; if she can't understand that..."

"I'll make sure to keep an eye on her, though without getting too close." Renji told him standing to attention.

"Good, now I have work to do and I don't want to be disturbed by anyone." Senator Kentaro told them before he walked off back to his office.

Renji waited until he had left the room before he did the same with Bernal beside of him but Lesharo stepped in their way still smirking as though he had gotten one over on him.

"That little brat is finally going to get a reality check." Lesharo said.

Renji grabbed hold of him by his jacket and shoved him against the wall.

"If anything happens to her, you'll be the one who'll get it do you understand me?" Renji warned him.

"You're taking this awfully personal." Lesharo said trying to sound brave, when really he was quite stupid for talking back while Renji was in such a bad mood.

"Of course I am, she's mine." Renji whispered leaning close enough so that only he could hear.

"What's that supposed to mean?" Lesharo asked confused.

"I'm sure that you're smart enough to figure it out on your own." Renji told him letting go of him with his right hand and then he punched him in the face letting him fall to the floor.

Renji sat waiting in Toria's room with his feet up on her desk, he couldn't believe how long he had to wait for her she had been gone hours; it had been going on like this for months since that Utenro had come. But tonight seemed different somehow, he was starting to get worried because she had been gone even longer than normal, when her door finally slid open he almost fell off of the chair, as he rushed to get to his feet.

Toria stood in the doorway leaning against the door frame for support, she looked up slightly knowing that he would be there as normal, her face was stained with sweat and blood and her sweaty hair struck to her neck; Renji rushed over to help her in, which she let him as she didn't really have much strength left to argue with him.

"Damn it...look at you; you look terrible." Renji told her as he helped her over to the desk to sit down.

"Thanks, that makes me feel great." Toria said sarcastically.

"I'll treat your wounds..." Renji told her as he pulled the med case out of her bottom drawer. "I'm sure they're getting worst."

"My body feels as though it's on fire...but it's different than those other times..." Toria told him as she leant her head on the cool surface of her desk.

Renji carefully lifted the back of her top so that he could treat her wounds, her back though was covered in cuts and bruises. He was surprised how she had managed to get back to her quarters on her own considering how badly her left side was hurt; he ran several scans to check if she had any broken ribs, which tonight it seemed as though she had three.

"Toria..." Renji started.

"I know...I know what you're going to say really I do...it's just..." Toria tried to explain, but she still wasn't sure how to explain to him that she wanted to continue even though it was killing her; she just felt as though this was important to her and she needed to do it.

"You don't have to do this, if you want vigorous; than I can give it to you." Renji told her as he touched her side slightly treating her wounds, but at the same time the flowers on the ledge above her caught fire; Renji looked up at them and blew on them making the fire go out. "See...you're losing control..."

"Actually I think that was you." Toria whispered into the desk but he still heard her.

Renji smiled slightly to himself. "Well I've still got it then it seems."

Toria leant back suddenly pulling her top down away from him. "I'm going to have a shower."

"I haven't finished healing your wounds yet." Renji told her as he tried to stop her.

"It's fine...just leave it there...I'll finish it off after." Toria told him as she got up and pushed him away so that she could get past. It was hard being so close to him even more so when he actually touched her; the only problem was that she didn't understand why. Or rather she thought she understood herself somewhat, but sometimes the things that he came out with; it would just throw her completely. "I just need some time to myself, it's not that I don't appreciate everything that you've done for me...it's just...well...you know, I'm not a little girl anymore I'm a young woman."

"I know that, I can see that; I'm not stupid." Renji said stepping closer but she moved away from him again.

"Please, just this once?" Toria asked him.

"Fine, just this once." Renji agreed. "If you need me for anything, all you have to do is just call."

"Thanks..." Toria said as she started to push him out of her room and locked the door behind him. "I think he is stupid, if he hasn't realized yet."

She stripped off as she walked through to the bathroom taking the healing device with her, she stood in front of the mirror turning slightly so that she could heal herself even though twisting at that angle actually hurt her even more but she would rather do it herself than let Renji do it for her.

It took Toria nearly half an hour to heal her side, but even then it was still sore but it was the best that she could do; it was getting late and she still needed to have a shower; she put the healing device in the drawer to the left so that it wouldn't get damp and turned the shower on behind her letting the water run for a moment before she got in.

She took her time stepping into the shower basin but even now the water hurt as it touched her skin, which changed her mind about having a long shower like she normally would have liked to relax after today's training, but in this state she wouldn't be able to.

Toria reached over painfully for the taps on the wall and switched the water off, after only being in there for five minutes. She stepped out slowly and carefully onto the thick bath mat; she picked up her towel which she had left close and wrapped the large soft purple bath towel around her and then her matching robe before she went back through to her bedroom.

She walked through softly drying herself but of course that wasn't working so she threw off the robe and towel on her chair, she stood there naked as though all the pressure had been released off of her body but she knew that she still had to finish getting ready for bed. She walked across to her drawers and pulled out a soft satin night dress, something soft on her skin she thought would be best.

She carefully tried to lift it over her head but it was still too painful to lift her arms, so she decided to step into it and pull it up slipping her arms through the holes; it didn't feel so bad against her skin kind of cool in fact because of the metal. She went back over to her bed and threw the covers back before she carefully got into bed.

"Computer lights out." Toria ordered as she lay down turning onto her right because it hurt too much to lay on her back and her other side. She closed her eyes and near enough drifted off straight away because she was so tired, falling into an uneasy sleep.

...Toria was walking down a corridor aboard a ship. There were wall consoles to the right and on the left was a view port looking over a beautiful red and purple nebula; she just stood there staring at it not even seeming to realize when a man walked up behind her. He wrapped his arms around her and softly kissed her on the cheek, Toria smiled to herself as her hair turned from purple to red.

"I can't believe that you once said that you didn't like me." The man said as he turned her around to face him...

Chapter Five

Toria could hear an alarm going off somewhere near by as she pulled her covers over her curling up into a ball underneath them hoping to block out the sound, but then something heavy suddenly fell onto her bed and over her legs and the alarm sounded louder as though it was nearer; she threw back her covers with her long hair astray and revealing the cotton short set pajamas that she was wearing.

"Good morning sleepy head." Renji said as he stood up off of her bed and stood over her at the foot of her bed.

Toria looked up at the sound of his voice, horrified that he was actually here. "What the hell are you doing here?"

She grabbed behind and then threw her pillows at him which he caught and threw back at her.

"Your father won't be pleased if you're late." Renji told her. "So we haven't really got time to play right now."

"What?" Toria said still a little sleepy and then she remembered what he was talking about and jumped out of bed. "Why didn't you wake me earlier? Why isn't my alarm loud enough?"

"You turned the volume down on your alarm." Renji told her as he watched her run into the bathroom. "And I'm not actually your babysitter."

"Really...then why are you here now?" Toria asked smiling at him as she leant out of the bathroom so that she could see him.

"Because if you're late, I'm late and then we're both in trouble." Renji answered turning to leave as Toria went back into the bathroom. "Not the best way to start off this month long trip now is it?"

"I guess not." Toria shouted through.

"I'll wait for you in the living room. Don't forget your bag the rest of them have already been taken aboard the ship." Renji told her.

"I'm not a child, so quit nagging!" Toria shouted at him.

Renji smiled to himself as he left her room.

Toria had a quick shower and threw her hair up hoping that it looked presentable enough, then she put on the outfit that she had left out the night before which of course was a good job considering how late she was getting up; it was smart but not over the top. She was only fifteen after all, a waist coat top with a matching knee-length skirt and shoes.

She stood in front of the mirror to make sure that she looked alright but as she did so she saw something move behind her, she spun around but nothing was there so she just shook it off as her imagination because she was still half asleep after just jumping out of bed; she walked over to the door picking up her bag off the set of drawers as she left to meet Renji.

Toria walked up the hall knowing that there wasn't anyone else left here only her and Renji because they had all gone ahead of them to the transport. She picked her pace up a little knowing if she was really late that they would both end up in trouble; when she reached the living room she stopped and stood against the doorframe and just stared at him seated there on the sofa with his head back as though he had gone to sleep himself.

"Well you look as though you really want to go." Toria said smiling.

Renji slowly rolled his head over to look at her and smiled back at her. He pushed himself up and stood staring at her for a moment before he walked over and joined her; Toria smiled up at him as she linked his arm.

"You don't mind do you?" Toria asked him.

"Just as long as no one gets the wrong idea." Renji teased.

"Please, an old man like you and a fifteen year old." Toria said smiling as they walked up the hall together out of the apartment.

"Hay, what's that supposed to mean?" Renji asked somewhat annoyed. "I may be a lot older than you, but it's not as though I actually look it, is it?"

Toria looked up at him. "How old are you then?"

"Well...that doesn't matter." Renji said dismissively as he opened the door; they both stepped out but Renji turned around slightly so that he could reach the console to lock the door. "Considering how late we are, we'll need to get a hover taxi to the transport centre."

Toria laughed at him as she pressed the button for the lift.

"What?" Renji asked her.

"You must be old if you're keeping it a secret." Toria said. "Or is it that you think that I'll think differently after knowing the truth?"

"You will do." Renji told her as the lift arrived and the doors slid open, he stepped in first and then Toria who still had hold of him.

"So what are you then?" Toria asked him looking up at him expectantly.

"What do you think I am?" Renji asked her.

Toria stared at him as though she was thinking this question over very carefully before she answered him.

"Well, to be honest I have actually thought about it of course since...well since years, even before I found out for sure that you were a Magic." Toria told him, which made him smile. "Well you're not a Tasian because you're not sensitive enough, see..." And she touched the left side of his face where if he was a Tasian he would have markings, but nothing; he just smiled at her. "It hurts me you know, even more for some reason being hit on my left... anyway back to you. So that means that you're a Ta'vaian."

"Does it now? There are other races that live a long time." Renji told her.

"Yes I know, but those two are the main ones and the ones that look most human." Toria told him. "And anyway, I think that you would suit be a Ta'vaian with all those markings all over you; making you look even tougher than you do now."

The lift stopped and the doors slid open before Renji could respond which he had wanted too, he lead them out past the other residents who were waiting to go up and through the quiet entrance hall even though normally this time of morning it was a lot busier with people going to work. Neither of them spoke as they walked through not wanting to be overheard; it wasn't really what you would talk about in polite society and being excited about it as well; at least not here.

The cool morning air rushed in as the front doors slid open with a slight wooshing sound, Toria moved a little closer to Renji feeling the cold more than normal. They walked down the front steps and then onto the walkway which lead to the end of the plaza which was surrounded by high rising apartment buildings and the open-air traffic at the end that would take you anywhere on the planet that you wanted to go.

"It isn't that cold and it's supposed to be summer as well." Renji told her.

"I know that, it's just that sometimes I'm really cold or I'm really hot as though my body can't make up its mind what it wants to do." Toria told him.

"You're at that age." Renji told her.

"What...hay..." Toria said swinging her bag at him and hitting him in the chest, but he grabbed hold of it and tried to pull it away from her, not that she would let it go of course.

"There wasn't any need for that, all I meant was that your body was changing into an adult so of course it would be..." Renji tried to explain but she cut him off.

"I know that...I don't need you telling me." Toria said blushing deeply now burning up as Renji smiled to himself flagging a hover taxi down.

"See that's better isn't it, you're all hot now." Renji teased.

"That's funny...ha, ha...can't you see me splitting my sides open laughing." Toria said sarcastically.

"Well I would have tested how sensitive your left side really is but we're in public, so perhaps later when we're alone." Renji teased as a hover taxi slowed down and stopped in front of them. It was green with black checks all over the body.

Toria's hair had changed from brown to red in matter of seconds, she reached out for the door handle but felt it melt under her touch and quickly pulled it away so that Renji could open it as she pulled her arm free of his; Renji slide over on the back seat though first pulling Toria into the taxi next to him touching her burning hand which didn't seem to bother him.

"We're going to the Senator Transport Centre." Renji told the driver as he leant over Toria making her flatten herself against the seat as he closed her door.

The driver looked as though he was three times Renji's age, well in appearance anyway making his once bright green skin look a dull muddy colour and his top knot with just a few stray hairs sticking out the top.

Toria made sure that there was plenty of room between them which Renji found funny but Toria found frustrating, considering that she already found it hard to keep whatever it was under control when she was around him but now with this teasing she didn't know what she was going to do; he had never teased her like this before but it didn't bother her as much as she let on that it did. It was the fact that it kind of felt familiar to her that made it seem even more strange in a way.

Toria sat in silence trying to ignore him seated beside of her and watched the passing hover and air cars outside of her window as they lifted up into the air and joined the air traffic lanes, hundreds of them flying through the air thousands of different lives going on beside her own.

"Have you ever wondered how many Magics there are on this planet right this moment?" Renji asked her breaking into her thoughts.

Toria turned around startled by his question. "No...no I haven't...would there be a lot?"

"Of course not...like they'd let those things on the planet, the Malarias Fleet are doing a fine job of rounding them up but they wouldn't let them here." The driver told her.

"Yes, it was on the news this week that three more Magical colonies have been destroyed and over five thousand captured." Renji said.

"Good." The driver said.

"Your people used to be part of their empire, one of the protective races before it fell you don't care that..." Toria started but Renji cut her off shaking his head at her, she crossed her arms annoyed and sat in silence again though this time angry with Renji for just letting that guy say horrible things like that about his own people.

"Foolish child, it makes you wonder what they teach 'um in school." The driver said annoying Toria even more.

Toria could feel herself getting more and more annoyed. She needed to get out of there before she exploded, not really a good thing to do, in mid air nor on her way to meet her father and half a dozen other senators.

Renji looked over at her knowing that she was getting annoyed with the driver. He was glad that she felt so strongly but this probably wasn't the best time or place to be expressing her views.

"If you don't mind but if we carry on at this speed we'll end up missing our transport." Renji told him.

"Right yeah...big shin dig for the senators getting to go anywhere they want." The driver said. "But us normal people, the hard working class can't even get off world for a week unless we save up for two years."

"That would be because there's a war going on. We need to make sure that you're safe when you go off world." Renji told him.

"There!" Toria shouted out suddenly pointing out the window at the large hovering platform in the air and the transport ships docked with it. "Just over there, there's even a space for you to get through."

"What, now you're in a rush?" Renji teased as the driver pulled out of the lane into the space that she had pointed out.

Toria looked over at him and then back out of the window as the taxi descended onto the platform into the taxi rank. Toria though opened the door as soon it landed and got out leaving Renji to pay for the taxi with his card; she stood waiting for him a couple of feet away as he walked over to her.

"The cool air really does help I take it." Renji asked her; Toria didn't answer him but linked his arm again as they set off across the busy platform.

There were senators of all different races dressed in formal clothes; some wore clothes of their world whereas some donned human clothes as if it was their way of saying that they supported them and their cause. There were so many people here, that Toria was glad that she had hold of Renji so that she wouldn't be separated from him; she noticed that quite a lot of the guards actually knew him or they at least acknowledged him as they walked by.

"Do you actually know all them or are they just letting on to you?" Toria asked him.

"I know some of them." Renji told her. "But in this business it's better to know as many as possible, you never know when you may need there help for something important."

"I guess." Toria said.

Renji could see their transport ship the second largest ship on the platform. He directed Toria over to where Bernal was stood waiting for them at the entrance to the tunnel which went down a flight of stairs.

"I'm glad that the two of you could make it this morning." Bernal said of way of greeting, eyeing the two of them stood before him. "You know in a strange sort of way...and I can't believe I've even thought about it, but you two kind of suit each other...perhaps in another lifetime though."

"What?" Toria said pulling her arm free and going first down the stairs.

"She's a little young." Renji said.

"She won't be in a couple of years, just three more years and she's eighteen." Bernal said staring after her.

"And still off limits to the guards." Renji reminded him. "Unless you're going to leave and try your luck."

Renji followed her with Bernal just behind him. He wasn't too keen on the conversation which Bernal was, but he was a little too distracted with his own thoughts to realize how annoyed Renji actually was with him for bringing up such a matter.

The stairs went down two levels with lights above on the ceiling, the corridors were just a bare metal shell with a door at the end and a wall console to monitor the docking processors. Toria walked through the open doors onto the transport ship, but to her despair Lesharo was waiting outside of the lift further down the corridor to take her to her father.

"Your father was going to have me put out a search order for you." Lesharo told her.

"We're not that late." Toria said as she walked over to him.

Lesharo didn't answer her but looked right past her at Renji accompanied by Bernal, Renji wasn't bothered that he was once again in a foul mood with him the only time that he would start to worry was when he wasn't; Bernal on the other hand didn't much care for the tension between them but he kind of understood it.

"It's probably his fault that you're late." Lesharo said as he hit the lift console behind him to call for the lift, which only took a second to arrive. "Get inside already."

Lesharo grabbed hold of her arm and pulled her inside of the lift Renji came in behind her and pulled her other arm stepping in front of her, while Bernal opted to stand against the other wall trying not to make eye contact with either of them, because it really did look as though it was going to kick off between them; again.

"You do realize that anyone watching you two would think that you're acting like children." Toria told them from behind Renji. "I can actually imagine the two of you coming into school everyday and fighting with one another every time the teachers' backs were turned."

Neither of them said anything because they both knew that she was right but of course they weren't going to tell her that, so they all stood in silence until finally the lift opened and Toria stepped out first on to a crowded deck of officials; Renji got out behind her then Lesharo who pushed Renji out of his way followed by Bernal.

"You should go and see your father." Lesharo told her.

"I'll take you to his office." Renji told her.

"Thanks." Toria said as she walked off with Renji once more. "Was I supposed to learn who everyone is?"

"Well most of the important ones at least, yes." Renji answered.

"Great...I think I've remembered about five." Toria said making Renji laugh out load surprising her and the others around them some stopping talking and looking over at them. Toria couldn't help but smile at him; she liked it when he was like this, able to be himself somewhat which was so hard considering that he had been working under cover for so long.

Toria wasn't looking where she was going because she was watching Renji and almost knocked a young lad to the ground. She turned around to help him but before she could he was being dragged to his feet by an older man who quickly bowed at them both; Renji took hold of her hand to carry on but she wouldn't as she watched this boy being dragged away.

"Blind fool! You should watch where you're walking!" The man shouted at the boy as they walked off.

"Renji?" Toria asked questioningly.

"I'm afraid that he is." Renji answered.

"What? But he's just a boy and did you see how they were treating him?" Toria asked him as her voice was getting louder with anger.

"Please, just come along." Renji told her quietly. "You're causing a scene where we'll both end up in trouble along with the boy."

Toria reluctantly carried on walking her mood not improving at all as though a black cloud had swept in and was hovering over her; Renji was angry also but he knew his limits especially on board a senate transport ship.

"There you are." A tall thin man said with greying brown hair which looked almost blonde, he looked about the corridor realizing that there was quite a commotion going on just behind them. "Has something happened?"

"Yes a sla..." Toria started but Renji cut her off.

"No not much, just one of the other parties getting a little overexcited." Renji told him.

"Yes indeed, they've been like that all morning." The man told them, and then he turned his attention to Toria and smiled at her. "Well haven't you grown up Lady Victoria, you might not remember me it has been a while since we last met."

"Aid Alec Fairhare." Toria answered stiffly.

Aid Fairhare smiled at her before he stepped aside for her to enter her father's office, Renji was about to follow her but was blocked as Aid Fairhare who rushed in front of him; Renji bowed his head slightly before he followed them inside.

"Father." Toria said as she stood in the middle of his office.

There were about half a dozen men rushing around all of whom looked very busy, but she didn't recognize one of them; Senator Kentaro sat in his chair at his desk which was the same size as her single bed back at the apartment full of work and several computers.

Senator Kentaro slowly looked up from his work at his daughter. "Victoria, I almost forgotten what you looked like. It seems as though we've both been busy lately, or late."

"Yes father." Toria said standing stiffly in front of her father as though she was stood in front of the head teacher at school. "My end of term exams went well father, I came in the top ten of all the exams."

"The top ten, not the top five?" Senator Kentaro asked sounding disappointed with her.

"I'm sorry father." Toria said. "I'll do better next term."

"I hope so." Senator Kentaro said and then turned to Renji. "See her to her quarters, they're joined with your own; I want to make sure that there's someone on hand all the time."

"Quite right sir, you never know with having so many Magics on board." Aid Fairhare said beside Toria.

"They probably didn't come by choice." Toria mumbled.

"What was that dear?" Aid Fairhare asked her.

"It's her first time being around them. She didn't realize that there was going to be some of board." Renji explained. "Don't worry I'll keep a close eye on her sir."

"Yes, see that you do; because if anything happens to her then it'll be your head." Senator Kentaro told him before he went back to his work.

Toria turned around and walked out of the room without saying goodbye to her father, Renji bowed his head again before he followed her; he slowly followed her down the crowded corridor easily making his way knowing that she would wait for him at the lift. Toria stopped by the lift and pressed the button knowing that Renji would get there before the lift arrived, and well she didn't want to be around all these people who think that it's alright to treat that boy like a slave all because he was born differently.

Renji put his hand on her shoulder making her look up at him, she had thousands of questions to ask him if this lift would only hurry up and arrive already; it seemed to take even longer than normal to arrive but finally the doors slid open and they got inside but as soon as the doors closed she started questioning him.

"Doesn't that bother you?" Toria asked him.

"Of course it does?" Renji answered irritably.

"Why can't you do something about it...I don't mean you over all..." Toria said. "Your kind...?"

"We can only do so much." Renji told her.

"What sort of answer is that?" Toria demanded rounding on him. "Would it be different if you knew him? If he was family? If he was your son?"

"It's an awful thing to say, but yes." Renji answered honestly. "Hopefully his family is doing what they can to get him back."

"What if they're slaves as well? What if they never see each other again?" Toria asked him. "What if...?"

"There's a lot of 'what ifs' Toria, the simple answer is that we can't save everyone." Renji told her.

Toria hit him in the chest suddenly. "Well that's not good enough, you have to save them all."

Renji grabbed hold of her forcibly. "How can I save them all when I can't even protect the ones closest to me?"

"What?" Toria said startled by his outburst.

Renji let go of her and turned around, he hadn't meant to do that. "It doesn't matter, just forget that I said anything."

"But...Renji..." Toria started.

"Just forget it!" Renji shouted at her startling her as she stepped back.

The door slid open and they both stepped out onto an empty corridor, Renji lead the way with Toria just behind him staring at her feet not daring to look up at him to see how angry he was with her; it was the first time that he had mentioned anything so personal and she had to go and upset him like that.

Toria thought that he wouldn't trust her with anything else, not that he had ever fully trusted her to begin with; now he never will.

Renji stopped suddenly outside of a door but she walked straight into him because she wasn't looking where she was going, he didn't say anything nor did he even look at her; but Toria stumbled backwards blushing deeply not wanting him to shout at her again.

"I'm sorry." Toria said.

Renji opened the door and went inside, Toria looked inside before she followed him and realized that her belongings were inside waiting for her like Renji had said earlier; she stopped two feet in the room and dropped the bag she had been carrying; the door closed behind her when she saw another door to the right. She looked to the left and saw her bedroom so that other door was to Renji's quarters like her father had said, they had joint rooms.

There was a four seated sofa under the view port with her bags on it and just in front the coffee table were two comfy chairs. On either side of the door through to Renji's room were paintings of space regions. There was a square table with four chairs around it with a vase of flowers atop, behind her on the other side was a desk with a computer so that she could do her homework while she was here.

Renji stood in-between the chairs staring out over the skyline listening to the docking clamps releasing the ship. It began to rise into the city sky above the air-lanes and the buildings far below; Toria walked closer to the view port around the chair so that she could watch them leaving the atmosphere since it had been so long since she had left The Dragon Senate.

The sky around the ship began to darken and clouds thickened as twinkles of light appeared in them, then as the ship pushed through the uppermost atmosphere there was blackness, a vast never-ending blackness with thousands of spots of lights; suns hundreds of thousands of light years away.

"I'm sorry about before, I had no right to say those things to you." Toria said turning to face him. "I just got carried away with myself..."

"It's alright." Renji said stiffly turning to leave.

Toria quickly went after him getting in front of him to stop him.

"Toria..." Renji said grabbing hold of her so that he could move her out of his way.

Toria just stood there as she watched him walk away, the door slid open and he went through to his own quarters without even looking back at her. The door closed behind him and he was finally alone; his quarters were identical to Toria's.

"Damn it!" Renji shouted as he reached for his shoulder a sword appearing suddenly, he pulled it off and sliced the table in half. "Why don't you understand!"

Renji glared at the destroyed table and smashed vase and then he looked over his shoulder at the adjoining door, knowing that she was upset on the other side while he was angry with himself.

"Damn it...it wasn't supposed to be this hard..." Renji said turning back around and going through to his bedroom, he waved his sword several times over his shoulder; the vase and table began to repair themselves as he sheathed his sword and it disappeared as though it was never there in the first place then he took his jacket off and threw it over the back of the chair as he walked pat it.

He went through to the bedroom taking his clothes off as he went to take a long shower to help him unwind.

Toria walked through the corridors of the ship on her own, she didn't feel like sitting in her room feeling sorry for herself and she did actually want to have a look around considering that this was the first time that she's been on such a large ship before. She had passed several officials who all had been polite to her, Toria thought that her father had probably told them all that he was bringing her as though they all had to have and extra briefing on it, it wouldn't have really surprised her; she had recognized some of them from their photos that she was studying but she couldn't remember all their names.

As Toria was approaching a corner she could hear several men talking. She stopped at the corner not wanting to go around and disturb them but just peered around the corner to have a glimpse of them; they were both officers in the Malarias Fleet, Captains. The one on the left was human in his late forties ageing well before his time, the man next to him was much younger his green skin still fresh looking.

"The Deturon system seems to have picked up activity recently; I've sent a team to investigate the situation." The human said.

"We have been trying to monitor the space around our system, but as you know there are in fact an awful lot of systems." The younger man said. "It's hard to keep track when they keep moving so often."

"Perhaps they don't move as often as we think they do. They just make it look as though they do." The human said. "It is after all a lot of hard work to keep moving all those people; though if we find one of those bases we'll make sure that this will be their last move, if they come willingly or not, either way it'll be their last time."

Toria couldn't believe what she was hearing. She had to tell someone; she turned around and ran back the way that she had came turning a few heads as she ran past them. She doubled over outside of Renji's quarter's breathing heavily as she pressed the button to beep her in but there was no answer, so she let herself in, he wasn't in the living room so she headed over to his bedroom.

"Renji...are you here?" Toria asked as she walked into his bedroom, she just stopped dead and stared not really meaning to but she couldn't help it as he stood there naked in front of her. She couldn't really keep her eyes focused in one spot as they kept moving up and down as if trying to take him all in.

"Yes?" Renji prompted as he carried on getting dressed.

"... What...? ... sorry..." Toria said spinning around on the spot blushing deeply suddenly realizing what she had done and began to leave.

"Wasn't there something you wanted to tell me?" Renji asked after her, pulling his trousers on.

"What?" Toria said distractedly as she tried to remember why she was there; then it suddenly came to her. "The Deturon system..."

"What about it?" Renji asked sitting down on his bed as he pulled his shoes on.

"I went for a walk and overheard these captains talking about sending some ships out to the system." Toria told him. "They said that they were going to find the Magics in the system...I'm not sure though if they're going to destroy them or capture them...perhaps both..."

"Great..." Renji said getting up grabbing his shirt and pulling it on as he walked past her into the living room and behind the desk sitting down, he switched the computer on and tapped the screen. "I haven't got any informants there...I'll have to contact someone else so that they could get the word out."

Toria stood with her back still to Renji unable to look at him her face still burning red; while Renji contacted an old friend encrypting his transmission so that it wouldn't be detected by communications on the bridge.

"Hopefully he'll be able to help." Renji said as he waited for the screen to connect.

It took a minute or so for the screen to come into focus though it wasn't a man but a Tasian woman who smiled brightly at Renji when she realized who it was.

"Well it's definitely been a while Pur, but I haven't got time to talk; will you pass a message on to your husband for me?" Renji asked her.

"Course, go ahead." Pur said.

"We believe that the Fleet is moving in on the Deturon system, I need him to take a couple of ships to check it out." Renji told her. "And if need be get as many out of there as he can."

"Another system, why can't they just leave us alone?" Pur said angrily.

"They won't be happy until they've caught every last one of us." Renji said looking past the screen at Toria who was still staring out of the view port. "I've got to go, but will you see to that?"

"Course and Renji be safe." Pur told him.

"And you." Renji said before he signed off standing up, he walked around the desk and turned Toria around to face him. "Did they see you, did anyone see you?"

"What? No...I don't think so..." Toria said.

"You need to be certain, it's very important that you remember." Renji told her as he tighten his grip on her.

"No...no one saw me listening to them." Toria told him. "People saw me walking around the ship though on my own, but not when I heard them talking."

"That's alright then." Renji said letting her go.

Toria suddenly realized that his shirt wasn't fastened and then she remembered seeing him naked a few moments ago, her whole body seemed to go into overload as this wave of fire erupted through her making her sway a little; the blast shot out of her body straight at Renji hitting him square in the chest with such force that it threw him over the desk and into the wall.

"Oh god..." Toria said panicked as she started to rush over to him as he slumped to the ground, but when she came to the end of the desk she changed her mind and shook her head; as though she didn't trust herself to get any closer to him. "I'm sorry...I didn't mean too..."

Toria turned and ran out of there too afraid to stay anywhere near him after what she had just done; and also too afraid to actually see what she had done to him.

"Toria wait!" Renji shouted as he pushed himself to his feet, he looked down at himself but there wasn't a burn mark on him; and then said to himself smiling slightly. "You just took me by surprise...silly girl..."

Renji fastened his shirt as he went after her, he didn't need to ask the computer where she was because he could sense her the Magic that had been sealed within her was pouring out of her; he just had to find her before she ran into anyone else and hurt them, they might not be as lucky as he was; though he was surprised that the alarms hadn't gone off since they left his quarters considering the discharge she was giving off.

Toria ran down the corridor making sure that she didn't touch anyone as she ran past them, but every so often a wall console would suddenly explode startling everyone around her; a security team arrived at the end of the corridor making her panic thinking that they had found out that it was her. Four consoles simultaneously exploded as she ran past them straight for the security officers who were knocked to their feet, the aids behind her were thrown to the ground by the shock of the explosion; the internal alarms finally sounded throughout the ship and the lights dimmed and changed to red and began to flash.

"Lady Kentaro this way!" A security officer shouted her, directing her towards them.

Toria ran in-between them not stopping, she could still feel the deep burning fire within her trying to overwhelm her so she couldn't be around anyone; she rounded the corner almost knocking into another security officer.

Toria ran she didn't know where she was going. There wasn't really anywhere on board the ship that she could go to and she couldn't get off the ship while they were traveling between systems. Screaming broke into her thoughts, it was a boy; she stopped and looked around trying to feel where it was coming from, which room was it? She began to walk slowly again listening out trying to block the alarms out that echoed through-out the whole ship, she heard it again and then she remembered the boy she had seen earlier; what was they doing to him to make him scream like that?

It was a different feeling now, a burning anger raged inside of her as her pace quickened her body taking over as though it knew where he was; she walked past several rooms until finally she stopped outside of one but the door didn't open automatically instead the console exploded and she walked inside.

The four security officers stood around the scared boy in the middle of the empty room, they all looked over at her surprised to see her there and also the alarms sounding outside of the room as they hadn't been turned on in there. The security officers were all human but almost twice the boys' size who was younger than Toria and a Tasian, his markings revealed down the left side of his body; but there was also blood stained on the back of his shirt and the guard behind him was holding a whip.

"Little girl you shouldn't be in here." The man nearest to her told her.

Toria's eyes flashed red as though small fires alight inside of them, her hair also like a wave flowing through it changing to red.

"Lady Kentaro..." The guard on the left said nervously.

"Get away from him." Toria told them.

They all looked at one another and turned back to the boy as though she wasn't even in the room. Of course this annoyed Toria even more as she stepped forward and grabbed the nearest man's hand; he looked down at her as he felt his hand burning then she suddenly kicked him in the chest and let go of him as he flew backwards.

"Sir!" The man facing holding the whip shouted. He looked at Toria and then pulled the boy out of the way who stumbled to the ground as he swung the whip around to strike her.

Toria grabbed the whip setting it alight, he tried to hold on as long as he could but he had to let go as the skin on his hand began to burn; Toria pulled and swung it around bring it down and across his face making him drop to his knees.

"Senator Kentaro and your officers to holding room five." The man to her left ordered through his com unit on his wrist.

"There wasn't any need for that." Toria told him as she swung the whip around again striking him across the face and across his chest ripping open his uniform.

He shouted out in pain as he dropped to his knee. Toria turned away from him and turned her attention towards the other two men stood in front of the boy. She swung the flaming whip around as two of her security officers ran into the room just in time to watch her bring the whip clean across the men's cheats tearing their uniforms.

"What...what's going on...?" The security officer on the left asked.

"Lady Victoria...?" The other security officer asked sounding unsure about what was going on.

The officer that she had kicked to the ground pulled a small blaster out of his jacket and shot at her but she dodged it as if she could sense it, but as she turned around she caught the blast in her right hand before it hit the wall; she held the ball of energy in the palm of her hand for a second as they all stared at her before she threw it back at him which seemed even more powerful as it threw him against the wall.

"What is she?" The security officer asked nervously stepping towards the door but was pushed forward suddenly and fell to his knees in front of her. He looked up at her fear in his eyes as he crawled backwards away from her.

"What's going on here?" Lesharo asked them stood in the doorway with Renji beside of him.

"That brat of yours...she's lost her mind..." The man told him stood behind her holding his chest.

"She's one of them." The man said holding his face on the floor.

"Toria..." Renji said calmly as he stepped forward.

"Stay away..." Toria whispered and brought the whip down setting the floor between them on fire and turned back to the men in front of the boy.

"Get her under control." The man ordered as she grabbed hold of him and forced him against the wall, his uniform began to burn away beneath her touch, his jacket, his shirt, straight down to his skin which began to burn away; he tried to hold in his pain but he couldn't help but shout out.

"Toria!" Renji shouted at her. "Don't...don't this...stop!"

"I want her under control, shoot her." Senator Kentaro ordered.

Renji looked over his shoulder at him, shocked that he would give such an order. "Sir?"

"You heard me." Senator Kentaro told him.

"It'll be a pleasure sir." Lesharo said smiling as he stepped forward but Renji put his arm up to stop him. "Hay...I can handle that little girl."

"You stupid men!" Toria shouted a wave blasted from her knocking everyone to the ground except for Renji who stepped forward.

Toria stepped away from him. She didn't want him to get any closer but he backed her against the wall the men moving away from her taking the boy with them as Renji reached out for her just as the guard shot at her again; Toria once again caught the energy blast in her hand and shot it back at him though this time intensifying the blast burning through his uniform and part of his skin.

Renji grabbed her while she was distracted pulling her into him, holding her as tightly as he could as she struggled to break free of him.

"Let go of me!" Toria shouted at him as a fire erupted in the palms of her hands as she tried to push him away burning through his shirt and down to his skin. 'Please!"

"Take her to the med bay." Senator Kentaro ordered stepping aside.

"Toria...calm down." Renji told her as he let go of her arm and scooped her up, he turned around with her in his arms and resting her head on his shoulder. "I'll take her."

"Are you sure...?" Lesharo asked him stepping aside when he saw that she was still burning his uniform away, his skin looked as though it too was burning beneath her touch; he could feel the heat radiating from her as Renji walked passed him, he couldn't believe that Renji could stand to hold her when none of them could even get close to her.

"I'll have the doctors aware of her condition." Senator Kentaro told Renji before he walked out with her, then he turned back to the officers in the room. "Nothing happened, do I make myself clear?"

"But...but...sir she's...she's....look what she's done..." The officer said still on the floor holding his face.

"Lesharo, I believe that we're going to have a few problems why don't you deal with them for me." Senator Kentaro told him polity before he turned and walked out leaving Lesharo to deal with the other officers while he went to check on Toria.

"Hay we're all in this together, what're you going to do?" The man further away asked who pushed himself away from the wall.

"Well the Senator wants to make sure that you don't talk." Lesharo told them simply.

Renji walked down the corridor with Toria in his arms, he had half a mind just to go to the shuttle bay and leave but there weren't a planet near by for days at the speed of what the shuttles go at. He just had to hope that she was strong enough to hold out until he could get her away; first of all he had to get her to sick bay then he suddenly remembered himself and looked at his chest.

"She's going to be upset about that when she wakes up." Renji said to himself not realizing that he wasn't actually alone.

"She can be overly emotional at times, as we found out today." Senator Kentaro said behind him.

The Senator startled him. He had been concentrating all his energy on Toria trying to help her to calm down that he hadn't even sensed his presence until he had spoken.

"You risked your life for her just now, she could have killed you." Senator Kentaro said questioningly as he joined Renji and they carried on walking side by side. "You trusted her feelings for you that much, when she wasn't in control at all, you still believed that she wouldn't have seriously injured you?"

"She isn't a killer." Renji told him and then looked over at him. "Did you know, I mean how powerful she was?"

"Of course I did, but she isn't to know until the right time for when I'm ready for her." Senator Kentaro told him. "But she won't be the problem, it seems that it could be you."

"My duty is to protect her." Renji told him.

"But she's one of them, that doesn't bother you?" Senator Kentaro asked him.

"No." Renji answered simply as the door opened to his right and he went inside, there were three doctors waiting for them stood around the middle medical console.

There were six med beds around the edge of the room and one in the middle next to the medical console where the doctors were waiting, above the beds were medical consoles which would monitor the positions. Renji walked over to the centre bed and carefully put Toria down on it but he didn't step back, the six foot golden skin doctor put his hand on Renji's shoulder and directed him towards the med bed behind to treat his wounds.

Renji reluctantly sat down, the doctor went to take off his jacket but Renji stopped him as the doctor in front of him pulled the head scanner over Toria's head making him jump to his feet.

"What're you doing?" Renji demanded.

"She isn't to remember what she has done, nor be able to use her powers yet." Senator Kentaro told him. "Are you going to be a problem?"

Renji knew what he meant, but he really couldn't do anything for her at the moment. "No...no sir."

"Good, then I want you to take care of her when she comes around." Senator Kentaro told him. "You'll be briefed on your new assignment in the morning."

"Yes...yes sir." Renji said, not fully listening to what he was told but staring at Toria.

Renji paced back and forth in front of Toria's bed in her quarters as she slept, he stopped every couple of seconds and looked over at her as if he was expecting her to wake up.

"Damn it...wake up already...it's been a whole week..." Renji told her but of course she couldn't hear him because she was still asleep.

Toria turned over suddenly pulling the covers close around, Renji turned around and went over to the chair in the corner and sat down to wait for her to wake up; he picked up the data pad on the ledge and started to flick through the pages again.

"I can't believe that he just came out and asked me to do this?" Renji said to himself, he looked up and over at her. "You need to wake up...we can't stay here any longer...Toria..."

Toria moaned as she turned over this time facing Renji seated by the view port. She smiled slightly at him as she blinked a few times focusing her eyes.

"Renji..." Toria whispered.

Renji jumped to his feet and rushed over to her side, he sat down beside her and pulled her into him hugging her tightly; she let him for a moment until she suddenly had a flash of what she had done the last time that she had seen him, throwing or rather blasting him across the room. She pushed him away throwing the covers off of her and crawling out of the bed away from him, Renji stared at her before he got up and walked around the bed over to her as she stepped back into the wall, she felt her way to the opening for her bathroom until finally she found it and dived inside before Renji could stop her and locked the door.

"Toria open the door." Renji told her. "We've been through this before, but this time it's different I'm not just going to walk away."

He disappeared from outside of the door and reappeared beside of her in the bathroom making her scream and stumble backwards into the glass shower door cracking it partly and cutting her elbow, Renji reached out for her but she still tried to move away from him.

"Toria..." Renji said with his hand out for her to take.

"I'm sorry...I didn't mean to hurt you...I...I just overreacted..." Toria said avoiding eye contact with him.

"I'm fine honestly." Renji told her as he grabbed her hand. "It isn't safe here for you anymore."

"I'm sorry." Toria said looking up at him. "I didn't mean too...Renji please...it's...it's just because I like you, I couldn't control it...it just consumed me...I'm sorry."

Renji smiled slightly as he pulled her into him. "You don't have to apologize for being who you are."

"But I hurt you..." Toria said and then looked up at him as though she had remembered something or rather that she couldn't remember. "I don't understand...what am I doing here? How did I get back here? What about you, are you alright?"

"You don't remember?" Renji asked her.

"Renji? What happened to me? Why don't I remember?" Toria asked worriedly.

Renji held her in his arms angry and pained that he couldn't tell her the truth. "All you need to know is that you're not safe here and that you can trust me."

"How can you say that...I mean after what I did to you?" Toria asked him as she pulled away slightly and touched his chest over his shirt. "I didn't mean to hurt you, you know that right?"

"Of course I do, you just get a little over excited from time to time that's all." Renji told her as he lifted her head to look at him. "You just took me by surprise that's all; I'll be ready for you next time."

"I don't want there to be a next time, I don't want to hurt anyone with this." Toria told him as she pulled away and walked around him unlocking the door to go back through to her bedroom.

Renji followed her and watched her as she went through the drawers for something to wear. She had to dress it wasn't as though she could go out in her pajamas and especially not in front of him, it wasn't really right.

"I'll help you if you'll let me." Renji told her. "We're in orbit of Telo-Sento, I'll meet you on the surface; it's a Magical settlement so I'll be able to take you away."

Toria looked over at him startled, she had imaged him asking her to run away with him but for him to actually say it to her she knew that the situation must be serious and she really was in danger here; but now that the time had come, what was she to do? Could she leave everyone behind, all of her friends and her school and her father the only family that she's got?

"I'll be waiting for you." Renji told her as he turned to leave.

Chapter Six

The ramp of the transport ship lowered as the tired-looking passengers approached it carrying several bags each, all of them were dressed in old dirty clothes as though they had been working in the mines; a young man stopped as though something or rather someone had gotten his attention.

He was in his early twenties and had short sandy hair with blue high lights and sparkling blue eyes. He looked straight at the senate guard who was watching him before he walked over to him through the crowd what was heading onto the transport ship.

"So you're him then?" The young man said.

"Yep, not what you imaged I bet?" Renji said smiling at him. "I don't always look like this, and if you really want to help out you'll have to change a little as well."

"I know that, that's why I'm leaving...I want to give them, my family, a better future than just this." The young man said.

"You really do look like a Titus I used to know." Renji said suddenly surprising him. "He died for his people; I hope that you don't have to."

"If it comes to it then I will." Titus said.

"You shouldn't be in such a rush to die, even though we're at war." Renji told him. "Remember you can do a lot more good alive than dead."

"Then why do you stay with them longer than you have to?" Titus asked him.

Renji smiled at him. "For someone special."

"I bet it's a girl." Titus said sounding annoyed.

"Isn't it always?" Renji said still smiling. "But hopefully we'll be leaving here also by the end of the day."

"You're taking her with you?" Titus asked him in disbelief. "Good luck with that one." He looked over his shoulder as the last passengers were boarding. "I've got to go, see you around."

"Good luck." Renji said.

"To us all." Titus said as he turned and walked off towards the transport ship.

Toria stood in the transporter room with Bernal beside of her and Lesharo it seemed trying to keep his distance from her, and making it quite obvious in doing so as well. The transporter officer stood behind the console waiting for Lesharo to stand on the pads to transport them to the surface where the Senator was waiting for them, Lesharo looked at Bernal who was watching him suspiciously and then at Toria as though expecting her to do something which of course she wasn't doing anything.

Toria moved uncomfortably on the spot, she knew that something had happened but what she didn't know and part of her didn't want to either. But she knew that it must have been something terrible considering how many people knew about it and was behaving so strangely around her, he knew the something that had happened to her and he didn't want to get close to her; she didn't blame him after what she had done to Renji but even after what she had done he still wasn't afraid of her and he even held her in his arms. Toria smiled slightly remembering being in his arms, the feeling of him holding her how safe she felt as though while she was with him he wouldn't let anyone hurt her even if she really did have the ability to hurt him.

Lesharo looked even more nervous now that she was smiling and her hair had lightened as well, it seemed a little more red than normal.

"Are you staying here?" Toria asked suddenly.

"What? Of course not, I've been ordered to take you down to the surface." Lesharo told her as he marched forward and turning around quickly stood in front of her. "Now, transport us now."

The transporter officer nodded and activated the pads, a bright light absorbed them as they disappeared and reappeared on the planet surface a moment later. They were stood at the end of the street in front of a large green and blue three-storey building; there was a terrace at the front of the main entrance and four security officers, two at the door and two at the bottom of the steps.

It was late afternoon on Telo-Sento yet it was still very bright and the clear blue skies had no clouds in them overhead. The only thing in the sky were what the people here would describe as birds, they were over a meter long with purple and blue feathers that seemed to glitter in the light as they flew over the buildings.

"I'm going to have a look around, tell my father that I'll be back shortly." Toria told them as she turned to leave but Bernal stopped her.

"What're you doing?" Lesharo demanded pulling him away. "Don't touch her."

"I wasn't going to do anything, just tell her to wait a while and then we'll go around with her." Bernal said surprised by Lesharo's behaviour, as he was probably the only person on her personal security that didn't know her secret yet.

"I can go by myself, I'll be fine and of course I know how to look after myself; considering who he's had me training against." Toria told them. "And anyway, I have a com and there's also plenty of security officers around here if I run into any trouble that I can't handle on my own."

"No...I mean...wait here and I'll get...Aba'rian, you can take him with you." Lesharo told her turning to leave before either of them had a chance to say anything.

"He'd rather Renji take over?" Bernal said staring after him as Toria started to walk away while he wasn't looking. "Now I definitely know that there's something wrong with him..." He turned back around to Toria but she wasn't there, she had gone; he couldn't see her anywhere. "Great...just what I need...to have lost her three seconds after we arrive."

Toria rushed down a side street so that Bernal couldn't see her, it was just that she needed some more time alone before she made her final decision because this was it; her chance to finally leave and be with the Magics, and to find out just what was really going on with her. Part of her was excited by the idea of course because it was such an adventure and then the other part of her felt as though she shouldn't consider that they were after all at war with them and they had killed her mother and tried to kill her also when she was younger; which when she thought about it she never fully understood if she herself was part Magic, unless it was because her mother had left them and gone off with someone from the other side. What if that was the reason that Renji had stayed by her side for so long to take her back to her Magical family, perhaps they had just been waiting for the right chance and if they knew that they could trust her; then that really would mean that she was just another assignment to him and perhaps the only reason that he had been so good to her all these years was so that she would trust him for this moment when he asked her to leave.

She walked down the empty back streets with doors into the buildings and rubbish outside of them waiting to be collected, and there were also fire stairs attached to the outside of the buildings.

She turned left walking towards the sound of people not too far away. She at least wanted to see some of the people while she was actually here; after studying about Magics for so long and only being told about them she actually wanted to see one of their colonies for herself even though she knew that she wouldn't see them use their powers, it was just a matter of actually being among them.

Toria knew that Renji would wait for her right until the last moment even if she had to turn him down, but whenever she thought like that she could see the disappointed look on his face which made her heart ache so much that she couldn't stand it; but she also thought about how her father would be, that then the disappointed look and reaction her father would have when he found out what she had done. She didn't know why but it felt different, she really did feel as though she would be letting Renji down more if she didn't go with him; yes she cared about her father, but she also cared about Renji as well.

Renji had always been more caring towards her, more concerned about her and her feelings then how well she does at everything, wanting her to perform better than everyone else. He had always been there for her for as long as she could remember and she knew that he would always try his best to protect her, if she went with him she knew that she would be safe. She didn't know why, but she was sure that she was more to him than just another assignment, she had to be, especially after all of this time; he must care about her as well.

She walked around for about ten minutes every so often there were people around but they kept their distance from her, Toria just put it down to that they didn't know her and of course they all knew that her father and Malarias Fleet officers were here with him; she didn't like the fact that they avoided her because she really didn't have anything against them but she did understand their behaviour considering everything that they have been through with non-Magics.

Toria turned the corner and found herself on a street full of children round about her age and a little older but there were also officers here pulling them up and questioning them.

"...you're old enough..." A man said further down the street.

Toria turned towards him to find out what was going on, the two officers had hold of a boy about her own age with sandy brown hair and with blue streaks in it; behind the boy were two girls who were younger than him, all of them were dressed in old looking clothes.

Toria walked over to find out what was going on. "Is there a problem officers?"

"Nothing that we can't deal with, now run along like a nice little girl." The officer on her left said as though she wasn't of any interest to him.

"That's nice, that you know who I am; so why don't you let them go." Toria said.

"I told you to run along." The man told her.

"They're Magics, we're only going to put them to work." The other man told her smirking at her.

"You mean you're going to make them work." Toria said as she walked between the girls. "You should go."

"I don't think so, we might just take them as well because of you." The other man told her.

Toria grabbed hold of the boy pushing him towards the girls out of the way and punched the man square in the face and then kicked the other man in the chest, she spun around and when she turned back to face them her long hair had flown out and flowed down her like a wave again and was now red; she smiled at them as she came at them again.

"The little brat knows how to fight." The officer said before she punched him in the face again finally wiping the smirk off of his face, as the other officer crawled on the floor and grabbed hold of Toria's legs pulling them out from under her.

He started to laugh as he pulled her towards him while the blue haired boy shot an small ice spear through his shoulder making him shout out in pain, he fell forward and grabbed hold of Toria's waist; Toria screamed out in pain as her body seemed to explode from the inside out, but this was different than anything else she had felt before and so much more.

Toria's whole body felt as though it was going to explode and there was nothing she could do about it, she combusted so suddenly that no one had a chance to do anything. The fire from her seemed to expand out and set fire to the man on top of her screaming in pain as he tried to move away but there was nowhere to go as the shock wave erupted outwards with such force to the other man and the children that none of them had time to react; the wave of fire raised into the sky and speeded through the streets and buildings destroying everything in its path.

Renji was walking down the stairs with Lesharo beside him when they both felt it, the whole building shook bits of dust fell from the rafters; they both quickly ran down the stairs towards the front entrance and that's when they saw it; a massive wave of fire expending from the centre of the city outwards destroying everything in its path.

"That's her...what's she done...?" Lesharo said as he looked on in horror.

Renji just stood there for a moment unable to believe that it was her, she wouldn't do something like that to all these innocent people; but there wasn't time to think about that at the moment.

"We need to get back to the ship before it gets here." Renji told him activating his com unit. "Evacuate! That's an order, everyone back to ship; there's an energy wave ripping through the city. All groups evacuate!"

As soon as Renji had signed off they disappeared in a bright light reappearing back on board the ship in the transporter room with Bernal, Senator Kentaro and several other security officers; they stepped down off the pad quickly as the transporter officer began again bringing aboard another team. Senator Kentaro pushed passed his security officers to get to Renji looking for Toria among their group and the ones being transported aboard.

"Where's my daughter?" Senator Kentaro demanded.

"That's the last of them...there, aren't anymore life signs in the whole of the city, not even animals..." The transporter officer reported sounding somewhat holo.

They all turned around and looked at him; there were only fifteen people in the room.

"How many did we get back?" Renji asked him ignoring the Senator's question.

"We got sixty three out of eighty five." The transporter officer answered.

"What about the people?" Renji asked. "Did we get any of them?"

"No sir, we were evacuating our own." The transporter officer answered somewhat surprised by the question.

"My daughter?" The Senator asked stiffly.

The transporter officer didn't answer at first as he started to check his records, but Renji became impatient and went over to the console pushing him out of the way checking them himself but he already knew the answer he just had to see it for himself; her name wasn't on the list.

"I'm afraid that she wasn't transported back aboard sir." Renji told him. "As soon as the wave has dissipated I'll take a team down to start looking for her."

"You do that, because if anything's happened to her you'll all pay with your lives." Senator Kentaro warned them. "I've waited too long, to lose now."

Then he left pushing his security officers out of the way, they looked at one another unsure whether or not to follow him; but it was still their duty to protect him.

"I want you ready to move out." Renji ordered his men. "She has a locator implanted within her, that's how we'll find her; we're not leaving until I've brought her back."

"I think you're taking this awfully personal Aba'rian." Lesharo said disgusted with him. "I think you got a little too close...to the brat."

"I'd gladly died for her." Renji told him before he turned to leave, and then continued talking to the other officers who were following him. "I want you kitted out ready to go back down in ten minutes, do I make myself clear; now get moving!"

The ground was burnt and smoldering the smoke still hung thickly in the hot night air, the city a burning ruin with no sound of life except for one breathing heavily laying on the ground without a scratch, without a single sign that she had been here when the fiery wave had ripped through the whole of the city. The girl sat up suddenly her long red hair falling over her face, she pulled it back and looked around wildly; she couldn't believe it the city was gone.

"What have I done?" Toria said as she just sat there trying to take in what she had done; to shocked to even cry at the devastation before her eyes.

Toria just sat there for over five minutes until finally she pushed herself up and bushed herself down, she looked around again now that she was on her feet it was even worst than when she was on the ground she could see even more of what she had done; the whole of the city as far as the eye could see was still a burning rumble. She slowly started to walk but really she didn't know where to go, she stopped again; where could she go?

Toria didn't think that it was such a good idea going back to her father, he had always been so strongly against the Magics and her turning out to be one, he may not want anything to do with her.

"Renji..." Toria suddenly whispered to herself. "I could...no...he wouldn't...not now..." She turned around on the spot looking at the devastation that she had done. "No...I can't...he'd never trust me again....not after what I've done…"

Tears started to cloud her vision and then she started to cry finally, she had killed all those people, all those innocent people and she had let Renji down after all those years of him looking after her; they had been so close to leaving together, but what if they would have left together and something like this would have happened she could have ended up killing him. Then she remembered, he was supposed to be here in the city along with her father and their officers, what if they're all dead as well what if she's killed them all as well?

Toria started to walk again this time in the direction that she had come from before any of this had happened, but she couldn't stay calm for long as she started to run down the back streets that she had come or rather what was left of them; she had to climb over the fallen walls of the buildings cutting her hands as she rushed and her legs as she slid or slipped over the rumble. It took her five minutes to get back to the governor's house where she had left Bernal and Lesharo, where Renji and her father had been inside; her paced slowed as she approached the building or rather what was left of the building.

The windows were blown out as well as the front door, the steps were blown apart and the whole left wing of the house had been completely destroyed collapsing in on itself.

Part of her wanted to go inside just to check to really see if she had killed the people that she cared most about, but the other part was too afraid and it wasn't as though there would be anything left because there wasn't any sign of anyone else, she hadn't seen anyone all this time as though they had been burnt so badly that it had left nothing.

"I have to go..."Toria said to herself as she started to run again, this time away from the governor's house.

As Toria ran down the main street stirring up the ash off the ground and the ash being carried on the wind and the destroyed buildings on either side, the sun was slowly setting in the quiet night sky clouds moving in as though to try and wash away the evidence of what had happened here. Toria tried to remember something anything about this planet, she needed to get off of it but she didn't want to contact her ship in orbit knowing that she would have to explain what she had done and how she had managed to survive when everyone else had been killed; she could image them taking her away and turning her so she would really become one of those 'modified traitors'.

Those that the Magics themselves fear, one of their own been reprogrammed to fight against their own kind not knowing the difference between the two sides or even knowing who they were themselves; she didn't want to live like that nor did she want this sort of power.

"Why...why didn't he do something...he must have known...?" Toria asked herself as she started to cry again, she rubbed eyes trying to stop herself from crying but she just couldn't and just ended up making the redness around her eyes even worse.

The doors to the transporter room were ajar so that the officers could come and go as they rushed about their duties preparing to go back down to the planet for the rescue mission. Bernal was stood over the transporter console running scans of the city still; he hit the console suddenly making several officers look over at him as Renji walked in finally his full length coat flapping behind him along with two more security officers.

Renji looked over at Bernal. "Have you found her yet?"

"No sir." Bernal said angrily. "The sensors can't find her...but shouldn't we be able to at least pick up the locator implant?"

"You would think so wouldn't you?" Renji said sounding annoyed, he wasn't annoyed with them but with himself for not being there for her, for not getting her away from all of this sooner, for not helping her enough when he'd had the chance to do so. "We're going down, we've given it enough time to cool down, down there; if she is alive we better get to her sooner rather than later."

"Yes sir." His officers all shouted as one.

Bernal came out from behind the transporter console which was taken over once again by the proper officer, he walked over to Renji's side.

"Why do you believe that she's alive?" Bernal asked him quietly but Lesharo walked in behind them and overheard him.

"Because it's probably her fault." Lesharo said angrily.

Renji turned around grabbing hold of him. He wasn't in the mood for his sly comments today; he forced him up against the wall making Lesharo wince from the impact.

"You don't know what you're talking about, she wouldn't do that...she isn't a murderer...she..." Renji told him.

"You seem to think that you know her pretty well." Lesharo said. "But truthfully none of us really know her, do we; not after the other day."

"What actually happened?" Bernal asked them.

"That was nothing." Renji said through gritted teeth.

"Why, you think that she's capable of a lot more; like what's happened to that city she was in?" Lesharo asked him.

Renji let go of him, but only to punch him in the face a lot harder than he had done last time; Lesharo sank to the floor as the other officers watched not daring to get between the two men.

"This isn't helping." Bernal said, thinking that this seemed to be happening an awful lot between the two of them lately; when once it had been near impossible to provoke Renji, but now it seemed to be quite easy for him too lose his temper, especially when it was about Toria.

"Well it's helping me." Renji said as he turned around and walked over to the transporter pad. "You're to stay aboard the ship and coordinate the search from up here, now get out of my sight."

"Please...everyone here knows that you're taking this awfully serious and it isn't just because you were in charge of her." Lesharo said as he pushed himself to his feet. "We all know that you've had a thing with her, all I need is the evidence and the Senator..."

"Do you even know what you're saying?" Renji said interrupting him. "She's under age, even if I thought about it, it's not as though I would actually act on it."

Everyone just stared at Renji they hadn't expected such an honest answer, nor an answer saying that he actually liked her.

"We're leaving, anyone coming with us better be on this pad in three seconds or I'm leaving you behind." Renji told them.

They all looked at one another and then rushed over to the transporter pad to take their places, the officer stood behind the console activated the pad and then the bright light embraced them all; they disappeared into the light and then reappeared moments later on the planet's surface in front of what was left of the governors house.

"Right I want you to split up into three groups and span out from this position, no one is to report to me unless they have found her." Renji ordered as he turned around and started to walk with Bernal at his side.

"Aba'rian...what if they don't find her...what if there really isn't anything left of her?" Bernal asked him. "I liked her as well...I mean...well you know what I mean..."

"I know she's alive...I just need to find her." Renji told him as he quickened his pace.

Senator Kentaro sat at his desk in his office with his aids rushing around trying to make themselves look busy and out of his way, Lesharo stepped into the doorway with his lip spilt and his uniform blooded but it didn't seem to bother him as he walked in and approached the Senator's desk. Lesharo stood in front of him for a whole minute before the

Senator even spoke to him, as if he was waiting for something.

Senator Kentaro looked up at Lesharo. "You seem to have upset Aba'rian again."

"I believe that he is too personally involved with your daughter." Lesharo told him.

"And you told him this fact it seems." Senator Kentaro said calmly. "He has a bit of a temper, but has always got the job done; and that includes looking after my daughter all of these years. It is only understandable that he has feelings for her, but they are not what you think they are."

"But sir..." Lesharo started.

"Aba'rian is a useful tool, especially when it concerns my daughter but it will go no further than that and he knows it." Senator Kentaro told him. "He will get my daughter back, and when she is returned to me he will be the tool to turn her against her own kind."

"I don't understand." Lesharo admitted.

"That is because you don't need to understand just obey my orders." Senator Kentaro told him. "Now leave, I have things to do and so do you. Clean yourself up and then take a team down to the planet and monitor all of the transports leaving the planet."

"Yes sir." Lesharo said bowing his head slightly before he turned and left.

The door slid closed behind him as he turned to his right and headed up the corridor past the officers stood outside of the senator's office, he pressed the com unit on his wrist.

"Lesharo to security unit five, meet me in transporter room six in ten minutes we're going to the surface." Lesharo ordered.

"Yes sir." A man answered through his com unit.

Lesharo pressed his com again and carried on up the corridor towards the lift, he really did need to change and clean up before he headed out and this time he was going to beat Renji to the prize.

Ten minutes later Lesharo walked into the transporter room changed and uninjured, with his security team ready and waiting for him; he smiled to himself quite pleased finally seeing an advantage to this situation that he could take he wasn't going to let it slip through his fingers.

"Right then men." Lesharo said as he walked over to the transporter pad his officers following his lead, he was dressed like they were now in his official uniform as a security officer and not in his senate uniform which was actually kind of hard to move in.

The young transporter officer activated the pad that they were stood on enveloping them in a bright light disappearing and reappearing in the over busy transporter center on the coast line of the of Terum; there was hardly any room to move as people crowded in trying to make their way through to the desks at the other end of the hall.

"It was lucky that we even managed to transport in here sir." The man to his right said. He was the same height but a couple of years younger and had short black brown hair. "The reports say that the population is in a state of panic considering that nothing like this has happened since the fall of the Tasian Empire a couple of centuries ago."

"If we wanted them dead, we wouldn't have stopped with just one city...fools." Leshara said as he pushed a child out of his way stepping forward to begin his search for Toria.

Just then at the far entrance Toria stood bent over leaning against the wall breathing heavily covered in dirt and ash from running out of the city, people briefly looked over at her as they rushed inside the centre and then not giving her a second thought only about themselves and getting off of the planet. Toria forced herself to stand up because she wasn't going to get anywhere just by standing there and the more time that she took getting off of the planet the more of the chance that they would find her and force her to go back home.

She knew it was no time to be polite. No one else was being, it was every person for themselves as she started to push her way through the crowds of people; it looked as though most of the people here were humans but she knew better than that after knowing Renji for so long as no one was ever what they appeared to be. They were probably Magics who have changed their forms so that they wouldn't be stopped.

Toria wondered if she would be able to do that one day, it would definitely come in handy, though to be honest that trick would come in handy today if she could somehow magically change her appearance so that no one would be able to recognize her.

A large man knocked into her from behind almost knocking her off her feet and into several other people trying to get by who also pushed her out of the way. She wasn't sure how considering that she was being pushed from side to side but she saw part of the security uniforms from the Malarias Fleet, it was no wonder that no one wanted to go that way or be signalled out. She lowered her head as she tried to quickly get past them, all the time thinking that she wanted to change or rather she needed to change. The blonde haired security officer looked over just in time to see a fifteen year old girl with long reddish hair walking by in the middle of the crowd, he pushed past the people as he tried to keep her in sight hoping that he had found her; it was only for a split second but he lost sight of her he couldn't see her. He almost threw the people out of his way as he grabbed hold of the nearest girl to him of the same age, but it wasn't her; she had short purple hair and purple eyes, she looked up at him fear in her eyes and those around her no one seemingly coming to her help.

A tall dark-skinned man with dark eyes in his early twenties walked up beside the girl and put his arm around her shoulder pulling her towards him, the security officer looked up at the man and stepped back considering that he was nearly a foot taller than him and more well built.

"Is there a problem here, I just lost track of her." The man said.

"Um...no...I thought she was someone else." The security officer answered nervously before he rushed past to carry on looking.

"You should be more careful." The man told her as he directed her through the crowd with his arm still on her shoulder so not to lose her.

"I'm sorry to have bothered you." She said looking up at him but he kept on looking ahead so to get through the crowd much easier.

"Not at all...you look as though you were close to the city." The man said.

"Yes...um...well kind of..." The girl answered nervously.

"Come on." The man said as he pulled her closer to himself to get through a denser part of the crowd to the ticket desk. He managed to get to the front of the queue with little effort. "Two tickets."

"What...but..." The girl said.

The man behind the ticket desk had scaly black skin and yellow eyes with just a robe wrapped around him loosely.

"Two tickets to Hav'erken'nash." The man said.

The scaly man behind the desk typed in the destination on his computer screen which beeped repeatedly before it printed out the tickets, the man handed them over and then the other man handed him a red plastic card which the scaly man took and swiped before he handed it back along with the tickets.

"Come on, we better get going the transport is leaving shortly." The man told her as he directed her away from the desk in the opposite direction where the crowd was so dense, this was the part of the building that only let the actual travellers through.

"But..." The girl said again.

"You want to leave here don't you?" The man asked her.

"Well...um...yes...but I didn't mean for you..." The girl said.

"That's fine, you can pay me back when you're ready." He told her. "No problem..."

She followed him closely never letting go of him as they made their way through the crowd and down the passageway towards the transport ship that was waiting to take them away, they couldn't see what the ship looked like because there were no windows in the small tunnel that lead them on board.

"I'll get you on board, but afterwards you don't need to stay with me." He told her as they passed through the re-enforced doors. He stepped to the side to let the others carry on through while he finished. "I don't mind if you want to go and look for your family now that you're on board."

"Well...um...I don't have any..." She told him.

He looked down at her sadly and held out his hand to her. "Then you'll want to strike around a little longer then, Lonac...that's me."

"To...um...I'm Touro." She told him.

"It's nice to meet you Touro." Lonac said as she took his hand and he lead her off to his quarters.

They walked to the end of the grey unfurnished corridor to get the lift up to their level with the three other humans waiting, they were all dressed like workers as though they had just finished and hopped straight onto the transport without even bringing anything with them, though neither did Lonac as though all these people just left with the clothes on their backs. Touro tried not to stare at them but it was hard because this was her first time being off world around strange people that she didn't even know.

It didn't take long for the lift to arrive and for them all to step inside once the door was open, Touro stood at the front beside of Lonac; he pulled out his ticket from his trousers pocket and quickly scanned it to find out what deck they were on then he pressed the third button on the small console after everyone else had already pressed their deck level. Everyone stood in silence as they waited for the doors to open up on their levels.

"Deck five, section three." The male computer voice told them as the lift stopped and the door slid open.

Lonac pulled Touro to one side so that the man behind them could get past, she looked up at him as he walked past her but he didn't look back at any of them as he walked out onto the crowded deck. The doors closed again and they set off for the next deck.

"Deck eight, section three." The computer told them as the doors slid open onto another corridor but this one wasn't as busy as the last one that they stopped at.

Lonac stepped out first with Touro at his side, she looked about at the bare corridor; nothing had been added to it in decoration it was just a plain corridor lined with doors.

"There's hardly anyone here." Touro said.

"That's because not many can afford the tickets for these quarters." Lonac explained as he lead the way.

"Considering that they're evacuating the population shouldn't they lower the ticket prices?" Touro asked him.

Lonac stopped and looked down at her. "There may had been a time that something like that may had been considered, but not anymore; we're still at war...I guess they're kind of thinking everyone for themselves..."

"Well...I don't like that kind of thinking." Touro told him. "You're all fighting together to save your people, but you're also willing to let your own kind die just to save yourselves; it just doesn't make sense."

"I never said that I..." Lonac started to defend himself.

"I know that you're not like that, or you wouldn't have helped me." Touro told him smiling. "I will pay you back when I'm able."

"Take your time." Lonac said staring at her wondering if she really was a child, he had never heard a child speak so strongly about their views before; even someone his own age could they be as strong in their belief's?

They walked down the corridor in silence which quickly emptied of the three people they had seen when the lift doors opened, which all had returned to their quarters. Touro was just about to ask Lonac something when he stopped and looked at his ticket again against the door panel; he held it out so that the panel could scan it and the door slid slowly open as the lights inside activated.

"Right this is home for the next couple of weeks." Lonac said as he went inside first followed closely by Touro.

Touro quickly looked around the room taking it all in trying to figure out why these quarters had cost more when there wasn't really much to them the carpet and walls were a light grey colour like in the corridors of the ship, to her right was a black metal square table with three chairs and a ledge behind it for their food; in front of her was the view port which was in place of the wall, beneath it was a full length greyish almost black sofa with two chairs and a small table set in the middle of them.

Touro looked to her left at the two doors. "Are they the bedrooms?"

Lonac looked over his shoulder at her and then walked over to the first door and pressed the button on the small panel, the door opened to reveal a very small bathroom; it had a cube shower, a toilet and a sink.

"Bedrooms must be through there." Lonac told her pointing to the other door. "Why don't you go and chose which one you want."

Touro looked over at him still a little unsure, but he seemed alright and she was here now; it was just that he was doing so much for her how was she every going to pay him back?

"It's fine, go on." Lonac told her.

He walked over to the nearest chair and sat down putting his feet up on the table while Touro watched him before she walked over to the other door which opened for her without having to press the door panel; she stepped into a small narrow hall with two dim lights overhead. A door facing her and a door to her right; she turned to her right and went into the first bedroom.

It had a view port facing the door with a single bed underneath it with plain grey sheets and a small side table, in the far corner on the wall of the door was the wardrobe and then a chest of drawers; she still couldn't work out why these were classed as more expensive. She stepped back out and down to the other door and went inside, it was a long narrow room which the view port was to the right over the head of the bed with a small side table and then at the other end was the wardrobe and a tall narrow chest of drawers.

Touro smiled to herself thinking that neither of them were much to chose from, but she would have this room considering how big he was, the other one seemed a little bigger; she turned back around and went back through to the main room the doors closing behind her.

"I'll have the one at the far end." Touro told him.

"Great..." Lonac said. "After we've left the system I'll show you around, and I'll see what I can do about papers for you."

"Papers?" Touro asked not knowing what he was talking about.

"Your id papers?" Lonac said. "I assume that they were destroyed along with your family."

"Well...I guess...I never saw mine; they must have done all of that." Touro said as she walked over and sat down on the sofa facing him. "I just seem to keep causing you more and more trouble; I don't mean to...it's just...well I don't really know much; that didn't come out right. Of course I know stuff, I was in the top five of my class at school...I mean...well I don't know anything about travelling out here."

"I get it, you don't need to explain." Lonac told her watching her closely. "One of the top five, in everything?"

"Yes." Touro answered.

"How's your Magical skills then?" Lonac asked her.

Touro looked away from him. "I've only ever used it the once...of what I can remember...and to be honest I don't know if I want to use it ever again."

Lonac didn't say anything, he didn't want to push the matter yet; so he'd just leave it for now.

Chapter Seven

A bright light flashed from within the room as the doors opened and two officers walked out talking quietly, but suddenly stopped when they saw Renji stood in front of them and stepped aside for him as he walked passed them and into the transporter room where Lesharo was stood waiting for him with his team; all eight officers stood silently trying not to make eye contact with either of their commanding officers.

"Right men, these are the last ships...I don't give a damn if there are Magics on board we just want the senator's daughter back; is that understood?" Renji told them.

"Yes sir." They all echoed.

"Please." Lesharo said as he walked over to the transporter. "We've searched everywhere for her. We were down there for hours; if she was going to get on any of the transports she would have left by now. That is if she's still alive, her tracker isn't even working."

"I have a team working on that, even if it's damaged they should be able to get something from it." Renji told him as he waited for his team to get onto the pad before he stood beside Lesharo.

Lesharo smiled suddenly. "Shouldn't you be waiting by your computer, you know in case she contacts you...you were her favourite after all."

"I modified my wrist com, so that it'll accept all my in-coming transmissions." Renji told him.

"What and pick up her tracker as well?" Lesharo asked him.

The floor began to glow and then they were enveloped in a bright white light and disappeared, reappearing in a large hall that had been cleared for their arrival; the table and chairs pulled back against the walls.

"Spread out." Renji ordered. "This is the last ship, I want her found."

Renji walked off before anyone answered him, nor did he wait for his back up; he didn't need or want any. He went straight for the far doors which opened for him onto a long destined corridor. He knew that no one would be about having been warned that they were coming aboard every ship that they had been on so far was like this, so they had to take up searching quarters which was taking up most of their time, time that he didn't have to waste.

Renji walked down the corridor as though he was a man on a mission without even stopping. He knew where he was going. He just had to get there without being seen by his officers; he turned to his right and carried on down the corridor to the fifth door which he stopped outside of and pressed the com button on the panel and it beeped inside before he went in without an invitation.

It was a spares room all in grey, a small black metal table to his right with two chairs, a set of drawers to his left next to another door to the bathroom then a single bed beside the view port and two chairs in the far corner; with a man sat waiting with his back to the door.

"You lost her again; this is starting to become a habit." Ichigo said.

Renji suddenly shot a ball of fire out of hands directing it just above Ichigo's head, as it hit the bulkhead it erupted leaving a black burn mark; Ichigo stood up still in his uniform and turned around to face Renji.

"I can't believe that I did it again...why does she keep running away from me?" Renji demanded punching the wall.

"You do know that I have to pay for the damage right, so if you don't mind unless you're going to give me the money after you've finished." Ichigo said calmly.

"You sound as though you don't even care." Renji shouted at him.

"And you sound as though you care too much for someone who is just a friend." Ichigo told him calmly.

"I...I can't fail her again." Renji told him.

"She's alive, so she'll come back when she's calmed down." Ichigo told him sitting back down. "She was probably just overwhelmed. You would have been as well if you would have been with her; and I think that would have been worse if she actually thought that she hurt you as well...she has a thing for you."

"That...that isn't the point." Renji said awkwardly.

"She told you..." Ichigo said rubbing his head, not sure if that was a good thing or not. "Damn it..."

"See...see why I'm worried, she won't come back..." Renji told him.

"I'll get the word out again, need to know only of course." Ichigo told him. "We'll find her."

Renji leant against the wall. "She's all on her own and she's just coming into her powers...she's going to get into a lot of trouble."

"She's strong..." Ichigo started.

"But she doesn't understand...and all those people...I should have been with her." Renji said. "I shouldn't have let her out of my sight...just when I had asked her to leave with me as well."

"What?" Ichigo said surprised looking over at him. "She agreed to leave with you?"

"She was going to...yes..." Renji answered and then looked away from him. "That's why I'm worried...she'll be afraid to come back...because of what she's done…"

A tall cloaked figure walked down the corridor with four guards behind him towards the opened-door room with two more guards stood outside of it holding black and silver blaster rifles, their uniforms were black apart from the silver zip of the jacket and the belt; they both had thick black visors that covered most of their faces. All the guards were dressed the same except for the man they were taking to the end room; nothing could be seen of this man except for a very small piece of dark midnight blue beneath his cloak.

Talking or rather shouting could be heard from the room ahead as the cloaked figure approached slowing his pace as if he wanted to hear what they were arguing about before he entered.

"I don't care...I'm not wasting my time looking for a child!" A man shouted angrily.

"I don't see how we can find her now anyway, it's been two weeks...and the tracker is out of the question...she fired it." Another man said a lot calmer than the first.

"I'll find her and when I do...I'll make her wish that she never ran away in the first place..." A third man said sounding amused. "I'd bet she'd be easier to make scream this time."

"This time?" The first man asked.

"You like torturing children?" The second man asked him questioningly as the cloaked man finally entered the room.

He walked into the room and over to the circular table with a straight head which they were stood around, the guard to his left followed him across the room as the other three took up positions by the view port one on either side and one in the centre; the cloaked man sat down and the guard took his place next to the other. The three men all look at one another before they too took their seats around the bottom of the table.

The man closest to the view port wasn't wearing his cloak but had it thrown over the back of his chair, he had a dark emerald green jacket with black trousers that had the same colour vertical stripes; he was slightly tanned and had almost black eyes.

The man next to him had a shaved head which was covered in tattoos and pale skin, he wore his cloak open revealing a metal chest plate which had a winged animal painted upon it and black leather trousers.

The third man had his cloak on but it didn't have sleeves nor did the white shirt which he fastened with black togs to the neck and a black wrap fastened around his waist with black trousers and high, dirty travel boots; he had thunder-bolts tattooed down his arms and had long greasy grey hair tied back in a loose pony tail.

"I don't want to hear that it can't be done, without her all my plans will be for nothing; so I want her found before she is taken in by Magics." The cloaked man told them.

"I found her once sir for you, and I will find her again." The man in the emerald green jacket told him. "I'll make her wish that she never crossed you, again."

"Just enough so that she knows her place." The cloaked man told him.

"So Zar-Jins was the guy then who brought her in the first time?" The man in the middle asked.

"I like a challenge just as much as the next guy...but six years...six long years to break her; but at least it'll be easier this time round." Zar-Jins told them smiling.

"Six years?" The man at the end asked amused as he clicked his fingers and sparks flickered from the ends of his finger trips. "She's just a little girl...even a grown man wouldn't have been able to last that long."

"She's very special and important to my plans, now you might understand why I need her so much Hul-Ercan." The cloaked man told him.

"My Lord, really...spending all this time on a child it isn't like you even if she is special as you say." Hul-Ercan said.

"She is the key to bringing the Magics to their knees and also the self-righteous Normals." He told him.

"They'll pay for what they've done to my kind." Hul-Ercan told them.

"They'll pay for everything, and regret the day that they crossed us." The man in the middle said smiling. "We're not playthings that they can throw away once they get bored."

"They took Karwan's wife to one of those worlds, My Lord." Zar-Jins told him. "They told him it was because he failed to follow their orders. It was only so that they could have a hold over him."

"I'll get her back and kill any man who has dared to lay a hand on her." Karwan told them.

The man in the cloak lifted his right hand and typed in a sequence onto the panel in front of him, at the other end of the table three slots opened and three data pads rose up out of them; the men reached forward and each took his own.

"Your assignments, find her." The cloaked man told them. "You will be rewarded greatly."

Zar-Jins smiled at this and stood up to leave. "I get to play with her and also get a reward for it. Not a bad job, not a bad job at all."

The other two followed suit while Hul-Ercan scanned over the first page of his pad walking slowly towards the door, but stopped and turned around making the other two stop also.

"We're all being sent to different regions?" Hul-Ercan asked.

"There were three regions which all those transports were going to, so you each have one to search." He told them. "Is there a problem?"

"No...no My Lord...of course not." Hul-Ercan said and then turned on his heel and stormed out of there.

His footsteps echoed down the corridor as he walked back to the lift followed by Zar-Jins and Karwan, the only one who looked at all pleased about their new assignment was Zar-Jins who had personal reasons why he was so excited about finding her.

"I'll find her." Zar-Jins told them again.

"Yeah, you keep saying that; but I'll believe it when you drag her back here." Karwan told him unimpressed.

"One little girl...she better be as special as Malevalus says." Hul-Ercan said leaning against the door-frame waiting for the lift.

"I doubt she's fully realized it herself..." Zar-Jins said smiling. "She'll be lost forever thanks to what we did to her."

They both looked at him wondering what he meant considering that he told them that he'll be able to find her.

"That part is none of your concern." Zar-Jins told them as the door opened to the lift and he stepped forward to enter but Hul-Ercan stopped him so that he could go in first.

"Damn it!" Renji shouted kicking his chair out from under him as he stood up.

His computer beeped at him as he stood there steaming with anger and frustration. He had been going over the sensor logs of what had happened on the planet; he had held out hope that she hadn't really killed all of those people but now he wasn't so sure.

He turned around and answered the computer even though he wasn't in the mood for talking to anyone unless they actually had news as to where she was; it stopped beeping and the screen changed; Ichigo appeared on the screen and he too didn't look at all happy.

"I can't find her; no one seems to have seen her." Ichigo told him. "She must have changed somehow...but how are we supposed to find her when we don't even know now what she looks like?"

"You'll know her if you see her." Renji assured him, he leant on the edge of the table. "I've gone over the results four times, there's nothing left...every one in that city is dead..."

"No...they can't be...there has to have been something..." Ichigo said. "I'll get them to look into it further back home...just don't tell Baron what you've found out."

Renji turned away from him. "She was having trouble for a while...I should have tried harder to help her...even if she didn't want it, it would have at least stopped this from happening."

"You're going to do it again, aren't you?" Ichigo said.

"I'll stay here a little longer, to see what else I can find out; but after that I'm leaving." Renji told him as he turned back around. "Even though I've been here over ten years I've still not figured out the link between Kentaro and Malevalus, how he got her in the first place. Nothing's going to change now."

"That isn't really our biggest problem at the moment." Ichigo told him. "I have teams keeping an eye out for bounty hunters."

"She's strong, but after what happened I don't think that she'll be able to stand up against them." Renji told him honestly. "I should have implanted her with a better tracker."

"They don't last long, even in me so why do you think it would have been strong enough for her?" Ichigo asked him.

Renji kicked the chair again, this time knocking it into the table.

"Be careful...they won't trust your motives if you carry on like this." Ichigo warned him. "I better get off; though...don't do anything too foolish."

"Yeah sure...speak to you later." Renji said before he logged off.

He looked at it again, the picture on his desk; he hadn't been able to stop looking at it. It was only taken two weeks before all of this happened, they were in the senate gardens under the trees; he was sat down on the grass and she knelt behind him with her arms around him smiling brightly just for him.

"I'll find you, no matter how long it takes." Renji told the Toria in the picture.

The sun shone down on the city, the buildings were nothing like that of the senate not even half their size; though it seemed just as busy as Touro and Lonac walked side by side down the road on the sidewalk which was full of people going about their every-day lives of spices from all over the galaxy.

The people seemed fairly happy but there was still a tense atmosphere about this world, which Touro had figured out as soon as she had arrived; it had a Fleet presence, though it wasn't as big as other worlds they were still here watching the people.

"My friend should be able to put us up for a while, that is until the next transport that we need." Lonac told her.

Touro wanted to ask where this transport went to, but she thought better of it not wanting anyone to overhear them talking; she knew better than anyone that no matter how normal someone looked it didn't mean anything.

"So is it much further to his place?" Touro asked.

"No, just another block." Lonac told her. "So what do you think?"

"It's very crowded...I know that I'm actually used to a busier city but..." Touro tried to explained, she looked around again as if trying to find the proper words to explain herself.

"It's because everything seems more closed in." Lonac explained.

Touro looked at him and then looked around. She smiled slightly to herself understanding what he meant, there were loads of buildings but they were all so closely built together; even the roads were narrow just enough for two lanes, and small narrow sidewalks as well; she wondered why she hadn't realized that on her own because it seemed kind of obvious now.

"Yeah you're right, I had been thinking about it but I couldn't put my finger on it." Touro said. "It kind of makes you think that it was built to keep you trapped, so that you can't do anything to break free...like a small prison cell with no room to more around to look for an escape route."

"That's just it." Lonac said looking over at her, somewhat surprised by her interpretation of the city.

Lonac also knew very well that no one was ever what they appeared to be especially nowadays, and of course he had picked up quite quickly that Touro wasn't what she appeared to be either; the only thing that he knew for sure was that she really didn't have anywhere else to go. Yes he wanted to know the truth but he didn't want to push the matter, not wanting to scare her off, as these were dangerous times and you didn't know who you could trust or not.

They carried on walking in silence for a while both hoping that they were doing the right thing.

Touro saw a group of Fleet officers on the other side of the road, which everyone was trying to stay clear of which was difficult considering how narrow the sideways were; panic seemed to fill her as if she believed that they had somehow found her already. She tried to carry on as normal, trying not to look so worried as her pace picked up slightly even though she didn't know where they were going but Lonac seemed to realize and also picked up his pace a little but not too much as to draw attention to themselves.

The doors to the building opened and several people came out dressed in suits. They had to stop to let them pass as there wasn't enough room for them all to go around each other unless you wanted to risk stepping out into the road which were just as narrow and busy as the sidewalks; when they finally passed they carried on until the end of the building and then turned left down another street.

It was a one way street with just one lane for the hover cars to go down, coming off of the main road. It wasn't as busy as the main road but there were still quite a few people around; they walked down to the crossing where others were waiting to cross also. Straight across the road were yellow straps and posts with lights atop of them; luckily they didn't have to wait long as the lights began to flash red signalling to the drivers to stop and then they stayed red and the traffic stopped so that they could cross. They all surged across on both sides of the road, a large crowd of people which if you weren't careful you would get carried away by; Touro moved closer to Lonac so not to be separated from him and well he did look a little scary being so tall and everything no one really wanted to get in his way.

Once they were across the road, they carried on down the street alongside the building which went quite far back until finally there was another entrance. It was just a double door which Lonac pushed open so that Touro could go in first before he followed.

It was just a small room with wooden floors and painted walls, the paint was a off-white and was peeling in places; to their right on the wall it was covered in grids with numbers on them for all of the apartments. On the other wall was the lift and a door next to it which Touro assumed was for the stairs.

Lonac pressed the button for the lift, a panel lit up above and slowly counted down from the tenth floor until it finally reached them on the ground floor; the door slowly slide open to the right and they both got inside of the small box lift. All four walls were mirrored with a gold tint, except for a long panel with buttons which were all numbered 1 to 26.

Lonac pressed the button 8, the lift jerked slightly before it started to move. Touro stared at herself through the tinted mirror, she still found it hard to believe that the face which was looking back at her was actually hers; though she had only looked like this for just over a week now but it made her wonder if Renji would still know it was her when he saw her. They had known each other for years and he was a Magic, would he be able to see through her? Would she want him to be able to see? The answer to that was still 'no', she still wasn't ready to face him because that meant that she would have to face what she had done.

"Is there something wrong?" Lonac asked her seeing that she looked a little upset.

"No...no I'm fine." Touro assured him, though she knew that he knew she was lying.

Neither of them said anything else as the lift carried on up and finally stopped at the eighth floor, the door opened sliding to the side once more; Lonac stepped out first with Touro just behind him. She looked up and down the long narrow corridor which barely had any light; the corridor was lined with doors about five meters apart.

"Are they all apartments?" Touro asked unsure thinking that they must be really small.

"Yep." Lonac answered as he turned to his right and straight down the corridor. "There not as small as you think they are, they're just narrow but long...but they're quite spacious as well, when you get inside."

"Oh..." Touro said as she followed him.

They didn't go down the corridor far before Lonac stopped again and knocked on the door. Touro stood beside him and waited staring at the door wondering what his friend was like and it only just dawned on her did he actually do this sort of thing often, rescue girls in trouble?

The door opened inwards and a man a couple of years older than Lonac stepped out of the shadow of the door. He wasn't as tall either probably just a couple of inches taller than Touro; he had short brown hair and brown eyes and was dressed in worn work clothes as though he was ready to go out.

"Good timing." The man said and then suddenly looked over at Touro and smiled. "She's pretty; no wonder you picked her up."

"Hay!" Touro said before Lonac had a chance to say anything. "He wouldn't do anything like that."

"Thank you." Lonac said calmly.

"You've only known him for a week, right?" The man said smirking. "You can't possibly get to know everything about someone in such a short period of time. And little girl, he isn't as innocent as you might want to believe."

"The whole galaxy is near enough at war, so how can anyone be called innocent?" Touro asked him.

"Are you going to let us in?" Lonac asked him.

He went back into the apartment so that they could follow him, Lonac went first and then Touro followed closing the door behind herself with a snap. Touro walked down the narrow hallway which had a door on the left into a room that was closed, she carried on into a large open plan living room and kitchen; there was a sofa and chairs with a coffee table in the middle and against the wall a dining table with four chairs set around it just before the kitchen started.

"It's a lot bigger than I thought it was going to be." Touro admitted.

"Yep." The man said and pointed to the far door. "Down there are three bedrooms. It costs a bit more but it's useful especially at times like this."

"So you do this often? I mean you help people with somewhere to stay while they're moving on?" Touro asked him.

"There are quite a few people on hundreds on planets, we need them...more really but it can't be helped..." Lonac explained.

"We do the best that we can." The man said.

"Oh this is After..." Lonac told her.

"It's Afton." He corrected him. "I'm sure he does that on purpose. And you?"

"Touro." Touro answered.

"Okay then...make yourself at home...I'm going to work." Afton told them as he was walking away.

"See you later then." Lonac said as Touro just stared after him. "I need to nip out as well, will you be alright on your own for a while?"

"Yeah, I guess so." Touro said.

"Okay then, make yourself at home." Lonac said before he too left.

The door shut behind him and Touro was left alone in the apartment. She just stood there looking around; yeah he had told her to make herself at home but how could she in someone else's place, and a person that she had only just met. She thought about going through to see what the bedrooms were like, but she had this sudden flash of Renji the last time that she had walked into his room; her whole body seemed to set on fire and she started to breath deeply.

"Perhaps this wasn't really a good idea after all." Touro said to herself.

She had tried not to think about it, but the way she is now anything could set her off and then; then she could end up hurting even more people. Tears started to build up in her eyes just thinking about what she had done, she wanted him to tell her that it was alright like he always did; even though this time she knew that it wasn't but she wanted to be that little girl that he would pull into his arms and tell her that everything was alright.

She looked around the room as if hoping to find a computer, but there was only a small wall console in the corner of the room; she walked over to it and activated it. A picture of the solar system that she was in, appeared on the screen before a menu appeared.

Menu
Travel Information
Accommodation Information
Local News
Galaxy News
Communications
Fleet Laws

Touro looked at the list for a full minute before she reached out and pressed Communications, the link appeared on the screen with options.

Local Transmission
Solar System
Inter Galaxy Message
Inter Galaxy Hook-up (5 Tarhrian's a minute)

She thought that this was better. He would hear her but she wouldn't let him see her because then he would know how she got away from his teams; she had to at least keep that a secret for as long as she could. She reached out and pressed Inter Galaxy Message and waited, it beeped three times and then the small button began flashing in the corner of the screen then it was ready for her to begin her recording.

"Hi, Renji it's me....I...I know that sorry will never be enough for what I did. Just...please...don't come for me...tell my father that you couldn't find me. You're probably thinking what a selfish brat she is, after what she did... But I'm afraid Renji, afraid of myself...of what's happening to me... Well that's it, thank you...for everything. And...I'm sorry."

Touro pressed the flashing button in the corner of the screen and the recording ended, she knew that she hadn't said enough but she also knew that she couldn't explain any of this or how sorry and grateful she was to him; how much of a traitor that she felt like. This was the best that she could do at the moment, to just give him something for she knew now that she didn't know at the time but he's still alive; she can't explain how she knows that he's alive she just has this feeling and that he will know that she is also alive which is why she has to do this.

"Computer how long will it take for the message to get to the Dragon Senate?" Touro asked it.

"Transmission will reach the Senate in three days." The computer answered.

"Great." Touro said. "Send the message to Renji Aba'rian head of security for Senator Kentaro. Send."

"Message sent." The computer told her.

Touro stared at the screen for a moment before she turned it off and turned around leaning against the wall, hoping that she had done the right thing; now that she had done it would it make him want to find her even more? She had after all told him that she couldn't control herself, he might think that she is a real danger that he has to stop; but he wouldn't hurt her?

"No...no of course." Touro told herself aloud. "He wanted to help..."

Touro sank down to the floor as the tears started to well up again, she wanted him to come for her but at the same time she was scared to face him because of what she had done; she really was a traitor.

Touro had been crying on the floor for that long that her bum had gone numb and that she couldn't cry any longer, she rubbed her red eyes dry and then pushed herself up; she had to do something to keep her mind off it which was of course harder to do when she was all on her own, which actually made her wonder how long Lonac was going to be because it already felt as though he had been gone well over an hour.

She walked over to the kitchen wondering what there was in to eat, not that she would take a lot because it wasn't her place and she still had the problem of not having any money; and she knew that she couldn't go into her account and take money out because then they would all know that she was alive and could probably track her through the transaction.

Touro opened the cupboards to see what he had in, all she could see were boxes with no labels on them; how was anyone supposed to know what was in them unless you pulled everything out and went through them all? She wasn't really in the mood to start searching through everything, and she wasn't really that hungry that she had to have something there and then; so she decided that she'd wait for Lonac to get back.

Considering that she wasn't going to eat anything she decided to have a look where she was going to be sleeping, she walked over past the table against the wall and the sofa, and pushed the door open and the lights came on overhead in the narrow hallway; on her left was a door for the first bedroom which she pushed open and had a look inside. The bed on the far wall was unmade and there were clothes hanging out of the drawers which were next to the foot of the bed; Touro closed the door realizing that it belonged to Afton.

"At least it's bigger than the transport ship." Touro said aloud to herself as she carried on to the next room.

She pushed the door open to the next room, it was laid out the same as the first room; but the bed was made and there were no clothes thrown about. She carried onto the last door which was at the end of the corridor, Touro thought that this was going to be the biggest of the three rooms which made her wonder why Afton hadn't clamed it for himself considering that it was his apartment after all; so she pushed the door open and went inside. It looked a little bigger because it was in a box shape but there was still the same amount of room.

"At least this time it doesn't matter which room I take." Touro said to her. "I'll have this one then..."

Touro turned around thinking that she heard something, she smiled to herself as she walked back through to the main room to see if Lonac had come back; but when she walked into the main room she was still alone.

There was mumbled shouting coming from outside the apartment, Touro stood on the spot wondering what to do; what if something was going on out there. Her heart started to beat a little faster as she stood at the back of the room looking up the hall at the front door, hoping that it was nothing.

Knock, knock, knock.

Touro almost jumped out of her skin and her heart started to pound against her chest, she couldn't open it, even though they never told her not to open the door to anyone.

Knock, knock, knock.

Touro stepped back into the wall, hoping that whoever it was would go away; her breathing started to increase as she took deep breaths her heart pounding so loudly that she was sure that they would be able to hear her.

Knock, knock, knock.

"Open the door!" A man shouted from outside of the apartment.

Touro just stood there, she didn't recognize the voice; she wasn't just going to open the door to a stranger.

"We know you're in there!" The man shouted through. "If you don't open the door then we'll be forced to open it."

Touro looked around the room wondering what to do, she still didn't know who they were; but they had said 'we'. What if they've found her?

"You have three seconds to open the door, then we're coming in." The man told her.

She didn't know any Magic which would help her, and what she had done before isn't really very helpful, not that she knew how to control it or anything.

"One...two..." The man started.

"Wait..." Touro said in little more than a whisper.

"Three!" The man shouted.

BANG!

Something rammed the door.

BANG!

She could see the door buckling under the strain; but she still had nowhere to go and hiding wasn't going to do her much use if they had scanners.

BANG!

The door flung open against the wall, security officers ran inside dressed in Fleet uniforms with blasters in their hands; their commanding officer walked in calmly behind them, his blond hair gelled back against his head.

Touro stood frozen to the spot as they rushed into the main room and spread out, blocking all routs of escape.

"Well lookie here lads...it seems as though we've just scored the big one." The commanding officer said.

Touro was scared that she had somehow changed back to her proper form, and they knew who she was. He walked over to her through the gap in his men; she looked up at him, into his dull grey eyes.

"Well you've been lucky to us...but I doubt that you'll see it that way." He told her. "You should have opened the door."

Touro couldn't say anything, even if she was able to think of something to say she was sure that she wouldn't have been able to speak.

"Come on now." The commanding officer said as he reached for a pair of cuffs hooked on the back of his trousers. "Don't make this any more difficult than it has to be."

He stepped forward with the cuffs in his right hand as he reached out for her with his other hand to grab her. Touro didn't move away from him because she couldn't. She was too afraid too.

"There now, that's all we want." The commander told her as he grabbed her arm and pulled her over to him.

He pulled her hands together putting the cuffs on her wrist activating them, which sent a small jolt through her arms; he smiled at her cruelly and then pulled her along.

"A pay raise is definitely in order now." The commander said to his men.

They all cheered in agreement to his suggestion; Touro though was just lead out of the apartment in a daze, dreading the moment when they brought her before Renji.

Chapter Eight

Touro stood cuffed to the wall in the commander's office. They had left her alone while they went to get who had come for her; she looked around the room to see if there was anything which would help her get out of the cuff's, but she couldn't see anything useful. There was a computer turned off on the desk and data sheets scattered across it, but there were no drawers that she could see underneath; and the only other things in the room were three chairs, one for the commander and two in front of his desk.

She had never seen such an empty office before, even Renji had more stuff in his not that she had ever really seen him do much work in it before.

Touro looked at the cuff's wishing that she knew some sort of spell that would unlock them, or if she could use that power to melt them somehow; but even though she was willing herself to do something nothing was happening unlike last time. She had really thought that she would be able to do something. She had changed her appearance and she was sure that was more complicated than unlocking something; so why can't she?

Touro though already knew the answer. It was because she still wanted to see him deep down inside, even though she was also afraid of what might happen when she did, she still wanted to see him.

"Damn..." Touro whispered to herself, willing herself not to cry.

"One little girl as you ordered sir." The commander said as he opened the door.

Touro looked up expecting to see Renji stood behind him, but he wasn't. In fact she had never seen this man before; he looked kind of out of place next to the Fleet Commander in his emerald jacket and his tanned skin. Touro was sure that she had never seen this man before, but somehow, just seeing him filled her with a dread that she couldn't explain.

"That isn't her." The man said glaring at the girl.

Touro stepped back, but she couldn't go anywhere as her hands were still cuffed to the steel bolt in the wall. The man suddenly smiled at her, seeming to change his mind about her.

"But Zar-Jins..." The commander began.

"Then again...I'll still take her...just incase." Zar-Jins said not taking his eyes off of her.

Zar-Jins walked over to her and grabbed her wrists over the cuffs and then pulled with such force that it pulled them out of the steel bolt; Touro bit the inside of her lip stopping herself from moaning in pain. He leant in against her pressing her against the wall, letting go of her with one hand bring it up to her lip and pressed them apart gently with his long fingers until he felt it.

"I'm going to enjoy this." Zar-Jins whispered into her ear and then licked her blood off of his fingers.

Touro was petrified at what he was going to do to her, and he could see it as well, which only made him more excited.

"You should be afraid." Zar-Jins told her. "I'll make you scream, until you can't scream anymore...and you know what? That doesn't mean that I'll stop there...it just means that I've broke you."

"You won't be doing that here though...sir?" The commander asked nervously.

"And what if I do?" Zar-Jins asked him smiling slightly as though he was actually willing him to challenge him.

"Well...um..." The commander said nervously.

"Don't worry, I've got my own place to do things like this." Zar-Jins said walking over to him leading Touro behind him. "We'll be going now. And remember...this never happened. I was never here and there was no girl."

"Yes sir...never here...never saw either of you..." The commander said stepping aside for them.

Zar-Jins walked out of the office with Touro trailing behind him, she didn't really struggle against him as if knowing that it would be pointless to do so; it was the fear that was consuming. She didn't know why but she had this uncontrollable urge, this need; to just shout his name as if hoping that Renji would just somehow appear and everything would be alright.

They walked down the empty corridor passing closed doors until they finally reached one that didn't have one, that's when he turned pulling her into the room with him; it was a transporter room.

"Nobody's going to come for you...just like nobody came for you last time." Zar-Jins told her as he pulled her onto the pad.

Touro didn't understood what he meant, she was kind of still sure that she hadn't met him before; but he seemed to think that they have and this dreaded feeling that she had about him, she couldn't explain where it was coming from.

"My ship now." Zar-Jins ordered as he dragged her onto the platform pulling her into him and wrapping his arms around her. "Can't you tell how excited I am to have you back?"

"Oh god..." Touro whispered horrified, as the pad was activated and they were enveloped in a bright light, the room disappearing and then another one appearing around them.

This room had no one in it and it was slightly smaller, the lights were set on dull which was somewhat misleading to begin with, before the light of the transporter went out completely.

"We're all alone now, no one to get in our way." Zar-Jins told her as he pushed her forward off of the pad.

Touro nearly trip down the step as she went forward but caught herself in time, he had let go of her now that they were aboard his ship; she looked over at the console wondering if she could get to it and then the pad before he could stop her? She looked over her shoulder slightly to see how close he was to her, he was still close enough to grab her; but this might be her only chance and then he surprised her when he walked around her to lead the way as though he didn't even consider her a threat.

Touro stared at his back and then over at the console again, for a second she didn't move as she made her mind up; she stepped to the side slowly over to the console not wanting to draw attention to herself, by making any sudden moments until she had to.

The doors slid open for him as he waited just outside of them, with his back to the room.

Touro didn't understood, why wasn't he watching her? She reached the console and tried to turn it on but it was just blank except for one button, which had LOCKED on it; she couldn't unlock the console if she couldn't turn it on then she would need more time to do it, a lot more especially seeing that her hands were still cuffed.

"Now that you know there's no way off my ship except for doing what I tell you, perhaps this time you'll just give in straight away." Zar-Jins told her. "Trust me, it'll be a lot easier for you if you just give in."

"I...I don't know who you think I am...but I'm not..." Touro told him bravely.

Zar-Jins smiled at her. "Yeah I know that. You'll never be as great as she was."

Touro just stared at him speechlessly, she was trapped with this mad man who kept referring to her as someone else who could do anything to her, and she was afraid that she wouldn't be able to stop him even after all that training that she did; she kind of felt as though it had all been a waste of time because now that she was in trouble she couldn't even use any of it.

Zar-Jins walked over to her. "I'll take you to where you'll be staying."

Touro still didn't move, she couldn't, even though she wanted to move away from him as he edged his way closer to her; he reached out and grabbed her wrists once more and pulled her along with him; she allowed herself to be pulled along by him out of the room and down the corridor.

There wasn't much light in the corridors either, which gave the ship an eerie closed-in feeling; she looked around as he pulled her down the corridor but it wasn't like other ships that she had been on before, there were no wall consoles and there were hardly any doors.

"Here we are. Your very own room." Zar-Jins told her as they approached the first door that she had seen.

The door had a small grey glass panel going across the right side with writing on it, but it was too small for her to make out at this distance; but she knew that it wasn't a good sign. This whole ship seemed to scream out in horror to her. The door slid open before she could read what was written on it; Zar-Jins went inside pulling Touro along with him, the lights turned on but only a little higher than the corridors.

The room was huge; she could see why he didn't have use for other doors. There were four large tables with straps on them and small tables next to them with instruments on them, there was a large console section set behind the tables. On the other side of the room were only what could be holding cells, six of them; they were all empty of occupants at the moment and the force-fields down.

"Like I said, your very own special room." Zar-Jins told her smiling cruelly at her, he pulled her into him. "There's only one thing that you don't have to worry about...little girls don't do a thing for me."

Touro stared at him, her eyes wide with fear.

"But depending on how long you have to stay, that could change." Zar-Jins told her. "You're not going to be a little girl forever."

Zar-Jins pulled the frighten Touro to the closest cell and then pushed her inside, she fell to the ground losing her balance as he activated the force-field behind her; Touro looked over her shoulder to see that he was still smiling at her. She couldn't look at him any longer as she turned away.

"I'll be back in a while." Zar-Jins told her walking away.

Touro quickly turned around when she heard him walking away and watched him leave the room, as he stepped out the lights went down except for the light in her cell; the door closed and she was left alone to imagine what he'll do to her when he returned. Wondering why he had come for her, sure that her father would never hire someone like him to come look for her, she was sure that he would have sent Renji, so why wasn't he here for her, why hadn't he come for her?

Zar-Jins pulled off his jacket and threw it over the back of the chair in his quarters; he wore a dark-blue sleeveless shirt leaving his arms exposed which were covered in burns. He looked over at his desk and the computer on it and then suddenly kicked the chair out from under it, sending it flying across the room into the dining table.

"Like hell I'm going to let her go." Zar-Jins told himself. "She'll regret ever running into me for a second time."

He walked around to the other side of the table and sat down, he tapped his fingers on the glass top for a moment as if he was debating what to do next; but then he reached out and activated the computer.

"Hook up a secure line to Karwan." Zar-Jins ordered.

The screen slowly went from black to white and then changed to a screen of a room, it seemed smaller than the one that Zar-Jins was in and he couldn't see anyone either. Zar-Jins glared at the screen as though thinking that it would help, he didn't really have much patience for these types of things.

"Hay! Answer me when I call you!" Zar-Jins shouted at the screen. "Idiot!"

The screen suddenly turned around and was facing the wall and a chair, Zar-Jins was about to say something when Karwan sat down.

"Is there a reason why you're getting yourself so worked up?" Karwan asked him warily.

"I found her." Zar-Jins told him. "But I've decided to hold onto her for a little while longer."

"Then why are you telling me that you've found her?" Karwan asked him.

"I want you too stall them...you know...say something like you picked up a lead or something." Zar-Jins told him.

"And why should I do that for you?" Karwan asked.

"You do this for me, and I'll help you get your wife back." Zar-Jins said smirking.

"You...you'll help me get her back?" Karwan said questioningly. "And why should I trust you?"

"Why not?" Zar-Jins said.

"It depends on how long you need." Karwan told him.

"Only a couple of weeks, this time." Zar-Jins told him. "She'll break a lot easier than before."

"I still don't understood fully about what happened...and I don't rightly care either." Karwan said nodding. "Two weeks. And then you've got to give up your toy."

"That's fine, it won't be worth playing with after that anyway." Zar-Jins told him smiling with this cruel look of delight as he logged off. "Just the two of us for two whole weeks..."

Touro sat in the cell with her hands in her lap just staring out into the black room wondering when he was going to come back for her, and what he would do to her when he did; she didn't know how long she had been there when her eyes began to feel heavy, she willed herself to stay awake not wanting to give in to how tired she was, but the lure of sleep was to great.

Her head began to drop and then lift and then drop again, until she finally fell to the side asleep; her body and mind too overwhelmed with everything that had happened to her.

The door slid open and the lights came up as Zar-Jins walked into the room, he walked over to her cell and looked inside at her sleeping before he deactivated the force-field and went in for her.

"You should never let your guard down with me, little girl." Zar-Jins warned her as he pulled her up almost dragging her to her feet.

"Wha...what're you going to do with me...?" Touro asked him.

"Brave of you to question me considering the situation that you're in." Zar-Jins said dragging her across the room to the nearest table. "I'll let you know shall I? I'm going to make you change back...into your other form...Toria..."

She looked up at him horrified, he knew who she was yet he was still going to go through with this; she didn't understand why.

"My father...he'll..." Touro began.

"Your father will do what?" Zar-Jins asked her mockingly. "Do you think that he's impressed with having a disgusting Magic for a daughter? He's against Magics; he doesn't like them...so do you know what that means?"

Touro struggled against him as he tried to pull her into him again so that he could lift her onto the table.

"I don't know why you're struggling...he wants this, to teach you a lesson." Zar-Jins told her.

"No...he loves me...he wouldn't..." Touro said as tears started to well up.

"Don't start crying yet, it takes all the fun out of it." Zar-Jins told her as he pushed her against the table.

He pressed a button underneath it with his knee that activated the top restrains, the restrains glowed brighter the closer she got to them as did the cuffs around her wrists; he grabbed her leg to lift it onto the table.

It only made things easier for him when she tried to move away from him, because the only place for her to go was in fact the table; he pulled her up his fingers digging into her skin through her trousers, as she tried to steady herself the cuffs got too close to the restrains and they were pulled up over her head and locked in place.

"See now, that wasn't hard was it?" Zar-Jins said as he tried to restrain her legs also, but she kept kicking them fighting against him. "Now, now...be a good little girl...cause if you are, I'll be able to let you go sooner."

"Let me go now! You just said that I wasn't wanted..." Touro said as she carried on struggling. "Then I'm not worth anything to you or anyone...so why are you doing this to me?"

"If you've got nothing or no one to go back to, why are you still struggling against me; why not just give in to me?" Zar-Jins asked her.

Touro stopped only for a second by his words, but it was long enough for Zar-Jins to get her tied down by the electro restrains; he walked around to the bottom of the table so that he could see her fully and she had to lift her head slightly so that she could see him properly.

"Now to begin." Zar-Jins said.

"I don't know how to change!" Touro shouted at him.

"That won't be a problem once we've started." Zar-Jins assured her.

He pressed the buttons on the small panel at the foot of the table below her feet, the lights in the restrains began to glow brighter until finally a bright white light shot through them sending an electric pulse through her whole body.

Touro screamed out as her body shook from the pulse.

"You're disappointing me Toria." Zar-Jins said. "Last time, you didn't scream for weeks...and here you go spoiling the fun by screaming as soon as we start. But there is still one good thing. You haven't changed back, so that means we carry on until you do."

The light went back to its perverse colour and Touro breathed deeply trying to catch her breath, but he didn't give her enough time as he pressed the button again sending another shock through her; she couldn't help herself as she screamed and her whole body jerked convulsing from the shocks.

Shouting could be heard from the lift as Bernal walked up the corridor towards the main security office where the shouting was coming from. He knew who they were and what they were arguing about they had been like this for the past couple of weeks.

"...the little brat has gone..." Lesharo shouted.

"She's fine..." Renji shouted.

"She's dead!" Lesharo shouted. "The sooner you accept that, the sooner the rest of us can get on with things."

"How dare you...she...she's the senator's daughter and he hasn't given up on her either." Renji told him as Bernal walked into the office and over to his desk ignoring the two of them.

"You're living in a fantasy world." Lesharo told him as he sat heavily in his chair putting his feet up on his desk which was empty of work.

"A fantasy world?" Renji said advancing on him, his hair somewhat astray showing how much the whole matter was actually getting to him.

Renji's computer started to beep loudly signalling an incoming transmission, he looked over his shoulder at the computer; it was like this every time wondering if it was her finally calling for him to come and get her.

"Oh, you better hurry...it might be her calling you for help." Lesharo said sarcastically. "Yeah, like every other call you get...it's sickening...you didn't used to be like this..."

Renji ignored him as he walked over to his desk and pressed the flashing blue button on the screen to accept the incoming transmission, the message didn't have a sender's name or address which he found strange considering that it was only a vocal recording, but he still pressed the blue button again and the recording began.

"Hi, Renji it's me..." Lesharo and Bernal looked up from their work and over at Renji when they heard the voice, neither of them seemed to believe what they were hearing. "I...I know that sorry will never be enough for what I did."

"Why is she just saying sorry to him?" Lesharo mumbled under his breath but they still heard him.

"Just...please...don't come for me...tell my father that you couldn't find me. You're probably thinking what a selfish brat she is, after what she did... But I'm afraid Renji, afraid of myself...of what's happening to me... Well that's it, thank you...for everything. And...I'm sorry."

"I don't get it...what's she afraid of?" Bernal asked him confused.

Renji stared at the screen for a second trying to take the whole thing in.

"Computer save recording." Renji ordered. "When and where was the message sent?"

"You don't think it's really her do you?" Lesharo asked him. "What if it's a trick?"

"The message was sent two days ago from the Pannos system." The computer answered.

"Where in the Pannos system...which planet?" Renji asked.

"It will take two hours and forty three minutes to locate the exact position the message came from." The computer told him.

"Then run the scan." Renji told it.

"Even if we find out where she sent the message from it doesn't mean that she'll still be there." Bernal told him.

"Yeah, she sent it you two days ago...I mean someone sent it to you two days ago." Lesharo told him.

Renji came out from behind his desk and walked over to Lesharo.

"I don't give a damn about you not liking me, I don't like you to be honest." Renji told him. "All I want you to do is your job, if you can't..."

"What, so my job is to get hard up over the brat like you?" Lesharo asked him.

Renji had to fight the urge to say what he really wanted to. "I've known her, her whole life...so I can..."

"She said it herself in the message, she's a selfish brat only thinking about herself." Lesharo told him interrupting him. "She doesn't care that it's our jobs on the line here to find her, as long as she's alright."

"She wants me to find her, or she wouldn't have sent the message." Renji told him. "Don't you get? If she would have stayed quiet, we would have had to give up on her; but this message is saying I'm alive and..."

"And what. Oh please Renji, please save me?" Lesharo said in a high pitched voice.

"That didn't sound like her at all." Bernal said calmly from his desk.

They both looked over at him as though they had actually forgotten that he was even in the room, Bernal looked at them both.

"It won't hurt to check it out, the Senator wants us to check all our leads." Bernal told them. "Personally I don't really want to be the one to tell him that we couldn't find her."

"Whatever." Lesharo said. "I just want to know how she got off the planet without any of us seeing her."

Renji didn't say anything to him, even though he wanted to know the same thing; he picked up his jacket off the back of his chair.

"Computer transfer the message and all information to my quarters." Renji ordered turning around to leave. "Nothing is to be said to the Senator until we actually know anything for sure, is that understood?"

"You're the one who wants to jump on a ship and go after her, not us." Lesharo reminded him, but he was ignored again. "Why don't you get yourself a real woman, instead of letting that little brat get to you so much."

"I'm actually engaged, but thanks for the concern." Renji said ready to leave the room, but Lesharo jumped to feet and stopped him.

"What do you mean you're engaged? You never said anything before." Lesharo said.

"That's cause it's got nothing to do with you." Renji told him walking away but Lesharo followed him.

"Does she know...Toria...?" Lesharo asked him. "Does she know that the love of her life is already spoken for?"

"Love of her life?" Renji said smiling slightly. "She's fifteen years old and has known me her whole life...she..."

"She told you...didn't she?" Lesharo said smiling. "That's what all this is about. You feel guilty because you're already spoken for and you're never had the guts to tell her the truth. Who would have thought it, hay."

"You can say whatever you want but it doesn't mean that it's true." Renji told him as they stopped at the lift, he pressed the button to call for the lift.

"So who is she then?" Lesharo asked him. "Anyone that we know?"

"...probably not..." Renji answered.

The doors opened and Renji stepped inside hoping that he wouldn't be followed any further, which he got what he wanted as Lesharo turned around.

"You'll have to bring her to the next function that we have, I want to know what type of woman you're actually into." Lesharo told him as he walked away.

The lift closed and he was finally alone to think about the full meaning of the message, he knew that part of her didn't want him to come because what she did but also she still needed him as well.

"Damn it!" Renji shouted punching the wall. "Why do you always have to make everything so damned hard?"

He leant against the wall as the lift moved upwards towards his floor, he shook his head wondering what he should do for the best; but the doors opened before he had begun to think of his next step. He walked down the corridor to his quarters and went inside locking the door behind him. He didn't used to because Toria used to just come in whenever she wanted no matter the time of day; he didn't mind really even if he told her that he did, because if he minded that much he wouldn't have left it unlocked for her.

Renji threw his jacket over the back of his sofa and went over to his desk.

"Computer replay my last message." Renji ordered.

The computer screen flickered on with just a flashing blue button in the corner of the screen, and then the message began.

"Hi, Renji it's me....I...I know that sorry will never be enough for what I did. Just...please...don't come for me...tell my father that you couldn't find me. You're probably thinking what a selfish brat she is, after what she did... But I'm afraid Renji, afraid of myself...of what's happening to me... Well that's it, thank you...for everything. And...I'm sorry."

"Why didn't you just tell me where you were?" Renji asked.

"Rephrase question?" The computer said.

"Not you...I wasn't asking you." Renji said irritably and then thought of something. "This message was sent on an unsecured line, so how many times has it been activated?"

"The message has been played three times." The computer answered.

"Someone read the message before I did?" Renji asked.

"Yes." The computer answered.

"Can you determinate who read the message and when it was intercepted?" Renji asked.

The computer didn't answer straight away, but took several seconds to reply. "The message was intercepted by a ship in the system, in the first hour that it was sent."

"Damn it." Renji said angrily. "Can you do a trace to find out what ship it was? Or even what type of ship."

"That information is not stored in the transmission." The computer answered.

Renji paced up and down his quarters wondering how he could find out who intercepted it and why. He needed someone who was posted out that way, but he couldn't remember anyone.

"Who would know?" Renji asked himself aloud and then stopped suddenly. "Computer open a secure channel to General Kasiya."

"Your request will take three minutes." The computer told him.

Renji waited impatiently to be hooked up, he went over and sat at his desk as he waited; he was sure that it took longer than three minutes before his screen came on and Kasiya appeared.

"Renji?" Kasiya said surprised to see him. "Have you found her?"

"Not yet." Renji told him. "I just got a message from her, she's in the Pannos system...it's two days old...she sent it two days ago, but that isn't the worst of it."

"What do you mean?" Kasiya asked.

"It was intercepted by a ship in the system." Renji told him. "What if Malevalus sent men after her? They've got her again, haven't they?"

"Renji you're over reacting..." Kasiya told him calmly.

"Over reacting? Perhaps, but I need to know who it was." Renji told him. "Who's in the system? I need someone there checking leads on that end until I can get there."

"I told you not to leave, unless Kentaro himself sends you to do something; that's an order." Kasiya told him.

"You just want me to sit here and do nothing, while they could be doing god knows what to her?" Renji demanded.

"We don't know..." Kasiya started and then broke off in mid sentence.

"What?" Renji prompted.

Kasiya did in fact look a little worried himself. "There was a report of a Fleet raid on an apartment building...it wasn't her...but thinking about it now...it does actually sound like her Renji. Purple hair and eyes."

"Wha...what?" Renji said somewhat surprised. "Do you think...?"

"No...they wouldn't have got her, would they?" Kasiya told him calmly. "I'm sorry Renji, but you still can't go. We still need you to carry on after this; I'll send Ichigo for her. She knows him and I'm sure that he can handle her and whoever has her."

"Purple hair and purple eyes..." Renji said smiling. "I was right not to lose hope, wasn't I? Or should I just forget and get on with things with how they are now?"

"We'll get her back and this time, we won't or rather can't give her back." Kasiya told him.

"So does that mean...?" Renji asked hopefully.

"In due time, just let us get this over with." Kasiya told him. "Why don't you do something useful on your side, find out how he contacted Malevalus."

"He transferred to a different ship on our way home, wouldn't take any of us with him; that's when he did it..." Renji said. "...they'll both pay for what they've done."

"I'll contact Ichigo and make the arrangements." Kasiya told him. "I'll contact you as soon as we've got her."

"Thanks." Renji said and smiled again now that he finally had his hope back that she was coming home.

Kasiya logged off his computer and sat back in his chair, his eyes fell on the picture next to his computer; he was stood with Renji who had his arms around a beautiful young woman who had long purple hair and bright purple eyes smiling up at the two of them. He reached out to pick it up but changed his mind looking away as though it brought a bad memory, even though he had kept the picture of the three of them on his desk since it was taken before the Empire fell several hundred years ago.

"Computer set up a secure line to Commander Ichigo Illiania." Kasiya ordered.

"Line secure." The computer replied.

The screen changed again, this time a living room appeared on the screen with toys all over the floor and a large teddy bear sat on the sofa staring at the computer.

"Just a minute!" Ichigo shouted from somewhere off of the screen. "One hour...it's been three..."

The screen was suddenly pulled around to Ichigo who's red hair was worse than Renji's was and didn't have his uniform on but a grey and white striped vest top.

"Is this a bad time, because I have an assignment for you?" Kasiya asked him.

"Oh yeah, great timing." Ichigo said sarcastically. "My granddaughter asked me to look after her kids, for an hour; that was three hours ago. But no, it's fine...what's the assignment?"

"I'll need you to leave straight away." Kasiya told him.

"Well...wait a minute...you've found her?" Ichigo said. "I'm surprised that Renji didn't demand to go for her."

"I told him that I'd send you." Kasiya explained.

Ichigo smiled slightly. "That can't be all."

"I told him that she didn't need to go back." Kasiya told him.

"Really? Is that because of what she did to that city?" Ichigo asked him. "Isidore has a team checking it out as we speak."

"I just want her here, it's better to have her here with us no matter how it turns out." Kasiya told him.

"What will you do to her, if she really did kill them all?" Ichigo asked him, but Kasiya could see that he already knew the answer. "You do know that Renji won't be the only one who won't let that happen."

"What are you saying? If you find her you won't bring her back?" Kasiya asked him calmly. "Do I need to send a team with you, to make sure that you do your job properly? We can't have someone like her out of control."

"Someone like her? You can say that because you don't know, but she's...she's not like that...nor will she ever be no matter what they do to her." Ichigo told him defensively.

"Well it seems as though you'll be betting your life on that then." Kasiya said. "Leave as soon as possible for the Pannos system, we believe that a Fleet ship picked up a message that she sent to Renji and then took her...two days ago."

"Two day ago?" Ichigo repeated. "I'd better get going then hadn't I?"

"Good luck." Kasiya said before he logged off and his screen went black, and then added sadly to himself. "I hope that it doesn't come to that."

The energy field came back over the cell as Touro curled to the back, wrapping her arms around her legs shaking from head to toe as Zar-Jins stared at her disgusted at the mere sight of her.

"You look pathetic." Zar-Jins said. "All you have to do is change back to your normal form, and then all of this will be over."

"I don't know how!" Touro shouted at him tears rolling down her face.

"You say that you want to give in, but really you're just being stubborn." Zar-Jins told her.

"NO! That's not it." Touro told him.

"Then do you want it all to be over and done with?" Zar-Jins asked her. "I have something that will change you back...but you have to beg for it."

Touro looked over at him horrified, she didn't want to beg, but she didn't want this to go on any longer either and also how did she know if he was telling her the truth or not.

"Oh well..." Zar-Jins said dismissively as though he didn't care about her response anymore. "Three days down... eleven left...just so you know I personally want you to hold out, that way it's more fun; for me at least. Sleep well, we'll be starting bright and early again."

Zar-Jins walked off as Touro watched him until she couldn't see him anymore, the doors opened and the lights went off once more and she was left alone.

She had been willing herself to change back the whole time, but she couldn't; she wondered if it was because part of herself didn't want to give into him still believing that Renji will come for her; she had sent him that message and he would have got it by now, she was sure that he would come for her. She kept telling herself over and over in her mind that Renji will come for her. He'll save her, even after what she had done.

Touro was still seated on the floor in the corner of the cell curled up in a ball, her eyelids feeling heavier and heavier as she tried to fight off the urge to fall asleep; but the lure to finally sleep after what he had done to her was just too great and finally she fell into an uneasy sleep.

She had only been asleep ten minutes though when the doors opened once more and the lights came back up, Zar-Jins walked in but this time he wasn't alone; there was another man with him who looked about the same age in the face yet his hair was greying much faster, he wore a floor-length coat which was fastened to the waist so that he could still reach his blasters which were fastened to his thighs.

They both stopped in front of her cell, Zar-Jins leant against the frame while the other man just stared at her unsure at why he had been called.

"She's a little…" The man said. "You never said she'd been a little girl."

"Does it matter?" Zar-Jins asked him.

"Yeah, I don't waste my time with children." The man said before he turned to leave.

"That isn't what she really looks like." Zar-Jins told him making him stop. "She's held it for three days. And you know me, I don't go easy on anyone."

"Three days?" He said turning back around.

"Yep, but the problem is I've only got just over a week...so I was hoping that you could give her something." Zar-Jins told him.

"My talents aren't like that, they're more of a long-term project." He told him going to leave again.

"So is she...for Lord Malevalus himself." Zar-Jins told him. "That's why I can't keep her for long. We just need something that will keep her in line, something that only your talents can provide."

He stretched his neck several times before he gave his answer. "How long term?"

"Just a couple of years." Zar-Jins said off handily.

"Years? How strong do you think she is?" He asked him.

"Oh she can handle whatever you give her, trust me." Zar-Jins assured him. "She won't even realize at first, but by the time that she does he would have worn her down to the point that she'll have to do everything that he tells her if she wants to stay alive that is. I just hope that I'm around to see it."

The man smiled slightly as he walked over to the table opening his jacket. "I haven't seen you this excited since you got yourself an Illiania, rumors has it she was a real Fire Elemental."

Zar-Jins stared at Touro. "I think she could be related to her."

"Really? Well we'll soon find out won't we?" He said somewhat more happier from hearing this as he pulled out several small black cases from the inside pockets of his jacket.

"How long do you need to set up?" Zar-Jins asked him.

"'Bout an hour." He told him.

"I'll be back then." Zar-Jins told him. "Oh Corcel, I can monitor everything that goes on in this room from any part of the ship."

"The only thing that interests me 'bout her is that she could be related to an Illiania. Nothing else." Corcel told him.

Zar-Jins looked over at him and then at Touro who was still asleep and then shrugged. He wasn't really overly bothered about what happens to her as long as he still gets paid for finding her; something that he has failed to mention.

The craft drifted silently in space alongside another ship, it wasn't much bigger but it was definitely more heavily armed with extra gun ports to warn off enemy ships. Which it didn't seem to work in this case as a bright light appeared in the middle of the cockpit, three men in black jumpsuits appeared and just stood there for a moment until the light had disappeared once more and then they came to life once more.

The man nearest to the front with red hair turned around pulling the chair out and sat down pressing buttons on the console. He had dull red markings down the left side of his face and over his red eyes. The other two men sat down just behind on either side of him, they too activated their consoles and just in time as the ship fired upon them; their shields had only just come up in time which deflected the blast and only shook their craft slightly.

"Get the engines up!" Ichigo shouted from up front. "The shuttle isn't moving!"

"It wasn't the bla..." The man to his left started as they were hit once more, his raven black hair was somehow still neatly in place which was the only part of him that seemed calm as his face was pouring with sweat.

The man on his right who had terracotta-coloured and spiked hair, wasn't listening as he lined up the targeting sensors and fired back at the ship, aiming for the exposed weapons ports.

"Damn!" The man on the left shouted as he hit his console. "I think they sent out some sort of deflector beam, to destabilize our engines...I need a couple of minutes..."

He didn't wait for a reply as he pushed his chair back and dropped to the floor pulling a metal panel off from under the console. There was a dull light which lit the wires and the access ports.

"We should have brought one of the Verno shuttles." The weapons officers said suddenly. "Their weapons are far more powerful...especially against something like that, and the other ship..."

"Yeah well, it's too late now to do anything about it." Ichigo told him. "If we had engines, it wouldn't matter what sort of fire power we had."

"I'm almost there..." The man said from under the console.

"Almost isn't good enough Mattie." Ichigo told him.

"I know..." Mattie said as he pulled a couple of wires out and then crossed them and then quickly replaced them in the circuit. "There try that."

Ichigo activated the engines. They roared into life as the ship fired at them but this time they were able to avoid the blast as they flew around the ship and off through the system closely followed by the other ship which continued to fire at them. The panel to Ichigo's right flashed signalling that there was more weapons fire coming towards them, which he avoided while activating the main engine and shot forward in a rainbow of colours, the stars just a blur as they left the system.

"Well that was close." The spiked-haired man said leaning back relaxing finally.

"Remind me next time to bring a better shuttle." Ichigo told them.

"Yeah sure, it's just a shame that we can't switch before we go on." Mattie said.

"They've pulled Corcel in, you know what that means." Ichigo told them. "Paul do you think it'll handle a little more?"

"Yeah, the shields are fine. We didn't take that much damage...weapons aren't as powerful as I'd like them to be, but they'll cause at least a little distraction." Paul told him. "The only problem is, how the hell are we supposed to get close enough to the ship to get on board?"

"Mattie, you can hide the whole ship right?" Ichigo asked him turning around to face him. "You can do right?"

"Yeah...but I won't be able to keep it up for long...five, ten minutes tops." Mattie told him looking a little pale wiping his face with his sleeve.

"Fine, you'll stay on board...we'll go over and get her." Ichigo told them.

Paul turned his chair. "So? Why is she so important?"

Ichigo looked at both of them before he turned back around looking out of the screen at the stars as they flew by them. They were moving so fast yet they couldn't feel a thing.

"Need to know." Ichigo answered. "Sorry..."

"That's fine...I mean as long as it doesn't get us all killed." Paul said.

"I promise..." Ichigo told them, even though there was a very small part of him that was worried that he wouldn't be able to keep it after what had already happened.

"We should be there in about six hours; I'm sure we can come up with a good plan by then hay...?" Mattie said.

Ichigo just sat there looking out into space, he wanted to find her; though perhaps not as much as Renji did who would forgive her in a heartbeat even if she had killed all those people; but he too did want to bring her back and make her safe again.

"Do you think she'll hold out until we get there?" Paul asked him. "She's what... fifteen years old?"

"She'll be fine." Ichigo said, even though he wasn't so sure himself.

They were almost to the system where they believed that Toria was being held, Ichigo took the engines off full power as they entered the outer system and everything came back into focus once more, along with a large yellow and orange gas giant with three moons orbiting it; they headed towards the nearest moon which was also the smallest.

"This should keep us concealed for a while." Paul told them.

"Okay...we move out in ten minutes when the moon moves close enough." Ichigo told them. "When I give the order, we move out."

Ichigo ran scans of the system to make sure that they were alone with their targeted ship; it showed up on their scanner screen three times the size of their own shuttle. Ichigo stared at the screen, hoping that they wouldn't end up in a shooting match with them because if they did, he knew that if they went up against it they wouldn't stand a chance; their only chance was a surprise attack. So they just hoped that they hadn't already been tipped off by the other ship that they had raided several hours before.

The ten minutes seemed to drag on as he watched the screen until they were in transporter range, and he keyed in their coordinates and then stood up; they both looked over at him before Paul stood up as well.

"Just remember five, ten minutes tops." Mattie told them again.

"We know, in and out." Ichigo said.

Mattie closed his eyes focusing as they both watched him shimmer slightly which extended outward from him engulfing the interior shuttle, Ichigo patted him on the shoulder and then disappeared with Paul at his side reappearing in a seemingly dully lit corridor aboard the ship; Ichigo reached behind and as his hand formed a grip on a hilt and sword appeared, it was bound in red and black leather with extra which trailed down his back. Paul stared at him as the whole sword appeared strapped to his back, he pulled the sword from its straps as though this was a completely normal act and began to walk.

"What you don't carry blasters like the rest of us?" Paul quietly asked him.

"Sometimes...but with this I can use my powers if I need to without worrying about breaking any of our laws." Ichigo told him.

"What?" Paul asked now confused. "If there's a way for us to use our powers without breaking the law then, why aren't we all allowed to carry swords?"

"You'd give everyone the power to break the law whenever they wish? Isn't that why we're at war to begin with?" Ichigo asked him. "Because they're afraid that's just what we'll do?"

"Only because they've pushed us to it." Paul told him.

"So it's their fault if we break the law?" Ichigo said and then held up his hand for them to stop as they came to the end of the corridor. He looked around the corner up and down but he still couldn't see anything because it was so dark.

Ichigo closed his eyes and reached out with his mind, he felt himself floating up the corridors and then through the deck plating onto the next when he couldn't find her; but it felt strange not that he couldn't sense her because he knew that he could feel something he just didn't know where it was coming from. It was as though there was some sort of barrier that was up around her.

"They've got a barrier up...but I can't locate where it's coming from..." Ichigo told him.

"Well it's not as though we can just keep wondering around blindly is it?" Paul said. "We need to access the ship's systems, so that we can find out where she is."

"I haven't seen one console yet, nor many rooms." Ichigo said.

"Damn it, what sort of ship..." Paul began but was cut off by an agonizing scream that echoed through the corridors.

Ichigo didn't say anything but just began to run with his sword in his hand still ready in a split second to use it if need be; he ran as though he knew where she was, that was all he needed just something of her to locate. Paul was at his heels not questioning him as they ran down the corridor towards the only door, Ichigo turned slightly not stopping and the door open for him.

Zar-Jins and Corcel was stood on either side of the table and looked up as the door opened, just in time to see Ichigo lift his sword and slice it through the air which sent a wave of fire straight at them, slicing through their clothes and torso knocking them to the ground.

"Make sure they don't get up." Ichigo told Paul, who seemed just as surprised as the two on the floor.

Paul nodded rigidly walking over to them with Ichigo, looking over at the table and the young girl tied up on it. Ichigo deactivated the restrains and then walked around the table so that he could get her off of it, she just lay there her purple hair a mess and her face stained with tears; he reached for her hands which were still in cuffs and only touched them slightly when she moved and kicked him in the side knocking him off of his feet.

Touro fell over the side of the table and tried to move away, but her body didn't seem to want to work the way she was telling it too.

"That wasn't very nice, seeing that I came all this way to get you Touro." Ichigo said pulling himself up holding onto the edge of the table.

Touro looked over at him, she knew his voice; and then his face came into focus but she wasn't sure if he was real. He walked over to her and bent down beside her.

"If Renji had come in person, I bet you wouldn't have kicked him." Ichigo teased her.

"Ichi..." Touro said trying to smile but instead began to cry and flung her arms around him.

He pulled her into him holding her tightly. "I'm sorry that I took so long."

Chapter Nine

Touro just lay there on something soft beneath her and over her keeping her warm. She didn't know where she was or how she had gotten there and at the moment she didn't really care; she didn't even have the strength to open her eyes to look around, all she wanted to do was rest.

"How is she?" A woman asked sounding quite concerned from somewhere close by.

"Has the doctor been yet?" Another woman asked.

"Yes...he's...he's just going over his scans." Ichigo answered sounding further away than the other two. "I'm going to contact Renji, he should know that..."

"N...no...no..." Touro whispered trying to make herself heard, but it seemed such a strain on her voice. It didn't matter though she still had to stop them from contacting him. "No...I don't...I don't want him here..."

Touro willed herself to open her eyes, there was light shining down on her, nice warm light from behind her somewhere. Her eyes were all foggy but she could still make him out stood at the foot of the bed staring at her.

"Please...Ichi..." Touro managed to say.

"Just until you're fit to travel, then I'll call him to come and get you." Ichigo told her.

She didn't say anything to him. She knew that she would have faced him if he was here; but she had too work up more courage after all of this to face him. She didn't know if she was strong enough to do that yet.

"Just rest, you're safe here." Ichigo told her leaving the room so that she could rest, closing the door behind him and standing out in the hall with the two women who were looking at him expectantly.

The two women looked about the same age, the one stood closest to Ichigo was almost the same height as he was and had long almost orange hair and green eyes which were quite sad; she wore a grey and blue strapless basque with a long flowing gathered skirt which had splits the whole way around. The other woman was about a foot shorter than them both and had layered, shoulder-length black and sliver streaked hair, her eyes were just as black as her hair was; she had a pale yellow vest top and matching trousers which had splits down the outside of the legs.

"She asked me not to contact him." Ichigo told them.

"What does that mean?" The black haired woman asked.

"She's upset about what happened." The orange haired woman told them stepping forward. "I'll go and speak to her."

"Lu..." Ichigo said gently. "Why don't we give her some time and then when she's ready to talk about what happened, we'll have figured the whole truth out as well. Rue where's the doc gone?"

"He's in the sitting room." Rue told him and then turned to leave.

"He's right Lutana. She needs time. And she's quite safe here after all."

Ichigo walked off first leaving the two of them, as he walked to the end of the hall with the only light coming from above in the ceiling and the rest of the bedroom doors closed; he went down the stairs so that he could speak to the doctor alone.

The stairs lead down into the sitting room which was flooded with sun light through the large panel windows behind the sofa which had half a dozen cushions thrown on it; the doctor was seated in the far corner chair with his bag next to him and equipment on the table.

He looked a couple of years older than Ichigo but was very handsome even though his long dark bags covered most of his face. He was dressed in a navy blue suit with white collar panels and cuffs; he looked up from his work when Ichigo stepped off the bottom step.

"So Ahtoury, what's the damage?" Ichigo asked him.

"Damage?" Ahtoury said staring at him. "You haven't told me everything, so how can I work out the damage?"

"The damage from what's just happened." Ichigo told him.

"Electro shock torturing to change her appearance, which to be honest I'm quite surprised at how she managed to hold it." Ahtoury said looking at a data sheet. "And there's this...you said that Corcel was there?"

"Yeah, we tied them up but by the time the other team got back to the system they had already gone; it looks as though we just got there in time, right?" Ichigo said.

"You didn't get there in time." Ahtoury told him. "She's infected."

"What? Infected with what?" Ichigo said angrily.

"It's only in the early stages, but I believe it's the Kovel virus." Ahtoury told him.

"What? How the hell would he get hold of that, there hasn't been an outbreak for nearly three hundred years?" Ichigo said. "It's...I mean...back then they couldn't find a cure for it..."

"We still haven't." Ahtoury told him.

"So? What're you going to do?" Ichigo demanded.

Ahtoury stood up suddenly lifting his bag onto the coffee table in front of him. Ichigo stepped forward ready to stop him if he tried to leave before he did anything to help her.

"Where the hell do you think you're going?" Ichigo demanded.

"I don't carry thing's like that around on me." Ahtoury told him. "I'll have to go back to my office, and go over the results and run a few tests...it could take a couple of weeks."

"Weeks?" Ichigo said unsure if he heard him right.

"You don't need to worry at the moment, if it really is the Kovel virus it'll take several months before she starts showing signs..." Ahtoury said and then broke off in mid-sentence while he finished putting the data sheets into his bag. He turned back around to Ichigo. "They didn't want her dead and it isn't contagious, that's why I need more time to study these results; it'll just take time."

Ichigo wasn't so sure if he believed him standing his ground not letting him past, it wasn't as though he could just run out and find a better doctor to check her over because Ahtoury was in fact the best doctor that he knew; so he finally stepped aside.

"She's lucky to have family like you." Ahtoury said picking his bag up. "I'll call as soon as I've found anything."

"Thanks." Ichigo said over his shoulder as Ahtoury walked over to the front door, which opened inwards.

"I'll see you soon." Ahtoury said.

"Yeah, soon." Ichigo said distractedly as he left, the door closing behind him.

Ichigo just stood there, he didn't know what to do; she had asked him not to contact Renji, yet it wasn't as though he could keep something like this from him. Ichigo knew that Renji wouldn't believe anything that he told him, he'd only accept that she was safe and that he could come and get her himself; he couldn't think of anyone he could contact to keep him away for a while.

Touro turned her head slightly on the soft pillows wanting to move her whole body to turn over, but it was still quite stiff; she had no idea how she had managed to sleep on her back since normally she couldn't, so she must have been really tired. She slowly opened her heavy eyelids, her eyes still a little blurred which she blinked a couple of times to clear them before she could properly see the room that she was in.

It wasn't what she was expecting. She knew that she was in a comfy bed and with Ichigo but she was in a little girl's room; the covers were covered in purple and pink flowers and facing the bed was a set of drawers with a dozen teddy bears sat atop of them watching her. To her right was a small table with a teddy bear shaped lamp on it and a small pile of data pads, as she looked around more just lying there as it was still hard to move about with her body feeling really heavy; there was a wardrobe on the far wall which looked about the same height as she was and then there was a desk next to it with a stool set underneath and a normal desk lamp set on top.

Touro wondered whose room this was. If it was one of Ichigo's daughter's; she had never thought about it before, but they must all have families of their own, all because she hadn't seen any of them didn't really mean anything.

It made her wonder about Renji as well since he was a lot older than she was, if he had ever been married or even if he was and has just never told her. What if he had children as well? What if he was actually old enough to have grandchildren? It wasn't as though she really knew anything about any of them.

Touro tried to push herself up so that she could at least sit up, since she had been lying down for longer than she could remember and not all of it were good memories; it made her stop suddenly wondering how they had found her and so quickly as well, but also if this meant that they were going to take her back home as soon as she was fit enough to travel; if it did than she'd just hold out for as long as she could until she could get away again, because she didn't want to go back there.

She had just finished struggling pushing herself up when there was a soft knock at the door, Touro looked over but before she could answer the door slowly opened and Lutana came in carrying a tray with food on it.

"Oh good, you're awake." Lutana said smiling. "Ichigo was getting worried."

"What? Why?" Touro asked her.

"You've been asleep for nearly four days." Lutana told her.

"Oh..." Touro said unsure of what else to say to her.

"I don't want to hear excuses! I want results!" Renji's voice boomed through the walls.

Touro looked around in a panic. "He's here...I didn't want to see him...?"

"No...no...he's not here, he's just very loud over the intercom." Lutana explained. "He's quite upset that he lost you, and that Ichigo still hasn't found you."

"He didn't tell him?" Touro asked slightly surprised.

"No, you asked him not to." Lutana told her smiling slightly as she walked around the bed and put the tray down on the side table and then sat down on the edge of the bed next to her. "He's getting into a lot of trouble covering for you, but he doesn't mind as long as you're well; Renji I'm sure will figure out what's really going on when he finally calms down, he normally does."

Touro smiled knowing what she met. "So it's alright...I mean if I stay a little...only until I'm fit to travel?"

"Of course, you're always welcome here Tour." Lutana told her smiling back. "I'm Lutana."

"Are you Ichigo's wife?" Touro asked her.

"Yes. One of them anyway." Lutana told her smiling.

"One of them? How many does he have?" Touro asked her. "I never really saw him as having more than one...but wait...doesn't that mean that he's a Tasian then?"

"Yes he is. And he only has one other wife." Lutana told her smiling. "Neither of us mind, though it was kind of strange to began with of course but we're actually quite good friends and have quite a big family."

"Oh yes." Touro said suddenly remembering. "This room, it's made out for a little girl...one of yours?"

Lutana smiled at her. "Our grandchildren's children when they stay."

"Oh." Touro said staring at her as she worked out what she just said. "Does that mean that you're like a hundred?"

"I'm actually over a hundred, but thank you." Lutana said smiling picking up the tray once more and putting it down on Touro's lap. "Now try and eat as much as possible. It'll help you to recover."

Touro looked down at the tray on her lap; there was a plate of fruit, a glass of juice and a blow of something grey which she didn't really like the look of.

"Do I have to eat that?" Touro asked pointing at the blow.

Lutana smiled and picked up the blow off of the tray and then stood up. "I'll send Ichigo in when he's finished with Renji. And just eat as much as you can."

"Thanks." Touro said as she watched her leave the room and close the door behind her.

She picked up the glass and took a long swing of it. She hadn't had anything to eat while she was being held by Zar-Jins and she couldn't really remember the last time that she had actually had something; but as she tried to remember she remembered something else. Lonac was probably wondering what had happened to her just suddenly disappearing and the Fleet officers as well, his friend probably wasn't at all impressed about coming home to a broken down door; but it wasn't as though she could do anything about it now, she kind of hoped though that she would run into him again some day.

Lutana walked up the hall still carrying the blow and softly knocked on the door to the next room before she entered, she went inside of the small office where Ichigo was sat at the desk under the window saying goodbye to Renji before he turned around to his wife as the screen went black; there were large computer consoles set up on either wall with solar systems and locations of ships for both sides.

"How is she?" Ichigo asked her.

"She's awake finally; I gave her something to eat." Lutana told him walking into the room and handing him the blow that she had left, which Ichigo took off of her. "She didn't want it, you should have seen the look on her face."

"I can imagine." Ichigo said smiling. "I'll have it. And then I'll go in and check on her."

"How's Renji?" Lutana asked him.

Ichigo stuck his head. "You know there's times that he's like this locked book, that you can't get anything from. And then there are times like this that you seem to think that you know why he's getting so worked up, but really you still don't know the whole truth with him. I've known him since I was fifteen years old, and you know what; I've still not figured him out completely yet."

"Except that he loves your cousin and doesn't know how to tell her." Lutana said smiling. "Just so you know, Touro likes him as well...that's why she's so upset about what she did."

"I'm working on it." Ichigo said hotly as though he already knew that, but knowing it wasn't really much help at the moment. "It's just...we can't seem to get a proper reading about what happened...only that it was a Magical explosion."

"I'm sure that you'll figure it out." Lutana said as she turned around and left him alone to continue with his work.

Ichigo ate while wondering what he was going to do next, either why he would be betraying one of them if he went along with this; he'd have to go talk with her, so he put the half eaten breakfast down and went through to her next door locking his office behind him, he walked along to her room and knocked on the door and waited outside for an answer.

"Come in." Touro said.

Ichigo pushed the door open and went inside. He was pleased to see her sat up in bed and actually eating something; he smiled at her as he walked over and sat down on the edge of the bed.

"So..." Ichigo started.

"I hope that I didn't get you into trouble with Renji." Touro said quickly.

Ichigo smiled at her. "He's always had a little bit of a temper. And also, I stand my ground against even him."

Touro just looked at him as though she didn't believe him, which Ichigo picked up on and laughed unable to stop himself.

"What?" Touro said surprised by his reaction.

"It's nothing." Ichigo told her smiling. "We were going to pull you anywhere considering that you were coming into your powers, he knows that. So I'll just tell him that's what happened and then it'll be up to you then when you want to face him."

"That's easier said than done considering." Touro said looking away from him. "You know what I did...all those people Ichi...I killed them all."

"We don't know that for sure yet, you might not have." Ichigo told her as he reached out for her hand, but she pulled it away from his.

"I might not have?" Touro said mockingly. "I'm not stupid. I was there, there was nothing..."

Ichigo moved closer and took her hand again. "I can't promise you that you didn't kill them, but we are looking into it. You might believe that you killed all those people, but I don't and neither does Renji who actually ordered the investigation so that we can prove your innocence."

"But there were so many...what if...what if I really killed them?" Touro said trying to hold back the tears as Ichigo moved the tray off of her and put it on the floor.

"You don't have to worry about that." Ichigo told her as he leant forward pulling her into a hug. "It'll be alright...cause it wasn't your fault."

Touro just cried into his shoulder, she couldn't take how nice he was being to her after what she had done but she didn't want to leave him either because then she'd really be on her own and she hated the mere thought of that; she wasn't strong enough to be on her own, not yet anyway.

Touro stretched across the bed to open the curtains behind them, the early morning sun brightened up the room even though her room wasn't on the side that the sun came up on; she looked out of the window since she had been stuck in bed for days she couldn't take it anymore and just wanted to look at something different. So she found herself looking out over a beautiful garden full of flowers of all different colours. There were plants that she had never even seen before and was looking forward to going down and seeing them properly.

She smiled to herself glad that she had gotten out of bed finally even if it was just to see the view, but now that she was up she might as well make the most of it. She got off the bed and turned around and found the clothes that they had left her out, which made her feel even better they were hoping that she would get up and join them; they were a perfect fit as well, 3/4 length grey almost blue trousers and a blue vest with pink stitching. She walked over to the wardrobe to have a look at herself opening the door for the mirror inside. It was still strange to see this other self looking back at her when she expected to see her real self; it made her wonder though how come she couldn't change back after what he had done to her because she didn't really know that much about Magic only that if you're put under a lot of strain that your spells and enchantments can be broken, so why didn't hers?

"This couldn't be how I really look, could it?" Touro asked herself, but she just struck her head she'd know if this was how she was really supposed to look because it'd feel right somehow, and it didn't feel completely right, but it did kind of feel familiar in a strange sort of way.

She closed the door and turned around to leave. She hadn't left this room since she arrived and hoped that they wouldn't mind if she did or at least go downstairs; she hadn't heard anyone come up for a while so she assumed that they were all downstairs knowing that they wouldn't leave her alone in case she just ran away again. Touro pulled open the bedroom door which lead out onto the long landing. She looked both ways to see which way the stairs were, but the only thing was there were two sets of stairs one which were right in front of her room which lead up to another floor and then at the far end the stairs went downstairs.

She came out of the bedroom and went right down the landing past a closed door which she assumed was Ichigo's office, because she had heard Renji's voice coming from it the other day; which made her wonder if she was doing the right thing by keeping him in the dark after everything that he had done for her over the years, and this is how she had repaid him, but no matter how long she thought about it she couldn't think of a way to apologize to him.

Touro looked down the stairs into a brightly-lit room, a little nervous now wondering if she really should be wondering around on her own; but it was too late now unless she just wanted to run back to her bedroom that they had given her while she was staying. No, she told herself and started down the stairs slowly as her heart started to beat faster; as the gap began to get wider she looked to her right and saw a large sitting room and only one person sat in it.

Ichigo looked up from his work suddenly and saw her at the bottom of the stairs, he smiled at her which she smiled back nervously at him.

"I'm glad to see that you're up and about." Ichigo told her. "But you can sit down if you want to."

"Oh right...yeah...thanks..." Touro said moving over to the sofa and sitting down in the middle of it, she leant back into the cushion thinking that it was actually somehow comfier than her bed; and said without thinking. "I could have slept here."

"Yeah, I know." Ichigo agreed. "I've spent many a night on there, staying up to all hours workings; but at least it was comfy."

Touro smiled at him. "So what is it that you really do? I mean I've meant you a couple of times because of Renji, you seem to work together; but with him being a Magic then that means that he isn't really a security officer but working undercover right?"

"Yes." Ichigo answered. "He's been there an awful long time. You want to know a secret?"

"About Renji?" Touro said smiling excitedly.

"He stayed because of you; he didn't want to leave you behind." Ichigo told her.

Touro just stared at him, she wasn't sure what he meant by it; why would he stay because of her? Was it because she was a Magic and was afraid of the sort of power that she had and what she would do with it? Well it seems as though he was right to be afraid considering that she destroyed an entire city killing thousands of people the first time that she really used her powers.

Ichigo had been expecting a better reaction from her, than just silence and wondered if he had said the wrong thing to her.

"Was it because of my powers?" Touro asked him finally. "Did he stay because he was worried about what I'd do?"

"No, not really." Ichigo told her kindly. "If he was afraid of what you'd do with them he would have pulled you out of there years ago, seeing that it's not just recently that you've been showing signs. I guess he was waiting for you, until he thought that the time was right to take you away."

"He didn't have to wait so long." Touro said irritably.

Ichigo burst out laughing, he couldn't help himself; Touro though didn't understand why he was laughing at her since she didn't think that she had said anything strange.

"He didn't want to." Ichigo told her when he finally calmed down. "It would have caused an awful lot of trouble, if he'd just up and left with you one day."

"Do you have any idea, how many times he had the chance to do it?" Touro demanded. "We've been alone loads of times...I...I would have been scared about running away, but if it was Renji...he wouldn't let anything happen to me."

Ichigo smiled at her as she just sat there frowning. There was a knock at the front door, Ichigo stood up putting his data pads on the chair before he walked over to answer it while Touro watched him wondering who it could be; he opened the door but Touro couldn't see who it was.

"Morning." Mattie said loudly.

"Morning." Ichigo said stepping aside for him to come in.

Mattie came inside looking around the room and then he saw her and made a bee line straight for Touro, he held his hand out to her but she didn't take it at first just stared at it until she realized what she was doing and gave him her hand to shake.

"I'm Mattie, Ichigo might not have mentioned it but I helped as well...I mean rescuing you." Mattie told her sitting down beside her as Ichigo came back over after closing the front door. "So how are you?"

"I guess I'm doing alright, still somewhat stiff I guess." Touro told him and then looked over at Ichigo.

"He's a friend and one of my officers." Ichigo told her.

"So how about I show you around?" Mattie suggested eagerly.

Touro looked at Ichigo and then at Mattie, she wasn't so sure about going off with someone she didn't know; and then she remembered Lonac who she had gotten on a ship with to a different solar system. It's not as though she hasn't done it before and Ichigo did know him after all.

"It's fine with me." Ichigo told them.

"Oh...I guess for a little while then." Touro agreed since Ichigo said it was alright also.

"That's great, let's go then." Mattie said getting to his feet ready to go already.

"Wait a minute; did you just come around to take her out?" Ichigo asked him.

"Yeah course, she's better looking than you." Mattie said. "And the guys will wonder where I found you, lucky me hay."

Touro smiled slightly, even more unsure now than she was before his explanation; but Ichigo seemed find with it as though this was quite normal behaviour for him.

"Just don't get into trouble; either of you." Ichigo told them both.

"What?" Touro said startled.

"It'll do you good to get out of the house, stretch your legs and get some fresh air." Ichigo told her. "And also this is a Magical colony, meaning that everyone here is a Magic; you could learn a thing or two."

"Okay." Touro said standing up, which Mattie quickly followed her lead.

"Come on then." Mattie said leading the way out. "I'll bring her back in a bit."

"Have a good time." Ichigo told them.

"See you later Ichi." Touro shouted at the door before she closed it.

Mattie and Touro walked up the front path through the garden, which was like the back one full of beautifully coloured flowers from all over the galaxy; there wasn't a gate so they just walked straight out into the street turning left and saw a couple of young children playing in the garden across the road, one of them was trying by cheating to climb the tree, he levitated into the air as the other boy struggled to climb up. Touro stared at them as they were the first she had ever seen use Magic so openly before; Mattie watched her with a small smile at such a small thing to surprise someone so much.

"Ichigo said that you were brought up as a normal?" Mattie asked her.

"Yeah, I was." Touro answered.

They carried on walking down the street past the other houses. There were more children about playing and using Magic; but Touro still couldn't understand how they could use it so openly even if this was one of their own colonies without being afraid that they were being watched, and also where did they all learn how to use their Magical abilities, do their parents teach them or is there a Magic school here which teaches you everything like a normal one would do.

"Where do they learn how to use their powers?" Touro asked.

"School." Mattie answered as though this was quite obvious.

"Really?" Touro said smiling. "I don't know how to use my powers, but I haven't really got all the time in the world to start studying like that."

"You have plans?" Mattie asked her.

"It's not like that...it's...it doesn't matter." Touro told him. "Anyway, where are you taking me?"

"Well if you want to learn a little about Magic, I've got just the place." Mattie told her.

He didn't say anything else on the matter but just carried on walking with Touro beside of him. She didn't question him instead just carried on looking at everything and wondering if things would have been different if she too would have grown up in a place like this; her mum must have been a Magic which she didn't understand why they would kill one of their own, unless she betrayed them by being with her father who was supposedly against Magics. But then why was he with her, unless he didn't know?

She couldn't help thinking that he must have known that she had powers as well which was why he was always so surprised that she was interested in them, but if he would have done something about it like explaining the whole thing properly or getting someone in to help her to use her powers then none of this would have happened. She also wondered about Renji, what things would have been like between them if she was raised as a Magic. Would she have even known him considering that he's been on this assignment for so long; then she remembered Ichigo telling her before that he only stayed for so long because of her. Why would he stay for so long just because of her? She was four years old when she met him and he hasn't aged a day; she had trusted him completely since the moment that she met him without knowing anything about him only that he was there to look after her.

They walked for about ten minutes in silence until they reached the outskirts of the city, Touro thought that it looked like some sort of base; a large five-storey building which was fenced off with vehicles parked up at the side but with no visible exit for them. She followed the fencing to see where it went but it didn't seem normal, or rather it seemed to shimmer in the sunlight.

"What's with the fence, is it an energy conducted fence?" Touro asked him.

"A Magic one, yeah." Mattie answered sounding surprised that she had realized that just after a few moments. "How did you know?"

"You can tell, just by looking at it." Touro told him.

"So are you related to Ichigo?" Mattie asked her.

Touro looked over at him. She had been taken off guard by the question as she hadn't been expecting to be asked something like that; it wasn't that she didn't like him nor the idea that they could be related it was just, well that she didn't know either way.

"You don't have to tell, if you don't want too." Mattie told her smiling slightly.

She carried on walking wondering why he had actually asked her, it must have been something to do with her question she would have to ask him about it later when she got back; as they walked around she could hear a lot of shooting that was coming from inside the grounds, making Touro wonder what sort of training they were doing inside and if she would be allowed to try it as well.

As they walked to the front entrance Touro couldn't see anyone but she knew that there were people inside because she could hear them, and also what she thought was strange was that she could see the entrance of the building but she still couldn't see the entrance in the fence; well not to begin with anyway but as they got closer she could see where the fence opened, she could actually see the lines in the fence where it swung back as though the gates were actually on hinges so she started to walk towards it.

"Where're you going?" Mattie asked her.

"There." Touro told him pointing at the fence. "That's where it opens like a gate, right?"

"Yeah, but how did you know that?" Mattie asked her.

Touro looked over at him wondering if it was a trick question, because it was quite obvious to see where it opened. They walked over to the opening which opened inwards at the very point that she had seen the hinges, but as soon as they were clear it snapped back shut not letting anything else in.

"You can tell my mate inside how you saw the opening, I'm sure that he'll like to know since he created it and the only ones who can normally see it are Ichigo's lot." Mattie told her.

"What do you mean, his lot?" Touro asked.

"Like his family and others like him." Mattie told her.

As they approached the building you could properly see it now, all the windows which there was actually twice as many as before and the entrance was also in a different place as well; it was more to the right.

"Does the fence make you see the building differently as well?" Touro asked him. "Or is that something done to the building?"

"That's enchantments on the building itself." Mattie told her. "Well we've got to protect ourselves."

"Of course you do." Touro agreed as the door slid open and they went inside.

They walked into a large foyer with a high semi-circle desk in the centre with four officers sat behind it; behind them were four doors, but the second on the left looked different and also had a different panel to open it.

"Morning." Mattie said as he walked over to the desk with Touro just behind him. "Do you remember Paul, he was with us when we rescued you as well?"

Touro looked at the four men sat before her, but she really couldn't remember seeing any of them before; though they thought that she did considering how she was staring at him but that was only because he was in his natural form, she had never seen a Tasian in their natural form before.

"Paul, hi." He said smiling at her. "Glad to see you're doing better."

"Thanks." Touro said smiling shyly.

The one on the far right had black scales instead of skin and no hair. His yellow eyes fixed on Touro as though he didn't approve of her being here. The man sat next to him wasn't human either but more like a large cat with grey and white fur and everything, he kind of reminded her of a tabby cat, he didn't wear the same uniform as the others though Touro thought that would be because he didn't really need to wear clothes like they did, just perhaps trousers. The man on the far side next to Paul was human, or at least he looked human but that didn't really mean much if you had Magical powers seeing that most learn how to change their appearance so that they aren't recognized.

"Oh Ag'nac she saw through the fence, you might want to give it a boost." Mattie told him.

Ag'nac's yellow eyes were still watching her seemingly with even more dislike than before, making her feel quite uncomfortable and then his tongue suddenly shot out hissing startling her slightly as he stood up.

"Come." Ag'nac told her walking around the desk.

Touro looked up at him over a foot taller than she was. She had never seen anyone of his race before and had no idea what to expect from him; but he didn't do or say anything, but just walked around her as if he expected her to just follow him without question. She looked over at Mattie who nodded to her that it was alright and she slowly followed him back outside.

Ag'nac walked over to the energy fence and stopped when he was three feet away waiting for Touro to join him. She slowly walked over but stood a little away from him since she didn't know what he was going to do.

"The entrance, where?" Ag'nac asked her.

Touro looked over at him and the fence and pointed to the point where they had come through as she could still see where the gate would open; she waited for a reply but he didn't say anything only stared at the point she was pointing at.

"How?" Ag'nac asked.

"How what? How can I see?" Touro asked unsure of his question.

"How?" Ag'nac asked her again.

"I don't know how I see it, I just can." Touro told him. "It's a gate, I can see the lines where the hinges are and where it would open...so what...can't everyone else?"

"No." Ag'nac answered.

"Oh." Touro said and then remembered. "Mattie said before that those like Ichi...I mean do you know Ichigo?"

"Yes." Ag'nac answered. "Family?"

"I don't know." Touro answered honestly. "Can he see it?"

"Just. Tested on him, I did." Ag'nac told her.

"Maybe it's lost power." Touro suggested but he just ignored her and held up his hand, she didn't know what it was for but just stood back out of his way.

He just stood there in front of her not saying a word or even moving, she wondered what he was doing if he was doing Magic without her realizing but she couldn't see anything different about the fence; she watched him for about five minutes getting quite bored at just standing around doing nothing.

"What're you doing?" Touro asked him but he still didn't say anything. "I can still see it, just as clear as before if that's what you've been trying to do."

Ag'nac turned around making her step back unsure of what he might do considering that she kept answering him back without showing any sign of respect. It wasn't as though she was talking with Renji and knew how far she could go with him before she crossed the line; he walked over to her but didn't say anything nor did he stop but just carried on back inside, Touro stared after him for a couple of seconds before she quickly followed him.

When she went back inside Mattie had taken Ag'nac's seat behind the desk and they were all watching one of the screens and hadn't even noticed that they had come back inside.

"Idiot!" Paul shouted.

"Jump over it, not fall over it." Huron said irritably. "No grace what so ever."

"What're they watching?" Touro asked Ag'nac.

"These are monitors for the system." Ag'nac told them.

"Roaring Torch are playing." Mattie told him.

"You're in my seat." Ag'nac told him as he walked back over to the desk closely followed by Touro to see what they were watching.

They walked around the back of the desk and Mattie still hadn't gotten up, Touro stepped around him so that she could see the screen but it didn't look like much to her just a bunch of people running around a forest shooting spells at each other.

"And what is this?" Touro asked them and then saw someone that she knew. "Lonac...what's he doing there?"

The four of them turned around to look at her.

"Vertigo, it's a game." Mattie told her.

"You know Lonac, but you don't know about Vertigo?" Paul asked her.

"Yeah so." Touro said. "Lonac's nice though, he helped me out before I was kidnapped."

"You've met him?" Paul asked. "Nice? He kind of comes across as being scary, he's massive."

"So what, who cares what he looks like...well he's quite handsome yeah; but I mean he was really nice to me when I was in trouble." Touro told them.

They turned back to the screen to carry on watching, but Touro still didn't know what they were actually watching only that it was called Vertigo and it was some sort of Magical game.

"So what side is he on then?" Touro asked.

"The Roaring Torch." Ag'nac answered.

"They haven't been doing so good lately since they lost their Rose Player." Mattie told her.

"My money's on Bane Axe." Jed told her. "They've got four werewolves, the most any team has."

"Werewolves?" Touro said smiling. "Wait a minute; they can change just like that without a full moon?"

"You really don't know much about Magic do you?" Mattie said.

Touro didn't like being in the dark about all this and being surrounded by people who take it all for granted thinking that she would know everything that they do, but she was sure that even other Magics don't know everything that's going on because it wasn't as though they could advertise what they're up to, with the Fleet watching near enough everything that they did.

She was watching the screen like the others when the players disappeared for a split second and then reappeared in a desert. She didn't know what had just happened but she was the only one that seemed bothered by this; she wanted to ask if it was normal for them to be suddenly transported somewhere else but they all seemed to caught up in the game and decided that she'd wait and ask Ichigo about it later when she got back to his place.

Chapter Ten

Fire sprung up out of the ground trying to circling Touro where she stood, she looked around wildly before the two points connected but she was too slow to stop it from forming a circle a round her; she tried to focus on what to do but it was as though her mind had gone blank. The fire rose even higher so that she couldn't see anything, but that wasn't the worst of it; she realized that the circle was getting smaller and the fire was getting closer to her.

The fire was only a foot away from her on all sides when she realized that she couldn't really feel the heat coming from it, it should be burning but there was nearly nothing coming off of it, or so she thought; so she decided to reach out thinking that it wasn't real but some sort of an illusion. She held her hand less than an inch away from the flames and still no different, it was warm but nothing that it should have been; she was just about to put her hand right into the flames themselves when they disappeared completely.

Touro looked around at the ground where the fire had been expecting to see burn marks, but it was as though nothing had just happened that the fire had never been there in the fire place; she was in a large empty store room that had an office at the far end which could watch the whole room through the windows that covered that wall.

"Idiot!" Ichigo shouted at her as he walked into the room. "Normal people don't try to put their hands into fire, even if they don't think it's real."

"It wasn't hot." Touro told him as she turned around to face him.

"That...that isn't the point." Ichigo told her irritably. "Remember the fire might have been real, and someone might have been suppressing the heat to make you think that it wasn't real but as soon as you would have touched it...do you know what would have happened? It would have burnt the skin right off of you."

Touro just looked at him thinking that he was overreacting once again, Ichigo seemed to pick up on what she was thinking as it was written all over her face.

"You wanted me to teach you about Magic, well these are important to know." Ichigo told her. "You need to know the difference between an illusion and the real thing, you need to know when the real thing is being manipulated. Do you understand what I'm trying to tell you, or am I just wasting my time?"

"Of course not." Touro told him. "Sorry. But can I just say that fire wasn't real, look at the floor; there's no burn marks from where it was."

Ichigo stared at her getting more annoyed by the second. "So what. It's not as though you can wait around to see what it'll be like afterwards, is it? You need to make up your mind there and then."

"So you're saying that I was wrong?" Touro asked him. "I couldn't help it...I just...I don't know..."

"That'll do for today, we've been doing it for hours and we're not really getting anywhere." Ichigo told her. "Come on."

"I'm sorry." Touro said as she followed him over to the office. "So what are Elementals?"

"What?" Ichigo said surprised by the question.

"I heard the others talking about it, and I'm sure that I heard it somewhere before." Touro told him. "You can see through the fence thing like I can, right? So what does that make you, a fire elemental?"

"Yes." Ichigo answered.

"They asked if we were related because I could see it like you, Ag'nac tried to change the setting on the fence but I could still see it." Touro told him.

"I wondered why it seemed more faded than normal." Ichigo said thoughtfully and then looked over at her. "And yes it does mean that we're related."

Touro stopped and then stopped him. "We're related?"

"Yes." Ichigo answered. "Is that a problem?"

"Yes." Touro answered him.

Ichigo was surprised and annoyed by her answer. "Yes? What you don't like me suddenly?"

"That's just it. I do like you." Touro told him. "I've known you for years through Renji, and neither of you ever said anything to me. And...and I've been staying with you now for a couple of weeks and you still didn't say anything to me; would you have if I hadn't have asked you?"

"Of course I would have." Ichigo told her.

"Please." Touro said walking off. "You can say that now after I asked you, but to be honest we'll never know will we?"

Ichigo followed her through the empty office to the back door. "No, I guess we won't."

Touro put up her arm to stop him from walking through the door which she had just opened, a cold breeze on her which made the hairs on her neck stand on end.

"What the hell is with that?" Touro said. "You're just going to agree with me?"

"There's no point in agreeing about it, you're right." Ichigo told her. "I have known all the time that we're related and so did Renji, at the time considering the situation we thought that it was best; it wasn't as though I could have been a real part of your life."

Touro wanted to know, now that they were on the topic she could ask him and since he was being honest with her perhaps he would be about this as well.

"My father...he knows right...I mean about me being a Magic, he knows doesn't he?" Touro asked him, even though she already knew the answer she just needed someone to tell her, someone to be honest with her.

"Of course he does." Ichigo told her watching her carefully.

Touro dropped her arm and walked out into the cool air on the base, they were in the far training building which was out of the way just in case one got carried away not wanting to hurt anyone else on the base and so that they wouldn't interfere with any of the equipment, which she had also found out that high pressure Magic can do. Ichigo followed a little way behind her to give her space, he hadn't just wanted to drop everything on her but he did believe that she deserved to know the truth or at least as much as he really was allowed to tell her; at least this way they'll know for sure which side she'd go with.

Touro walked across the stone covered yard back up to the main building. She wasn't really in the mood to talk to the rest of the officers like she normally did after training so she changed her pacing so that she would walk around the outside of the building and could go straight back to Ichigo's place; she knew that he would understand without having to explain to him. She had wondered for a while now about her father knowing the truth about her, and she had always thought that he had but why would he hide it from her, if he would have just told her the truth then none of this would have happened; he could have gotten someone into help her instead of her just losing control like she did do.

Touro stopped suddenly, what if that was it, that was his plan all along since he knew that she was a Magic and what type she was; what if he wanted her to turn against her own kind? She would end up killing millions of them at a time with her power if she got it under control, if she could already kill thousands just losing control for a few minutes.

"Do you think this is what he wanted me for?" Touro asked.

Ichigo came up beside of her. "We don't know. But I do hope that it wasn't."

"But there's a chance that it is, considering that he knew." Touro said almost in tears. "He must have known all this time. I've been coming into my powers for a while now, feeling strange and everything...he could have used one of those Chip thing's that suppress your powers on me all my life; if I would have just told Renji everything then he would have been able to do something sooner to help me wouldn't he? He wouldn't have to hate me because what I did."

"He doesn't hate you." Ichigo assured her. "Trust me. He's just worried about you because I won't tell him where you are. Perhaps if I told..."

"No." Touro said. "He'll come won't he? I can't face him, not until I know for sure what I did to those people...I can't. I feel...I feel as though I've betrayed him more than anyone else, more than even my father for running away and not telling him anything..."

Ichigo smiled at her and took her into his arms. "You silly girl, you fell for him didn't you...of all the people you could have fallen in love with and you chose him."

"It's so stupid...he's probably hundreds of years old...but...it's so stupid." Touro said trying not to cry and then pushed him away suddenly. "You can't tell him."

Ichigo laughed at her. "Cause not."

Though he already knew that she had told him that she liked him, and even if she hadn't it wasn't as though one wouldn't be able to tell how she felt; he knew though that Renji wouldn't hurt her, not on purpose; break her heart perhaps.

Renji paced back and forward impatiently in Kasiya's quarters as he waited for him to return; he was still in his human form the only thing that was different was the length of his hair, he had returned it to its full length tied up in a pony tail. He started to breath heavily as his anger was getting the better of him, he sat down suddenly on the edge of the desk knocking a photo over; he reached back and picked it up. He was just going to replace it when he decided to have a look instead. He just stared at the picture, it had been such a long time since he had seen it and this was the last place he had been expecting to see it again; it was of the three of them when he was much younger.

He gently touched the face of the woman and whispered to himself, or rather the woman in the photo. "We should have been married by now."

The door slid open next to him and he quickly put the picture back as Kasiya walked in and looked around. He didn't look surprised to still see that Renji was there.

"You're still here, I thought that you would have already left." Kasiya said walking over to the chairs with the door closing behind him, but Renji stayed where he was. "You're already this far out, just a little further and then you could go chasing after her." He smiled suddenly.

"What the hell is so damn funny?" Renji demanded.

"I was just remembering something." Kasiya told him.

"Well, where is she?" Renji asked the question to why he was there in the first place. "What happened on that colony?"

"My ship's been investigating along with several others." Kasiya told him calmly. "All we can make out is that it was done by a very powerful Magic. I've sent teams down to check the place out seeing that I have Magics on board that I can trust, but even they couldn't sense anyone. Renji, I don't want to give up on this either...but we just can't find anything."

"They said that after Tasia and Ta'via was destroyed didn't they?" Renji said. "It was done by Magics, it was the first real time that our own kind had betrayed us; and since that day it's only been getting worst."

Kasiya looked over at his long time friend, it had become a regular thing it seems to see him like this and he didn't like it; he was normally so strong.

"It's like losing her all over again." Renji said suddenly. "I keep losing them, I live on and the people that I care about I just keep losing them."

"You haven't lost Toria, she's still here." Kasiya assured him.

Renji just laughed bitterly. "I lost her. And she'll lose herself no matter what anyone says to her, if she believes that she killed all those people; she's not a murderer, and no matter what anyone tries she'll never become one, that's why I know I'll lose her to this."

"If we're being honest with one another, I didn't think that you would stay for as long as you did." Kasiya told him smiling slightly to himself. "I thought that as soon as you earned her trust that you would have taken her away and brought her home to her real family."

"So did I." Renji told him. "And I hate myself for not doing it."

Kasiya looked out of the view port and then over at Renji. "She said that she doesn't want to see you, not yet anyway."

Renji looked over at him; he got up and walked over sitting on the chair next to him. "I knew it, I knew you knew where she was...he knows, Ichigo knows as well doesn't he? She's with him, isn't she?"

"Where else would she be?" Kasiya said. "She's upset like you said because of what she did. She can't face you until she knows the truth; this is her choice."

Renji leant back in the chair, his whole body just relaxed; it seems that was all he needed for now, just to know that she was safe he could solve everything else later as long as she was safe.

"Perhaps I should have told you that from the start, if it would have gotten you off my back." Kasiya said. "It was just that I didn't want you running off half cocked."

"I don't do that...not that often anyway." Renji said smiling to himself.

"She got you good didn't she?" Kasiya said looking over at him for some sort of reaction, but to his surprise it actually looked as though he had fallen asleep; this annoyed him slightly but thought that he'd let him be for now.

The doors slid open to the busy cargo bay, where the crew was readying Renji's shuttle to leave with supplies; his was the largest shuttle in the bay twice the size of the three which had to be moved to fit his, the cargo itself had to be moved to another hold as there hadn't been enough room for everything in there.

Renji walked in with Kasiya at his side, he had changed his hair again so that it was short since that was how he had arrived and how everyone in the Fleet knew him; though their own people knew what he looked like in both forms, of course, just in case they ran into him or if they needed his help.

"I'll contact you when she's ready to see you." Kasiya told him.

"Perhaps I'll just drop by." Renji suggested.

"And upset her again, probably not the best thing to do right now, is it?" Kasiya said. "Just give her time, she's just come into her powers and coming of age; she needs space to clear her mind. You hovering around definitely won't help her."

Renji smiled. "You'll see, she'll come running back to me."

"Just be careful how you act when you get back, you're coming across as being too attached to her." Kasiya warned him. "They'll start to think that you have feelings for her that you shouldn't have. That is if they haven't already."

"Lesharo..." Renji answered.

"Then you should be careful." Kasiya told him.

"I can take him." Renji assured him.

"And everyone else that the senator will send after you?" Kasiya asked him.

"You worry too much." Renji told him off-handily as though he wasn't worried at all about the situation anymore since he had been reassured. "I better get going, they'll start to wonder what I'm up to especially if don't come back with anything."

"See you next time then." Kasiya told him as he stopped.

Renji turned around smiling at him. "See I knew you liked me, who wouldn't; I grow on people."

Kasiya just smiled at him as he turned around and waved at him from behind. Renji laughed to himself as he walked over to his ship ignoring the rest of the officers looking at him; probably shocked that anyone would speak to their captain like he was doing, but he had known him since he was boy and he has always been his commanding officer but he's also one of his oldest friends. Renji actually enjoyed talking to him even though they were complete opposites at times, they were still good friends at the end of the day.

Renji walked around to the side entrance which was open, a younger man quickly moved out of his way lowering his head so that he wouldn't be seen; he never did like being on Fleet ships too long with the way that they behave and treat their officers. He walked into the small cargo hold that he had that they had filled with supplies and a few gifts also for the senator for his continues support with the war against the Magics. Renji pressed the button on the console behind him and the door closed from above locking out the sounds of the ship, he checked that his own cargo was secure before he went through to the cockpit; on his left in the bulk head were bunk beds and on his right was a desk with the chair securely fastened underneath it.

He walked up to the front where there were only two seats, one for navigation where he normally sat and a seat at the weapons station though he could always transfer them over to his own console if he really needed them; it wasn't as though he couldn't handle both. He had been fighting in this war now for a few hundred years since before they destroyed his home world. He pulled the high back chair out and sat down resting his head against the back of it, it might not be how he wanted to go back without her but at least he knew she was safe wherever they were hiding her for the moment; that would have to be good enough.

Renji shook himself mentally before he sat up straight and started the per-launch systems, knowing that Kasiya was right that he better get going or the senator will really start to wonder if something was going on. He reached across the console for the orange button at the top and pressed it.

"Right I'm ready to go." Renji said.

"Cargo bay two will be clear of personnel in a minute." Kasiya told him. "I hope you enjoyed your stopover."

"Of course, I'll give the senator your regards." Renji said smirking to himself, he was only keeping up appearances for the rest of the crew so that they didn't think that there was anything strange going on, after all this wasn't really the first time that Renji had come knocking on his door for help; it was just that there were new crew on board that he hadn't seen before but he trusted Kasiya to have everyone properly checked out before he let them serve on his ship, he didn't want to be compromised after all.

He waited until they signalled him from the bridge, his console flashed that the bay was clear and the hanger doors began to separate opening slowly, the blue energy field flashed slightly as the doors opened locking the atmosphere inside and the vacuum of space out; he waited until the doors were wide enough for his ship and then activated the engines and lifted of the deck slowly heading out through the field and out into space between the engines of the ship. He turned sharply to port and over the engine before he carried on his way.

"Senate security shuttle one, clear." Renji reported.

"Safe journey." Kasiya said over the intercom.

"Thanks. You too." Renji said before he logged off and set a course back to the senate.

Renji set the auto pilot not seeing the point in flying it all the way back himself as there wasn't really anything to do, he activated it and then pushed his chair back to have a look at the supplies that they had given him hoping that Kasiya had given him something a little special for his good behaviour. He walked through to the cargo hold, there were two boxes for the senator and a large container for him, he couldn't see it being in there so he stepped behind the boxes breathing in so that he could squeeze through the small gap; he had too push himself through and almost fell as he reached down for the handle on the case resting in-between the bulk-head and boxes, he grabbed it and held onto the top box for support pulling himself back squeezing through the gap again almost falling out from trying to hard.

Renji straighten himself up and put the case on top of the boxes to open it, there was just one bottle inside which made him smile.

"I knew you wouldn't let me down old friend." Renji said as he lifted the bottle out and read the label. "Tas'vian Wolf Whiskey; the best stuff in the galaxy...I'll have a small one since it's such a long way back."

He carried the bottle and case back through to the cockpit and put them both down on the desk as he pressed the button on the drawer which opened revealing two glasses inside. He picked up one of them and then closed the drawer again; he opened the bottle and poured himself one out and then closed the bottle again before he picked up his glass and went back to his seat putting his feet up on the console as he leant back to relax.

He had only just taken a sip of his whiskey when alarms started to beep, he sat up straight and took the ship off auto pilot activating the sensors; it was a ship, but it wasn't just any ship but the senator's ship.

"Lesharo senate security officer to shuttle one, reply." Lesharo said through the intercom.

"Idiot." Renji mumbled to himself before he activated his intercom. "What're you doing all the way out here then?"

"You said that you had a lead, so the senator wanted to meet you; hoping that we could take the both of you home." Lesharo told him. "But our sensors are only picking up one life sign."

"That would be because I'm alone, don't you think that I would have called ahead if I'd found her?" Renji told him angrily. "You know, so that you could meet up with me."

"Prepare to come on board as we lock onto your ship." Lesharo told him.

The shuttle shook suddenly as they locked onto him from behind, he knocked the whiskey back in one burning the back of his throat and as it went all the way down as he stood up and went over to get the case not wanting to leave it behind; he put the bottle back in the case and stood ready to be transported aboard. He disappeared in a flash of light, the shuttle fading away and then another room started to appear around him; he was stood in a small security office with Lesharo in front of him looking quite smug with himself.

"I told you not to tell him." Renji told him.

"He asked." Lesharo said and then smiled evilly at him. "I knew you wouldn't find her because there's nothing out there to find."

Renji didn't even bother to say anything to him as he turned around and walked out the door which slid open for him, it began to close again and then opened with Lesharo quickly following him wanting to know what was going on.

"Hay...what're you...what're you doing?" Lesharo demanded as he tried to keep up with Renji.

Renji turned the corner to the right and then carried on for a minute before he stopped outside of a door which he pressed the button to open the door and went straight inside, Lesharo hesitated for a moment before he too followed him inside.

They had walked into the senator's quarters. He looked up from his work not at all pleased to see either of them. He was sat in a large high-back comfy chair underneath the view port with his desk in front of him piled high with work that he had brought along with him; the sofa was set in the corner to their right with a small coffee table, and to their left was another room which was the bedroom and bathroom.

"I'm sorry for intruding sir, but I thought that you would want to know what I found out." Renji told him.

"That does not give you the right to just walk into my quarters, no matter what you have to report." Senator Kentaro told him sternly not at all pleased, especially with Lesharo who was stood slightly behind Renji.

"I'm sorry as well sir, I tried to stop him...but I couldn't." Lesharo told him quickly.

"I couldn't actually find her sir, but I did find out that she is still alive." Renji told him. "She's well..."

"Alive? But you couldn't find her?" The senator asked him. "Leave us."

Lesharo looked from Renji to the senator furious that he was the one being kicked out, but he reluctantly bowed his head before he turned around and left them alone.

"I thought that we had an agreement." Senator Kentaro said evenly.

"Yes sir." Renji said calmly. "I...I did think about it, it does seem the best course but at the present time in her condition I believe that it's unwise to force anything on her."

"So you believe that it was her who killed them all?" Senator Kentaro asked him watching him carefully. "Did that small accident change your mind?"

"From what you told me about her, it seems the most logical assumption that it was her since she herself is still alive." Renji said calmly. "She ran because she was scared of what she did, which is another reason why I believe that we should give her some space instead of forcing her back straight away. And no sir, it did not change my mind if you still believe that it is best."

"If you believe that is best." Senator Kentaro said calmly.

"For now sir." Renji answered.

"Then for now I'll give her some space, but you must understand that I will still continue my search for her; I'm her father after all, I need to know where she is." Senator Kentaro told him.

"Of course sir, if you believe that best." Renji said even though he didn't really want him to continue searching for her, he also knew that he probably shouldn't have told him that she was alive but it gave him an excuse now for leaving more often, if he was actually helping to find her. Since that he did have a lot to gain once she returned. "Oh yes sir, Captain Kasiya sent you his regards and apologies that he was unable to find her but it was with his help that I found out that she was still alive."

"Yes I was told that you were on board his ship." Senator Kentaro told him watching him as if he was expecting some sort of reaction. "I didn't realize that the two of you were friends."

"Yes, we've known each other for years; we just went in different directions with our careers." Renji told him, he wasn't pleased that he already knew where he had been because that meant that Kasiya had Malevalus' men on board his ship; he had to find an opportunity to warn him. "If you'll excuse me then sir, I'll head back to my own ship and follow you back to the senate."

"Yes that's fine, dismissed." Senator Kentaro said as he turned back around to his work as though he had already gone.

Renji turn around and walked out, he wasn't at all surprised to see that Lesharo was still stood outside of his quarters as if he had been expected to be called back into arrest him; it would have made his day, no his year.

"I'm heading back to my ship, if you need me." Renji told him as he walked back up the corridor with Lesharo at his side.

"That's it, he's not going to do anything to you considering that you didn't bring her back?" Lesharo demanded outraged.

"Doesn't look like it does it?" Renji said off-handily.

"I don't believe it; he wouldn't just let you walk like this." Lesharo said. "What did you really tell him?"

"I'll go and get her when she's ready to come back." Renji told him. "He was fine with that, see he has more sense than you; doesn't want to scare her off again, making her run."

"Please, he's not going to let it go." Lesharo told him stopping. "And you're a fool if you think that he will just because you told him to."

Renji didn't reply, he just carried on walking he had actually thought the same thing but hoped that he would stand by his suggestion, but why would he if he was afraid that he would lose her to Magics after spending all this time trying to turn her against them; and Lord Malevalus defiantly wouldn't let her go so easily so he couldn't go against him, he had known them both a long time now but he hasn't actually seen him truly bond with her as though she was really his daughter but it was more of an act for her and for everyone else around them so that they wouldn't know that there was anything going on.

Renji hurried back to the transporter room so that he could get back to his ship and warn Kasiya that they may have trouble, they had to be careful though so that they don't figure out that it was him who tipped him off about it; he just hoped that Kasiya would be able to do something considering that he had a spy on board his ship.

When Renji got back on board his ship he put his case down on the desk and went back over to the main console, they still had his shuttle held with a tracker beam so that he couldn't go anywhere unless he opened fired on them, but if he did that then they might know that he wasn't really who he appeared to be all these years; the real problem wasn't about getting away but getting a message back to Kasiya without them intercepting it.

Renji sat there tapping the console trying to figure out what to do and wondering if the order had already been sent.

"Computer have any messages been sent from the senator's ship in the last ten minutes?" Renji asked hoping that the reply would be no.

"Yes, two messages have been sent." The computer answered.

"Damn it." Renji said slamming the console. "Computer encode this message and send it on wind channel to the Orihan System, to Colonel II; danger for fires the lord may know. send."

Renji just hoped that it would be enough and would get to them in time, if not then Toria wouldn't be the only one captured from this.

The hot steam filled the room as Touro opened the glass shower door grabbing for the towel off the rail. She wrapped the large fluffy bath towel around herself as she walked over to the fogged up mirror over the sink not that she could see through it; she picked up a small towel and dried her hair with it partly before she wrapped it around. She looked around for her robe but couldn't see it, she must of left it back in her room since she was so used to having it joint as an en suite.

It didn't bother her too much as her bedroom was only two doors down and she still had the towel, she opened the door and stepped out leaving it slightly open to let the cool air in.

Touro looked around wondering where she could hear a beeping sound coming from, she walked closer to Ichigo's office door and pressed her ear up against it thinking that was the only place that it could come from; she was sure that Ichigo wasn't up here or he would have heard it himself so she turned back to the stairs.

"Ichi, you're office is beeping!" Touro shouted down to him.

A moment later Ichigo appeared at the bottom of the stairs and started up them.

"How long its been going on for?" Ichigo asked her.

"I don't know, I just got out of the shower and heard it." Touro told him as she stepped aside for him, she followed him over to his office.

Ichigo put in his accept code and the door slid open, they both went inside and over to his desk where the computer screen had tornados ripping across the country side; the beeping seemed to have gotten even louder the closer they had got.

"What is it?" Touro asked him as he pulled out his chair to sit down touching the screen. "Is it a weather warning?"

"No, but it's still a warning." Ichigo told her.

The beeping stopped. "Danger for fires the lord my know." Renji's voice said.

"That...that was Renji right, I know his voice...that was him." Touro said her worry sounding in her voice. "What does it mean? If he's sending us a warning? Fire's and the Lord? Lord who?"

"Us, he means we're in danger." Ichigo told her pressing another button. "Ag'nac we might have been compromised, deploy the teams."

"Yes sir." Ag'nac answered.

"Get dressed, now; quickly." Ichigo told her.

Touro stood there for a moment, not sure what was going on; everything had been fine one moment and now they were deploying teams and they were in danger. She just didn't understand how everything can change so suddenly. She slowly turned around and walked back out to get dressed, she went through to her own room pushed the door to and dropped her towel and grabbed the nearest clothes to her; a short purple and red panel dress with matching knee socks, she grabbed the nearest pair of shoes which were purple with a big heel.

She left the towels on the floor as she went back through to Ichigo but he was already coming out of the office and heading for the stairs to leave.

"Come on, we need to get to the base." Ichigo told her.

"On foot?" Touro asked him.

"I'll transport the two of us." Ichigo told her as she followed down the stairs.

"I've never done that before...are you sure it'll be alright...I mean considering that my powers aren't stable?" Touro asked him nervously.

"You won't need to do a thing, it'll be all me...so don't worry." Ichigo told her as she stepped off the bottom step where he was waiting for her, holding out his hand for her to take.

"Are you sure...what...what about you're family...shouldn't you be more worried about them?" Touro said looking at his hand unsure about taking it.

"You are my family." Ichigo told her as he grabbed her hand and pulled her into his arms.

They were both suddenly engulfed in flames which caused a strange tingling sensation as they were transported out of the house and onto the base outside of town, into the main hall where the officers were preparing for an attack.

Touro looked up at Ichigo slightly surprised by what had just happened. She had seen him use his powers before but somehow this felt different kind of familiar in a way that she didn't understand and knew wasn't the time to start to question him about.

"So what do we know?" Paul asked him as he rushed over.

"All the message said was that the lord may know." Ichigo told him as he let go of Touro and walked off with Paul into the crowd of officers, leaving her stood alone while everyone else rushed about around her.

"Who sent it, can you trust them?" Paul asked him.

"Completely." Ichigo answered.

Touro just stood there not knowing what she was supposed to be doing. She didn't know how she could help even though she had been training a little with them for the past couple of weeks; but perhaps this was because of her, they had found her somehow and was going to take her back to that guy, she didn't want to go back nor did she want to put all these people in danger she just didn't know what to do for the best.

Someone touched her softly on the shoulder, she turned around to see who it was but she didn't recognize him; he looked human with brown hair and eyes, he smiled kindly at her.

"You should come over here out of the way." He told her.

"Oh right...yeah...sure..." Touro said following him over to a side room away from everyone else.

He went in first and then she followed, the door snapped shut behind her which made her jump; she looked over her shoulder to see him stood by the door blocking the way.

"What're you doing?" Touro asked him.

"I was told to keep you in here until it was all over." He told her.

'Ichi...Ichigo told you to look after me, even though I don't know you?" Touro asked him somewhat unsure now if she had done the right thing, what if they actually had spies here it wasn't as though she actually knew any of them and considering what was going on would Ichigo really want her somewhere where he couldn't keep an eye on her?

"It'll all be over soon." He told her.

"You're not with them are you?" Touro said stepping away from him.

"Who do you think I'm with?" He asked her smiling slightly at her.

She knew, she knew that she had made a mistake she needed to get out of there; but how was she supposed to do that?

"Move." Touro told him, but he didn't; he just kept smiling at her. "I'll make you."

"You're a little girl, what do you really think that you could do to me?" He said smirking at her.

"They didn't tell you much about me did they?" Touro said as she stepped forward and punched him the face, kicked him in the chest and then again punched him in the face making him fall backwards into the door; and with one more kick he fell through the door making those close by stop and turn around to her direction. "He...he was working for them!"

"Was he now?" A man close by said as he stepped forward.

Touro noticed that there was something different about his uniform, there was a small badge pinned to it of a black shield with two swords crossing; she stepped away from him.

"He's with them as well!" Touro shouted pointing at the man making him stop as did everyone else turning around to find out what was going on. "Spies, we have spies...he's one of them!"

"Don't be draft...she's overreacting." The man tried to say as calmly as he could as the man next to him reached out to grab him, but he wasn't quick enough as he was shot by a hidden blaster.

The alarms sounded and he fired again at anyone who tried to get close to him, Touro didn't know what to do she didn't want to just leave them to be hurt by him but how was she supposed to defend herself against a blaster; they hadn't got that far yet in their training and if this carried on she never was going to either.

"Tour!" Ichigo shouted form somewhere in the crowd, but she couldn't see him.

Touro looked around for him and then back at the man, she had to do something; without thinking she ran over to him and grabbed him from behind making him drop his blaster, he tried to shake her off but she wasn't going to let him go until they had got him.

"Weapons fire detected, prepare for transport." A man's voice said quietly from somewhere in his uniform.

Panic struck her about what was going to happen, but she still couldn't let go of him because if she did then she'd be letting them all down; if she just gave up perhaps that would save them even though she didn't ever want to go through that again. She could feel the beam locking onto her before the light appeared around them.

"Tour...let go!" Ichigo shouted as he pushed past several officers to get to her, but it was too late as they were both engulfed in the bright light.

Her eyes began to burn with tears realizing that she was leaving them and not wanting them to be taken as well. Her whole body began to burn in this light that was taking her away from the life that she had so longed for; even the man that she had hold of seemed to disappear in her gasp as they started to reappeared. She could see the transporter room starting to appear and know that if she did appear in there even Renji when they took her back wouldn't be able to save her. She willed herself to somehow at least appear somewhere else on the ship so that she could hide, anywhere as long as they wouldn't find her; the last thing that she remembered was once again being engulfed in flames as her tears fogged her vision and then nothing as everything went black.

Touro woke up several hours later blinking slightly on a cold hard floor in a dark room. She pushed herself up rubbing the sleep and dried tears out of her eyes as she looked around; she was in some sort of cargo hold. It was as though her memory was on fast forward as it quickly replayed what happened to her and she realized that she must have somehow transported herself on board the ship with the help of their transporter, it must have worked because they hadn't found her. She just hoped that Ichigo and the others were also alright; she was just about to push herself up when the lights came on and the far doors opened and she quickly made sure that she was out of sight

"I'm glad I'm not the captain." A man said.

"Yeah I know, who in their right mind would tell Lord Malevalus that they failed." Another man said.

"She's been lost twice, a little girl..." The first man said almost amused. "But at least the Magics are dead, hey?"

"Yeah, the cap will take credit for that even though we don't actually know how it was done." The other man said stopping as he strained to pick something up. "Some sort of explosion which ripped through the colony, all burnt alive...well that's what they get for trying to hide from us right?"

"Yeah..." The first man said before the door closed behind them.

Touro just sat there, she couldn't believe it they had all been killed just like that; one moment they were there and then the next they weren't; it couldn't be. She had only just found her family and now they were gone; but it was there again, what if it was her when she was transporting aboard the ship she hadn't used her powers properly. She remembered it feeling so warm. What if she had killed them, her own family; Ichi who had tried so hard to help her, she could still see him as he tried to get to her but she wouldn't let go and stay with him? Thinking about it now, she would have rather have stayed with him, than be here all alone.

Her own tears seemed to burn her eyes as though her body was telling her that if she had killed them then she had no right to cry over it since she had been the one who had murdered them, but what else was she to do now; where was she supposed to go now?

She couldn't find Lonac and put him in danger after he had tried to help her, nor could she go to Renji who had tried to warn them of what was going to happen and she had killed his friend and more of his people; he really was going to hate her forever.

Touro leant back against the bulkhead wanting to cry but it hurt too much to do so, so she just sat there hoping that they would land so that she could get off the ship not knowing where she would go to next; where it would be safe for her to go.

She felt as though she had sat there for ages when the ship began to shudder and the engines sounded as though they were straining somewhat, the cargo containers shook but none of them fell as the ship landed heavily.

Touro pushed herself up and looked around the room, she needed to get off the ship but if she opened the doors herself then they would know that there was someone down here that wasn't supposed to be; but she knew that she didn't have any other choice if she wanted off the ship she would just have to risk it. It wasn't as though she had much left to lose considering she had lost everything that has ever meant anything to her, so why was she still trying to hard to get away?

Touro made her way across the cargo bay to the hanger doors, and quickly scanned the access panel before she entered the code in; nothing seemed to happen for a moment and then they began to open, she ran over to the opening and straight out rolling several feet to ground cutting her knees and hands not landing very gracefully, making her think that Hurrin wouldn't be impressed with her as he always said that you should land on your feet.

She pushed herself up and ran for it across the dusty field going behind the other ships so that she wouldn't be seen by anyone. There were so many ships and the dust field seemed to go on for miles but she had no other choice if she wanted to get away; she couldn't hide on any of these ship because they might be working for that Lord guy as well who was looking for her. She didn't want to be found by any of his men, nor did she want to be found by any of her own kind either.

After ten minutes of running between ships she finally saw

buildings to the right. She made her way over to them without it seeming as though she was making sure that she went the long way around in case she was being followed; if she had no idea if she was or not because she didn't stop to check as she just wanted to get as far away from that ship as she possible could. Finally she reached the edge of the field and the buildings were only a few feet away from her, she ran across the open field and down the first narrow alleyway; the buildings weren't as tall as she was used to but they were still at least four storey high. She turned down the next ally and then the one facing when she felt it, there was someone else close by but she didn't know if they had followed her or if they were already here before she was; her pace slowed down as she looked over her shoulder to see if there was anyone there when she was grabbed.

She was grabbed around the middle with one arm while the other tried to cover her mouth, pulling her back; she bit down as hard as she could on his hand and stomped on his foot pushing him back as she almost fell forward to get away from him; she was just about to start running again.

"Wait..." Ichigo said out of breath behind her.

Touro slowly turned around at the sound of his voice, it looked like him and it also sounded like him but they had said that they were all killed so that must mean that this wasn't really him, it was a trap.

"Tour...it's me...Ichi..." Ichigo said seeming to see that she wasn't sure.

"No...no...they said...they said that you were all killed..." Touro said. "Then that means that you're not him...you're not Ichi..."

"Tour it's me, I'm fine except from the bite; you bit me." Ichigo said frowning at her. "Would you prefer that I told you that you destroyed my colony just like that other, because I will; because you did."

"What?" Touro said stepping away from him.

"But I was there; I know now what happened; what you really did." Ichigo told her smiling at her. "You really are special, they'll never find us unless we want them too; you hide us from them. It's still there, but they can't see it; even the spy's that they had gotten into the colony are locked away except for the one that you had hold of."

"But...I don't understand." Touro said confused at what he was talking about.

"You never wanted to hurt us, yet you didn't know what to do for the best as your power overwhelmed you." Ichigo explained. "What you wanted most of all in your heart matters most of all. You wanted to help your people not hurt them; considering what was happening to you at the time this was the only thing that your body could do. It may seem completely over the top, but in truth it's actually a lot of help."

"I...I still don't understand." Touro said.

"Touro these people they believe that they are dead, but they're not; they won't be bothered by the Malarias Fleet." Ichigo told her.

"So, they're not really dead but in a kind of hiding?" Touro asked him slowly as she tried to make sense of what he was telling her. "So...well I mean...um...what if I did it purposely, would it still have the same effect?"

"Yes, it should do...why?" Ichigo asked her unsure why she wanted to know, but she didn't answer him only turned around back the way she had come from. "Where are you going?"

"I said to Renji once that why couldn't he do more to help, why couldn't he help more people..." Touro told him without stopping. "At the time, I didn't realize how offensive I was being because he was helping as much people as he could do. So it's me now, if I can help no matter how small after what you lot have done for me, how could I turn my back."

Ichigo stopped her. "What? What the hell are you planning to do?"

"I'm not completely sure yet, but I know if I go back that I'll be able to help you more." Touro told him finally changing back into her proper form, her short purple hair growing out reddish brown down her back and her eyes turning brown once more. "I'll contact you when I've figured out what I'm going to do. You know that it's best not to tell anyone that you're alive...even Renji...he especially can't know."

Ichigo let her go, he knew it was for the greater good even though it was the last thing that he wanted to do; but at the same time he didn't want to stop her as though he knew in a way that she needed to do this to find herself.

"We'll stay hidden until we're needed." Ichigo told her. "You can contact me on the elemental encoded channels. Be safe."

Toria now back to her normal form, no longer Touro for the moment didn't look back nor say anything to him as she headed back to the ship that she had only just run away from; it was time for her to go back and to finally begin the life that was meant for her, but doing it her way.

Chapter Eleven

The wind rushed past her face blowing her long hair back as she walked calmly over to the guards stood at the bottom of the ramp to the cargo hold. They both looked over at her when they realized she was walking towards them and then looked at each when they actually realized who she was; they held their position as though they weren't sure if she was real for some reason or some sort of trap, until she finally stopped in front of them.

"You're here to take be back?" Toria asked them.

"Um...yeah..." The guard on the right answered.

"I'm ready to go back now." Toria told them as she stepped forward and took her first step up the ramp; she wanted to look back knowing that he was still back there watching making sure that she was safe for as long as he could and also that she was doing the right thing.

At the moment she didn't really know herself if she was doing the right thing, because she hadn't completely figured out what she was going to do when she got back. All she did know was that this was her chance to do something for her people finally.

"Holleb to the bridge, we have her." The guard on the left said through his intercom.

"Repeat last message?" A man replied.

"We have her sir, she just walked over to us and said that she was ready to come back; and then walked on board." Holleb told him.

"Are you sure that it was her?" The man asked.

They both looked up the ramp just in time to see her disappear around the corner but she still looked just the same.

"Yes sir, it's her." Holleb answered.

"Right then...take her to her quarters, we'll be leaving for the senate." The man told them.

"Yes sir." Holleb answered.

He looked over at the other man before they too went back up the ramp, where the low buzzing noise began to get a little louder as they walked through the hanger doors; once they were past the threshold it started to grow quiet again and the ramp raised back as the doors began to close. They walked across the room through the cargo containers to where Toria was waiting for them; she just stood at the door waiting.

"We'll take you to your quarters for your journey back to the senate." Holleb told her.

"Thank you." Toria said.

Holleb went first and the doors opened onto the corridor, Toria was glad to see that it was properly lit unlike the last ship that she was on; she followed him up the corridor towards the lift with the other guard closely behind her. They didn't have to wait for the doors just opened for them as they approached. They all went inside with Toria at the back of them both and the doors closed.

"Deck three." Holleb ordered.

The lift began to move upwards but it didn't take long until they stopped once more and the doors opened up onto another deck, Holleb stepped out first so they followed him along the corridor to the fourth door which they stopped at once more; he pressed the button on the door panel and the door slide open to her quarters.

"We're here." Holleb told her.

Toria stepped forward but before she had stepped over the threshold he stopped her.

"You'll understand, but considering what happened you'll have to remain in your quarters until we get back." Holleb told her.

"Of course." Toria said as she walked into her new quarters and the door closed and locked behind her.

Toria just stopped, not to look around but to take in what she had just done and to tell herself that it was the right thing to do. She had to keep telling herself, that it was the right thing; that she couldn't keep running away, because everyone gets a chance to do something and this was her chance and she really did believe that she could do more good for them if she returned now. She just hadn't worked out all the details yet.

Toria looked around her quarters, they seemed alright considering the situation; living area with a view port that at the moment looked out over the dust field and other ships and to her right was the bedroom and bathroom, they were actually quite big compared to the other quarters of the ships that she had travelled on while she was with Lonac. She wonder what he would think of her for doing this, probably not being brave but being stupid, foolish even for going back alone without fully coming up with a plan of what she was going to do with this new found power of hers.

Lord Malevalus sat at the head of the table in his conference room, two guards at both doors dressed in black robes carrying blaster rifles and three more along the view port that was the full length of the room; he wasn't alone though at the table for Hul'Ercan had arrived but he didn't seem as relaxed as the last time that he had been called here over a month ago.

They both sat there in silence as they waited for another five minutes until finally the doors slid open, Zar-Jins and Karwin walked in together and over to the table to take their seats next to Hul'Ercan who was watching them to see if they knew why they had been called back but they weren't giving anything away.

"I'm glad to see the three of you." Lord Malevalus said from beneath his black cloak. "I've come for an update on the small assignment that I asked of you."

"Small?" Hul'Ercan said bravely. "It's a big galaxy, how do you expect us to find one little girl?"

"I've had several reports informing me that she is alive that she has been located and apprehended." Lord Malevalus told them. "That report later changed when she was rescued by Magics, I didn't want her making contact with them as they could bend her to their will against me; but it seems as though my hopes of having her all to myself were dashed because of you; Zar-Jins."

Hul'Ercan looked over at him whereas Karwin stayed facing his Lord having no reaction, to his statement.

"Sir, I apolo..." Zar-Jins began but was cut off.

"You failed because of your desires, I trusted you to complete this task because you knew her best; yet you let her slip through your fingers." Lord Malevalus said.

"Sir, if given another chance I'll..." Zar-Jins tried again.

"As I was saying, I've had several reports." Lord Malevalus continued as though he hadn't had his conversation with Zar-Jins. "She has been sighted, we were in the process of apprehending her once more when she had another accident; at the Magical colony that rescued her, it was destroyed. As of five hours ago she returned to our custody once more willingly and is returning to me."

"She's willingly coming back?" Zar-Jins asked him unsure if he believed what was being told to him, since the time that he had spent with her he hadn't thought that she would come back without a fight.

"Yes." Lord Malevalus answered and then once again returned his attention to Zar-Jins alone. "I have one more assignment for you and if you can't complete this one then I'm afraid that you will no longer be in my service."

"I understand sir." Zar-Jins said.

"I want you to visit her once she has returned, and ask her to join me." Lord Malevalus told him. "I do not want you drawing attention to yourself or to her by doing this. No one should know that you have approached her; but I'm expecting a positive result considering that you held her for some time before she was rescued, I'm sure that she won't want to relive whatever it was that you did to her."

Zar-Jins didn't say anything knowing that it wasn't appropriate to do so, only to follow his orders knowing that he had been given a second chance whereas if it would have been anyone else they would have been dead before they had even walked through the doors.

"She'll arrive back at the senate before the end of the day." Lord Malevalus told him. "I want you to give her a couple of days to make her believe that it's all blown over and then I want you to approach her, just make sure that her guards aren't around to see you especially Aba'rian; but I don't want any of them harmed."

"Yes sir." Zar-Jins answered.

"And what shall we do sir?" Hul'Ercan asked him.

"I want you to go to the colony just to confirm that it was her that destroyed it. We can use that to our advantage to make her join us." Lord Malevalus told him.

Toria sat patiently in her quarters for the captain to come down to her. She had asked to see him over an hour ago and he still hadn't come down to her; she didn't want to push the matter too much as she didn't know who the crew was really working for only that she needed to do this before they got to the senate.

She had made up her mind, to what she was going to do, all she needed to do now was to put her plan into action and contact Ichigo knowing that he wouldn't want her to put herself into such a dangerous situation; but she believed that it was the best course of action for her to take considering the situation.

Then finally she was beeped telling her that he was here, she took a deep breath and then stood up; it was her first opportunity and she didn't want to fail.

"Come in." Toria said.

The door slid open and stood in the doorway was the captain dressed in the uniform of a Malarias Fleet officer. He looked about the same age as her father though with more grey hair; he stepped inside and the door closed behind him.

"You wanted to see me?" He asked briskly as though he didn't have time for her.

"Yes, thank you." Toria said politely. "I have given this a great deal of thought sir. I don't want to be dropped off at the senate."

"Then why did you come with us?" The captain demanded.

"But instead I'd like to be dropped off at Rinsac IV." Toria told him.

He just looked at her as if he was trying to read her mind, but she didn't give into him and stood her ground; this is what she wanted to do.

"I know you must think my decision sudden, but it isn't; in fact I have been thinking of this for some time." Toria told him. "After what happened to me with the Magics, I finally understand why we're at war with them. They tried to turn me against everything that I believe in and everyone that I care about. I can't let them get away with that and to be able to do it to others."

"This isn't what you're father wanted." The captain told her.

"Actually in a way it is, he always wanted me to truly see what they were; and I have." Toria told him. "Now I want to help him, and this is how I believe I can."

The captain smiled at her, though it was cockaded. "Very well."

He turned around and left without another word. Once the door had closed and locked behind him she just fell back into the sofa; she couldn't believe that she had just done that. Now all she had to do was convince her father and everyone else she was going to meet, she had no idea how she was going to have the strength to do this; but even though her path ahead wasn't completely clear to her she felt somewhat at peace with the thought that she was finding her place finally, as it had always been clouded and unknown to her, as to what she would do with her life once she had left school. She knew if it was up to her father she would stay close by and probably marry someone of high status to help them in the war against the Magics, but that was never what she wanted to do; she always felt as though she wanted to do something important it had just eluded her until now.

Toria smiled slightly to herself as she sat back and waited for them to arrive and for her new life to begin. She was glad for her father's attendance to her training as she believed that it had prepared her a little to withstand the endurance that she would need now.

She didn't have long to wait until they arrived in the outer system of the Dragon Senate's home. She leant on the back of the sofa as they approached the moons of Rinsac; you could actually see the academy training bases in high orbit as they were the only buildings on the moon.

Toria stood up and walked over to the door which opened. Holleb still stood outside with the other man waiting for her; she went out and once again followed them up the corridor though this time not towards the lift but to a different room on that deck. They didn't walk far until Holleb turned into another room; she followed him into the small transporter room and onto the pad while he went behind the console.

"They've been informed of your arrival." Holleb told her. "But you know you can't just say that you want to join and they'll let you in; you have to pass the test, which you'll sit when you arrive."

Toria knew that there would be a test but she didn't think that they would make her take it as soon as she arrived. She hadn't studied for anything like that actually, nor had she done any of her school work since she left the senate two months ago; thinking about it now she had missed the final exams because of what happened and she wasn't actually sixteen just yet, so she was actually under age which wouldn't go in her favour either, so she had to make sure that she gave a good impression for them to want to take her on as an officer.

Holleb didn't wait for a reply from her before he activated the transporter. She was taken from the ship and transported down to the moon's surface and into the lobby of the new recruit base where there were three training officers waiting for her.

"You must be Victoria Kentaro." The man in the centre said looking over a data sheet in his hand. He was the shortest of the three but the most muscled wearing his jumpsuit open showing the sweat down the front of his vest, as though he had just come straight from training.

"I was surprised by your request. You didn't really seem the type of person who would want to join the last time that I saw you." The man on the right said looking down his nose at her, as though she was beneath him; he was the tallest of the three and had his brown hair brushed back off of his face. "I thought that you seemed more suited to life in the senate court, wearing pretty dresses."

"You're age maybe a problem." The third man said casually as though he was the only one who hadn't already formed an opinion about her.

"Yes I am aware that I'm a few months early, and that I was raised to be a lady in the senate court; I know all of this." Toria told them calmly. "But even though I was supposed to be safe there in the heart of our empire, I wasn't; I fell victim to the Magics because I wasn't prepared. They tried to take advantage of me as they've done to many others in the past. I finally understand why you do what you do; I was hidden from the galaxy and those in it but no longer. I want to be able to protect all those that I care about so that they don't have to live in fear any more."

"Brave and noble words, but that's all they are; words." The first man said finally dropping the data sheet to his side so that she could properly see his face.

She was sure that she had seen him before perhaps at a function like the other officer.

"I know that they are only words now sir, but that's why I want this chance to prove that they're not." Toria told him.

"We'll see." The middle man said. "You will sit the entrance exam with Commander Prem and then you'll come with me for the physical part of the exam."

"Depending on how well you do in these exams, we may well overlook your age." The third man told her. "Commander Zo'hora will be waiting for you outside of the changing rooms after you have finished the written exam. You're clothes aren't really appropriate. You'll need to change."

"Yes sir." Toria said trying not to take her eyes off of them, even though their staring was getting to her; but if she couldn't stand this then she wouldn't be able to get through whatever came next. She had to keep reminding herself to be strong.

"Then come with me." Commander Prem told her walking off to his right.

Toria quickly followed after him leaving the other two officers just standing there. She wondered now that she was here if it really was the best plan that she could have come up with at such short notice; well she was about to find out.

Prem pushed open the large set of doors that were placed in the wall so that they wouldn't be seen unless you knew that they were there. Toria wondered why she hadn't seen them like she could see the gate in the fence back at the Magical base; then she wondered, what if there was something wrong with her powers, how was she supposed to carry on now with the plan then without them as it all rested on her having those special powers?

They had entered a large hall with small tables set in rows the whole length of the hall. She assumed that this was where she would take her written exam; it was kind of overwhelming the only person before the commander going to be in this huge empty hall.

She followed him to the front where he stopped with his back to her and pointed to the desk to his right. She quickly pulled out the chair and sat down the clattering of the legs echoing off the walls making the hall seem even bigger than it actually was; he walked over to the desk that was facing all of the smaller ones and picked up the only data sheet that was on it and brought it over to her with an electric pen.

"You have two hours." Prem told her placing the data sheet on her table before he walked back over to his own desk; Toria watched him pull out his own chair and sat down before she looked down at the data sheet.

Name:
Age:
Race:
Gender:

1) What are the Malarias Fleets' main objectives?
2) What is the difference between a curse ship and a system patrol ship?

The questions went on and on, some of them Toria didn't even see the point of as they weren't really questions to test your knowledge but your opinion on the war with the Magics. She answered them to the best that she could, hoping that she had lied enough to get through without seeming as though she was trying too hard; the general knowledge questions crossed a wide range of subjects to probably figure out where to best place the officer, if they don't know themselves where they wanted to be.

Toria hadn't really thought completely where she wanted to be placed, perhaps security where she would be on the front lines the most; but the only problem with that was that she might not be able to work up through the ranks the same, she'd just have to see how it went on here for a while and figure out the rest as she went along.

The two hours seemed to just fly by, making her worry if she was actually going to finish in time; she was just trying to finish writing her answer for the second to last question when Prem stood up and walked over to her and grabbed the data sheet out from under her.

"Your time's up." Prem told her. "I knew you wouldn't finish it."

Toria looked up at him restraining herself from saying anything. He just smiled at her as he started to walk down the row that they had come from earlier; Toria pushed her chair back getting up knowing that she was supposed to follow him because now she had the physical part of the exam, not really in the mood as she was actually quite tired which as she thought about it following him she couldn't really remember the last time that she had really felt tired, yeah she got tired when training but it felt different not as much as this.

She shook herself as Prem opened the doors back out the lobby which was empty of all personnel. She could see the doors at the far end with glass panels in them and saw that it was dark out and wondered just what time it was; she had been travelling all day and then before that when staying with Ichigo, she had been training for a few hours before all of this actually started, she wasn't even sure if it was even the same day, it couldn't be since it had been so long.

"You go down this corridor and take your first left and then right, it's the first door on right; did you get that?" Prem asked her.

"Left then right, first door on right?" Toria repeated hoping that it was right thinking that he wouldn't tell her even if it wasn't, though she might have remembered now but when she started walking down there it was another matter.

"I'll mark your exam." Prem told her. "You'd better hurry; Commander Zo'hora doesn't like to be kept waiting."

Prem walked off with her data sheet across the lobby leaving her alone, to find her own way in a place that she had never been in before with only a couple of directions that she didn't even know were right.

Toria started to walk down the corridor that met up with the lobby looking around noticing that there were actually quite a few corridors going off to the right but none so far to the left, but then she remembered that would be because of the exam hall; she carried on walking thinking that she should have come across it by now, when finally she saw it and quickened her pace.

164

Toria thought that this corridor was strange as there were no doors on either side and again she had to walk a couple of minutes before she came to her first turning, she went down the corridor which was only dimly lit compared to the other hoping that she had gone the right way when she saw Commander Zo'hora stood outside a door waiting for her; panic filled her thinking that she was late as she approached him.

"Get changed quickly." Zo'hora told her, he had taken the top part of his jumpsuit off and had tied it around his waist revealing his hair-covered arms.

Toria went inside the brightly lit changing room which was lined with lockers and benches. On the front bench was a dark navy jumpsuit for her with a white stripe down the arms and under them down the body line and legs; she undressed leaving her dress on the bench and putting the jumpsuit on and then the boots. She stood up and looked down at herself; this was who she was now even if she didn't like what she was wearing.

Toria opened the door and went back out to where Zo'hora was waiting for her. He didn't say anything to her as he started to walk off, which again she followed knowing that he expected her to do so without a word from him; she followed him down the middle of the corridor wondering what he was going to do.

They didn't go far, only to the next doors which when he opened them the lights came on inside illuminating the full length of the gym. It was even longer than the hall she had just been in; there were climbing frames on the left floor to ceiling high and ropes hanging from the ceiling. Red circles were painted on the floor for sparring, and mounted up on the wall were training swords of all different sizes.

"Right then, how about we start with the basics." Zo'hora told her. "Have you ever climbed a rope before?"

"No." Toria answered honestly, not thinking there was any point as he would want her to prove that she could do whatever it was she said that she could do.

"How disappointing." Zo'hora said. "But it's not unusual, there...now's your chance."

Toria looked at him and then at the rope. He was actually being serious so she went over to the rope and grabbed hold of it no idea if she could actually do this or not; she looked up at the rope and then jumped making sure that she had a good grip of the rope but she couldn't get a hold of them with her feet and just kicked about as she tried to pull herself up but in struggling so much she lost her grip and fell to the floor on her bum.

She got up and tried again, she wasn't going to let it beat her; but she still couldn't get hold of the rope properly with her legs and feet and her arms felt too heavy to lift her completely on her own, she fell a couple more times before he finally stopped her.

"That's enough for now, girl." Zo'haro said sounding somewhat annoyed. "The frame, can you at least manage that? If you can't at least show that you have any strength at this point then you're saying that you have nothing to work with."

"We never really did climbing, it was more fighting." Toria told him as she went over to the frame and reached for a hand hold, she had just started to climb when he grabbed her from behind and pulled her down onto the ground; she landed with a thud and a slight groan.

"Fighting?" Zo'haro said smirking at her. "Well that'll do, lets see what you've got; girl."

Toria pushed her body up and kicked him in the chest and with the momentum pushed herself up onto her feet as he stumbled backwards taken by surprise. It seemed as though he hadn't expected her to make the first move. She made to kick him again but as he put up his arm to stop her she bent down and took out his legs and kicked him in the face; he rolled over trying to stop himself as Toria calmly waited for him but he was taking too long.

She made to go for him again but he reached out thinking that she was going to kick him but she jumped over him and grabbed the rope behind him, swung around kicking off the frame to give her more speed as he got to his feet, she turned around as she kicked him as hard as she could in the face, then she let go, turning around in the air and landed gracefully in front of the fallen commander.

"There's a room ready..." Zo'haro said heavily from the floor as the blood poured out of his nose and mouth.

"Thanks." Toria said walking away just leaving him on the floor. "I'd call for a doctor but I haven't got an intercom, yet."

Toria walked out of the gym with the doors closing behind her, she looked up and down the corridor no idea where the dorms might actually be but wondering if there was even any point seeing that everyone would be up fairly soon anyway; she leant against the wall and smiled to herself, as she had actually gotten in.

Toria had wandered back to the lobby thinking that there might have been a base map, which luckily for her there was; she found out where Captain Nandor's office was so that she could get her room assignment and timetable. By the time she had finished everyone was up and coming down to the food hall for their breakfast before lessons started.

She was to be in the first year classes until the new semester started and then, of course, she couldn't move up with them but she would have to start the first year properly, but Toria didn't like the idea of that if she could somehow actually catch up with them then perhaps they would consider moving her up to the second year as well; but to do that she'd have an awful lot of work to do.

She walked into the loud and busy food hall which was full of students from sixteen to twenty years old. They were all sat in their own groups of friends and she was sure she didn't even know one person; she was pushed to one side by a couple of older students carrying trays of food.

"Do you mind?" The girl said walking off with the lead lad with black hair tied back.

Toria looked around for an empty table and also where they had gotten their food from. She saw a queue at the one on her left and thought that there must be a computer port for the food there; she started to walk over but walked straight into someone else.

"Watch where you're going." A lad said pushing her back out of his way.

Toria wasn't really in the mood to start making friends after the last couple of days that she had had.

"Maybe it's you who needs to look where they're going, because I wasn't the only one walking." Toria said looking up at him, there was no going back. Now this was who she had to become; she had to become strong, strong enough that everyone knew.

He smiled at her and Toria couldn't help but think that he did in fact look quite handsome with blonde hair and blue eyes, so it wasn't really a surprise to see that he was surrounded by friends that would probably strike up for him if things kicked off but she was a girl after all and even they wouldn't all try it on with her even if she did take him out.

"You must be new here, just transferred?" He asked her pleasantly enough.

"Yeah that's right, my first day." Toria said, it wasn't a lie. "Do you know if Commander Zo'hora is alright, I left him in the gym bleeding and unconscious after the test was over?"

They all started to laugh at her. Toria smiled at them and before they knew what had she done, she had moved so fast punched the lad twice in the face and then kicked him in the chest knocking him into his friends who stumbled backwards into the table behind them; they all just looked up at her in disbelief, as though they couldn't actually believe that she had just done that to them.

"I don't like it when people laugh at me." Toria told them. "You laughed at me, that isn't very nice."

The guys tried to struggle to their feet, the one on the left pushed his friends off of him and got to his feet first; he was about a foot taller than her and had a shaved head his cold blue eyes zoned in on her but she just smiled at him.

"What, it's your turn now?" Toria said.

"I don't care if you are a girl; you're going to get what's coming to you." He told her, as everyone was struggling to see what was going on; it seems as though it had been a while since something like this had happened and a fight always got everyone's attention.

He made to kick her with a round house kick but she dodged bending backwards out of his reach, as she came back up he had picked up a chair and swung it at her; she held up her arm to block it stinging slightly but after all she was used to a lot worst, with her other arm she grabbed the chair out of his gasp and broke it over her knee. She kept hold of the metal bars that held the legs together and used them as extra protection as he kept trying to hit her. He looked past her for a moment but that was his mistake as she took his legs and kicked him in the head; he didn't get back up.

"Kyo...get her!" The first lad shouted.

Toria smiled to herself as she turned around to face him, for she knew who he had shouted suddenly remembering that he had also joined the Fleet academy; he though was surprised to see her and especially after what she had just done because that wasn't his Toria.

"Toria?" Kyo said questioningly.

167

She smiled at him. "So you're going to do what he says, that's not like you."

"I was just going to say the same thing." Kyo said staring at her. "What's gotten into you?"

Toria had to be convincing especially to those who knew her before. She had to make them believe that she's really changed; the only problem with Kyo though was that he was just as good as she was at kick boxing. She stepped forward slowly to begin with and then her pace quickened to a run and she came at him with everything that she had. He managed to block and dodge several of her blows but not all of them and he didn't really want to hit her back; but she had to make him think that she was a real threat to him. She turned around grabbing his arm pulling it up behind him and into her.

"You shouldn't have held back." Toria whispered.

She brought her leg up slightly and then into the back of his, she heard it snap and he shouted out in pain as he doubled over but she wouldn't let him go; with her other hand she grabbed his hair and slammed his face into the table and then let go of him to slump to the floor. All anyone could do was look on. She had just taken them all out even without breaking out into a sweat.

"It's not too much to ask for a few manners now is it, a gentleman is supposed to apologize to the lady even if he isn't at fault." Toria said as she walked back over to the blonde lad. "I'm sure you'll remember that for next time won't you."

"She took Kyo out."

"I think he knew her."

"Who was she?"

"She took all three of them out."

Toria walked out of the hall amongst whispering of what just happened, she held her head high since someone who just did that wouldn't be bothered by a few whispers; they made a clear path for her as though they didn't want to try their luck with her after what had just happened, she finally reached the door and was out in the quiet of the corridor.

It might have been somewhat of a good way to get noticed and to break her ties with Kyo but, on her first day she just hoped that they wouldn't kick her out. Toria unzipped the breast pocket and pulled out her timetable to see what lesson she had first. She wasn't bothered if they all hated her because she wasn't here to make friends. They were after all the enemy; she just hoped that she would be able to make it up to Kyo who had always been a good friend to her, and of course she hoped that she hadn't hurt him to much.

Toria went to her first lesson and walked into the classroom as though nothing at all had happened, the students who were already in the room looked around as she entered and then quickly turned away and started to whisper; she knew what they must be talking about as she walked up to the front of the class and took the seat in front of the teachers desk, she didn't really want to watch them all whispering about her all lesson and it kind of showed that she wasn't scared of what the teacher was going to say to her either by sitting right in front of them.

168

She pulled out the chair and sat down to wait for the lesson to start, no one took the empty seat next to her and to everyone's surprise including Toria's nothing was actually mentioned about the little fight over breakfast when the teacher finally arrived.

Lessons weren't really that exciting considering that they were supposed to be coming to the end of the semester and starting to prepare for their exams, they should be going over everything from the whole year, which she was going to start doing as soon as she found her quarters after she had eaten something; and the only place to do that was the food hall.

She had been the talk of the academy all day, even though she didn't go for lunch but it didn't really say much if she didn't go back; she followed her classmates inside who were trying to keep a bit of a distance between them and her as they all went inside.

They broke away and headed off for a table so that everyone could see her, silence fell over the whole hall as they stared at her; she turned and headed over to the computer port to finally get something to eat. There were a couple of girls stood around the port as she came up behind them, she was just about to go around them and join the back of the queue when they all moved out of her way realizing who she was; that was easy Toria thought picking up a tray from the small table in between the two ports.

"Warm chicken salad, no tomatoes." Toria ordered, a moment later on the ledge through sparkling light a plate of salad appeared with pieces of chicken on it; she picked up her plate and went to find a table.

"Did you hear...about Kyo?"

"What about him?"

"He left a couple of hours ago."

"Don't be daft."

Toria stopped at the side of their table and they fell silent again. She wanted to know if it was true but it didn't really sound like him to just up and leave even after what she had done; she had actually thought that he would have come looking for her as soon as he had left the med bay, she was sure that he wouldn't just run away, that didn't sound like him one bit.

Renji flicked through the computer monitors hoping to pick her up on one of them, but he still hadn't spotted her and she should have been back yesterday and no word yet; he was sure that the Senator would bring her back here.

Bernal and Lesharo had just returned from a session at the senate walking into the office hoping for some good news, as the atmosphere seemed to be going from bad to worst; even Lesharo wanted her to come back at least it would get Renji out of this depression that he seemed to be in.

"Anything yet?" Bernal asked as he pulled out his chair to sit down.

Renji was just about to answer him when he stopped flicking at someone that he recognised in the hanger below, he was sure that was one of Toria's friends even though he was wearing a Fleet cadet uniform.

Renji pushed his chair back and headed out there, Lesharo and Bernel both looked at each other before they followed him, both thinking that she must have finally returned; they went down to the end of the corridor and then turned heading for the lift.

Renji went inside and tried to shut the door before they could get in but Lesharo slammed the door shut so that they could both get inside glaring at Renji, he ignored them as though they weren't there and typed in a sequence of numbers into the lift panel before it started to move; it took a little longer than normal before it stopped and opened but it opened up into the hanger.

"I didn't know it could do that." Bernal said surprised.

"It must be a new thing." Lesharo said as they followed Renji out.

"It's in case of emergencies." Renji told him looking around for him; he heard a scuffling sound behind the parked hover cars and headed towards it.

Kyo was leant up against the red and black hover car with his lower leg in an electro cast, he looked up at Renji his worry written all over his face.

"I need to know what's happened to her." Kyo demanded breathing heavily.

"Her? Her who?" Lesharo asked him.

"Toria? You've seen her?" Renji asked him.

"Well it looks as though I've seen her, doesn't it; seeing that she did this to me." Kyo told him. "How could you let her...?"

"Where is she? She was supposed to be coming back here." Renji demanded.

"Rinsac IV." Kyo answered.

"The little lady did that to you and joined the Fleet?" Lesharo said quite amused by all of this.

Renji stared at Kyo waiting for him to deny this but the look on his face told him that it was true, he didn't understand everything seemed fine; something must have happened.

"I'll sort this, I want you to go back until I can get out there myself and get her." Renji told him. "Make sure she doesn't do anything too foolish."

"Renji, it...it didn't seem like her for some reason; the way that she smiled at me she enjoyed it." Kyo told him reluctantly.

"NO!" Renji said hotly. "She'll be fine, go back and watch her; I'll sort everything."

Renji walked off before Kyo could say anything else about her. He didn't want to hear it because he couldn't believe ever that they could have gotten to her. She was too strong too stubborn for that; they went back up to the apartment leaving Kyo to make his own way back. Renji marched down the hall closely followed by Lesharo and then Bernal who was quite clueless still about what had really been going on.

Senator Kentaro looked up from his work when they entered the living room, Lesharo and Bernal stood by the door while Renji went in and stopped in front of the senator.

"Sir, it appears that she has been dropped off at Rinsac IV; I'd like your permission to go and bring her home...sir." Renji asked him.

"Rinsac IV?" Senator Kentaro said thoughtfully and then slowly. "That is an academy base is it not?"

"Yes sir, that's why I want your permission to go and get her." Renji told him. "It appears that she has somehow joined, even though she is under age."

"She probably beat up the instructors; she's capable after all her training here." Lesharo said off-handedly.

"Don't speak unless you have something constructive to say." Renji told him.

Lesharo stood there stiffly fuming that he'd dare speak to him like that and especially in front of Bernal and the Senator, and to make it worse the senator didn't even seemed bother at how he spoke to him.

"You can go." Senator Kentaro told him. "I want her brought straight home. The army is no place for her, is that understood; make sure that she is clear about this. She doesn't have a choice in the matter this time. She's coming home; bring her to me Aba'rian and our agreement will be fulfilled."

"Yes sir." Renji said and then turned around on his heel and marched out of there without another word said, this time he wasn't followed as he went straight for the door to leave.

The classroom once again was only half full as Toria arrived and headed for the front table. They were still talking about her in whispers as this must have been the most exciting thing to happen for a while; she sat down as the door opened and the class fell silent but she didn't bother to turn around to see who it was thinking that it was only the teacher who was here early. The empty chair beside of her was pulled out and Kyo sat down beside of her leaving his broken leg out in the isle, Toria looked over at him and tried to hide her surprise to see him and especially next to her considering what she had done to him.

"He's coming for you." Kyo told her.

Toria didn't need to ask him who he meant because she knew, though she had hoped that she would have a little longer before he came; but she thought that it was best to be done sooner rather than later, the only problem was that she still didn't know what to do to prove to him that she had really turned and she was running out of time.

Chapter Twelve

It was the end of the lesson not that she had paid much attention to what had been said during it, she had more important things on her mind as she leant into Kyo to give her response.

"Tell him that I don't want anything to do with him, that it's his fault that this has all happened to me." Toria told him. "Ichigo who was supposed to save me, I killed him and his family; he can send who ever he wants to check it out for himself if he doesn't want to take my word for it."

Toria stood up to leave but Kyo grabbed her forearm to stop her.

"Neither of us believe that you can change so suddenly, nor do we believe that you'd actually kill anyone." Kyo told her.

"Then why don't you pass on my message, and if he can prove that I didn't do it; but if not then what does that actually mean?" Toria said smiling as she pulled her arm free and walked off but before she left she turned back around. "I don't want anything to do with him or his kind, they destroyed my life so I'm going to repay them in kind."

Toria walked out with the rest of the class wondering what was going on, she just hoped that it was enough that he'd want to know what was going on with Ichigo since they hadn't actually found any proof until she did it the second time and that was only because of Ichigo himself; she was sure that he would keep up his end of the deal and keep her secret even from Renji as they both knew that he wouldn't let her go through with this if he knew the whole truth.

Kyo wasn't sure about what she had just told him, he couldn't believe that she would ever kill anyone and he knew that Renji would never believe it either but he'd still pass on her message; he got up slowly because his leg still hurt, he still found it hard to believe that she'd actually hurt him because the Toria that he knew wouldn't do that to anyone.

He ignored the rest of class who all wanted to know what had happened, why he had sat with her after what she had done to him and he just acted as though nothing at all had happened between them just like the teachers had done; Kyo looked up and down the corridor but he couldn't see her so he went off to the lobby knowing that it wouldn't be long until Renji arrived, it was hard to believe that she'd just turn her back on him as well. It dawned on him suddenly, she knew what he was, what both of them were but she hadn't actually turned them in even though she was supposed to be giving up on all that what was Magic; he knew there was something else going on but until he knew the full length of the situation he'd just go along with her for now and for now she wanted or needed to get ride of Renji.

Kyo didn't have to wait long in the lobby before Renji arrived, he was stood up against the wall so not to put so much weight on his leg while it was healing; Renji marched over to him with such determination that Kyo had no idea how he was expected to convince him to leave without her.

"Where is she?" Renji demanded.

"She said that she didn't want anything else to do with you, that you've caused her nothing but trouble since you entered her life." Kyo told him and saw just from those words that Renji's face softened somewhat. "She said it's all your fault that she ended up like this."

"Did she now?" Renji said trying to stay calm.

"She said that she'll repay your kind back for what they did to her." Kyo told him. "Icihgo who was supposed to be saving her, or so you both said; she killed him..."

"What?" Renji said. "She wouldn't."

"That's what she said." Kyo told him. "And also, if you carry on trying to force her to come back; she'll tell them just what you really are."

"I don't believe you.' Renji said.

"And you think that I'd want to believe that she'd betray us to them, look at what she did to me." Kyo said. "Would she do this if she was only pretending? Of course not, she cares too much about those around her to really want to hurt them; they got her. You...you were supposed to be protecting her, you lost her to them."

"No, no I didn't...I can't..." Renji said distractedly. "And Ichigo, she wouldn't...he's her...she just wouldn't..."

"Then why don't you go and prove her wrong, because I want to believe as well that she hasn't been turned; but from where I'm stood, they've got her good." Kyo told him.

All the anger in Renji seemed to just empty out of him as though he had lost the only thing that was keeping him going, Kyo wondered if he had done the right thing by lying to him now; but he had to believe in him that he'd make all this right whatever she was doing that he'd figure it out and help her with it as he himself would as much as he could without drawing too much attention to himself as well if she supposedly was going against all Magics.

Renji just looked at him, it had been such a long time since he had felt like this; the last time that he had lost the woman that he loved, he felt as though he wouldn't be able to go on without her by his side but he had to. He told himself that he had to carry on, he'd go and see Ichigo and find out just what had happened while she was staying with him for her to change so suddenly. Something must have happened; Renji turned and left without saying another word to Kyo because to be honest he didn't have anything to say to him.

Kyo just watched him walking away really hoping that he had done the right thing.

Kyo went to find Toria to tell her what had happened, but he didn't ask the computer where she was since he had been told that she was spending an awful lot of time in the library; he stopped by his own quarters on the way as he had something to give her, he walked into the library which was pretty empty of students considering the time of year and that exams were only a month away. There were a dozen isles with only half of them filled with books, four of the isles had data sheets and data pads with ports so that you could make copies; on the last two isles were computer consoles all along the walls with small out ports so that whatever you found would be printed out for you.

Kyo headed up the first isle and then along the top to the table where there were a handful of students studying and in the corner Toria was sat with her back to the room and her desk covered in data sheets and data pads. He walked over to her and pulled out the chair next to her since he was here he might as well rest his leg it was still quite sore and he was pushing himself getting around so much.

Toria looked over at him annoyed that he had sat down next to her, she'd definitely wouldn't want to sit next to someone who had just broken her leg on purpose even if they were a friend; but it seemed as though it didn't bother him.

"He left for now, he really looked upset after I finished talking with him." Kyo told him.

"But it seems that I didn't upset you enough, strange I would have thought it would have been the other way around." Toria said and then smiled suddenly. "Perhaps if I break your other leg as well?"

"If you really feel as though you need to." Kyo said placing the data pads on the table that he had been carrying with him, from his quarters. "They're copies of my notes for the whole year, I thought that you might need them I mean if you want to get through this as quickly as you can."

Toria just stared at him unsure why he was doing this.

"I don't know who Ichigo is, but he didn't seem to believe that you'd killed him...and to be honest I don't really believe that you would kill anyone either." Kyo told her. "But Renji still left, I guess to find this guy you said that you killed to get some answers. I also told him that if he carried trying to get you to come back you'd tell them what he is, which means that you would end up betraying a lot of people; I guess for now he doesn't want to push his luck."

"What you want a thank you for passing on a message, a child could do it." Toria said as she picked up the top data pad he had given her.

"I'd help out with getting you up to stretch with the physical training." Kyo added ignoring her last comment. "But it seems as though an angry little girl put me out of commission for a while because she doesn't know how to ask for help when she's in way over her head."

"What? I know enough." Toria said hotly.

Kyo smiled and relaxed a little. "He would have seen right through you wouldn't he? I'm glad I was right, I was getting a little worried there though."

"I don't know what you're talking about." Toria said gathering up all her data sheets and pads, she didn't think that it was a good idea if she stayed and carried on talking to him as it was he didn't believe her anymore.

"Strangers might believe you, especially if you keep up that tough act but those who know you won't believe that you've turned." Kyo warned her. "I figured it out didn't I?"

"Well then, I'll just have to be more convincing then won't I?"

174

Toria said getting up to leave and then changed her mind. "How did you get in, I mean you walked around showing off some of your markings and when you took your medical they must have noticed...?"

"See I can be useful." Kyo said smiling at her. "Their scanners are supposed to detect when Magic is used especially to cover up what spices you are, but the trick is to only use a little just enough to confuse the sensors, they pick up on it but they just put it down to background interference."

Toria laughed she couldn't help it, something so simple, meaning that there could be loads of Magics in the Fleet and they wouldn't know about it.

"You know a little friendly advice, most Magics who want to get into the Fleet try and keep a low profile even those working themselves up the ranks so that they're in places of influence and information." Kyo told her.

"I don't have that sort of time." Toria told him. "And for what I'm going to be doing, I'll be noticed pretty soon by both sides."

Back at the senate they were still waiting for Renji's return dragging home the normal somewhat well behaved senator's daughter, but he was a day late and they hadn't heard anything from him since he left.

Lesharo was in-charge of security whenever he wasn't around which was actually quite often nowadays; he was quite tightly wired up as it was him who would be in trouble if neither of them returned, as it was his responsibility to check up on them to make sure that they were in fact doing what they said they were doing.

"He's probably eloped with her, that bastard when I find him I'm going to kill him." Lesharo told Bernal, who was sat at his desk on the computer only half listening to him. "What, have you gone deaf?"

"Renji wouldn't elope with her, he's engaged to be married remember?" Bernal said while reading the report off the computer screen. "He left, he arrived at the academy but didn't talk to her but to someone else and then left soon after his arrival without filing a flight plan. Lady Toria herself is still at the academy."

They both looked at each other knowing that there was something wrong with that, they knew that Renji wouldn't leave without her especially leaving her there of all places; so all they needed to do was figure out what was really going on.

Toria walked down the corridor ahead of Kyo who was carrying a handful of data sheets, he was quite far behind her because he was having trouble keeping up with seeing that she wasn't taking into consideration that he had broken his leg earlier that week; the rest of the class was still giving her a wide birth not wanting to get in her way, they probably thought that Kyo was running around after her because she threatened to break his other leg; which truly was actually the opposite way around.

Toria saw the blonde lad and his friends from the first morning that she had arrived, he was still with a large group even after he had gotten beaten up by a girl who was two years younger than him.

"Kyo, what're you doing?" He shouted over to him when he saw him behind her.

"He's being a gentleman and carrying my work." Toria answered for him.

He started to say something back to her while Kyo carried on trying to catch up to her breathing heavily, but they all looked past her to who was walking up the corridor behind them; this of course annoyed Toria she didn't like too be ignored especially by stuck-up guys like them.

"Victoria!" Senator Kentaro boomed up the corridor.

Toria slowly turned around to see her father walking towards her with Lesharo and Bernal, but no Renji still, which she found strange and was of course partly relieved as well.

She walked calmly over to them pushing Kyo out of her way making him stumble into the wall, but no one helped him instead their attention was on the senator and his guards who had come for her. Toria stopped a couple of feet away from Lesharo who looked as though he wanted to murder her on the spot where she stood.

"Father it's so nice to see you." Toria said pleasantly. "You didn't need to come all this way to wish me luck."

"You stupid brat, we're here to bring you home." Lesharo told her unable to control his anger.

"But this is where I belong, where I believe I can do the most good for our cause." Toria told her father ignoring Lesharo as though it hadn't been him who had spoken to her.

This of course pushed him over the edge finally, he tried to grab her but she just smiled at him as she grabbed him instead and threw him over her shoulder turned around kicked him in the stomach and then the face.

"I never did like you much." Toria told him. "I never did understand how someone like you could become a senate security officer, it's not as though you're smart enough to bribe your way in either after failing all the tests except for one; you can just about fire a weapon at a target. You always blame your problems on everyone else when really, you're the problem. You should have sent Renji to get me, see now he's a real man...whereas you're something else unworthy to be even classed as one..."

"Victoria." Senator Kentaro said behind her, she turned around to face her father as though nothing had just happened. "Why do you suddenly want to join the Fleet when you've never had any interest in it before?"

"You need to ask, after what they've done to me; I'm just sorry that it took something like this to open my eyes to what they're really like." Toria said. "Tricking me, holding me prisoner...but when the Fleet officers came to rescue me they even tried to stop them. But I wanted to come home, I'm not sure how I did it but all the Magics are dead just like from that city; they hurt me, so I hurt them back."

Senator Kentaro just looked at her as though he was trying to tell if she was being truthful or hiding something from him, but if she was hiding something from him, he couldn't sense it at the moment though that didn't mean that he wasn't going to keep a close eye on her.

"For the moment I'll let you stay here then." Senator Kentaro told her. "But you must return home during your leave periods, which if I remember correctly is in a month's time after the exams."

"Of course father." Toria said. "Thank you, now I should be getting to class."

"Good luck with your training." Senator Kentaro said to her and then turned his attention to the speechless Bernal next to him. "You're in charge of security until Aba'rian returns, I'm sure he won't be gone long; but in the meantime you'll need to find a replacement officer as you can't do all the work yourself."

"Sir?" Lesharo shouted from the floor trying to get to his feet as Toria walked past him smiling. He grabbed her ankle and tugged but with her free foot she kicked his hand away.

"Your behaviour is inappropriate for a senate guard and towards my daughter." Senator Kentaro told him before he turned and left.

Bernal looked over at Lesharo on the floor one last time before he quickly followed after the senator.

"Oh, what a shame." Toria said before she carried on walking grabbing hold of Kyo's arm and near enough pulled him along.

Everyone just stared at her even more curious than before, now that they knew who she really was; but that just seemed to make her that much more of a puzzle as she could change so suddenly from being really nice to beating someone up and getting them fired also.

"I guess that was somewhat convincing." Kyo said struggling beside of her. "I think you enjoyed beating that guy up though a little too much."

"I've never liked him and he's never liked me. It helped my case though." Toria said. "Renji didn't like him either."

"Yeah, now you'll be known as the crazy senator daughter." Kyo teased, smiling a little especially from the last comment about Renji.

Toria smiled at him. "Seriously though, do you think he bought it?"

"He's leaving you here isn't he, so he must have." Kyo said nodding. "Oh by the way, I know that you don't actually pay attention to this sort of stuff; but you'll have to start to get into the bigger circles. The guys you beat up, the blonde one is Macallister; the senator's son for the Husterian system. The guy you fell on is the grandson of General Kersan, the lads called Rian. And the stupid one who actually tried to fight you is Cletus, the son of Senator Iokia's first aid, Makah."

"Okay, thanks you're right I do need to know all this stuff." Toria agreed looking at him strangely. "But how do you know it all?"

"Some people actually like you knowing who their family is, they think it means something." Kyo told her.

"I guess it does in some cases." Toria said thoughtfully.

"Your dad's a big player, all you need to do is give your name and they'll fall over themselves for you." Kyo told her. "I'm trying not to, but I've still got this problem with my leg."

Toria smiled at him. "I am sorry about that you know."

"Yeah I know." Kyo said.

Toria wasn't sleeping much lately, even though she felt tired from all the extra work and would like to just relax properly, but her body didn't seem to want too; she tried to look at the positive part of this, that at least she had plenty of time to study for the exams that were starting that morning. She sat on her bed against the wall trying not to think about how sore she was while she read through her data pad on Fleet ship protocols. She was quite surprised when she started reading about all the rules that they were actually quite lax on how the commanding office punished a member of the crew as though they were leaving it up to their discretion; Toria thought that would be quite helpful if she did get a command.

She looked up from the data pad at the clock on the dresser drawers, it was only 03:37; she still had hours before they had to get up because they didn't have their morning run today with the exams. She didn't think about going out for a run to kill some time as she wouldn't be bothering anyone because she didn't have a room-mate. They had offered to put her with someone but she'd told them that she wanted a room of her own. She was glad that she did really in case she used her Magic without realising; something else she hadn't managed to do or rather figure but to turn the sensors off in her quarters so that they didn't pick up on Magical energy. She had been reading that many engineering books about so many different things that her brain didn't seem to be able to hold much more information at the moment, but she needed to do more especially in these exams to make sure that she passed them but there was still no promise that they would put her up with the rest of the year if she did.

Toria somehow made it through all of the exams with everyone else and all they had to do now was wait for the results in a week's time, but for now she could relax a little on the transport ship back to the senate sat next to Kyo who was now cast free.

There were quite a few empty seats in the many rows of students, as not everyone lived in the same system, though those who lived further away didn't all decide to go home but went to stay with friends who lived closer as the travelling time in these slow transports was a bit much if you had to go all the way in one of these, that was little more than a bus.

"So what're you doing for your birthday tomorrow?" Kyo asked her.
"Having a few friends round."
"Friends like who?" Toria said. "Anyway my father would have probably planned something with it being my sixteenth."
"What you're not even sixteen yet?" Macallister demanded turning around in the seat in front of them and kneeling on it so that he could be seen. "Just how the hell did you get in then?"
"I'm sure that I mentioned it, but I took down Zo'hora." Toria told him calmly. "You might not remember though because I hit you in the head, you should get that checked out in case you've forgotten anything else before it becomes too serious."
"There's nothing wrong with me, and by the way I only let you win because you're a girl." Macallister told her.
"That's so sweet, I'll remember to mention that to your uncle that you're such a gentleman." Toria said trying not to smirk too much.

Macallister's face contorted with fury as Rian pulled him back into his seat, while over on his other side Cletus looked as though he was ready to go a second round with her until she smiled at him surprising him as she did everyone else when she switched like this.

"If I am having a party, you'll be attending won't you?' Toria asked him. He weren't bad looking when he wasn't deciding the best way to attack her; not that he was her type or anything but it gave her an idea.

"Well...I...I don't know..." Cletus stammered.

"It'd be such a shame since my father was going to visit Senator Iokia on the weekend." Toria said sounding disappointed.

"I'll be there." Cletus said quickly.

"What? Why?" Macallister demanded grabbing hold of him to pull him over to speak to him. "It's not as though she has any say in anything that goes on..."

"I am glad that we're finally getting a new guard. I didn't like him much and the other one who was with my father got a promotion out of it." Toria said airily pretending that she was talking to Kyo who knew she wasn't.

Cletus pulled his arm free and sat back smiling at her as though that settled the matter, even Macallister didn't have an argument because he had seen what had happened with his own eyes.

"They could be useful after all." Toria whispered to Kyo.

"Okay you've picked up on this whole being bad thing too quickly, it's kind of scary to be honest." Kyo told her whispering back.

Toria just smiled to herself, it had gotten a little easier but it was still hard work, always trying to remember that she has to be this other person now, and knowing that it was in fact only going to get harder especially with what she was really planning to do as a Fleet officer; but she also knew it was going to get a lot harder when she has to face her friends and convince them that she wasn't the same person as before.

Toria was dreading bumping into Renji the most, who she was sure would be able to see through her even if he hadn't been able to find anything to clear her name, which she knew he hadn't because Ichigo hadn't contacted her recently after she had told him the basic outline of her plan.

The transport took an hour to get back to the senate, they landed on one of the high transport platforms where they all started to get off with their luggage, but those from the upper-class families didn't need to carry it for long before it was taken off of them and loaded into the back of their hover cars which would take them home.

Toria watched them all fussing around, it still annoyed her at how they acted as though they were better than everyone else all because they had money and a title; she knew that she couldn't say much because she had never wanted for anything but at least she was willing to change to actually help people even though most would never realise what she was up to until it's too late to do anything about it.

"I'll see you tomorrow night." Kyo told her breaking into her thoughts.

"Oh right, yeah; see ya tomorrow." Toria said as Bernal rushed over and tried to take her small bag off of her but she wouldn't let go of it.

"So did you find a replacement for that idiot?"

"Miss, you really shouldn't have done that...it's not like you." Bernal said sounding worried for her.

"This isn't the real me you say, but to be honest I feel more alive being like this than I ever did before." Toria told him as he lifted the boot and she put her bag inside. "So if I feel more of myself like this, then that means that little girl you all thought you knew was just a shell until I found my real self; wouldn't you say?"

"I still prefer the other you, and I bet Renji does as well." Bernal said opening the door for her to get into the car, she got into the car and he closed the door before he walked around to get into the drivers seat.

"That isn't his job to decide which of me he likes better." Toria told him as he started up the engine.

"He cares about you, he's been worried..." Bernal tried to tell her.

"It isn't his job to care about me, and to be honest he has good reason to worry about me." Toria told him leaning forward. "If anything was to happen to me on his watch, he'd be in a lot trouble; and that's putting it nicely."

"Now I know I like the other you better." Bernal told her. "She'd never want anything to happen to Renji."

"Really? How sure of that are you?" Toria asked him.

If things had just been normal and nothing at all had changed then Toria would be very disappointed now, she hadn't seen Renji since she had got back home and even Bernal hadn't heard anything from him which she didn't need to ask because he just kept telling her; she did think he had become quite brave speaking out so much and especially after what she did to Lesharo but it might also be because of that since he did get promoted out of it.

She stood in front of the mirror and smiled sadly back at herself, she did love the long straight pale blue dress that cut slightly down the front below her cleavage line but showed nothing and gathered at the bottom of her back, the silver embroidery glittered slightly when she moved as did the silver thread in her hair which she wore up wrapped around in sections.

Part of her wished that Renji could see her dressed like this, because at this moment in time she didn't look like a little girl but a young lady; though part of her knew she was being foolish knowing that he could never like her like that and especially after what she was going to do.

Toria took a deep breath knowing that it was going to be a very long night, her father had invited nearly everyone that he knew; normally she hated this sort of thing but at the moment she'd put up with it because she'd need these people's help in the future the only thing was that they wouldn't know what they were really helping her with.

Her father had hired out the great hall in the Granrio Sector which normally held the senate functions, though considering everyone who was attending it might as well be an actual senate function as there was going to be more of them than people her own age.

Toria walked down the beautiful corridor towards the hall with her father beside her and Bernal with the new guard just behind them, he looked as though he was at least ten years older than Bernal in the face but he still looked pretty fit and able.

"Thank you father, I was surprised that you organised something like this on such short notice." Toria said as they neared the hall and could hear the music being played inside and a large crowd of people talking just beyond the doors.

"Nonsense, I've been planning this all year for you." Senator Kentaro said as though it was nothing. "I do believe though that you'll enjoy tonight much more since your new out look on the galaxy. If you truly wish to be an officer then there are plenty of people here tonight that will be able to make that dream come true."

"I am glad that you support my decision on this." Toria said.

Two foot-men stepped forward wearing long black jackets with gold embroidered around the edge, their top hats were black with long beautiful golden feathers in them; they bowed before they opened the doors onto the ball.

"Happy birthday my daughter." Senator Kentaro said smiling at her as she just stared.

Toria had been to these functions before with all these people, but tonight seemed different, it seemed more overwhelming because they were all here for her; or rather they were here to curry favour with her father through her but she could use that to her own advantage.

"Why don't I introduce you to a few people before you go off with your friends." Senator Kentaro said.

It wasn't a suggestion, which she knew, she walked off into the crowd noticing that they all looked quite eager as though hoping that the senator will come over to them and some who actually remembered who she was and why they were there were quite surprised by her appearance considering what she normally wore; for she wasn't a little girl any more.

Toria spent over an hour mingling before Annyetta walked over to her, her long dark purple hair back but still worn down; she was also dressed in blue, a dark blue basque with thick straps and a flowing blue skirt. She smiled at Toria as she always did; Toria didn't see the harm with still being friends with her and smiled back.

"Annyetta you look lovely." Toria said.

"I was actually going to say the same thing to you, Lady Toria." Annyetta said.

"You don't mind if I spend a little time with my friends?" Toria asked her father.

He seemed a little disappointed that she wanted to go off already which Toria noticed.

"I'll still speak to everyone that I recognise." Toria assured him. "And then I'll come and find you again."

"For a little while then." Senator Kentaro agreed and watched his daughter walk away, he signalled his hand calling Bernal forward.

"Yes sir?" Bernal asked.

"Aba'rian isn't here yet?" Senator Kentaro asked him.

"Not yet sir, but he should be here soon." Bernal told him. "Do you think that he'll be able to find out what's going on with her?"

"There's nothing going on. She's just finally grown up and seen sense." Senator Kentaro said.

"So how have you been?" Toria asked.

"I was going to ask you that." Annyetta said. "It was supposed to be kept a secret, but we still heard that you disappeared; and then later they found out that you had been kidnapped by Magics? Is that true?"

"Yes, I escaped or I wouldn't be here...a Fleet ship." Toria explained simply enough, not wanting to go into great detail especially here of all places.

"And why would Magics want to kidnap you?" Siren asked stood behind her suspiciously.

Annyetta smiled brightly at her as they both turned around to face her, she would have looked quite beautiful if she wasn't so angry glaring at Toria; her blond hair was styled to make it look shorter with silver intertwined through it to keep it in place. Siren was also wearing a long flowing dress which gathered at the front and lower back, it was in a lovely shade of midnight blue with fine silver embroidery.

"Anyone looking at us would think that we all dressed to match, when really we didn't even know what the other was going to wear." Annyetta said smiling ignoring the tension between the other two.

"Well are you going to answer my question?" Siren demanded.

"I don't know, perhaps to use me as a bargaining chip...they didn't explain their plans to me." Toria told her as she linked Annyette's arm and started to walk away, but Siren stopped her.

"What do you think you're playing at, and now you're just walking away from me?" Siren said. "We're supposed to be friends, best friends."

"I was wrong to become friends with someone like you." Toria said pulling her arm free.

"Someone like me?" Siren repeated slowly. "Then what about yourself?"

"I'm disgusted that part of me is like them, but that's why I joined the Fleet." Toria told her.

Siren stared at her for a moment. "You joined the Fleet so that you can fight the Magics?"

"Yes." Toria told her. "They were quite happy to accept me, since I've already destroyed two Magical colonies. It was so easy, no wonder that they're losing."

"How dare you." Siren said through gritted teeth grabbing hold of her roughly. "What're you up to...?"

"I don't know what you're talking about." Toria said calmly smiling at her.

"Of course you do, you love everything about the Magics...especially...especially Renji..." Siren said upset.

"There's Renji now, by the fountain." Annyetta said pointing towards him stood next to the fountain looking around the room for her, but he wasn't dressed in his uniform like Bernal had been but a suit as though he was just any other gentleman there.

"Damn it." Toria said under her breath thinking quickly, the fountain; but she'd need Siren's help. "Stop him."

"What?" Siren said now confused. "No, I think we should call him over here to sort all of this out; perhaps he could knock some sense into you seeing that you've lost it suddenly."

"There's nothing wrong with me, but I can't have him getting in my way." Toria told her. "If you want to make yourself useful, use the water to stop him."

Siren considered her for a moment and assured herself that it wasn't a trick to get her caught, but there was something really big going on and this was the only way for her to find out and perhaps help. Siren concentrated on the water in the fountain imagining it moving out of the basin and straight for Renji, as she opened her eyes the water seemed to come alive and lunge at Renji making several women close by scream as it covered him from head to toe; everyone just stared as the water fell to the ground slashing those closest to him who was unable to move away in time.

Renji just stood there as stunned as everyone else, Bernal ran over to him slipping on the wet floor and sliding into him; Renji caught him pulling him to his feet fuming.

"Are...are you alright?" Bernal asked nervously.

"Do I look alright?" Renji asked him as calmly as he could, Bernal though couldn't form the words to answer him but somehow managed to shake his head. "Tell the senator that I had to get changed."

"Um...yes sir..." Bernal managed to say as Renji let go of him and carefully walked off the way that he had come.

Bernal stared after him for a moment before he carefully turned around and headed back to find the senator to tell him what had happened, but of course by the time he had reached him the senator had already been informed of what happened.

"Sir, I'm sorry." Bernal said. "But Renji had to leave after what happened, he said that he was going to get changed."

The senator didn't look at all pleased by this news which made him wonder if he actually expected Renji to walk around here wet to the bone, though what he found even stranger is that Toria hadn't appeared at all thinking that she'd be more concerned, but then remembered this new her who supposedly didn't care about him in the same way as she did before.

Annyetta closed the doors to the balcony after they had checked that it was all clear, Toria walked over to edge looking out over the city with this empty feeling deep inside of her; Siren rounded on Toria for answer now after what she had just done for her.

"So come on, I want to know why we just humiliated Renji in front of everyone?" Siren demanded.

"Cause he'd just get in the way." Toria answered.

"In the way of what, you trying to declare war against the Magics?" Siren asked sarcastically. "I need a better answer than that. You were supposed to be different from the rest, especially after I found out..."

"That's why he'll get in the way, it's his fault, he's the main reason that I like them so much that I'm willing to lose everything just to pay him back." Toria told her.

"I don't understand." Siren said confused now not keeping up with what was going on.

"I destroyed two Magical colonies with my powers because I couldn't control them." Toria told them. "I ran away because I couldn't face him, I'd betrayed him..."

"But you didn't mean too, he'd understand." Siren told her. "So why are you doing all of this?"

"I joined the Fleet to fight the Magics, to kill as many of them as I can the same way that I destroyed those colonies." Toria told them. "They were destroyed, nothing left; yet they're still there alive. Do you have any idea what that means? All those people living in fear can finally disappear until we're really ready to fight back."

"But..." Siren said slowly as the whole of her plan became clear to her. "You know what will happen to you...it's not as though you can do this for a while and then go back...the Magics will want you dead. God the Fleet will want you dead if they ever figure out what you've done."

"Lady Toria, perhaps if you think about this some more." Annyetta said beside of Siren also worried about her friend.

Toria smiled at her kindly, but she had already made up her mind.

"Renji...he'd help you...you should tell him." Siren told her wanting to help her in some way.

"You think he'd help me?" Toria asked her sadly. "He would never willingly let me do something like this where the odds were in favour of me being killed by both sides. And I don't want his help, because he'd be classed as a traitor if they ever found out that he was helping me. So that's why I can't see him. He'd be able to figure out that I'm only acting especially at the moment and try to talk me out of it, which I'm afraid that he'd be able to do...so that's why I can't see him."

"Fine, but I'm helping you as well." Siren said suddenly. "Not like what you're going to be doing of course, but I'll be here if you need me...which you'll need someone on the inside of the Magics to get you information."

"I have help on that front...and I think I know how to get some more without putting anyone in danger." Toria said smiling. "Do you fancy going on a trip?"

"Why not." Siren said.

"Perhaps I shouldn't, its not that I'm going to abandon you but..." Annyetta tried to explain.

"You can come if you want, I'm not sure yet where I'm going to tell them that we're going though." Toria said.

"Yeah because we'd have to stop off there on the way and coming back." Siren said thoughtfully and then smiled at Annyetta. "You can help us out with that, you know cover for us."

"Yes, I can do that." Annyetta said smiling pleased that she could help in her own way.

"We'll leave tomorrow, so pack quickly." Toria told them.

"Will you be alright tonight?" Siren asked her.

"Hopefully." Toria said even though she was unsure, it was going to be pretty hard to keep away from him in the same apartment, but she'd have to.

Toria almost fell backwards as she pulled the smallest travel bag off the top shelf of her wardrobe slipping on the hem of her dress, thinking that it might have been better if she would have changed her clothes first before trying to pack; her hair had already started to fall out with all the messing that she was doing. She reached up to pull her hair down properly when she saw a dark black figure in the mirror stood behind her, she screamed and stumbled back into the open door of the wardrobe as she turned around to see who was there; but there was no one or nothing that could have made such a large shadow or whatever it was in the mirror.

"Toria!" Renji shouted outside her bedroom door, startling her. "Open the door! Are you alright?"

"I'm fine, relax already will you!" Toria shouted back at him as she stepped in front of her mirror, but there was nothing there now.

"Toria! If you don't open this door in five seconds I'm going to break it down; do you hear me?" Renji shouted.

"I'm fine." Toria told him turning to the door hoping that he wouldn't actually break the door down. "It was nothing."

"Let me come in and see for myself then." Renji told her.

"No I will not." Toria said stubbornly.

"Stop being so childish and let me in." Renji shouted.

"I'm sixteen years old and...and I'm in the Fleet now, how can you still think of me as a child?" Toria said.

"Because you're still acting like one now, keeping me out when I'm only trying to do my job; or is it that you're hiding something in there?" Renji said.

"What?" Toria said. "What, you think that I brought someone back to my room and then was stupid enough to draw this much attention to myself?"

"What's going on?" Senator Kentaro asked outside of her door.

"I heard her scream, so I came to find out what was wrong." Renji told him. "She won't let me in."

"Victoria, are you alright?" Senator Kentaro asked.

"Yes I'm fine, I just startled myself...stupid really..." Toria said as calmly as she could. "And anyway I can't really let him in, I'm not really dressed properly."

"Well okay then, I'll let the matter drop this time." Senator Kentaro said. "Come with me Aba'rian."

"Yes sir." Renji said.

Toria hoped that she hadn't gotten him into too much trouble for not letting him do his job, but he'd ruin everything if he saw her now.

Renji followed the Senator into the living room that was dimly lit considering the time. Renji stayed standing as the senator sat down studying him for a while before he spoke finally.

"Is there a problem with my proposal Aba'rian?" Senator Kentaro asked him.

Renji looked away, there was a problem of course there was, but if it was the only way then he'd go ahead with it.

"No...no sir." Renji answered.

"You took a long moment to think about that then." Senator Kentaro said. "You missed quite a treat tonight considering your misfortune with the fountain. It is a shame that you missed seeing her tonight, she looked most beautiful; I'd expect that she would have even broken through that thick exterior of yours."

"Sir?" Renji said questioningly.

"I have given her this, because I believe that it is best for her as well, after much consideration." Senator Kentaro told him. "But for her to get what she wants she must give me what I want in return."

"You want her in a position that you can control her?" Renji said.

"You I thought would be the perfect choice since she trusts you completely...but considering her behaviour towards you recently..." Senator Kentaro started to explain.

"I believe it's just with everything that has happened." Renji told him quickly. "She just needs some space. I was being too pushy for her; she needs to come around to this on her own to make it think as though it was her idea to begin with."

Senator Kentaro looked at him as if trying to read his mind, but nodded slowly. "I'll give you some more time. But don't disappoint me again."

"No sir." Renji said.

Chapter Thirteen

Toria had gotten up extra early to pack her bags, which she was now somewhat used to getting up so early, with the month that she had spent at the academy getting up running even before classes started to keep everyone in shape. In the beginning she had hated it because she had never had to do anything like it before, but she took her time until her body got used to it and she wasn't too bad now though it helped that she actually had so much extra energy built up sometimes.

Toria had managed to sneak out of the apartment without anyone seeing her and without setting off the motion alarms, mainly because she had overheated them so that they wouldn't work; though she had been surprised that Renji hadn't camped outside of her quarters waiting to interrogate her. Especially after what had happened last night, but now that she had had time to think about it, she was sure that it must have just been her imagination it's not as though there could have actually been something in the mirror one moment and then nothing the next. Normally when something strange like this happened she would ask Renji, but considering the new situation that wasn't really possible any more; she just reassured herself that it was nothing, that she must have just been seeing things.

She was out and in the transport centre standing with Annyetta waiting for Siren who was late, which they both knew wasn't like her, they just hoped that she hadn't run into any trouble getting away, but they were sure that she would have found a way to contact them if she had.

Ten minutes more had passed since they arrived, but it still wasn't very busy for those going to work would probably start arriving in an hour or so; which is why Toria decided on this time so that they wouldn't be seen by anyone that they knew. She didn't even have to worry about getting transport off world because that was where Annyetta came into it, her father would take her anywhere that she wanted including her friends; so Toria could wait until she actually arrived to tell them what she had done and they couldn't kick up a fuses since her father was just as well known as her own.

"Do you think she's alright, Lady Toria?" Annyetta asked concerned.

"I'm sure she's fine, she might have just missed her transport over here." Toria said. "There should be another one in a couple of minutes. But if she's not on that then, we'll have to call."

"I'll call her for you, Lady Toria." Annyetta told her.

Toria smiled at her and then turned her attention back to the arriving transports, partly wishing that she had worn a jacket because it was actually quite breezy up here; and she seemed to be feeling the cold a lot more since she had started coming into her powers. That actually made her think of the doctor that Ichigo told her about, the only problem was that she couldn't remember his name; but it would be a lot of help if she could get in touch with him since he actually knows so much about Fire Elementals.

Her list of thing's to do on this so-called holiday seemed to be getting longer all the time, and she was also looking forward to having perhaps a little bit of fun with her friends; since they had never actually gone away together before.

They could see the transport bus approaching the stand with only a couple of people on it, but neither of them could see Siren as they were looking for someone with blonde hair; there wasn't even a human that they could see. Toria held her ground as if hoping that somehow she'd be on it, when they saw a huge bag pushed out of the door.

"That isn't her is it?" Toria said irritably watching.

Another slightly smaller bag fell out beside of it, a moment later a blond head appeared wearing a short red paneled dress with flaw cut sleeves with a white shirt underneath and matching red paneled trousers; she picked up the smaller bag and dragged the other bag along looking around for them.

"I'm sure I said pack lightly." Toria said. "And isn't she supposed to be the sensible one?"

Annyetta just stood there not sure what to say as Siren struggled over to them with her bags neither of them going over to help her, which Siren found quite annoying and stopped about four foot from them.

"What are you just going to watch me struggle?" Siren demanded.

"Yes." Toria answered.

"Okay enough with the cold shoulder act..." Siren started.

"I'm being serious." Toria told her. "It's alright going to Annyetta's but you'll have to leave most of it behind, we can't be lugging all that around with us."

Siren glared at her and then looked down at her bags, they were kind of big but she didn't know what to bring as she wasn't told where they would be going; so she decided that it wasn't her fault.

"Fine, when you tell me where we're going, I'll take out what I don't need." Siren told her stubbornly.

Toria smiled at her picking up her own bag, Annyetta's were already on her transport; Toria walked over to Siren and picked up the smaller bag which was actually quite heavy itself.

"I'll help this once, but you have to get that one on yourself." Toria told her. "Annyetta you can go on ahead, we'll only be a minute behind you."

"Okay Lady Toria." Annyetta said. "I'll tell them to prepare to leave as soon as you're on board."

Annyetta walked off towards the largest transport on the platform, it was a slick reflective bronze with small view ports along the hull. They slowly followed her over to the ship, watching her walk up the ramp and then out of sight.

"I was starting to get worried that you might have had second thoughts." Toria admitted. "I know that I set out to do this on my own...I guess when you said you'll help, it made me feel...well stronger in away."

"Why would I back out on helping a friend and my people?" Siren said. "Please I thought that you knew me."

Siren sat on the sofa under the view in the main lounge, Toria and Annyetta had a chair each facing her with their drinks on the table set in the middle; the other seats in the lounge which were set out like these as well, were empty as they were the only ones travelling today.

"So what's the plan?" Siren asked finally.

"You've heard of Vertigo right?" Toria asked her.

"Of course I have." Siren said indignantly.

Annyetta looked between the two of them as she didn't know what it was and was hoping that they would fill her in; though as it was Toria didn't really know what it was either which was why she had brought it up.

"Well I don't really know much about it, but the guy that I'm hoping to meet, plays." Toria explained. "So why don't you tell me about...it'll be a good way of getting to know my other self if they think I'm interested in it."

"You're meeting a guy, you never said that...so come on who is he?" Siren asked her.

"Lady Toria I think this is the first time that you've said that you're interested in a guy." Annyetta said giggling.

"I didn't say that I'm interested in him like that." Toria said hotly.

"She likes Renji remember." Siren reminded her.

"He's a little old for her though." Annyetta said.

"Hay, I'm still here." Toria told them. "He's called Lonac from the Roaring Torch."

Siren stared at her for a moment. "That big scary guy?"

"He's nice, he helped me; I'm sure that he will do now." Toria told them. "Well he helped Touro out."

"And what does Touro look like?" Siren asked her suspiciously.

"The same age as me. Purple hair and eyes. Of course my face is a little different as well." Toria told them, Siren though didn't look as though she believed her. "So come on, the game?"

"Oh right, yeah." Siren said distractedly. "Right, there are seven players on every team; most teams have at least three reserves. There are four Walkers, the captain is normally one of them but not always. They move around on the five platforms scoring the points avoiding the other team and the Magical traps which if you're caught in them you lose points. There are two Defenders, which do as their names say, defend their teammates and try to get the other team. Oh, you can do nearly any kind of Magic as long as it's legal of course; even if you're a werewolf you're allowed to change and bite someone. They have to call a time-out afterwards so that they can be treated with the cure, then it goes on record and they can't be bitten for over a month."

"They actually allow them to bite other players?" Toria asked surprised by this.

Siren though just continued as though it didn't matter. "Now then, the last player is the Rose; the secret weapon. The Rose player is said to be able to do anything, can play as any position and is allowed anywhere on the platforms; they normally have some sort of power that gives them the upper hand that helps the team to win. They keep their powers a secret of course, 'cause you only have to tell them if you can change into anything like a werewolf that's dangerous to others."

"All powers can be dangerous though, if they're not used properly." Toria said thoughtfully.

"Yeah, well." Siren said off handedly and carried on again. "Right the game itself is played on platforms that are suspended in the air. They start off as just one large one and then spilt into five small ones; they can move up and down through each other and also tilt knocking you off your feet. That's not all, each platform has its own environment, which can be anything. When the platforms pass through each other you can be transported to another, there are also portholes to travel through."

"So is this popular?" Toria asked her.

"I don't really get it." Annyetta said.

"I'm still talking, and yes it's been popular for a couple of thousand years." Siren said getting annoyed that they don't seem interested in it and that they kept interrupting her. "Right, scoring points through the four pockets which sometimes move; you can hardly see these so you've got to have a good eye for seeing things that are kind of there but not; oh yeah, you get ten points for them. To end the game you need to find the special Rift pocket which is even harder to see than the normal ones, you score through this and you get one hundred points; normally whoever scores that wins; but there have been times that the other teams won. Energizers are these two balls that travel through all the platforms after the players, the Defenders can use them to help; you get hit by one of these and you lose five points and also get an electric shock."

"I don't really like..." Toria started.

"Do you mind, you asked me to tell you and you keep interrupting me." Siren said irritably.

"I didn't think that it would take this long." Toria said.

Siren once again ignored her comments and continued. "There are also Grids and Nets; they lock you inside for two whole minutes. There's an anti-gravity field around the platforms in case you fall off or get transported off, then you've got to make your own way back onto the platform. That's basically it, and it is a good game...you just have to see it for yourself."

Toria nodded slowly. "It doesn't really sound that hard to play."

"You're being stupid again. And...and you haven't even seen a match before." Siren protested.

"Relax already will you." Toria told her thinking that it might help to get to know the players and the people better if at least one of them could get on a team, but she had to admit that it wasn't as though you could just walk up to them and say you could play; especially if you've never even seen a match. "What about you?"

"What about me?" Siren asked her, but Toria only looked at her until she realised what she met. "NO."

"Anyway, there's plenty of time to work out your plans when we get to my place." Annyetta said calmly. "You'll be staying for at least a day right?"

"Actually...I think there's a match tomorrow night." Siren said thoughtfully. "So if we leave tonight we should be able to get there, the only problem is getting somewhere to stay as all the rooms are normally taken."

"We'll just have to risk it." Toria said. "You don't mind do you?"

"No of course not, I know how important this is to the both of you; I'm just glad that I can help in some way." Annyetta said smiling kindly at them both.

"And anyway, if we get this done early we'll be able to stay with you longer." Toria told her smiling back.

Toria knocked on Siren's bedroom door to see if she was ready considering that they hadn't seen her for the past hour. Toria had never really thought that she was this girlie needing to spend hours to get ready; she didn't though perhaps if she was seeing someone then she would make more of an effort like for her birthday she put a lot of effort into that. That made her think that she would really have to start doing it soon, she wanted to be notice even in that way so that she could have strong connections throughout the Fleet.

"Come in." Siren said from inside.

Toria opened the door and went inside from the hall; the whole of the double bed was covered in clothes. It actually looked as though she had completely emptied the bags that she had brought and was trying to repack them; but she wasn't really getting very far. The wardrobe was open but empty as if she was only using it for the mirrors on the inside of the doors, the dresser was also unused; as though everything that she had brought with her was on the bed.

"It can't be that hard." Toria told her. "We're not going to need anything formal, just a few things to wear during the day and perhaps at least one nice thing if we go out at night. We're only staying a couple of days."

"I know that." Siren said irritably.

Toria smiled at her as she passed her a couple of outfits and then the shoes. "It's the shoes with me, I like matching shoes to my outfit. But the trick is to pack clothes of the same colour so you don't have to bring as many."

"And just how long have you been doing this sort of thing for then, hay?" Siren asked her.

Toria smiled. "This will be my first time, and I'm actually looking forward to it. Hopefully it'll be the first of many."

"Doesn't it bother you that you'll be lying to them all?" Siren asked her seriously.

Toria sat down on the only free part of the bed.

"Of course it does, but it's the only way...we don't really know who we can trust and to be honest the more people that know about this then I've got less chance of it working." Toria told her. "If someone's caught or if they slip up...there's just too many lives to risk..."

"God, you sound way too grown up." Siren said as she closed her bag.

"It's going to take a few years to get to the position that I need to, to be able to make the effect that I want." Toria told her. "But I'll get there...hopefully a little sooner if I can get through the academy in record time."

"You're really going to push yourself aren't you?" Siren said.

"I've got to." Toria said standing up grabbing her bag off of her to see how heavy it was and then gave it her back. "That's much better than before."

"We better go through to Annyetta." Siren said as they walked over to the door. "What are we going to do about money?"

"My father's paying for us, my birthday money." Toria told her. "I took nearly a quarter of my money out, even though I don't need it now; but I will need it as Touro."

"What are you going to do, open an account in her name?" Siren asked sarcastically, but Toria was nodding as she opened the door. "Are you allowed to do that?"

"That's what you're worried about." Toria said laughing. "I'm going to be saying that I've killed thousands of people. Opening an account in a different name doesn't really worry me the same."

"Well I guess putting it like that." Siren agreed smiling slightly as they walked down the hall. "Do you think she'll mind me leaving all my clothes like that?"

"It'll actually make it look as though you're staying." Toria told her. "Your room gets like that as well, doesn't it?"

Siren glared at her, but didn't answer as she knew she was right. They carried on down the hall until they got to Annyetta's rooms; her door was still open so they both went inside to find her stood at the balcony doors looking out over the sunset that was being masked by the rain clouds.

"Annyetta." Toria said softly.

She slowly turned around to face them and tried to smile even though she was partly sad to see her friends leaving, though she knew this would only be the first time in their long journey ahead of them. Toria smiled back at her and then bent down and picked up her own bag which she had left at the door.

"Thanks." Toria told her. "We'll be back soon."

"Stay safe." Annyetta told them both.

"We will." Siren assured her.

And with that, they both turned around and left; they walked down the hall not looking even though they both knew that Annyetta had run out of her bedroom to watch them leave. Toria opened the side door which lead out into the garage, they were going to borrow one to get them to the transport centre.

There were three hover cars though none with hoods and one rector speeder, without even thinking Toria walked over to the rector speeder her appearance changing to that of Touro surprising Siren slightly, she knew that she could change but she hadn't been expecting her to do so, so suddenly like that.

"Do you know how to drive one of these?" Siren asked her as she watched her opening the seat hatch and putting her bag inside.

"We'll soon find out won't we?" Touro said smiling holding out her hand.

Siren gave her bag to her and squeezed it inside somehow closing the hatch again, Toruo mounted the bike swinging her leg over the side as though she had done it hundreds of times before; though in truth this would be her first time.

"You get us there in one piece and I'll make sure that we don't get wet." Siren told her as she carefully got on behind her and put her arms around her waist. "I can't believe that we're doing this."

"The adventure starts here then." Touro said pleasantly as she pressed the large silver button on the handlebars and the engine started. "That was a good guess."

"We're going to die before we even save anyone..." Siren said holding her even tighter. "Renji probably would have been good to have around, at least he could have saved us if we got into trouble."

"Yeah, I keep saying that to myself as well. But we have to start learning how to do these things ourselves, because there may come a time that we're all alone and we have to save ourselves." Touro told her kicking off the hand break and they safely hovered off the ground half a foot, she smiled to herself as she revved up the engine and they started forward.

"Not to fast...we have to get out of here first remember." Siren told her worriedly.

Touro moved them through the largest gap as the shutter opened for them to leave, as soon as Touro was clear of the hover cars she gunned the engine and shot out down the steep path turning sharply out onto the main road with Siren holding onto her for dear life.

"That was so much fun." Touro said excitedly. "It's as though I already know how to drive it, even though I've never been on one in my whole life."

"You're going to get us both killed." Siren said into her back not daring to lift her head to see where they were going.

"Actually I think if you hold me any tighter, you might break a couple of my ribs." Touro told her.

Siren reluctantly loosened her grip but not by much, she had never been on a rector speeder before and Touro had never driven one before; her brain had told her not to be so stupid and again she had ignored her own advice, and got on.

Touro seemed to pick up speed when she realised that the road was empty except for the odd hover car that didn't provide much of a trouble for Touro as she would move around them with ease; even the rain didn't seem to make it more difficult, but Siren had kept up her end of the deal and was keeping the rain off of them even though she was so worried; the rain was like an inch away from them as though there was a cover over them and when the rain hit it, it just rolled off but still leaving a clear view for Touro to see where she was going.

"You're going to be annoyed with yourself later." Touro told her over her shoulder.

"No...no I won't..." Siren said briefly looking up to see the houses passing by in blur. "How...much longer...?"

"About ten minutes at this speed, 'cause of the weather or I could go faster." Touro told her.

"Don't you think that you're going fast enough to start with?" Siren muttered into her shoulder.

Touro didn't hear what she had said, but she knew that she had said something and chose to ignore it as she knew it would probably be some sort of complaint.

She carried on at the same speed watching the road ahead and everything going by in a blur, unable to shake off this feeling that it wasn't by far the first that she had driven one of these; she wished that it wasn't and that it wasn't going to be her last either, it was so exhilarating to be moving so fast as to give you a strange sense of freedom, to be able to do anything.

The ten minutes just seem to fly by, Touro half wished that it had been longer as they approached the large box shape transport centre turning to a storage hanger on the right of the main entrance along the road that lead up to the front; the barrier came down in front of them as Touro slowed right down and Siren finally loosened her grip properly and looked up.

There was a toll booth on the left with a pocket where you put your money with the amount written over the top, 2,70 Purvinian's; Touro reached into her pocket and pulled out a handful of coins and counted out the smallest pieces as she didn't really want to be carrying around so much but making sure that she had enough for parking. She threw the coins into the pocket and the barrier suddenly lifted up to let them pass, so Touro slowly drove them inside the darkened hanger; the nearest lights came on when they got close enough to them, they both assumed that at this time of night they worked off of sensors.

Touro turned them into the next empty alcove, as there was quite a few more hover cars here than both of them thought that there would be. Once the engine had been turned off completely, Siren near enough jumped off the back and quickly stepped away, Touro though reluctantly climbed off looking longingly wanting to get back on and do it all over again, but she knew that she didn't have time.

Touro opened the seat compartment and pulled out their bags handing Siren's to her and then shouldering her own slamming the lid shut and stepped back, Touro walked over to the pocket in the wall in front of where she had parked the speeder and put in 5 Purvinian while Siren walked off first the light in the next booth came on and then Touro followed her over to the door as their transport was waiting.

There was a large empty gap next to the booth where the door was, the light flashed on as they approached and the doors swung out towards them revealing the brightly lit ticket room that wasn't actually very busy; just a few aliens here and there carrying lots of luggage.

"That's what you would have looked like." Touro whispered to Siren.

"I didn't have that much." Siren protested.

"Yeah but you would have been struggling that much." Touro told her looking around for a ticket machine, their tickets were already ordered so they just needed them to be printed out.

She spotted one to her left that wasn't being used and quickly went over to it as the group of four men seemed to be looking around for one as well. She didn't want to be held up now, just get on the transport and then they would be on their way. Siren stood by her shoulder as they looked at the machine, neither of them had never actually used one before; and everything was written out in four different languages.

"Right, I think all we need to do is type in our order code...I couldn't really borrow her card, nor use my father's cause he can trace where it's been used." Touro told her.

"Do you think that he's being a little paranoid?" Siren asked her.

"I left home without telling him, and before that I ran away for over a month without calling him once." Touro said.

"Fine, I guess with you doing that." Siren said. "But didn't he do that before hand as well?"

"He just liked to make sure that I was safe." Touro told her.

"What he didn't trust Renji to look after you, after all these years?" Siren asked a little surprised. "Or it was perhaps he was worried about you running away with him."

"I was going to, before all this happened." Touro told her as she typed in the order number off the small print-out she had taken off the data sheet. "He asked me, I think he was worried because of my powers...I would like to think, if everything had worked out to plan...that I would have left with him. But I wouldn't be doing this, I would never have been given a chance to help..."

"I don't mind you know, if you go on at me about all this; especially Renji." Siren told her smiling slightly. "Seeing that you haven't really got anyone else to talk to."

"Thanks." Touro said just as their tickets were printed out on small clear blue data sheets, she pulled them out of the slot at the bottom of the machine reading them as she straighten up.

Two young adult tickets
Deck 5, Room 58
Transfer point 7
Onto Argandar
Deck 7, lounge 10

"It's a good job that we know where we're going, as this is actually in code." Touro said as they walked off to the transport tunnels on the left side of the desks, with only two operators working.

"I know." Siren said. "But I'm surprised that they haven't picked up on it yet."

They walked past the group of four men who were now questioning the operator, trying to all talk at once and not making much sense; they hurried past them and down the tunnel towards the stairs at the end. There were five sets of stairs, the two end ones went down and the three in the middle lead into three different tunnels; over the top of each entrance was a sign theirs was the third stairs going up. They went upstairs and then down the tunnel that bent right.

"Oh, I didn't mention it before but Kyo knows a little of what's going on." Touro told her. "But he doesn't know about Touro."

"Oh right." Siren said.

"I'm surprised that he's still talking to me since I broke his leg, the first day that I arrived." Touro told him.

Siren looked over at her as though she didn't believe her and was waiting for her to tell her that she wasn't serious.

"I said I was sorry...but I guess I went a little over the top." Touro told her. "He went to tell Renji what happened...but I guess that's when it twigged..."

"If you had really turned, you would have turned us all in." Siren said nodding her head understanding.

"Renji will figure out what I'm up to as well, it's only a matter of time; but..." Touro said. "I...I don't know if I could do what I really need to do..."

"Well we'll figure that problem out when we come to it, one thing at a time." Siren told her. "Like getting to this Vertigo match and seeing your friend."

"Yep." Touro said smiling as they showed their tickets to the three foot women at the entrance, who waved them inside.

They walked down the corridor, it reminded her of the one that she was on with Lonac; though she had thought that it would have been a bit more luxury since it was coming from a summer holiday world for the rich, but they weren't travelling anywhere like that after they left here, so it wasn't as though they had to keep up the appearances of those sorts of fine things.

Touro was just about to carry on walking when Siren stopped her so she turned around to see why, it was for the lift which opened for them with one other already inside, a Serwa with pale blue skin and four head tails tattooed in green.

"Deck five." Siren ordered, but nothing happened. "Deck five...is it broke?"

Touro smiled at her, she had thought the same thing the first time that she had travelled on one of these transports; but now she knew differently and pressed their deck number on the small panel.

"Oh right...my brother normally does these sorts of things." Siren said airily.

"Yeah and people think that I'm helpless." Touro said sarcastically.

"I heard that." Siren said.

"You were supposed to since we're stood next to each other, I'd be worried if you couldn't." Touro said smiling slightly.

"That's funny." Siren said.

The lift stopped on their deck first, Touro went out first closely followed by Siren who was still glaring at her from behind; Touro though seemed to ignore her and turned left looking at the door numbers that were painted on the full length of the doors, they didn't have to go far until they saw their room number on the third door on the right, number 58.

Touro slotted the card into the port above the panel and the door opened, they both went inside and were surprised to see that it was actually much bigger than they had first thought it was going to be; there was a small lounge area with a table and four chairs and a computer food port set behind it. There was only one other door to their left which they went through to find the only bedroom that had two single beds with one small table set in the middle of them, two wardrobes on either side in the room with three drawers at the bottom of each of them; there was one other door in the far left corner which Siren headed for dropping her bag on the bed as she past.

"It's only going to be the bathroom…" Touro told her.

But Siren wasn't listening to her and opened the door to find out for herself, to find out that Touro was right; she slowly turned around and went back over to her bed and sat down.

"So what are we going to do now?" Siren asked her. "We're on our own now."

"Yeah I know, it's kind of scary but also exciting at the same time." Touro said putting her own bag on the other bed and opening it up, she pulled out a large t-shirt and dropped it on the bed.

Siren watched her, partly thinking the same thing and also wondering about the t-shirt. "That looks like a mans t-shirt."

"What…?" Touro said innocently, but it didn't work.

"No way...how come you have one of his t-shirts?" Siren said smiling at her. "What are you now, a stalker?"

"No I'm not." Touro said picking up the t-shirt and walking to the bathroom but Siren grabbed it off of her as she passed.

"Come on now...I know you like him; but really." Siren said holding up the t-shirt, which was massive. "He's quite big isn't he…"

Touro grabbed it back. "I can't actually remember how I ended up with it...but I sleep in it now and then...so what…"

Touro started to walked off and push the door open to the bathroom.

"You should be careful, since you know nothing at all about your Tasian side." Siren told her.

"So what if I don't." Touro said dismissively.

Siren stared after her friend shaking her head, a little worried and amused at the same time.

...Touro walked down the paddock with a group of officers, they were all dressed in the same uniform which was basically like a second skin; a tight fitted black cat suit with red straps.

"This'll be fun." Touro said smiling excitedly.

"I always feel worried for some reason when she's enjoying herself." A Ta'vian man said beside of her nudging the other man next to him.

"I'm not complaining." he replied.

"Fine, I will." The first man said. "These suits are horrible...I can hardly move."

"You don't like them?" Touro asked them turning around, so that they could see her at every angle in her own.

"I think you look great." The tall crimson-haired Ta'vian man said next to her. "I think he meant on the guys."

"I can see that, as they don't suit all of you." Touro said heading towards the newest bike stood next to the instructor, but before they could stop her she had mounted it and turned the engine on; spun it around and was moving off. "I'm just going to take it for a quick spin before the lesson."

And with that she speeded off out of the paddock out of sight, leaving the others to deal with the fuming instructor.

Touro speeded around the paddock as fast as she could, it had seemed like an age since she felt so free; she had missed being able to ride since she had arrived here, but at least things were starting to look up now.

Touro came back up the path five minutes later spun around on the front hover pad and parked up the speeder just where she had found it, she turned the engine off and dismounted; she headed straight over to the crimson-haired Ta'vaian, who had been waiting for her patiently. She couldn't make out his face but she smiled at him as though she knew him well enough, and felt that he was smiling back at her even though she couldn't see it.

"That was fun, but it felt a little sluggish on the right turning." Touro told him as though she knew quite a bit about how they should handle.

"That was probably because you weren't driving it properly!" The instructor shouted at her angrily. "These are new, that means that they are different to the ones that you're used too."

"I think she did quite well." The Ta'vian man said as he tried to wrap his arms around her waist but she struggled against him.

"Don't touch me there!" Touro protested setting the nearby bush on fire...

Touro almost jumped out of bed burning from head to toe and her waist especially from where he had been trying to hold her was still tingling, but in a kind of a nice familiar way.

"Don't touch you where?" Siren said sleepily turning over to face her.

"What?" Touro said blushing.

"That's what you just shouted out." Siren told her. "You were having dirty dreams about him, wasn't you?"

"No I was not." Touro said firmly turning back over so that she couldn't see her and pulled the blanket over her as well, even though she was still burning up; she wasn't going to tell her about her strange dreams, and they weren't about Renji because if they were she would have been able to see his face; wouldn't she?

Ten hours after leaving Annyetta's summer house they finally arrived on the planet Ardergat, they walked out into the bright busy square from the hover bus centre; there were races here from all over the Magical galaxy, all here just to see the Vertigo match that afternoon.

They had both changed their clothes so to fit in more. Siren had a blue shoulder dress with what looked like a purple one underneath it and blue knee boots; Touro had a lilac shoulder dress with a pink shorter one over the top with cut-out panels on the one side shoulder. She wore matching pink sandals that tied up her legs.

"People are looking at us." Siren said pulling her bag in front of her, she wasn't really used to dressing like this.

"That's cause we're just stood here." Touro told her. "Or perhaps they're checking us out."

Siren decided to ignore her and started to walk with Touro at her side, as she tried her hardest not to look around so much at everything. There were groups of people talking excitedly about the match and catching up, as this is the only time that they see most of these people and are allowed to be somewhat publicly open about what they are.

Touro was sure that she sensed something running towards her quickly, she dropped to ground startling Siren who stumbled backwards as whatever it was jumped right over her and skidded across the ground; stopping itself and made ready to try again as Touro looked up to see what had tried to jump her.

She just stared transfixed at the large furry wolf the size of a grown man, with dirty blue and silver coloured fur; he looked at her staring and then ran at her again. Touro panicked forgetting where she was as she tried to push herself up as much as possible and when he got close enough she kicked him as hard as she could, grabbed his arm pulling herself up completely and pinned him down on the ground with a husky groan.

"Tour...what're you...?" Siren tried to say speechlessly next to them.

"Inker, what the hell are you doing?" A man demanded making his way through the crowd, with Lonac beside him.

"She likes to be on top." Inker teased still lying on the ground being held by Touro.

"Let go of him." Siren told her pulling her off of him forcefully.

Touro almost tripped as she tried to stand up properly. He changed back before her eyes; he looked partly human with tanned skin and brown hair but his eyes were golden through of a Neszenrain.

"He...he jumped me." Touro protested.

"Do you know who he is?" Siren asked her irritably. "He's playing this afternoon."

"Playing what?" Touro asked confused.

"I don't believe it; I let you out of my sight for one second and look...you attacked someone." The handsome young man said as he grabbed Inker's tail making him howl out in pain, he had sandy brown hair and blue eyes that was full of fury at the moment but that didn't make him any less handsome.

"Touro." Lonac said surprised to see her stood before him.

Touro smiled at him. "Hi, I'm sorry that I haven't been able to contact you to tell you that I'm alright; thing's just got a little crazy."

"Wait a minute...you know the big guy?" Inker asked her nervously.

"Yes she does." Lonac answered for her.

"You've been holding out on us again, haven't you?" The handsome man said smiling teasing him. "Who wouldn't, considering how Inker reacted...and so far away as well."

"How did you see him anyway?" Siren asked her blushing slightly in front of the three men before her, which Touro noticed but didn't understand completely.

"I didn't...I just kind of sense his presence coming towards me." Touro explained.

"That aside, why don't we go for breakfast...he'll pay to make up for what he did to you." Lonac told them.

Touro was about to look over at Siren to see if she was alright with this, but it seemed as though she didn't need to worry.

"Really...oh thanks..." Siren said walking over to the handsome young man who still had hold of Inker's tail. "So you're Vi, from Vikas...hi...I'm Siren."

"Hi, nice to meet you, as well." Vi said smiling at her as they started to walk off among the staring crowd.

"I was worried about you." Lonac told her.

"I'm sorry..." Touro said.

"It's been almost two months, but you seem to be doing alright." Lonac said.

"I was rescued by my family...the only problem is now..." Touro told him. "He was on the colony in the Orihan system, that was destroyed...they say that the Malarias Fleet had like half a dozen spies there, at all different levels so it was only a matter of time before something happened...but they were the only family that I had left that I knew about..."

Lonac looked down at her and put his arm around her shoulder pulling her a little closer. "You'll be alright...I have quite a large place this time; you and your friend can stay while I'm here. Then after it's over..."

"You don't have to do that." Touro told him as they followed the others turning the corner onto a much quieter and emptier stretch of road.

"I'd like to, unless you already have somewhere else to stay." Lonac said.

"We don't actually." Touro admitted.

"Right then that's set..." Lonac started.

"You didn't offer to share your place with any of us." Inker said over his shoulder, who was walking in front of them. "You just wanted to keep them to yourself, don't you?"

"And if I did?" Lonac said off-handedly.

"Okay...that's enough." Vi said stopping suddenly and then pushed the shop door open and went inside.

They all followed him inside of the cafe, it wasn't packed but those inside did look up at them as they all walked in together and found a large booth to sit in; Inker sat at the back with Vi on his left and Siren next to him. Lonac sat on his side making sure that he couldn't get to Touro.

"S'not far..." Inker groaned.

A holographic menu appeared in the centre of the table in a square shape so that they could all see it, wherever they were sat; Touro was a little unsure about some of the things that she had never even heard of before, Berzen, Mursar with or without a Turanne and Utoran; and there were many more that she had never even heard of. She looked around the side to see if Siren was having any better look, but from the look on her face she was in the same situation.

"So what do you fancy?" Vi asked them.

"What...?" Both Touro and Siren said together.

"It's alright, I think that we're ready to order." Lonac said.

Before anyone could say anything, a bronze coloured robot wheeled out from the back of the counter and over to them, to take their order.

"We'll have three mursar's and on the side of them turanne's, and we'll have a pitcher of juice for the table." Lonac said.

The robot nodded and then waited for the rest of the order.

"I'll have vercot." Inker told it.

"And I'll have a full opyistan." Vi told it.

"Thank you, five to ten minutes wait." The robot told them before it wheeled back into the kitchen.

"So what did you order for us?" Touro asked him.

"You'll have to wait and see." Lonac told her.

"So you're Touro?" Vi said staring at her. "So what happened to you?"

"What?" Touro said nervously. "After the officers took me away? I was held on a ship before I was rescued, stayed with family before I..."

"She's staying with me, my brother's an officer stationed near the Dragon Senate." Siren told them.

"You're very strong." Inker said smiling at her.

"What?" Touro said not sure how to respond to that.

"He's right you know, he was in his proper wolf form; which means that he's at least four times stronger than a normal fully-grown man." Lonac said.

"Yeah, it takes a lot for a fully-grown man of any race to take a wolf down...but you're what...?" Vi asked.

"I just turned sixteen the other day." Touro said.

"Anything else we should know about?" Vi asked her.

"Not really." Touro said a little unsure on how this line of questioning was going.

"Oh yeah, Vi is a specialist in potions." Lonac told her. "I'm sure that he'll be happy to help you out a little, you said that you don't really know anything about Magic."

"I guess I could give you a few lessons, after the match." Vi said glaring at Lonac.

"That's so nice of you." Siren said beside of him. "I am looking forward to watching the match, we have to watch it on one of those big holo screens; our trip idea was kind of last minute so we didn't have time to buy a ticket."

"Sorry." Touro said pouting.

"That's alright." Lonac told them. "I haven't got tickets either, a few friends are coming around to my place. Why don't you come as well, they're all Magics so they'll be able to give you a few pointers as well."

The robot rolled out with extra arms to carry the plates of food, he put the pitcher in the middle of the table and the stack of glasses before he poured them all a glass each; then he shared the food out to who had ordered what. Inker's was a kind of porridge, Vi's was a roll with what looked like a breakfast on it; theirs were sandwiches which tasted an awful lot like bacon with blue eggs.

"This isn't bad, thanks." Touro said.

"I thought that you might like it, just something simple." Lonac told her.

Siren opened the door to the wardrobe that they would be sharing and just dumped her bag inside, while Touro stood at the window on the other side of the room looking out over the city full of Magics, free just for a little while; it made such a difference being around them here, they all seemed so different as though they could relax without looking over their shoulder worrying about doing or saying anything wrong.

"It'll be nice won't it?" Touro said. "To be able to come to these worlds every so often, just to relax a little."

"We're here on a mission, not to relax." Siren told her snapping the door shut.

"And then why were you flirting with Vi?" Touro teased turning around to face her.

"I wasn't flirting, I don't flirt." Siren told her indignantly.

"Yeah, you keep telling yourself that." Touro told her smiling as she went back over to her bed and sat down.

They were sharing a room again but they didn't mind as it was easier than keep going to each other, this way they could talk to one another all they wanted without it seeming odd.

"He seems nice." Touro said. "Wavy of course because he doesn't know us; I'd be more worried if he just accepted us straight off."

"Didn't Lonac do that with you, and look where you ended up." Siren pointed out.

"No, he's a good guy." Touro said standing up going over to the door. "I don't get that from him, he wouldn't betray his own kind."

"Some don't have a say in the matter, they're just made to." Siren told her as she followed her down the carpeted hall into the main lounge.

Lonac was sat in the largest chair at the side of the holo screen against the far wall, on the opposite chair sat a young woman in her early twenties with blonde hair with a slightly older man sat on the arm of the chair; there were two men on the sofa with their backs to them so that they couldn't be seen, but one had green hair in a top knot and the other had golden hair.

To their right stood around the table with snacks on it were two more men, one looked human with dark brown hair and black eyes making him look a little scary; the other man looked part Neszenrian smartly dressed with his black hair pulled back and his yellowish skin looked a little off in the light of the room.

"So you're Lonac's friends." The black eyed man said pleasantly walking over to them. "I'm Leka and he's Delky, we're from Roaring Torch as well."

"Normally I would say that we're the better team, but at the moment we're not doing too well.' Delky told them.

"Yeah, but you're practically at the bottom of the table." The man on the sofa said turning around to face them, he was a full Neszenrian with golden hair, eyes and even skin; it was rare to see one of this colour; he was still very handsome even though he was much older than them both.

"You're Zad'di from Yudan." Siren said excited. "And you two as well are from Yudan right, Ta'di and Karly?"

"Yep that's us." Zad'di said smiling at her.

"She doesn't know anything about Vertigo." Siren told them nodding at Touro beside of her making them all stare at her.

"Hay, so what." Touro said defensively.

"It doesn't matter." Lonac said.

"Yeah, he told us how you took Inker out; so what else can you do?" Leka asked her.

"Well, just that really...my Magic isn't very good, because I've never used it." Touro told him.

"She was chipped, until about two to three months ago." Lonac told him.

"Well that won't do, you could go around blowing anything up." Leka told her.

"What?" Touro said honestly sounding panicked, since she really was capable of doing that and actually had already done that.

"It's alright, how about I teach you a few things, while they watch the match?" Leka offered.

"Don't you think you're moving a little fast there, you'll end up scaring her; your face is scary enough without you being so pushy." The man next to Karly said.

"She'll be fine, if you hear pleading screams for help, they'll probably be his." Siren said off-handedly, making them all look at Touro again who just blushed deeply as Siren walked over to the sofa. "Can I sit next to you Zad'di?"

"Yeah sure." Zad'di said moving over for her to sit down.

"Remember don't hurt him, and especially don't kill him." Siren told her.

"Like I would." Touro said as Leka took her hand leading her off into the other room.

"Now I'm interested to see what you can do." Leka said.

"You know, you can say no Touro." Lonac told her as he leant over watching them walk into his room.

"You need to be more firm, he's a Tasian after all; they say that they can have any woman that they want." Zad'di said teasing him.

Lonac had a double bed with blue and white cross covers, a table on either side of the bed and double drawer wardrobes on one wall and facing was the window, which Leka walked over to and closed the curtains.

"Lights on." Leka ordered and the lights came on.

"So...um...what're you going to teach me?" Touro asked him nervously, she had never been alone in a bedroom with a man before beside from Renji, and she never actually felt this nervous perhaps awkward.

"What are you?" Leka asked her.

"What?" Touro said.

"Your race." Leka said.

"Oh...um...well...." Touro said not sure if she should tell him.

Leka though seemed to pick up on her nervousness and changed into his true form; she couldn't help think that he was very handsome, his black markings over his left eye and down the side of his face and neck disappearing underneath his clothes.

"I don't have to change as well do I...I don't seem to be able to change out of this form at the moment." Touro told him.

"No, that's fine; in fact it takes quite a bit of practice to be able to change your form." Leka told her. "It's not as though you could just change right now on the spot with never having done it before. And you have been locked in this form all of your life."

"Oh..." Touro said, but she didn't understand then how she could have changed her form if normally it took quite a bit of practice; unless that was her special talent, being able to change her appearance, she'd have to try it later on. "Well I'm human...with a bit of Tasian as well, I don't know how much though."

"Good, that should make things a little easier." Leka told her. "Tasian's and Ta'vian's are the strongest of all the Magical races in the galaxy, and the oldest. In a way, it just kind of comes naturally; what they learn is how to control their powers so not to hurt anyone or use their powers without realising."

"Okay..." Touro said.

"How about we start off with something simple to get you going." Leka suggested smiling slightly at her, which made her feel even more nervous. "We'll start with moving and lifting."

"At least it's not perception; I don't really do too well." Touro admitted.

"Why what did you do, put your hand in the fire?" Leka teased, but Touro blushed deeply. "Oh...well...um...this won't be as bad as that, at least you can't hurt yourself."

"I didn't hurt myself, I just couldn't figure out when it was real or not; but I didn't hurt myself." Touro told him.

"Really?" Leka said seemingly more interested in her now. "Well then, we'll do some more of that after this. Now to lift something or yourself, to levitate; Tollevare."

"Tollova..." Touro said.

"Tol...lev...are..." Leka said slowly for her pronouncing the word out simply.

"Tol...lev...are..." Touro repeated. "Tollev...are...Tollev...are... Tollevare...Tollevare..."

Everything in the room suddenly lifted a couple of inches off the ground, as Touro had been repeating the spell wondering what she had done and if she was meant to lift everything all at once.

"Well...um..." Leka said somewhat speechlessly.

"Hay, is there a reason why we're all off the ground in here?" Zad'di shouted through from the other room. "You said simple Magic, remember!"

Touro in a fit of panic lost her concentration and everything fell back down to ground in both rooms; Leka looked around the room and then back at Touro as though trying to figure her out.

"That can't have been your first time." Leka said.

"I'm sorry...I didn't mean to..."Touro told him. "I've never done this before...I wasn't really focusing on everything...actually wasn't focusing on anything at all, just trying to get the words right."

"Are you playing me?" Leka asked her. "Most people find it hard enough just to lift one thing, let alone everything in two rooms; without even trying."

"I assure you this is my first time." Touro told him, thinking that he didn't fully believe her.

"Well since you can do that, how about calling something to you?" Leka suggested, looking at her suspiciously.

Touro didn't see how she had learnt that spell already since she had no control over it, nor did she actually know how she had manage to do it in the first place; but he didn't seem to believe her at the moment that she had never done Magic before, and he definitely wouldn't believe her if she told him that she could change her appearance without knowing how to do it.

"To move something is mo 've 'a which is different than calling something to you, which is venadve." Leka told her. "Now this time just concentrate on one thing, or you could end up hurting yourself. Um...the pillow, think about moving the pillow; it's soft, so it won't hurt you."

Touro stared at the pillow trying to concentrate only on the pillow, she had to move just the pillow; move only the pillow. This time though before she had even said anything the pillows that she had been staring at just shot off of the bed, Touro looked at them on the floor and then back at Leka who looked just as surprised as she was.

"I don't think I did that...did I?" Touro said. "I was thinking about moving the pillows and then they just shot off the bed..."

"That's very good, I think you'll do just fine...why don't we leave it there for now though, hay." Leka said as calmly as he could. "Um...why don't we go back through to the others."

Leka rushed past her to the main room, Touro though was quite disappointed that she wouldn't learn anymore spells; she also wanted to know how come she could do those so easily making Leka worry and doubt that this was in fact her first time using Magic.

"I don't think she really needs lessons." Leka told the others. "She's fine..."

Touro walked back into the lounge behind him, Siren and Lonac seemed the most concerned but the others seemed more bothered about the match that was playing on the holo screen.

Nothing was mentioned until everyone had left, Touro didn't want to talk to Lonac about it but waited until they went to bed and her and Siren stayed up for hours talking about it; but neither of them could actually figure out how or why she would have such power, Siren told her that they would have to pick up some spell books before they left for her to practice on when they got back.

The desk stuck as it was bumped into and the boxes on top of it fell over spilling all of their contents over the floor, data sheet, pad and chips scattered across the floor of the office.

"Damn it!" Renji said angrily on the other side of the table. "As though I haven't got enough to do already."

Renji walked around his desk careful not to knock into anything else, the six screens behind him on the wall showing different parts of the senator's quarters; but these weren't of Senator Kentaro's apartment but someone else's.

He was just about to bend down and start to pick up the contents, when his computer started to beep, he stood up turning around looking at the screens but couldn't see anything going on in any of the rooms or corridors; so he made his way over to the other desk where the computer was beeping and turned the screen around to face him pressing the flashing button in the bottom corner.

The screen changed from black to that of Siren sat on the balcony in the city, Renji was quite surprised to see her calling him, since she had never done such a thing before.

"It took me a while to find you." Siren said calmly. "I didn't think that you would just give up on her like that, neither did she to be honest."

"My assignment with the Kentaro's ended when she joined the Fleet." Renji told her.

"You were only there for her?" Siren said surprised and then smiled at him suddenly. "Well then, I'll let you know that I'll keep a close eye on her as much as I can anyway."

"You still believe in her after what she did?" Renji asked her.

"I want to believe that she can be saved from all of this, one day, yes." Siren answered honestly.

"That day my come too late." Renji said. "As I was."

"I'll send you something, something to think nicely of her." Siren told him and pressed the screen on her side.

Renji received the file from her, making the whole screen change, it was a picture of Toria; she was laughing and smiling her long hair down her back over a white flowing dress being swept in the light sea breeze, he smiled slightly to himself as he touched the screen, his whole heart seemed to contract seeing her like this; she was so beautiful and innocent.

"I think she'll be able to be saved one day." Siren told him. "For now she just needs some space to figure herself out."

"Thank you." Renji said.

"I'll keep you updated shall I?" Siren told him before she logged off.

Chapter Fourteen

The library was quite busy with students studying for their mid-term exams. Kyo was making his way past a large group of fourth years, carrying a stack of books trying to get back to his table where Siren and Toria sat with their table already full of books, data sheet and pads. They had been studying for weeks now, but after all this was very important. Kyo dropping the books on the table in the only free space left startling them both.

"Did you need to do that?" Toria snapped at him.

"They were heavy." Kyo said as he sat down.

Toria just looked at him and then went back to her own work, she was working harder than everyone else wanting this more than everyone else.

"I think you're just a little too obsessed." Siren said.

"Of course I am, do you know what this will mean if I can get this posting?" Toria said. "I already got into the second year, straight off; so I'm not going to give up the chance to get a position on a ship even if it's just for a short while. As long as I make a good impression..."

"So that means you can't beat up your commanding officer." Siren said.

"No... but I can of any Magic that I come across." Toria said smiling slightly.

Both Kyo and Siren looked at her, it had been strange for the last six months to get to know this new Toria; as though they had met a whole new person and was learning everything about them for the first time.

It was still hard to believe sometimes when they heard her talking in public to others about her dislike of Magics and how she would fight during class, it was as though no one stood a chance against her; this was her own personal mission and no one was going to stop her until she had done as much as she could possibly do.

"I know it's hard to get these places but there's only five remember." Kyo reminded her. "And they are open to everyone from the second year to fourth year in all six academies throughout the galaxy."

"I know, you keep saying that my chances are slim...but I might have to do something about that." Toria said thoughtfully.

Siren looked at her not sure if she believed what she was hearing. "He wouldn't agree to do that, would he?"

"If it's what I really want, he would." Toria said smiling and then gathered up her things. "I better give him a call."

"Now?" Siren asked.

"I've already left it too long, and I want to keep him on my good side remember; I'll need his help in all of this as well." Toria said before she walked off leaving them staring after her.

She made her way through the library easily as everyone moved away from her not wanting to get in her way; well it seems as though she has already made quite a name for herself even in this short time, but she still had a very long way to go.

She made her way back to her quarters without being disturbed by anyone, she walked down the dimly lit corridor with the lights activating when she got close; finally she arrived at her quarters and went inside, she put her books down on her desk and activated her computer hoping that her father would still be up working late as normal.

It took a couple of minutes before her computer screen finally changed and her father was looking back at her, seemingly pleased to see her.

"Victoria, I'm pleased that you decided to contact me." Senator Kentaro said; he didn't have his normal formal robes on but a plain shirt. "It's always nice to hear from you."

"I'm sorry that I haven't contacted you recently, but I've been studying for the exams; there's a placement opportunity out of it." Toria told him.

"Oh yes, I've heard about that." Senator Kentaro said.

"I've been working really hard, I believe that I have a good chance; beside from being the youngest of course." Toria said leaning back in the chair looking somewhat disappointed. "I know it's hard with only five places open, and I'm probably thinking too highly of myself; but I am looking forward to it...it'd just be such a disappointment...you know working so hard and then...and then having it all taken away from you."

"I understand Victoria." Senator Kentaro said. "I believe in you, and that you'll do well. I'm sure that it'll go well, and when you get your results you can come home to celebrate for a while before you have to leave."

Toria smiled at him. "You think too much of me father."

"You are my daughter; of course I'll think that you're more capable than any of those other officers." Senator Kentaro told her. "Good luck."

"Thank you, and I'll call again soon." Toria said. "Oh...um...I was wondering about Renji...well I mean I know he hasn't come back..."

"I know you liked him dear, he was a good friend to you growing up; but the two of you are better off where you are now." Senator Kentaro told her. "I have new officers, it'll take you a while to get used to them, since you don't spend that much time here anymore; but at least you know Bernal."

Toria smiled. "Okay then, good night father."

"Good night." Senator Kentaro said and then logged off.

Toria sat in her chair hoping that she had said enough without actually saying what she wanted, but she knew deep down that her father had in fact always given her what she wanted and knew that he wouldn't fail her this time either; it's just a shame that she had to do it like this, but being a senator's daughter had its advantages.

She had been disappointed when she had heard that Renji had left, she really had thought that he would stay for her, but it looked as though she was the only reason why he had been staying as long as he had done; and since she wasn't really around anymore there was no point in him being there. She was sure though wherever he was that he would still be looking out for her. She couldn't explain why she felt like this, she just did.

She turned her head slightly and caught a glimpse of something in the mirror, she jumped to her feet knocking the chair over ready to fight, but again there was nothing there.

Toria slowly walked over to the mirror and looked into, but there was no shadow just her reflection and that of her room; was she going mad? Or was someone trying to contact her, through the mirror itself?

"I'm being paranoid." Toria told herself turning back around and began to unfasten her top, when she felt it again.

As she turned around to look over her shoulder she was thrown to the ground hard with someone on top of her breathing heavily, she kicked against him trying to break free but her legs were tied together Magically and then she felt her arms being pulled up, she tried to fight against it knowing that she couldn't be caught; with all of her strength she kneed the man in the chest and crawled out from under him still trying to break free of her restrains.

"You little brat." The man said angrily and swung his arm in her direction.

Toria was lifted up off her feet and across her small room into the wall, she used her arms to try and push herself off but the pressure was too much as the man walked over to her; she looked up at him finally, he had white patchy skin as though it didn't see much sun light and his eyes were black, everywhere there should be white, they were black, his hair was straggly and grey; his clothes old and worn as though he hadn't brought new in years.

"I'm glad that you put up a fight." The man said eyeing her up from head to toe, with this strange look that Toria had never seen before, but she didn't like it, it made her feel nervous and sick at the same time. "I have an offer for you..."

"Is this how you normally propose an offer to someone?" Toria asked bravely even though she was scared to death of what he might do to her pinned Magically against the wall.

"My master believes that you are ready to finally join us." He told her. "After you killed all those people...all those Magics."

"I'm not working for your master, I'm a Fleet officer...how dare you!" Toria said. "I want to fight the Magics, not work with them...or perverts like you..."

"Perverts like me?" The creature asked smiling slightly at her, then he stepped forward and reached out to touch her but pulled back at the last moment. "I'm not allowed to touch you...not in that way."

"I don't want anything to do with you or your master." Toria told him. "And stop watching me...I see you watching me through the mirror."

"Only someone with powers of their own can see the world within the mirror." The man said pleasantly. "My master's offer will remain open until you accept it, this remember is a friendly warning; the others aren't as nice as I am."

He looked her over one last time with his cold dark, unseeing black eyes before he turned around and began to fade away into nothingness as he approached the mirror and was gone, as soon as he had disappeared Toria fell to the ground looking around wildly for a moment before she jumped to her feet and grabbing the sheet off the bed and threw it over the mirror covering every reflected surface she could see.

He had been watching her for months or even for years, in her room getting changed, sleeping, doing everything; the mere thought made her feel sick to her stomach.

After that night Toria became awfully paranoid, wondering if every reflective surface had someone watching her; she stopped talking to her friends about what she was planning and got rid of every mirror that she owned.

She wasn't really bothered if anyone thought that she was acting strange, which many did because she seemed a little jumpy; strange and scary were quite a combination which for both, the rest of the students still wanted to stay well away from her.

Siren did try and talk to her but Toria kept blowing her off, so Siren gave it up for now knowing that there must be something going on for her to be acting like that, so she just decided that she'd wait until it all blew over.

Toria studied alone for the exams which she took, hoping that she would pass with or without her father's help; but in the end she would never know how she had gotten the position. The bigger problem was that she didn't know how to contact Ichigo without anyone finding out, or this guy who had been watching her; hoping when she got off the base and on a ship he wouldn't be able to watch her because she wouldn't be in a fixed position and then, hopefully be able to get him a message.

Toria walked down the corridor wearing her academy jumpsuit next to an older officer, he wasn't long out of the academy himself and this was his posting; he had short brown hair and blue eyes and Toria thought that he was quite handsome. She had been told at the briefing that he was called Harding and would be her personal tutor while she was here.

"You know the captain said that you're the youngest to ever get the training posting." Harding said.

"I was put up a year, when I passed the end of year exam." Toria told him. "I've been studying for both hoping to get a chance to do this."

Harding smiled slightly at her as they walked down the corridor towards the lift passing other officers who just ignored her, well she was a nobody to them, but that wasn't going to be for long.

"So, I was told that I would be with security; learning about the ship and away mission protocols." Toria said.

"Well, not anymore." Harding told her kindly. "On your record it looked alright...I mean you seemed capable...but well...the captain doesn't think that you're best suited to security."

"What?" Toria said stopping putting her hand up blocking his way. "Because I'm a girl, because I'm the youngest student he's ever had, because I was brought up as a lady in the senate court? Well then, it seemed as though I've been posted with the most stupidest captain in the Malarias Fleet history."

"You...you should keep your voice down...you'll get into trouble." Harding told her quickly looking around making sure that no one had heard her, no one seemed to have heard and even if they had they had totally ignored her.

"Idiots, the lot of them." Toria said walking off in a bad mood, this wasn't what she wanted; it was going to be even harder now to get the notice that she needed on this assignment. "So where am I being placed?"

"Engineering." Harding answered

"Great, at least my grades in the subject might go up." Toria said sarcastically hitting the panel to call for the lift.

"I am sorry." Harding told her kindly. "But truthfully, you don't really seem the type who belongs in security with those brutes."

Toria smiled at him. "That's because you think I don't look the type, not because I'm not...you don't know me."

"I'd like too." Harding told her.

"What?" Toria said startled by his statement. It had been the last thing she was expecting him to say to her.

"Why don't you come to mine tonight, for dinner I mean." Harding told her. "We can go over everything, and I can start to get to know you."

Toria blushed deeply feeling herself burning up, and knowing that she had to get it under control or something awful might happen; she stepped back away from him into the lift that opened for her and he stepped inside with her; this was awkward for her as this had never happened before.

"Well...um...I...don't know...I mean...well...um..." Toria said nervously.

"You can just come to have something to eat, so you're not on your own; it's hard when you first get posted somewhere not knowing anyone." Harding told her.

"Well, okay then." Toria said, her body still on fire, but had somehow managed to keep it under some kind of control.

"Engineering." Harding ordered.

The lift began to move, while Toria tried her hardest to calm down while he stared at her making her feel even more uncomfortable; she wished that the lift could go faster but it seemed to take forever and she herself could feel that the temperature was rising and see the sweat coming off of his face, she wasn't controlling her powers at all.

"There must be something wrong with the environmental controls..." Harding said wiping his face with his sleeve. "It is strange though, how it suddenly got really hot in here."

Finally the door opened into the busy engineering sections and Toria almost ran out of the lift the cooler air helping a little. Harding followed her out and grabbed the first person that walked past; an older man reading a data sheet.

"The environmental controls don't seem to be working in the lift; the temperature has gone up too high." Harding told him.

"The computer hasn't picked anything up." The man said as he went into the lift. It was still warm so he pulled the panel off and turned the lift off. "I'll get a work team on it...the chief's down there just finishing off handing the daily assignments out..."

"Thanks." Harding said.

Toria looked down the corridor where the man had pointed; the walls were covered in consoles showing different parts and systems of the ship, making sure that everything was operating correctly. As she walked past the console she tried to look at as many as she could, but there was just too much to take in all at once; it would take ages to properly get used to all of this.

Toria saw a group of people stood around a large squared console desk, probably the main console in the engineering section and these were the ones in charge of the different systems with the chief stood at the end; he looked about twenty years older than her, his dark hair was already grey and showing lines on his face.

"Thanks, that'll be all." The chief said.

The other officers began to walk away with their assignments talking quietly among themselves, Harding lead Toria over to the chief who didn't look at all pleased that he was getting one of the cadets assigned to him; though what he didn't know was that the feeling was mutual.

"Chief Tokon, this is Cadet Toria Kentaro." Harding introduced.

"Kentaro?" Chief Tokon said thoughtfully trying to remember where he had hard the name before.

"My father is Senator Ramiro Kentaro." Toria told him calmly.

"He's your father?" Chief Tokon said staring at her as though he wasn't sure that he believed her. "The senator?"

"He was yesterday when I spoke to him, unless something's happened in the last couple of hours and no one's been polite enough to tell me." Toria said pleasantly.

He didn't seem impressed by her sarcastic comment as he waved Harding away.

"Sir." Harding said before he left giving Toria a reassuring smile.

"You may think that you can say whatever you what, cause of your upbringing; but here you do as I say." Chief Tokon told her. "Is that clear?"

"Somewhat." Toria answered.

He smiled at her cruelly. "Why don't you go with Righton?"

A young thin man stopped walking past them with others behind him, they were all wearing dirty overalls and looked very tired; Toria smiled politely at her commanding officer before she left with Righton who didn't speak to her as they walked across engineering everyone keeping their distance from them, which Toria knew why because they smelled of something rotten. Toria had a bad feeling about this, and as they approached the rear of the engine room and the doors slid open Toria knew why they smelt so much; they had just entered the main core engine room, where the actual engine was.

"You didn't make a good impression on the chief." Righton told her as he picked up a hyper scrubber. "Clean."

"What?" Toria said.

"Clean." Righton repeated.

Toria locked the door to her quarters and was very careful not to touch anything as she began to undress in the middle of the lounge for the second week in the row. She couldn't believe that he was still making her do this; she stank of rotten sulfur and was covered in dirt and grime from the waste that the engines were giving off onto the circuits.

The dining table was untouched, still the same as when she had arrived, as she hadn't yet used it; though that didn't mean that she hadn't eaten, she had had quite a few meals with Harding who in fact seemed quite nice even though he was a Fleet officer.

She put her boots on the computer port ledge and then quickly took off her jumpsuit trying to keep her balance not wanting to fall over, that would mean that she would have to start cleaning the carpets from her uniform.

She stripped down and then placed it on top of her uniform wrinkling her nose at it, disgusted that she was being made to do this type of job; she was better than this and they were going to regret ever making her do it.

"Clean and repair uniform, then clean ledge." Toria ordered.

She walked past her suite and through to her bedroom naked, untying her hair letting it fall down her back; it didn't feel soft and smooth like it used to but harsh and greasy, she'd had enough. She walked past her bed which already had clean clothes laid out for her, which she had left that morning when she had showered.

She went through to the bathroom to shower, to scrub herself clean; she seemed to be spending longer and longer everyday in the shower just to get rid of the smell and dirt that was trying to stick to her skin.

Toria spent nearly half an hour in the shower, before she finally felt as though she was clean and got out wrapping a robe around herself and went back into her bedroom out of the hot steam-filled bathroom; she sat down at the top of the bed and pulled lifting her feet up as though didn't bother to re-arrange her robe which was now showing most of her legs, well it wasn't as though she was expecting anyone, she was all alone.

She picked up the data pad off the side table and smiled slightly to herself, cleaning hadn't been a complete waste of her time. In fact she had found quite a bit of information out like on their next assignment to a small Magical colony which she wanted to be apart; but at the moment with how things stood she wouldn't be a part of the engineering team that would go down to the surface, but hopefully by this time tomorrow her plans will be back on track.

Toria was nervous and excited all at once. This was going to be her first really big plan, if she could get through this then she knew that she had a chance to do the rest of it.

Toria arrived for her shift on time as normal unlike Righton and the rest of them. She didn't like the work that they were doing but they still had to get there on time; but she didn't really care that much especially today since Tokon had started the ship wide dialogistic, which meant that most of the ship's systems were just working at basic functions for the next couple of hours.

Toria walked. She wasn't allowed to go anywhere on her own, so like any other morning she started to study the wall consoles that were giving out readings of the ship's function and operating systems, telling you that everything was working properly; but that's when she saw it again, the third morning on the row.

"This is still there..." Toria started to tell the older woman next to her, with short bluish green hair.

"Like we told you every other morning, it's fine." The woman told her irritably.

"But the readings have changed, they've gotten higher." Toria tried to tell her. "Don't you think it's a little strange, that the power output has increased on a system that is normally stable?"

"Its fine, they're allowed to be out to this percentage." The woman told her dismissively before she walked off.

Toria frowned and turned back to the console. She knew that the woman was right, but it shouldn't have lasted for three days and even they should have done something about it before now. She watched the screen of the power flow to the conduction, they'd be taken off to basic functions in a moment when their dialogistic started fully; the level bar started to climb again slowly at first and then faster, the screen flashed before it burnt itself out and then a chain reaction started along the line of consoles, one after another exploded.

There was man behind her at the other console stood too close, she turned around just in time and dragged him to floor out of range of the explosion; he looked up at her white as ghost and nodded slightly unable to actually say anything to her as the red alert alarm sounded through the ship and the lights dimmed to an off-flashing red.

Toria scrambled to her feet jumping over the man ducking under the rents of hot smoke leaking out of the conduits, she could just make out Tokon pulling someone off of the main desk console; she made her way over to him.

"Sir...I..." Toria started.

"I'm busy!" Tokon shouted at her. "I need to find the problem...damn it...it seems to be coming from all over the ship...how the hell am I supposed to...?"

Another conduit exploded behind him nearly knocking him off of his feet, Toria was holding onto the edge with one hand while trying to access the main systems with her other to take the dialogistic off-line, believing that it would help.

"What're you doing?" Tokon demanded.

"Sir, we need to get the main systems back on line...the dialogistic..." Toria tried to explain.

"I know what I'm doing...damn brat..." Tokon said tapping the console trying to figure out where the problem emanated from, while Toria continued on the other side messing around.

"There've been too many systems burnt out, to disconnect it from here..." Toria told him. "It has to be done from the main engine room, but the temperatures already started to rise too quickly."

"What're you talking about?" Tokon asked her walking around to her side of the console, looking over the readings, the computer core temperature was steadily getting higher to a full-on reaction. "I don't believe it...how could I have missed something like that...?"

Toria walked off but he grabbed her.

"Where do you think you're going?" Tokon demanded. "Stay here and monitor the readings while I send a team in there..."

"They'll have to get suited up, it'll take too long...I've been working in there since I got here, I know the lay-out pretty well now." Toria told him. "As long as you have a med team waiting for me I should be alright."

She pulled her arm free and walked off as he just stared after her, she knew somehow that she wouldn't be hurt but she would have to at least fake it for now. Toria was actually kind of surprised that he didn't try again to stop her from going inside, but he just let her go; no one said anything to her as she forced opened the door just enough for herself to squeeze through so that it would shut as soon as she was through.

She could feel the heat of the room already and the door slowly opened for her as she prized it open with her bare hands and then squeezed through almost falling inside, she quickly straightened herself as the door slid shut; it was a lot hotter than she thought it was going to be and it was already making her feel light-headed, but she couldn't understand why, the heat had never really bothered her before. What if there was actually something wrong with her? But Toria didn't have time to think about that right now, she had to find the right outlet and turn the energy supply off to the conduits.

As she walked around the edge holding onto the rail for support, which itself was hot but she needed to hold onto something because her eyes were starting to unfocus.

"Pull it together...this is...supposed to be your thing." Toria told herself.

She pushed herself off the rail and into the console, the air smelt even more rotten than normal it was almost sickening; she tried to push that thought out of her mind while she concentrated rerouting the circuits while her eyes became more and more blurred, if she didn't do this then she might as well give up on it all, if she wasn't strong enough to withstand a little heat then she would be no good to anyone. It didn't matter though, her head was getting lighter and she fell against the console hitting several buttons before she fell heavily onto the hot metal platform.

Toria woke with a start almost falling off of the med bed, but Harding caught her jumping off of the stool next to her; she looked up at him and then around the room wondering what had happened and why she was in the med bay.

The med bay was actually quite busy with every bed full with someone injured upon it, with the doctors and nurses still rushing around treating people; the supply trolleys nearly empty from being used already on the patients.

"Toria, are you alright?" Harding asked her.

She looked back over at him and suddenly realised that he had hold of her hand. She quickly pulled it free and then realised that she wasn't actually burning up anymore in fact she seemed a little colder than normal; now she knew this wasn't good.

"I don't know...the last thing I remember is being in the computer engine core room...then everything went black." Toria told him as she pulled the off bluish blanket closer around her.

"You fixed it." Harding told her smiling. "Just before you passed out."

"Really?" Toria said feeling a little better after hearing that and lay back down.

"Tokon was in a lot of trouble trying to keep everything under control, they found out what caused it...the captain wants to speak to you when you're feeling up to it." Harding told her. "And also, tonight why don't you come around to mine...for something to eat, you shouldn't really be on your own after what happened."

"Thanks." Toria said shyly.

Even though it wasn't the first time that she would be going to his quarters for something to eat she still felt really nervous about it, she smiled slightly thinking that this must be what it really feels like to like someone; she had thought that she liked Renji but perhaps that was only because he was or had been the only guy in her life, perhaps it wasn't really love but more like a brotherly love.

Toria was a little worried though now, she had gotten the "all clear" from the doctors saying that she was fit for duty and now she had to go and see the captain; she just hoped that he hadn't figured her out, perhaps the doctors had when she was unconscious somehow, but then she thought that they wouldn't really be letting her walk around the ship freely.

She walked down the corridor towards the lift, noticing quite a few of the computer wall consoles had been blown out and started to imagine how bad it must be all over the ship; everyone seemed really busy, which they were because there was an awful lot of repairing to do.

The lift doors opened slowly and she stepped inside as she felt this sudden wave of dizziness, she tried to focus herself holding onto the wall as it passed, but she also knew that she needed to be looked over as well by a proper Magic doctor; the only problem was that she didn't in fact know any and couldn't remember the name of the man that Ichigo told her about. She wouldn't mind using the man if she could remember who he was, he was a friend of Ichigo's and he did check her after what had happened. This could be some sort of side affect to what they did to her.

The lift took a while to get to the bridge, but what surprised her was that it didn't stop on any other level; the doors finally opened out onto the bridge, it was even larger than her quarters. On the back wall next to the lift was a wall of consoles, which most of them were blown out. Another door facing, the weapons station in front of the consoles with three officers trying to get it fully operational. Just below the weapons' station was the captain and first officer's chairs, which at the moment both of them were empty; the navigation station seemed to be worse off than anything else she had seen so far, to the point that they were pulling it out completely and replacing the whole thing.

Toria just started to walk down to the front when she was stopped from behind a hand on her shoulder. She turned around a little startled by it to see the first officer; he was much taller than she was, dark hair which was already greying and grey pale eyes, he was a little big around the middle making it look as though his uniform was either too tight or belonged to another

"Sorry sir, I'm cadet Toria Kentaro." Toria told him standing to attention.

He nodded slightly and then walked past her and down the slope, but before they reached the bottom he turned towards a door that Toria hadn't been able to see from the lift; he pressed the square button on the panel and it beeped inside of the room.

"Come in!" A man said inside of the room, and then the door opened for them.

The first officer went in first and Toria quickly followed. She stood to attention in front of the captain's desk in the middle of the room trying not to look around since she had never been here before; on the wall behind the captains desk was a beautiful painting of a solar system which she had never seen before, seven planets with moons and the sun, but there was something else not a ship, but a creature flying through the system.

Toria couldn't help but stare at it, everything else in the room seemed to have faded away she didn't even notice that the first officer had left, and she was left alone with the captain who was watching her and her entranced outlook at his painting.

"It's beautiful isn't it?" The captain finally said breaking into her thoughts.

Toria tore her vision away from the painting and looked at the captain. He had a scar from his head over his right eye and down the side of his face, his hair was shaven and he wasn't really in his uniform but a vest top showing off his muscular arms.

Toria couldn't help but stare at him as well, she wanted to tell herself that he wasn't really what the captain should look like but the Malarias Fleet is really only after war and domination, so this type of captain should really be what she was expecting to see a lot more of; though she had to remind herself that some might not look it on the outside like she doesn't but it will still be there on the inside.

"I'm sorry sir." Toria said.

"Not at all, most are interested in the painting when they see it for a first time." Captain Jasp'erat told her. "It's of a Magical system long ago, before the war that they started with us. Looking at it you wouldn't believe that they were capable of deserving thousands of races, and using them all for their own purposes."

Toria had to fight the urge to say what she really wanted to, but instead said what she was meant to say. "The seemingly innocent ones are the worst; they're the ones that do the most damage."

"Yes, you are right." Captain Jasp'erat agreed, then waved his hand as though none of that mattered. "Well I don't really give a damn about them. I wanted to ask you what happened down there, a few of the officers mentioned that you noticed the levels rising but nothing was done."

"Well...um..." Toria said reluctantly as though she didn't want to get anyone in trouble.

"Come on...I need to know what happened." Captain Jasp'erat told her. "A lot of people are injured and my ship is dead in the water, if we were attacked now; we wouldn't stand a chance."

"I just mentioned...for the past three days that the levels seemed to be getting higher in the power conduits." Toria told him. "They were still within safety margins, that must be why no one listened to me...but today...they just got out of control when they were running the systems' dialogistic."

"Idiots the lot of them." Captain Jasp'erat said angrily. "The chief has lost his rank and position. It seems as though he wasn't really worth such a position. The other officers in the situation are also being dealt with accordingly; you...cadet will help with the repairs and will also accompany us down to Darslun. I want someone who looks at everything, who sees everything no matter how small the problem might be."

"If you think that I'm the right person sir, thank you; thank you so much." Toria said smiling gratefully for the opportunity.

"Make sure that you've studied up on the system before we arrive." Captain Jasp'erat told her.

"Yes sir." Toria said quickly.

"Dismissed." Captain Jasp'erat said waving his hand for her to leave now.

Toria bowed her head slightly and then turned on her heel and left, she couldn't believe how easy that was and just hoped that the rest of the mission would be this easy.

Toria reached out and pressed the button on the door which beeped inside. She stood nervously outside with her long hair down and wavy, almost in curls; she wore blue trousers with a short purple embroidered dress over the top of it. The door opened and Harding stood there, he had a white and grey shirt on with black trousers; he smiled at her and she shyly smiled back.

"You look beautiful." Harding told her.

"Thank you." Toria said. "And you look very handsome."

"Come in." Harding told her, stepping aside so that she could enter.

Toria walked past him and went inside of his quarters which were basically like hers except that he had more personal belongings because he was posted on board the ship, as she was only here for a couple of months and they were already starting their second month; this wasn't the first time that she had come over, but had been coming over a couple of times a week since she arranged to come on the ship.

There was a problem though, they both liked each other; but every time that he got close to kiss her she moved away from him. Toria was a little afraid of how off she had been feeling lately, her powers seemed to be all over the place and she just didn't trust herself not after what she did to Renji; she liked him and didn't want to hurt him, but unless she could figure out what was wrong he might not wait around forever to at least get a kiss from her and he was a grown man, this kind of behaviour kind of really showed in a way that she really was just a child.

"I got us a bottle of wine." Harding told her.

Toria was a little surprised. It wasn't as though she had never had any before but she was still under age.

"Just a little mind, I don't want to get into trouble and you're going down to Darslun in the morning." Harding told her.

"I guess so, just a little then Kole." Toria said as she walked over to the sofa under the view port which overlooked the planet below, the atmosphere brown and orange dusty clouded the planet's surface from view; she had found out that it was because of all the mining that was done down on the planet's surface and how it was extracted.

Harding opened the bottle of wine at the table which was already set for the two of them with lit candles. He poured two small glasses and then carried them over; he handed one to Toria which she took and then he sat down next to her.

"So are you nervous about your first away mission?" Harding asked her.

"A little yes of course, but also excited." Toria told him. "I know that I've had a long time to prepare for this because of all the damage the ship took, and that normally I wouldn't have so long to prepare; but I was glad in away, so that I could fully study everything about this world and the system as well."

"To be honest, I've noticed that all you do in your spare time is study." Harding told her.

"Well, I've still got a lot to learn." Toria told him and then took a sip of the wine, it was dry but not too dry, but a little fruity as well. "This is nice. Anyway, I like it here; being out here doing something to help. But when I go back, I've still got years to go..."

"I don't want you to go back either." Harding told her putting his glass of wine down on the coffee table and taking Toria's glass off her as well. He reached up and touched her face softly with the tips of his fingers.

Toria felt his fingers against her skin, for a brief moment they felt so soft and gentle before they burnt into her skin making her jump back away from him; her face was burning red as though she was blushing deeply.

Harding just stared at her wondering if he had done something wrong again, as she kept doing this every time.

"I...I'm sorry...perhaps...um..." Toria tried to say, but she just didn't know how to get out of this without offending him again. All she seemed to do is keep running away when really she didn't want to; he wasn't like the rest of them even though he was an officer in the Fleet, perhaps in time she could earn his trust enough to tell him everything but if she carried on like this then it wasn't going to go anywhere at all.

"Toria...I don't want to push you into anything you don't want to do; but you need to know that I like you, I like you a lot." Harding told her.

"I know, I like you as well." Toria told him. "It's not...well...truthfully, I've never actually dated before."

"Oh." Harding said leaning back as though he understood now. He smiled to himself. "Okay, that's fine...slowly, I can do that. But you need to sit back down and relax a little; I won't jump you...not until you're ready anyway."

Toria smiled shyly at him still quite red in the face.

"So no pressure." Harding said to himself making Toria laugh at him as she sat back down. "Well I don't really want to put you off guys now do I?"

Toria felt a little more relaxed with him now that he kind of understood why she wanted to go slow, but she couldn't understand why it had hurt so much when he had touched her. She had wondered if he had felt the same thing but she was sure that he would have said something to her about it; she tried to put it out of her mind for the rest of the night now that there was no pressure whatsoever, at least for the moment.

The wind blew around them as they gathered up their supplies, the dirt off the ground getting everywhere, hitting the goggles which they wore over their eyes to protect them from the storms that the planet was so susceptible to.

The dozen man-away-team was stood outside of the main building carrying the supplies through the open door, the only thing that they could properly see because of the light that was coming from inside. It was hard to see anything, as it was so dull and with the storm blowing all the dirt around wearing the goggles didn't really help or make you want to look up and look around at your surroundings; though there wasn't really much to see anyway just a mass of nothing behind them and the main mining building in front.

Toria struggled through the door with the wind at her back and two heavy cases, one in each hand; she carried them over to the officer talking to Captain Jasp'erat who had his back to her, but she felt somehow that she knew him even though she hadn't met him yet.

"Oh yes, this is cadet Kentaro; you can use her." Captain Jasp'erat told the man.

He turned around to face her finally, but she couldn't hide her surprise to see him; because she did know him, well she had only met him a couple of times but she still knew him.

"This is Commander Delky." Captain Jasp'erat told her.

"It's a pleasure to meet you sir." Toria said as calmly as she could, even though a part of her was excited to see him.

She couldn't wait for them to be alone so that she could talk to him, but there was something different about him that she couldn't put her finger on, she just shook it off as nothing because they all had to be different when they were playing the part of Fleet officers.

"This is quite a treat for you, you're actually getting to see what you'll be helping us to do." Delky told her. "Why don't I show you to the labs where we've been having our problems and then I'll show you around?"

"Thank you sir." Toria said.

Captain Jasp'erat didn't seem to think that there was anything else for him to do, so he just walked off without even saying another word to either of them to check on the rest of his men; Delky lead Toria away to the right past the security point and over to the white corridor which was quite a contrast to the rest of the place that was grey.

They walked down the white corridor that was lined with doors, Toria hoping that it wasn't far as the cases seemed to be getting heavier;

they turned right down another corridor which looked just as long as the last one, but Toria thought that was because everything was white and the lights seemed so bright, you couldn't judge the distance of anything properly.

Toria stopped, she had to just for a moment to put down the cases and flex her fingers; Delky though didn't stop to see if she was alright but carried on walking. Toria was sure that he wasn't normally like this, even though she didn't really know him very well; she told herself that it must be because he was an officer, so she picked up the cases and quickly went after him.

He stopped finally outside of a door and waved the palm of his hand over where a door panel normally would have been, but at first Toria couldn't see anything and then when she got closer she could just make out a hand scanner.

"Do the Fleet often use things with Magical properties?" Toria asked him.

He didn't answer her straight away but went into the lab, Toria followed him into the room; there were consoles on the walls, tables with equipment all over them. At the back of the room in cages were animals, small ones and a few just a little bigger; Toria walked further into the room staring at the animals, not sure that she wanted anything to do with what they were doing here but she couldn't back out now.

Delky finally took one of the cases off of her and lifted it up onto the lab table, he opened the case and inside of it was medical equipment; this made Toria even more worried about what was really going on in these labs.

"So...um...what are all these thing's for then?" Toria asked him.

"There's still a great deal that we don't actually know about Magic and the people who can use it." Delky told her. "That's what this place is for, we have plenty of Magics to study; and it's not as though we won't get replacements."

"Replacements?" Toria asked.

"For the ones that can't work anymore, there are still plenty of Magics out there; one day we'll get them all." Delky told her and then looked over at her directly, that's when she noticed his eyes they seemed glazed over.

"Are you alright?" Toria asked him.

"I'm fine." Delky answered and started to unpack the equipment.

Toria wasn't sure what to do except carry on with what she was supposed to be doing. She lifted the other case up using her leg for support and then slid it onto the table and opened, there was even more equipment and data pads; one of them caught her eye titled Reprogramming.

"What's reprogramming?" Toria asked him.

Delky didn't answer her, in fact it was more like he hadn't heard her question. He just carried on as though she hadn't said anything at all.

"What are they hoping to be able to do with the Magics?" Toria asked him. "I mean, they want to win the war...I mean...we want to win the war...but how can we do that 'cause they'll always be fighting back."

"Not if they don't want too." Delky answered. "Not if they're told they don't have to."

"I don't under..." Toria started and then she suddenly understood what he meant and what reprogramming was. "But that can't be done on such a massive scale."

"Not yet." Delky told her. "But with what's going on here, it shouldn't be much longer."

Toria was horrified. She hadn't been able to concentrate on anything all day, just the idea that they would be able to control Magics on a massive scale, and she had no idea what to do; she was basically in the middle of nowhere with no resources and her powers weren't working properly, not that she knew how to use them properly. But she had to do something, just what she didn't know; she turned the corner and stopped when she heard a group of men talking.

"So you know when?" A familiar voice asked.

Toria was sure that she knew who it belonged to.

"Yes." Delky answered stiffly.

Toria risked looking around the corner to find out who he was talking to, she couldn't believe it; it was Lonac with two other's that she didn't recognise.

"Good, I'm glad that you're here." The man on Lonac's right said, he was a little shorter with brown hair brushed back.

Delky nodded slightly and then walked off without another word, none of them seemed to think that this was strange, except for Toria who couldn't help herself; she changed her appearance and walked out and down to them as Touro.

"This is a restricted area, only Fleet officers are allowed here." Touro told them.

Lonac turned around surprised by the sound of her voice, the others looked ready to attack if they needed to but Lonac held up his hand to tell them to hold off.

"Touro, what're you doing here?" Lonac asked her.

"I got the academy placement program." Touro told him. "So what's up with Delky?"

"What're you talking about?" The brown haired man asked her eyeing her up. He didn't seem to trust her, as he of course didn't know her.

"So you noticed as well." The other man said.

"His whole manner seems to have changed and he's so stiff." Touro said. "And his eyes, did you notice his eyes?"

"Yes." The man said.

"What're you saying; you think that they got to him?" Lonac said not wanting to believe it. "He's strong; he'd fight them all the way."

"What if it didn't matter how much you fought, they could still get to you." Touro said and then it all came together. "You need to step up your plans, I'll find out for sure about Delky staying away from the other student here...and...um...deal with any problems on this end. How quick can you get out of here?"

"We've already done half our mission." The brown haired man told her. "Two hours tops."

"Right, so when were you supposed to go ahead with Delky's plan?" Touro asked them.

"Just as the morning shift was starting, when the workers were switching over." The other man told her.

"That's great, that gives me quite a bit of time actually." Toria said. "I'll come and visit next time you play Lonac, see ya."

"I play as well, Ze-Siro." The brown haired man told her, sounding a little annoyed that she didn't know who he was.

"Ignore him; he thinks that all the pretty ladies should know who he is. I'm Rui-Lin; good luck." He told her.

"And to you as well." Touro said before she walked off the way that she had come from, feeling a little better now that she had a basic plan; she stopped suddenly and turned back around. "Can I ask a small favour, could you make me an appointment to see a doctor when I come and visit...it's nothing serious...I just want a check up to make sure?"

"Yeah sure...are you sure you're...?" Lonac started.

"I'm fine, it's just I never got a chance when I was staying with my cousin." Touro told him. "With everything that's happened, I..."

"I understood." Lonac told her.

"He's a big softy really, isn't he?" Ze-Siro teased him.

Touro smiled slightly before she walked off leaving them to finish off their mission and for her to start on hers finally. Right so all she had to do was figure out how she was going to get rid of the lab without it looking as though she had anything to do with it, and also how was she supposed to help Delky with whatever they've done to him; firstly she had to find out if he could be helped enough to actually get off of the planet safely. After she had set up the base, she would have to confront him and see how he would react to her.

She changed back to her normal self knowing that it wasn't really a good idea walking around as someone else, though she just hoped that Lonac and the others didn't check up on her because they wouldn't find anything at all about her; but that gave her an idea which she would have to do when all this was over with, she'd have to at least make a basic record of her other self incase the others did actually check up on her, they were after all at war and didn't or rather couldn't just trust anyone that they met.

Toria walked up the corridor to the control room, she had been asked to look everything over to make sure that everything was running properly so she might as well at least do that and get a few ideas of how to destroy the labs at the same time. She didn't see anyone the whole time, when she reached the room she waved her hand over the scanner twice because the first time she missed; she really did need to see a doctor when she had time, she was sure that this wasn't normal.

She entered the computer room, the walls covered in consoles which gave you the complete layout of the labs and also of the mine and mining quarters.

Toria studied them for hours trying to figure out how she could connect the whole place, when it finally dawned on her; the ore that they were mining was kept at a regulated temperature because it was highly dangerous in its natural state when it was over-heated, she had read the reports of the accidents they had during the summer months here and how many miners have been killed.

There were six holding pounds for the minerals not wanting to keep them altogether incase something happened, which of course was the wise thing to do; but it also helped Toria with her plan as well to get the whole of the lab. If she could set the temperature gauges simultaneously to start going up so that it doesn't set the alarms off until it was too late, but that would be too slow.

She went over to the main console and logged in to find out about the temperature ranges, they seemed pretty normal not having many problems with them only when the doors were opened; when the door is opened the computer starts changing the temperature of the room, but what would happen if the door didn't close but the computer thought that it had closed? This could be it, she carried on working hoping that Lonac and others had finished and were well on their way by now; it was all up to her now.

Toria had been at it for hours trying to reprogram the system without leaving a trail that she was up to something. It had taken her much longer than she thought it was going to take; she knew that she had to have it done by the time that Delky came for her and she still hadn't had a chance to confront him to see if he was still in there somewhere fighting to break their control.

The door opened behind her startling her suddenly as she pressed the last button just in time as Delky and several officers walked in behind him.

"You've been studying in here all night?' Delky asked her.

"Yes, I was looking over the storage systems wondering how you controlled the temperatures." Toria told him honestly, she didn't see why she should lie considering that was what she was supposed to be doing anyway.

"Yes, why don't I show you around then?" Delky told her stepping aside so that she could leave the room and leave an officer to monitor the controls. "If you're interested, why don't I show you the storage rooms myself?"

"That's great." Toria said, it wasn't really what she wanted to do straight away but it would actually help in the long run. "So commander, have there ever been any problems with the storage?"

"Most systems have a few problems of course when they first start up, but to be honest the system's done quite well." Delky told her.

"What about the temperature though, isn't it hard to keep it under control when you have to keep going in out when the temperatures in both rooms are so different?" Toria asked him as Captain Jasp'erat arrived looking quite pleased about something. "I mean, doesn't hot air interfere with the room temperature?"

"Only for a couple of seconds when the door is first opened." Delky answered. "Then the computer begins to balance the temperature out, then it returns to normal once the door is closed once more."

"It always reads if the doors are closed properly, how often do you run tests to make sure that everything is working properly?" Toria asked him.

"I assure you that everything here is working how it should be." Delky told her irritably.

"So you don't actually run system checks?" Toria asked him, this was what she wanted to know and what she wanted the captain to know as well.

"There is no need to run system checks like you do on board star ships." Delky told her dismissively.

"Because you always have someone sat at that computer monitoring the system, so they would know if the doors were open or closed even if it didn't read on the computer?" Toria asked him.

Delky stopped suddenly. "Is there something you're getting at here?"

"Yes, I was just going to suggest that you put camera's in the entrance rooms to the storage rooms; just so you know..." Toria told him.

"It would make sense." Captain Jasp'erat agreed. "I'll have a team help with that later. But now these Magics...I'm glad to see that you came through."

"Magics?" Toria asked sounding confused. "He came through with what?"

"Oh yes, this would be your first time working alongside a Magic." Captain Jasp'erat told her pleasantly. "He's been working here undercover, but they found him out when he tried to smuggle out the research that they were doing here. They used it on him, took a couple of weeks from what I was told; but they got him. Turned his friends in...we're going to get them now."

Toria didn't know what to say, Delky didn't seem to care on the surface and she couldn't sense anything from him that he might try and do something to help them; the only problem now is that it is going to look as though he betrayed them because they hopefully listened to her and were long gone.

Captain Jasp'erat pushed the end door open grabbing the goggles off of the wall and handing them out, Toria looked out over the wind-swept landscape of people slowly walking almost dead of their feet, and others walking the other way as though reluctantly to go but still somehow carrying on. They walked out the wind blowing the dirt up scarring their skin but their eyes were protected, Toria remembered that there was a storage room to their left and looked over at it.

"Isn't that one of the storage rooms?" Toria asked.

"You can have a look, after we've gotten the Magics," Captain Jasp'erat told her.

"They should be here somewhere, trying to make a pass for him." Delky told them.

A security officer ran over to them somehow able to see them through all of the dirt being blown about.

"Sir, we haven't been able to find the Magics...and sir...the Magic he told us that they would come for..." The officer told him. "We can't seem to find him...perhaps it's because there's so many of them, or they've already been and gone."

"Well now, I've got to give you credit if you really did pull that off." Captain Jasp'erat said pulling his blaster out of the harness off of his thigh. "Why don't you tell me honestly where they are?"

Toria stepped back away from Delky, it's not that she wanted to abandon him it was just that she couldn't really do anything to help him only hope that her plan would still work.

"I spoke to them, this was when they were supposed to be doing it." Delky told them.

"Well they're not here." Captain Jasp'erat said.

Toria could feel heat on her back, it wasn't much but it still felt strange; she turned around and walked off in the direction of where it was coming from, the storage room doors were open and she could actually feel the heat coming from inside. That wasn't really how hot she had actually wanted them to get, not yet anyway; she ran back around as quickly as she could.

"Sir, the storage room..." Toria said.

"Not now!" Captain Jasp'erat shouted at her.

"But sir..." Toria started but was cut off as the alarm sounded, he finally looked over at her and she told him calmly. "It's going to blow."

"What?" Captain Jasp'erat said.

Toria reached for Delky but he grabbed her and pulled her into him and pulled his own blaster out pointing it at her, she couldn't believe it he was actually going to use her as a hostage; the captain didn't seem to care what happened to her by the look on his face.

"I want a transport and your word..." Delky started.

"She's just a cadet." Captain Jasp'erat told him. "Not even worth the trouble."

"Actually I am." Toria said and elbowed in the chest making him drop his blaster, she kicked it out of his reach. "Sir we don't have time, the alarm means that this storage point is going to explode."

Captain Jasp'erat smiled at Delky cruelly before he pressed his com-unit. "Three to transport aboard."

"Aye sir." The man in the transporter room answered.

Toria focused all of her remaining energy to the explosion, all of her will to protect her kind but to destroy the lab; she could feel herself being pulled away too soon but she had no choice and just hoped that she had done enough as she was transported back on board the ship. They appeared in the transporter room, the man behind the console looked deathly white staring at the three of them and then slumped over.

"Useless the lot of them." Captain Jasp'erat said angrily as the door opened and his first officer and medic's rushed in. "What's going on?"

"You're alright?" He asked.

"Of course I am." Captain Jasp'erat answered.

"It...the lab just exploded..." He told them. "From the first explosion there was a chain reaction, there's nothing left just a crater in the ground."

"What?" Toria said and just slumped to the ground.

"I want a full investigation of what happened down there, she can head it...seeing that she noticed there was something wrong." Captain Jasp'erat said nodded at Toria on the ground beside of him not listening to what he was saying but hoping that she had really done the right thing and it hadn't somehow been messed up.

Chapter Fifteen

Toria sat in the high back chair, almost drifting off the data pad in her hand which she had been reviewing about the labs of Darsslun, but she still hadn't been able to find anything to say what had happened down there; she had been awake for two days straight and was finally starting to feel the need for sleep, especially as her powers hadn't recovered either.

Her lure to sleep was helped by the fact that she had also been working all alone on this research, they had even given her her own office with a desk that she was sat at and computer consoles that could study the surface of the planet and analyse them all from the comfort of this room; but the loneliness just kind of made the lure to sleep even more, as the data pad slip from her hand and she finally drifted off.

...Touro walked down the brightly-lit corridor, the lights were on overhead and the sun was shining in through the door behind her and several open office doors along the corridor also. There were other officers going about their duty, but they weren't part of the Malarias Fleet but these officers were Tasian's and Ta'vaian's; she was kind of unsure about which uniform they were wearing, the women wore a long flowing white and gold skirt and a matching bodice and attached sleeves, the men wore a white suit trimmed in gold.

She noticed a few people stare at her as she walked down the corridor, but she didn't really know why and looked down at herself she was in fact dressed like they were; it didn't make her feel uncomfortable but actually more like herself as though this uniform felt more right on her than that of the Malarias Fleet uniform. She smiled to herself that there was still hope for her.

Touro started to slow down as she was reaching her destination, when the door was suddenly flung open hitting the wall which echoed throughout the corridor; a young man with long red crimson hair walked out with black Ta'vaian markings on his face over his forehead and the back of his neck, the only thing was that she couldn't make out his face clearly but she knew him somehow. She could feel herself burning up as she just stood there staring at him as another man joined him, they both stared at her until finally his friend dragged him away.

Touro tried to shake off the burning feeling that he had caused, as she went into the office; she stood to attention in front of the commander's desk while he finished his work and finally looked up at her. He had shoulder-length brown hair which fell partly over his face as it wasn't tied back, his eyes seemed a little cold but there was also warmth in there hidden away; he was very handsome still even though he was much older than herself, but Tasians' did have a very long life span.

"Touro Toria Illiania, reporting from Filort in the Rigeant system." Touro told him handing her transfer papers over.

"Thank you." He said as he took the papers off of her but didn't look at them, instead he stared at her for a while as though he knew that she wasn't who she said she was and was trying to see through her disguise, making her feel quite uncomfortable.

"Have we met before?" He asked her finally.

"No sir, I'd remember if we'd met." Touro said pleasantly

"Really?" He said trying to hide a smile. "Well yes, these seem to be in order even though I wasn't informed of any transfers. So you have the unlucky posting of ....'s team, the man who just left this room before you entered. He is to put a team together and train them, even though he is only the same rank as yourself; there are six teams in total and they will be competing against one another for the next two years........ will fill you in on the full details as it's his job as the commander of his team."

"Yes sir." Touro said wondering why she had to be on his team, even though she was a little pleased that she would get to work with him...

Toria woke with a start, she looked around the room trying to remember what she had been doing before she fell asleep; but the dream was bothering her, she didn't hear whose team she was going to be placed on but she didn't seem to mind being put on his team. And also the commanding officer kind of looked familiar as though she had seen him before, but she was sure that she would remember if she had met someone as handsome as him and a Tasian as well; the name though she had given him wasn't in fact her name. She was using the name Touro whenever she changed into a Magic, but Toria wasn't really her name but what every one called her for short instead of Victoria; the family name she had given wasn't her own name either but Ichigo's name. She was related to him but why would she have given his name?

Toria found it hard to keep her mind on the job after that so decided to go and visit Kole to get her mind off of everything, maybe it was because she was over-tired and worked that she was having such strange dreams.

She walked up the corridor reading the data pad of the readings from the site, or rather the crater in ground; all there was left to do was to confirm that it was a malfunction and not foul play. They had left the planet and system a couple of days before and met with another ship that wanted the results of their report.

Toria was getting very nervous about the whole thing, even though she had been over it several times and hadn't been able to find anything that would suggest that Magic was involved; see they wanted to rule that out but she needed to know that it was there to tell her that she hadn't killed all those people.

"Miss Kentaro." A woman said behind her kindly.

Toria stopped and turned around to the woman who smiled at her, she was human with shoulder-length brown hair and was a couple of years older than her though looking at her you wouldn't know that; she wore a Malarias Fleet uniform but instead of trousers she wore a pencil skirt.

"Maya, sorry I was in a world of my own." Toria said smiling back.

"That's alright, I know that you're putting a lot of effort into this report; it is your first official report and very important as well." Maya said. "So how's it going?"

"Well, I've done it to be honest; I was just going over everything making sure that I haven't missed anything out." Toria told her.

Maya smiled at her as she reached her hand out for the data pad. "I'm sure it's fine."

"Yeah, you're right." Toria said handing the pad over. "It's like you said, I guess I just want to make sure that it's alright."

"So did the Magics have anything to do with it?" Maya asked her.

"No, I didn't think that I would find anything to be honest; it's not their sort of thing." Toria told her. "I mean from what I've read, they would be killing too many of their own; and they to also need the ore that was being mined there."

"You're right of course." Maya said.

Toria noticed that she didn't look her normal cheerful self for a moment, as if the thought of all those people being killed saddened her; and then as though it hadn't happened she was smiling again.

"I'll let you get on." Maya told her. "You were going to see Kole weren't you?"

"Guilty as charged." Toria said smiling.

"Have a nice night then." Maya said before she walked off.

"Thanks." Toria said and carried on towards his quarters.

Toria pressed the door panel which beeped inside of his quarters and waited for him to tell her to enter, but there was nothing; disappointed that he wasn't there she was about to leave when the door opened and he was stood there smiling at her.

"I thought that you might come over tonight." Harding said.

"Am I that predictable?" Toria said as he stepped aside for her to enter.

The table was all laid out for the two of them, she really did enjoy this special treatment that he gave her, making her feel that she was wanted for herself and not for anything that he could gain from her, which is all she wanted.

"So I take it that you've finished your report?" Harding asked her as he pulled her chair out for her to sit down.

"Just, I gave it Maya on the way over here." Toria told him.

She watched him open the bottle of wine and pour them both a glass each, she of course only had a small glass; she wasn't really in the mood to drink a lot of it anyway incase it just sent her straight to sleep.

After they had finished their meal they took their drinks over to the sofa and sat down to finally relax, Toria leant back while Kole just stared at her making her feel very nervous and a little hot, she could actually feel herself blushing.

"The captain seems impressed with you, perhaps he'll let you stay a little longer." Harding said.

Toria looked up and over at him. "Am I allowed to do that, since I'm still at the academy?"

"I think so, I mean as long as you're still studying; and you'll be getting first-hand experience as well out here." Harding said. "And you'll get to stay here with me."

Toria smiled shyly at him as he leant forward and softly caressed her face, they both moved forward together until finally their lips met softly at first and then more passionately. For a moment everything seemed to melt away, and it was only the two of them; but it only lasted for a moment before her whole body felt as though it was on fire and she felt something explode out of her knocking her back. She still saw it though, Kole was lifted out of his seat and thrown across his quarters and into the wall; he fell to the ground smoking and shaking.

Toria rushed over to him, she bent down to help him but he just moved away from her; fear and horror etched into his face, but there was also pain as he continued to shake.

"Kole..." Toria tried but he pulled away from her again.

"Stay...away...Magic..." Harding said as he tried to reach for his com-unit on his wrist.

Without thinking Toria grabbed his wrist and pulled it off, it just melted away in her hand; she couldn't believe what she had just done. She fell back pushing herself away from him looking around the room wondering what to do. She had to do something or he'll tell everyone what she is.

"I'm sorry." Toria said as she got to her feet and ran out of his quarters trying not to bump into anyone and trying to stay calm, which was quite hard to do when her body kept trying to run which drew too much attention to herself.

She finally stopped and leant against the door frame as she banged on the door, but they weren't answering quick enough so she melted the panel and went inside; Maya just stood there staring at her somewhat surprised to see her and so upset.

"I didn't know who else to turn to." Toria told her. "I don't know why...but I kind of felt as though I could trust you...I need your help..."

"Has something happened, did you have an agreement with Kole?" Maya asked her moving towards her but Toria moved away from her.

"I didn't mean too, you need to understand that...I couldn't control it...I wouldn't really hurt him..." Toria told her almost in tears.

"I don't understand, hurt who?" Maya asked concerned.

"He hates me...I...I don't blame him...he's in his quarters." Toria said sounding as though she had just been defeated terribly. "I never meant to hurt him."

"Okay...um...you stay here...I'll go check on him." Maya said and then rushed out leaving Toria alone in her quarters.

Toria had just sat in Maya's quarters all night, wondering what was going on with Kole and wondering why no one had come back to arrest her for being a Magic; all she could think of was what they could do to her, she didn't really have clue of how they dealt with Magics that they find out have become officers, well except for Delky and she was sure that they didn't do that to them all. But then she wondered, what if they did; no one would really know if you had switched sides until it was too late and it wasn't as though she could ask anyone for help since she had told them all that she didn't want anything to do with Magic and had supposedly turned against them all. Part of her wanted Renji, she always thought of him whenever she was in trouble; at the moment she didn't care about how much he would shout at her just as long as he could make it all better, but would he help her considering that she had hurt him like this as well; even though he said she hadn't she was kind of felt as though he had lied to her.

The door finally slide open and Toria looked up expecting security teams to take her away, but it was just Maya who came inside and the door closed again behind her; she looked a little tired with black rings around her eyes, she sat down facing Toria.

"I...I didn't mean too." Toria told her again.

"I believe you." Maya told her. "He's been transferred onto my ship, I'll have him picked up so that no one will find out what you are."

"You're really helping me?" Toria asked her a little unsure. "So...so you really are...?"

"Yes." Maya answered. "You need to be very careful. Which means that this sort of thing should never happen again, there won't always be someone around to help you out; remember that. But also, why should we trust you as well?"

"I...I guess I understand..." Toria said as the real meaning of her words hit her, it wasn't just relationships in the Fleet but outside it as well; with her powers that she couldn't control, how was she ever supposed to be with anyone?

It was almost a month later and Toria was still finding it really hard to control her powers, as there had been several small explosions on board the ship; no one had managed to trace it back to her but they were putting it down to the fact that they had somehow managed to get a Magic spy on board and they were trying to sabotage their ship.

Toria was in charge of investigations, which weren't too bad, as she could say it was anything that she wanted.

She had only been partly pleased when the captain had approached her and asked her to stay on after her training period was over, part of her had wanted to go back to the academy and be with her friends and hide away for a while for what she had done and what she needed to do; but she forced herself to carry on, she had started now and still had a long way to go.

It was going too be even harder than she thought it was going to be, but the worst part was over; she was sixteen years old and would be seventeen in a couple of months and already had a place aboard a Fleet ship, without having to go all the way through the academy, she couldn't waste this chance.

Siren had been worried about her especially after she had told her what had happened to Kole, Toria had wanted to take some leave so that she could go to a doctor but if she left too early than she could miss something important and the captain might change his mind about her.

Toria was going through the damage reports that all the sections had given her, she was making sure that they were done properly and that she could put the data into her simulation with the consoles that she had in her office did; she didn't care that some of the other officers didn't like the fact that they had to report to a cadet, she was only doing her job at the end of the day. She was just inputting the last of the reports into the computer when the door beeped.

"Come in." Toria said.

The door slid open and Toria turned around to see who it was, the first officer Commander Slater; he was carry a data sheet and looked just as unpleasant as he normally did and seemed to have managed to put a little more weight on.

"The captain has a treat for you." Commander Slater told her and handed her the data sheet.

Toria took it off of him and read the top of it, but it didn't really mean anything to her.

"I don't understand, Ruc've, O'ca'tis and Losendian; aren't they all solar systems?" Toria asked him.

"Yes, they're Magic systems; or rather kind of like slave systems now." Commander Slater told her. "The only one which is still kind of free is the Losendian system, but they give us slaves."

"Okay, but how is this a treat?" Toria asked him a little confused.

"He's taking you down with him, make sure everything's okay; and you can also relax a little yourself." Commander Slater told her smiling slightly.

This worried Toria even more, she had never actually seen him smile before. "Relax, how?"

"We'll be visiting the pleasure parts of the system." Commander Slater told her, but she just looked blankly back at him. "You'll find out soon enough, we arrive the day after tomorrow; so better get studied up. The prices are in there also."

"Prices?" Toria asked, but he didn't say anything else, he just turned and left, leaving Toria alone and very confused about what had just happened.

Toria went back to her desk to read through the report that he had given her, and to find out just what he meant by a pleasure world and why she would want to check out the prices; what would she want to buy on a slave world?

She also wondered if there could be anything that she could do while she was there to help them, she knew that she couldn't keep doing things in secret and had to start making a bigger show, that it was her who was doing all this; but she had to be careful, she had to make them think that she did it for the best and not just to kill them, this would take more planning than the others.

The only problem was that she only had less than two days to come up with something; she just hoped that she could do it in time.

She had spent a couple of hours reading up on the Ruc've system, they had a couple of mining colonies throughout the system; but what she couldn't understand is that Viter was classed as a pleasure world, it didn't actually give much detail to what the world offered. Toria assumed that it was a world which you would go if you wanted a holiday of a sorts, but would be waited on by Magic slaves she guessed, she wasn't really looking forward to it; but it was kind of better than working in the mines.

Toria had come to this conclusion and then she had found the price list what Commander Slater had mentioned.

One night

1 female - 25.50 Purvinian's
1 Ta'vaian female - 88.00 Purvinian's
1 Tasian female - 250.00 Purvinian's
1 male - 22.50 Purvinian's
1 Ta'vaian male 65.00 Purvinian's
1 Tasian male 200.00 Purvinian's

2 females - 45.00 Purvinian's
2 Ta'vaian females - 165.00 Purvinian's
2 Tasian females - 550.00 Purvinian's
2 males - 40.00 Purvinian's
2 Ta'vaian males - 120.00 Purvinian's
2 Tasian males - 420.00 Purvinian's

2 females & 1 male - 95.00 Purvinian's
2 Ta'vaian females & 1 Ta'vaian male - 220.00 Purvinian's
2 Tasian females & 1 Tasian male - 750.00 Purvinian's
2 males & 1 female - 70.50 Purvinian's
2 Ta'vaian's males & 1 Ta'vaian female - 200.00 Purvinian's
2 Tasian males & 1 Tasian female - 650.00 Purvinian's

Packages available for more than one night, and for other combinations on request; Tasian's do not come in packages and are always at full price listing.

This gave Toria a horrible feeling, she hoped that it wasn't what she was thinking but part of her kind of knew what they were, and why it was called a pressure world; she was disgusted at the mere thought.

She knew that she had to put on the impression that she supported the Fleet in their war against Magics but it didn't mean that she had to support this, and she definitely wasn't going to; the only problem was that she still needed to go down there, so that she could try and help them, these were the ones that needed her help the most.

She would have to go down there so she could figure out the layout of the place because they didn't have the plans in their records, well they didn't just want anyone getting their hands on them because then they would be able to break in and rescue or steal the slaves.

Toria also needed to find out who else was going to be a part of this, and who had put in requests for shore-leave. So she hacked into the system which didn't take much doing, and was horrified to find out that nearly most of the ship had requested shore-leave, but of course not everyone would be able to take it. She printed out a list of all those who would be taking leave and those who had been refused this time, and of course those who would be going down to begin with, with the captain to greet the governor.

Toria had hardly slept for the past day or so trying to prepare herself for what was to be done down on the planet, she walked up the corridor towards the transporter room to go down to the planet with the rest of the first team.

"Hay, wait up...you're Toria right!" A man shouted up the corridor.

Toria turned around to see who was shouting her, she was surprised to see that it was the security chief of all people; he ran over to her looking a little out of breath and red in the face, he was much taller than she was and very muscular with a shaved head .

"What can I do for you sir?" Toria said pleasantly.

"Now that's the kind of response that they'll give down there as well." Security Powa said smiling at her, he put his arm up against the bulkhead to stop her leaning in to whisper to her. "You could always join me tonight, you know for a little fun."

"I don't think so." Toria told him as she lifted his arm out of the way.

"It'll be fun, I've been saving up all year for this." Security Powa told her as he grabbed her again.

Toria turned around and punched him in the face before she pulled her arm free, and carried on walking towards the transporter room; she could hear him grumbling behind her but neither of them said anything as they carried on walking.

They entered the transporter room where the others were waiting, the captain and the first officer along with two other security officers; they all noticed that Powa's nose seemed a little swollen but didn't say anything. They all stepped up onto the pad to be transported down to the planet's surface.

"So are you looking forward to your first time on a pleasure world?" Captain Jasp'erat asked her.

"I don't know." Toria answered honestly.

The transporter officer activated the pads and they were engulfed in a bright white light, everything around them began to disappear and then again reappear down on the planet in a beautiful garden just outside of the open patio doors, where the Governor Lavam and his wife Sike stood waiting to greet them.

The building wasn't like that back at the senate but made of brick, like they used to make them centuries ago; it was only four storeys high but it was huge going off in either direction, with the gardens surrounding it the whole way around as far as the eye could see.

"Welcome." Governor Levam said smiling.

As soon as the words had left his lips, half a dozen beautiful Tasian women stepped out of the shadows to greet them also; they all had long beautiful hair flowing down their backs, their markings visible from head to toe; they were all different but similar in different colours. Toria didn't mean to stare at them so much, but one couldn't help it; they were all so beautiful and near enough naked, except for the beautiful nearly see-through material draped over them.

The women came over to them; one each, and began to act intimately towards them. Toria though wasn't really into the whole women on women thing, even though they were very beautiful.

"No thanks." Toria said politely pushing her away slightly but she didn't seem to want to take no for an answer, and kept trying to touch her; this probably wasn't such a good idea since what she had done to Kole and that her powers were still overreacting at the slightest thing.

"Oh, I'm sorry...you can go; send out one of the others." Governor Levam told the woman stood with Toria.

"No, that's fine...I don't need..." Toria tried to say, but it was no use no one was listening to her.

The Tasian woman walked back inside; Toria wasn't sure but she kind of felt a certain sense of relief coming off of the woman, which Toria understood why now that she was here. A moment later another appeared, this time a male Tasian; he was very handsome with short brown hair his front bangs part covering his face, but they still didn't hide much; all he had on was a pair of silk green and blue shorts which were almost the same colour as his markings.

He walked over to her and reached out to touch her but Toria stepped away from him, panic setting in; she knew that she couldn't let herself get carried away with this and needed to stay away from him and everyone else here.

"She's probably feeling a little scared, this being her first time and all...and her boyfriend just dumped her as well." Powa told him.

"Hay!" Toria shouted turning around and kicked him in the ribs.

Everyone just stood there staring, shocked into silence as he doubled over; the woman bent down to see if he was alright. The Tasian man took advantage of her distraction seemingly not put off by her temper and scoped her up into his arms, and began to carry her away.

"Don't touch me! Put me down!" Toria shouted.

"I'll look after you, don't worry." He told her kindly. "You're so tense."

"That's because I don't like to be touched by strangers." Toria told him.

"Who shall I make the payment out to?" Governor Levam asked as they were walking past.

"I'm not paying for something I don't want!" Toria shouted at the Governor as she struggled against the Tasian, also trying not to touch him anywhere that she wasn't supposed to.

"She's Senator Kentaro's daughter, I'm sure that she can afford to indulge a little while she's here." Captain Jasp'erat told the governor as Toria was taken inside.

"Wait...I don't...this isn't why I came here..." Toria tried to tell him, but he just carried her down the corridor, other slaves from other races stepping out of their way to let them pass.

"This is why everyone comes, to say that you're different is just a lie." He told her kindly. "I understand why people come here. I also understand what it is that I have to do..."

"But that isn't what I want." Toria told him.

"It isn't much further to your room; he said that you're Kentaro." The man said.

"What?" Toria said not knowing what to do, she hadn't expected this kind of thing to happen; she had hoped that she would be left alone to have a look around.

She was in too much of a panic that she never noticed how beautiful everything was, the carpets beneath them, the curtains hung up at the windows, the paintings on the wall and the flowers in the large vases.

He opened the door waving his hand over the scanning and then carried her inside of the large luxury room, there was a four-poster bed layered with pillows; facing the bed was the five door built-in wardrobe with mirrored doors. There was a dresser and stool to the right and on the other side was the door that lead to the bathroom.

"What...what...?" Toria said unable to say anything.

He closed the door behind them and then carried her over to the bed, he carefully placed her on the bed; Toria finally free of him pushed him away rolled over and off the bed backing into the wall well away from him as he just sat down on the bed seeming somewhat confused by her behaviour.

"Well, you're not like what I normally get." He told her.

"I'm sixteen years old, why would I be?" Toria said.

"Sixteen?" He said to her. "Well, you'll be the youngest that I've had."

"What?" Toria said. "I'm not doing anything with you...nor am I going to pay 200 purvinian for you."

He smiled at her. "Even though you say that you're not interested in this sort of thing, you still checked out the prices?"

"What?" Toria said. "I...I wanted to know what was going on here. I've never been to a pleasure world, nor does anyone I know ever talk about them; so why would I know..."

"You didn't know about these places?" He asked her a little surprised.

"You heard my captain, I'm a senator's daughter; it doesn't really come up in conversation...well none that I've heard anyway." Toria told him and then stepped away from the wall. "So...um...who are you anyway...and how long have you...I mean...?"

"How long have I been here, doing this?" He asked her seriously before he smiled at her. "I was brought here at the same age that you now, before you were even born."

"Seriously?" Toria asked.

"When you turn sixteen, you're old enough to take part." He told her. "My name, if you really want to know it...most just call me what ever they want me to be called; it's Alvi."

Toria just stared at him, she didn't know what to say to him; it's not as though she could tell him why she was really there could she? Would he help her if she asked him, why would he though they had only just met.

"Well Alvi, not to hurt your feelings; but I'd prefer you to leave." Toria told him walking over to the foot of the bed.

"I'm not your type; I can change my appearance to that of anyone you like?" Alvi asked her standing up and walking over to her.

"I didn't come here to buy you, or anyone else." Toria told him firmly. "Now, where's the computer?"

She turned around to look for a console but couldn't see one anywhere; Alvi came up behind her and gently moved her hair back and leant in to kiss her upon the nape of her neck, but she swung around and blasted him in the chest and flew into the post of the bed which the whole canopy collapsed on top of him.

"I told you I wasn't interested, see now that's what you get..." Toria told him. "Now...where's the computer?'

"In the mirror of the dresser." Alvi said as he pushed the canopy off of him and slid off of the bed onto the floor, he looked over at her a little shaken about what she had just done. "Are you here to help us?"

Toria laughed, she couldn't help it, but she didn't answer him; instead she sat down and activated the computer that was also built into the mirror.

"These mirrors don't record people doing stuff in secret do they?" Toria asked him looking over her shoulder while she waited for the complex system to upload.

"Not unless you want them to." Alvi answered. "You know to take away with you, for personal use."

"Okay...I don't actually need that sort of detail." Toria said, she was disgusted enough with this place she didn't need to know everything else that went on here; or perhaps she did, people would pay a lot to keep those sorts of things secret. "Can you fix the bed?"

"If you want me to fix the bed." Alvi said. "Why, might you change your mind later on?"

"Don't be daft." Toria said off-handedly turning back to the screen, it now had the whole layout of the place including the slave quarters and the transport hangers. "This is great."

"I'm glad that you're enjoying yourself." Alvi said staring at her briefly before he began to fix the bed, the pieces slowly began to lift up into the air and return to where they belonged once more; until finally they were all one piece and everything was back to how it was to begin with. "I was wondering about your hair, but you answered the question for me without having to ask."

"My hair?" Toria asked turning around to face him a little confused.

"It changes colour, turns more red than normal." Alvi told her.

Toria smiled to herself turning around. "I guess it does sometimes. I'll have to learn to control it somehow...I don't just want anyone picking up on it."

"What're you looking for?" Alvi asked her.

"Away to kill you all, and to make it look as though I had good reason to do so." Toria told him honestly.

"What?" Alvi said marching over to the dresser and pulled her to her feet. "Kill us?"

"If you don't let go of me, I will hurt you." Toria warned him. "That before was nothing compared to what I'll really do, but if you'd like to carry on cause it'll just give me more of a good reason to retaliate."

"Please, as if I'll play along with you..." Alvi said letting go of her and going to leave.

This time it was Toria who stopped him, she kicked him in the back and then in his ribs as hard as she could; she even heard a couple of ribs actually break as he fell to his knees.

"Sorry, but I can't let you get in my way." Toria told him and then pressed her com unit. "Toria to security, I had a problem with my guest...he's been dealt with but I'm going to take him over to the holding pound in the slave quarters."

"Are you alright?" The man on the other end asked sounding quite concerned. "Perhaps I should send a team to help you out."

"It's alright, I've dealt with him; he just didn't like me saying no..." Toria told him. "It's fine...as long as I can get my money back."

"Okay then, I'll log it down." He told her. "And contact us if you need any extra help."

"Thanks, Toria out." Toria said smiling as she turned Alvi over, turning her com unit off. "See you're helping already."

She held out her hand and the ties off of the four poster bed untied themselves and then flew over to her, she tied his arms behind his back and then gagged him before she pulled him to his feet.

"Not bad for a little girl, though perhaps I should have mentioned that I've already killed over eight thousand Magics." Toria told him pleasantly opening the door. "This place is nothing compared to those colonies, and just think that you helped me kill your people."

He tried to struggle against her as she dragged him down the corridor, the other slaves that were left quickly moved out of the way wondering what was going on, but of course none of them would dare to ask incase they ended up in the same position; three doors down the corridor the door opened suddenly and a woman stepped out who she knew.

"Toria what're you doing?" Joset asked her, her dirty blonde hair was a little astray and she only had a towel wrapped around her.

"Oh...um...I taking him to the lock up; he attacked me." Toria told her.

"Really?" Joset said surprised as a Ta'vain man came up behind her naked.

Toria blushed deeply as she looked away. "I should be going..."

"Shame that you didn't have a good time, these two are great." Joset told her as Toria walked away.

"Yeah, that's great for you." Toria said distractedly, and then when the door closed and there was no one else around. "Does he have to walk around like that...what are all Ta'vian just not bothered if they're seen naked or something."

Alvi couldn't answer her but just made a groan as though he was trying to say something to her, but she chose to ignore him and carried on dragging him down the corridor towards the slave section; knowing that he couldn't put up much of a struggle since where she had hit him, and that he was probably already finding it hard to walk.

It didn't take them long before they reached the slave quarters and quite a few people had seen her taking him there, and she had informed her security team what he had supposedly tried to do as well; so at least she was covered for that, now the other problem. She turned him around roughly almost throwing him into the door, his hand hit the scanner panel and it slide open making him fall inside; she nudged him the rest of the way in and then bent down at his side.

"How about I let you in on another secret, I kind of already figured out how to kill you all just before I got here." Toria told him. "You were just the icing on the cake."

She kicked him in the face knocking him out and then stepped over him the door closing behind her, she quickly walked down the corridor; these were almost bare compared to just beyond that door, there was nothing nor no one only doors to quarters where the slaves would sleep while they weren't working.

Toria knew that she had to hurry she didn't have long to complete everything that she needed to do, fifteen minutes tops before someone found Alvi, which was starting to make her think that perhaps she shouldn't have just left him there like that.

Almost twenty minutes later Toria slumped against the bulkhead outside of the transport hanger, ready to go with her plan; she pressed her com-unit signalling it three times. A moment later the engines started up in the hanger and her com sent a message to the ship, then Toria herself activated her com.

"Toria to security, there's a transport ship here trying to take off..." Toria told him.

"What?" The same man from before said.

"I saw these guys acting strange so I followed them, they went to the hanger." Toria told him. "I tried to contact the ship but they haven't responded."

"We'll try from up here." The man told her.

"I'll contact them again, telling them that if they don't turn their engines off then I'll destroy their ship." Toria told him.

"Do you think that's necessary?" the man asked nervously.

"Yes, they're trying to escape; it'll set an explain to the rest of them not to try anything." Toria told him and then logged off, and sent another message through her com unit. "Right then...here goes..."

Toria concentrated all of her energy at the ship's engine to overload, and for the explosion to the quarters; but for everyone to be alright, willing everyone to be alright; just as her com unit started to beep.

"Toria...wait...!" The security officer shouted through her com unit.

"I can't..." Toria said.

"The whole place is rigged to explode...prepare to come aboard..." He told her.

Toria smiled to herself briefly as the white light engulfed her and the smile faded away just as she reappeared in the transporter room, the security officer stood waiting for her; he was a about six years older than she was with three head tails and pale blue skin.

"Dovi...what happened?" Toria asked him as she stepped down off of the platform.

"The slave quarters, they were all destroyed." Dov told her. "We contacted the governor to tell him what was going on, and he told us that they were rigged to explode incase anything like this were to happen."

"Well then, his system works." Toria said pleasantly making to leave. "I better get my report ready for the captain; he'll want to know what's happened."

"Um...yeah...I guess..." Dov said somewhat speechlessly as he watched her walk out as though the whole thing didn't bother her at all.

Toria's heart was pounding inside of her chest as though it would explode, she was scared half to death that they would figure out what she had done; but she had to make sure that her report and everything down there said that she did everything by the book it was just the governor's system in the end that was completely over the top and that her who wanted to destroy just the one transport ship would have been enough.

Toria stood nervously in the lift as it took her to the bridge to hand in her report to the captain of her version of the events. She knew that she had to come across calm as though she had nothing to worry about, that she had acted properly and followed protocol; she had gone over all the reports and all the evidence which also supported her. All she had to do now was give it to the captain and hope that he didn't send her back to the academy, they still had a few more Magical systems to visit; and she felt as though given another chance that perhaps she could do just as well as she did this time, as long as she wasn't actually caught out.

The door slid open and Toria stepped out onto the bridge, she quickly looked around to see if the captain was there but she couldn't see him so she assumed that he was in his office going through the reports that everyone was giving him; she walked down the slope ignoring the other officers whispering about her and beeped the captain.

"Come in." Captain Jasp'erat called from inside his office.

The door slid open and Toria went into his office, he didn't look up to begin with so Toria stood to attention in front of his desk until he looked up; she was sure that she had been stood there a whole two minutes before he finally stood up.

"What the hell did you think that you were doing, thinking that you could take charge in the situation of the slaves escaping?" Captain Jasp'erat demanded.

"I followed procedures sir, I call it into security just like I was supposed to sir." Toria told him. "I didn't know that the governor had rigged the whole of slave quarters to explode if some tried to escape. But I do agree with him, they need to know that they can't get away with trying to escape; and you know considering that everyone was distracted they would have wouldn't they?"

"And just what is that supposed to me?" Captain Jasp'erat asked her through pressed lips.

"I've written my report sir." Toria stepped forward and handed it to him. "I'm giving it to you first, before I officially send it off. It says that the command staff were preoccupied by Magics; though I haven't said how, but I could do if you think that it might help?"

"Are you threatening me girl?" Captain Jasp'erat asked her.

"I'm just telling you what's in my report." Toria told him calmly. "It's up to you how it ends. I'm just telling you what happened down there and how they'll see this at the Malarias Command Centre, they'll see it as an example to the others not to do the same thing; but if they don't then they'll just end up the same way."

He looked at her for a moment as if considering what she had said, or if he was wondering if this girl had actually come up with what just came out of her mouth; he slowly nodded as though he agreed with her.

"Shall I send the reports off sir?" Toria asked him.

"Yes, they were killed trying to escape and with the governor's counter measures the whole slave quarters was destroyed." Captain Jasp'erat agreed.

"Very well then sir." Toria said turning to leave.

"Just remember that this is the first and last time that you threaten me." Captain Jasp'erat told her. "I agree with what you said, but how you went about it..."

Toria turned back around to face him. "I know that I'm only a cadet still sir, but I have helped you out on several occasions now; I was only doing it again. I didn't want you and your senior staff looking foolish, how do they say it...caught with your trousers down?"

Captain Jasp'erat didn't say anything as Toria turned and left, she walked back up to the lift the bridge officers still whispering among themselves probably wondering what had happened to her; though even Toria was wondering the same thing, she couldn't believe what she had just done and said to him. It was as though something had completely taken her over and she really had turned into a different person, it was the only way that she could explain it to herself; not that she didn't kind of like this other self because she needed to be strong with men that she was going to meet. Especially with how quickly everything seemed to be moving she had to make sure that she came across that she could handle whatever was thrown at her and she herself needed to know that she could cope with it as well.

She did know though that the captain was going to be a problem, he didn't like how her attitude had suddenly changed towards him; but she kind of knew that she was right in away, he had been compromised and she had gotten him out of trouble, it was just how she had gone about it. She would have to deal with him at the first opportunity that she got; though that may just be at the next port of call which happened to be another so-called pressure world which they would be arriving at the following week.

An alarm was sounding somewhere in the distance, it seemed so far away but kind of near at the same time, as Toria rolled over pulling the covers around her trying to keep her eyes closed even though she knew that she had to get up; then she seemed to suddenly remember something very important and sat bolt up right making herself dizzy.

"Damn it." Toria said looking around in the dark throwing the covers off of her, revealing cotton striped shorts and a vest. "Computer turn the alarm off and turn the lights on."

She couldn't believe that she had slept in again, normally she didn't have much of a problem getting up in fact she had more of a problem actually getting to sleep in the first place; she just put it down to that she was over-tired with using her powers so much, her body wasn't used to using them yet after all these years it was probably putting a strain on her. She just hoped that after this assignment she could get some leave because she had asked Lonac to see if he could get her a doctor's appointment and she still wanted to get checked out to be on the safe side, as she didn't really know much about Magics or Tasian's and she was one or rather both now properly; it wasn't as though she could go to the ship's doctor and ask him if she was working properly, she might get arrested or worst.

Toria went into the bathroom to have a wash; she had decided to take a shower the night before which she was glad for now considering that she had still managed to oversleep even though the alarm had been going off.

Once she had finished she went back through to her bedroom and grabbed her uniform off the chair, she was about to turn around when she saw someone in the mirror that was stood in the corner of her room; she looked over her shoulder but there wasn't anyone behind her and when she looked back into the mirror there was nothing.

"He couldn't be...this is a ship...a mirror hopping or whatever it is that he does...no...it's stupid..." Toria told herself, but she grabbed her bathrobe and threw it over the mirror all the same just incase, not wanting that strange guy watching her.

She pulled on her jumpsuit and was fastening it up when the computer in the other room started to beep, signalling that she had an incoming transmission; she had a bad feeling that she knew who it was, well he had been trying to call her for the past week. She walked through to the other room and turned the computer around to face her on the desk, it still had the black screen.

"Computer, can you tell me who the transmission is from or where it's from?" Toria asked.

"The caller id is not listed. The transmission is from the Dragon Senate." The computer answered.

"Disconnect transmission, I don't want to accept unknown callers; wait...can you send the caller that written message that I won't accept from any unknown caller's?' Toria asked.

"Yes, sending transmission and disconnecting." The computer told her.

Toria turned the computer back around, she didn't need to answer to know who was trying to contact her since the mission report had been sent off; she knew that her father wouldn't hide who he was from her so it was only one other person and she still didn't feel as though she could talk to him even over a subspace channel. It was best this way, for them both; especially now that she had started her plan for real and her name was now being used, if he was to side with her then he'd only end up in trouble with his own people and she didn't want that.

"Sorry Ren, but you'll understand one day." Toria said before she left her quarters without tying her hair back and just leaving it free down her back.

Toria walked along the corridor a few officers looking at her, but she tried to ignore them and also wondered why they were staring at her;

it wasn't as though she had done anything yet.

"Pretty." Powa said as he joined her from the adjoining corridor. "Going even more for the sweet and innocent look are we?"

"What're you talking about?" Toria asked him confused about what he was talking about.

"Your hair, not really regulation; but you look nice." Powa told her. "And by the way, I don't think that you could take me off guard again like last time."

"Really?" Toria said stopping suddenly, he turned around to see what was wrong.

She made to punch him again but giving him enough time to block, but she didn't even connect with him instead she kicked him in the shins making his legs buckle and him fall to his knees; Toria stepped away him smiling.

"I do like to lead people into a false sense of security." Toria told him as she walked away. "But so do you, you make it seem as though you can do your job; but really you can't."

"That little bitch..." Powa said gritting his teeth as he pushed himself up holding onto the bulkhead for support as Toria carried onto the transporter room.

Toria arrived at the transporter room, again the captain was already there waiting along with three security officers; but this time Commander Slater was staying on board the ship to monitor everything that was going on down on the surface, they didn't want the same thing to happen to them twice.

"Powa seems to be having a problem with his legs." Toria told the captain.

"What?" Captain Jasp'erat asked confused, but when the door slid open again and Powa struggled inside his legs seemingly unstable he understood. "Really, you should have just said that you weren't fit to come down...get to the med bay..."

"I can always go over the security reports until he's fit enough to join us." Toria said stood slightly behind the captain smirking at Powa.

"Fine." Captain Jasp'erat said annoyed with his security officer.

"But that little..." Powa tried to explain, but he knew that he would look even more stupid if he told them it was her who had done this to him and she knew it as well.

"She'll be fine...just go...and hurry up about it..." Captain Jasp'erat told him stepping up onto the transporter pad next to Toria.

The other three security officers joined them while Powa limped away steaming about what she had just done. Toria though hoped that she hadn't pushed him a little too soon.

They were all engulfed in the bright white light which transported them down into a grand waiting room; there were luxury sofas that had beautiful woman lying across them waiting for them and male musicians playing in the corner by the doors that lead out onto a balcony, with the setting sun colouring the sky an inky blue with a dash of red.

"I'm glad that you still managed to make it, after what happened on Viter." Governor Harjas said as he came up behind them, he was of the same height as the captain and was a round man quite red in the face and balding; he seemed to notice Toria straight away and made to greet her personally. "Well aren't you just the prettiest little officer I've ever had the pleasure of meeting."

"Thank you sir." Toria said kindly shaking his hand briefly and then pulling it away, as he seemed really creepy and it was kind of sweaty as well.

"She may be little and look sweet, but believe me she isn't." Captain Jasp'erat told him. "She was the one who called it, the slaves trying to escape."

"Oh, so that's why you brought her down here; to make sure that mine don't try anything." Governor Harjas said smiling at her. "Well you don't need to worry about that little one, none of my slaves have ever escaped; nor could they."

"Actually sir, that isn't true now is it?" Toria said. "I've read quite a few reports about this, I mean since I was told that we were coming here; and actually you've managed to lose a couple of hundred slaves somehow. No one seems to know how they manage to get away. Perhaps they do their Magic thing on your guests, you know make them take them away from here and you supposedly wouldn't know anything about it."

"I really don't know what you're talking about." Governor Harjas said trying to hide his anger, and his new dislike for her.

"I'm just going to be looking over your records, you know trying to figure out how they got away; so that you don't lose any more of them." Toria told him. "You don't want to lose any more of them do you sir, or is it that you're the one who has been helping them escape?"

"How dare you." Governor Harjas said angrily nearly spitting at her.

Toria smiled kindly at him as she stepped around him. "I'll go and find your security office, then shall I?"

Toria walked off before he could say anything to her, even her captain didn't bother saying anything since she had brought this up with him and she had persuaded him that it was for the best that if he turned a blind eye when he knew about it that he too would get into trouble for helping him to set these Magics lose on the galaxy.

Toria walked down the corridor even though she had no idea where she was going, she knew that she was walking pretty fast but she didn't really like that the walls had mirrors hung on them in-between all of the rooms; though what was worst, was that she could feel that someone was actually watching her, but every time she looked into the mirror there was no one there or rather she couldn't see anyone.

Toria carried on walking just focusing ahead pretending that there were no mirrors, and that there was no one watching; when she saw someone, a man, at the end of the corridor watching her and then quickly disappeared around the corner. She couldn't help herself, she ran after him down the corner and then turned right she could see him ahead of her; she tried to remember the spell to move something but she couldn't remember the words properly. It didn't matter what the words were, she just concentrated on the carpet to be pulled, to knock him off of his feet.

"Damn it...move!" Toria shouted and the carpet was ripped up from under his feet and he fell forward flat on his face.

She couldn't believe that she had done it, she hadn't really expected the spell to work considering she didn't know the actual words only what she wanted to do; which she guessed was also part of it, she'd have to ask Lonac or Leka next time she saw them. Toria walked over to him, he had hoped that she could have more time to figure out how to do this place but it looks as though her plans had been brought forward again and she had once again found someone willing to help her out; the only problem was that she might get a little too used to this happening and wouldn't know what to do if she was faced with a real problem.

Toria was only two feet away from him when two men appeared behind her and the alarms sounded, she spun around to face them but the one on the left lifted his hand and she was lifted up into the air and thrown against the glass framed windows smashing them open and slumping to the ground. She tried to push herself up but she couldn't, there was a shard of glass in her back on the lower left; she needed to get up not matter what, she had to do this without letting anyone else get in her way. She forced herself to ignore the pain as she pushed herself to her feet and activated her com.

"Toria to Captain Jasp'erat..." Toria started but was hit in the face from somewhere by something that she couldn't see and then everything went black.

The first thing that Toria realized was that her back was in agony, and then she remembered what had happened; the guy that she had been chasing and then two other guys that had just appeared but she couldn't remember what any of them looked like because it had all happened too fast.

She opened her eyes to find herself in a small dark room with her hands and feet tied, she crawled on her back toward the door and kicked against it as hard as she could as she focused her anger into burning the ropes, which just fell apart as burning ash; while still trying to ignore the pain of her back.

"Just be quiet!" A man shouted through to her.

Toria wasn't really one for doing as she was told, so she kicked the door as hard as could until it finally gave way and fell forward onto the man who was stood outside keeping guard; she struggled to her feet and stumbled out of the storage room not bothered about the man on the floor anymore, she needed to find the others. She had no idea where she was as she wondered over to the computer console but it didn't come on, it wasn't working; they must had taken it off line Toria thought but why?

"They couldn't be...idiots..." Toria said as she went back over to the man who was still underneath the broken door; she pulled it off of him and shook him awake. "Where the hell are they? Tell me...no wait, take me to them."

"Please...like I would." The man said to her a cut upon his forehead where the door had hit him.

"Our star ship is in orbit, a Malarias Fleet star ship." Toria told him. "They already know that something's happened to me...you must be stupid to think, that you could still get away...take me to them and they'll...well lets just say that they'll get off a little lighter meaning that they won't be killed."

"I don't believe you." He said stubbornly.

"Take me to them!" Toria shouted at him her temper getting the better of her, she could feel that she was getting hotter and knew that he would be able to feel it as well; but at the moment perhaps it was the only way to make him do what she wanted.

"What...what are you...argh!" The man said and they disappeared suddenly and then reappeared in a dimly lit damp hanger.

The hanger doors were open with a breeze coming through, Toria let go of the man and stood up slowly as it hurt too much to rush; she had no idea what she was expecting herself to be able to do in this condition, but she needed to be able to do something.

"Sorly...!" The man shouted behind her.

No one appeared though, not what she could see anyway; she didn't have time for this as she slipped forward and grabbed the ship for support. Toria knew that she had to do it, she had to risk it; she focused the last of her strength at the ship, she spun around just in time to see the back of the man again who had run away from her appear and then disappear with the other man.

Her grip slipped off of the ship and she fell to the damp cold floor as the ship slowly moved out, she watched it leave the hanger and began to gain speed and altitude; it wasn't long until it was out of view but she could still hear the engines and then a deafening explosion which shook the whole building, but Toria couldn't keep her eyes open any longer as she just gave into the tiredness of her body.

Chapter Sixteen

Renji pounded the desk with his fist knocking over his hot tea, he jumped up so not to get burnt from it as it slipped over the edge of his desk; his data sheets were covered but he didn't seem to care only turned the computer screen around another angel so that he could carry on talking.

"Renji, you need to calm down." Kasiya told him for the hundredth time.

"Calm down, she won't answer any of my calls." Renji told him again. "If the reports are right, that's her fourth colony; fourth Kasiya!"

"Have you even heard yourself?" Kasiya asked him calmly.

"I don't care; I can't lose her this way..." Renji told him. "This last time she was injured, I was hoping to go out and meet her when she took her shore leave but I have no idea where she's gone to."

"Renji, she isn't your responsibility." Kasiya told him kindly.

"Of course she is, she always has been...and I failed her." Renji said leaning against his desk with his back to the screen. "I need to be out there doing something, finding out a way to help her come back from this."

"Renji if our people find out what she's done, then she may never be able to join us." Kasiya told him.

"That's why I need to get out of this place; I'm not the paper work sort of guy." Renji told him turning around finally getting to the real reason that he had contacted him. "You don't really need me here any more and you've got Blaze here, he's more than capable on his own. Me...I need to get back out there; Kasiya come on, I need a ship."

"I believe that you are a capable officer, you're a General after all; but the way that you are now..." Kasiya started.

"What if she really has turned, do you honestly think that any of the tracking teams will be able to bring her in; especially if she really is using her powers?" Renji asked him, he had a look of regret but he was sure that this was the only way. "I'll bring her in if I need to, if she really has turned against us."

"Renji, no one expects you to..." Kasiya told him disappointedly.

"Her powers don't effect me, well they didn't...either way I've got a better chance than anyone to bring her in." Renji told him. "So how about I get another ship?"

"The Silver Star, just lost her captain; I'll have them meet you." Kasiya told him. "Renji, find out what she's up to before going after her. You want to save her, but you can't do that if everyone believes she's a Magic traitor.

"Thanks, I owe you one." Renji told him smiling sadly.

"I'm not the one who owes you anything." Kasiya told him. "I'll have the Silver Star meet you in the Ori System at the weekend, I'm sure that's plenty of time for you to get yourself together."

"Thanks again." Renji said and then logged off.

He stood up straight and looked around the room. He'd finally be leaving this world and getting a ship of his own again; it had been twelve almost thirteen years, but he'd finally be leaving. This wasn't how he had imagined leaving, he had hoped that he could have left with her not to go after her like this; he still didn't want to believe that she had turned against them but the first two colonies he couldn't find anyone left alive. His heart was filled with dread and fear of what he was going to find on these pleasure worlds, but most of all on the mining colony where there was just a crater left behind; he just hoped that all this wasn't really her, because if it was he had no idea how he was supposed to save her.

...Toria was lying on a bed in the med bay, wearing a grey med grown; she heard the door at the far end of the room slid open, so she looked up to see who it was. It didn't surprise her to see the captain stood there talking to the doctor about her, she had been waiting for him to come down to her since she had woken up; she pushed herself up so that he could see that she was awake, he dismissed the doctor and then marched over to her.

"The Senator, your father wishes me to congratulate you on a job well done." Captain Jasp'erat said angrily. "But honestly, you went against my orders again..."

"I didn't go against your orders, sir." Toria told him. "I was attacked, I tried to call for back up and then before you could answer I was knocked out. I remember very clearly, no one came to give back up and that ship with escaping with Magics on board trying to escape; so I did what was needed to be done. If you can't see that then I guess that you're not fit to wear that uniform."

"A face of an angel, but a soul of a devil; you'll go far in the Fleet." Captain Jasp'erat told her. "But I warned you girl, not to cross me; I'm sending you back to the academy."

"That'll look good for you won't it?" Toria said smirking. "You're shipping off the one that stopped the Magics from escaping twice, as if people won't notice what you're really up to. And when they find out what I've done, I doubt that they'll want me to stay at the academy for long."

"You think that all of this is a game, what do you want your daddy's attention; doesn't he give you enough?" Captain Jasp'erat said. "I won't be made a fool out of by a child."

"You didn't need me to make a fool of you, just think; if I hadn't been around then you would have been stripped of your rank for letting those Magics escape." Toria said pleasantly. "Doesn't that mean that you owe me one, and believe me; I'll come back to collect when I need a favour. Now if you don't mind, sir, but I really should rest a little more."...

Touro woke with a start, almost falling off of her chair and elbowing Rui-Lin sat next to her; she looked around the waiting room full of Magics trying to shake off the dream that she had just had and remember why she was here.

"Are you alright?" Rui-Lin asked her.

"Yeah...sorry about that; I've been really tired lately." Touro told him.

"That's alright, I'm pretty tough." Rui-Lin told her smiling slightly. "Lonac said that he'll meet us afterwards, he had a meeting about the team."

"Oh right, yeah I think I heard that they're supposed to be playing tonight right?" Touro asked him.

"Yep, the only problem is that they're down a player, I mean with Delky." Rui-Lin told her.

"Oh...right...of course..." Touro said looking away from him, she still felt guilty that she wasn't able to help him and that he had been killed.

"It isn't your fault, you explained what happened...and those sort of thing's happen; even to the best of us." Rui-Lin told her kindly.

"He didn't turn on you though; I mean he didn't give your names or description." Touro told him again, Rui-Lin smiled at her.

"Touro." The lady behind the desk said, she had purple skin and silver eyes and wore a white nurse's dress with no sleeves.

"I'll wait here for you." Rui-Lin told her.

"Thanks." Touro said standing up, she had a red knee length dress on with one strap which was a purple panel fitted across the top matching the waist band and the attached piece from the top panel to her arm which draped down slightly; she also had red matching boots on.

Touro walked past the other patients who were waiting to go through and see the doctor, some of whom had been waiting longer than she had; but she did know that there were four doctors working today so they could be going to see any of them. She pushed the door open and went up the corridor looking from side to side for the number 3, she had been told when she arrived that was the room that her doctor was working from today; though she still didn't know who Lonac had booked her in with she just hoped that they would be alright and able to figure out what was actually wrong with her.

It was the second door on the left; she knocked on the door and waited to be called inside.

"Come in." A man said inside the room.

Touro pushed the door open and went inside of the office, the doctor looked up from his work and just stared at her for a moment before he stood up relief spreading across his face as though he was pleased to see her. She just stared at him, she didn't actually know him, or rather she couldn't remember ever meeting him before.

"I was hoping that it was going to be you when I saw the name." He said to her.

Touro didn't know what he was talking about still stood at the door, unsure now if she should actually go any further inside even though there was a desk and chairs between them; though she couldn't help notice the med bed in the far corner with the curtains partly closed around it.

"I don't..." Touro started.

"Of course, yes sorry; I'm Athoury." He told her.

"Seriously?" Touro said a little surprised and relieved herself. "You were my cousin Ichigo's doctor right?"

"Yes I am." Athoury said smiling slightly and pointed to the chair in front of his desk. "How are you feeling?"

"Truthfully, like hell." Touro told him. "I thought that it could be because I've been using my Magic a lot more, perhaps my body is drained."

"It only has a little bit to do with that." Athoury told her. "When I came to visit you and Ichigo I examined you, he wanted to make sure that you were alright; I've spent all this time trying to find something to help you and then to find you."

"Help me?" Touro asked a little unsure. "You mean, there's something wrong with me?"

"Unfortunately yes." Athoury answered. "The man who was holding you captive, he infected you with a genetically engineered strain of the Kovel virus. It was changed just for you, I'm still not sure how they managed it; though I did hope that I would be able to find a cure...but to begin with there wasn't one."

"Wait a minute, what're you saying?" Touro asked him. "This Ko...what ever is going to kill me or will I be able to live even with it?"

"At the moment, with the medicine that I'm going to give you; you'll start to feel your energy coming back to you." Athoury assured her. "I'll continue to work on it, until I find a cure; but you must understand that even though this wasn't meant to kill you straight away but last longer...it will in time kill you, no matter how much medicine I give you to keep it at bay."

"No..." Touro said shaking her head, she didn't want to believe that she already had a death sentence; she knew that doing what she was doing that she could be killed, but this was different actually being told that she was going to die, and it was only a matter of time. "Well...erm...I mean...do you know how long?"

"A couple of years." Athoury told her. "I want to run a few tests while you're here today, hopefully I'll get a better understanding of how it's working in your body. Touro, I don't want you to give up; you still need to fight this just like you would with anything else."

"Right...yeah...course..." Touro said distractedly as Athoury stood up and walked around his desk to do the blood tests.

Touro couldn't even remember leaving the doctor's surgery with Rui-Lin nor walking through the city to meet Lonac and the others in the bar. Rui-Lin opened the door for her and she went through first and was near enough pounced on by Leka, but backed away holding his hands up when Rui-Lin glared at him; Touro walked over and sat next to Lonac at the bar.

"So how did it go?" Lonac asked her turning around.

Touro still looked quite pale and didn't answer him, he looked over at Rui-Lin but he just shrugged as she hadn't told him anything either.

"Hay, you know how to play Veritgo right?" A large guy asked sat in the first booth, his hair was shaved but with swirls marked into it.

"Yeah course, but I've never actually played a proper game before." Rui-Lin answered.

"So what can ya do?" A tall man asked with tanned skin wearing a vest top so that you could see the white lines, he looked just as bad as Touro did.

"Why, what's going on?' Rui-Lin asked.

"We're two players down, Delky and we don't have a Rose player." Lonac explained then nodded to the guy stood behind him. "Jo-Mi's been calling everyone he knows, even if it's just to cover for today."

"I don't care if I can get someone just to stand in as the Rose player, they don't actually have to do anything." Jo-Mi told him. "But I need someone strong...someone who knows the game to fill in as Defender."

"Hay I don't mind, if you don't mind having a werewolf on your team for a change." Rui-Lin said excitedly.

"We could do with a wolf, seeing that we're the only ones who don't actually have one." The woman said on the other side of Lonac, she was quite beautiful with her long hair tied back; but she also looked quite strong and was dressed in leather.

"You're a werewolf?" Touro asked finally speaking, seeming to come out of her trance.

"I think you could help and also help pay back on the favour you owe me." Lonac told her.

"What's that supposed to mean?" Touro asked worriedly.

"Yeah, she could stand in...she's pretty strong; well her Magic is anyway." Leka agreed understanding where Lonac was going with this.

"I don't know...I was kind of hoping to hear back from Kyo..." Jo-Mi said.

"Kyo?" Touro asked a little surprised wondering if it was the same she knew. "He's got the shuttle training at the academy this weekend; he told me that he won't even get to watch through the com videos."

"You know Kyo?" Jo-Mi asked her eyeing her up.

Touro knew that she didn't look like much especially considering how she was dressed today, really girlie for a change; it wasn't that she wanted to play or anything but she also felt as though she owed these guys something considering how much they had helped her out when she needed it and they didn't even know who she was.

"She'll be fine." Leka assured him.

"Wait a minute..." Touro said. "You do remember me telling you that I haven't even seen a match before right?"

"You said that you know basically how the game's played though." Lonac said on her other side.

"But..." Touro protested.

"You don't have to do anything, just make up the numbers." Jo-Mi told her. "I can't believe I just said that...but this is it; if we lose today or can't find the players we'll be demounted to the lower league. Now Tour, you won't know this but the Roaring Torch has never been in the lower leagues before and they're not going to go in them while I'm captain; so you know what that means?"

"I have to play." Touro said filled with dread.

"Come on, I'll take you over to the stadium; you'll need to get measured up." The woman said standing up, she was the same height as Jo-Mi; Touro nodded and got down off the stroll over a foot shorter than her. "I'm Kima-Na, nice to meet you."

"Hi." Touro said.

"I'm Rox, welcome to the team." The guy sat in the booth said. "We'll see you later then."

Touro left with Kima-Na while the others stayed to discuss the match later on, Touro didn't think that she was the right person even if it was just to cover; she didn't know anything about the game except from what Siren had told her months ago, and to top it off she hardly knew any Magic. Though one good thing, she was feeling a little better after her first dose of medicine, but he did tell her that using too much of her Magic could be a strain on her and if it wasn't for her bigger plan of saving as many people as she could then she didn't know if this was really such a good idea.

"You really looked as though you didn't want to join." Kima-Na said as they walked up the road side by side the passers by staring at them, well they did look kind of odd together but also they knew her from Vertigo. "I know that we're not doing so well this year, but we've just had some bad luck that is all."

"I don't know anything bout all this." Touro told her.

"There are a lot of people like you out there, some just look forward to these days." Kima-Na told her. "Yeah we're fighting in a war, hiding from them; however you want to put it. But what's the point if we give everything up, these matches that we carry on playing; they kind of give our people hope that we haven't lost yet."

Touro looked over at her, she hadn't thought about it like that; but she did have a point there were different ways of saving a people, and this was one of them. She could give a little of her power to help this way, it wasn't as though it was going to be every time only until they got a new Rose player.

"So erm...what does I Rose player do?" Touro asked her. "My friend said that they're the secret weapon in a way."

"Yeah, they can play every position and they don't have to tell the Players Board what their powers are; well only if they're a wolf." Kima-Na told her. "So Rui-Lin will have to register. He's probably already registered, he's a pure wolf I think." Kima-Na added thoughtfully, and then noticed that Touro didn't seem to know what that meant. "You really don't know much do you? He was born a wolf, like most on his home world."

"Oh, I think I've heard of a few worlds like that; but aren't they heavily monitored?" Touro asked.

"Unfortunately." Kima-Na answered.

They turned the corner and Touro saw the circular open topped stadium up ahead, it was massive, so overwhelming; she had heard that it could fit nearly ten thousand people.

Touro was sat on the bench in the changing room, wearing a full body suit of armour in purple and red like the others on the team who were all quite excited; Touro just sat there nervously still no idea about what she was supposed to do when she was out there.

"Oh, I didn't tell you; we're playing Vikas." Lonac told her.

"That doesn't actually help me." Touro told him looking up to face him.

"Inker and Vi are on the team." Lonac told her.

"Great, that's all I need a wolf who likes to jump me." Touro said sarcastically.

Rui-Lin leant through the gaps in the clothes which were hung up over the benches. "You don't like wolves?"

"I never said that...I have nothing against them...except him." Touro told him. "You're nice."

"Thanks." Rui-Lin said smiling slightly.

"Oh, so you like older guys do you?" Kima-Na teased her.

Touro blushed deeply, her skin and hair both turning red which everyone noticed.

"Seriously?" Kima-Na said laughing. "Well, Rui...it looks as though you have a fan; poor Lonac though."

"What?" Touro said getting to her feet shaking her head trying to get her hair to change back. "I...it doesn't matter...I'm just not interested in anyone at the moment or ever..."

"You'll have to tell me about it after the match..." Kima-Na told her putting her arm around her waist towering over her.

"I don't really care about any of that, only that we're going to be called out there any minute now." Jo-Mi told them and stared at Touro's hair. "Is that the only thing you can change?"

"When I get embarrassed, yes." Touro admitted. "I try not to set people on fire, I think I've done quite well the past week..."

"What?" Jo-Mi started.

"And here comes the Roaring Torch!" A man shouted through the speakers and they all disappeared in purple smoke reappearing out in the middle of the platform in the stadium.

Touro stood there in the middle of the empty plate with the rest of the team on either side of her, the Vikas team facing them; she only knew two of them and knew nothing about the other players; the platform hovered in the centre of the arena a hundred feet off the ground, thousands of people from all over the galaxy cheering for them.

"Welcome for this evening's match between Vikas and The Roaring Torch." The commentator shouted. "The Roaring Torch have several new players, with them today. Finally the team has a wolf, Rui-Lin their new Defender." A howl suddenly echoed throughout the stadium and the fans seemed to cheer even more. "They also have a new Rose player, Touro!"

The stadium still cheered even though Touro knew that none of them of course knew who she was, it was just the whole part of it. She looked across at the other team and saw Inker looking very excited to start, part of her wished that he wasn't part of the team.

"On the count of three." The commentator shouted.

Beep, beep, beep!

"Vertigo!" The commentator shouted.

Inker transformed in an instant and charged for Touro as the platforms began to change and separate, she saw something falling to the ground from high above them that none of the others had seemed to have seen yet; Touro ran forward before Lonac could stop her, she leaped up onto Inker using him as a kind of spring board pushing herself even higher catching the ball.

"Look at Touro go, the caught ball to Roaring Torch; ten opening points." The commentator shouted excitedly. "It's been a couple of matches since I've seen anyone actually catching it... what a way to start out; we'll all be keeping an eye on this Touro from now on."

Touro landed on soft grass and rolled a couple of feet before she stopped and looked around getting to her feet, she was in some sort of meadow with trees and fence over near the edge of the platform; she couldn't believe how real it all seemed.

"Tour, behind you!" Jo-Mi shouted.

She turned around and was about to throw the ball to him, but something didn't seem right, there was something in front of him but she couldn't make out what it was.

"Tour!" Jo-Mi shouted.

Touro was about to throw it to him when the blurred imagine in front of her suddenly shone brightly blinding her making her stumble backwards over something on the ground, she heard something howl coming towards her from the left; it was coming quickly so she threw the ball at it hitting him in the face making him howl out in pain.

"Got it!" Jo-Mi shouted.

Touro turned over squinting from the bright light and came face to face with a very angry wolf, he had a deep red glossy coat so she knew that it wasn't Inker; no one had told her that they had two wolves...or did they she couldn't remember, his brown eyes looked as though they were ready to kill her.

"Sorry..." Touro whispered.

His eyes seemed to soften, but she didn't understand why since he was on the opposite side; she didn't care at the moment only about somehow managing to survive this game in one piece.

"I thought that they had finally found a good Rose, with your opening but after that I guess not." A man said behind her somewhere in the bright light.

Touro didn't care what he thought of her, she just wanted to get rid of that light so that she could still see; she waved her hand in the direction where he was stood, he lifted off the ground and flew over towards the tree hitting the truck with quite a thud.

"I hope that was a little better." Touro said getting to her feet, she looked at the wolf hoping that he wasn't going to do anything to her; which he didn't only ran off and then disappeared but she couldn't see where he had gone. "Great."

"Vi seems to be enjoying himself today, it seems as though he brought his little bag of tricks with him as well." The commentator said. "Lonac looks as though he's going to be tied up in the jungle for a while, I guess the beach would have been the better place to be caught up in; more sun."

Touro had no idea how to get to the other platforms, she knew there were gateways or doors, but the problem was that she couldn't see them; she had hoped that they would kind of be like that fence thing, or perhaps they were and her powers haven't come back yet. Touro looked around knowing that she probably looked stupid to all those people watching, she wasn't really doing anything to help just standing around filling in the numbers; but that wasn't really what she wanted to do, now that she was here she wanted to be able to help in some way.

Lonac needed help, she focused on him knowing that he was on the jungle platform and that she needed to find the door; she looked over at the guy who was still lying under the tree and then looked up on its lowest branches, there it was. She ran over to it, jumped up and swung around near enough throwing herself through the doorway.

She appeared up another tree almost falling out but caught onto the branch and swung around again, kicking Vi in the face making him drop a vial of something; he looked up to see who was there and was quite surprised to see Touro.

"Sorry, but I can't let you do that." Touro told him.

"No need to apologise." Vi said pleasantly.

"Ready?" Touro asked Lonac who was hanging from the vines in the tree next to her.

"For what?" Lonac asked still struggling against his bindings.

Touro reached out and touched the vines, they set on fire dissolving into ash; he fell to the ground in a heap while Touro jumped down gracefully beside of him. He looked up at her and smiled slightly.

"I didn't quite see how she got him down, but I believe that our new Rose player might just have a few tricks up her sleeve after all." The commentator said excitedly. "Now let's see if The Roaring Torch can get back any points since Vikas have already scored three times."

"What, when did they do that?" Touro asked.

They both looked at her as she shrugged and then carried on walking past them both, through the densely packed jungle.

"Does she even know what she's doing?" Vi asked Lonac who was getting to his feet to go after her.

"We'll find out soon enough." Lonac said as he followed after her and Vi went off in the other direction. "Wait up...do you even know where you're going?"

"There's four people just up ahead, can't you see them?" Touro said as she quickened her pace pushed the branches out of her way.

"You can see people through this?" Lonac said unconvinced.

"Yeah there." Touro said pointing ahead but went right as though to circle around them.

Lonac had no idea what she could see, he couldn't see anything but still decided to follow her until he could find the door to get off of the platform; that's when he heard someone ahead shout out in pain and the buzz of an energy field.

"It doesn't sound very high..." Touro said remembering her encounter with Zar-Jins.

Lonac walked a little faster looking through the coverage and saw Zuyo caught in the electric net, her long golden hair which was all braided was shining, but behind her were three others Jo-Mi and Rox and also the captain of the Vikas team, Ida holding the ball; she didn't seem to be doing so well two against one and it was going to be soon four against one.

Touro and Lonac pushed away the branches when the whole of the platform shuddered and faded away for a moment, Lonac beside of

Touro disappeared and she reappeared on a beach with Jo-Mi and Rox who still had Ida cornered. Touro wasn't sure what had happened only that she was now on the beach platform and that there was a warmish breeze on her back, but she didn't have long to think about that when something green ran at her and she fell back into the ocean head first.

Touro's head went under the water, panic filling her as she had never been very good at swimming and couldn't hold her breath even if her life depended on it; she kicked out at who had knocked her over and saw that it was a woman with green skin and hair. The two of them seemed to slash around as they struggled against each other, Touro wanted to get out of the water as she couldn't really swim nor could she use her powers properly in the water either; the other woman though didn't seem to care about being in the water as long as she kept her distracted long enough for her captain to get away.

"Ida!" A man shouted as he jumped down from the rocks behind Rox, he turned around and seemed to blast something at the rock face causing a rock slide; he jumped out of the way just in time. "Hay...damn it!"

Touro pushed her away noticing something high in the sky, it was a door; but she didn't understand why it was so far out of the way. She could only think of one way up there, but she didn't know if she could do that; but if she could at least get the ball through it and to another team member who wasn't having so much trouble. She focused her energy on heating up the water as quickly as she could, she could feel it herself; now she needed to get out as the steam started to rise.

Touro managed to push the other woman off of her and grabbed onto a kind of ledge which was made out of hot air, she pulled herself up and seemed to be just sat in mid air.

"Well it seems as though we're just going to have free for all today guys." The commentator said. "And Touro, she's just sat there watching; in the air...even we don't see that, that often."

"Throw us the ball!" Touro shouted as she stood up.

Jo-Mi looked out at her, at first he wouldn't have even considered it and then he seemed to have seen something as well.

"Venadve!" Jo-Mi shouted.

The ball shot out of Ida's hands and went straight to Jo-Mi who had called for it, something so simple but still effective; he gave it to Rox and pointed to Touro who was a couple of feet above the ocean and out of reach of the other woman who was still slashing around trying to get her. Rox threw it as hard as he could, Touro prayed that she would catch it after what they were doing; she stepped forward holding out her hands and it just fell into them, she quickly pulled the ball into her and then turning around she threw it up into the air straight at the doorway she had seen.

Touro suddenly fell back into the ocean further out this time, she started to flail her arms and legs about trying to reach the bottom to stand up but couldn't reach it; her head went under the water again making her choke and then suddenly it was all gone. She was lying on the platform that they had started on, she looked around wondering what was going on as Jo-Mi held his hand out for her; she took it and allowed him to help her up.

"What happened?" Touro asked him.

"Well...The Roaring Torch wins!" The commentator shouted.

"We won?" Touro said confused.

"Yes." Jo-Mi said looking at her dripping wet.

Leka put his arm around her smiling, pulling her closer to him, even though she tried to pull away from him; they were suddenly engulfed in the purple smoke again disappearing and then reappeared in the changing room.

"What just happened?" Touro asked.

"We won." Leka said excitedly.

"You scored the winning point." Jo-Mi told her.

"What through that thing in the air?" Touro asked him pulling away from Leka finally her boots squelching. "Seriously?"

They all looked at her as though wondering if she was the one joking that she hadn't realised what she had done, but they could see that she had no idea.

"You scored, we won." Jo-Mi told her smiling. "You can play in our next game, just get a little more training before-hand...I mean about the game."

"Wait, you want me to play again?" Touro asked following him across the changing room as he took his armour off and she left wet foot prints behind. "But..."

"You don't want to?" Jo-Mi asked her turning around suddenly.

"Well, that isn't it...I thought I was just covering?" Touro said.

"And you can do, for the next couple of matches; we'll see how you go." Jo-Mi told her. "If you don't mind, I want to get changed unless you want to watch me?"

Touro went bright red and her whole suit just steamed up, all the water evaporated and she was born dry.

"That was interesting." Jo-Mi said smiling at her. "I think you'll do just fine."

"But..." Touro said turning around going over to Kima-Na to avoid Leka who looked as though he wanted to embrace her again.

Toria sat at her desk in her quarters dressed for bed in a yellow vest top and trousers, her long hair down her back and partly over her shoulder; the computer screen showing Siren and Kyo who seemed just as excited as she was.

"I can't believe that you actually played." Siren said.

"I can't believe that you won for the team." Kyo told her. "He was going to ask me as well."

"Yeah I know, he said." Toria said off handedly. "Sorry, but he also asked me to stay on for the next couple of matches... To begin with I didn't want to do it, and just after it was all over; but now I'm actually looking forward to the next time."

"Well who would have thought it, hay...Touro the Rose player for the Roaring Torch." Kyo said smiling. "I'm glad for you."

"Okay, so come on tell us what happened next." Siren told her. "I mean with your new position."

"Oh right yeah, well after everything that's happened since I was on board Jasp'erat's ship; they thought that I did well spotting all those incidents with the Magics." Toria told them. "So they're sending me to talk to this Lord Zebulon guy, he sells his people off as slaves; they want a good deal to make up for the ones that they've just lost."

"So they're sending you?" Kyo asked a little confused.

"I know, I found it strange as well, and to be honest I'm not really looking forward to meeting a guy who is willing to sell out his own people just to save himself." Toria told them. "But that's what they want me to do, they want me to sound him out to make sure that he's still working for them; and to get them a good range of slaves. To be honest, I refused to begin with, telling them that I didn't approve of what they made them do on those pleasure worlds; Colonel Web said that he understood where I was coming from...I didn't believe him and he probably thought that I was being soft."

"After what you did?" Kyo said. "I don't really think that anyone can call you soft."

"Yeah well, anyway I'll be there in an hour." Toria told them.

"Then why are you dressed for bed?" Siren asked her.

"Because...well I've been trying to get some sleep for the past couple of days but I haven't been able to...perhaps I'm just too excited with everything that's been happening." Toria told them.

"Well as soon as this is over, you should be able to get some sleep; it's probably 'cause you're just over excited about everything like you said." Siren told her. "I'm glad that everything's working out for you. To be honest, I didn't really think that you would be able to do so much and so soon as well...good luck and be safe."

"And to you too as well, see ya soon." Toria said before she logged off, she leant back in her chair spun around before she got up to get dressed.

She walked through to her bedroom and scowled at the jumpsuit that she had to wear, it wasn't very nice and how was she supposed to get to this guy who was supposedly a ladies man dressed like that; she picked up the jumpsuit off of the bed and walked over to the mirror to hold it up.

The mirror though wasn't reflecting her, but instead an arm came out of the mirror and grabbed hold of her trying to pulling her inside, Toria fought against it dropping her uniform and kicking the mirror shattering it into a hundred pieces falling to the floor though not before several of the pieces cut her bare leg.

"Damn it." Toria said carefully stepping back trying not to step on any of the broken pieces of glass, since she didn't have anything on her feet.

She couldn't believe it, an arm had actually tried to pull her in there; she would never have been able to go through though would she? She really didn't want to know, only that every mirror she had was covered.

It had solved her problem about what to wear, she wore a normal Fleet uniform only with a pencil skirt instead of trousers which she had explained to the captain why and that she hadn't had time to get it sorted out by their doctor.

Touro walked up the high ceiling corridor following one of the

Lords security officers, who wore a brown jacket with gold buttons fastening the front and trimmed around the edge at the back of the jacket, he had black trousers with knee boots and like her, their heels echoed against the walls that didn't hold a single piece of art work.

Along the corridor there were vases every so often which were almost as tall as she was and filled with beautiful long stemmed blue and silver flowers. Which she wished that she actually had some herself, though she knew that she couldn't really ask this Lord guy if she could have some.

"Lord Zebulon is waiting for you in here." The security officer told her as he stopped at the end of the corridor and pushed it open just enough so that Toria could go inside but not enough so that she could see clearly.

"You're not coming in?" Toria asked him.

"He asked to speak with you alone." The security officer told her.

"Very well then, thank you." Toria said and went inside.

It was another huge room with high ceilings, a long table with sixteen chairs set around it but only two places made at the very top where a man was sat with long blonde hair waiting for her. She stepped further into the room, but didn't rush over to him as she glanced around the room taking everything in; there were thick beautiful embroidered fabrics hung from the ceilings to the floor every couple of feet and all along the back wall behind the Lord, but there was also a engraved wooden throne with gold melted into it along with jewels.

Toria stopped and stood to attention and then at ease, she waited for him to look over at her but he just carried on drinking his wine; he wore black armour with a red cape and skin-tight trousers with sliver metal boots.

"Lord Zebulon, I am Toria Kentaro; I've been sent to discuss the amount of slaves that we wish to purchase from you." Toria told him.

Lord Zebulon put his glass down on the table and finally looked over at her, he seemed amused by her presence, but she didn't know why it wasn't as though she had done anything only enter the room.

"Well you're not what they normally send me." Lord Zebulon said finally. "They normally send stiffs, I could get used to you coming around though."

"I'm not here for your amusement sir. I'm here to do my job." Toria told him.

Lord Zebulon smiled at her as he pushed his chair back and stood up, he was almost a foot taller than her. Toria couldn't help but think that he was very handsome and understood why he was such a ladies' man, he could just smile at them and they would probably throw themselves at him.

"Why don't you make yourself at home?" Lord Zebulon told her as he stepped closer to her as though he was going to do something and then changed his mind and walked over to his throne, as he sat down on it the front under part slide out as a foot rest and he put up his feet.

Toria looked over at him, sat on his throne and then pulled out the chair of the place that was set for her and sat down, though turning her chair slightly so that she could still see him; she crossed her legs so that he could see the cuts on them along the side.

"What happened?" Lord Zebulon asked her. "You didn't follow your orders?"

"Nothing like that." Toria said smiling at him. "I had a little accident with my mirror; I guess I didn't like what I saw."

"Most Fleet officers just pretend not to see anything at all." Lord Zebulon told her.

"Maybe I'm not like the rest of those old fools." Toria said pleasantly watching him carefully trying to read him, wondering how she could use him. "So, unless you want me to stay; why don't we get down to business?"

"I'd like you to stay very much, then in the morning we can solve your business." Lord Zebulon told her.

"It's the Fleet's business; I'm here to do my job which I did mention." Toria told him pleasantly. "And I won't be staying the night. All I want from you is slaves. I killed too many; so they need replacements."

"You? You killed them?" Lord Zebulon said shaken by her comment.

"Yes, I believe there was someone called Sorly." Toria told him turning to the table to pick up her goblet of wine.

Lord Zebulon rose from his seat and was across the room in a matter of seconds, he pulled her chair around to face him forcibly knocking the goblet out of her hand and spilling it over the table spoiling the food; he put his hand on the back of her chair as he leant in to her.

"I don't believe that such an innocent little thing such as yourself could kill so many of them." Lord Zebulon said calmly as he brought his hand over her shoulder, his finger gently stroked her face.

Toria felt a gentle shiver where he had touched her, but there something else as well; something different than normal, something that she had never felt before. She pushed him away and quickly moved away from him, but he turned around and smiled at her as he followed her while she backed up into the wall.

"Well they have sent me a real treat this time." Lord Zebulon said smiling at her as he advanced on her.

"I'm sixteen years old, a cadet...do you really think this is suitable behaviour?" Toria demanded looking around wondering what she could do and if she could take him down, without getting into too much trouble for it. "I told you that I'm not here..."

"Perhaps you'll change your mind, if I can get you to change into your Tasian form with just a touch?" Lord Zebulon asked her as he got closer and she backed into the wall.

"Touch me, and I swear..." Toria warned him, but he didn't seem to believe that she was capable of hurting anyone.

He reached out to touch her again, but this time she grabbed him and pulled him closer and then kneed him in the groin before she pushed him off of her; she walked around him out of reach as he watched her going to leave.

"I don't want many more than normal, just perhaps one hundred more." Toria told him. "I'll wait for your reply on the ship."

"You're just going to leave me here like this, what if I tell them that you're a Tasian?" Lord Zebulon asked her.

"I've had quite a few medicals since I joined the Fleet, and no one's really going to care especially if I'm killing my own kind." Toria told him. "And just so you know, I'm not."

"I'll keep your secret if you help me out with something, I'll also give you the extra slaves that you want." Lord Zebulon told her.

"Whatever, as long I get the slaves; send me the info to the ship." Toria told him and then smiled suddenly. "I'm already looking forward to next time."

"So am I." Lord Zebulon told her.

Toria breathed a sign of relief when she finally got back into her quarters and locked the door behind her, she couldn't believe that she just fell apart like that and she had almost transformed into her natural form even though she hadn't even seen herself in it yet; it wasn't as though she didn't find him kind of attractive but he was a traitor, why the hell would she like someone like him. Then it dawned on her, that would be how others thought of her.

Toria shook herself, she wasn't really a traitor unlike him who was selling his own people off just to make sure that he lived a comfortable life; yeah well he wasn't going to be comfortable for much longer not if she had anything to do about it.

Her computer started to beep, she looked over at it wondering who it could be hoping that Renji wasn't starting to pester her again; then she remembered that Lord Zebulon had told her that he had wanted her help with something, perhaps he was sending her the information on it already. She walked over to her desk and around to sit down, the screen read that there was a message waiting for her; she activated the message.

It wasn't a message, but information; she read through the whole of the data twice just to be sure what she was looking at, it was tracker codes. She didn't understand why he was sending her tracker codes and how many of the slaves had them.

"This couldn't be..." Toria said to herself. "He couldn't be trying to do the same thing as I am...?"

She wasn't sure what to do with this, he was either trying to do what she's kind of doing also; or it could be a trap, he was trying to figure out just what side she was really on considering that he knew what species she was.

"What the hell am I supposed to do?" Toria asked herself.

Toria had had nearly a week to come up with a plan; she had managed to call Ichigo to inform him of the situation or rather part of it that she might need his help evacuating the slaves earlier than normal; she didn't tell him that she might be being tested by someone else because she didn't want him to get caught up in the middle of all this.

Toria was still wearing the Fleet uniform with the skirt, she actually felt more comfortable dressed this way, even though it had caused a little problem with the captain of the ship; but as she reminded him she wasn't actually out of uniform and also she'd look better while talking to the new governor of Ra'sa'tis.

She sat in the waiting room in one of the large comfy chairs, that looked out over the grounds through the floor to ceiling windows; she had been shown into the room by an officer and then left alone; this was ten minutes ago. She hadn't been expecting a warm welcome since what happened last time that she was here, but this was actually quite annoying; she would only wait a little longer before she went to find the governor herself.

Toria waited another five minutes before someone finally decided to come and see her, he was about the same height as she was and had pale blue skin with two head tails tied together; he didn't wear a shirt only a loose pair of grey trousers and was bare-footed. She was quite surprised, he wasn't really like any official that she had met before and she knew for a fact that her father definitely wouldn't want anything to do with him, considering how he dressed.

"So you're the little girl who's been giving everyone so much trouble lately." He said smiling at her, quite amused that the rumours were right. "Well, I didn't want to believe it; but here you are."

"I don't really care what you think of me to be honest, I'm only here to give you more slaves; though considering that this place won't be operating as a pleasure world for sometime they have to go to the mining colonies." Toria told him. "It's a shame isn't it, that you got to become governor and you can't keep any of them; not until the whole place is rebuilt. What a shame for you."

"It won't take long." He told her. "Your slaves are going to help, the ones that you're bringing..."

"Actually you can only have two dozen, the rest have to go to the mining colony; it's all in the transit reports." Toria told him.

He looked as though he was ready to spit fire at her, a little girl getting one over on him like this.

"I've already had the ship transport down the workers that you'll need here." Toria told him standing and picking up the data sheet off the chair arm. "All you have to do is sign here, saying that you've reserved them."

"I'll get them all, you count on it." He told her as he snatched the data sheet out of her hand. "I'll make this place even better than it was before."

"Really, and if there's nothing left; then what?" Toria asked him smiling slightly.

"What? Is that a threat?" He asked her. "I'm going to contact your commanding officer..."

"There's no need for that, we've already received word that the complex has been reporting problems of overloads in its systems since the explosion." Toria told him.

"No we..." He started but wasn't given a chance to finish as she pulled out a blaster from under her jacket and shot him, he just looked at her, his eyes wide as he fell to the ground.

"Toria to security..." Toria said as she activated her com unit.

"Security here, we detected weapons fire; report." The man said through her com as she walked over to the wall console, and activated it logging into the main system since they hadn't changed the access codes.

"He attacked me, saying that I ruined his big chance...wait a minute

262

I can hear something...I'm not sure what it is though..." Toria said sounding worried.

"It's another overload, we're getting you out of there..." The officer told her.

"But wait..." Toria protested, but still allowed herself to be transported back on board the ship reappearing in the transporter room; she pressed her com. "Toria to bridge...what just happened down there sir?'

"The whole complex blew, section by section it just overloaded; we didn't realise that the problems were so bad..." The first officer said sounding quite shaken.

"I'll start to analyse the data, to find out if there was anything that we could have done to stop this from happening." Toria told him before she signed off and left the transporter room feeling quite pleased with herself.

The large heavy door to Lord Zebulon's throne room was thrown open banging against the wall knocking the vase over which smashed, water spilling out over the floor, as Lord Zebulon marched in and over to Toria who was sat at the top of the table in his chair smiling at him.

"It really is nice to see you again." Toria said pleasantly.

"What've you done?" Lord Zebulon demanded waving his hand behind him closing the door with another bang.

"Are you supposed to use your powers so freely like that?" Toria asked him. "You should be careful, my ship may pick up on you and you'll end up in a lot of trouble just like those people you sold out to be slaves; though now they're dead, short lived slaves I should say."

"How dare you speak about my people like that." Lord Zebulon told her grabbing hold of her and pulling her to her feet. "I asked for your help..."

"You mean you asked a complete stranger for help, someone who told you that they like killing Magics." Toria said pushing him away easily as he had loosened his grip on her, suddenly realising what she was saying. "You had no idea who I really was, yet you thought that I'd help you all because you think that I'm a Tasian. Why the hell would I help someone who sells out his own people, just so that he can live a better life?"

Lord Zebulon slapped her across the face, the slap stung more than anything she had felt before; she felt herself feeling light on her feet and sway slightly and also her form changed, but only for a moment before she regained control of it.

"Sir, wait!" A man shouted from the door.

They both looked over to see who it was, Toria was just as surprised as Lord Zebulon was to see who it was.

"Are you Sorly?" Toria asked him.

"You said he was dead?" Lord Zebulon asked her.

"I did kill him, he doesn't know how to stay disappeared when given the chance." Toria answered.

"Wait a minute..." Lord Zebulon said turning back around to her a little confused.

263

"If you're really trying to somehow save your people then I'll help where and if I can, but you have to help me out in return." Toria told him. "I can make them to disappear to begin with, but I can't move them all...it takes too long."

"Now you're asking for my help, after you just said that I shouldn't trust a stranger." Lord Zebulon said.

"I trust him, I didn't say that I trusted you completely yet." Toria told him.

Lord Zebulon looked over at Sorly who nodded and then back at Toria who was holding her face where he had just hit her.

"I'm sorry about that." Lord Zebulon told her. "Why don't you spend the night, while I have my men take care of a few supplies you may need."

"Supplies?" Toria asked a little confused to why she would need supplies and from him of all people. "Perhaps next time about staying over, my captain wants me where he can see; well on his ship anyway but we'll be leaving in a few hours."

"That'll have to do then, but I'll hold you to that; next time you'll spend the night." Lord Zebulon told her.

Toria smiled at him as she walked past to leave, Sorly smiled kindly at her as he stepped aside; he only looked a couple of years older than her in his face but she could see it in his eyes that he was much older because of everything that had happened.

"I hope to see you again." Toria told him.

"Be careful, the galaxy is a cruel place to our kind." Sorly told her.

"I know, I intend to become one of them; just don't tell anyone what I'm really up to." Toria said smiling at him before she left.

Toria felt relieved when she got back to her quarters and flopped on her sofa underneath the view port, she didn't bother looking out as her quarters weren't on the planet side and just looked out into the system; she hadn't realised properly that there were crates next to her desk. She looked over to see if she was seeing things, which she did from time to time, but they were really there; she got up and went over to find out just what he had sent her.

"My so called, much needed supplies." Toria said smiling to herself as she unlocked the first crate.

She couldn't believe what was inside, several small rectangular devices that fitted into the palm of the hand; she knew what they were, she just couldn't believe that he had given them to her and the energy pack with recharges.

"Body shields..." Toria whispered to herself. "I'll definitely need these. Thanks."

Toria just sat on the floor going through the crates that he had sent her, wondering how she could have been so wrong about him to begin with; but partly understanding now why he is the way that he is, because she's doing it as well. They both know how it'll probably end, though for Toria if Ahtoury's right she might not need the Magics to find her.

Chapter Seventeen

Two security officers walked up the corridor towards the training arena, they had two torn beige coloured long sleeved tops and black trousers; they were Magical security officers. The one on the left was carrying a data pad in his purple hand while his head tails swung slightly with his movements; the other man looked somewhat annoyed frowning, his dark eyes narrowed upon his grey face, he pushed his white hair back out of his face roughly.

"I can't believe that I missed another match, and now they won't be playing until the tournament starts." The white haired man said angrily.

"You still following Roaring Torch? They've had a crap year." The purple man said amused by his friend. "Come on Dalal, see sense. They're new Rose player was injured in her second match, she couldn't even finish playing."

"That could have happened to anyone." Dalal told him. "She came back, and did alright in the next match..."

"They still lost." The purple guy reminded him.

"Not by much, and it wasn't her fault." Dalal protested hitting the panel on the door.

The door slid open into the dimly lit arena, that was echoing blaster fire from their captain who was doing target practice; they walked over to him keeping to the safe path that was marked out on the floor with reflective markers.

"Sir, we've just returned." Dalal said aloud trying to talk over the blaster fire.

The blaster fire stopped and the lights became a little brighter, Renji returned his blaster to the holster which was strapped to his thigh; his long red crimson hair was tied back in a pony tail out of his way. His uniform was slightly different, he wore a vest in two tone red because he was the captain; but also the vest showed off his native markings more, across his chest and down his arms; thick black patterned lines.

"Did you find her?" Renji asked them, but they just stood there as if they didn't want to report their news to him. "Dalal, Kayro; I asked you a question?"

"Well sir, we found her; that part wasn't really very hard." Dalal told him.

"She didn't want to come along with us, she put up quite a fight." Kayro told him nervously. "Sir, she's either a Magic able to deflect our spells or she has a properly functioning body shield."

"What?" Renji said a little confused. "The Fleet don't just hand them out, especially to cadets..."

"Oh, she also had some good news sir; she's an ensign now." Dalal told him. "They probably think that she's done such a good job out there that she doesn't need to go back to finish her training, bastards."

Renji smiled suddenly surprising them both, they looked at each other and then back at him.

"Sir, she'll be returning to the senate for the late summer events and then for her new posting." Kayro told him.

"They haven't decided where to put her?" Renji said thoughtfully. "I think our luck has just changed."

They both looked at him confused, wondering why this news had pleased him when really the whole thing was actually bad news; but he didn't seem to want to explain himself to them just yet.

Music was being played by the grand staircase where everyone made their entrance from above through the engraved golden dragon doors, below couples danced gracefully to music their gowns sweeping across the marble floor making it look as though they were merely floating. Those that didn't want to dance sat at the tables around the edge of the hall, making small talk and also learning the latest gossip and information; this was actually the main reason why these functions were so popular, so that people could find out what was really going on because being stuck on a star ship, you didn't really get to find everything that was going on.

Kasiya had his shoulder length brown hair down, but slightly pulled back out of his face and wore an elegant double breasted jacket suit; he was stood with his first officer Neil who was in his dress uniform and their security chief Rylan who was also in his dress uniform.

"So sir, are you going to tell me now why we came all this way?" Neil asked him, he looked at his captain and then out among the sea of officers, lords, ladies and officials.

"I've come to get a new recruit." Kasiya told him finally.

"And why did you come all the way here to meet them in person?" Neil asked.

"Because it's been a while since I last saw her in person." Kasiya told him still searching himself for her through the sea of people before him.

"Her? A woman?" Neil said smiling. "Well it's about time sir."

"She's seventeen years old; the only interest that I have in her is as an officer." Kasiya told him firmly, which was when he saw her; there was no mistaking her even at this distance.

He watched her enter beside her father, her hair was half up and half down with part of it over her shoulders; she wore a pinkish red halter-neck grown which was slit up the center to reveal the under grown which was a lighter shade. She took her father's arm as they walked down the grand staircase, Kasiya watched them as he made his way across the room not seeming to look where he was going but not bumping into anyone either; his two officers followed him as quickly as they could but they weren't as graceful as he was moving through the crowd of people.

Senator Kentaro stepped down first and was then followed by Toria, he was ready to lead them off to the right to begin the rounds; but she stopped for a moment as if she felt someone, she looked over towards the nearest table and saw him.

Toria was a little surprised to see him, it had been several years since the last time that she had seen him; but also she couldn't get rid of the thought that she had dreamt about him being a Tasian, and how much more handsome he would be if he would stay in that form.

Senator Kentaro seemed to notice how distracted she was and looked over to see what had caught his daughter's attention, he was pleasantly surprised to see Kasiya himself; so he lead her over to greet him.

"She's seventeen?" Neil whispered, but Kasiya ignored his question.

"Captain Kasiya, it's a pleasure to see you again." Senator Kentaro said shaking his hand and then introduced his daughter. "I don't know if you remember my daughter, Victoria."

"How could I forget, especially after recently reading all these reports about her; they are about you?" Kasiya said looking at her alone.

"Yes, I only joined the Fleet last year; but I seem to be given opportunities to shine." Toria said smiling slightly at him.

"Yes, I heard that you've already been made an ensign and are just waiting for your first posting." Kasiya said.

"I'm sure that you could put a good word in for her with your friends, Captain." Senator Kentaro said.

"Father please." Toria said shyly.

"Despite your age, your record is very good; it speaks for itself, I'm sure that someone will snatch you up quickly enough." Kasiya told her.

Toria smiled wondering if he knew about her, she couldn't get rid of the feeling that he was a Tasian and then she remembered, he knew Renji.

"Would you mind if I steal your daughter away, for a while?" Kasiya asked the senator surprising them all.

"Of course not." Senator Kentaro said smiling, quite pleased for her.

"Victoria..." Kasiya said his arm out for her to take.

She smiled at him even though she didn't like how he had called her Victoria, then she took his arm and walked off with him leaving her father behind; he waved his officers back as he lead her out onto the balcony through the heavy burgundy and cream curtains. It was still quite mild even though it was quite late but it had also been a very hot summer so far. There were a few small tables set outside by candle light, only two of the tables were occupied; Kasiya lead Toria over to the furthest one by the edge of the balcony, he pulled her chair out for her and then sat down himself.

"So do you prefer Victoria now, or do you still prefer to be called Toria?" Kasiya asked her.

"Toria." She answered.

"Are you worried?" Kasiya asked her.

"And why should I be worried?" Toria asked him smiling, but she partly was by his line of questions.

"That I might know your secret." Kasiya told her.

"Secret? I don't have any secrets." Toria told him calmly.

"You know that I'm a friend of Renji Aba'rain's?" Kasiya asked her watching her carefully.

"I think I remember seeing the two of you together a few years ago, the Magics attacked that night." Toria said. "The two of you seemed quite well prepared."

"We were." Kasiya told her.

This threw Toria slightly, she wasn't really expecting him to just come right out and say it; but she calmed herself, though not quick enough as he had noted her surprise.

"You were wondering when we met, I could tell." Kasiya told her.

"What, you used your powers on me?" Toria asked him, not bothering to dance around the matter and just bringing it straight up.

"I didn't need to use my powers, it was written all over your face." Kasiya told her. "You just wanted to know for sure."

"That you're a Tasian?" Toria said.

"Yes." Kasiya said looking at her questioningly. "How did you know that I was a Tasian?"

"And wouldn't you love to know that." Toria said standing up to leave, but he didn't try to stop her.

"So are you, so why are you doing what you do?" Kasiya asked her.

"They're the enemy, isn't that what we do?" Toria said turning around to answer his question. "And for the slaves, it was an example to the rest of them not to try it again. Though to be honest, at least this way they're better off considering what they do to them there."

"Do you honestly believe that they would chose death?" Kasiya asked her.

"I wouldn't want that life, if I was them...so yes I do believe that they are better off." Toria told him before she walked away.

"You still care for them in your own strange way." Kasiya said to himself as he watched her walk away back inside.

Toria still couldn't get over Captain Kasiya the night before, how he had just come out and told her that he was a Magic and that he knew she was; she definitely didn't want to get on board his ship even though if things were different and he didn't know about her then perhaps his ship would have been her first choice, since it would see a lot of action.

She wore her hair up tonight in gathered buns, with a lilac dress the top fitted out like a corset and the bottom layered like her other dress had been, only that this one had a frame underneath it.

She had been distracted the whole night so far while her father lead her around another night of introductions, she could hardly remember anyone that she had spoken to let alone what they had said to her.

"Good evening Senator." An Admiral said cheerfully as he walked over to join them, he was the same age as her father but was already going bald on top and his hair turning grey.

"Admiral Persius, I didn't realize that you were coming tonight." Senator Kentaro said shaking his hand.

"I had some business that I need to take care of." Admiral Persius told him, turning his attention to Toria; but he didn't shake her hand but kissed it instead. "It's pleasure to finally meet you, after hearing so much about you. Your father was worried that the Fleet wasn't the place for you, though it's turned out to be the best place by far."

"Thank you sir." Toria said.

"Now, I know you've been waiting for this news since you got your promotion." Admiral Persius told her. "You've actually had quite a bit of interest, but there was one captain that seemed to want you more than any of the others."

"Seriously?' Toria said smiling unable to hide her excitement. "Who is it, what ship is it...sir?"

"Well, considering that he couldn't make it down tonight; I'll leave that as a surprise for you." Admiral Persius told her smiling back. "Though the ship is in orbit and you're allowed to transport aboard whenever you want."

"So I could go up now?" Toria asked excitedly.

"You're not in your uniform dear." Senator Kentaro reminded her.

"The captain did say she could come aboard tonight if she wanted, and her belongings in the morning." Admiral Persius told him.

"Father?" Toria said turning to him.

The senator smiled then nodded, giving into his daughter; she hugged him and then gave him a kiss on the cheek. "I'll have Bernal send up your things, and expect you to call a little more often this time."

"Of course father." Toria said smiling. "Thank you Admiral Persius, I won't let you down."

"I hope not, but you have kind of set yourself up rather high already." Admiral Persius said. "Good luck dear."

"I'll call." Toria told her father before she walked off; bumping into an older man who she smiled at before she walked off.

He turned around to her father making himself a part of their group, he was dressed in a midnight blue green suit with silver buttons; his hair was dark brown and brush back.

"General Conoab, enjoying yourself?" Admiral Persius asked him.

"Yes, though I would enjoy myself more if I knew of the young lady who just left." General Conoab said smiling.

"My daughter, and a little young for you at the moment." Senator Kentaro told him evenly. "Though personally I think she has her eye on someone else, I mean if he plays his cards right that is."

"Old fashioned man, Ramiro; you need to approve of her choice of a man?" Admiral Persius said amused.

"Well then, I'll just have to prove that I'm the better man then won't I." General Conoab told them.

Toria turned the corner into the transport room, the two men stood behind the console were talking and didn't seem to notice that she had entered the room; she cleared her throat as she walked over to the pad, they both stood to attention even though they didn't know who she actually was.

"Admiral Persius has sent me, Toria Kentaro." She told them.

"Oh, yes...right..." The man on the left said accessing the console looking for the data, before he activated the pad. "The captain will be waiting for you when you arrive."

"Thank you." Toria said before she was engulfed in the bright white light and everything around her disappeared for a moment.

She felt herself reappearing and the light fading, she could make out another transporter room; she couldn't make out the officer stood in front of the console to begin with until the light faded completely. She just stared at him, he wasn't really what she was expecting.

"Miss Kentaro, welcome to the Ake'cheta. I'm glad that you decided to come aboard tonight; you look beautiful." Kasiya told her.

"What?" Toria said still confused at why he wanted her on board his ship, but the more that she thought about the more it actually made sense; he'd want to keep a close eye on her and stop her if she tried anything, well that just meant that she would have to try even harder than before. "I mean...sorry...I was startled for a moment, surprised even that someone such as yourself would ask for me personally."

"You intrigue me." Kasiya told her. "Why don't I give you the tour?"

"I don't need special treatment, sir." Toria told him as she stepped down off of the pad, she knew that she couldn't turn this down because there would be too many questions; she'd have to tough it out.

"I don't mind, and you are special...fresh out of the academy after just a couple of months." Kasiya said motioning for them to leave together. "I'd like to know a little about you while I tell you about your duties on board my ship."

"Very well then sir." Toria said following him out of the transporter room and into the corridor. "Perhaps I should change? I rushed up here, without thinking much of my appearance."

"You're not on duty yet, and I won't take you anywhere that you're not allowed dressed like you are." Kasiya assured her.

Toria thought that the ship looked like the other two she had been on, though corridors did all look the same after all there wasn't really much you could do to them; she knew that the quarters would be the same as well as they were standard throughout the Fleet. It was only the actual layout of the ships that were different, hopefully it wouldn't take her long to figure out where everything was; it wasn't as though she had to sleep much so she had the extra time to study up on the ship and its crew including her captain.

"So what class of ship is this then?" Toria asked him.

"Battle ready three." Kasiya told her.

"So it's capable of going up against low-level Magics?" Toria said. "I couldn't find out what was the type of ship that a Battle ready one would be able to go up against."

"They are mainly run by Storms, they're capable of attacking fully capable Magical ships." Kasiya told her.

"But I don't understand, I thought that the Magics no longer had anything that could withstand our attacks...unless they've been building new ships in secret?" Toria asked him.

"During war there are times like this one, that both sides have to step back from the fighting to regroup; that's what the Magics are doing." Kasiya told her.

"They'll lose if they don't start fighting seriously against us, won't they?" Toria asked him stopping at the lift. "Does that upset you, that it doesn't seem to matter what you do it never seems enough? It upsets Renji, he wants to do more than he is doing; but he can't."

"Does it upset you, that you've betrayed him; after he risked so much for you?" Kasiya asked her.

270

Toria smiled at him briefly. "What did he risk for me, his life to take me away and turn me against my family...my father the only family that I've ever known? And I haven't really betrayed him."

The lift doors opened and Toria went inside but Kasiya didn't follow her, she turned around to face him; his composure had changed to that of a cold man not welcoming at all.

"You betrayed Renji." Kasiya told her.

"Then why wasn't he arrested, I know what he is; I've known for years." Toria told him smiling. "If I'd really betrayed, I would have turned him in."

"Or perhaps you seem to think, keeping him free and having to read about you doing all these crimes against his people is more fitting?" Kasiya suggested, but Toria just struggled. "Your quarters are on deck seven section thirteen, you've been assigned to security; report to Rylan at 09:45 in the morning."

"You don't want to give me a tour after all?" Toria asked him.

Kasiya didn't answer her, but closed the doors. Toria breathed heavily, she couldn't believe that she had just got away with that, or rather for now she had gotten away with it; but she thought over what she had said to him and thought that it was a little too much if he gave it proper thought. She'd have to be careful of what she said to him, enough not to think that she was up to something that she didn't want him to know about but enough to make him wonder still.

Toria hadn't slept at all that night, instead she got up everything she could on the ship and the officers that she would be working with; well she needed to know as much as she could about her environment and those around her. She needed to learn the layout of the ship, especially if she needed to act quickly incase an opportunity presented itself to her.

She also felt as though considering this was Kasiya's ship that he wouldn't leave himself without a few loyal Magics on board, she had to be careful of what she said to people; she just hoped that Renji didn't turn up now that she was on one of his friend's ships.

Toria was glad that she didn't have to wait long for Bernal to transport her belongings on board, she wanted to get out of her dress; she really needed to think about this whole looking-nice thing, what if she had been attacked suddenly she wouldn't have been able to defend herself, only perhaps tried to run away unless she used her powers. Which sounded good in theory being able to use her powers to defend herself, but she still wasn't very good at that; she somehow manage to destroy but not, and also do a few simple spells but she needed to start learning them more. Which is the real reason why she hadn't slept, Zebulon had also given sensor plug-ins; you hotwire them into the sensors of the room which scans for Magic use, but it doesn't alert anyone when some is used but it does continue to send a signal that it's working.

Toria stood in the doorway of her bedroom, it looked a mess; she had shoes and clothes scattered all over her bed and the high back chair in the corner by the view port, she had spent that much time with everything else that she hadn't really sorted any of her own things out.

Though the reason why it was such a mess, was that she had packed her uniform at the bottom of her truck; which now stood open and empty at the bottom of her bed.

Toria turned around and looked into her living room, the three crates that Zebulon had given her were next to her desk at the far end of the room; next to her on the floor to her left were two more crates with her personal belongings in them. She wondered if she had packed too much, it wasn't as though she would be living here all the time; just most of it while she was posted here, but she was kind of hoping to get an apartment on Ardergot where most of the Vertigo matches took place. It wasn't about being able to play, because she would still want to visit so that she could at least get away from here, and try to be a little of her true self.

"I think it's about time, for my new challenge to begin." Toria said to herself walking over to her door to leave, she had decided to go with trousers for now and she didn't think a skirt really look the same on a security officer.

The door slid open and she stepped out into the corridor which was a little busier than when she had arrived, her door closed and locked behind her; she had also set up her com to signal if anyone tried to enter her room, with Magic or without. She walked up the corridor past the other officers, who were all much older than her and even in her uniform you could tell; though she thought that was more to do with how she had put her hair up, she had done three pony tails and then turn them into buns going down.

As she thought about it she wondered if she had done the right thing, normally she wouldn't spend so much time thinking about how her hair looked unless perhaps she was going somewhere with her father; but this was different, she wanted them to think that she wasn't a threat but at the same time still able to have a little responsibility. She was definitely thinking over the whole thing, and in future she was just going to brave it all.

A group of officers stopped by the lift, two women and three men all much older than she was, she stood behind them and waited for it to arrive with them without saying a word to them; the doors opened and it was empty inside so they all got in with Toria standing at the front of them.

"Did you hear what Kasiya did?" The woman on her right asked them.

"It's just rumour." The other woman told her.

"Nope, Rylan said it's true; and she's starting this morning." The man behind her said sounding quite smug that he seemed to know more than the others.

"She's supposed to be a little girl right?" The first woman asked.

"Yeah, I heard that she didn't even finish at the academy." The man to her left said.

Toria smiled to herself and then turned around surprising them all, she looked at the man who had been stood right behind her; he had bluish green hair parted in the middle and pasty colour skin.

"Hi, I'm new on board I was wondering if you could show me to the main security office; Lt Rylan is expecting me?" Toria asked him pleasantly.

"Your...you're new?" He asked her.

"Yep." Toria answered smiling at him sweetly.

The door opened behind her and Toria stepped out followed by the other man as the others were going to a different deck than they were, he stared at her while the door slid closed again and they were left alone.

"Toria, and you are?" Toria asked him.

"What? Me...oh...erm...I'm Sakay." He told her.

"Nice to meet you Sakay." Toria said smiling at him as she carried on walking in the direction of the office; she did know where it was because she had made a point of finding out where it was located of course when she was studying the ship.

"So...erm..." Sakay tried to say.

"I did graduate early, to be honest I didn't even spend a year there." Toria told him leading the way now as he just stared at her. "I got the placement program onto Jasp'erat's ship; and I guess you've heard the rest."

"Those slaves...did you really kill them?" Sakay asked her.

"Yes, they were trying to escape." Toria answered as though it was the obvious thing to do in that situation.

She pressed the button on the door that Sakay almost walked past and went inside, he quickly doubled back and followed her inside of the office; it was the same size as her quarters with five desks around the room that would seat four though not all of them were taken at the moment; except for the desk facing the door where Rylan sat alone and only he sat there.

Sakay walked over to a desk which was the one on her left on the other side, she walked over to Rylan's desk ignoring everyone else staring at her who had probably heard the rumours about her; she stood to attention in front of his desk as he looked up at her.

"Ensign Toria Kentaro reporting for duty, sir." Toria said.

"Nice to see you again, I hardly recognised you in your uniform." Rylan said smiling at her.

Someone almost choked behind her, she turned around as their cup of coffee was knocked to the floor and they almost fell off of their chair; the woman next to him jumped up patting him on his back.

"Don't worry, they've just got overactive imaginations." Rylan told her.

Toria turned back to face him wondering if he had said that on purpose, to see what sort of reaction he would get from them all.

"I know that you've had a little experience with security, so that's why you've been sent to me." Rylan told her. "It's a large team over all, but they're split up into sixteen sub teams which you'll head one."

"Wait a minute, me in charge of a team?" Toria said sounding unsure, but it was only because she was so surprised and she had never actually done anything like that before.

"You don't think that you're up to it?" Rylan asked surprised. "It said in your record that you dealt with escaping slaves and the investigations that followed them. So if that's anything to go by, then you should do alright."

"If that's what you believe." Toria said.

Rylan smiled at her kindly. "Anything new just takes a little time to get used of."

"Yes sir, thank you sir." Toria said.

He pointed to the empty seat at the desk behind her to her right, she turned around and went over to her desk sitting down next to a dark-skinned man who appeared to be growing out an afro; he just stared at her as if wondering what she was and why she was sitting next to him.

"Don't mind Abner, he's like that with everyone; I'm Wira and he's Lords." The woman facing her told her, she had black bobbed hair with a fridge that made her face look square and very pale; but she seemed quite nice.

The man sat next to her was the oldest out of the four of them, he was even older than Rylan though it was kind of hard to tell if you hadn't met anyone of his race before; his scales were flaking which showed that he was at least three decades old, which was quite old for someone of his race as most didn't live past forty.

"Hi, its nice to meet you." Toria said smiling at them all.

"I'll take you on my rounds and show you around your sections, before you meet your team." Wira told her. "I'm actually glad to have another woman to talk to...actually I'm just glad to have someone else here, they don't really talk much...just sit there."

"Deep in their work." Toria said.

"They must be, even though the rest of us never seem to get as much as they do." Wira told her smiling and then she pushed her chair back suddenly. "We'll be going out on our rounds sir, want anything brought back?"

"Just the usual." Rylan answered.

"Come on then." Wira said leading the way with Toria just behind her.

Toria was actually glad that she didn't have to sit in there while they all tried and failed to whisper quietly to each other about her, this way they can talk about her without having to worry about being heard and she gets to have a proper look around; she also gets to meet her very own team, which if she was being honest she wasn't expecting especially after her run in with Kasiya, or even if it had never happened. It just means that she's made an even better impression than she had first thought, she only hoped that she could keep it up, or do better.

"So, what do you think?" Wira asked her as they walked down the corridor.

"Seriously? I wasn't really expecting all of this." Toria told her.

"Rylan, said that you did a good job with those Magics; even the captain's interested in you." Wira told her. "See now, that alone has got everyone talking...he's not really the type of guy who'll get personally involved if he can help it. Or rather, that's how he comes across."

"Or maybe that's how he wants everyone to think he is, but deep down he's a sensitive caring man." Toria suggested. "Do we need the lift?"

"Oh yeah, thanks." Wira said calling for the lift. "So do you know him, the captain I mean; that's why you got the posting?"

"No. I just met him a couple of years back through my bodyguard." Toria told her, she didn't really want to give out his name incase she knew him and so that loads of people don't find out who he is, he is supposed to be working undercover.

The door slid open and Wira motioned for Toria to go in before her, which she did and the door closed behind them; Wira typed in deck ten section five and then the lift started to move again.

"Oh..." Wira said.

"My father's a senator, so I've always had a couple of body guards; but I also learnt how to defend myself as well." Toria told her. "You know just incase one day I'm alone. I can't always be depending upon others to look after me, and it's a good job as well since it got me through a few tough times over the past year or so."

"You'll have to show us what you can do, this weekend we're having a small tournament." Wira told her.

The doors slid open onto their deck and they both walked out and turned right, to follow the corridor around.

"Well I guess I could turn up." Toria said. "Or is it too late to put my name down?"

"Nope, all security officers names go down, it's mainly for us but other officers take part as well." Wira told her.

"I'll have to get in a little more training...wouldn't want to show myself up." Toria said.

"Wira!" A young man shouted as he ran towards them, he had dark brown almost black hair and mocha coloured skin and he wasn't much taller than they were. "Hay, you've seen our new chief?"

"Yep." Wira said smiling.

"Well?" He prompted.

"This is Dai, he might not act it; but he's about three years older than you and the youngest in your team. That is apart from yourself." Wira told her.

"Hay, I'm Toria." Toria told him holding out her hand.

"You?" Dai asked her staring at her suspiciously.

"That's what I'm told." Toria said smiling. "So what's the problem?"

"Well...erm...Osaxe...he kind of got into a fight..." Dai told her reluctantly.

"Great." Toria said. "Where is he and is it still going on?"

"Yes, and he's this way in cargo bay three." Dai told her, he looked between the two women before he turned back around and lead them back to the cargo bay. "We were going to use the space today...with you sir...miss...erm..."

"Toria or Kentaro is fine." Toria told him. "What so someone else tried to use the space as well?"

"Yes." Dai said walking quickly. "He has a bit of a temper."

"Great." Toria said.

"Osaxe, well he's not human, not fully anyway...he has a bit of giant blood in him." Wira told her sounding worried. "I don't know how you expect to get him under control, maybe we should call Rylan."

"NO." Toria said firmly seeing the cargo bay door up ahead and picked up her pace over taking Dai. "He's the biggest guy in there right?"

"Yeah..." Dai said worriedly.

Toria tried to prepare herself, telling herself that this would be like fighting Utenro; she'd be fine and get to show her new team that she does deserve the position that's been given to her. She walked into the cargo bay, the doors sliding back for her; the whole area had been cleared out so that they could train, most of the containers had been moved against the bulkheads out of the way, except for the ones that had been thrown into the middle of the open space. Her team was stood back away from the fighting to her right whereas Osaxe, who was three foot taller than her and probably also over a foot wider as well; he was picking up another cargo container with ease as though it was nothing at all to him and raising it over his head, the man on the floor looked up horrified.

"Stand down!" Toria shouted as she walked over to him, but he just ignored her. "I told you to stand down, that's an order!"

He still ignored her, he was either choosing not to hear her or he couldn't; Toria knew though that he didn't consider her his commanding officer because he believed that she was beneath him.

"Argh! He's crazy!" The man shouted from the floor his arms up over his face.

"Move!" Toria shouted at him, but he couldn't he was too scared to do anything.

Toria sighed deeply, then she kicked the side of Osaxe's leg as hard as she could; but it hardly did anything to him, just made him buckle a little but still held onto the container. Toria jumped up, grabbing hold of his large arms and lifted herself up kicking the container out of his grip and swinging herself over his head and landing behind him; the container echoed loudly throughout the bay. Osaxe turned around to face her, even more angry than he was a moment ago at the other officer.

"What is it my turn now?" Toria asked him lightly as though it didn't bother her either way.

Osaxe swung at her but she ducked out of his way, turning and then bent down to take his legs out from under him, his legs gave way making him fall backwards heavily, shaking the deck plating. She walked over to him and bent down as though to speak to him but instead she grabbed his arm pulling it up and kicking over so that he was lying on his front. She twisted his arm around his back as hard she could and stood on his lower back.

"Now, Osaxe is it? When I give you an order, I expect you to follow it; is that clear?" Toria asked him.

"Osaxe don't take orders from little girls." Osaxe told her in a deep but child-like voice.

"Okay then." Toria said and bent his arm back out of place, while pressing her foot into his back; it wasn't long before they all heard the sickening break. "You will follow my orders or we'll do this everyday until you decide that you don't want anymore of your bones broken. Today, I'll break one, tomorrow I'll break two and then so on; it's up to you. Though perhaps you should be warned that I've trained against a half giant nearly everyday for several years before I even joined the Fleet, so it'll just feel like light training going up against you."

"Argh!" Osaxe shouted trying to roll around to get her off of him, but she dropped down to her knee now pressed into his spine.

"Just a little more weight, and perhaps I could break even your back." Toria whispered to him.

Osaxe stopped struggling, but Toria didn't get up straight away just incase he changed his mind; but after a minute she got up and walked over to the other officer who was still on the floor with two more officers trying to pull him to his feet.

"Perhaps you could do with a little more training yourself." Toria told him. "What do you think would have happened if I wasn't able to resolve the situation?"

"Well...erm..." He tried to say.

"That isn't really an answer." Toria told him. "I'll be speaking to your commanding officer, about some additional training."

"What?" He said looking at the two guys pulling him to his feet.

"You can go now." Toria told them.

Toria turned around to face her own team, who looked just as speechless as the guy being carried away; she looked down at Osaxe still on the floor and then at Wira who seemed to have gone even paler than she was before.

"Osaxe, med bay now." Toria ordered, before she turned back to the rest of the team and said much more pleasantly. "And we can start on a light excise to get to know one another."

They all looked horrified at the mere thought of going up against her now after seeing what she had done to Osaxe, who was slowly getting up off of the floor holding his broken arm; none of them looked as though they were going to offer to go first against her, as their hopes and dreams of an easy life just faded away.

Toria knew now why she had been given this posting, it was a test; to see if she was up to commanding others and also to see if she was using her powers for anything. She had known that he would want her on board to keep a close eye on her, but it seemed as though it was going to be a little harder than she had first thought; she needed to regain some ground.

Rumours of what had happened that morning were probably well about the ship by now, Toria thought as she walked towards the holo arena where the computer had told her that Kasiya was training inside. She'd decided that she confront him head on, or at least find out what he was really up to; she might as well do it like this so they didn't need to hold back. This time she had braided her hair so that it was out of her way and so she knew it wouldn't fall out of place, if things did get a little rough between them. She had also changed out of her uniform into a red vest and burgundy red leggings with black boots, she looked as though she could go a couple of rounds; all she needed now was a partner.

As confidant as she could she walked into the arena, her head held high as she walked over to the centre as Kasiya sliced off the arm of his holographic opponent; which then disappeared.

"Freeze program." Kasiya ordered as he stood up straight returning his sword to its sheath on his belt.

Toria thought that he looked so different in normal clothes, he still looked just as handsome and intimidating in a vest and casual trousers.

"Evening sir, I thought I might join you when I heard that you were having light workout." Toria said pleasantly.

"Haven't you been training all day, starting off with putting one of your officers in the med bay?" Kasiya asked her calmly.

"Yes, but for some reason I've still got plenty of energy left over; it is very strange how there's days that I don't seem to tire and others I feel it even more so." Toria told him. "And about Osaxe, he attacked another officer to begin with before I even arrived."

"So you decided to break his arm, to stop him?" Kasiya asked her as he stood ready to begin.

Toria smiled at him and went for him first trying to punch him, once, twice and then a third time but he blocked them all as if he knew what she was going to do before she did.

"His kind, you need to show strength...they only listen to you if they know...that you're just as strong as...they are..." Toria told him as she tried to connect with him, but he was much faster than she was. "Damn it...Renji at least let me get in a punch once in a while..."

"He was too easy on you." Kasiya told her before he waved his hand and she was lifted off of her feet and thrown several meters across the room.

Toria landed heavily on her side, but still pushed herself up. "You're using Magic against me...how's that fair...? And just so you know, he didn't go easy on me!"

Toria ran across the room, she tried to kick him and punch him but nothing; he didn't even move this time and she still couldn't hit him, it was as though he had some sort of shield up protecting him just a couple of inches away from his skin.

"You're angry with him?" Kasiya asked her.

Toria tried to kick him again and again, but she still couldn't get through his shield.

"He never told me!" Toria shouted at him. "I killed all those people... 'cause he didn't tell me what I was!"

Toria was angry with him, she knew she was but she was also angry with herself as well for not realising and letting him; just for a second she kept that angry and let it consume her as she made to punch him again, but this time she broke through his shield and almost hit him. She hadn't even seen his hand move to stop her blow, she tried to push against him using the anger that she had just felt until she felt herself burning and there was even smoke from her hand; she pulled it away from him and stepped back unable to look at him.

"Is he the reason why you're doing this?" Kasiya asked her softly.

Toria smiled sadly. "In a way yes."

"You want to hurt him, the way that he hurt you?" Kasiya asked her. "But you won't see him?"

"I can't see him...he'll ruin everything that I've done!" Toria shouted at him turning to leave, but she was stopped by invisible biddings and lifted up into the air.

278

"What will he ruin, your desire to kill your own kind?" Kasiya asked her. "Your anger towards him? Your resolve?"

"My resolve...hanging freely...so thin that the slightest thing could destroy it." Toria said suspended up in the air. "You said the other night that I had betrayed him, well he betrayed me as well...making me do this all by myself...making me care for him so much that it torn my heart to pieces...when I thought that I had betrayed him..."

Kasiya lowed her to the ground, she just sat there with her back to him.

"You should talk to him." Kasiya told her. "He's just as angry and confused as you are."

"I can't see him, he'll see through me...he'll see the truth that I'm not ready to show." Toria said.

"Instead of entering the tournament, you'll train with me; every day for at least two hours." Kasiya told her.

"You'll help me improve my Magic as well, even though I'm not going to promise you that I won't kill anymore of your own kind?" Toria asked him looking over her shoulder.

"I believe in you." Kasiya told her simply. "We'll start tomorrow."

"Just what I wanted, Magic lessons." Toria said smiling slightly to herself as she stood up, she couldn't look at him; she had wanted to get him but he got her.

She walked out of the arena in a kind of daze, she had known that all those feelings had been inside of her; but she hadn't let any of them out properly since all this had began. Toria went back to her quarters, not wanting to run into anyone but just lock herself away; her door slid open for her and then locked again behind her. The first thing she saw as she walked in was a holo-picture that she had pulled out and put on her desk, she marched over and picked it up; it was of her a couple of years ago, she had sneaked up behind him and thrown her arms around him while Siren took the picture.

"Damn it!" Toria shouted and then threw the picture across the room, smashing against the wall. "It's all your fault!"

She just sank to her knees and cried.

Toria had been on board the Ake'cheta for over a month now, she had found it hard in the beginning working with Kasiya and doing the training with him as he had kept trying to poke holes in her shield to break her down to find out what she was up to; but after a couple of weeks thinking that he had nearly broken her. She realised that in truth everything that he said was right but what she was doing, wasn't completely right as she was taking people's choices away from them; but she was actually helping in the long run more than she could if she had left with Renji when he had offered to take her away. If she would have left then, then all the people that she had saved and all the people that she could save, they would still be living in fear and as slaves; she was doing the right thing no matter what it meant was going to happen to her in the long run.

Toria though had decided on one thing, she had made him a message that would be sent out to him upon her death; it explained everything that she had done and those who had helped her, as she also wanted their names to be cleared as well. She told him that he had to wait though to clear her name until the time was right. She of course, also apologised for doing everything that she had done and not telling him the truth; and how she loved him and that he gave her the strength that she needed to carry on every day, dreaming of a better future for the day that their people no longer had to live in fear.

Toria sat at her desk in the security office her mind not really on the job, well there wasn't really much for them to do again; just go about their normal duties. The others seemed just as bored as she was, though they weren't showing it as much; she would have even gone a couple of rounds with Kasiya for something to do as she was getting better at not taking the bait that he tried to lure her out with.

She had been more disappointed when she was told that she wouldn't be a part of the away team to go onto the Station, she had done all the research and everything on it; well she was interested to know more about the Bosik as they hadn't taken a side in the war, well that's what they said.

Toria though couldn't see how anyone couldn't take sides in this and now because she wasn't one of the higher ranking team officers she wouldn't get to go aboard herself and meet these so-called neutral Bosik.

"So Toria, aren't you taking some leave next week?" Wira asked her. "Where're you going?"

"Just visiting friends." Toria answered, it was true she was visiting friends; she was also going to get herself an apartment, find out if Jo-Mi still wanted her on the team and if he did she'd also have a Vertigo match to play, which she was actually looking forward to.

"I'm surprised that your father wouldn't want you back at the senate, to show you off some more." Wira said teasing her.

"He'd like that, but I had this planned before hand; he'll just have to settle with a call for now." Toria said.

The door to the office opened and Rylan looked in, scanning the room looking for someone.

"Kentaro, you busy?" Rylan asked her.

"No." Toria answered getting up and going over to him, hoping for something a little more challenging to do.

"Why don't you come along, for a little experience?" Rylan asked her as he walked up the corridor with her.

"Seriously?" Toria asked excitedly. "Is that really alright?"

"Yeah, course." Rylan told her. "And besides you looked as though you were going a little crazy in there with nothing to do."

"Just a little, the most excitement I get is with the captain at night." Toria told him.

He stopped dead and just stared at her, Toria carried on walking not realising and then it suddenly hit her what she had said and how it had sounded.

"No...I didn't mean that...I mean..." Toria told him quickly. "We've just been doing some work out...wait that doesn't sound right either...it's only extra training, fighting...that sort of thing."

"Oh right." Rylan said seeming a little relieved. "The Captain?"

"Yeah, I was surprised as well...but he's very good." Toria said and realising that everything she said seemed kind of out of context. "Okay you know what I mean, so I'm just going to stop now."

Rylan laughed at her. "Okay. So back to the station. It's just routine, when ever we come across one of these; we go aboard and scan for Magics just to make sure that they're not hiding any."

"You mean that the Fleet don't really trust them, when they say they haven't picked a side?" Toria said.

"Officially no, unofficially yes." Rylan answered.

"I was actually wondering that myself." Toria told him. "Considering how big this all is, it's hard not to choose a side; nearly everyone else in the galaxy picked a side."

"Yeah well, some don't like to draw themselves into other peoples conflicts." Rylan told her as they approached his team who were waiting for them outside of the transporter room.

"Kentaro, I bet that you're looking forward to getting off the ship?" Neil said as they entered the transporter room, he threw her a hand scanner which she caught even though he had taken her by surprise."

"It'll be nice, to see different bulkheads yeah." Toria said smiling.

"Yeah I know what you mean." Neil said.

They all got on the transporter pad, Neil stood at the front with the security team at the back of them; Rylan stood on his left and then Toria. She had wanted to go on board the station, but this was different than the other times, as she had a little more freedom considering that the other officers she had been with wanted to be left alone. Well she'd just have to make the best of the situation that she could.

"Transporting." The officer told them, just before they were engulfed in the bright light and disappeared reappearing on board the station's transporter pad on the main operational deck.

The transporter pad was at the top of the stairs that lead down into the operational center of the space station, there was a main console in the centre of the room with four officers sat around it; they all looked human even though they weren't, but there were quite a few species that looked alike. Facing them, up the opposite stairs were more stations with more officers working at them and the captain's office which was empty as he was stood at the bottom of the stairs to greet them.

Even before Toria had stepped down off of the pad her wrist com unit started to beep strangely, they all looked at her while she started to fumble with it; a small screen appeared on the face with a small map and flashing blue lights.

"Late for something?" Neil asked her smiling.

"Actually no, I think we're just on time." Toria said smiling back. "If you don't mind me asking, Captain Iker; but do any of your crew have Magical abilities?"

"Of course not." Captain Iker told her looking as though he had just been insulted.

"Perhaps you don't know about them, or perhaps you've had Magical guests recently." Toria said.

"Kentaro!" Neil said in a warning.

"What is the meaning of this?" Captain Iker demanded.

"I'm sorry sir, she's new; her first..." Neil began to explain.

"My com can pick up Magics, it was a present from a very good friend." Toria told him.

Neil and Rylan looked at her and then back at the captain as though that had settled the matter, the captain actually looked a little thrown, lost for words.

"Teams check the station, they could still be on board." Neil ordered.

"You can't..." Captain Iker began.

"Actually we're allowed to search your station and ships, its part of our agreement and yours to stay out of this conflict." Neil told them. "Rylan go with Kentaro."

"Yes sir." Rylan said leading her off to the left towards the lift while the other teams went to the opposite lift after checking over the center officers; they called for the lift which didn't take long to arrive and then went in. "So how close do you have to be to know if they're a Magic?"

"I think it depends on how powerful or how many there are." Toria lied, it didn't pick up Magics like that only those who had been implanted with homing chips and if you knew the right signal. "I think they're on one of the lower decks."

"Probably one of the cargo holds." Rylan suggested.

"No, I don't think...they wouldn't want them in a room that they could just be blown out into space; would they?" Toria said.

"That makes sense I guess." Rylan agreed as they got out of the lift onto an empty corridor, it only had bare metal decks and bulk heads.

"Well I wanted to see different bulk heads." Toria said smiling.

"That you did..." Rylan said as he pulled out his blaster. "The crew's not about...they must have been warned..."

Toria didn't have a blaster, as she was only a junior security officer; something she would have to bring up when they got back to the ship.

"Stay close." Rylan told her. "The captain's probably been warned of the situation, but we're on their turf; remember they have the upper hand."

"They have Magics." Toria said as she followed him closely.

The lights went down and everything went black for a few seconds before the emergency red lighting came on; Toria a little worried that things could get quickly out of hand and that perhaps she had alerted them too soon, she still hadn't found them herself nor a way to blow up the station to hide them; and the most important part of this plan is that she didn't have anyone coming to get them to explain what was going on.

"I need an access panel." Toria told him suddenly.

"What?" Rylan said confused.

"We need to find out where they're being held right, so I need an access panel." Toria told him.

They walked on a little further until he stopped and pulled off the bulk head plate and threw it on the ground behind him, he stood guard while Toria bent down to access the main systems; it was only a small screen with a couple of dozen wires and chips around it.

"This might take a couple of minutes." Toria told him.

"As long as we find them, before they find us." Rylan told her.

Toria worked as quickly as she could. She needed to find out where they were being held and also a name of a ship that could have brought them; she needed something to give them afterwards. The only problem was that the information was in a kind of code, and she didn't have time to break it so she just downloaded it into her com to figure out later making sure that Rylan couldn't see what she was doing. Now for the main event, she cross-wired some of the circuits hoping that she was using the right wire and moved a couple of the chips around and throwing the odd one out completely; she hoped that she had done it right as she pressed the activate button.

"Kasiya to Rylan, we've just picked up the self destruction has been activated." Kasiya said through his com.

"I think it came on when I accessed their location..." Toria said looking up at Rylan.

"Can you turn it off?" Rylan asked her.

"Not from here." Toria answered.

"Sir, we can't shut it off here; nor do we know how long until it goes off." Rylan told him talking into his com. "We didn't even know we'd activated it, it must be running off a silent alarm."

"We've already started to transport the teams back, we'll try to hook up to their systems from here." Kasiya told them.

Rylan pulled Toria to her feet just as they were transported out of there, they were transported directly onto the bridge just to the side of the navigation station; Rylan rushed around to the weapons station where Neil was trying to hack into the station's systems.

"Can we transport any of the...?" Kasiya started but was cut as the station began to explode on their view screen. "Move the ship to a clear distance."

They moved back from the station as it carried on exploding, section by section until it was just floating debris.

"I want a full report on what just happened, by 1700hours." Kasiya told them as he walked off to his office.

The lights were on dim in the arena just the way that Kasiya liked it, though Toria didn't moan as it didn't really matter to her because she could see fine however they had the lights set. Kasiya wasn't in the mood for taking prisoners tonight as he came at Toria relentlessly, who was just managing to stay clear of any serious blows; but once again she wasn't able to get past his shield unless she really harnessed her powers.

"Someone seems to be upset." Toria said as she blocked his fist with her foot kicking it out of the way. "Are you upset that we found out what the Bosik were really up to, or that everyone was killed?"

"Perhaps both." Kasiya told her.

"Perhaps you knew some of them, some of the Magics I mean...it's possible isn't it considering you've lived such a long time like Renji?" Toria said.

"The reports say that the self-destruct came on when you tried to access information about the Magics?" Kasiya asked her.

Toria smiled at him. "And you want to know, if that's true or if I was the one who did it? But truthfully, if you actually think about it. I did kill them either way."

"How can it not bother you?" Kasiya asked her angrily.

"Does it bother you, that it doesn't bother me?" Toria asked him as she came at him while his guard was down, she managed to connect but still not properly as his shield was still up protecting him.

"You're still just a child...how can you...?" Kasiya tried to ask her.

"Kill people?" Toria said and then added thoughtfully. "It must have reached at least ten thousand by now, right? Including my cousin and his family."

Kasiya just stopped suddenly as did Toria.

"What you've had enough?" Toria asked him.

"Ichigo cared deeply for you as if you were his own sister." Kasiya told her.

"He wasn't really a part of my life before, so it's not as though I've lost anything. I still have my real family, my father." Toria told him.

"He was the one who called bounty hunters after you, he didn't want to lose his greatest prize." Kasiya told her.

"I know what you're doing, and it's not going to work anymore...I've had enough of games." Toria told him. "And I'm sure that you've had enough of me. We both know where we stand, you with the Magics and me here. It's not going to change the more that we talk."

"Here?" Kasiya asked. "What does that mean?"

Toria smiled at him but didn't answer his question. "This is going to be our last night together until I get back; you'll miss me right?"

"Of course." Kasiya told her. "Be careful, as Renji has his men looking for you."

"So they were Renji's?" Toria said smiling as she made to leave, she had been wondering; but at least she knew for now.

Chapter Eighteen

The computer beeped loudly from the other room as Toria sat on the edge of her new double bed, on top of the thick soft lilac covers, rushing to pull on her purple boots over her pink tights, she had just finished getting dressed and had to change back to herself as it appeared that the call she had been waiting for had finally gotten through. Once she had pulled her boots on she got up and straightened her sleeveless high neck purple and pink panel short dress out as she went through along the hall that lead into the spare bedroom and the bathroom, until she finally came into the living room where she had a three piece suite, a desk with her computer on it and the dining table at the far end where the computer panel and a preparation table was. She went over to her glass desk and sat down as she activated her computer to accept the incoming transmission, the screen turn from black to that of Lord Zebulon smiling back at her.

"You took your time." Toria said by way of greeting.

"Sorry, but I've been busy." Lord Zebulon told her.

"I know what you mean, normally I'd have given you more notice; but it was a kind of spare of the moment thing." Toria told him. "But did everything go alright?"

"Yes, fine; you've been a great help." Lord Zebulon said smiling at her.

"Not at all Lord Zebulon..." Toria started.

"You can call me Zebul." Lord Zebulon told her.

Toria smiled at him, he was flirting again with her; she didn't mind they weren't in the same room so he couldn't distract her the same way.

"Zebul then, thanks." Toria said. "I'm glad that you were able to get them all; but I don't mean to be rude but I'm running late, you kind of caught me on the way out."

"Not at all." Lord Zebulon said. "Until next time, and remember you don't have to just call me on business."

"Thanks, I'll remember that." Toria said smiling. "See ya later."

"Most definitely." Lord Zebulon said smiling at her before he logged off, turning the computer screen black again.

Toria smiled to herself as she changed back into Touro, as this was her new apartment; she had arrived a couple of days ahead of the team so that she could properly move in her things, this place looked more like her than her quarters back on Kasiya's ship. That was probably because she was more free here to be herself not having to worry about someone finding out who she was, though she had brought some of Zebul's things with her just incase not wanting to be caught off guard.

An hour later Touro was sat in the cafe bar that the team had their meetings in, they were still waiting on Leka; though Vi and Inker had arrived along with another man that Touro hadn't meet before, but somehow he seemed familiar. Touro sat on one of the bar stools next to Lonac who was drinking a brownish liquid from a short glass, Jo-Mi was getting more and more impatient making him keep turning back to her, to give her lectures on how bad she had been in her last two matches. Inker seemed to be able to sense her a mile away, as it was the only reason that he had come along and made a beeline straight for her.

"How's my pretty rose?" Inker asked her.

"I'm not yours, or anyone's." Touro told him.

"You can be if you want." Inker told her.

"She said no; she must have some sense." Vi said sitting down next to the other man who had sat down next to Touro.

Touro smiled and turned her attention to them ignoring Inker. "So who're you?"

"Excuse me?" The man asked her startled by the question. "You don't remember?"

"No..." Touro said a little unsure, she was sure that she would remember meeting him; brown hair and a caring face with brown eyes, his eyes seemed kind of familiar somehow.

"When we played in your first match, you threw the ball at my face." He told her. "I'm Romas, you saw me in my wolf form."

"What...I'm so sorry about that." Touro told him.

"That's alright, it's all part of the game." Romas told her smiling kindly at her.

"Hay, you don't need to apologise to him." Jo-Mi shouted at her.

"What about me?" Inker said behind her. "You stepped on my face."

"You were running straight at me...it kind of makes me feel, to stop you before you get anywhere near me." Touro told him as she picked up her glass without looking behind her, and then took a swig before Romas could stop her; he just stared at her as if waiting for something awful to happen. "What's wrong?"

"Are you...alright?" Romas asked her.

"She just knocked it back in one." Vi said.

"That was my drink." Lonac told her.

"Really? It's kind of boring, doesn't taste of anything." Touro told them off-handedly as they all stared at her.

"Boring?" Lonac asked staring at the other two who seemed just as bewildered as he was.

"Sorry, I'll get you another." Touro offered.

"That's fine." Lonac told her. "I'd probably had too much anyway, to remember anything of Jo-Mi's speech when he finally gives it."

"At this rate I won't be!" Jo-Mi shouted from behind them in the booth next to Rox, he was sat facing the door watching it still like he had been for over an hour, waiting for everyone to turn up.

Touro turned around when something caught her attention out of the corner of her eye, it was strange; she saw someone walking towards her but from outside of the bar, and what was even stranger is that she knew who it was even though she could only see them from their body heat.

"Leka's coming, and I think with the reason why he's so late." Touro told them, and surprising then as well with her announcement.

"What are you now, a seer?" Jo-Mi said sarcastically.

"No, but I could see him...right there." Touro said pointing at the door just as it opened and Leka walked in with a woman right behind him. "See."

"How did you do that?" Vi asked her.

"Don't you dare tell him, what type of Magic you can do." Jo-Mi warned her. "You're our Rose player, our secret weapon...so don't tell any of the others anything."

"I don't actually know how I did it." Touro whispered to Lonac on her other side.

"He might mean that sort of thing as well." Lonac suggested.

"Sorry guys, so have you decided if we're keeping Touro or not?" Leka asked as though this was the only reason that he had bothered to turn up for.

"Yes, for now." Jo-Mi answered.

"That's great, I just got a new place." Touro said excitedly.

"You got a place? Where'd you get the money to get a place here?' Lonac asked her.

"I found out that my family had some money saved up, when you know...it came to me..." Touro told him.

"Oh right." Lonac said.

"I have a spare room, so I don't ever mind putting one of you up." Touro told them.

"Can I stay?" Inker asked her excitedly.

"No." Touro answered flatly.

"She likes me really." Inker told Romas. "She just doesn't want anyone else to know."

"Yeah keep dreaming." Kima-Na said as she stood up towering over him, he looked behind as if to say something to her and changed his mind; but she had lost interest in him and turned her attention to Touro. "You said that you have a spare room?"

"Yeah, you want to stay?" Touro asked.

"Only if it's alright, I was going to look for a room in the Vertigo building." Kima-Na told her.

"I think it's fully booked up." Vi said thoughtfully.

"Yeah, even we're tripling up." Romas told them. "But it's always like that when there's a match on."

"Well I don't mind helping out when I'm here." Touro told them, though she wouldn't want them staying all the time even though it'd be nice to have a bit of real company; the only down side was that she had to stay in this other form all the time while she was here.

Cheers and shouting echoed throughout the Vertigo stadium as Rui-Lin and Romas charged at each other in the muddy marches on the third largest platform, normally both men were so calm and gentle but they were after all wild animals; and today they were showing their true nature for all to see, as they crawled at each other while their team mates were left to fight over the ball for themselves.

Touro had been quite startled by them, she knew what they were but had never really seen them actually act like animals; the only one who actually came close was Inker who tried to pounce on her every time she was near.

Touro could hardly move through the thick march around the river as she tried to get closer to Rox and Leka who seemed to be having a lot of trouble getting the ball off of Ida and Cerse, she definitely would have thought that they wouldn't have been a match against two women, or maybe that was why they were going easy on them. Touro though didn't need to hold back because she was a girl as well; the only problem was getting to them through all of the mud as her armour was actually slowing her down.

"Tour...!" Rox shouted.

"I'm trying!" Touro shouted back.

"Our Rose isn't up to much today." The commentator shouted. "She's seems to have lost her touch since her first match, perhaps she was just a one time wonder after all. It's been almost half an hour and the points are practically even...we need some big scoring if you want to win out here today. First match of the new season, both sides need a big opening game, but the real question is; who's going to give it to us."

She slipped forward almost ending up face first in the mud, wishing that there wasn't thousands of people watching her make a fool out of herself once again; she tried to push herself up her hands in the mud when everything suddenly went black and she couldn't hear anything either. The blackness only lasted for a moment and then it began to change, everything around her began to change; at first she thought that she might have been transported to another platform but this was different and she still couldn't shake the feeling of being surrounded by darkness.

She tried to move but something was holding her back as though she was being restrained by something, she didn't like that feeling at all; nor how everything was changing around of her, it kind of seemed as though it was changing to that room of Zar-Jins. As she fought against the restraints she could feel them getting tighter but also as though she was being lifted up off the ground, she knew that if he got her again she might not be able to escape from him this time; she had to risk using her powers, even if it meant showing what she really was.

Touro was lifted up off the ground and was being moved as she struggled concentrating all of her energy, but everything around her shimmered violently before it had even fully focused and she fell to the ground landing on a hard stone floor; the room was gone and the feeling of darkness was gone as well, all that was left was warmth from the hot springs that were spread out across of the fourth platform, which was also the second smallest.

"Are these things supposed to be this warm?" Vi asked from somewhere behind her.

To begin with Touro didn't turn around, she was actually staring at Zuyo who now had the ball from her captain Ida; but there was something just above as well which she kind of recognised from her first match. They were both stood close to a hot spring, probably a little too

288

close considering how hot they were at the moment and how hot they were going to get as well.

Touro knew that she had to do something to make up for her last couple of matches, so if she could somehow score; then perhaps that could help, but all she had to do was get across to the other side of the platform before they realised what she was doing and get the ball off of them.

She slowly started forward knowing that Vi was at least three feet away from her, she didn't want him getting in the way so she concentrated on the two closer springs to him making them heat up so that the steam would cloud his vision.

"Damn it! I can hardly see...we need to get out of here!" Vi shouted from behind her. "I think there's something wrong with the platform."

"Yeah, but I can't see a door." Zuyo shouted over to him as the steam got hotter and thicker.

Now that the steam was so hot that they couldn't actually see though Touro could move freely, she could see the hot shots of the steam but also Zuyo and Ida who was giving off a different type of heat; it wasn't that much further and she'll have it.

"Wow, that platform looks as though it's out of control." The commentator said. "We might have to shut it down...though it's been well over a century since something like that's been done. Players will be transported to another platform as will everything of importance that is located on the hot springs platform..."

Touro had heard the announcement, she had to move quickly before everything was moved; she didn't know how long it would take her to find another scoring point.

"Tour...damn it...where have you gone?" Vi asked her sounding concerned.

She couldn't help but smile, even though they were on opposite teams he was still concerned about her since he knew that she was here as well and supposedly not to far away from him.

"We can't locate all the players on the platform...little Miss Rose seems to have disappeared...or she could have become part of the steam!" The commentator said excitedly. "It'd be nice to have another fire on the team, since they haven't had one since the fall of the empire...just a little history there for everyone."

If the situation was different Touro would have been quite interested in what was being said, but she needed to get the ball knowing that time was running out; they had moved closer together and the ball was between them, she still had to risk it though.

"Ignite!" Touro whispered focusing her energy at the spring behind them.

The water began to bubble and spit, higher and higher; they stumbled away from it straight into Touro who grabbed the ball before they had even realised what was going on and stepped on the hot air particles in the air and threw the ball straight at the shimmering hole. The siren didn't sound for the end of the game but the platform did shudder violently, those stood on the platform could hardly keep their balance even Touro who was stood on the hot air above them was actually finding it difficult as though the spot she stood on was trying to cool down too quickly.

"Player transfer in progress!" The commentator announced. "Wait...there's something else going on..."

All four of them shimmered off of the platform, Touro fell to ground landing in front of Zuyo and Ida; she just looked up as the platform below them exploded shaking the whole of the platform knocking everyone off of their feet as the destabilizers were damaged, the whole of the platform slid to the right at an angle. Touro who was already on the floor felt herself slipping, she tried to use the heels of her boots to grip the ground but there was nothing to grip to as they were all back on the starting platform.

"Losing platform controls!" The commentator shouted in a kind of panicked voice; this of course didn't help the situation.

Screams had replaced the cheers and shouting as the players struggled to get to the higher side of the platform, Touro slid some more as she couldn't stop herself as she didn't have anything to hold onto; but then she felt a large strong hand grab hold of hers, holding onto her tightly as they pulled her back. She looked up to see who it was, part of her couldn't believe it but another part of her wasn't surprise as he had always been nice to her.

"Hold on, they'll transport us soon." Vi told her as he tried to pull her further away from the edge.

He was right, ten seconds later the platform was covered in coloured smoke which transported them back to their changing rooms; normally they would have been transported to their separate rooms but considering the situation they were all transported to just one, the Roaring Torches. Vi loosened his grip on Touro and then helped her to her feet.

"What the hell just happened?" Jin-Drah shouted, he was the Vikas Rose player and had a bit of a temper.

"Something happened to the hot spring platform." Vi told him.

"Yeah, it just started to overheat." Ida told them.

"I've never seen anything like it before." Ceres said next to Kima-Na.

"The game's over though." Kima-Na reminded them. "That means that someone still managed to score."

"I scored." Touro said, but not very loudly as though she didn't want them to actually hear her; but of course Vi did who was stood right next to her.

"Did you now?" Vi said quite loudly. "Is that why I couldn't find you on the platform?"

"You were going to help her?" Jin-Drah demanded. "She's on their side!"

"Sorry." Touro said. "I...didn't mean for the platform to explode...but I did over heat the springs..."

"She's out of control...!" Jin-Drah shouted.

Touro moved a little closer to Vi who still seemed to be on her side, as Jo-Mi marched over to her and pulled her away from him suddenly.

"Are you ever going to listen to what I tell you?" Jo-Mi demanded. "I told you not to tell them, or anyone else what you can or can't do."

"What?" Touro said a little confused.

"Roaring Torch wins by one hundred and fifteen points!" The commentator shouted through the annoucer speakers.

"We won, why would I be angry?" Jo-Mi said smiling putting his arm around her shoulder. "We won our first match of the season and everyone's going to be talking about this for ages; it'll even make the other teams wonder how you managed to pull it off."

"You're famous now." Rui-Lin told her.

"Little Rose, Touro scored the winning point!" The commentator announced. "Still trying to figure out how she managed to find the scoring port through all of that steam."

"See, this is going to be great." Jo-Mi said excitedly. "This is going to put us back on top."

"I didn't really want to be famous." Touro told them, but no one was listening to her as they were all talking excitedly planning where they were going to have the party to celebrate their victory; anyone would think that they had just won the galactic cup.

The atmosphere back on board ship had seemed a little on edge for the past month since Toria had returned from her shore leave, she didn't know what she had missed while she was away as no one was talking about it; she knew that it couldn't have been about her that they had found her out because they still wouldn't be letting her roam the ship so freely, unless they were hoping to catch her out doing something.

Zebul had missed her as well wondering what was going on since she hadn't contacted him in so long, and she had to explain to him that it wasn't as though it was her ship and she could do whatever she wanted, at the moment she had to wait until an opportunity presented itself; and that meant an awful lot of waiting around. Though there was some good things with having a lot of time on your hands, it had given her a lot of time to plan situations out, so that she wouldn't be so caught off guard like she had been in past; it also gave her time to practice a little of her Magic.

Toria was on her way to the security office to hand in her weekly report, he had asked her to come last as he had wanted to talk to her about something important; this of course aroused her interest making her wonder why he would want to talk to her of all people. As she was approaching the office Wira was just leaving, she looked quite tired from all of the extra training that her team had been doing lately.

"Evening." Wira said trying to sound cheerful.

"You look as though you need an early night." Toria said smiling kindly at her.

"Just as soon as I finish my work." Wira told her. "You're leaving yours to the last minute aren't you? That's not like you."

"I guess he won't mind then, just this once." Toria said; not sure if she should mention that he had actually wanted to speak to her. "So anyone else in there?"

"Nope." Wira answered. "I'll let you get on, and see you in the morning."

"Good night." Toria said carrying onto the office.

She didn't need to press the caller button, as they were all allowed in and out of the office whenever they wanted. Toria thought that it was kind of strange being here when it was so empty with just Rylan here, she had never been in here when there wasn't anyone around; she had tried it but she wasn't able to get around the sensors so she tried other ways of getting into the security network.

"Sir, I've got the weekly reports for my section." Toria told him as she walked over to the desk.

The side door opened suddenly startling her, Neil walked out and around the tables grabbing the nearest chair to sit down in front of the desk and indicated that she do the same; she grabbed her own chair and sat at the other corner of the desk not wanting to be too close incase they tried anything.

"I'm glad that you came." Neil told her, he seemed quite serious for a change when normally he was kind of acting the joker.

"Am I in some sort of trouble, that you both have to be here?" Toria asked them.

"No, actually quite the opposite." Rylan told her.

"Remember the station that you blew up?" Neil asked her.

"Yes." Toria answered.

"You gave us the name of the ship that had been running the slaves, well we've been tracking its activities for the past month." Neil told her.

"Oh, I wasn't told about that; I just thought that since no one had said anything that nothing was found on the ship." Toria told them.

"Oh no, we found it; and where it's getting its slaves from." Rylan told her.

They both looked at her as though this was the real important part.

"The captain though isn't willing to do anything, he thinks that we should carry on watching it." Neil told her.

"We think like you do, they should be showed that they can't get away with this." Rylan agreed.

"You mean, that if we show them that we can find them and that we know what they're up to they'll think twice before trying to escape again." Toria said. "It makes sense of course, so what's the problem?"

"Like I said, the captain." Neil told her. "He doesn't want to destroy them."

Toria smiled surprising them. "He's hoping to find out where they're taking them then?"

"NO. He's not even doing that." Neil said outraged. "Normally I wouldn't say this...but...what if...?"

"The captain?" Toria said smiling. "Well if you want to know for sure, why not just push his hand? Find out one way or another. How close are we?"

Neil and Rylan looked at each other and then at her.

"We'd been able to catch them by this time tomorrow if we carry on at our covert speed." Neil told her. "I have the night shift, so I could make a small detour without drawing too much attention. The only problem is that I need to know that I can count on you."

"You want to bring down the Magics, and perhaps get a promotion out of it at the same time; I guess if all goes well." Toria said. "I'm going to the arena for a couple of hours, if you want me to keep him distracted for a while?"

"By the time that you've finished your training, we should have caught up to the Magics." Neil explained.

"Just make sure that you don't tip him off to what we're up to." Rylan warned her.

"Course." Toria said standing up and turning to leave, leaving her chair where it was; she wanted to get out of the room as quickly as possible.

She had worked on a few plans for when she came across Magics, but mutiny wasn't part of any of those plans and she didn't actually want Kasiya to get arrested. She carried on walking up the corridor, with no idea of what to do except go along with them for now; she knew that if she tipped Kasiya off too soon then she could lose too much from both sides. So she went to the arena as normal where Kasiya was waiting for her, well she had already told him that she was going to be a little late.

The arena doors slid open and she went inside to find the captain practicing alone with his sword, she had wondered why he carried it around with him and brought it here if he wasn't going to actually teach her how to use it as well.

"Captain, hope I haven't kept you waiting too long." Toria said by way of greeting.

Kasiya stopped and sheathed his sword. She walked over to him wondering why he hadn't replied; partly wondering if he already knew what was going on and if he had really set the whole thing up to test her.

"It's not like you to leave your report to the last minute." Kasiya said. "Unless something's going on."

"Like what?" Toria said smiling. "You're the captain, if there was anything going on; wouldn't you be the first to hear about it?"

"I'd hope so yes." Kasiya answered. "Now, we've done basic defense; you still need some work."

Toria laughed, she couldn't help it; even though she had been training for over ten years most of that time against Magics even though Magic wasn't actually used in the training, she wasn't too bad.

"Did I say something amusing?" Kasiya asked her sternly.

"Sorry." Toria said smiling. "Shouldn't you have said, I'm not good at defending against Magics when they use their powers on me?"

"No." Kasiya answered. "That isn't your only problem. Everyone needs different types of training, you can't just say I've been trained and expect to be able to go up against anyone; they might have different abilities to your own. You need to understand that, that's why we're having these lessons."

"That's so nice of you, you still want to help me; even though I'll probably end up using all of this to kill more of your kind." Toria told him.

"I hope that you'll see the errors of yours before it's too late." Kasiya told her.

Toria looked away from him. "It's already too late, that day that I could have left with Renji; I killed all those people. That was my point of no return, even if I didn't mean to do it; even if I really did only lose control of powers. I still killed them Kasiya, all of those people...there was nothing left...even the city was in ruin. You think that I can be saved from that?"

"Do you regret what you've done?" Kasiya asked her.

Toria shook herself mentally, she needed to get off this subject for a while. "So how about we have a sword lesson today?"

Kasiya looked at her questioningly, there had been many times like that one when he had thought that he was getting to her and then she would change the subject; he'd play along a little while longer but he couldn't wait forever for her.

"If that's what you want." Kasiya said mildly.

Just over an hour later and still not getting anywhere, Toria was panting heavily bent over holding her side, her hand cut in several places and her holographic sword once again on the floor after being knocked clean out of her hand. Kasiya on the other hand was perfectly calm as though this whole exercise had done nothing for him.

"What the hell!" Toria shouted at him. "I've never used a sword before, and you're treating me as though I'm supposed to be at your level...or at any level come to that."

"I thought that you might at least learn how to use your own powers." Kasiya told her calmly.

Toria though didn't get a chance to ask him what he meant as the red alert sounded and the lights came up to full power in the arena, Kasiya looked at her as though she had something to do with it even though she had been with him this whole time.

"Can I ask a favour?" Toria asked him. "Your sword, can I borrow it?"

Kasiya looked at her questioningly for a moment and then handed it over to her, she took it from him and smiled slightly at him as she turned to leave.

"When you place it on your waist it will disappear, but you'll still be able to feel it." Kasiya told her.

She didn't say thanks as she left, she'd wait until it was over and done with; for now she needed to get to the transporter room to be part of the away team. She near enough ran down the corridor everyone moving out of her way, she rounded the last corner as she saw Rylan going into the transporter room; she was going to make it in time.

"Sir!" Toria shouted as she ran into the room just stopping short of him, looking a little flushed; the rest of the security looking at her as though they didn't think she was needed.

"I thought that you might've wanted to come with us." Rylan said. "Neil will be here in a minute, he's just informing the captain of what happened."

"I don't understand." Toria said.

"It seems as though we were in luck and came across the Magic smuggling ship that we've been looking for." Neil said walking in calmly behind her.

"He bought that?" Toria asked as though she didn't believe that he would.

"Well it doesn't matter if he does or doesn't now that we're here." Neil said motioning them all onto the pad.

The security team stood behind them while the three of them stood up front, Rylan handed Toria an extra blaster; she looked at the weapon in her hand and then up at Rylan who nodded his approval of her. They were engulfed in the bright light, disappearing for a moment as everything faded away and then reappearing in an empty corridor on board the smugglers' ship; the lights were on dim and like their own ship the red alert siren was on and red lights flashing over head.

"Spilt up, but be careful; who knows what they're capable of." Neil told them. "You can come with us."

Toria followed Rylan and Neil as they went off in the opposite direction, Toria brought up the rear wondering what she was going to do; she'd still help them but they weren't part of Zebul's people and she hadn't talked to him about this yet properly, maybe on this one she'd have to get Ichigo's help as he was somewhat more likeable among his own kind.

"So is that sensor thing of yours working?" Rylan asked her impatiently.

"It doesn't seem to be, but that doesn't really mean anything..." Toria told them. "They could have a way of blocking it or I could have damaged it while training with Kasiya just now...he cut up my hand pretty good...it's kind of sore to be honest."

"I hope it isn't too sore for you to use that weapon." Neil told her. "I need to pull this off, now that I've gone against the captain; and if I do you'll have a new captain."

"Does that mean that I'll still be a mere junior ensign?" Toria asked him.

"That depends on how well you do here." Neil informed her.

She wanted to move up in the ranks, but there were some things that she wasn't willing to do at the moment and hoped that she would never be willing to do them in the future.

They heard a door opening and shutting up ahead, Rylan signalled that they all stay back. Toria was worried since she was the furthest one back she couldn't see what was going on up ahead so she wouldn't know if anyone was in danger of these two, they were both ready to shoot whoever came out of the room; Toria had her blaster ready. She saw it, a small figure behind the bulkhead; she'd have to risk it.

Toria shot Rylan's hand making him shoot before he dropped his weapon, the child never came out; Neil turned outraged that she'd do such a thing and with his own blaster he hit her across the face making her change into her native Tasian form.

"You little bitch!" Neil shouted disgusted with her.

Without a thought she reached for the Kasiya's sword on her belt, as soon as she touched it, it appeared startling them both but neither of them had time to react as she brought the sword up and sliced through Neil's neck in one stroke; his lifeless eyes just stared at her for a moment before he just collapsed in a heap. She then turned her attention to Rylan, she could plainly see the fear etched across his face but that didn't matter at the moment; only saving her people mattered.

"Wait...stop please...you won't get away with this..." Rylan tried as he reached for his com.

"The captain will support me, considering what the two of you tried to do here." Toria told him as she stepped closer, but he didn't move away from her too scared to even move; she brought the sword up again and swung even harder than the first time.

His head rolled off, but his body stayed standing for two seconds before it collapsed bleeding from the wound. She turned around and went back the way that she had come from replacing her sword, she couldn't be found with it then the rest of the team would know what she had done. She needed an access panel, just so she could hook up to the main system incase that Kasiya wouldn't give the call, she'd need a back up plan; she pulled the panel off to access the circuits inside. Toria thought that she really needed to do more studying on engineering as she only knew the basic's, she moved a few of the chips and replaced some of the wires hoping that it would work pouring her own energy into it as well; before she activated her com.

"Toria here to any team leader, Neil and Rylan are injured and I'm out numbered request assistance." Toria said on an open com link that also went through to the bridge.

"Fall back." Kasiya ordered. "We'll transport you back on board..."

"But what about the Magics sir?" Toria asked him.

"Fall back, then we can take care of them." Kasiya told her.

"Yes sir." Toria said turning her com off and was just about to move off when she was transported back to the ship, she had appeared on the bridge; but alone without the rest of her team. "Where is everyone?"

"They're aboard but we couldn't lock onto Rylan and Neil." Kasiya told her. "Take the weapons station."

"Yes sir." Toria said pushing the other officer out of her way and accessing weapons, three missiles ready to go on his order. "Sir?"

"Fire." Kasiya ordered.

"Firing." Toria said pressing the command button, the missiles launched into space straight for the smugglers' ship hitting it directly as they didn't have any shields. "Direct hit sir, scans picking up an overload...we should move the ship to a safe distance."

"Yes of course." Kasiya said. "My ready room, now."

Toria gave the station back and followed Kasiya into his ready room, with everyone staring holding back until the door closed behind them. Kasiya rounded on Toria as soon as the door was closed, she didn't give him a chance to say anything as she pulled his sword off of her belt and handed it over to him still stained with blood; he looked at the blood stained sword and then up at her.

"What happened?" Kasiya asked her.

"Their eyes...they...so..." Toria tried to explain, but words seemed to just fail her.

"Toria?" Kasiya said gently.

"They were going to turn you in as a sympathiser." Toria told him. "They thought that you weren't handling the situation properly...they preferred my way..."

"But, you're not..." Kasiya said.

"Do you have any idea what they would have done to you?" Toria shouted at him. "You really are too soft, if you show them any weakness; any..."

"Toria..." Kasiya said reaching out to her but she just pulled away from him.

"They really did seem nice to began with." Toria said. "They...I knew which side they were on...of course I did. And I knew what I would have to do, have done...but to really do it with my own two hands...to see the life in their eyes just fade away...but it doesn't, not straight away, they still look at you the same don't they? Their eyes locked on you."

"Toria..." Kasiya said gently.

"Well you're smart enough to figure it out now right?" Toria said smiling sadly at him. "Renji, he would have seen through me straight away; that's why I just wanted him reading the reports. You still can't tell him, cause I won't be able to do what I need to do... If he was here now, I'd probably run to him and cry my eyes out and beg him to never let me do anything like this again. But I'm not the only person in the galaxy, I have a chance to help them...I just need to be stronger. I just need a little more time."

"My help to you, can only go so far." Kasiya told her.

"I wouldn't want to put you in danger with your people or with the Fleet." Toria told him. "You know, you're quite a bit like him; like Renji I mean."

"Really?" Kasiya said sounding amused.

"You wanted to believe even after what you heard and saw, that I was able to be saved." Toria told him smiling; she turned to leave and then stopped suddenly. "Do you think that he'll forgive me, for not telling him everything?"

"In time, when he fully understands why you had to do this." Kasiya told her. "For now, he'll just be broken hearted. You meant a lot to him, you still do. He'll hunt you down, and find out what you're up to."

"As long as I'm not discovered too soon." Toria said smiling at him. "We're not ready for them yet, are we?"

"Not yet, no." Kasiya answered honestly. "Before you go, I need someone to fill in for my first officer until we get back to the senate; I'll need someone who I can trust that won't stab me in the back."

Toria smiled at him taken back, her surprise showing making him smile also. "Are you serious?"

"I wouldn't ask you, if I wasn't." Kasiya told her. "If you need to sleep on it..."

"No, yes...I mean yes I'd love the job...actually I mean I kind of would like the job." Toria told him.

It had sounded great to begin with, but she didn't know anything about commanding others and she was still an ensign without even spending a whole year at the academy; would anyone really take her seriously, would any of them want her as their commanding officer after what had happened? She didn't have a clue, only that this was a great chance for her and she'd be stupid to give it up now.

"I'll transfer everything that you need to your quarters." Kasiya told her. "And don't worry, I don't expect you to get everything overnight; even though you don't actually need to sleep much."

"What?" Toria said, she was surprised that he knew that and she thought of something herself. "Do you know Athoury?"

"Yes." Kasiya answered.

"Can you contact him for me, tell him that Touro needs some more and that I'm on board your ship?" Toria asked him.

"You're not going to tell me everything then?' Kasiya asked.

"It's best that those who know, don't actually know everything." Toria told him. "And also to that, I can't tell you who knows."

Kasiya seemed to understand this and didn't question her, she left his office feeling a little lighter after telling him that she really was on his side. The bridge crew seemed to be waiting as though they were expecting her to tell them something important, but she decided that she'd wait to tell them when she started her duty shift in the morning.

It had been a full week since Toria had agreed to take over as acting first officer, and of course it hadn't completely gone alright; some didn't mind as they had thought that she had done everything she could to save both the first officer Neil and Rylan, though if they knew the truth then they definitely would like her even less than they already did.

She should have listened to Kasiya when he had told her that it wasn't going to be easy, she had no idea how much work was really involved considering that Neil never looked as though he did anything just sit around on the bridge. She'd been around to all the different departments, gotten their weekly reports and maintenance updates; but the thing was she wasn't sure about the whole confronting them if there really was anything wrong.

Toria was sat in her new office alone as normal going through all of the reports the desk full of them, as she was transferring them onto the computer so that she could then send them off to Kasiya. The whole of the office was bare except for the furniture, it was as though it didn't belong to anyone only someone who did too much work; she hadn't bothered putting anything of her own in there as she had this horrible feeling that she wouldn't be allowed to stay with Kasiya once they returned to the senate.

Her computer started to beep, this was all she needed when she had so much to do; unlike normal she just switched the screen instead of finding out who was trying to contact her first.

"I thought that I better call you, considering that you didn't seem to be getting around to telling me the good news." Senator Kentaro said.

Toria quickly turned around smiling at her father. "I'm sorry, I've been really busy...I was going to call you with the good news; but there's been so much to do."

"Of course, that's what I thought; it's not as though you didn't want me to know." Senator Kentaro said.

"Of course I would want you to know, I told you this is what I wanted to do." Toria told him. "It's just all happening so quickly, I guess it's kind of overwhelming but in a good way. It's shown me that even though I've still got a long way to go, it's really what I want to do. Those officers were killed...and there wasn't anything we could do about it. But the worst thing about it, which you must of heard is that we lost our only lead on the Magic smuggling operation."

"Yes, of course I've been informed about that." Senator Kentaro told her. "That's why I wanted to talk to you. When you get back here, I believe that great things will soon be coming your way."

"Even more great than this chance now?" Toria asked him smiling. "I know that I can't stay the first officer, but it's a great opportunity for me to learn..."

"This, will be even greater." Senator Kentaro assured her.

"Wait a minute, I don't understand." Toria said a little confused. "How can there be anything else, considering that I'm only an ensign?"

"You'll have to wait and see." Senator Kentaro told her.

Toria smiled even though she was quite unsure about what her father considered to be good for her, she knew that she couldn't stay with Kasiya for long because it wouldn't look good to his people if she carried on getting away with killing their kind.

"I look forward to seeing you when you return." Senator Kentaro told her.

"Yes, of course." Toria answered, not as sure as she was about returning anymore.

After he logged off she just sat there for a while staring at the black screen wondering what he could be up to this time and why he was supporting her so much when he really didn't want her to join the Fleet. Part of her wondered if she should ask Kasiya about this, if he had heard anything that was going on; he had more people in higher places with that sort of information, but at the same time she didn't want him to think that she was worrying over something that could turn out to be nothing.

Music could be heard throughout the corridors of the main building in the Granrio Sector, with the Diun Orchestra playing as they always did for these types of official functions. Officers were in their dress uniforms, but Kasiya was in a suit of his own; wearing a knee-length open jacket with a blue silver pin striped shirt and matching tie.

Kasiya walked down the corridor with Toria linking his arm; she was wearing a purple reddish dress with a small slit at the bottom left that showed the under dress that was a lighter shade to the top dress, it draped down the back and then gathered at her lower back. They seemed to surprise quite a few seeing them together as most had never seen Kasiya arrive with a woman before, but normally his senior staff; but those who knew who she was, were especially interested to find out if there was anything going on between them.

"People are staring." Toria whispered.

"I didn't notice." Kasiya said calmly.

"What, now you're lying to me?" Toria said irritably. "These things are so annoying."

"They are, aren't they?' Kasiya agreed. "Though at least I've got interesting company tonight."

"I'm interesting?" Toria teased. "You do know that we'll be the top topic of conversation, since we're arriving together."

"Well at least I'll have something different to talk about than normal." Kasiya said lightly as the guards opened the doors for them, and they entered the grand hall at the top of the stairs.

"Is that why you asked me here?" Toria asked him.

"We were both coming tonight, so why not arrive together." Kasiya answered. "And remember I said that I get to have some interesting company tonight, someone finally who will say what's on their mind to me."

"Don't worry, I always do." Toria told him smiling as they made their way down the stairs.

Even though there was quite an age gap between them they did in fact look well suited to one another, especially when they were out of uniform and with Toria smiling at him, he actually seemed like just any other man. They walked down ignoring the whispering and staring, Kasiya lead her off to the right as though he knew just where he was going.

"I think we should get your father out of the way first." Kasiya told her. "Especially from what you told me."

"You don't like him?" Toria asked him.

"Do you know what it is that your father does?" Kasiya asked her.

"...I know that he opposes the Magics, and that a lot of people follow him and his views about what should be done..." Toria answered.

"Have you heard of Lord Malevalus?" Kasiya asked her quietly. "He is said to be a very powerful dark Magic, and has been around for nearly as long as I have; or perhaps even longer. The rumour is that he is really behind the Malarias Fleet, the only problem is that we've never been able to get any proof."

Toria couldn't look him in the eye, she had heard of him but she hadn't known that he was such a key player in all of this; she knew at the moment that she wouldn't be strong enough to also work for him, it was hard enough doing what she was doing now.

"Your father works for him." Kasiya told her.

Toria was about to say something to defend her father, but words seemed to fail her as doubt seeped into her heart.

"Victoria." Senator Kentaro said cheerful as he walked over to his daughter with General Conoab on his right and another senator, who smiled broadly at her and held out his arms to hug her.

Toria let go of Kasiya while she hugged him, and then stepped back towards him but still smiling. "Vande-An, it's been such along time."

"I know too long, my dear. Look at you, a beautiful young woman." Senator Vande-An said smiling at her, before he turned his attention to Kasiya. "And this is?"

"This is Captain Veiko Kasiya, he's my captain." Toria told him smiling.

"It's a pleasure to meet you senator." Kasiya said shaking his hand first and then turned his attention to her father. "Your daughter is very special; she's been a brilliant asset to me; especially after losing my first officer and head of security."

"Magics, we'll all be better off when we finally get them all under control." Senator Kentaro said.

"Yes." Kasiya said rather stiffly.

General Conoab stepped forward so that he could be noticed, especially by Toria. "Victoria, it's a pleasure to finally meet you; I've been looking forward to this day for quite some time now."

"Really?" Toria said; she had no idea who he was and was hoping that she wasn't expected to know.

"General Conoab has the good news that I was telling you about." Senator Kentaro told her as he seemed to sense that she didn't know him.

"I was hoping..." Kasiya started but was cut off.

"Yes, we considered your request and thought that this would be a better use of Victoria's talents." General Conoab said cutting him off shortly.

"Request?" Toria asked him, but he didn't answer her.

General Conoab grabbed her arm and began to try and lead her off, but Toria didn't want to leave until Kasiya nodded that it was alright, but this just seemed to annoy him even more.

"You know I outrank him." General Conoab told her, as though that was supposed to impress her somehow.

"So I'm not going to be staying aboard Kasiya's ship?" Toria asked him ignoring his statement about rank, as she didn't care about it.

"No." General Conoab told her leading her towards the balcony through the crowd, trying to put his arm around her waist to make it look as though they were there together but she moved away from him.

She couldn't believe this guy, she didn't want him touching her in anyway shape or form, even if she wasn't overly sensitive it didn't matter. The only reason why she was even bothering was because he had her new assignment, she just hoped that it wouldn't be with him or anyone else like him; she wasn't going to use that sort of thing to get what she needed no matter what happened.

"So, where will I be posted next?" Toria prompted him.

"Why don't we talk about that outside so we're not disturbed." General Conoab told her.

Toria didn't really want to be alone out on the balcony with him, but at least if anything happened there would be no witness and she'd be able to get away with anything if she just said that they were attacked by Magics. He pushed the doors open and allowed her to go out first, it was a lot chiller than the last time that she was here; but it was now winter which made her think of Renji since it would be his birthday this weekend, she couldn't believe that she had almost forgotten. It would be two of his birthdays now that she had missed, she normally got him something along with a chocolate fudge cake which they both would normally share.

"Well then." General Conoab said closing the doors behind him.

Toria turned around keeping on guard the whole time, but her attention was taken away from him when she noticed all of the gold-tinted mirrors that was placed between the doors; she was sure that they weren't there last time she was here, they seemed to make her feel even more nervous than before.

"We don't believe that being with Kasiya is the right place for you." General Conoab told her. "Yes, you've done very well; even showing that you're able to lead at your age. We want to give you an even better opportunity."

"Better than that?" Toria asked.

"Yes." General Conoab answered. "You know that there are of course special task force teams within the Fleet that deal with special situations?"

"Yes, I've heard...kind of." Toria said.

"Well, that's what we want you to be a part of." General Conoab told her excitedly. "You won't go in straight away as a team leader of course, but perhaps like second in command to see how you go; and then we'll proceed from there."

"You want me to join a special task force team?" Toria repeated as she tried to take this in.

"You'll be leaving at the end of week, you'll be given training of course for what you'll be expected to do." General Conoab told her.

"The end of the week?" Toria asked. "I guess I could have all my things off the ship..."

"You'll only be able to take the basics with you, as you won't be posted aboard a ship, but moving between ships to get to wherever it is that you're needed." General Conoab told her.

"Okay." Toria said sounding very unsure, and seemed to realise considering how he was looking at her. "Sorry, I'm just surprised. I wasn't expecting anything like this. I...erm...could I have a minute and then I'll follow you back through?"

"Sure..." General Conoab said looking at her questioningly, but he still left her alone.

Toria couldn't believe it, this was way beyond anything that she could have hoped for in a year and a half; no way could she had imagined that she would have come this far in such a short time. Yes this was kind of what she wanted, but really she did think that it would have taken her longer; even with killing the Magics like she has been doing. The whole thing was kind of overwhelming; if she wasn't careful she could end up losing herself along the way.

She turned around to go back inside knowing that she couldn't stay out here or he would probably come looking for her and she was quite cold as well, when she saw that her path was blocked by half a dozen men; they all kind of looked the same with patchy white skin and all black eyes, they all had grey hair but different lengths.

Toria knew this wasn't good, she didn't fair to well against one of them let alone six and especially wearing this dress; the only good thing was that she had managed to remember to wear her own body shield tonight.

"We've come with an offer, from the great Lord Malevalus." The man she had met before said stepping forward so that she could see him better.

He had come out of the mirror that she had passed with Conoab, which made her believe that they knew what they had just been talking about.

"I already said that I'm not interested in severing a Magic." Toria told him standing her ground even though she was scared half to death.

"You are already severing him, all you will be doing is announcing it to the rest of his followers." He told her.

"And I said no." Toria told him firmly.

"Then you give us no other option." He told her gravely.

The other five seemed quite pleased by this as they advanced on her, the man on her far right pulled a jagged edge sword off of his back and smiled at her as he charged; Toria dodged his first blow and tried to kick him but her dress was too restricting so that she couldn't lift it up. He hit her in the face with the hilt making her stumble backwards; she needed to do something or the others won't need to do anything this guy would just be enough. Toria felt blindly behind her knowing that she wouldn't be that far from the edge and then would be pinned, but she felt something metal and remembered that there were chairs and tables; she turned slightly so that she could grabbed the chair and swung it at the guy holding the sword knocking it out of his hands, she threw the chair at the other guys knocking them over.

She bent down quickly and grabbed the sword slicing a long slit up the side of her dress so that she was able to move more freely, she had only learnt the basic's with a sword and this one was much heavier than the one she had been using, it was even heavier than Kasiya's; but it was the only thing that she had and she had to make the most of it.

"Come on now, we don't really want to hurt you." He told her still stood behind the others.

"Is that why you're attacking me with a sword?' Toria shouted swinging the sword to stop them from getting any closer. "I might not be very good, but I'll start slicing until you decide to leave."

"Don't be stupid!" The man shouted at her. He was who she had just taken the sword off of.

He came at her as if he was ready to take his sword back, but she could move a little better now, she turned around bringing the sword over her head and down again slicing off both of his arms making him scream out in pain. The others backed off, but this gave her an idea; she didn't care about using her powers in front of them because she was sure that he, this lord guy must already know that she had them.

Toria focused her power on the chair she had thrown at them, making it lift into the air and straight at the far mirror shattering it.

"Now I can do that to every mirror that you've had brought here..." Toria told them. "Or you can leave now, unharmed. Well the rest of you unharmed."

"We were told not to leave without you agreeing to join us." He told her.

"Do I honestly seem as though I'm going to change my mind?" Toria asked him, but she didn't give him a chance to answer as she used the chair to smash the next mirror along. "You should start leaving."

"We'll always find you." He warned her as his men started to edge back.

The man she had wounded holding his stub like arms close to his chest, blood pouring out of the wounds all over his clothes and the floor; they made their way back through the mirrors, stepping into them as though they were liquid and slowly fading away. Toria wasn't in the mood to be nice, she used the chair to smash the mirrors going along one by one making them hurry back afraid to be trapped without an escape.

"I liked this dress." Toria said to herself looking down at her now ruined dress, and wondering how she was going to explain what had happened; but she couldn't think of anything, so she activated her com. "Kasiya, I'm heading back to the ship; I'm feeling a little worn out."

"Are you sure?" Kasiya said sounding concerned.

"She was fine a moment ago." General Conoab said angrily. "I hope that this sort of thing doesn't happen often."

"No, of course not." Toria told him. "I'll see you back on the ship sir."

"Good night then." Kasiya said.

"Toria to Ake'cheta, one to transport." Toria told them.

"Just one?" The transporter officer asked.

"That's what I said." Toria told him.

He didn't say anything, but followed his orders, as she was engulfed in the bright light and disappeared off the balcony covered in fragments of broken mirror.

Chapter Nineteen

A Magical officer in a gold coloured uniform walked up the corridor carrying a long box, that they had just received and was delivering it to its intended recipient; he didn't stop to talk to anyone as he walked past his fellow officers who was probably wondering who the present was for. He finally slowed his pace as he was nearing the end of the corridor where two officers in red stood, outside of his destination; they both had their backs to him as they were pressing the panel which beeped loudly inside of the office.

No one answered to begin with so the man on the right pressed it again while the other officer leant against the door frame impatiently, but he seemed to notice that there was someone coming and turned around; he looked as though he was in his early twenties with dark reddish hair and orange-brown eyes.

"Is that for him?" He asked.

"Yes sir." The man answered.

"We'll give it to him." The red haired man told him.

"But...erm..." The officer said as though he was unsure of giving it over to anyone other than his captain.

"Renji, open the damn door!" The other man shouted.

The shouting seemed to work as the door slid open, the three of them went inside; the two who had arrived first stepped aside so that the other officer could give him his present. Renji seemed quite surprised by it, standing up to see who the card was from.

To Renji

Happy Birthday
I hope that you have a nice day
Sorry that I missed it last year,
but I'm sure that this will make up for it.

Love from
Toria
xxx

"I don't believe it." Renji said snatching the box off of the officer. "You can go...no wait. Who sent this? How did it get here?"

"A carrier of General Kasiya sir." The officer answered nervously hoping that he hadn't done anything wrong.

"I want that confirmed." Renji told him.

"Yes sir, right away sir." The officer said nervously, before he quickly turned around and left the door finally closing behind him.

"You don't think that he sent it?" The red-haired man asked him calmly as he pulled the chair out from the desk and sat down.

Renji though didn't seem to have heard his question as he stared at the message wondering if it was really from her, and also wondered why Kasiya would help her to send it to him considering that he hadn't said that thing's had changed; he hoped that they hadn't changed.

"Damn it!" Renji shouted angrily sliding the box onto his desk and sitting back down; still acting as though he was on his own.

"Baron do you think we're invisible?" The red haired man asked the other.

"I know you're there Isidore, I can see you just fine." Renji told him.

"So what's with the present?" Baron asked him calmly pulling out the other chair sitting down.

"Toria...it's from Toria..." Renji told them.

"So you've sorted it out then, she's back to normal?" Isidore asked excitedly. "So where is she then?"

"I don't know where she is, and no she isn't back to normal." Renji told him angrily. "If it was that simple don't you think that this would have been sorted out years ago?"

"So what, you're just going to give up on her?" Isidore demanded.

Renji laughed bitterly. "She's given up on us. I've sent men to bring her in, but somehow she still manages to get away. Just the other day I sent a team...they couldn't get her. But do you want to hear the funny part, she didn't kill any of them nor did she call for help. After she was done taking them all out she just left them there. Kasiya won't return any of my calls, like she wasn't. I feel as though I'm doing this all on my own, while she's making everything more difficult for me...she's tormenting me."

"She's tormenting you?" Isidore repeated as though he didn't believe it.

"I think you just need to step back, and try to look at this from a different angle." Baron told him calmly. "I really don't believe that she'd kill all of these people, not unless there was something behind it; someone controlling her."

"Well that's just it, I haven't been able to see her or I'd know one way or another." Renji told them. "Kasiya won't confirm much, only that she was responsible for the station and the ship...beyond that, I got nothing."

Isidore leant forward to grab the present but Renji stopped him pulling it away, making Isidore knock the photo off of his desk; they both made to pick it up but of course Isidore was closer and picked it before Renji could stop him. He turned it over and was surprised to see who was on the other side, it was the picture that Siren had sent him of Toria on the beach.

"Is there a reason why you have this on your desk?" Isidoro asked him as he passed it over to Baron to have a look at.

"Someone sent it to me." Renji told him.

"So you kept it as a keepsake?" Isidoro asked.

"This is why you're holding back?" Baron asked him.

"She...it doesn't matter, I know what has to be done." Renji told them holding his hand out calling the picture over to him and putting it into his drawer without even looking at it himself. "She's crossed the line, and I will take care of it. She was my responsibility, and I failed her; so it's up to me to deal with her."

"You say that, but if you came face-to-face with her; could you really kill her?" Baron asked him. "We've known each other quite a while now, I..."

"I said that I'd do it, so I'll do it." Renji told him and opened the box finally to find a ridge-edged sword inside of it. "She sent me a mirror sword."

"What? How the hell would she get her hands on one of them?" Isidoro said outraged. "She could have at least sent me one, instead of you."

"I never told her that I collect them...swords I mean." Renji told them.

"What if..." Isidoro started but Baron stood up to leave.

"We should be going, we only came to find out the situation with Toria; we'll leave it to you then." Baron told him. "Come on Iss, your wife said that she'll kill us if we're late again."

"Yeah...sure..." Isidoro said reluctantly not really wanting to leave yet, but he still stood up.

"You'll keep us updated of the situation?" Baron asked him.

"Yeah." Renji answered as he watched them both leave, he waited until the door had closed behind them before he opened the drawer again and pulled out her picture. "I hope that I don't have to kill you to save you from yourself...but I will do if it comes to it, I hope that you understand that?"

Rain pelted down through the grey and black clouds, making the already dangerous terrain even more so; the muddy slopes along the river banks were sliding down causing the soldiers who were trying to climb it, to slip down into the river.

Toria tried not to swallow the water as her head went under, she pushed herself out and over to the bank again as the other officers once again tried to climb up it, but there wasn't any hand holds to help them. She was wishing that she had never agreed to do this, no one told her anything about crawling through mud in the rain; she was so dirty and wet that she thought that she would never be clean again.

"Get moving!" The officer in-charge shouted down to her only a quarter of the way up; you couldn't really tell because he was covered in dirt also, but he had blond hair and was normally white with rosy cheeks.

"You better do what he says." The man next to her said; he had dark brown hair with mud in it and slightly pointed ears.

"There was a better way to go, but no...he wanted us to walk right into their trap." Toria said angrily as she tried to climb up the bank, the rain clouding her vision as it was coming down so hard.

"Do you have a better plan?" He asked her.

Toria looked over at him, she only hesitated for a second. "It's no use coming from this direction; and it'll only take a little longer but we have to go around. Going over the bank is going to take too much of our energy. Get a handful of men, who'll follow you and we'll go around."

"Gotcha." He said, turning around signalling to a couple of officers close by who made their way over to him.

"We're going around." Toria told them. "Volic come on."

Toria lead the way through the river with Volic and the other two officers trailing behind them, the water was up to their waists but it was a little easier to get through than trying to climb the bank.

"So do you know how many there are?" Toria asked Volic beside of her.

"The captain said four." Volic answered.

"So all of them will be concentrating on keeping up this storm right?" Toria asked him nearly slipping on a rock in the water.

"No...he didn't brief you on them?" Volic said surprised. "It'll only take the one, to keep all of this under control. The rest are to keep us occupied when we get closer."

"Remind me not to agree to do training assignments with Storms in the future." Toria told him.

"I'd rather not work with them myself to be honest; at least I know I have one sensible commanding officer." Volic said pointing to the opening in the bank where they could climb through more easily.

They waded across the river onto the bank slipping on the mud, but at least there wasn't any climbing they could go straight through the gap which was just big enough for them; they could hardly see much ahead of them with the passage being so high and the night sky coming early, but they still couldn't risk using their torches not wanting to be spotted. It only took them a couple of minutes to come to the end of the passage, when they did they stopped to see if they could see the rest of their team; but there wasn't anyone about.

"Right, keep to the edge and go slowly...we don't want to be spotted by any sudden movements." Toria told them. "Unless they can see in the dark and through all of this mud, we pretty much blend in quite nicely; even better than the camouflage they gave us to wear."

Toria headed out first, then Volic closely followed by the other two; she just hoped that her powers would be of some use to see anyone out there, the only problem was that she might not be able to tell them apart. They kept close to the rock face but not close enough to disturb it so that they would cause a mini slide, but so that they wouldn't be seen.

There was a half uprooted tree in their path, Toria stopped for a moment quickly scanning around to see which was the best way around; she was about to carry on when she saw something odd, it was kind of like a cold patch. She didn't know much about her powers, but she had learnt enough; cold wasn't good.

"Get down." Toria said as she pulled Volic to the ground, the other two following her order slowly.

Though the rain she saw it, a rock but it didn't completely seem as it was aimed for them, as it smashed over head causing a rock slide; she had to move quickly or they would be caught by the falling rocks so she pulled him to his feet almost dragging him along slipping and sliding herself as she climbed over the roots sticking out of the ground.

"That was close..." Volic said following closely behind her. "How the hell did you see that?"

"I don't know...I just kind of felt something coming towards us." Toria lied.

Toria stopped suddenly making Volic bump into her and then the other two officers bump into him, she couldn't see the cold spot anymore, it had moved somewhere else; perhaps it was a Storm after all and decided to change its location as they had missed the rock which might have really been aimed for them.

"Stay here." Toria ordered and then started out on her own, she couldn't see anyone but she still knew that they were out there.

The wind started to pick up pushing her back so that she had to push her way forward sliding on the water-logged ground, she slipped and fell forward putting her hands out to stop herself; that's when she saw it again and quickly rolled to her left as several rocks fell out of the air. Toria was sure that she had been told that this was just training, so she didn't know why they were seriously trying to kill her.

She pushed herself up and carried on forward with no idea of what she was going to do when or even if she ever managed to come face to face with one of the Storm's, she was sure that her body shield wasn't that strong as it didn't seem to be repelling the weather so far and she had the shield on just incase she was attacked by one of them. It started to get windier again and Toria felt herself being lifted up off of the ground, with the wind rushing around of her; they had her.

Toria reached for her blaster that she had had securely strapped to her back, so that she wouldn't lose them and so that they wouldn't end up in the water; she pulled them out and started to shoot blindly in the direction that she had seen the cold patch; the wind faltered for a moment, meaning that she was kind of shooting in the right direction. She replaced one of the blasters and this time pulled out a knife; knowing that she couldn't see her target but still willed the knife to find it.

"Find the source..." Toria ordered and then threw her knife out through the cyclone that was forming around her as hard as she could, hoping that it would hit a target or at the very least come close so that they would lose their concentration.

She hung there for about ten seconds thinking that it hadn't worked and was about to start firing randomly again when the wind gave way and she fell slightly, but was caught up again for a moment before she was thrown across the valley over the river bank and into the water; her mind a blur as she flew through the air straight into the water and her head hitting against the rocks. Everything went hazy and then black, slowly going quiet unable to hear the rain and the rushing water as she slipped further beneath the surface; and then nothing.

...Toria was sat in a class room and was a couple of years younger than she is now, she was seated next to a boy the same age as herself; he had white greyish hair and grey eyes. She didn't know why but she knew it was very important to keep quiet, while he showed her something.

He held out his hand in the shape of a fist facing up. He seemed to be concentrating, then he finally pushed his hand up releasing what he had been holding in his fist. Hovering a couple of inches above his hand were black storm clouds, they shot a bolt of lightening that didn't seem to bother the boy and then a clap of thunder followed.

"That was brilliant." Toria said excitedly.

"Hopefully I'll be able to do that for the test tomorrow, just on a bigger scale." The boy said nervously.

"You'll do great." Toria assured him. "It's who you are; everything that you need is inside of you."

"Thanks." He said smiling at her...

The first thing that Toria felt as her mind came back around was pain, her head was banging, she had no idea how she had managed to sleep. She slowly tried to open her eyes but they felt so heavy and everything was blurred out of focus, she had to blink a couple of times before her eyes started to adjust but even then she still couldn't see properly so she lifted her heavy arm and rubbed the sleep out of her eyes. She tried to turn over, wondering where she was as her eyes focused and realised that she wasn't in her bed, this bed was kind of stiff and she only had a thin blanket over her.

"Oh, you're awake." A man said somewhere nearby.

Toria couldn't sit up so that she couldn't look around to see who was talking to her, she tried to remember what she had been doing last but nothing except rain and water, why couldn't she remember.

"So she's alright?" Volic asked also somewhere nearby.

"Where...where am I?" Toria asked.

"That doesn't sound as though she's alright." Volic said angrily.

"The head injury was pretty serious, and we had to revive her." The first man said.

Volic walked over to her so that she could see him. "Do you even remember who you are?"

"Toria..." Toria answered. "What happened?"

"The Storm training." Volic said. "You were thrown into the river and knocked out, you almost drowned."

"I don't really remember much...just lots of water and it being dark." Toria said thoughtfully.

"Well there was a lot of water and it was dark, so you pretty much remember." Volic told her. "You got one of the Storms by the way, that's why they went all out on you."

"I got one?" Toria asked confused, as she didn't remember going up against a Storm.

"Yeah, you injured one with your blaster." Volic informed her. "They didn't seem to like a kid getting the upper hand on them. Neither did the captain. He got a right dressing down."

"Captain Ja'tin? The idiot who didn't know what he was doing?" Toria asked.

"That's him, see she's fine." Volic told the doctor behind him. "So when can she be released?"

"How long have I been here?" Toria asked.

"Nearly three days, we were starting to get worried about you." The doctor told her behind Volic.

"Three days?" Toria said thoughtfully, trying to strain herself to remember something important. "Don't I go on leave today?"

310

"That's if you're fit to go." The doctor told her. "But to be honest, I wouldn't mind keeping you in a bit longer..."

"That's fine, there's a doctor where I'm going; I'll tell him what happened and he can give me a check up." Toria told him trying to push herself up, she really needed to get out of here, she didn't want to miss her transport.

"You can't leave until you've done your report." Volic told her.

"What?" Toria said. "Can't I do it while I'm on leave and just send it back here?"

'Well...' Volic said thoughtfully.

"How about I write it on the transport, and send it by tonight...that way everyone gets what they want?" Toria suggested.

"You really want to get out of here?" Volic said half smiling at her. "I can stall for a while, saying that you're working on considering the situation...but no later than tonight."

"Thanks." Toria said swinging her legs over the side of the bed, she still felt a little dizzy but she had to get out of here; she couldn't let them down they were all counting on her and she could always sleep a while before it started.

"Are you sure you're fit to go?" The doctor asked her unsure about releasing her so soon.

"I'll bring your things to our next assignment. It hasn't changed, but if it does I'll contact you with the new info." Volic told her.

"Thanks." Toria said slipping off the bed a little unsteady on her feet, but still determined to go without any help from anyone.

Toria turned over in her nice comfy bed pulling the thick covers around her, willing herself to go back to sleep even though her head was still a little sore but that was because of how she had been lying and the report she had forced herself to write on the transport over here, she didn't even remember finishing it or let alone sending it off but she was sure that she had done.

She heard banging again, wondering if it was just her head but had a horrible feeling that it could actually be time to get up already; she slowly threw the covers back and crawled out of bed as the door was banged on again. She walked through her apartment changing her appearance into Touro, glad that she hadn't agreed to let any of them stay before-hand considering she didn't think that she would have been able to hold her form.

She was wearing lilac pyjamas with silver stitching all around the edging, the jacket only had three buttons which were all close together just covering enough.

She walked through to the living room and over to the front door on the left, she opened it to find Lonac and Ze-Siro stood there a little surprised by her. They kind of just stared at her stood before them, while Touro leant against the door frame looking half dead.

"Are you alright?" Lonac asked her.

"I guess." Touro answered. "Is it time to go already?"

"Yes." Lonac answered.

Touro turned around leaving the door open for them as she went back through to get dressed. They both looked at each before they went inside, Ze-Siro closed the door behind himself and then had a quick look around while Lonac just sat himself down; Ze-Siro picked up a few pictures of her friends and places that she had been too while they waited for her to come back through.

"Is she normally like this?" Ze-Siro asked.

"No, she's nervous and excited normally." Lonac told him. "She would have said if there was anything wrong."

"She did ask you to come round and pick her up, perhaps she knew that she'd be like this." Ze-Siro suggested.

"She'll be fine, don't worry about the match." Lonac assured him.

"So how old is she, did you say?" Ze-Siro asked him.

"Seventeen." Lonac answered

A couple of minutes later Touro came back through dressed and as ready as she ever would be considering how she felt, she had a short, sleeveless v-neck short pale blue and turquoise panel dress on, with turquoise leggings and blue boots. Ze-Siro tapped Lonac on the shoulder nodding towards her as they were ready to go, he made his way over to the door leaving first with Touro and Lonac just behind him.

"So working too hard at the academy?" Ze-Siro asked her.

"Training's pretty rough, especially when you're almost drained." Touro told him. "I really don't like water...mainly because I can't swim very well, barely that is."

"Did they know this?" Lonac asked her.

"It doesn't matter, you have to be able to keep up." Ze-Siro said. "How about tomorrow if you're feeling up to, I'll give you a few lessons?"

"Seriously?" Touro said smiling. "You don't have to run off straight after the match is over?"

"Not this time." Ze-Siro said. "I've got a week off, and my date doesn't get here until tomorrow night; so I don't mind."

"Thanks." Touro said.

"I'm surprised that the two of you aren't married yet, since you've been going out for years." Lonac said.

"Yeah I know, but there's plenty of time for all of that." Ze-Siro said off-handedly.

Ze-Siro planned his day with Touro as they walked over to the stadium going in through the back entrance so not to be seen by the fans arriving, they weren't normally too bad but on match days they did get overly excited.

"Don't worry, I won't tell the rest of my team that you can't swim." Ze-Siro assured her before he went off to his own changing room.

Touro smiled at him as Lonac lead her into their own. She had only gone two feet when Jo-Mi appeared in front of her blocking her way.

"And what time do you call this?" Jo-Mi demanded.

"I overslept." Touro said.

"You overslept?" Jo-Mi repeated. "It's the middle of the afternoon."

"I...it doesn't matter..." Touro said distractedly staring at the wall blinking an awful lot as she thought there was something wrong with her eyes. It looked as though it was on fire but she knew that it wasn't because no one else seemed to notice it. "Is that the way to the stadium?"

"Yes." Jo-Mi answered staring at her.

"Great..." Touro said putting her hand over her eyes walking around and everyone else, she couldn't see them as normal but through their body heat. "If anything happens to me...like I collapse...tell the doc that I've got a concussion, almost drained and they had to revive me..."

"What?" Jo-Mi shouted.

"You didn't say that walking over." Lonac said coming around from the other side of the benches half-dressed.

"Well, I thought I'd better mention it...you know just incase." Touro said sitting down.

"What sort of training were you doing anyway?" Lonac asked her.

"You can still play right?" Jo-Mi asked her.

"I can kind of see...or rather I can see the body heat that people are giving off." Touro answered him and then turned to Lonac. "They were Storms."

"And you're still alive, not bad." Rox said sounding impressed.

"Did I mention the part that I nearly died...I was unconscious for three days..." Touro told him. "I woke up last night and got here as quick as I could."

"See now that's the type of effort that I expect everyone to put into this, do you understand; even if you're on your death bed I need you here. Fit to play." Jo-Mi told them, seeming to be very impressed all of a sudden with Touro.

Ten minutes later everyone was changed and waiting to be transported out onto the platform.

"The Roaring Torch!" The commentator shouted through the speakers.

They were suddenly engulfed in purple smoke and transported out onto the main platform facing the Nezer team, Touro had only ever meet Ze-Siro and knew hardly nothing about the team only that their Rose player was also a woman and of course they had wolves as Defenders.

"Nezer and Roaring Torch, this is the first time they're going up against each other since Touro and Rui-Lin joined the team." The commentator said excitedly. "Lets hope that these two will make things a little interesting, considering their last match."

"Why what happened?" Touro asked Jo-Mi next to her.

"Nothing...I don't want to talk about it." Jo-Mi said.

"That bad?" Touro said worriedly, she was hardly in a proper fit state to be playing to begin with but knowing that it went terribly last time just seemed to make her feel even worst.

"I can't believe that you're letting a little girl play Rose for you Jo-Mi!" Ko-Dero shouted over who was the captain and a Walker.

"Are you part-Storm? You seem to have the same coldness that they do." Touro asked him surprising everyone.

"What? How dare you?" Ko-Dero said outraged.

"So he is then?" Touro said.

"You don't really need to upset him anymore than he already is." Lonac told her.

"But I can see how his temperature is different from everyone else's, it's like a Storm's; and his hair colour is like theirs as well." Touro said matter-of-factly.

"When the buzz sounds; lets play Vertigo!" The commentator shouted, and the buzzer started.

Beep, beep, beep!

"I'm going to take your little Rose down." Ko-Dero warned.

The platform began to change and they were all transported to different platforms, Touro had been too distracted to look for the ball, but she had more important things to worry about when she arrived on the third largest platform facing Ko-Dero smiling at her as she was alone with him. It was just after sunset on the platform and there were a few trees throughout the clearing, she couldn't see a doorway that she could get through.

"Now be a nice little Rose while I pluck your petals." Ko-Dero said as a low ground-mist rolled in behind him.

"Well Ko-Dero is starting off early for us today and he's not giving anything for one of our newest players." The commentator said.

"Now, lets see if you can find me before I find you." Ko-Dero said.

Even though she had no idea how she did it, she could still see him through the thick damp mist that hung in the air; he wasn't giving off much body heat but she could still see him. Now she knew where he was all she had to do was get past him and find a way off of the platform. She'd have to get ride of the mist.

"Grow and hold him!" Touro shouted as she concentrated all of her energy heating up the air, pushing the water, heat and light at the trees; and they did just that.

Ko-Dero had noticed what they were doing behind him, he was between amusement and anger; she watched as the trees grew out of control, their branches stretching out as they tried to grab hold of him the closer they got.

"You should watch your back." Touro warned him smiling.

He looked over his shoulder just in time to see the branches rushing him and being scooped up into the air upside down, he was bound tightly as he was pulled back into the centre of the trees. Touro saw her doorway to her right, she waved goodbye and then ran over to the doorway leaving him to sort his own mess out.

"What was that?" The commentator shouted excitedly. "Touro, the Rose; really seems to have control over the plants...they just came to life. I thought they were going to eat him at one point."

"Eat? Eat who?" The Nezer Rose player said worriedly to her own wolves, who were stood either side of her; they both looked identical with dark blue fur and black eyes.

"Well I didn't know she could do anything like that." Rox said casually stood atop of the facing grassy hilltop. "She's just full of surprises that one."

Leka was just below him edging away out of sight holding the ball, heading towards the doorway, while he left Rox to handle himself as it was his job.

"So who's going to move first?" Rox asked them as he didn't care, as long as he actually got to see some action this time.

"If that's what you want, I'll leave these two to play with you then." She said before she turned around and slid down the slope to find another way off of the platform.

She had reached the bottom but she could still hear the growling from up above; as could Leka, part of him felt as though he should go back and help but he had to get the ball to somebody else as they hadn't managed to score yet.

Touro seemed to take a while before she emerged on the other side of the doorway, but when she did she wished that she hadn't. She gasped for breath as her mouth started to fill with water, she was under water and there was nowhere to go as the whole platform was under water; she didn't know how to create a spell so that she could breath nor could she see anyone.

"Touro doesn't look too good now, the water took her by surprise." The commentator said. "They might have to net her out of there, if she can't create an air bubble for herself soon."

She didn't know how but she could still just about hear the commentating, and hoped that someone else on her team had heard it as well and were close by so that they could help her, because she really had no idea how to create an air bubble; she was waving her arms around madly to stop herself from sinking which was making her swallow even more water and choking. She couldn't see anyone and she could move to look around, there were dark areas covered in seaweed not that she wanted to get any closer to them either.

Someone grabbed her arms from behind trying to pull her along, she couldn't see who it was though because she couldn't turn herself around properly; they pulled her into them and put their hand over her mouth. She seemed to panic even more struggling to break free, so they let her go but she could breath now somehow; they turned her around to face them and saw Ze-Siro.

'You alright?' Ze-Siro mouthed.

Touro nodded; he pointed for her to follow him so she did though swimming much slower hardly moving at all, he seemed to realise that she was struggling and slowed his own pace a little so that he didn't get too far ahead.

"Touro rescued by Ze-Siro, at least someone was around to help her out...I thought that it was going to be bad there for a moment." The commentator said. "Now it seems as though they're working together to get off of the platform, though who could blame them. I wouldn't want to be on that one today."

Touro was getting tired quickly, she had already used quite a bit of her Magic on the other platform and trying to swim so much when she wasn't used to it, it was a little too much straight after being discharged the day before; she couldn't see the force field nor the edge of the platform but she knew roughly where they would be, so take away the force field and take away the water. She focused her energy at the shield, trying to over-power it as she carried on swimming without over heating the water, she didn't want to cook them both.

"Oh what's this, there's something wrong with the holding field." The commentator said. "The field is about to go off line...yeah look at that!"

The shield around the platform flickered and then went down, releasing all of the water inside spilling over the edge, cascading down like a waterfall for a couple of feet before it was caught up in the anti gravity field around the platforms. The water separated and seemed to form into floating blobs looking a little eerie.

Touro and Ze-Siro had fallen to the sandy ground of the once ocean-like floor the sea weed lying dead on the ground beside them, they looked around at the almost empty platform able to see the water floating out in the stadium.

"What do you think caused the overload?" Ze-Siro asked her as he removed the spell.

"Who knows...?" Touro said swaying on her feet, but Ze-Siro caught her.

"Please tell me that you didn't do that, especially when you're not even feeling well?" Ze-Siro said angrily.

"Fine...I won't then..." Touro said allowing herself to be helped along.

"You reckless little...what if you were hurt....what if something would have happened?" Ze-Siro questioned her as she pointed to the doorway, he looked over to where she was pointing but he couldn't see anything. "There's nothing there."

"It's a door...I can see it..." Touro told him.

"How nice for you." Ze-Siro said.

"Rox, somehow managed to get away from Keon and Teon, the Nezer twin wolves." The commentator said. "Normally no one stands a chance against them, but Rox is used to standing up to wolves alone as it's only recently that Roaring Torch have gotten themselves their very own wolf. Leka got away safely and scored on the crashed down platform but has been unable to get away from it since, but that's where most of the scoring has been going on this game; but perhaps not all of the action. Nang-Ya seems to be trying to get a hold of Kima-Na but she's too strong to be held by any of her bindings, as she throws herself over the top of the wreckage catching the ball in mid air and throwing it...high...she threw it high! She must have seen something!"

"Do you think that...?" Touro started but her question was already answered, as the platform faded away and they were transported back up to the main platform.

Ze-Siro still had hold of Touro, Kima-Na landed gracefully nearby and Ko-Dero landed in a heap behind them, trying to get to his fight pushing his team mates away while they tried to help him up.

"You're not supposed to help her!" Ko-Dero shouted at him.

"But she..." Ze-Siro started as Kima-Na took Touro off of him leading her back over to their side while he went to deal with Ko-Dero.

"The Roaring Torch WINS!" The commentator shouted. "It looks as though they could be back on top, despite a few little problems here and there."

"You scored." Touro said smiling up at her.

"You almost drained I heard." Kima-Na said.

"How did the platform overload?" Jo-Mi asked Touro rounding on her before they were engulfed in purple smoke and transported back to the changing room.

"I...it just did..." Touro said vaguely

"What tried to eat Ko-Dero?" Rui-Lin asked her.

She wasn't really in the mood to be answering their questions; she just wanted to get back to her place to rest but knew that there would be an after match party and she couldn't really skip out on it altogether but it didn't mean that she had to stay for the whole thing, especially since she was also meeting Ze-Siro tomorrow if he was still up to teaching her to swim.

Renji sat in the back of the shuttle as it descended through the atmosphere and over the ocean of the planet Tandro, he couldn't figure out any other way than to come for her himself, none of the other teams had been able to get close enough; he knew that he was stronger than she.

"Well she's going to get a surprise this time won't she?" Dalal said sounding a little more positive than he had done last time. "I missed another match though, you do realise that you keep making me miss all of these matches."

"The Roaring Torch won, no thanks to the stupid Rose player." The woman next to Renji said, she was in her mid twenties and looked about the same age as Renji though of course they weren't; she had shoulder length layered black hair and soft brown eyes. "So are we still going to the New Year party?"

Renji didn't answer her, he wasn't in the mood to make small talk with them; Dalal looked back over his shoulder when he didn't hear an answer.

"So does that mean that the rumours are true, Jessa?" Dalal asked her. "You and the cap?"

"If he says yes, instead of keep ignoring me." Jessa answered.

"What, sorry did I miss something?" Renji said distractedly.

"No sir, just that we've already completed the mission; got her locked up in the back and heading back so that you two can have a nice New Year together." Dalal said sarcastically.

"Together? Who's together?" Renji said wondering what he had missed looking from Jessa and Dalal.

"Obviously the whole conversation." Jessa answered.

"I have more important things on my mind." Renji told them. "This is serious. I want you both prepared for anything, but you must not kill her; is that understood?"

"Yeah sure, we take her back to be put on trial." Jessa said.

"That...that's after..." Renji said.

"After what? She's helping them hunt us down and kill us. So what if she's still a child." Jessa said angrily.

"I know, but those are my orders; alive and as unharmed as possible." Renji told them, even though he didn't believe it himself; he knew that they would have to use force on her, that she wouldn't come back with them willingly, especially not with him.

Volic couldn't help but stare at Toria stood next to him, he and his fellow officers were in their dress uniforms while Toria, well she had been given something different to wear by the governor. She had spent over an hour arguing with the captain that she hadn't wanted to wear it, but in the end she had lost the argument and finally agreed to wear the outfit.

Captain Ja'tin was sat at the top of the high table, with a glass of wine in his hand looking quite smug with himself; Toria thought that he kind of looked like a lord in his castle who had just gotten what he had been waiting for, for so long and hadn't been disappointed by it.

She thought that it was too put her on show as she was the only woman on the team, and why Ja'tin had agreed as though to get her back for the reprimand that he had been given over their training assignment with the Storms.

She couldn't believe what she was wearing, a dark blue thin strapped butterfly shaped top with a short off-cut skirt, cut off above her knee at an angle to the floor until it was nothing.

"I look...well I shouldn't have to wear this." Toria said angrily.

"It'll please the governor, and if he's in a good mood perhaps I'll get a good offer on a couple of pretty little girls like you." Captain Ja'tin said smirking at her.

"Disgusting." Toria said unable to look at him.

"If you don't like this sort of thing then why did you agree to come?" Captain Ja'tin asked her.

"Cause I was ordered as part of the team, but that doesn't mean that I have to like..." Toria started but she couldn't think of a word that could describe the place.

"We're just taking pleasure out of what the galaxy has given us." Captain Ja'tin told her.

"You mean, what you've enslaved." Toria said angrily. "You make them do what you want, they're forced to do these things...death or forced to be with bastards like you."

"Now, now; you should watch what you say." Captain Ja'tin said. "I'm your commanding officer, remember I'm in charge and I give the orders. If I order you to do something, what do you say?"

"That all depends on what it is." Toria said stiffly. "I'll never do to you what you'll be making those poor girls do to you later."

"Don't worry, I've made sure that your room is next to mine so that you can listen to them moaning in pleasure." Captain Ja'tin told her smirking even more broadly.

"You mean scre..." Toria started but was cut off as the alarms sounded, she ran off towards the door before anyone could say anything; the door slid open and she was gone.

"And just what does she expect to do in that?" Captain Ja'tin said staying just where he was as though it didn't concern him that the alarms were sounding.

Volic, on the other hand, ran after her signalling that the others follow him as well, which of course they did; Ja'tin though didn't seem bothered that his officers were doing their own thing just as long as it didn't interfere with his plans for later.

Toria ran down the corridor in her high heeled slip ons, thinking that at least this dress was easy to move in as there wasn't really much to it; she could hear the others behind her not that it bothered her one way or another she would still deal with the situation the same way. She turned the corner and came face-to-face with an older woman in a Magical uniform holding a blaster rifle, pointed straight at her, she fired; the shot came straight for her, Toria just had enough time to throw herself to the ground missing it only by an inch but she still felt the heat almost burn her skin.

"They said that you were good." Jessa said, turning to take another shot.

"Yeah, well...I don't like to brag" Toria said wrapping her legs around her bringing her down next to her.

She kicked the rifle out of her hands up the corridor, then got to her feet; but she wasn't on them for long as she was lifted off the ground and was thrown back into the wall and then off it and into it again. Jessa got to her concentrating on Toria, as she beat her against the wall; but Toria kicked her shoes off into her face and was dropped to the ground but still on her feet.

"I'm not taken that easily." Toria told her as she punched and then kicked her pushing her back all the while until she fell over the blaster rifle.

Jessa tried to grab the rifle but Toria had already put her foot on it and kicked it backwards out of reach again, blaster fire could be heard further up the corridor.

"Do you think that I came alone?" Jessa said.

"So who cam...?" Toria started but was cut short as she was hit in the left shoulder, she stumbled backwards slipping over her own shoe into the wall.

"Jessa! Grab her!" Dalal shouted from further up the corridor.

Toria's arm felt as though it was on fire and twice as heavy as normal, she tried to push the pain out of her mind as she tried to push herself up while Jessa was making another move on her.

"Kentaro we've got them cornered!" An officer shouted from the same corridor that Dalal had shouted from.

"It sounds as though you're out numbered." Toria said kicking her in the stomach. "Do you really want to die trying to bring me in?"

"I'm not the one who's going to die here, Renji might want you back alive; but I don't." Jessa told her.

"Renji...Renji's here...?" Toria said more to herself than to Jessa, she looked up the corridor knowing that he was only there; she knew if she shouted for him right now even after he thought what she had done he'd still come running for her. But she had to give him up, it was for both of them, for their people's future.

Toria pushed herself up, she had to make this convincing without actually killing her; she palmed her in the face and then grabbed her hair swinging her around smashing her face into the wall. Jessa fell to the floor in a heap unconscious.

"This Magic is taken care of, send a med team." Toria said into her com to Volic, who she knew would be where Renji was. "We want them alive, to find out some useful information from them."

"Yeah course." Volic answered. "Do you want to interrogate them yourself?"

"No, but I know someone who'd like that job." Toria said pleasantly. "Throw them into a holding cell."

"Yes sir." Volic said before he logged off.

Toria picked up her shoes as she walked back, but she didn't put them back on. She also bent down and picked up the blaster rifle thinking that it could come in handy. She walked back to the dining room where she had left her captain, knowing that he'd still be there. She flung open the doors startling Ja'tin who had had two young women sent to him, one was straddled on his lap with the top of her dress untied revealing her breasts and the other by his side with his arm around her waist.

"Care to join us?" Captain Ja'tin asked her.

"Get out." Toria told the women, but they didn't move; so she shot and blew up the empty chair next to woman stood up.

They both covered themselves as they rushed out past her, Ja'tin didn't get up from his seat or bother to fasten his trousers he just looked furious but so did Toria and she was the one holding the blaster rifle.

"This place was under attack and you're here taking pleasure in the slaves." Toria said. "I already told you that I don't approve, but you still decided to rub it in my face."

She aimed the blaster at him ready to fire, he didn't seem to think though that she would fire; but he of course was wrong. She aimed ever so slightly lower, shooting off the chair legs instead; he fell backwards onto the hard marble floor.

"You think that I'm going to let you order me around or anyone else come to that, you must be joking." Toria told him. "They don't mind their officers indulging themselves as long as it doesn't get in the way, your indulges got in the way. And you've upset me personally; you can say goodbye to your commission on the special task teams."

"You don't have a say in what goes on here!" Captain Ja'tin shouted at her.

"I have some very important friends, how do you think I got here in the first place?" Toria said smirking. "You should pack your things; they'll be a ship here shortly to take you back to Sanctus."

"You...you can't do that!" Captain Ja'tin shouted at her.

Toria though wasn't listening to him, she pressed her wrist com. "I need a security team to confine Captain Ja'tin."

"Don't listen to her...she isn't in charge...I am!" Captain Ja'tin shouted outraged as he struggled to get up from the broken pieces of the chair.

"Move, and I'll shoot you saying that you made me; giving me no other choice to stop you." Toria warned him.

This time he seemed to believe her and stayed where he was until the security team came and took him away, Volic arrived just after they had taken him away; Toria knew that if she was going to have any problems that they would be with him as the men trusted his word more than the captains.

"The Magics are in the holding cells, the woman will be fine when she wakes up." Volic told her. "Though probably regretting to take on this mission."

"They came for me." Toria said walking around the table, she switched on the wall view screen logging it into the holding ceils. "They've sent others before."

Toria couldn't believe what she saw, she had never seen him so beaten up before; Renji was in his native form, his long red crimson hair partly out of his pony tail and a cut on his forehead bleeding over his eye.

"I think Kasiya is in the area, he can give us a lift and handle them also." Toria told him turning around unable to look at him anymore as it hurt too much to see him like this when she couldn't tell him why she was doing what she was doing.

The lights were dimly set in the restaurant with candles lit on every table, couples sat together throughout making Toria feel very uncomfortable seeing that this was the first time that she was alone with General Conoab and on a date after her father had pushed her into it seeing that they were on the planet; she was going to meet up with Siren and Annyetta before the New Year, but they understood.

She had a purple reddish one strapped top showing off her mid-riff with a long skirt which had a slit up the left leg and layered. Conoab were his dress uniform, still thinking that it impressed her to be seen with a General; she might not be impressed with it but it seemed that everyone else was and they couldn't do enough for him.

"I am glad that we happened to bump into each other." General Conoab said again.

"Yes, my father did mention that you would be stopping over here." Toria said smiling slightly.

"So how's your training going?" General Conoab asked her, as though he didn't want to talk about her father at the moment.

"I guess it's going alright, a few bruises here and there of course." Toria told him. "You must of heard about our captain...disgusting behaviour wouldn't you say?"

"Well, considering the situation...but other than that, they don't mind." General Conoab told her.

"So you go to them, then?" Toria asked him.

He looked around nervously as if wondering how to answer her question, but Toria didn't need for him to give her an answer as she had already figured out what type of guy he was.

"Well, I don't really approve of them; nor would I considering going out with a man who liked that sort of thing." Toria told him.

"Yes well..." General Conoab said.

Toria's com beeped loudly making those sat close by look around wondering who it was. She answered the com before Conoab could object.

"Toria here, go ahead." Toria said.

"I regret to report that Captain Kasiya's ship was attacked by Magics and rescued those who attacked Tandro." Volic informed her. "Another ship is on its way to help with repairs on the Ake'cheta, as she was badly damaged in the battle."

"Is Kasiya alright?" Toria asked him sounding very concerned.

"Yes, it was he who sent the message personally to inform you of the situation." Volic answered.

"Thank you." Toria said and then logged off of her com.

"Well that isn't something you hear everyday, the Ake'cheta out gunned by Magics." General Conoab said. "She's one of the top battle ships..."

"She's third class isn't she?" Toria asked him.

"Exactly." General Conoab said.

The rest of the conversation for the night was all on business, how they both thought that there was going to be another full on war before long.

Chapter Twenty

On board the Silver Star, most of the senior officers were taking a couple of hours off and went down to the rec room which was full to busting as normal, of those who were off-duty during the Vertigo match to watch it on the large holo screen; today was Yudan vs Roaring Torch. Most were there to follow their own team, but some were there to see what the Roaring Torch Rose player got up to, seeing that every match she had shown some sort of different power.

Renji was sat with Dalal, he was still angry about what had happened with Toria how she hadn't even come to see him. He just found it lucky that she had called for Kasiya otherwise they would probably still be in the Fleet's custody.

"I know she's only young sir, but she seems alright." Dalal told him.

"The word is that she blew up the platform a couple of matches ago, you know with the hot springs." Labon said turning around from in front of them.

"She does sound interesting, I mean from how you lot talk about her." Renji said.

"She's just a little girl." Jessa said squeezing past a couple of officers so that she could sit down next to Renji.

"So what, Touro's just getting started." Dalal said.

"What you have a thing for little girls now?" Jessa teased.

"Touro..." Renji said thoughtfully, it had been bothering him for some time now; he knew the name. "Bring up a close up of Touro!"

This order caused a few raised eyebrows and a scowl from Jessa next to him, but they still did what he asked. Renji just hoped that he was over reacting and seeing something that wasn't really there, but no such luck; purple hair and eyes, she looked just like her only younger like when he had first meet her.

"Damn it!" Renji said angrily getting up to leave.

"Hay the match isn't even over yet!" Dalal shouted after him.

"I just got here." Jessa protested.

Renji though didn't care about them this was far more important, he needed to find out everything that he could on her knowing that it wouldn't be easy; just as long as he could find out when she joined the team and where she was staying so that he could at least go and see her, that way he could clear up this whole mess. But there was something nagging at the back of his mind, telling him that it wasn't going to be that simple.

Music blared out of all the halls in the Vertigo quarter building, along the main corridor hung a huge banner HAPPY NEW YEAR; every room was crowded with people dancing and drinking, screens up on the walls showing the most recent matches including the one that Touro had played the day before.

Touro had told her team mates that she'd meet them all at the party as she was coming with her own friends; the only problem was that this place was so big she didn't know if she'd be able to find anyone that she knew. This was her first really big party with the team as she hadn't gone to last years party, she had been to a few of the after match parties; but this was a proper party so she wanted to dress right. Even though she felt as though she hadn't over-dressed she still felt as though she had somehow, she wore a short pink reddish dress with thin silver straps and trousers, there was silver line embroidery running up the front of the dress that matched the body paint that Siren had done for her.

Siren walked in beside of her, she had been looking forward to this party for a month not just that she got to see her best friend but also so that she could just relax and let her hair down; she wore a blue and silver sleeveless top and trousers which had a sliver line of stitching swirling up her right leg then around the middle. Annyetta stood nervously on Touro's other side, it was her first time around so many Magics; it had actually taken them weeks to convince her to come out with them and then all day to get to wear the dress that Touro had gotten her. Annyetta was used to wearing elegant gowns for the official senate functions, so this dress wasn't really what she was used to wearing but she still looked beautiful as normal; she wore a deep-red wine coloured boob-tube dress with a lighter coloured waist-band, from the knees it striped off into different lengths.

"See it's not too bad." Touro said as she started to make her way through the crowd.

"Touro!"

"Hay Touro."

"The Torches' Rose!"

"You're quite popular here." Siren teased. "Who would have thought it, since you knew nothing about the game."

"I know tell me about it." Touro said smiling. "It's kind of strange that all these people know who I am."

"But they don't Miss Toria...sorry Miss Touro..." Annyetta said.

"That...I meant her...this me." Touro said squeezing past a couple of guys to get into the hall facing the main entrance. "And while we're here, actually all the time...just call me Touro, with no titles."

"I don't know, it doesn't seem right." Annyetta said still feeling uncomfortable keeping very close to Touro.

Siren smiled to herself as she spotted one of the holo screens showing Touro's match from the day before, she had been impressed with it herself how well she had come on with her Magic but to be able to completely break through an Electro Net without being hurt, well she didn't know of anyone who could do that.

"Can you see any of the team?" Touro asked Siren.

"No but I can see you on that screen." Siren told her. "You still haven't explained how you managed to do it yet."

"No she hasn't, has she." Ko-Dero said behind them. "Like I believe that someone of your ability could pull something like that off, it had to be some sort of trick."

"I bet that Ze-Siro showed her how to do a few illusions', you know when they went out that time after our match." Nang-Ya said smiling at the three of them. "Nice of you to bring friends."

"Ze-Siro's been helping you use Magic? I'm going to kill him." Ko-Dero said angrily before he marched off into the crowd to find him.

"You said that on purpose." Touro told him.

"I might have, then again I might not." Nang-Ya said still smiling. "They're over by the balcony."

"Thanks." Touro said and then walked off, she didn't really know him that well as she had never actually talked to him before now.

"Well, you've definitely sparked a lot of interest among the teams." Siren said.

"I know, I only really wanted to learn some Magic and get to know what was going on here..." Touro told her. "Even if I only used it as somewhere to escape to, from everything that...you know?"

Touro walked straight into the back of someone not looking where she was going while talking with Siren, he turned around to see who it was and was surprised to see that it was Touro; she was also surprised to see Romas wearing a smart emerald green shirt.
"Tour..." Romas said.

"So you finally found us." Vi said turning around himself, but was surprised to see her as well. "You look..."

"Wow, Touro you look great; how'd you afford such a pretty outfit?" Kima-Na asked her pushing past the two speechless guys, and taking her and her friends out onto the balcony where the rest of the team was. "Hay guys, Touro's here!"

They all turned around and was meet with the same dumb-founded looks that Vi and Romas had, who had in fact followed them out; Touro was starting to feel a little awkward herself wishing that she had worn something else.

"Tour, is that really you?" Jo-Mi teased. "I wouldn't have recognised you."

Touro smiled shyly.

"You look great." Lonac told her and handed her a drink.

"Thanks." Touro said blushing deeply, but Siren grabbed her and dragged her off towards Kyo to get their own drinks.

"I don't want you to start setting fire to everything, all because he said that you look good." Siren told her.

"He said that she looked great." Annyetta corrected her.

"You know what I mean." Siren said.

"So that's why you wanted to keep her to yourself, I knew there had to be a reason." Rox teased Lonac.

"I hardly recognised her...well I did of course...I meant...she surprised me." Vi said.

"She isn't seeing anyone is she?" Leka asked them and received some very scary looks from them all, warning him off. "Okay then."

"She's off-limits, especially to you." Jo-Mi told him. "I know what you're like."

"Hay, comments like that hurt you know." Leka protested, but they all knew what he was like.

"What if she is seeing someone?" Rui-Lin asked, making them all look at him as if he was going to tell them something; so he quickly added. "Not me...I'm just saying."

"She isn't." Kima-Na told them. "She would have said something, and anyway her place didn't show any sign that there was a guy staying. And remember she said that we could stay as well, if we ever had any problems getting a place; as long as she had the room."

"Well then, where's she gone to...I need to talk to her about the game..." Jo-Mi said turning around trying to see her.

"That was strange; it was as though she just acted on impulse." Lonac told them. "I don't even think she realised what she had done until after she had done it."

"Well I definitely got it right with her, didn't I?" Jo-Mi said proudly.

"You asked her to play, just to fill up on numbers." Rox reminded him. "And you were going to kick her off the team before this season started; only you couldn't find anyone else."

"Yeah, well; everything worked out for the best didn't it?" Jo-Mi said dismissively.

No one seemed to care what he thought; it didn't seem to make any difference what they said to him he was going to believe that it was his brilliant idea to have her join his team. Lonac went off with Vi and Romas to find her and her friends.

Dalal near enough had to run down the corridor to keep up with Renji, who was marching ahead of him out of uniform and wearing a long-sleeved blue rimmed v-neck t-shirt with shirt bands on both arms with a blue and white belt around it, over his dark blue trousers.

"Sir...erm...the New Year parties should be over by now..." Dalal told him again.

"That isn't why I'm going." Renji told him. "I'm going to meet someone...alone. Just stay in the system, and be prepared to transport me back when I say so."

"But sir, this is kind of sudden." Dalal said.

Renji stopped and turned around, not a man to be questioned. "I'm asking you to follow a simple order."

"Of course." Dalal said still sounding unsure that he was doing the right thing.

Renji carried on walking and went into the transporter room; Dalal followed him standing next to the console while Renji got onto the pad. The officer activated the pad, only doing as he was told and wasn't in any sort of position to question his captain even if everyone thought that this was kind of strange him disappearing all of a sudden.

Renji concentrated as he was engulfed in the white light, he wanted to change his appearance but not before he had left the ship but before he reappeared on the planet's surface; when the light had vanished and he had appeared in the busy market square filled with people and aliens from all over the galaxy shopping for a bargain.

He no longer looked like himself, well not completely as he was still quite tall and muscular, but he had short light brown hair and dark eyes, but they had a gentleness about them; his whole facial features had changed into that of a different man but he was still Ta'vian and looked as though he was in his early twenties.

The easy part was over, now the hard part began; he had to find her without making it appear as though he was actually there looking for her. He had found out which apartment block she lived in, so if he headed over that way then perhaps he could make it look as though he just bumped into her.

He walked through the market square watching out for her, as this was the closest market to her apartment; he hadn't wanted to arrive that close but close enough so not to waste too much time incase she was leaving as most did straight after everything was over.

Renji had been walking around for over an hour, getting a bad feeling that he had missed her; perhaps he should have checked the transport logs to see if she was flying out today. In his position he did have the clearance to check the manifest of the ships. He wouldn't have used names of course not wanting anyone to find out what he was up to; but it might have been easier instead of wasting all of this time.

He had just finished debating with himself whether or not to go back when he saw a girl with purple hair, his heart started to pound in his chest; he had to be calm as he made his way over to her without making it look as though he was doing so. He could see her, she looked just like her at her age, except perhaps for the clothes that she was wearing; she had a pale blue and turquoise block panel baby doll top with matching wrap-over skirt and knee socks, one in each colour. He couldn't help but smile to himself, seeing her there, so close; he didn't even realise how close he was to her, but if he reached out he'd actually be able to touch her.

Touro seemed to be in a world of her own as she made her way through the crowded market square, until she was pushed out of the way by a Targratullan; they were twice the size as humans and four times stronger. She fell straight into the arms of a man who had rushed forward to catch her, he held her in his arms as she looked up at him blushing deeply feeling herself burning up inside by his touch.

"Are you alright?" He asked her.

Touro just stared at him as though she didn't hear his question.

He was just as taken off-guard as she was, but perhaps for another reason; he knew who she was, how could he have not known.

"I'm so sorry..." Touro said pushing him away abruptly.

"No, it's alright...I mean as long as you're alright?" He asked her.

"What? Oh yeah...I'm fine...thank you." Touro said smiling at him.

He smiled back at her, realising that she hadn't noticed; this had worked out even better than he could have ever imagined.

"Sorry about that." Touro said still blushing deeply, finding it hard to look him directly in the eye.

"That's alright...I'm...Liko." He told her, it was the first name that had popped into his mind; his father's name, it's not as though he could use his own.

"Liko...well it was nice bumping into you, but I'd better be getting off." Touro told him starting to walk off.

Liko quickly joined her, not wanting to give this chance up; but Touro seemed a little wary of him.

"Do you mind if I walk with you?" Liko asked her.

This question seemed to startle her, making her bump into someone else and her hair flashed red for a moment but he still saw it; he knew why she was so nervous and couldn't help but smile at her.

"Nice trick, with the hair." Liko told her. "So I'll take your answer as yes then."

"What?" Touro said.

"You need to work on your Tasian features, especially if you don't want people to know what you are." Liko told her as they walked along together.

Touro looked up at him, not sure that she knew what he meant; she hadn't really looked into her Tasian physiology, but perhaps she should considering that a complete stranger was able to tell what she was, if only her hair changed colour.

"Don't I know you from somewhere?" Liko asked her.

"What? Me? No...I think I'd remember meeting you." Touro said.

"You would now, would you?" Liko teased, causing her to blush again and her hair to strike red. "Oh I remember, you play Vertigo...The Roaring Torch."

"Touro." She told him. "I know it sounds stupid, but I forget sometimes just how many people actually follow the game... and have seen me play."

"You don't sound like the rest of the hard core fans or players." Liko said.

"Truthfully, I'm still just learning about the game...I don't know much about it." Touro told him smiling.

"I wouldn't have guessed that by watching you play." Liko told her.

"You mustn't have watched all of my matches then." Touro told him. "Some have been quite embarrassing."

They walked out of the market square together and into a much quieter street, Touro thought that he seemed nice but she didn't trust herself to be alone with him let alone any guy she thought was nice, especially considering that her hair kept changing to red as well which meant that she still didn't have control over her powers, which made her worry if she would ever be able to control it so that she would be able to be with anyone.

"I really should be getting off." Touro told him.

"You're in a rush, heading back?" Liko asked her.

"No, I'm staying hopefully for a couple more days as long as I don't get called away; you know how it is." Touro told him.

"Then, why don't you let me take you for a drink?" Liko asked her.

Touro just stared at him as she took in what he had just asked her, no one had ever just asked her out like that before; but she didn't know him, it wasn't as though she could just go off with a complete stranger, but then she thought isn't everyone a stranger until you actually get to know them, and she could be missing out on something if she turned him down.

"Well...I don't know..." Touro said sounding unsure.

"How about I give you my card, then that way you can contact me, when you're ready for that drink." Liko told her getting a contact card out of his pocket.

Touro took it off of him; it was on a data sheet with his ship and channel to contact him on.

"I'll call then." Touro told him smiling shyly.

"I'll be waiting." Liko told her smiling back.

She slowly turned around and walked off, leaving him stood there watching her walk away; part of her was already regretting just walking away like she had done, and wondering if she could actually call him after she had basically blown him off like that. She had never called a guy before, well not like that before, no one who had asked her out; then she wondered if it was as a date thing or he was just interested in her because of Vertigo. She knew she was thinking too much about it and if she always did then she would end up getting no where.

Toria had gone back to her apartment and changed back into her real self, she was sat on the sofa turning the card over that he had given her still wondering what to do about it. Part of her wanted to go, and then she would remember what she had done to Kole. One part of her mind kept telling her that it might be alright considering he was a Ta'vian and a Magic, which meant that he was a lot stronger; but another part kept saying that it didn't matter what he was because she could still hurt him. Renji was Ta'vian and she had blasted him across the room, but he had said that she didn't hurt him. She had wanted to believe him but it was hard.

Her computer started to beep in a staggered pattern; she had changed the tone so that she would know who was contacting her before she answered so she could change if she needed.

She got up and walked over to the desk sitting down before she turned it on, Volic definitely didn't look well-rested after the New Year celebrations, in fact he looked even more agitated than normal.

"What're you wearing?" Volic asked her.

"What?" Toria said looking down at her, suddenly remembering that she hadn't changed her clothes knowing that they would never imagine her wearing anything like this; but she kind of liked it, being able to dress more fun like. "Does it really matter what I'm wearing?"

"No. Of course not." Volic answered and then moved on to why he was contacting her. "We've picked up a lot of activity in the Coldar system, we're being sent to check it out. As you know it's a mixed system, which still has a lot of Magics living there trying to pass themselves off as Normals."

"So when are we moving out?" Toria asked him.

"You need to meet up with us, within two hours." Volic told her.

This was going to be a bit of a problem, since where she really was; he didn't know where she really was and believed that she was quite close by from where she had told him she was spending the New Year.

"I might be a bit longer than two hours." Toria told him.

"I can send a ship to get you, if that's what you need." Volic told her.

"That'll be fine...I'll get to you as soon as I can." Toria assured him and logged off.

She got up and went down the hall to her bedroom, went over to the far corner and opened the closet grabbing her bag putting Liko's card inside; she had no idea how she was going to meet up with him since that Siren's ship had already left, she couldn't ask any of the team because she would have to answer too many questions of why she was just running off and then if there really is an attack. Well she'd just have to head back over to the transport centre and try and get herself a seat off the planet and meet Volic in time.

She changed back into Touro and rushed over to the transport centre expecting it to be bombarded with people trying to get off world, with word of an attack but as she walked through the entrance she didn't hear one person mention it; in fact they were all still in high spirits from the three matches and the New Year parties that had been held throughout the city the day before.

Touro walked over to the departure screens to see if she could get a transport off world and was horrified to see that they were still sending ships to the Coldar system, that meant that they didn't know that the Fleet was moving in on them; she looked around the room wondering what to do hoping to see someone who could help her knowing that no one would listen to her if she suddenly told them that there was an attack about to happen.

The last person she had been expecting to see was stood at the information booth questioning the harsh looking woman behind the screen, she didn't know him but he was the only person who she recognised; she made her way over to him trying not to bump into anyone or hit them with her bag even though no one else seemed to be giving her the same consideration.

"Liko, isn't it?" Touro said as she came up behind him.

He didn't turn around straight away but seemed to ignore her, so she tapped him on the shoulder thinking that he hadn't heard her; he turned around to see who it was and was just surprised to see her as she was him.

"What're you doing here...and with your bag?" Liko asked her. "I thought you said that you were staying a couple more days?'

"Something's come up with work." Touro told him. "I was wondering if you knew the fastest way I could get to the Coldar system, without arriving there on a Magical marked ship?"

"You don't want anyone to know where you've come from?" Liko asked.

"No one does really, do they?" Touro said. "There's a problem and I need to get there, my ship will be expecting me there in two hours."

"You won't get there in two hours on any of these transports." Liko told her.

"Seriously?" Touro said even more worried than she was before.

"By the sounds of things you'll be in a lot of trouble if you don't make it back in time." Liko said. "I could ask my captain to give you a lift."

"What?" Touro said looking relieved even though she hadn't accepted his offer.

Liko smiled at her stepping away from the information booth, giving the woman a chance to make a break for it. Touro didn't care who he was at the moment as long as he could get her there, but she still felt the need to tell him why she was in such a rush. Liko put his arm around her waist pulling her slightly into him, surprising her slightly as she looked up at him; but he had lifted his other arm for his com.

"Dalal, two to transport when you're ready." Liko told him.

"Erm...yeah...sure..." Dalal said slowly.

They were both suddenly engulfed in the bright light of the transporter surprising a few passersby, they disappeared and then reappeared on the pad of the transporter pad aboard The Silver Star; Dalal just stared at the two of them strangely.

"Oh god!" Dalal shouted suddenly.

Touro just stared at him hoping that he didn't recognise her as she had him, he had been apart of Renji's team who had tried to capture her, in fact he had been a part of a couple of the teams sent to take her.

"Is there something wrong?' Liko asked him.

"You...you know Touro?" Dalal asked.

Both of them was relieved that he didn't say what they thought he was going to say.

"We just bumped into each other down there." Liko told him. "She said that she needs a lift to the Coldar system, and I said that we might be able to do that."

"Yeah...everyone's up now...you were the last..." Dalal told him staring at Touro making her feel very uncomfortable.

"I'll take you to my quarters so you're not mobbed by the crew." Liko told her leading her past the red Dalal, who was ignoring the angry glare that he was giving him.

"So you work on one of the big Magic ships?" Touro said walking beside of him now giving them both a little room, because whenever she got too close to him she felt her temperature double. "I've never seen a proper one before, let alone been on one."

"This is The Silver Star." Liko told her, more like testing her reaction to see if she had really heard of it and her captain.

"The Silver Star, it kind of sounds familiar....as though it reminds me of something, but I can't put my figure on it." Touro said thoughtfully. "I like the name though."

A few of the crew stared at them as they walked through the corridors, as they were surprised to see Touro on board those who actually followed Vertigo which was most of the ship in fact and some wondering who she was with as they didn't recognise him. Liko was actually glad that none of them stopped him considering what he was doing, but he was also annoyed at the same time that they didn't ask who he was seeing that none of them had seen him like this before; he could be a spy for all they knew and they were just letting him roam about the ship; apart from Dalal who he had informed a couple of minutes before Touro turned up that he's coming back looking a little different.

"So why are you in such a rush to get to the Coldar system?" Liko asked her as they walked down the corridor towards his quarters.

"Well, the ship I'm on...well...they've picked up a lot of Magical activity..." Touro told him. "It's a Fleet ship you see, so they want to check it out as soon as possible."

"What?" Liko said grabbing hold of her roughly and nearly throwing her against the bulkhead. "And just when were you going to tell me this, when they start firing on us?"

"No of course not; I didn't think that you would take me all the way there yourselves..." Touro said trying to struggle against him but he was much stronger than she was. "I told you that I couldn't arrive by a Magic ship, so why would I want you to turn up in your ship putting everyone in danger. The people in that system are in enough danger."

"And why should I believe you?" Liko demanded.

"Why would I lie?" Touro asked him.

"I'll check out what you're saying." Liko told her.

He let go of one of her arms and nearly dragged her the rest of the way to his quarters, he opened the door and waving his hand behind her making everything that showed him as Renji disappear.

"Wait in here, I won't be long." Liko told her.

"I'm sorry." Touro said not turning around to face him, and she really was sorry for getting him caught up in all of this mess that was her life. This kind of solved the problem of her calling him for that drink, she really couldn't get involved with anyone. It was too dangerous for her and too dangerous for whoever else might be involved.

Renji had changed back into himself on the way up to the bridge, the doors slid open and he stepped out between the engineering and science consoles; Dalal turned around from the weapons station looking a little disappointed to see Renji alone.

"We've set a course for the Coldar system." Dalal told him. "So you went down to meet Touro?"

"I told you that I just bumped into her." Renji told him sternly. "I want you to check out what's happening in the Coldar system, and also find out who's our closet contact so that our guest can jump ship."

"Oh, she works undercover...that must be tough for her." Dalal said turning back around to start on his requests. "It'll take about ten minutes to log into the Coldar network, and then to find out who's nearest. Anyone that you would want especially?"

"Kasiya." Renji answered simply.

"So what's she like?" Dalal asked him typing on the console and looking over at the pacing Renji.

"Do you know, that not one person stopped me in my other form." Renji informed him ignoring his question. "Not one. What if I was spy here to destroy the ship?"

"With Touro, of course not." Dalal said dismissively.

Renji looked over at him, he hadn't thought about that; she did seem pretty harmless like this and earning everyone's trust, what if that was part of her plan and then turn on them all they wouldn't stand a chance. But it was still hard to believe, especially after seeing her finally after so long; yeah she might look different but she still seemed like the Toria that he knew, he just couldn't figure out what was going on.

The lift door opened again and Jessa walked out looking rather angry about something herself, she marched over to Renji stopping right in his path making him stop his pacing.

"Someone said that you brought Touro from the Roaring Torch on board, and took her to your quarters?" Jessa asked him. "Is it true?"

"She's quite pretty, though I didn't think that she would be his type... but seeing that I'd never actually seen him go out with anyone beside you; I don't really know his type." Dalal said.

"I'm not going out with anyone, since I lost my faïence." Renji informed them before Jessa could say anything. "And Touro just needed a lift. She's in my quarters so she isn't bothered by anyone."

"But...Renji..." Jessa tried to say.

"Send the information to my quarters, I need it quicker than ten minutes." Renji told Dalal ignoring Jessa once again, walking past her and back into the lift to his quarters where she was waiting for him.

He needed to know what was going on, but without ruining this chance; if for some reason she is telling the truth and giving him the heads up then perhaps he could still save her as there is a part of her in there who still wants to be saved. Maybe that's what they actually did to her, they split her into two different people; he just hoped that he could save them both.

He stood outside of his own quarters, unsure about going inside and finding out the truth that he didn't want to hear.

"Dalal to Renji, I have the info that you wanted." Dalal told him through his com. "There's a mass of Fleet ships converging on the system, Kasiya is on his way and will meet us half way."

"Thanks." Renji said. "The system has been warned?"

"Of course, but...I don't know how many we can actually get out in time." Dalal told him. "There's ten planets and six dozen moons, we'll never be able to get them all out in time."

"I'll see what I can do, Renji out." Renji said before he turned back into Liko and going into his quarters where Touro was sat waiting for him.

"So, am I under arrest?" Touro asked him.

"No, you're not." Liko told her walking over to the facing chair and sitting down. "We've warned the system, but to be honest...there's nothing we can do except a full out attack."

"An all out attack?" Touro said worriedly.

Liko could see how worried she was.

"You could help us, if you're on board a Fleet ship." Liko suggested.

"How, when I'm only in the academy, I'm just an observer." Touro told him.

"Are you sure?" Liko asked.

"I'm sorry...I really am..." Touro said and she really was; and both of them knew it.

"It's alright, we'll find a way." Liko assured her, it really made him worried if she really was two separate people and if he could keep her here then perhaps she wouldn't change back into her other self.

"I hate it...do you? I mean, being so powerless unable to help them?" Touro asked him.

"We can only help as many as we can." Liko told her.

Touro transported over to Kasiya's ship alone, she changed back before she reappeared with Volic and the team waiting for her, staring at what she was still wearing as she still hadn't changed into her uniform yet; which she couldn't because it wasn't a cadet uniform like she had told Liko.

"I've got time to change it?" Toria asked.

"Yes." Volic answered walking out with her. "So who'd you get to give you a lift?"

"What didn't Kasiya tell you?" Toria asked.

"No." Volic answered simply.

"Are you going to come with me, while I get changed?" Toria asked him changing the subject wondering why he was following her the whole way.

"Yes." Volic answered.

"That's kind of you, but I can dress myself thanks." Toria told him.

"I just want to make sure that you're up to this, seeing as it'll be your first big confrontation with the Magics." Volic told her. "I'll stay close by so that..."

"So that I don't lose my head?" Toria finished for him, she stopped him in the corridor a couple of doors away from her quarters. "What exactly are we supposed to do, considering that it's a whole system?"

"There's a military outpost, that's what we'll be attacking." Volic told her.

"With the ship, then why were we needed?" Toria asked, even though she still wanted to be apart of it; thinking that if she worked at the weapons station then perhaps she might be able to save some of them.

"We're going down to the surface." Volic told her. "Now shouldn't you change?"

They were going down to the surface, Toria repeated to herself; she knew that Kasiya would do what he could but she'd be able to save more people if she was on the ship. Yeah she'd hide the military outpost, which is of course helpful, but all those innocent people.

"I'll be fine on my own, I'll be there in twenty minutes after I speak with Kasiya." Toria told him; she needed to do something she just didn't know what to do.

She went into her quarters, or rather what used to be her quarters and started to unfasten her top.

"You might want to wait to do that." Kasiya told her coming out from the bedroom.

Startled Toria shot a fire ball at him, he hit the deck as it flew past him and into the wall above her bed.

"What're you doing?" Kasiya demanded.

"You...you scared me!" Toria shouted at him. "You don't just jump out like that."

"I didn't jump out, I stepped out; then dropped to the ground." Kasiya told her looking over his shoulder at the burn mark, as he stood up once more. "How am I supposed to explain that?"

"I don't know...I..." Toria said still confused about what to do.

"So, you got a lift from The Silver Star." Kasiya said causally.

"Don't you think that we have more important things to talk about than how or who got me here...he...he...it doesn't matter." Toria said all flustered.

"Is there something the matter?" Kasiya asked her calmly.

"Of course there is!" Toria shouted at him. "How can you just stand there like that?"

"One has to be calm and collected in these types of situations." Kasiya told her.

"I don't know what to do." Toria told him. "What am I supposed to do? There's so many people, and I know that I can't save them all...I know if I go down to that base then so many people are going to be killed...I...I don't know..."

"Do you still want to help them?" Kasiya asked her. "If yes, then it doesn't matter how many you can save just as long as you try. They may not know today or tomorrow how you helped them, but one day they will know and be grateful for everything that you could manage."

"But it isn't enough!" Toria shouted at him.

"The base is important, we need it." Kasiya told her. "That's what our ships will be trying to protect."

Toria walked around him to get changed, she knew he was right but she still couldn't forget about all those innocent people and Liko putting their lives on the line and she couldn't really help them.

"I know that you'll do the right thing." Kasiya told her before he left her alone.

Yeah it was alright that he thought that, but she didn't; she couldn't save them. She finally understood what Renji had felt when he wasn't able to help that boy several years ago; as it didn't matter how powerful you were there are still limits.

The news report played on the computer screen, with the sound down; she had been watching it over and over since she had come back to the ship and locked herself in her quarters. Ships, Magic ships, Fleet ships fighting firing at one another, flying in and out of the weapons fire and being hit by it, whole sections of ships being destroyed.

They had taken what ships that they had out to protect the people, drawing the fighting away from them so that the Fleet would just concentrate on the military outposts that they had built; which they did do.

Toria had gone down with her team on foot, they had to fight their whole way inside; she could only save the ones that she shot herself since she still didn't know how to use her powers more effectively, but that meant that dozen's more people had to die because she wasn't good enough, wasn't powerful enough to save them. She should have been stronger, she should have been able to save them.

Kasiya was giving her a wide birth, knowing that she needed her own space but Volic on the other hand had to be ordered to stay away from her by him when they had returned to the ship.

She dropped her feet and kicked her bag that she had left here before it had all happened, she suddenly remembered what was inside of it; she slowly bent down and opened it, there it was on the top of her clothes. She smiled slightly to herself as she picked it up and sat back up, holding it in her hand wondering if she should call him; did she have the right to contact him after what she couldn't do. She didn't feel as though she should, but she also just needed someone to talk to who wouldn't judge her, knowing what she wasn't able to do for them.

Toria stared at the card for ten minutes before she finally turned the news report off changing her form and contacting Liko, hoping that he was alright since his own ship had been involved in the fighting.

Renji painfully pulled his long white and pink flowered robe on as he stepped out of the shower, his long hair wet and down his back; he looked drained as though he hadn't slept for days. He heard a beeping from the other room and slowly went through to answer the computer, to yell at who ever had disobeyed his order about contacting him; he had only wanted a couple of hours but he couldn't even get that.

He turned the computer around and saw that it was encoded, and that it was from Touro; he was so surprised to be hearing from her and also somewhat pleased as well that she was alright; he changed into Liko before he accepted the incoming call. Touro appeared on his screen looking just as terrible as he did, he sat down turning the screen around again.

"You're alright...I'm glad...I was worried." Touro said trying to smile, but she couldn't manage it; instead she looked close to tears.

Liko felt his heart clench, he hated seeing her sad. "Don't...if you cry, I won't be able to able to wipe them away..."

"I'm sorry...I'm just glad that you're alright...so many people...there were so many people killed..." Touro said unable to stop the tears from flowing. "I couldn't help...I couldn't do anything to help..."

"You said it yourself, that you couldn't do anything...I...I...don't blame you..." Liko told her, he really didn't blame her; even as her other self she wouldn't have been able to do anything as there were so many ships fighting one another. "One person, wouldn't have been able to make a difference."

"You say that...but it doesn't help...it...it still hurts knowing that they were all killed..." Touro told him. "They...us. We're all fighting to save our way of life...they're even willing to die...I thought that I was strong enough to do this, but now I don't know..."

"We all feel like that, especially after days like this one." Liko told her. "We never give up...you must fight, remain strong."

"Strength is a hard thing to hold onto, especially when you're alone." Touro said.

"You're not alone, you'll never be alone." Liko assured her and smiled kindly. "You have me to talk to, and whenever I'm in the neighborhood I'll be glad to drop by and buy you that drink that you refused me."

Touro smiled at him. "I'm sorry about that as well. I'll definitely call..."

They talked for an hour about nothing until finally Touro let him go, promising that she'd keep in touch with him.

Renji had never been so pleased to hear from her in his whole life, it had been the moment that he had been waiting for; he knew now that he could save her, he just wasn't completely sure how he was going to do it.

Chapter Twenty-One

The door slid open to the briefing room, Volic went in first with Toria behind him and then the rest of their team, which were made up of four other officers all men of course and all of them older than Toria. It was a long room with a table that fitted down the middle with fourteen chairs sat around, on three of the bulkheads were wall consoles with the ships' design and layout, except for one at the top of the table which was blank at the moment. Along the facing wall behind the table was a full length view port, broken up into sections or there would have been too much strain on the pressure.

The top three chairs were taken by officers Toria hadn't seen before, all of whom were Admirals. The one sat at the top of the table had almost white hair and deep lines set in around his face, his uniform also looked as though it was kind of tight on him like he was still trying to get away with a size that he would have worn as a much younger man.

The man on the right was the youngest of the three probably in his late forties, a few lines around the eyes but his short brown hair hadn't started to show signs of ageing, only in his face. The third man on the left just sat there, his thin face not showing any sign of emotion and his once dark eyes seemed kind of dull; his greying hair was brushed back neatly in place.

Toria followed Volic to the empty chairs along the left side as the other members of the team went around the other side to sit down, the admiral seated at the top of table seemed to wait until they had all just sat down and then stood up himself pushing his chair back and turning the screen on behind him; it showed all five of them and their records.

"Before we begin how about a few introductions, as I'm sure that not all of you will know us." The man on the right said. "I am Admiral Vonash Lownato." Then he gestured to the man stood up. "Admiral Lash Sankar and lastly Admiral Wanika Everardo."

"You all know we've been called here today." Admiral Sankar said as he sat back down, before Lownato could say anything further. "We all know that you have been operating recently without a captain or commanding officer."

"From what we've heard you have all done quite well." Admiral Lownato said.

"Yes, considering." Admiral Sankar agreed. "But the team needs a leader. We have gone over all of your records, and of course Volic should be the one next in line but if it was that simple then we wouldn't be having this conversation."

"Miss Kentaro, you also stand out as an impressive officer; able to take orders but also to work alone to solve problems." Admiral Lownato said. "We have been very impressed with your work so far, especially from someone so young."

"Yes well." Admiral Sankar said dismissively. "There can only be one of you who gets the position, over the next couple of months you will be working together still as the units' commanding joint officers; and then at the end of the review we will decide who is best suited to the role."

"This is not a competition." Admiral Everardo said. "We just want to know who is best suited to lead and to making the hard decisions, so far Miss Kentaro has shown on more than one occasion that she can do this. Even at great personal risk to herself."

"For now you will remain on board the Palladin, train to prepare for your next assignment." Admiral Lownato told them.

Volic returned to his quarters once the meeting was over, turned the lights down and took a small black holo projector off of his desk and placed it on the floor in the open space before he stood back and waited for it to be activated. He didn't have to wait long before the small lights around the edge flickered on and a light beam shot out of the center, it shimmered and then changed to that of Lord Malevalus in his long black robes and the silver pin fastening them together; Volic dropped to one knee and bowed his head.

"My Lord." Volic said. "I thank you for replying to me so quickly."

"My only concern is with how the meeting went." Lord Malevalus told him.

"They didn't decide on a commanding officer." Volic told him not daring to look up. "They said that they're reviewing how we do over the next couple of assignments."

"Toria Kentaro, must get the position." Lord Malevalus informed him. "I'm sure that if she carries on the way that she is doing, then that won't be a problem. But I still need for you to make sure that she pushes herself, any signs that we could be losing her then you must contact me straight away."

"Yes, my lord." Volic said.

The lights were set to dim and Toria's computer was sat on the coffee table in front of her, with the training timetable still on the screen; she sat on the chair with her feet up in her bath robe and her long hair still damp from the shower she had taken an hour before. She was just about to drift off after waiting so long for a reply when finally her computer beeped signalling that she had received a message, she almost jumped out of her seat as she grabbed the computer and pulled it back onto her lap, changing the screen over so that she could read the new message.

> Sorry that I couldn't speak to you tonight, you're not the only one who's been run off their feet these past weeks.
> I'm glad though that you decided to take me up on my offer,
> and yes I can get this weekend off to visit.
> I'll meet you at the Wild Foxglove, Friday night, 19:45.

Make sure you don't have anything to eat before hand.
Dress there at night, is smart casual.
See you Friday.
Liko

Toria smiled to herself, she was going to meet him again in person; it felt like she hadn't seen him in ages but really it had only been a couple of weeks since New Year. It wasn't as though they hadn't talked, she had been calling him near enough every other night; part of her was surprised that he still wanted to see her after she had gone on at him for hours on end every time that she called.

She was excited and nervous at the same time of meeting him again, she wanted to, and to get off the ship finally and away from Volic who seemed to have turned into a mad man pushing them all with extra training when he himself looked as though he was going to pass out from exhaustion.

"What am I going to wear?" Toria said realising that she didn't have anything to wear for a date as Touro, and all of her dresses were probably completely over the top.

She put the computer down and got up to go through to her bedroom and opened the wardrobe looking inside at all of the dresses she had, they really was too much just for dinner. She wanted to look nice but not look as though she had put too much effort into, incase it wasn't a 'date' date, but a date as friends; she wasn't even sure herself if she should be doing this even though she felt herself getting more and more carried away, but she couldn't help herself.

A blue-skinned man with three head tails dressed in a waiter's uniform carried a tray of drinks in one hand as he carefully moved through the sofas of waiting couples, waiting to go through to their table; he took a glass of wine off the tray and placed it in front of Liko who was sat alone.

Liko was dressed quite smartly in a grey shirt with a blue side fastened waist coat and black trousers with boots.

He sat somewhat nervously wondering if she was going to turn up, he hoped that she did and didn't let her fear of what if got in her way. He hadn't been waiting long when he heard a fuss at the main door and turned round to see what was going on, as it was his night off he wasn't really in the mood for trouble; but it wasn't the fuss that he thought it was, in fact it was Touro who had drawn a crowd considering that she was well-known as a Vertigo player here.

Liko put his drink down and walked over to meet her as she seemed a little overwhelmed by all the fuss they were all making over her, he didn't mean to take his time but he didn't seem to help it as he stared at her with her hair pinned up and wearing a sleeveless knee-length yellow and orange wrap dress, normally no one would have put the two colours together but she really did somehow manage to carry it off.

"Is there a problem?" Liko asked as he gently put his hand on her waist.

"Oh...erm...no sir." The head hostess said politely. "I'm sorry to have kept you waiting..." She clicked her fingers a couple of times before a waiter came over. "They need to be seated."

"Our table won't be ready for..." Liko started to explain, but it seemed as though it was ready as the waiter showed them through to the main part of the restaurant. "I'm sorry that I didn't think about that."

"No...it's alright...I didn't think that I'd cause a stir like that either." Touro said smiling as she followed him through the tables, to the one set by the fireplace with long stemmed blue flowers decorating the frame.

"Is this alright?" Liko asked her.

"Yes...thank you." Touro said.

Liko pulled her chair out for her, she sat down then he walked around and sat down facing her; the waiter handed them both the menu each which were on data sheets.

"We'll have a bottle of Frosted Rose wine." Liko told the waiter.

"Yes sir." He said sounding very pleased before he rushed off.

"You look lovely by the way." Liko told her.

"Thank you." Touro said blushing, feeling even more nervous now than she had done before for some reason.

"I am glad that you came." Liko told her. "I was worried that you might change your mind."

"Truthfully, I was surprised that you still wanted to meet me after the last couple of weeks and all the messages that I sent you." Touro told him. "I kept you up all night some of the time, just talking about nothing...I..."

"Its fine, I enjoyed talking to you or I wouldn't have wanted to meet you like this." Liko told her. "I know how hard it is when you first start off doing undercover work."

"You kind of feel as though you're two different people, which you kind of are really." Touro said. "When I'm her, the me that they expect me to be...sometimes it's like I'm watching myself from a distance, just being swept along in a storm that I can't control."

"I'm sorry to say, but it's only going to get harder the deeper you get." Liko told her.

"I know...a lot more will be expected of me...like I said I hope that I'm strong enough." Touro told him.

"I'm always here, if you need to talk." Liko assured her.

"You'll probably end up regretting that you said." Touro said smiling at him. She thought that he really was nice and understanding.

"What, I only need a couple of hours sleep a night; then I'm right." Liko teased her.

"If you keep letting me talk the way that I do, you probably won't even get that." Touro told him.

"That's fine, it gives the crew something to talk about wondering why I'm up all night." Liko teased.

"Even though you're alone in your quarters?" Touro asked.

"They don't know if I'm alone or not." Liko teased.

Touro laughed at him as the waiter brought their bottle of wine over in an ice blanket stand, the bottle was completely frozen over but as soon as he opened it and tipped the bottle sideways to pour their drinks, the pink liquid just poured out freely.

"It's Magical." Liko told her, seeing the surprised look upon her face. "I thought that you might like seeing that, that's why I ordered it."

Touro smiled at him; she was still nervous but at the same time she felt oddly comfortable as well being with him, as though he wouldn't mind if she really was herself with him.

A large blow of cereal appeared on the computer panel, Touro picked it carrying it over to the chairs when there was a knock at the door; she looked over at the clock on the screen and then down at herself horrified. She wasn't dressed yet, and was still wearing her little vest top and shorts that she wore for bed. There was another knock, she couldn't believe that she had overslept when she had made arrangements; she slowly went over and opened the door holding the bowl of cereal and still dressed for bed.

"Morning." Liko said brightly, before he had taken in fully that she wasn't ready to go out. "You know I would have had you as a morning person, first one up considering that you don't need to sleep; but I guess I was wrong."

"That's why though...I mean that I overslept this morning." Touro told him as she turned around going back through and over to the chair to finish her breakfast without even inviting him inside; Liko luckily seemed to take the hint and followed her in closing the door. "Because I don't sleep much, when I do I kind of want to stay in longer."

"Wanting to make the most of the time that you have." Liko said.

"Yes." Touro said smiling at him. "So I'll eat this then get ready."

"That's fine, take your time." Liko told her sitting back on the sofa next to her in the large comfy chair. "So you live here alone?"

"Yeah, my own little get away." Touro told him smiling. "I let my friends stay over of course if they need a place, but yeah mostly this is all just for me."

"That surprises me, since you said that you don't like being alone." Liko said.

Touro looked over at him. "It is lonely, and this seems to make it worse. But I normally just come here when there's a game or something like that, so I'm not really alone."

"What about your family?" Liko asked her.

"My family?" Touro said surprised by the question. "I don't have one...anymore..."

"I'm sorry, I didn't mean too..." Liko said.

"It's alright, just ask me about it some other time." Touro told him.

"So are you still up for the grand tour weekend?" Liko asked her changing the subject.

"Course I am." Touro told him smiling. "So where are you going to take me?"

"It's a surprise." Liko told her leaning back crossing his leg over his knee.

"Fine, I'll hurry a little...it's still early and we have two days." Touro told him getting up as she carried on eating while she walked through to get dressed.

The holo arena doors open onto a deserted sand plain program with the sun almost at its highest point in the sky, with the team looking worn out and wishing that they were anywhere but here, which was the complete opposite to how Toria felt.

"Good morning all." Toria said cheerfully, she felt well-rested after her weekend break even though they had done so much sightseeing.

"What's good about it?" Reloco asked sat on top of the dune, his mousy brown hair blowing in the breeze.

"You didn't have a good weekend?" Toria asked him as she walked over to join them. "Shame, I did. I feel better for it. So let's start with laps, to wake up and then some hand-to-hand."

"You want us running on this program?" Volic asked her.

"Yes, the nice hot sun on our back; a bit of sand to make us work a little harder." Toria said taking her jacket off and unfastening her shirt, as she had a vest top on underneath it; then she started to run.

Even if they didn't need it, she definitely did after her weekend; she had enjoyed it but her powers were so overwhelming she had no idea how she had managed not to set more fires than she had done and somehow managed to gloss over the whole thing.

"How is this a little sand?" Reloco asked staring after her thinking that she was mad. "Can't we run on a different program while she does this one?"

"Come on..." Volic said taking his own jacket off and throwing it down beside Toria's and started to run. "Consider it a warm up."

"More like a roasting." Reloco said as he slowly got up and started to run himself with the other two officers behind him.

Half an hour later Toria finally stopped by the pile of jackets and shirts looking as though she had only just arrived. She waited for the others to join her; slowly Volic came over the top of the dune and slid down the other side panting doubled over beside of her.

"I'll let you off, you're only a couple of laps behind me." Toria told him.

Normally he would have argued with her, but at the moment he didn't even have the strength to look up at her. They waited another five minutes until Reloco finally appeared crawling over the top of the dune and then rolling down the other side, Toria moved Volic out of the way as Reloco landed in a heap on their uniforms; his vest was soaked with sweat and his hair was stuck to his face in parts.

"This'll help...but slowly." Toria told him bending and getting the bottle of water that she had dropped underneath her jacket.

Reloco took the bottle and tried to drink it too quickly but just ended up choking and spitting most of it back out, Toria didn't bother saying anything as she turned back around to wait for the other two to join them.

"So what did you say that we're doing next?" Volic asked her.

Reloco moaned loudly next to them, as words were still failing him while he tried to drink a little water. Toria frowned, she had wanted to go onto training after the run, but it looked as though that would have to wait a while, while they all rested.

"I guess we can do that after lunch." Toria said. "Computer end program."

Everything disappeared instantly, returning to the bare holo arena; a couple of metres away were the other two officers lying on their fronts looking pretty well baked.

"I'll go sort out our next program while you sort this lot out." Toria told Volic grabbing her jacket and shirt from underneath Reloco, before she walked out of there. "I want them ready for 13.30hours."

"Yes, sir." Volic said as he looked up watching her walk out of the holo arena, wondering how she still managed to look as though she hasn't done anything.

Later that week, after pushing the men as far as they seemed willing to go, Toria sat in her office finishing writing her weekly reports with Volic sat in the facing chair, he had been sat there for five minutes and hadn't said a word to her, which of course was annoying her especially since she knew why he was there.

"I'm leaving in half an hour, even if you haven't told me why you've come to see me." Toria told him finally as her patients had finally ran out. "But if you're here to moan about the training, I don't want to hear it."

"But you should hear it, the men aren't happy with your supposed way of doing things." Volic told her.

"I changed the program, so that they're not running through the dunes." Toria told him pleasantly. "Yes I know that I keep changing, but that's only so they and I can get used to different environments; in this sort of thing that we do we have to be ready for anything. We go up against Magics, some of whom might actually use their powers on us; and in those cases we all need to be strong enough to be able to handle that. And besides, the running is nothing since we all had to do it in the academy."

"Well, we did yes." Volic said as he couldn't argue with that, and the rest of what she said also made sense as well. "I know what you're saying but there has to be an easier way of going about it."

"That's the thing; we don't know when our next mission is going to be; so we can't just sit around and do nothing." Toria told him. "The running is only for half an hour, then we have hand to hand, blaster practice and shuttle practice. It isn't as though I'm working them to death."

"All the same..." Volic tried to explain again.

"We've got the weekend off again, while I'm away; I'll think of something so that you don't have to listen to them complain for hours at you." Toria assured him.

"That's all I want." Volic told her.

"A quiet life?" Toria said smiling at him. "You don't seem the type, you seem like you prefer the action."

"Yes, sometimes." Volic answered and then changed the subject. "So where are you going this weekend?"

"I'm visiting friends again, making the most of the time that I have since I don't get to see them that often with how everything is." Toria told him, it was only a part lie as she was going to see a friend just not the ones that he'd think she be seeing.

The sun was shining high in the sky over the lush green fields with purple and red flowers, the trees outlining the edge of the fields as though nature's own fencing; gracker birds flew overhead their black features contrasting against the blue of the sky that seemed to make them change colour to a silver blue almost disappearing from view. Around the corner onto the field two fully grown Kura's ran in with riders astride, they were fully grown at ten feet tall and just under five feet in length stood on two crawl-like feet; they were both a mucky blue colour with floppy ears and large green orb-like eyes.

"You know I was kind of worried at first." Touro shouted over to Liko who was ahead of her. "But, it's kind of fun."

"I told you that you'd enjoy yourself." Liko told her turning his Kura around pulling on the reins. "I have another surprise for you as well."

"Another surprise? Out here, in the middle of nowhere?" Touro asked smiling, her disbelief showing.

"You don't believe that I could pull off something like that?" Liko asked sounding offended.

"Well I don't know, since I don't really know you that well yet." Touro answered still smiling at him.

"Come on, this way." Liko told her as he pulled on the reins again, they turned around and started to run in the direction that they had been going to begin with.

Touro's Kura wasn't as fast, so couldn't keep up that well; which is kind of what she thought he wanted, to get to wherever it is that they're heading to first. It actually made her wonder if he really did have a surprise for her, all the way out here. They strung along behind him following his path as he turned out of sight, when she finally caught up to him he had dismounted and tied his Kura to a tree and a couple of feet away was a picnic; Touro couldn't believe that he had gone to all of this trouble for her.

She slowed down as he walked over to her taking the reins off of her and walking her over to the tree, tying her Kura next to his own; she swung her leg over to climb off seeming to forget how high she really was but he stood there his arms out ready to lift her down, she slid a little off the saddle and he caught her pulling her into him his large hands against her bare skin, seeming oddly familiar in away that she couldn't describe and a burning surge throughout her whole body. She practically pushed him off of her and she stumbled away from him breathing deeply as she tried to control herself, to stop the fire within her from taking control.

"I'm sorry...I didn't mean too..." Liko said trying to reach out to her, but she kept moving away from him. "I forgot...I guess since you don't show yourself in your proper form..."

"What?" Touro said almost doubled over trying to control her breathing.

"You're a Tasian, it was wrong of me to touch you in such a manner." Liko told her.

Touro looked up at him, he did look sorry as though he had offended her in someway; she smiled at him and waved her hand dismissively.

344

"It's just...kind of overwhelming..." Touro told him. "I didn't used to be able to feel anything like this...yes they were a little sensitive I guess where my markings are...but nothing like they are now..."

"With some, it comes with age and depending on who touches them." Liko told her.

Touro blushed deeply unable to control the fire within her any longer, setting alight the lower brushes of the tree.

"Oh god...I...I..." Touro said panicked, no idea how to put it out.

Liko though calmly raised his hand and the flames started to fade away, she looked over at him a mixture of fear and panic threatening to take over wondering what he was going to say to her childish outbursts and that she couldn't control herself.

"Are you alright?' Liko asked her gently.

This was too much, him caring, when he should be angrily shouting at her.

"Alright?" Touro said mockingly. "How can you ask me that? After what I just did, what I could have done to you...I...do you have any idea how hard it is...? You act all calm and collective because you don't know...!"

"Tour...it's alright." Liko said gently as he stepped forward his hand out stretched to her, but she just swept it away.

"It's not alright...it hurts...it hurts so much that I feel as though it's going to consume me...!" Touro shouted at him. "You...you're just like him! You don't understand!"

"Tour...please..." Liko said worriedly, but it was too late she just erupted in flames and disappeared scaring the Kura who went wild pulling on the reins to free themselves. "Damn it!"

The lift door slid open and Renji stepped inside wearing his white dress uniform, Jessa followed him looking quite annoyed since he hadn't paid her any attention all night; she had gotten herself a brand new dress as well, just for him; long flowing turquoise with a blue waist corset and it didn't matter, she might as well not have been there for all the good it had done.

Renji just stood there still thinking about how he could have done things differently, she hadn't called him in two weeks nor was she accepting any of his calls; he hadn't meant to scare her off, but he hadn't realized or rather hadn't predicted how uncontrollable her powers would be. It was his fault, he kept telling himself, if he would have done more to help her when he had the chance then none of this would be happening now.

"Renji?" Jessa said, but he didn't answer her as though he hadn't even heard her. "Renji, we just had a report that Tasia has just reappeared."

"That's nice." Renji said distractedly.

"You aren't even listening to me!" Jessa shouted at him, finally breaking him out of his thoughts. "Sir, Renji...you've been like this since you got back early the other weekend; perhaps if you told me what happened then I could help."

"You can't." Renji told her brutally. "I'm not even sure if I could."

"Well that's kind of hard to believe, something that you can't handle." Jessa said smiling kindly at him.

"This has always been somewhat tricky, but this time I don't know if I'll be able to handle it." Renji admitted leaning against the bulkhead.

"Well if you've done it before, then you can do it again." Jessa assured him.

"I wish that I felt that confident." Renji said. "I'd at least give it another try, if only I could find..."

"You lost it?" Jessa said surprised. "Maybe if you told us..."

"No, this is something that I have to do on my own; it's my responsibility." Renji told her, he had to do it on his own to make up for everything that he had done wrong so far; if he could just do this one thing then perhaps, but he knew that it was still just hopeful, wishful thinking.

Lord Zebulon sat on his throne, his long blonde hair down as usual and wearing his black armour; he didn't seem as happy as normal but who could blame him since Toria hadn't arrived alone, like he had wanted her to.

She stood by his throne while Volic and the others sat at his table eating, not really seeming to be paying much attention to the two of them, but they still couldn't really risk it.

Toria wasn't in her uniform, instead she wore a wrap-over dark blue jacket with buckle fastenings over her chest across the large v shape plunge neck, and a matching pencil skirt with a long slit up the back and knee boots; definitely not standard uniform, but no one was complaining as long as she got her job done.

"So..." Toria said.

"Look at you, commanding your own unit." Lord Zebulon said.

"That isn't really true, I'm joint with Volic at the moment." Toria told him. "Where I go, they go."

"Except on your weekend breaks." Reloco added.

"Why would I want to take you, to show to my friends?" Toria said.

"I'm hurt; you don't consider me a friend?" Lord Zebulon said making it sound as though he was offended by her remark.

"If you weren't a friend, then I wouldn't have come all this way when you asked." Toria told him smiling. "I don't mind helping you when I can, and since things have been a little dead at our end."

"Yes, I heard about the attack." Lord Zebulon said handing her a data pad. "Just a little information that I found out, that you might want."

Toria looked through the data pads information, it was a lot of help telling her where quite a few of the ships had gone when they were evacuated and that there were several Fleet ships out looking for them already.

"We don't really have a ship to do this sort of mission, you see the ship that dropped us off here isn't really a taxi service." Toria told him.

"I'm always happy to help out the Fleet, which includes a ship for the five of you if you need it." Lord Zebulon told her.

"That's generous of you." Volic said not sounding as though he was convinced that he really wanted to help them.

"Anything to help out the beautiful Miss Kentaro." Lord Zebulon teased her.

"That's nice, thank you." Toria said stiffly, she wasn't really in the mood for flirting as she was still angry with herself for how she had handled the situation with Liko, completely over-reacting like that and now ignoring all of his calls.

"Maybe when we're alone then, we can talk like that?" Lord Zebulon added.

"Yes." Toria said not listening to what he had said as she turned around to leave, but the others had heard perfectly fine what he had said and her answer.

"If he gives you a ship of your own, you'll be able to visit him even more than just on the weekends." Reloco said as he got up following her out with the others.

"What?" Toria said not sure what he was talking about.

"You seemed a little distracted." Volic said beside of her. "We didn't think that he would be your type, since he's a Magic."

"What?" Toria said feeling as though she had missed something important somehow. "My type, what do you mean?"

"He likes you, its plain to see; I'm surprised that you let him..." Volic started to explain.

"He's like that with everyone, and I might as well play along as long as he keeps giving us what we want." Toria told him.

"Does he give you what you want?" Reloco teased.

Toria stopped suddenly and pulled a blaster out from underneath her jacket and pointed it straight at him. "My personal business has nothing to do with you, is that understood? And just so you know, there is nothing going on between us."

"Of course not, he's a Magic traitor." Volic said as though the matter had been settled.

Toria lowered the blaster and carried on walking while Reloco just stood there frozen to the spot, while everyone else walked on leaving him behind.

"Reloco don't just stand there like a statue." Toria told him. "We have thing's to do, Magics to capture and kill."

"So we finally have an assignment?" Volic said. "I bet it doesn't involve doing a lot of running though does it?"

"That's funny." Toria said sarcastically, and then added a little more seriously. "But no it doesn't. The ship will do all of that, but the flight practice will come in handy."

"So the rest of it was all for nothing?" Reloco shouted up the corridor.

Toria stopped again and turned around making him stop and step back away from her. "Reloco, is this your last-ever mission with the Fleet?"

"What? What does that mean?" Reloco asked worriedly.

"It means, are you leaving after this is over?" Toria asked him.

"No." Reloco answered.

"Then, the rest of the training will come in handy on other assignments." Toria told him, then turned around again and carried on walking. "It seems a lot of hard work, and that's before we even get anything done."

"They probably thought that you liked a challenge." Volic told her.

Toria sat on the edge of her bunk aboard the ship that Zebul had leant them, it was a small transport ship with very cramped quarters; this had been the only single quarters on board and as she was the only woman of course it had been hers, but these were the smallest quarters that she had ever stayed in. The bed was in a kind of hole in the wall with a small view port, above it was a cupboard probably the largest thing in the room, a ledge for her computer on the right side of the bed; on the other side was a small sink and a box-in shower. She couldn't believe that he had given her such a tiny ship; she'd definitely have to have a word next time that she saw him.

The computer finally signalled next to her that she had an incoming transmission, she picked it up and put it on her lap; Siren looked worriedly back at her.

"What's wrong?" Siren asked her.

"Sorry...it's just that I needed to talk to someone." Toria told her.

"Okay, but don't do that. I thought that there was something really wrong with you trying to contact me so much." Siren told her. "So what's the big problem?"

Toria had been trying to contact her since she had ran out on Liko, but now that she had her here to talk to she didn't know how to tell her best friend that she ran away from a guy; scared.

"Okay, if you don't actually speak...you know, tell me what's going on, then I can't help." Siren told her.

"Well, it's kind of embarrassing..." Toria told her. "I...I kind of ran away from this guy while I was on a date with him."

"What?" Siren shouted at her. "You were on a date with someone, after what happened with Kole; which I might add you still can't control your powers. And you ran away from him, let me guess because they were getting all heightened cause you body was responding to his."

"Okay I get all that, especially about Kole." Toria said. "That wasn't the worst part."

"There's more?" Siren asked.

"Well...I kind of pushed him away from me, yelled at him...set a tree on fire, yelled some more...and then to top it all off, I combusted...that's the running part, when I disappeared." Toria told her. "You can say it...I've been thinking it myself. I lost it, freaked out. And you know the worst part of it is, he's a nice guy; he's a Ta'vian."

"Seriously?" Siren asked her, seemingly a little more positive after hearing this part. "He knows you're a Tasian as Touro, so he'll understand. I mean that is if he really liked you."

"So what?" Toria said.

"When did this happen?" Siren asked her. "Have you spoken to him since?"

"About two weeks ago, and no." Toria answered. "How could I? After what I did, he's tried though...I mean to contact me...but I haven't accepted any of his calls."

"What are you, stupid?" Siren told her angrily. "He must still be interested, or at the very least worried about you."

Toria though wasn't sure, how could she do this; she was stupid to begin with.

"Next time that he calls you answer it." Siren told her firmly.

"It's been two weeks; he's probably not going to." Toria said trying to sound dismissive as though it didn't bother her, but of course they both knew better.

"Fine, if he doesn't call you, you call him and apologise for being an idiot." Siren told her firmly. "You wanted my advice, well that's it."

"Thanks." Toria said sarcastically, but she was still unsure or rather afraid of what to do; she had never been in this sort of adult situation before.

Tired and sore Touro walked over to her front door dressed for bed in her shorts, vest, sporting quite a few cuts and bruises; she reached out and opened it expecting to see Lonac or one of the others from the team.

"I hope that I'm not disturbing you?" Liko asked her.

"What're you...what're you doing here?" Touro asked him.

"Well I didn't think that it was such a good idea turning up before your match, I didn't want to upset you." Liko told her.

"Upset me?" Touro said expecting the worst.

"That...that isn't what I mean..." Liko said quickly. "I mean, well last time that we talked...you kind of left upset..."

"I...I...damn it..." Touro said as a door opened down the hall, she grabbed him and pulled him inside startling him a little, but it was so that they wouldn't be overheard and closed the door. "I...erm...okay, right this is kind of hard to say. I haven't really got a clue about my whole Tasian side, which I might have mentioned before but at this point in time I can't remember if I have or not. I know that I've told you that I haven't got a clue about Magic. So if you put them together, I'm quite scared of myself and what I'm capable of...and trust me...you really don't want me too lose control...I...I..."

Liko dropped his bag as he stepped forward and pulled her into his arms hugging her tightly.

"It's alright; I'm not going to make you do anything that you don't want to do." Liko assured her. "We'll take things really slowly, and work at controlling your abilities."

"You make it sound so easy." Touro said as she held him also, it really did feel nice being held in someone's arms, that they cared about you; but she could still feel it inside of her slowly building. "Okay...that's enough...you need to let go..."

Liko let go like she asked and she moved away from him around the chair and sat down, breathing heavily as she regained herself; Liko walked around the other side and sat down on the sofa but the opposite end so that he'd give her space to calm down.

"I'm sorry..." Touro said.

"You don't have to be." Liko told her smiling. "I never had such a strong reaction from a woman that's liked me before, of course I'm not just going to run away."

"What?" Touro said wanting to say something else in her defense but words just failed her.

"It's nothing to be embarrassed about, you're a Tasian; their bodies give off signs when they're attracted to others." Liko told her.

"It's still embarrassing, especially when you don't have any control over yourself." Touro said leaning back staring at him.

"You didn't think that I'd turn up." Liko said smiling at her.

"Truthfully no, considering how I acted and what I did." Touro told him. "And then afterwards ignoring your calls; which my best friend told me that I should reply to."

"Well I definitely like this best friend of yours." Liko said smiling at her.

She smiled back at him, this is what she liked about being with him, just being able to talk to him normally; yes there's an odd moment now and then when she feels as though she's going to lose control but that's all because she likes him, and kind of comes with being who and what she is.

"So what happened, I saw the game and I know that you didn't end up that badly injured." Liko asked her.

"A mission, that didn't go as well as I would have liked." Touro admitted. "Even after all the training we did; the real thing..."

"It's always different." Liko said.

"Yeah." Touro agreed. "We did it, we completed the mission but with a few injuries; and I didn't have time to stay to get patched up, as normal."

"That's 'cause it's hard living two lives, trying to fine a good balance between them." Liko told her.

Touro nodded in agreement and then suddenly remembered something and sat up so that she could see over the sofa, she hadn't imagined it; she sat back down and looked over at him.

"You didn't book a room anywhere did you?" Touro asked him.

"Well I wasn't sure if I was going to catch you before you left." Liko admitted.

"And of course everywhere is booked up because of the match today." Touro said somewhat reluctantly. "This is only because I wasn't...well just to say sorry...if you wanted I do have a spare room."

"You don't have to do that." Liko assured her. "I know how hard it is for you, and if I'm here..."

"I said the spare room, not with me; so I'll be fine." Touro assured him.

Liko smiled at her, he had been teasing her. "Thanks."

They talked for a while longer, before Touro said that she had to go to bed, though she showed him through to his room and where the bathroom was; she was a little unsure about him staying over but they were staying in separate rooms as she had told him, it was probably just because she had never had a guy stay over before in any way.

Liko got changed for bed and waited for a while until he thought she had gone asleep and then quietly came back through to the living room, now was his chance to find some hard proof to clear her name; he was so sure that she was innocent, but his word wasn't enough. He pulled her chair out at the desk and sat down, there was a picture of the two of them when he had took her out to the Tak'quan Forest; they both looked so happy, smiling and laughing riding one of the giant floating leafs.

"You could at least make this a little easier for me to help you." Liko whispered to himself.

Baron walked down the corridor to Renji after being told that he was on this deck, he wasn't impressed by the situation and how things were progressing; he turned right and finally saw him, so he quickened his pace to catch up to him.

"You still haven't found Kentaro." Baron said a little way behind him, making him turn around.

Renji had known that he was on board but he had hoped that it would have taken a while longer before he had found him; he'd definitely have to do something about the ships' sensors next time.

"How hard is it to find one person?" Baron asked him as he slowly turned around to face him.

"We have found her and tried to bring her in, but she isn't too willing to come with us." Renji told him. "I've gone myself, but still haven't been able to get close enough to her."

It was a half truth in a way, but he still couldn't do it to her.

"She...she really is a danger." Baron told him. "You've heard of the recent attack, of those who tried to escape? She had Lord Zebulon's help; well that's what the rumour is considering the ship she was spotted aboard. They captured seventy percent of those who escaped."

"Lord Zebulon?" Renji said somewhat surprised that she would be working with him, seeming not to hear the rest of the report. "He's a Magic, why would she be accepting help from a Magic if she doesn't want anything to do with them?"

"Good question, but that makes you think of Lord Malevalus if he's approached her and if she's agreed to join him as well." Baron said.

"Do you believe that she would?" Renji asked him, not wanting to believe it himself but considering everything that was going on, he really couldn't afford to dismiss anything any more.

"Truthfully, I don't know." Baron answered honestly. "I want to say no, just like you; but I don't know."

"I'll save her." Renji assured him.

"I want to believe you, but with how things are going...I can't..." Baron admitted.

"I'll deal with it, somehow." Renji told him.

Renji marched up the corridor towards the throne room, two security officers lay unconscious at the other end of the corridor who had tried to stop him from entering; he pushed the door open and walked in to find Lord Zebulon sat on his throne drinking a glass of wine as though he didn't have a care in the galaxy.

"General Renji Aba'rian." Lord Zebulon said pleasantly. "Well I heard a bit about you, though I never thought that I would have the pleasure of actually meeting you in person. And especially not on a day like today, since there are three Fleet battle ships in orbit of my world."

"If you were a true Magic, that would cause you fear." Renji told him.

"Why?" Lord Zebulon said casually. "I help them, so they leave us alone for a small piece."

"You call selling your people a small piece?" Renji demanded.

"Is that why you've come, to stop me?" Lord Zebulon said surprised. "You know that if you kill me, there's no guarantee that they'll let my brothers rule. Then my whole planet and system will fall into their hands. A few lives to save billions, you don't think that it's worth it at the end of the day?"

"That...that isn't the point, especially with what they have some of them do." Renji argued, but he knew that he was right, that if they killed him that they would lose the whole of the system right out. "But no, that isn't why I'm here."

"Then why?" Lord Zebulon asked now sounding interested.

"Toria Kentaro." Renji told him.

"Oh yes, she is beautiful; deadly but beautiful." Lord Zebulon said smiling. "Oh, to be able to capture such a heart; if it's even possible for someone like myself, being a Magic...wishful thinking on my part I guess, for now at least."

"So...the rumours of you helping her are true then?" Renji said trying to control the anger that was building inside of him.

"I gave her a ship, which she needed to track down a few stray Magics." Lord Zebulon told him. "I'm surprised, that they would send someone like you to bring in a child; even though she has killed a few thousand Magics."

"It's personal." Renji told him.

Lord Zebulon laughed out loud, which echoed throughout of the large hall.

"Well...she does have a way about her doesn't she?" Lord Zebulon said. "That soft smile of hers and then that sad look which breaks your heart, and would make you do anything to make her happy..."

Renji lost control drawing his hand back a fire ball forming in it and shot it at him.

Toria was just about to step up onto the transporter pad when she felt something odd inside of her, pain, anger; but it wasn't her.

"What's wrong?" Volic asked her.

"Find out if there's something going on down there, now." Toria ordered the officer behind the console.

"Did I miss something?" Volic asked her.

"And don't let the admirals go down until we know it's safe." Toria continued ignoring Volic, which of course annoyed him making him grab hold of her but she just pulled her arm free of his.

"Erm...sir...a Magic has broken into the palace and the throne room." The officer reported.

"How did you...?" Volic started

Toria stepped onto the pad pulling her blaster out of the holster on her thigh below her jacket, the transporter officer activated the pad and they were engulfed in a bright white light disappearing out of the room and then reappearing in the throne room; the intruder alarms sounded throughout of the palace, but there wasn't anyone in the throne room beside from Lord Zebulon.

Toria almost ran over to him when she saw the burn mark on the wall just above him, he smiled at her seemingly pleased that she was so worried about him.

"Are you...are you alright? What happened?" Toria asked him all at once.

"You seem to have upset General Renji Aba'rian, probably not a very wise thing to do of an Imperial Ta'vian officer." Lord Zebulon whispered.

"Renji...he was here?" Toria whispered as her heart tightened, she had been so close to seeing him, but what would she have done if she really would have come face to face with him?

"Kentaro...the Magic...he's gone already." Volic told her.

"Don't you think that it's strange that she knew?" Reloco said.

They all turned around and looked at him, he did for once have a good point.

"Perhaps it's me, perhaps she sensed that I was in danger." Lord Zebulon suggested. "I haven't kept my feelings for her a secret...and Magics create a bond with whom ever they're attracted too..."

"How nice for you." Volic said not at all bothered about what he had to say.

Toria was kind of glad that she hadn't had to come up with an excuse, but she wished that he could have come up with a better one than that, they were already thinking that there was something going on between them and this was only going to make matters worst.

Liko was clearing away the pots that they had eaten on as Touro came back through, already changed for bed wearing a pinkish red colour vest and trousers with stitching and patterned embroidery up the leg. She couldn't believe that he was doing it again, after she had told him that he didn't have to clear up. She walked over to him and reached for the same plate that he was going for.

"I told you...you don't have to..." Touro told him as he took the plate out of her hand and put it with the rest on the panel surface.

He grabbed her hand pulling her into him and gently ran his finger tips down the side of her face where her markings would be and then leant in and kissed her, softly to begin with and then more passionately, his hand moved over her back as he pulled her closer into him; and then suddenly turning them both around so that she was the one pinned against the wall.

Touro's mind was in a spin as he seemed to devour her senses, taking over her as she seemed to lose herself in his arms and lips, as her body began to heat up rapidly; but it didn't do anything as though there was something keeping it at bay before it completely took her over, she didn't know what it was nor did she care at the moment just wanting to be lost to him and this moment.

Liko suddenly just pulled away from her, her senses still seemed to be out of focus as she looked up at him blushing slightly and unable to say anything to him.

"I'm sorry...I shouldn't have done that..." Liko said turning away from her increasing the distance between them. "I...I guess I just got carried away..."

"It's alright..." Touro said still leant against the wall, feeling as though if she moved away from it she might actually collapse.

Liko looked over at her finally, unable to hide the look of uncertainty on his face.

"Oh..." Touro said moving along the wall trying to stay away from him, and still needing some form of support.

"It isn't like that..." Liko said thinking that she had gotten the wrong idea.

"It isn't like what?" Touro shouted at him. "How dare you! You knew...you knew...!"

"Tour please, just calm down." Liko said as he moved between the chairs and sofa to get to her, but she just kept moving away him.

"Don't...if you don't mean it...then don't...it'll kill me..." Touro told him almost tripping over the table leg as she tried to get past it while he tried to grab hold of her.

"I don't want to hurt you." Liko told her.

"Then quit screwing with me!" Touro shouted.

"We haven't gone that far yet." Liko said somewhat teasing her, but it just made things worse as the holo screen behind him on the wall exploded. "Okay...sorry....but you really do need to calm down."

"I was calm...just fine...and then you...you!" Touro shouted at him. "You decided that it was all a bad idea."

Liko just stared at her for moment, then he reached his hand out to her but she didn't take it, so he stepped closer until she had back into the wall.

"I won't hurt you, nor will I do anything to you." Liko told her.

Touro didn't know why, but she did trust him and she gave him her hand; he lead her out of the living room pushing the door too slightly and then all the way to the end of the hall to her room. She stopped in front of her own door as he pushed it open and stepped inside, this wasn't what she had meant, but she didn't know what to say without sounding as though she was freaking out again.

"I just told you that I won't do anything to you." Liko assured her and lead her into her own bedroom.

He let go of her hand and she just stood there in front of him, he though began to undo his shirt. Panic started to set in which he saw on her face, but he just carried on and pulled his shirt off and then sat on the edge of the bed and took his shoes and socks off; he picked them up and carried them around to the other side of the bed, putting his shirt on the chair and his shoes just underneath. He threw the covers back far enough so that they could both get into bed, then looked over at her staring at him still.

"I wouldn't just kiss anyone, it has to mean something; nor would I ever force myself on anyone." Liko told her. "Just get in."

"What?" Touro said. "Get in there...with you...but you just said..."

"How're your powers holding up?" Liko asked her. "You feel it don't you, burning inside of you to the point where you think its under control...but it could still erupt."

"How do you...?" Touro said unsure. "How could you possibly...?"

"All I'll do is lie with you, as you fall asleep until your body calms itself." Liko told her.

Touro just looked at him, he was still being so caring to her even after how she had acted; he knew what she would be like.

"I'm sorry..." Touro whispered.

"Fine." Liko said sitting down before he put his legs under the covers and pulled them up over himself.

"I don't know." Touro said staring at him in her bed, part of her wanted to get in alongside of him and the other was worried that she could explode just lying there with him. "I...erm..."

Liko turned onto his side staring at her making her feel even more uncomfortable than she already felt, she turned around so that he couldn't see her face and then sat down on the edge of the bed and flopped down pushing her legs under the covers; Liko pulled the covers over her smiling to himself as she lay on the very edge of her own bed.

"You know, you'll end up falling out." Liko told her.

"I'm fine." Touro lied, she was uncomfortable but she didn't want to get any closer to him than she already was.

"Just move a little further over, and relax." Liko told her.

"I'm fine." Touro said lying again, but this time he wasn't having it and grabbed her hand turning her over so that she was on her back. "Hay!"

"I said relax...you can't calm yourself if you don't relax." Liko told her.

"How am I supposed to relax with you lying next to me, in my own bed?" Touro asked him leaning up so that she was looking down on him.

"Like that, just be yourself." Liko told her as he stretched out his arm which if she lay back down would go underneath her.

Touro was still a little unsure, but she knew that she had to calm down so she slowly lay back beside him with his arm around her; she didn't know why but something about this kind of felt strangely familiar in away but she didn't know how it could considering this would be the first time that they would have slept together, the first time that she would have slept with any guy; well except for Renji when she was little but that of course was completely different.

Chapter Twenty-Two

Toria and her team had been assigned to another ship, one which was a little more suited to transporting them around on their missions and of course offering assistance if they require it. As normal Toria had spent the first couple of days kitting out her quarters with sensor dampers and alarm sensors to tell her if someone had broken into her quarters, that one was very important since the attacks on her life by Magics were still going on; though what had surprised her was that they still hadn't been given the order to kill her only to bring her back alive. Toria knew that was to do with Renji, he was always too soft on her; which part of her was glad but it also meant that he still wasn't taking her seriously even after everything that she had done.

Toria had just finished putting the blows of snacks out on the coffee table in her new quarters when they signalled, that she was here.

"Come in." Toria said standing up straight.

The door opened and Siren stood there holding a bottle of wine dressed in a Fleet uniform like Toria's with a slightly longer jacket than normal, that covered more of your bum; she came in so that the door could close behind of her.

"Hi, you wouldn't believe the trouble I went to, just to get a bottle of wine." Siren told her.

"Considering that you're under age, I can imagine." Toria said smiling at her.

"Yeah, well we all don't have older boyfriends who can get us these things." Siren teased her walking over to large comfy chairs under the view port, noticing that she had already gotten two wine glasses out for the both of them. "You knew that I'd still get the bottle?"

"Of course, you always do everything that you say that you're going to do." Toria told her, sitting down and finally taking her boots off and putting them down beside the chair. "You can take them off as well, just make yourself at home."

"You say that, as though it's the easiest thing to do." Siren said as she sat down and opened the bottle before she poured them both a glass.

"Well it isn't that easy, especially since I met Liko." Toria admitted.

"You've been slipping, since you met him you know." Siren told her. "You've hardly done anything, just a couple of small jobs here and there. He's got to you hasn't he?"

Toria reached forward for her glass. "He...he isn't like any guy that I've met before. I think that he really likes me, well he must do considering everything that he's put up with. But I don't know if that will go as far to dating me if he knew I was a traitor."

"But you're not." Siren reminded her.

"In my true form, I am to the galaxy." Toria told her. "He doesn't even know who I am really am. Even if my name is cleared, he still might not like the real me."

"I think, you're over-thinking the whole thing." Siren told her. "The way that you are with him; that's who you really are, you can't pretend all of that."

Toria put the glass on the arm of her chair and grabbed a blow of the pink chocolates, and ate a couple of them while she decided to tell Siren everything; she seemed to gather that there was something else with how she sat there waiting for her to go on.

"He doesn't mind that I'm Fire Elemental, like you said he understands." Toria told her. "When we kissed for the first time...it was...it was incredible...the bit after it we don't need to go into details about that. But he gets the whole fact that my body can't seem to handle a lot of that sort of thing, but...he's really good with me not expecting, but just waiting until I'm ready. Even when we sleep together..."

"Wait a minute, the two of you are sleeping together? For how long now?" Siren asked her, wondering how she could have missed something like that.

"A couple of months now...but..." Toria tried to explain.

"Wait a minute...you just said that nothing was happening and that he wasn't rushing you." Siren said. "So how come you're sleeping with him?"

"Can I answer?" Toria said. "I was trying before you over-reacted."

"Fine, explain." Siren said sarcastically. "And here I thought that you still didn't have control."

"Nothings happened, we've just slept." Toria told her. "I know that it must be hard for him, god it's hard for me as well. I'm trying, I really am...but it's just so hard and especially with all the strain that I'm putting my body under to begin with. He's really great..."

Siren didn't look convinced by her explanation, but Toria didn't have anything else since that's how it was with them.

"Okay, I don't want to sound all paranoid; but I'm going to say it and then we can move on." Siren told her.

"Why does that make me feel nervous?" Toria asked.

"Right, you two just happened to bump into each other one day when you're out; he's really nice to you and helps you out." Siren said. "He's really understanding about your outburst and controlling your powers. The two of you start dating, but nothing happens between you and he's fine with that even though the two of you are sleeping in the same bed. I'm sorry, but I have to say that it does kind of sound strange. Perhaps he really is an understanding guy, who doesn't mind taking things slowly; but...what if he's working for Renji? You always said that you thought that he would recognise you even in your other form, what if he found out since he has to watch Vertigo as well?"

"No. He wouldn't do that. Renji wouldn't do that to me, even after everything I've done...he wouldn't." Toria told her.

"Liko kind of sounds like Renji, I mean...well they kind of sound the same in their behaviour not that I know how he would be to date of course." Siren said. "But his way of treating you...they both care about you a lot and understand an awful lot about your powers. Please, just be careful."

"Fine." Toria said, but she was a little worried now even though she didn't want to be.

There was something to what Siren was saying especially since she didn't know who was Liko's captain, nor did she know what Renji himself was up to nowadays or where he was posted. She didn't want to ask Siren incase she did know, and it did turn out to be Liko's ship, it wouldn't mean that they were working together but it would still kind of feel that way.

Toria was just about to walk out of her quarters carrying a couple of data pads that she had been studying all night on when her computer started to signal, it sounded like it was from Lord Zebulon; she didn't mind hearing from him but this meant that he had something for her to do and she already had her hands full with her new assignment from the Fleet.

She went back into her quarters and turned the computer around to her accepting the transmission, he smiled at her pleased to see her and then his features changed more seriously.

"What's wrong?" Toria asked him.

"Some of my officers failed to transmit at the times allotted to them." Lord Zebulon told her. "We haven't heard anything from them for over a week. I was hoping that you could look into it."

"Any other time, and my answer of course would have been yes." Toria told him. "But I've just been given a new assignment. It's quite a big one as well, in the Peduian system..."

"That's great, that's where they are on the sixth planet part of the mining slave group there." Lord Zebulon told her looking a lot happier about this. "They were sent to negotiate a supply to us secretly, with promise that we could help get some of their people off world; just the ones that are too weak to work any more of course."

"This is going to be a problem, I can't keep blowing up their mines without them doing anything...but of course I can't just leave them there either." Toria said.

"Thank you." Lord Zebulon said smiling at her.

"You should hold off on the thanks until I've actually completed the mission." Toria told him, and then thought of something. "Have you heard of Senator Cullter's aid...erm...I think the report said he was called..."

"He's called Orji, a right slave lover; meaning that he loves having young slave girls." Lord Zebulon said. "Yes I've heard of him. Sick bastard. I doubt many would mind if you killed him."

"What now you're asking me to kill people?" Toria asked him.

"Isn't that what you do anyway?" Lord Zebulon told her. "But no, I wouldn't ask you to kill anyone with your own two hands."

"It's alright, my childish innocence was lost a few years ago." Toria told him, even though she didn't like to say it out loud because it always made everything seem more real than it was. "I'm not going to be on board over the weekend, but it doesn't start until I get back anywhere."

"I hope that you're not cheating on me?" Lord Zebulon teased her.

Toria smiled at him. "I'll contact you again when I know a little more of what's going on."

"Thanks." Lord Zebulon said. "Be safe."

He logged off and the screen went black again, she smiled slightly to herself; everyone kept telling her to be safe or careful as though they all sensed that something awful was going to happen.

The water was running in the bathroom telling Liko that he still had time to think of how to confront her, he had given her plenty of time to earn her trust and now she had to give some back and it would hopefully tell him as well what side she was really working for. He sat there waiting for her to finish in the shower and to come back through even though he was still unsure about how to ask, other than just coming right out and asking her.

His time had run out though as he heard the water being turned off, knowing that she'd come through in a moment; Touro walked through with her hair up in a towel and wearing a big fluffy pink bath robe with blue flowers printed over it randomly. Touro smiled at him as she walked around to the other side of the sofa and sat down beside of him, not realising just how tense he really was.

"I feel much better, well I always do coming here...being with you..." Touro told him.

She wasn't going to make it easy for him, he noticed; but he still had to do it. He turned around so that he was facing her with his leg up on the sofa, Touro turned around and smiled at him.

"What?" Touro said.

"I need a favour." Liko told her.

"Really?" Touro said.

"We've just gotten intelligence that the Fleet is moving into the Peduian system, it's a Magical system." Liko told her. "They've already got them basically imprisoned on their own worlds, and enslaved them in the mines..."

"And what do you expect me to do?" Touro asked him unsure, she already had so much riding on this and she didn't need him asking as well; since she still hadn't figured out how to help Zebulon yet.

"We'd like you to sabotage Aid Orji's ship, then our team on the ground will deal with him." Liko told her. "There's more..."

"More?" Touro said. "How do you expect me to get to his ship to be able to do anything to begin with and then you want me to do more? Wait a minute...what makes you think that I could help anyway?"

"Well you already told me that you can, because you know what I'm talking about." Liko explained.

"That wasn't what I meant. Have you been spying on me?" Touro demanded, a little worried at how this was going.

"I just wanted to know where you were...you know incase anything happened..." Liko assured her.

Touro though wasn't sure if she believed him, she couldn't help but think about what Siren had said to her, what if he really was working for Renji?

"We need you to help the miners to start a revolt, to distract the Fleet officers to what we're doing." Liko went on. "Hopefully also helping some of them to actually escape."

"Are you insane?" Touro asked him. "How the hell do you expect me to get away with all of that, without being caught?"

"It can be done, if you do it properly." Liko assured her.

"Then get one of your own people to do it then." Touro told him angrily. "I'll help, but that doesn't mean that I want to be executed or worse...you know what they do to our kind."

"I would never let them do that to you." Liko assured.

"Yeah well you can't promise something like that, 'cause you're not always around." Touro told him getting up, but he grabbed her wrist stopping her.

"Tour...we need you..." Liko told her.

Touro pulled her hand free and went through to the bedroom, to change and to calm down while Liko stayed on the sofa, to think about what he had just done wondering if he had gone too far; part of him didn't think he had since she had told him that she did want to help, but another part thinks that he could have since if they had done something to her and she was kind of two people, making her do this could tear them both apart. There was also a problem with that as well, since he still hadn't found hard proof to say that they were two different people or if she was just pretending, and was up to some greater plan that he still hadn't managed to figure out yet.

Touro came back through ten minutes later in her pyjamas and a robe, she still looked agitated but walked over and sat down beside him, who hadn't moved from the same spot.

"I don't want to put you in danger, but you must have realised when you agreed to this undercover assignment that there would be a lot of risk involved." Liko told her.

"Well it kind of chose me really." Touro said as she leant back and then pulled her feet up and rested on Liko as he put his arm around her. "I can't promise that I'll be able to do everything that you're asking, but I'll try and do something to help."

"That's all we want really." Liko assured her as she snuggled up closer.

This is what he found so hard being with her, taking advantage of her like this; but as himself he would have never been able to get this close to her. When he looked down her, he saw that she had closed her eyes and was already asleep, she always looked so peaceful and calm when she fell asleep with him; but also what had made him wonder the first time was if she really knew who he was or was it just a subconscious reaction of hers. She had done it again as she moved a little closer to him, she changed back into her native and true form; it was as though she knew that she was safe with him and could let down all of her defences.

This was why he had found it so hard to give the order; it was as though she was asking for his help.

"You're going to get me into a lot of trouble." Liko told her.

"Ren..ji..." Touro whispered in her sleep.

He pulled her closer into him.

Touro slept the whole night on the sofa with Liko, but of course before she woke up she had already changed back into Touro again never knowing that she had even done it. She looked up at Liko and smiled at him, feeling an awful lot better than she had done when she had gone to sleep as though everything that had happened, had been forgotten.

"Morning." Touro said smiling up at him.

"Morning." Liko said smiling slightly back, he still needed to know one way or another what she was going to do; even if he really did have to push the matter this time.

Touro sat up slowly stretching her legs as Liko stood up beside of her, he went through to the bathroom while Touro went over to the computer to get a drink and something to eat since she had to sort herself out incase she had to leave early for her mission and she wouldn't be back here for a while.

Liko came back through from the bathroom and saw that Touro had set them both breakfast out, it was a kind of eerie feeling; it was as though they were really together doing couple things. He really did need to sort this out before it got completely out of hand.

"So have you given my plan any more thought?" Liko asked her.

Touro dropped a glass, it shattered all over the floor; Liko rushed over to her since she didn't have anything on her feet.

"Don't move." Liko told her, and then he waved his hand; all the pieces started to come back together again and remade the glass in his hand. "See good as new." He said as he stood up and put it down on the table and sitting down in his place.

"I told you last night, that I couldn't do what you asked." Touro told him. "I'm sorry."

"Do you mean that you can't or that you won't?" Liko asked her.

"I said that I can't do your plan...that..." Touro tried to tell him.

He'd have to show his hand. "What if Renji asked you?"

Touro just stared at him horrified, Siren had been right about him; he'd just been using her. He could see that he had struck a nerve.

"You said his name again in your sleep." Liko told her.

"What, I don't talk in my sleep." Touro assured him. "Do you...do you know him?"

"You call me Renji in your sleep." Liko told her calmly, thinking that he might as well go the whole way. "Yeah I know him, and he knows what you're up to."

Touro shook her head confused, she was still trying to get over calling him Renji in her sleep and the fact that he works for him; but what was more confusing is that if Renji really knew what she was up to then he wouldn't be doing all of this, and hopefully Kasiya would have told her that he knew the truth, that was if he had told Kasiya to begin with.

"Really? Well I don't know what you're talking about." Touro said walking away from the table.

His patience had just gone far enough with her, he had given her every chance to come clean with him; his anger had really gotten the best of him. He had gotten up in a flash and grabbed hold of her forcing her up against the wall roughly, stopping her from going anywhere.

"Why don't I explain to them, what's going on here." Liko told her.

Touro was kind of too startled to react to his sudden change of behaviour, but before she could really do anything her com started to beep; it was signalling that Volic was trying to contact her.

"Answer it and I swear." He warned her as he tightened his grip on her, and changing back to his normal form of Renji.

Touro was horrified to see him stood before her, that they really were the same person; that he had tricked her this way. But also at the back of her mind, a small thought formed; she still fell for him even though he was in a different form.

"If I don't answer, then they'll think that there's something going on." Touro told him.

"That's because there is, focus!" Renji said angrily. "I thought that you trusted me, Tour. But at the first sign of trouble you run away from me, without even trying to ask for my help."

She couldn't say anything to him because it was true what he was saying, and also she was kind of still in shock at him changing right before her; that she hadn't known that it was really him.

"Damn it! Explain yourself now, or you really have gone too far." Renji told her. "I really will deal with you myself."

Touro panicked, she still couldn't tell him; now that she was face to face with him and she had her chance to tell him, she couldn't. She still had to carry on through; she had to prove to him at least for now that she really wasn't on his side; no matter how much it hurt her to do. She concentrated her energy and shot a fire ball out of her right at him, throwing him off of her and clean across the room, she stumbled past the chairs to try and get past him before he got back to his feet.

"Damn it, Tour!" Renji shouted as he got to his feet, a little shaken by the surprise attack; but he wasn't going to let it slow him down as he reached for her to stop her from leaving. "What are you, stupid! Thinking that you could take me, even with your powers."

Touro turned around and shot another fire ball at him, but he dodged and disappeared reappearing behind her, grabbing hold of her and pulling her into him as she tried to struggle against him.

"So this is dealing with me?" Touro shouted at him as she tried to break free, but of course he was always a lot stronger than she was.

"You're not even trying." Renji told her.

Touro stopped struggling, surprising him somewhat making him wonder if he should tighten his grip more on her or not.

"Neither are you...after everything that I've done." Touro told him as she turned her head slightly to him, but couldn't see his face clearly as her hair had fallen obstructing her view.

"It's just..." Renji tried to explain to them both, because he knew that he was holding back as though he knew that there was something he was missing, something important especially after spending so much time with her; somehow he knew deep down that she wasn't evil, perhaps scared but not evil.

Touro knew that she was slipping, and that she had risked to much already; she had to get out of there before he fully figured out what she was up to, she had come too far now to just turn back.

Renji seemed to wait for her to tell him something, but she wasn't going to which just made him even more angry. Touro slammed the back of her head into his face, forcing him to let her go as she stumbled forwards turning around to face him.

"I always considered you to be a great man, but to sink this low just to find out what I was up to...that's sick." Touro shouted at him. "You used me...praying on my feelings for you...knowing that I'd fall for it...for you..."

"If you can say that so openly, that you have feelings for me; then I know that you're still in there, that I can save you." Renji told her softly reaching out his hand for her. "Why don't you let me save you?"

"You're too late." Touro told him smiling, as she concentrated all of energy and shot it out at him blasting him across the room.

She ran past him to get to her bedroom, but Renji turned over and grabbed her ankle making her lose her balance and fall into the door frame cutting her lip open; he pulled at her trying to pull her towards him but she just kept trying to kick her legs free. Renji grabbed both her legs and near enough pulled her underneath him pinning her down.

"You know, if the circumstances were different, this could kind of be fun." Touro teased putting him off by her statement, so that she had room again to move and kneed him in the stomach.

She pushed him off of her and ran through to her bedroom, with him just behind her; she ran over to the closet and grabbed her bag from inside and struck her hand inside to pull out the small flashing transporter beacon.

She turned around and smiled. "See you next time."

Then she was suddenly engulfed in the bright white light disappearing before his eyes.

"Damn it!" Renji shouted angrily shooting a ball of fire at the spot where she had just been stood.

The door slid open and Toria walked into the briefing room having just arrived back and everyone was waiting for her; she had managed to change her clothes but not heal her cut lip or bruises that had now formed around it since; she walked over to her chair next to Volic who was looking as though he wanted to know every detail of what had happened to her. He of course wasn't the only one who wanted to know what had happened, Senator Cullter and his aid Orji was sat facing her with looks of disapproval.

They were both much older than she was, probably old enough to be her father; and Toria thought that they probably actually knew her father, though this didn't make her feel better since what she had heard about them.

"Why's there a little girl sitting in on this meeting?" Senator Cullter asked the captain next to him.

"Is she supposed to be a gift?" Orji asked looking a little more interested in her, as this new idea formed.

"Please, as if I would do something so disgusting." Toria told him.

Orji looked outraged by her statement, while the rest of her team was trying not to laugh; even their captain was amused but had to calm himself to settle the matter.

"This is Commander Toria Kentaro, she is the commander of the special forces team." The captain told them. "Young she may be, but she is more than capable to handle this situation."

"Kentaro?" Orji asked.

"She isn't Ramiro's daughter, is she?" Senator Cullter asked.

"Yes I am." Toria told him, before she turned her attention to Orji. "Shall I tell him when I speak to him next that you wanted to turn me into one of those slave playthings, that you carry around with you?"

"I'm sure that you would have enjoyed yourself." Orji told her smirking, not seeming at all worried. "You look my type; I would have given you an excellent memory for your first time."

"I doubt that." Toria assured him, she actually looked sickened just by the mere thought of it. "Personally I feel sorry for the other girls that you force yourself on."

"No more than they deserve." Orji told her.

"They don't deserve that, no one deserves that!" Toria shouted at him angrily as she stood.

"Now, if you'll all just calm down." The captain told them. "I asked you all here today, 'cause we're heading out to the system earlier than planned; just incase that they have anything planned. One way or another, we will get this ore. We've be given permission to use force of course, meaning that their so-called protective treaty is basically worthless."

"They all are, just something to give them to lure them into a false sense of security." Toria said, not meaning to sound as though she disapproved of the situation so much; but she couldn't help it, she was still so angry with Renji and this smug guy sat in front of her.

Renji marched down the corridor with Dalal and Jessa trying to keep up with him, he had been like this since he returned; neither of them knew what had happened nor do they know why he kept disappearing nearly every weekend.

"The mission still goes ahead, but our timetable as been brought forward." Renji told them as they took notes and tried to keep up with him. "Toria Kentaro will also be apart of this mission, as she'll be heading up the special forces team. I want two separate teams dispatched to bring her in, but alive."

"Why alive sir?" Jessa asked him. "I mean after everything that she's done."

"She must answer for her crimes against us, just killing her on contact is too easy a punishment." Renji told her.

"Can I ask you a question?" Dalal asked.

Renji didn't refuse or agree, which meant that he could ask, but it didn't really mean that he'd answer his question.

"I didn't mean to...but...the picture on your desk..." Dalal said curiously, this made Renji stop in his tracks. "Why do you have such a picture of her?"

"What? The girl...they say that she's smiling on the beach playing in the water." Jessa said, seemingly confused about what this meant.

"She...she was the one that I lost." Renji told them, without turning around to face them. "My mission was to keep her safe from harm, to make sure that she wasn't turned. But I lost her, I failed. And yes, it was Toria."

"You still think that you can save her?" Dalal asked him.

"No one will accept her, being here...even if she is under the influ..." Jessa started but stopped when Renji finally turned around to face them.

"I know, that she has gone too far...she knows that as well." Renji said stone-faced; it really did break his heart to be saying it out loud like this to them, but it was true, she had gone too far and now he really didn't know if he could save her, even if she wanted to be saved.

"She's a fool, to let them do this to her and to you." Jessa said angrily. "I'd never betray you."

This didn't make him feel any better, he just turned around and carried on walking; he needed something, anything to find out what they had done to her. He also had to wait to find out what she would do, now that she knew what their plan was; this he thought would be also her test if she would blow their cover, as he hadn't told anyone that she knew because then he'd have to tell them that she was also Touro.

Renji couldn't bring himself to do it, it was his only way to get to her to see her as she was really meant to be; he couldn't lose that part of her as he had already lost too much.

Renji's office had been converted into the main centre for investigating Toria's movements, over the last couple of months they had been travelling all over the galaxy gathering information on all the attacks she had instigated herself. There were three more wall consoles and his desk had been changed as well, but even with all of this extra space to gather and analyse the information he still hadn't come up with anything useful.

Renji was tapping his finger on the wall console when the door opened behind him, he didn't seem to notice the man who had walked in and over to his desk pulling out a chair and sitting down; he looked about the same age but that didn't mean anything especially to Ta'vians, which he was one also. He had short black hair and soft coloured brown eyes, with a scar that ran across his left cheek over his nose, though it didn't make him any less handsome; he was dressed in the same command uniform as Renji; only his rank was different.

"I still can't figure it out." Renji told him. "I've been over everything that she's done, for the past couple of years and I can't find any sign that she could still be working for us in some strange way. Accept for one time, I really did think that she was going to help us...the plan had been going great, just how it was supposed to...and then it suddenly went wrong. They revolted like we wanted them to, but the colony was destroyed... it's strange...why would she pretend to help and then betray us. I need something..."

"Unfortunately I haven't been able to find out much of anything, from when she first ran away...except for the time that she was held prisoner by Zar-Jins." He told him.

Renji turned around. "Hazner, you did find him didn't you?"

"Of course." Hazner told him. "We've held him for nearly a month, and he hasn't changed his story once."

"And what would that be?" Renji asked him.

"He said that he didn't have enough time, this time to do anything to her." Hazner told him. "I didn't understand what he meant, nor would he tell us; only that it was part of Malevalus' plan. She was his most important part."

"She is, and he already did something to her before this?" Renji repeated to him.

"He seemed quite proud of what he had done to her." Hazner told him. "It's strange though isn't? Perhaps they got her back then at the battle, and made this Toria out of her hoping that she'll have her powers..."

"No we've already run tests like that and she isn't a clone nor..." Renji explained, but stopped in mid-sentence.

"You still hold yourself responsible don't you, for losing both of them?" Hazner asked him.

"I was supposed to keep them both safe!" Renji shouted at him. "I lost them both, when they both trusted me to keep them safe...I failed them and my duty."

"It isn't your fault, you've done everything that you could do." Hazner told him.

"But it wasn't good enough, was it?' Renji said.

The door beeped and then opened, they both looked over at the man carrying a long package; he stopped suddenly when he saw the angry look on Renji's face. Renji walked over to him and took the box off of him and handed it to Hazner, who seemed pleased to take it and while Renji was reading through the letter that had come with it, Hazner opened the box to find a very rare three-bladed sword inside.

"Who'd send you a Triple Crawl Sword?" Hazner asked him, as he looked over watching him read the letter. "Why can't I have friends like this?"

"How did this get here?" Renji asked the man, who seemed very nervous.

"One of General Kasiya's men, sir." The man answered.

"I want you, you personally to contact him and to confirm that he sent it for this person." Renji told him. "Now go."

The man quickly turned around and left the room, not really wanting to stay while his captain was so angry, which to be honest not many people would.

"Dear Renji, I'm sorry that I haven't been able to see you recently; you know how busy things have been." Renji read from the letter. "I'm still angry about what you did; I really didn't think that you were that type of guy. But I'll let it go, since I know what you were trying to do; and of course I've done worst. I've sent you the latest report of what I've been up to, since I know that you've been looking into me for nearly half a year now. But also, I thought that you might like this present. Happy Birthday, love from Toria."

"Did I miss something?" Hazner asked him. "She sends you rare swords for birthday presents. And is also helping you investigate her. Oh and wait, what was that, that you did to her?"

"It...it doesn't matter..." Renji said not looking at him, and trying to make it sound as though it was nothing.

"You don't have to tell me then, if you don't want to." Hazner said, knowing that it must be something considering that he won't mention what it was.

"She was responsible for destroying another colony, five thousand people this time." Renji said angrily as he carried on reading the report. "She must have caused a lot of damage as they won't be able to rebuild or have slaves there for at least five years."

"Five years?" Hazner asked him thoughtfully. "There's been a few reports like that, where it'll take an awful long time to rebuild; making the places unable to resume as slave holdings."

Renji looked over at him, wondering if this actually meant something or if it was just a coincidence; he'd have to go over everything else just to confirm it, but this could have been what he was looking for and she had just handed it to him. But that thought made him stop, why would she just hand it over to him, making it too easy, so did that mean there was more to it?

"Renji?" Hazner asked staring at him, as he just stood there staring at the report in his hand. "Do you want us to go back over the damage reports?"

"Yeah, just incase." Renji said distractedly. "It couldn't be this easy."

"If it was, she wouldn't tell you; unless she needed your help with something." Hazner suggested. "She still cares about you, it seems."

"What?" Renji said startled.

"She's still thinking about you, remembering your birthday; making sure that you're keeping a close watch over her." Hazner told him. "What if she's doing it to keep you close, 'cause she needs you."

"You're thinking too much about the whole thing." Renji told him dismissively, but he also knew that he had a point; the only problem is that he didn't know how to see her as she was still going to play Vertigo as Touro but he hadn't been able to get close to her, as though she knew when he was around so that she could avoid him.

He had also looked into her apartment, nothing had been coming up about it; it didn't even say if she still owned it or if she had sold it on after her last visit with him.

He just wanted to see her, as if he could then he could finally figure out what was going on with her; but mainly so that he could just see her.

Chapter Twenty-Three

The music started to play from the orchestra in the far side of the hall, all dressed in the same golden suits. The noble people stood up in their grand clothes and made their way onto the dance floor, to begin to dance to the music; it was still quite early so there still weren't a lot of people here, and there was plenty of room for the couples to dance.

Renji though had already arrived with Jessa and his team when he had heard that Toria was going to be here. He wanted to talk to her about what was going on since he'd had plenty of time now to go through all of the reports; he really thought that he would be able to help her finally. He couldn't of course tell his team that was the reason that they were here, as they still believed that they were there to take her into custody given the chance.

Jessa stood beside of Renji wearing another new dress that he hadn't noticed, a one-piece blue suit, that looked as though it was dress but was in fact trousers, just incase she needed to defend herself after the last time that she had ran into Toria and was beaten by her even though that she had used her powers on her.

Renji was in his human form wearing a basic suit not wanting to draw too much attention to himself; he was watching everyone in the room, while he also looked for Toria not wanting her to spot him first so that she'd run away.

"Are you sure that she's coming?" Jessa asked him.

"Yes." Renji answered simply.

"Perhaps...you know we should dance...so that you could have a better looking around, while you're moving." Jessa suggested hoping to get a chance to actually dance with him.

Renji seemed to consider this for a moment, but the idea went straight out of his head when he saw Senator Kentaro and knew that Toria wouldn't be far behind; there was also another man, who was in his dress uniform, with the senator but he didn't know who he was, he seemed quite interested in looking around the room than paying much attention to what was being said as though he was actually looking for someone.

Renji finally spotted her, entering the ball alone; he couldn't help but think that she looked beautiful with her hair up and wearing a pinkish red dress with a very low v-neck below her breast line. As he stared at her, he realized that he had missed her change from a child into woman; even after spending all that time with her, it just wasn't the same as seeing her as her true self.

Without even realising what he was doing, he started across to her; Jessa beside of him thought for a moment that he was taking her up on her suggestion until she saw Toria and knew better. He made sure that he didn't go near the senator so that he wouldn't have to stop and talk to him, but it kind of looked as though Toria was doing the same thing after she had spotted her father, which made Renji wonder just who that man was if she didn't want anything to do with him.

Toria saw Conoab talking with her father and she really didn't want to spend the night listening to him going on about himself, after all the only reason that she had come tonight was in fact to see her father, but it looked as though that would have to be put off for a little while. She tried to head off in a different direction before he saw her, but it was too late as he had spotted her as though he had been looking just for her; she still turned hoping to flag someone else down to put him off for a while, which is when she saw Renji in his human form heading straight for her.

Seeing him coming towards her, almost made her stop in her tracks, wondering what to do for the best. The big question was, who did she want to avoid most? She quickened her pace being careful not to bump into anyone dancing and headed straight for Renji, she grabbed his hand startling him somewhat and pulled him towards her onto the dance floor.

"Dance." Toria told him.

"You do realise that it's normally the guy who asks, the lady to dance?" Renji told her calmly, seeing the annoyed look on the mans face when he saw the two of them dancing. "You know, I'm not sure how I should take it."

"Take what?" Toria asked him, not looking up at him but at his chest.

"That you would rather dance with me, than that guy who looks seriously pissed off now." Renji told her.

"That would be General Conoab, someone who's trying to get in my father's favour and is also interested in me. Though probably only to further his own ambitions." Toria told him as she finally looked up at him, into his handsome face that didn't show a pleasant smile of greeting as it used to. "He's also just returned from a slave pleasure world, so I've heard. Probably best to stay away..."

"Why, would he expect the same from you?" Renji asked her disgusted by the mere thought, of that man laying a finger on her pulling her a little closer without realizing that he was doing so, as in a protective gesture.

"Please, as if I would. Especially with the likes of him." Toria told him, a little surprised by his behaviour; but she didn't fight, pull away from him as she still felt it, even after what she had done, that need from him to protect her to keep her safe. She smiled at him suddenly. "Any road, I would have thought that you would have realised what my type is by now."

Renji chose to ignore her last statement, as he knew very well what type of man she was interested in. He pulled her a little closer into his arms as they danced to the music, as though he had forgotten that his team was probably watching his and her every move just incase something happened; and also wondering why they were being so damned friendly with one another.

"Toria...I...I don't know what they did to you...but if you're in any kind of trouble..." Renji tried to tell her.

Toria looked up at him and smiled softly at him before she rested her head gently on his chest, the music changed to that of a slow dance it seemed just for them.

"So you'll come for me, you'll come and save me; when it's time?" Toria asked him.

"I'd take you right now if you'd come." Renji told her. "If you're using your powers, then we'll always be able to find you and get you out."

Toria looked up at him a little surprised, but also pleased that he'd still come and save her after everything that she had done.

"Thanks." Toria said. "But I doubt that your crew would be too pleased with that."

"I'm their commanding officer, they have to do what I tell them." Renji told her.

Toria smiled at him. "Well at least you've found someone that does, finally."

"Tour...please...can you give me something?" Renji asked her.

"I've already given you too much." Toria told him as he turned her around, and she saw Jessa who looked furious. "Perhaps I should go, your girl friend doesn't look to happy...though considering if she knew everything she'd probably want me dead even more, right?"

"She isn't my girl friend." Renji told her as she pulled away from him, but he didn't want to let her go, he just wanted to keep holding onto her like this.

"Until next time." Toria said before she walked away.

Jessa rushed over to him and grabbed hold of him, also dancing with him so not to draw any unwanted attention to herself; Toria looked over her shoulder and saw them together, she didn't know why, but it made her heart ache. She knew that she could never really have him, that they could never be together but it still hurt; though she did feel a little relieved after Renji telling her that she wasn't his girl friend.

"What was that?" Jessa demanded.

"We couldn't just take her here, there were too many people around...and..." Renji told her.

"Sir...Renji...the way that you held her...she…she seems to mean..." Jessa tried to say, but she didn't want to say it either.

"A lost soul, that I would have wanted to save...and she knows it..." Renji told her. "I've known her all her life, it's hard to see, to believe what she has become. I mean what they've done to her. She wasn't always like this."

"But she is, so she has to be punished." Jessa told him firmly; but Renji didn't say anything as he looked past her and over at Toria with her father, who was also looking over at him.

It had been a while since he had spoken to her father, actually the last time that he had spoken to him was when he had left the senator giving up his offer of Toria; a small part of him regretted it, but he also knew that it wouldn't have made a difference even if he would have stayed.

On board the Nightshade, Toria was sat in the captain's office, in his chair with Volic and Reloco sat in front of the desk going over the damage reports still; it had changed quite a bit over the past month or so since the attack and Toria had taken over the running of the ship.

"You would have thought that they would have appointed a new captain by now." Toria said irritably.

"What you don't want it?" Volic asked her.

"Yeah, he's right...you could get it." Reloco told her eagerly. "You've been running the ship for the past month...I mean since the captain was killed in the attacks by those Storms."

"Yeah, well that's because I had to, since there wasn't anyone else to do it." Toria told them. "We still haven't found out what happened to the Storms."

"No, but we know that they're not on the Magics' side..." Volic said.

"Perhaps they're on that Lord Malevalus' guy side." Reloco added.

"Actually you could have a point there, it would make sense to why they would seem to be on our side; lure us in and then attack us." Toria agreed.

"No, I don't believe that they would do that." Volic said defensively. "From what I've heard Lord Malevalus doesn't support the Magics, but us; so he wouldn't have one of his own attack us."

Toria looked over at him, it made her wonder why he would stick up for Lord Malevalus, she just hoped that he wouldn't be stupid enough to actually work for him; but if he did turn out to be a spy for him, it wouldn't really surprise her much, nor would she lose much sleep over it either.

"Okay, we don't know who they're really working for." Toria told them. "But I still put in the report that Captain Kaseem Gerik, attacked us knowingly."

"Let me guess, they didn't seem to care considering the ship is still in one piece and still has someone to run it for them." Volic said.

"You're right of course." Toria said. "You know sometimes, I really don't think that they care one way or another, what actually happens to us out here."

"Why should they be bothered, you seem to have proven yourself once again that you're capable of doing this." Volic told her.

"Yeah, that's right." Reloco agreed. "They'll probably end up making you the captain. I doubt that anyone will mind considering that you've kept everyone alive; you saved us all from the attack, when you took over after the captain was killed."

Toria wasn't sure that she believed that completely as she was still only eighteen years old, and of course she never finished at the academy but just came straight out here, and of course the most important factor was that she was a woman. These type of men, don't really like women running things, as they don't think that they have the stomach for it; but she could keep up with the best of them, though the only thing that she doesn't approve of is the sex slave worlds and she wasn't going to change her mind about that either.

Toria's computer started to beep, signalling that she had an incoming transmission, even the screen had changed to show that it was coming straight from the Malarias base; she had a horrible feeling that this was the call that she had been waiting for.

"If you don't mind, but I should take this call." Toria told them. "I'll tell you as soon as I know who the new captain is."

"Tell them that the men will only follow you, that way you'll get it for sure." Reloco told her as he stood up to leave.

"I don't believe that you'll have to do something like that." Volic assured her as he followed him out of the office, and then the door closed behind them leaving Toria alone to answer the call.

Toria activated the screen and was surprised to see Admiral Wanika Ever'ardo.

"Well, you've definitely surpassed all of our expectations of you." Admiral Ever'ardo said. "You stopped a Storm ship from destroying yours after taking control of the Nightshade after her captain was killed. And then afterwards have been running the ship as though it was second nature to you."

"I don't think I would say it was second nature." Toria told him. "It's hard work, since I've never done anything like this before; I feel as though I haven't had a proper night's sleep since it happened."

"No one would know that though, because you don't let anyone see your weaknesses." Admiral Ever'ardo told her. "We believe that you have done an excellent job so far, and are willing to give you a trial period as Captain. That way, you have full say over all of the missions and also get to train the crew, the whole crew for special assignments. To be honest we have wanted a ship that could be just focused on this for sometime, but have been unable to do so with how the conflicts have been of a late. But now with you here, it seems as though we'll have a ship that will put the fear back into those Magics."

"Wait a minute, you want me to train them all up? Or just those that I'll actually send on missions?" Toria asked a little confused and overwhelmed at the same time, not knowing how she was expected to train a whole ship.

"They are yours to do with as you see fit." Admiral Ever'ardo told her. "If you believe that you need the full crew trained, then do so."

Toria didn't know what to say, or what she was going to do with a ship of her own; it would be more helpful of course but also dangerous as she wouldn't have anyone else to blame if something was to go wrong. She would have to make sure that each attack she committed herself to, was justified and that she would be able to follow it through. Things may seem in one respect to be a blessing but in another she had a great challenge ahead of her again.

"I look forward to accepting your challenge sir, and hope that I don't disappoint you." Toria told him.

"Well then, I have a mission for you." Admiral Ever'ardo told her, as though he knew she would accept.

"Already? But what about the training I was supposed to do here?" Toria demanded, wondering if this was a test to see if she could really pull off something like this.

"It is only a rescue and recovery mission, but if you don't want it then I'll give it to someone..." Admiral Ever'ardo started.

"No, that's fine; I'll accept it." Toria said, knowing that there had to be more to this than met the eye, as there always was with most of their so called missions.

"I'll send the full details over to you, but this is the basic outline of your mission." Admiral Ever'ardo told her. "One of our ships have gone down in the Ventearian system."

"I've never heard of it." Toria said thoughtfully.

"No, not many people have since there isn't really anything there." Admiral Ever'ardo told her. "It's only got four planets and both sides have never took any interest in it until now, the ship went down after tracking another Magical ship. No one knows that we have found them, so if this is leaked then we know for sure that it'll be you or one of your crew who let the Magics know of our plans."

"And why would I betray you?" Toria asked him calmly. "I can't say that I can vouch for all of my crew yet, since I don't know them all personally...but at least I'll be able to after this mission is over with. But why the big secret?"

"There are five Magical officials on board that ship, one is supposed to be working under cover at the senate." Admiral Ever'ardo told her. "We would like to know who they are of course. And also, we have found out that most Magics don't even know about this ship; which means only one thing of course they're hiding something very important from us on board. We want the ship and everyone and everything on board. Is that clear?"

"Yes of course." Toria told him.

"You have a month, hopefully that will be enough time to get your crew ready for the planet." Admiral Ever'ardo told her.

"A whole month?" Toria said, this definitely didn't make her feel any better if they were giving her so long to get ready; there must be something seriously wrong with the system if they needed that long to prepare for one rescue mission. "I'm sure that the next time that we talk, that I would have completed the mission and you will have what you need."

"I hope so." Admiral Ever'ardo said before he logged off, leaving Toria to wonder of the mess that she had gotten herself into now.

Toria decided to call her senior staff together for their first meeting, this of course included her team members so the briefing room was quite full unlike normal, even though there were only an extra four people at the table. She was nervous as hell as she sat at the top of the table with them all looking at her, as of course they had all heard the rumours that she had been made captain over their first officer Maska; Toria hoped that they would do as she said as this would be her first proper meeting like this.

"Right then, I want to clear up the matter about captain." Toria told them. "I was appointed captain, and I wasn't told that there have been any changes made to the first officer. So Maska you will still hold that position. But my second officer will of course be Volic. Everyone else still holds the same positions, but my security team will have a say if they wish to join missions that I don't personally assign them to."

"Why?" Maska asked.

"They are still trained for special operations, like bringing in Magics." Toria explained. "This extra training of course will now apply to all of the security teams on board the ship. But also everyone on board this ship, has to under go extra basic training as we will often be put in danger by Magics; if we are boarded I need to know that we will succeed in beating them back."

"They want the whole ship to become a special task force?" Volic asked her.

"Yes." Toria said smiling. "We will become the most feared Fleet ship, helping to bring down the Magics once and for all. If anyone has a problem with this, they should speak up now and I'll have you reassigned...well in a couple of months after spending it in the brig, seeing that we already have our first assignment."

"You'd throw them in the brig until this is over?" Maska asked her a little surprised.

"Of course, this is a top secret mission; that will not leave this room." Toria told them. "So, like I said if you have a problem with how things are going to be I expect you to speak out now; it'll be worst afterwards, I assure you."

She waited to see how they all reacted, but none of them seemed to want to leave even though she was sure that they probably didn't want her as captain; but seeing how important the ship and they were going to become, they didn't want to run away just yet.

"Right then." Toria said. "We will be going to the Ventearian system, but before you say anything; I know that there's nothing normally there. This time there's something that requires us. Two ships have gone down on the third planet's second moon. The Fleet ship In'orcan and the Magic ship Mercury Daze, we of course want our own ship back, but we want the Magic ship as well. We don't want to miss the chance of finding out as much as we can about their technology, and there's also a few people on board that we want."

"So it's a rescue and recovery mission?" Maska asked her.

"Yes, basically." Toria answered. "But since that the Magics don't seem to know about this, we're keeping it top secret so that they don't get in there before us."

"Fair enough." Maska agreed.

"I want you and Parkila to help train your men, we're not sure what to expect down there." Toria told him. "Volic and the rest of my team will help of course. Training will be done in every environment that you could think of, against Magics; who knows what they might use against us."

"Basically be prepared for the worst." Maska said. "Consider it done. It's about time, that this crew saw some real action."

"Okay then, the six of you will head up the training teams; I will come down every so often to add in a few programs of my own." Toria told them.

"They're never very nice ones." Reloco told them.

"The rest of you, will research as much as you can about the system and its planets and moons; just incase there is something in there to why those ships came down." Toria told them. "If anyone asks, we're just doing routine spot checks for Magic bases."

"Simple, but quite normal thing for us to do; since your new posting of course." Maska agreed. "No one would think much of that."

Toria was quite pleased with herself that the meeting had gone so well, and they all supported her on this mission; but she knew it wasn't just because of her but because of what it meant for them all if the mission was a success.

The night before they were due to go down to the planet finally, it had been a very long month with everything that they had to do to be prepared; but they had somehow managed it all in time. Toria was sat in her quarters in her pyjamas, reading through the reports from the team leaders, she was actually quite pleased with how things have gone.

She of course kind of wished that things were different and this was really a Magic ship and they really were going to rescue the Magics, but it wasn't; and she still had no idea how she was going to get the Magics off of her ship and to someone who could help without drawing too much attention to herself or to them. She knew that she couldn't ask Kasiya, because she was already getting him into too much trouble with his own kind, considering that he had helped her out a lot recently. She also knew that she couldn't turn to Lord Zebulon because the Magics thought that he was a traitor as well, and if he was seen helping them then his cover would be blown and all of his people would be in danger.

The door beeped suddenly startling her somewhat, she looked up putting her data pads down.

"Come in." Toria said.

The door opened and Maska walked in, he looked a little tired with all of the extra training that they had been doing for the last month, but she knew that they would all be fit and well to start for real in the morning. The door closed as he walked over to her and sat down on the facing chair, just staring at her.

"Is there something wrong?' Toria asked him.

"I was just wondering how long we will be able to keep all of this secret, now that the men know what they are to do." Maska said.

"We knew that we would have to tell them, but we didn't tell them everything of course; just enough." Toria told him. "The problem won't be the rescue but when we are finally told where we are to take the prisoners."

"You still haven't been informed?" Maska asked surprised.

"I guess they don't want it leaking, they'll probably tell me like an hour beforehand so that no one has time to react." Toria said somewhat annoyed, because then if that happened she wouldn't be able to do anything herself.

"I also came to say, that I'm quite impressed with how you got them all motivated...the crew, even though that most of them don't actually like taking orders from a child." Maska told her.

"I know that they don't like me, but they like what I can bring them; so they'll put up with it." Toria told him and then smiled suddenly surprising him somewhat as he had never seen her smile like this before, so kind and gentle. "I won't be a child forever, and I'm nineteen this time around."

"Yes, you are." Maska said smiling slightly back at her. "You know that you're the youngest ever captain in the Fleet's history?"

"Yeah I know." Toria said still smiling. "I'm quite proud of myself really of what I've done over the past couple of years, I just hope that I'll be able to keep it up."

"You have a ship of your own now, and we won't let you down." Maska assured her.

"Good, I'll be counting on you all an awful lot." Toria told him. "But if you don't mind, I wouldn't mind a bit of rest seeing that we have a long couple of days ahead of us. And you should get some rest as well, seeing how hard you've been working."

"Yes, of course." Maska said standing up. "I'll see you in the morning then, captain."

"Yes... see you in the morning." Toria said as she watched him leaving.

She didn't know why, but it kind of made her think of Renji when he was Liko and they had spent all of that time together; she knew it had all been a trick on his part, but she really did miss him. She missed spending time with him, and also of course the way that he held her in his arms. She didn't know why, but part of her couldn't believe that he would pretend that he cared about her in such away; kiss her the way that he did, and sleep with her as well.

Toria wanted to talk to him about it, but she knew that she couldn't consider the situation between the two of them; and even if they were on good terms she didn't know if she would have the courage to just come out and ask what she wanted to.

Toria had swallowed her resolve, as she didn't have any other options; she had changed into Touro and walked out of the transporter room and up the corridor with a slight limp to her left leg. She wore her purple hair braided which was now just below her shoulders, she wore a green vest top with matching trousers, that had a kind of yellow embroidery that ran all the way up the legs.

She knew that she was risking an awful lot by coming here, especially after what had just happened; but she had no one else to turn to, this was all she had left.

Everyone stared at her as she walked up the corridor surprised to see her again on board the ship, and probably wondering what she was doing there and who she was there to see, and of course why she was injured.

It did hurt her, every time that she put weight on her leg the pain shot up it threatening to buckle and give way, but she knew that she didn't have much further to go and then hopefully she'd be alright even for a little while.

She knew she had to be strong and hold it together, with so much riding on this; she just hoped that she would be able to do something. She finally reached the end of the corridor to the mess hall; the door opened into the loud and busy hall, which was twice the size as the one on board her own ship. She looked around briefly as she carried on walking noticing that everyone was staring at her again, once they seemed to realise who she was, which she tried to ignore it was hard to have all those faces looking at you.

She near enough saw him straight away, sat alone; though he wasn't really hard to miss with his long red crimson hair. She'd know him anywhere, well near enough as long as he didn't change his form of course. She walked over to him and around to the other side of the table and carefully sat down as her leg hurt even more as she bent it to sit down; Renji looked up from his work unable to hide his surprise.

"Hi." Touro said pleasantly.

"Well...hi." Renji said staring at her, wondering why she would risk coming all this way to see him.

The hall seemed to have actually gone a little quieter, as they all tried to listen to what was going on without actually seeming to, but it wasn't as though they could hide their interest in seeing the two of them together.

"I need a little help." Touro told him coming straight to the point.

"And just how much is a little?" Renji asked her, not sure why she would come to him now even though he had told her that he still wanted to help her.

"My ship is holding Captain Decha Ansis and most of his crew, they'll be killed Friday." Touro told him calmly, but she couldn't hide the worry from her face.

Renji stood up and walked off with his data pads still in his hand, Touro got up and followed as quickly as she could, while everyone else just looked on wondering what had happened as they hadn't heard what was said between them.

They went back to Renji's quarters, she had walked behind him the whole way there unable to keep up with his pace; neither of them had said a word not wanting anyone to hear what they had to say; Touro was a little surprised that they were the same quarters that he had taken her too last time that she was here.

Renji went into his quarters first then Touro followed, she changed back into herself as the door closed behind her and just before Renji turned around and grabbed her by the throat forcing her up against the wall. She let out a loud groan as she hit the wall; she had known that he wouldn't just listen to her, and knew that she wasn't in any condition to fight him today.

"I need to know the whole truth, before I can...that I'll help you." Renji told her and then let her go and stepped back.

"Renji please believe me, when I say that I'm sorry." Toria told him touching her neck gently. "I...I couldn't tell you...and even now I...I can't go back but only carry on."

"No...you can end it right now and stay here with me." Renji told her as he reached out an uncertain hand for her. "I'll keep you safe here with me."

Toria smiled at him as she stepped aside not taking his hand and just leant against his desk since her leg was hurting her so much. "I still have things to do, but I did tell you that when I'm ready I'll ask for you to come and get me."

Renji didn't want to accept that as her answer, but he knew that he had too for now, especially considering why she had come; she pulled out a data pad from under her vest top and handed it to him.

"I need your help with this." Toria told him.

"What you can't handle it?" Renji asked her unable to hide the sarcasm in his voice.

"No, not how I would normally." Toria answered surprising him somewhat as he briefly read through the data pad.

"This...this, you can't expect me to do this?" Renji said angrily. "I couldn't guarantee your safety."

"That's why it needs to be done like that." Toria told him. "They can't know that I came to you. But they need to be rescued."

"Tour...there has to be..." Renji tried to say.

Toria stood up to leave. "You must have figured out what I've been doing by now, which means that it won't be long until the Fleet or rather Lord Malevalus also figures out what I've been up to. This is why it needs to be like this."

"Tour..." Renji said reaching out to her but she moved away from him.

"Please don't." Toria said sadly. "It hurt you know, thinking that I had killed all those people...betraying you..."

"But you didn't, and that's how I can prove to them..." Renji tried to tell her.

"No." Toria said angrily. "You don't understand. You can't tell them until it's time, not before..."

Toria turned to leave, even though it hurt to leave things like this with him, but it also felt a little better now that he knew the truth.

"Can I still visit you as Touro?" Renji asked her.

Toria turned around and smiled slightly at him. "Of course not."

Renji quickly stepped forward without thinking before she could get away from him and wrapped his arms around her, Toria let him and leant back into him as she had missed his embrace also.

"You won't leave it too long, until you let me bring you back home to me, will you?" Renji asked her.

"Home with you?" Toria said smiling to herself.

"I know that I shouldn't but I do care about you." Renji told her holding her tightly, not wanting to let her go.

"You better not tell anyone, or you'll be classed as a traitor as well." Toria teased him.

"A price that I'm willing to pay for you." Renji told her.

"I wish you wouldn't." Toria said. "I mean talk like that...it's as though you know just what to say to me... to get to me, to get my barriers down."

"That would be because I've known you forever." Renji told her and kissed her upon the cheek over her markings, sending a red hot tingling sensation throughout her whole body and into his own.

Renji stood in the transporter room with his security teams and the alarms sounding overhead with the red lights flashing. Dalal and Jessa stood behind him, waiting for the order to move out; none of them had asked how he had gotten the information as they knew better in these times with having so many spies on both sides.

Renji felt quite nervous and worried, not for himself and his crew but mainly for Toria since this was her first real mission as a captain and she was risking so much for them, and he really couldn't do anything to help her. He was worried about the Fleet and of what his officers will do to her, he had told them that she still wasn't to be harmed, that he wanted her back alive but he really couldn't guarantee that in the heat of battle.

"When you're ready." Renji told the officer behind the console.

"It's a good job that we had someone on board Kentaro's ship." Dalal said.

"I still can't believe that they made that little girl a captain." Jessa said angrily.

"You're still upset because she beat you." Dalal told her.

"I'll deal with her personally, the rest of you get the Magics." Renji told them. "The attack has already started so they'll be ready for us, be on your guard. They'll be ready for Magics."

"Great, just what we need a whole ship trained to fight us." Dalal said sarcastically.

"So are you still going to bring her back alive?" Jessa asked him again.

"If I can yes." Renji answered her.

The pad below their feet began to illuminate, they all stood ready with blasters in their hands ready for what ever awaited them aboard the Nightshade; they were all engulfed in a bright white light disappearing off of their ship and reappearing in the dimly lit corridor somewhere aboard the Nightshade. The lights were also flashing red with the alarms sounding.

"Intruder alert, intruder alert!" The computer announced throughout the ship.

"Right we won't have long, split." Renji ordered and ran off down the corridor to his left with Dalal and Jessa and two other security officers right behind him, he just hoped that none of the others actually ran into Toria and that she decided to stay on the bridge this time since she was the captain, but he knew her better than that.

It wasn't long before they ran into officers, but none of them needed to use their Magic only their blasters to defend themselves; but also something else, his com started to beep.

"Go ahead." Renji said.

"We've found the holding cells...but we're under heavy fire." The man said through the com. "She's here as well..."

"Toria..." Renji whispered to himself, before he disappeared startling his team.

He reappeared in the corridor just behind his men who had rescued the survivors, they weren't using their blaster but their swords to deflect the blasts; that's when he saw Toria pinned down, cut and just knocked to the ground. His heart seemed to clench in his chest at the mere sight of her in trouble, he had to do something; he disappeared again and reappeared directly in front of the officer who had been ready to bring his sword down on Toria, but instead sliced through his uniform and skin into his shoulder. He gritted his teeth from the pain as Toria looked up at him, he could see how worried she was for him but that only made him more angry, since he thought that she should be thinking of herself in a situation like this.

He brought the hilt of his sword up and stuck her over the head with it, knocking her out cold; she fell to deck before him. Part of him wanted to pick her up and take her back with him, but he knew that wasn't what she wanted yet, so he'd wait a little longer for her.

"Pull out!" Renji ordered; they had gotten what they had come for after all.

Toria reached for her head as she slowly woke up blinking at the bright lights that met her eyes in the med bay, everything came back to her of how she had ended up there; Renji had been injured right before her eyes still trying to protect her, she just hoped that they had gotten away safely.

"Captain, if you're awake...I'll fill you in on what you missed after the Magics attacked you." Maska said stood over her; she nodded slightly for him to continue. "They escaped, with the prisoners and the information that we had about the ship. I've got a team looking into how they had found us, but to be honest I think that we could have several traitors on board."

"It would explain how they responded so quickly." Toria said leaning up. "They got us to rescue them, so that they wouldn't have to do all the hard work and then they just come along and take them back."

"There's another ship coming to meet us, they're going to interview all those with knowledge of the mission." Maska informed her. "We of course are included on their list."

"Of course." Toria said, she wasn't expecting them to respond so quickly but she should have known better.

Her head still hurt so much that she was unable to think clearly; she couldn't help though smiling slightly as she thought that he had really made it look real. But she knew better, she knew that it had cost him a lot to not take her with him, leaving her behind here wondering what they would do if they learnt the truth about her.

When Toria finally made it back to her quarters later that night she had several messages waiting for her, from Kasiya, she really wasn't in the mood for him to lecture her especially from a recording but she knew that she still had to listen just incase it held important information about what was going on, as he would have probably been informed of everything that had happened by now.

Toria slowly walked around her desk and sat down, activating the screen and the recorded message from Kasiya.

"Toria, I hope that this message finds you well." Kasiya said. "For I fear that you may not be, after this recent failure. I'm not sure how Renji and his men managed to get past you, but I fear that he may have discovered what you are really up to. If that is the case, then perhaps now maybe the time to ask him for help to return to our own kind."

"You could at least have some faith in me, after everything I've done." Toria said irritated by his message, she then activated his second message; but she was surprised to see that it was Renji, she was so pleased to see him that she couldn't help but smile.

"Toria I'm sorry, for what I had to do to you." Renji told her. "But you know that I had to, to make it look real. I hope that you are alright, I'll try and see you soon. Everything went alright on our end, so don't worry."

Toria just smiled, she couldn't help it; she was looking forward to seeing him also, she just hoped that it wouldn't be as long as it was last time, but it also made her feel better that she didn't need to hide from him anymore.

Chapter Twenty-Four

Renji walked wearily into his office, after spending the last couple of hours being debriefed on what had happened on his last mission; he still had an awful lot of work to do even though he would have preferred to have gone straight to bed. But there was also someone waiting in his office for him, Hazner had come to see him again, he was sat waiting in the chair at his desk.

"You couldn't have waited until the morning?" Renji asked him as he walked around his desk.

"I came to see how you were holding up." Hazner told him. "I've been hearing an awful lot of rumours about you, and that Toria person."

"Really, good for you." Renji said sarcastically sitting down and leaning back in his chair, not really in the mood to start explaining himself again.

"They say that you had her, but you just let her go. Is it true?" Hazner asked him.

"It wasn't part of our mission." Renji told him.

"But, she is of course." Hazner told him. "You know that's why you're in so much trouble, because it kind of looks as though you just let her go. I've known you a long time, and I know that you wouldn't just turn your back on your people, even for a woman."

"Actually...I might do...depending on the woman in question." Renji told him as he opened the locked draw at the bottom of his desk; he pulled out a blue flat jewellery box and slid it across the table. "For her, I'd give up my life."

Hazner looked up at him somewhat surprised, he grabbed the box and opened it; inside was a beautiful white gold necklace with red and pink gems set in it, along with a matching ring.

"But she's dead, the woman that you were going to give this to...ten years before this Toria was even born." Hazner told him. "She is...dead I mean...isn't she?"

Renji didn't answer him, he just stared at him.

"Have you fallen for this little girl, after all that time you spent with her?" Hazner asked him. "That's not like you."

"I've only ever loved one woman...but she...if thing's were different..." Renji tried to explain, but he couldn't not even to his friend, not about this.

"You fell for the little girl." Hazner said smiling slightly. "You could have at least picked someone that you could have been with. But I guess that's something you do as well; always go for the hard to reach women. Even if you do somehow manage to turn her to our side, our people won't accept her and you also will be classed as a traitor; you really do have to ask yourself if she's worth it."

"You mean worth giving up everything for, I think so." Renji told him smiling. "It isn't her fault that she's lost her way, I'll just help her find it again, no matter what I have to do."

"This is all going to end up in tears." Hazner said frowning; he had wanted his friend to be happy but with someone that wasn't like this girl, he really didn't understand him at times.

Toria was dragged into a dark room by two security officers, one on each arm and then thrown onto the cold hard floor, she looked around wildly wondering what was going on, as they had just come to her quarters and grabbed her telling her that it was her turn to be questioned. A pair of men's hand next to her grabbed her and pulled her to her feet again, as she heard what only could be chains falling from the ceiling just behind her.

Toria couldn't believe it, they weren't just going to ask her questions but were actually going to interrogate her; she wanted to struggle but she didn't know what to do for the best, if she put up a struggle would that make her look more guilty? She didn't really have much of choice as the electro chains were activated and she was pulled back and her wrists locked into them; she heard the two men leave the room but no one else came into her.

A spot-light lit up over her head illuminating the space around her, but everything else in the room was still in darkness as though she was the only person in there.

"Good morning." A man's voice said overhead through a com channel. "For the record, state your name and rank."

Toria didn't like this one bit, but she knew that she had to go along with it. "I am Captain Toria Kentaro."

"Wrong." The man said.

An electric volt was sent down the chains and into her, but she didn't shout out in pain as she was really used to a lot worst than this; considering what had happened to her when she had ran away from home several years ago.

"Try again." The man told her.

Toria regained herself before she answered his question. "Captain Victoria Kentaro."

"Very good, we don't really like nicknames here; only real names." The man told her. "Now then Captain. Why don't you give us your account of events, when the Magic ship attacked and why you think that they didn't kill you."

"How am I supposed to figure out what's in the mind of a Magic?" Toria shouted, but she shouldn't have lost her temper as they sent another electric volt down the chains to her.

"I want it in order, no skipping to the end missing out the important parts." The man told her sounding somewhat amused.

Toria wasn't at all amused, but she'd tell him what she knew none the less. "We had just been told to wait for orders, while holding the Magics..."

"But why did you leave the ship while you were holding such valuable prisoners? That alone looks suspicious." The man told her.

"I had gotten permission to leave the ship, and I had been injured during the rescue by...well we weren't really sure what it was only that it was very big, hairy and had very sharp claws." Toria told him. "I went to visit friends as I normally do."

"That of course is being looked into." The man told her.

This worried Toria, as she had put that she was visiting Annyetta and she didn't want to get her into trouble.

"She has nothing to do with this investigation." Toria told him. "If I was going to do something don't you think that I would have gone somewhere out of the way so not to be spotted by someone I know? My father is very well known, which means that so am I. I wouldn't be stupid enough..."

"So you say." The man said calmly. "Well then, why don't you carry on...with just before the attack then."

"Fine." Toria said. "Everything seemed fine, we had interrogated the prisoners and was analysing the data that we had gotten from the Magic ship, while in orbit of a gas giant. At this point we didn't know that we weren't alone, nor do we know how they managed to avoid our sensors. They came out from the other side of the gas giant and opened fired on us, we took quite a bit of damage before we were able to put up our battle shields as we had only been using our atmosphere shields of course."

"Why? Since you knew that you were transporting such important guests, you should have been ready for anything." The man asked her and sent another electric volt down her chains but she still didn't scream out in pain for him, but managed to keep it in.

"No one was supposed to know what we were doing." Toria strained to tell him. "Considering how things went after the attack, I would be lying if I said that they hadn't come for the prisoners as they went straight for them. I took a team to head them off and came under heavy weapons' fire, but they also had swords...I don't really think they were normal swords either..."

"Magical swords..." The man said thoughtfully. "I'm surprised then that you're still alive after coming face to face with someone who wields one. They were known as part of the Imperial Guard when the Magical Empire still stood; I am surprised that there are still so many left. We will have to do something about them."

Toria was starting to regret mentioning them now, but she knew that she had to as the others from her team would have mentioned them when it was their turn and she would have ended up in even more trouble for leaving important information out, they'd definitely think that she was hiding something then.

"Did you recognise the man who dealt you the blow over the head? The one who appeared to be in charge?" The man asked her.

"Of course not." Toria said angrily. "Why would I know any Magics?"

"I didn't ask if you knew him personally, but recognised him as you had had many attacks on your life recently." The man told her. "Had he ever been apart of the teams that have tried to attack you?"

"He could have, I guess." Toria answered, she didn't just want to come out and say yes. She knew that he had been, but they would have to at least do a bit of work this time to find out if he really had attacked her before. "It all kind of happened really fast, and he just appeared suddenly and hit me...meaning that I didn't really get a good look at him."

"That is a shame, since the sensors in that area were damaged because of the Magic that was being used." The man told her. "I just hope that one of your officers might be able to give us a description."

"So do I." Toria said irritated, wondering how much longer she would have to be held like this.

Toria stood out on the balcony looking over the city, letting the cool breeze wash over her; finally glad to be off of her ship now that the interviews were over with. She was still quite sore with everything that had happened lately, but had decided that she would let her injuries heal normally not wanting to draw too much attention to herself, after finally clearing her name.

Music was playing inside the great hall just beyond the doors, but she wasn't really in the mood for dancing tonight as there wasn't really anyone here she would want to dance with; which made her remember last time when she had ran into Renji and they had danced for a couple of minutes. She hoped that she would get another chance, to be able to really dance with him.

She had her hair down and wavy but pulled back out of her face and she wore a lilac thin strapped dress with a long knee length silver necklace.

She had been called home by her father after what had happened but had decided against staying with him and decided to stay with Annyetta just incase the Fleet decided to drop in on her. It had been a rough couple of months for her since she had been made captain, she knew that it wasn't going to be easy but she really did have to be more careful now with so many people watching her every move.

"I was worried." Kasiya said behind her.

Toria turned around startled by the sound of his voice; he smiled kindly at her as he walked over to her and stood by her side.

"You don't seem the type to worry, that much; especially for someone like me." Toria said smiling at him, partly teasing since he knew what she was really doing.

"Of course I worry." Kasiya told her. "I had a wife once, she made me worry all the time doing reckless things."

"You had a reckless wife?" Toria said not sure that she believed him. "That type of woman doesn't really seem your type. I would have thought that you would have liked a proper well-mannered woman."

"She was that as well." Kasiya told her. "Our daughters are very much like her, they still make me worry even though they have children and grandchildren of their own. It is just something that I do."

Toria smiled at him, she had never once heard him speak of himself like this before, it was nice to finally find out something about him even if it was sad that he no longer had a wife.

"Renji is worried about you." Kasiya told her. "His type hasn't changed. He likes strong independent women, even though all he would really want secretly would be to keep them all to himself."

"I don't understand." Toria said confused, not sure why he was telling her this about Renji.

"You may not have realised, but even though you are just a child compared to us; you are still very much a woman...especially to Renji, even though he may hide it." Kasiya told her. "Be careful. I know you didn't want him knowing what you were up to because you feared that you wouldn't be able to carry on properly, but I don't believe that it would be you, but he wouldn't let you. He would do everything that he could to pull you out of the fighting so that he could have you by his side."

"I think that you're reading too much into...whatever it is you think is going on." Toria told him, a little confused.

"You must put him straight." Kasiya told her. "When you see him, make sure that you tell him that there can't be anything between the two of you."

"Of course there can't be." Toria said indignantly, but part of her was actually kind of heart-broken at the mere thought that Renji could actually like her, but she wasn't allowed to be with him because of the mission that she had already given herself. She didn't know why she was so upset, since she already knew all of this, but she had never been told by anyone else.

"Just as long as you understand that, you have to make him understand it as well." Kasiya told her. "He has to be clear, as he is Ta'vian and they need to be told out straight without any doubt for them to question. Can you do that?"

"I...I...don't know...I truthfully don't know..." Toria told him honestly. "I've always cared about him, for as long as I can remember...I can't just turn those feelings off. I had thought of him when I was little as a kind of big brother...but..."

"If you must love him, then that is the only kind of love you can give him for now." Kasiya told her. "He will understand one day when all of this is over."

"He'll be angry with the both of us, for doing this." Toria said sadly.

"It's for the best." Kasiya told her before he turned and left.

Toria stood there alone once more, but this time she felt even worse then she did before; she really did have to give him up this time. She hadn't been able to, she knew that even if she hadn't been able to see him because he had still always been in her heart and especially when she had met him as Liko; she had fallen in love with him again.

He had told her that she knew who he was, perhaps she had and she just didn't want to admit it to herself as she was hoping that he really could take her away from all of this; but she knew better, she knew she was doing a good thing for her people, no matter what it meant for her. She knew that she was giving up on everything that she had wanted, but she was giving that chance back to millions of people; what more could she really want?

Toria felt someone behind her, but she didn't bother to turn to see who it was as she recognised them, it was someone that she knew; she smiled to herself thinking that Kasiya had come back to talk to her some more. She heard an energy discharge of a blaster and turned, but not quick enough as she was hit by the blast; her head felt heavy for a moment before she passed out without seeing who had shot her only knowing that it was someone that she had trusted.

Toria woke suddenly with a start and somewhat disorientated, she was sat in a comfy chair; she opened her eyes looking around the somewhat familiar room. She couldn't believe it. She didn't know if she was angry or pleased to be here, especially how she had actually gotten here.

"I'm glad to see that you're finally awake, you've been asleep for hours." Renji told her pleasantly behind her, leaning on the top of the chair.

"What?" Toria said somewhat annoyed with him, but when she looked up and saw him smiling at her she couldn't really stay angry at him for long. "You know if you wanted to see me, all you had to do was ask."

"I've tried that remember, you have a nasty habit of ignoring me when I call." Renji told her as he put his arms around her, happy now that she was back here safe with him.

Toria liked this feeling as well but she knew that she shouldn't, especially after what Kasiya had just told her. "We're both going to end up in a lot of trouble for this."

"I don't care." Renji told her.

"But you should care about what happens." Toria told him as she turned around to face him, but their faces were so close that if they moved just a little more they would actually kiss, the mere thought of kissing him again though kind of ignited a fire inside of her and she pushed him off of her and near enough threw herself off the chair away from him.

"What's wrong?" Renji said partly amused and partly confused about her behaviour.

"I don't...I don't like getting so close." Toria told him.

"You're being silly, it's not as though you could hurt me." Renji told her as he walked around and sat down himself. "You didn't used to complain."

"That...that isn't the point...you tricked me!" Toria shouted at him, but he only smiled at her as she sat down at the other end of the sofa.

"It hurts you know when you push me away, especially since I know how you really feel." Renji told her.

"Please...I've heard the rumour...well part of it." Toria told him. "You have a girl friend. It better not be that stupid woman who tried to attack me using Magic, and still lost."

"What, she did?" Renji said a little distracted and then smiled suddenly at her. "Actually the rumour is that I'm going out with Touro."

"What?" Toria shouted at him getting to her feet. "What the hell is with that?"

"Everyone knows that we're serious about each other." Renji teased her.

Toria didn't find his joke funny, she didn't need this.

"There's nothing going on between us, idiot." Toria shouted at him as she went back over to him.

Renji reached out and grabbed her, pulling her down into the chair onto his lap with him; she struggled a little against him and then gave in when she realised that he wasn't going to let her go, unless she used real force.

"Renji...come on..." Toria said.

"Come on what?" Renji said playfully as he softly turned her face to him.

She pulled her head back out of his hand. "You shouldn't...what if someone came in?"

"No one's going to come in, what're you afraid of?" Renji asked her.

She was afraid of getting too close to him, of hurting him and giving him her heart and then losing him, having to walk away from him. She pushed his arms off of her as she stumbled getting down off the chair while he still tried to grabbed her and pull her back.

"It isn't a game." Toria told him. "Stop it! Let go of me!"

She stumbled behind the other chair so that there was something between them just as the doors opened behind Renji startling them both as Dalal and another security officer walked in.

"What's the meaning of this?" Renji demanded standing in front of her.

"Sir, transport has arrived for her." Dalal told him.

"I didn't contact her, telling anyone that we had her." Renji told them.

"Well it wasn't as though you could keep her a secret for long." Dalal told him. "It wasn't as though you actually wanted to keep her here."

"That's what I was planning to do." Renji told him angrily.

"What?" Toria shouted at him angrily. "What the hell, is with that? I'm not some plaything!"

"You could be, if you would just stop complaining so much." Renji told her before he could stop himself, he hadn't really meant to say that out loud especially in front of his officers.

Toria blushed deeply embarrassed by his statement, as for his officers they just seemed confused by their captain's sudden change in behaviour, as they had never seen him act like this before towards any woman, let alone someone who was classed as their enemy.

Renji turned around to face her, ignoring his officers. "What do you say, will you stay here with me?"

Toria just stood there speechlessly, she really didn't know what to say to him; she knew he was risking so much right now in doing this for her, but if she stayed then she wouldn't be able to carry on and those that she had saved might also end up in trouble if everyone found out the truth about her.

Renji seemed to guess what her answer was when she didn't answer him, he disappeared from in front of the chair and then reappeared in front of her and pushed her up against the wall.

"Damn it..." Toria mumbled. "What have we moved on to me trying to pretend to fight my way free?"

Renji suddenly smiled at her, but that faded as quickly as it had appeared as she disappeared out of his gasp and the alarms sounded overhead.

"Get her back, now!" Renji shouted as the ship was hit with weapons fire. "Damn it! Battle stations!"

The three of them disappeared from his quarters and reappeared on the bridge, just as the ship was struck again from weapons' fire.

"Sir, it's a Storm Battle Ship." Dalal reported behind the weapons console.

"Intruder alert!" The computer announced.

"They just transported through our shields sir, teams have been dispatched to their location." Dalal told him as he continued to fire back at the Storm ship.

"As soon as there's a hole in their shields, get her back...is that understood?" Renji told him just as two Storms transported onto the bridge behind him.

Renji barely missed the lightning bolt as it shot past his face, grazing it slightly and giving him black dots before his eyes; but he had trained blind folded before so it didn't matter to him as he moved around pulling his sword over his shoulder bring it down to bear on the first Storm, but as he came for the second one he just disappeared as though he thought better of going up against him.

"Sir...are you alright?" Jessa asked him at the navigation console before him.

"I'm fine." Renji told her.

The view screen changed from the battling Storm ship to that of it's bridge with the captain holding Toria, and an Ice Spear to her neck; Renji was furious at the scene before his eyes and it showed as well.

"Well, I can tell by the look on your face that I found the right person." The captain said pleasantly. "Who would have thought that she was the Magical spy that we've had such a trouble finding."

Renji didn't know what to, he knew what he had to do but it was just doing it, that might be the problem.

"Sir...the ship...it's imploding." Dalal said somewhat surprised.

Toria smiled at him just before the captain threw her to the ground, and consoles exploded on the bridge behind him.

"Damn it!" Renji shouted as he gathered all of his energy and transported himself over to the Storm bridge.

The captain was too surprised to do anything as he appeared next to him, and bent down grabbing hold of Toria's hand pulling her to her feet and into his arms; she allowed him to take her as they were both engulfed in flames disappearing off the ship just as it was destroyed and reappeared back on Renji's ship and on his bridge in front of his officer.

"Anyone would think that you wanted me dead." Toria said sarcastically as she stepped back away from him.

"What the hell is that supposed to mean, I saved you just now; why would I want you dead?" Renji shouted at her angrily.

"Exactly." Toria said smirking at him. "They'll probably be wondering why you saved me, considering that I'm on the wanted list by the Magics."

"Don't get smart with me!" Renji told her pointing his finger at her. "You always have to make things difficult."

"Technically this is your fault for kidnapping me in the first place and not turning my locator chip off." Toria told him.

"I turned it off." Renji told her.

"I have three." Toria told him calmly.

"What?" Renji said staring at her angrily, but it didn't last long as his whole expression changed. "Well at least that's settled, you'll stay here with me."

"What?" Both Toria and Jessa shouted together.

"Her?" Jessa said angrily. "She's with them. What ever you think she's done, it must be a trick to get to you...Renji..."

Toria ignored her as she turned her attention back to Renji. "I can't stay, you know that. I can still go back as no one knows the truth about me."

"My crew know." Renji protested.

"Renji, think about this." Toria told him.

"I have thought about this." Renji told her. "Wait in my quarters, while I talk to Kasiya."

Toria stepped forward and kissed him softly on the cheek making Jessa even more angry, and a murmur spread across the bridge staff; Renji though looked more surprised than them all put together.

"I'll be in your quarters for Kasiya to take me back." Toria told him sadly.

"He'll let you stay." Renji told her, but she didn't say anything as she walked away which made him wonder if she knew something about Kasiya's position on this that he didn't. "Everything that you have seen and heard is classified until further notice, is that clear?"

"Yes sir." His bridge crew answered though they kind of sounded unsure.

"Renji, I don't understand...why her? Why do you want her?" Jessa demanded. "She's just some stupid girl, out to kill us! She's using you, can't you see that?"

"She can use me however she wishes." Renji told her as he walked off to his office to contact Kasiya; leaving Jessa to just stare at his back to wonder what he meant by that last statement.

Several hours later Toria walked into the transporter room with Renji by her side, he looked sadder than she did for leaving but that was because he knew something that she didn't, it was just that he didn't have the heart to tell her.

They had hardly spoken much, or at least of what they had really wanted to say to one another before she was to leave and she was running out of time. Toria stopped just before she was to step onto the pad and turned around to Renji and hugged him tightly.

"I'll just stay in the Fleet a bit longer, then you can come and get me." Toria whispered. "I don't want that to be my only life. I want to be free as well, to live, to be able to be in love and not have to hide and to have a family of my own."

"I'll make it all happen for you, I promise." Renji told her as he hugged her back.

"Can I tell you a secret?" Toria whispered into his shoulder too embarrassed to look at him. "I like the name Naru."

Renji's eyes went wide, he couldn't believe it.

"Then I'll have to make sure that we have a little girl then." Renji promised her. "I'll be waiting."

Toria kissed him on the cheek and then pulled away from him, she would love to be able to be with him but part of her knew that he was only being kind to her as he always was; she couldn't believe that he really loved her for some reason, probably because she didn't want her heart to be broken; even after everything that he had promised her.

She turned around and smiled at him on the pad, before she was engulfed in the white light of the transporter and disappeared off of his ship, not knowing when she would see him next.